George C. Lewis

Essays on the Administrations of Great Britain from 1783 to 1830

SALZWASSER VERLAG

George C. Lewis

Essays on the Administrations of Great Britain from 1783 to 1830

Reprint of the original, first published in 1864.

1st Edition 2022 | ISBN: 978-3-75259-097-5

Verlag (Publisher): Salzwasser Verlag GmbH, Zeilweg 44, 60439 Frankfurt, Deutschland
Vertretungsberechtigt (Authorized to represent): E. Roepke, Zeilweg 44, 60439 Frankfurt, Deutschland
Druck (Print): Books on Demand GmbH, In de Tarpen 42, 22848 Norderstedt, Deutschland

THE

ADMINISTRATIONS OF GREAT BRITAIN

FROM

1783 TO 1830

ESSAYS

ON THE

ADMINISTRATIONS OF GREAT BRITAIN

FROM

1783 TO 1830

CONTRIBUTED TO THE EDINBURGH REVIEW

BY THE RIGHT HON.

SIR GEORGE CORNEWALL LEWIS, BART.

EDITED BY SIR EDMUND HEAD, BART.

LONDON

1864

Engraved by J. Hall from a Photograph.

G C Lewis

PREFACE.

During Sir George Lewis's life-time, many persons, including the accomplished author of the *Life of Pitt*, expressed to him the wish that the Essays now brought together in this volume might be published in a collective form. No one but the author could have done this as he would have wished it to be done: my part has been simply that of endeavouring to place them before the reader in the best shape which they can now assume without his revision and superintendence. The reader will remember that the articles themselves do not profess to give a continuous narrative, or to contain a complete history of the period to which they relate. They are, in fact, a commentary on the ministerial history of England, and they require to be read with a certain previous knowledge of the general outline of that history.

In the Review, for want of space, passages were omitted, and notes and references were curtailed. Where the original proofs exist (which is not the case with all the articles), these passages and notes have been restored. On the other hand, the text of the Review, where it differs from that of the proof, has, as a general rule, been considered as embodying the author's last corrections, and expressing his final opinions.

In the beginning of one of these articles, Sir George Lewis has, with much ability and judgment, discussed the various sources and the different kinds of history, and weighed their relative value. The practical teaching conveyed by any narrative, and its utility to us as a history, depend, of course, very much on the similarity which exists between the circumstances with which it deals, and the circumstances under which its lessons have to be applied. No history can be more valuable than that which supplies us with the key to the present action of our Government, and which explains the moral working of the laws and polity under which we live. To understand the nature of the English Constitution, and appreciate its results, the student must have traced its origin and watched its growth. The last motto applicable to it is the one adopted by Queen Elizabeth, 'semper eadem.' Every decade has made, and probably will make, some change in its action, if not in its principles, although the movement itself, like that of the hands of a watch, escapes the notice of those who see it only in their own time, and do not look backwards or forwards. At the end of fifty years, however, the effect of changes now going on, of which men are hardly conscious, will be seen, and their results will be felt to the benefit or the sorrow of our descendants. This progressive character of the English Constitution—which is, in fact, its excellence, and which accounts for its length of life—is peculiarly illustrated by the history of the times covered by these articles of Sir George Lewis's. The last half of the eighteenth, and the first quarter of the nineteenth century were fertile in those silent changes of which I have spoken above. Moreover, they stand from us just at that distance which enables us to draw from the contemplation of them the most complete and useful inferences. The circumstances are so similar to those under which we live, that we have little difficulty in understanding all the allusions relating to persons and things which occur in memoirs or in history. Many of us remember the events, or have heard them discussed when we were children; yet now we stand far enough from the time to enable us to take a general view of the facts, and to estimate impartially, if we choose to do so, the relations of men and parties to each other. When we are far removed by time or place, facts are doubtful and allusions unintelligible; when we are close upon the scene of action, and well acquainted with the persons concerned, our vision is distorted by our proximity or our prejudices—some points assume an exaggerated importance, and appear of vital consequence, which will hereafter prove to be secondary in their character, and will, when looked at in history from a distance, sink into comparative insignificance. On the other hand, circumstances which to the contemporary appeared trifling and unworthy of notice, may hereafter afford the historian and the statesman the real clue by which he will trace out the maze of politics and diplomacy. A contemporary record of facts and opinions is one thing; a contemporary judgment on the real meaning and value of those facts and opinions is another.

For these reasons then the period embraced in these Essays, illustrated as it is by letters and memoirs, is one of deep interest and instruction to all Englishmen; and it can hardly be doubted that the mind of Sir George Lewis was eminently adapted to the task of treating this history with profit to the reader. A narrative, or a comment on such narrative, even when the events themselves are interesting, is only instructive in the hands of a writer who can carry his reader with him, and who is conversant with the acts and motives of men in a broad and philosophical sense. In addition to these qualifications, and to his practical statesmanship, Sir George Lewis was singularly acute and industrious, as well as singularly impartial and fair.

He had opinions in politics; he was a Whig, and all his tendencies were liberal, but he was quite incapable of allowing his own feelings to taint a recital of facts or warp his judgment of motives. The reader will find many examples of this fairness in the articles themselves, and it never would have crossed the mind of the author that it was admissible to write on any other principle. Indeed, the striking feature of his character in politics, in literature and in private life, was his honest and straightforward simplicity. Trick or contrivance of any kind was alien from his nature. He never suffered party or personal motives to affect his judgment in any question, whether of literature or politics. He would not have thought of outwitting an opponent in public life by subterfuge or stratagem, any more than he would have tampered with a Greek quotation for the purpose of supporting a favourite philological dogma. He never failed to give what he thought its due weight to an argument because it was offered by an opponent, though he might differ from him as to the proper value to be assigned to it. Personal likings and personal enmities had as little to do with his opinions or conduct as personal interest. He rarely formed an opinion without looking at all sides of the question before him, or without having recourse to all accessible sources of information, which few knew so well where to seek as he himself did. He was deluded by no prejudices and jumped at no conclusions, without testing them by the application of sound common sense. When he had thus formed an opinion he adhered to it steadily, but not obstinately. He was ever open to argument, and he never refused to listen to it because it conflicted with his own view of the case. He had none of those crotchets or fancies lurking in his mind, which so often taint the reasoning of men of the highest abilities.

These peculiarities, as they struck an impartial observer, are well described by an American of the greatest intelligence and cultivation, in the following extract from a letter written to myself after Sir George Lewis's death :—

I knew him but little, but there was one quality in his mind of vast consequence to him as a statesman, and to his country, which was quickly apparent; I mean his *instinctive* fairness. He was singularly able and willing to change his opinion when new facts came to unsettle his old one. He seemed to do it too without regret. This struck me the first time I saw him, which was at breakfast at Lord Stanhope's in July 1856, and it was still more strongly apparent the next morning at breakfast at his own house, the conversation on both occasions having been much on American affairs, at the period just before Buchanan's election, and when Walker was making his wild filibustering attempts on the isthmus. And so it continued, I think, every time I saw him that summer and the next, down to the last dinner at his house, when we were together. I remember I used to think he had the greatest respect for FACTS of any man I ever saw, and an extraordinary power of determining from internal evidence what were such. I suppose this meant that the love of truth was the uppermost visible quality in his character.

Sir George Lewis's love of work and his diligence in research were no less remarkable than his impartiality and fairness. Such books as those on the Roman History and the History of Ancient Astronomy are wonderful proofs of industry, especially when we consider that the latter, like many others of his productions, was composed by way of relaxation from the toils of office. He could not be idle, and he could not waste his time on frivolous or trifling subjects. His scholarship was the result not only of early study and constant exercise, but it bore the stamp of that good sense and accuracy which characterised his whole mind. In a notice of *Paley's Theocritus*, inserted in the *Saturday Review* of October 10, 1863, the critic says:—

It comes forth as a finished edition, deserving a place in the same class and rank of editions as the Babrius of Sir G. C. Lewis, which is generally admitted to be a model and pattern of a compendious edition. This is no mean merit, for few professional editors of the classics have either that love of conciseness, or that abhorrence of waste of words, which characterised the scholarly productions of that most learned, yet withal most practical mind.

I will add to this testimony the few words prefixed by Dean Milman to the 3rd edition of his *History of the Jews*, which was going through the press at the time of Sir George Lewis's death:—

I may now express my full admiration of a man whose

recreation during the leisure afforded by his arduous and parliamentary duties — duties discharged as few can discharge them — were feats of scholarship which might try the erudition and research of the most recluse student. It is rare that a man who might have aspired to the very highest dignity in the State, might have done honour as Professor of Greek to the most learned university in Europe—*His saltem accumulem donis.*

My own knowledge of Sir George Lewis began about the year 1831, and I owed his acquaintance to a dear friend who died many years ago—one whose high character, gentle nature, and great abilities, would, if he had lived, undoubtedly have won for him a place by the side of his distinguished brothers. Had Edward Villiers survived to see this time, he would have mourned for a friend as deeply and as sincerely as his widowed sister now grieves for a husband. To me, at this moment, it is a painful task to attempt to describe Sir George Lewis's character, because at every word I feel how impossible it is to convey to others a true and adequate conception of him, whilst the endeavour to do so renews the sense of my own loss. An intimacy and constant correspondence of more than thirty years enables me to vouch with confidence for all that is stated in this preface.

Sir George Lewis might appear to strangers to be cold and reserved; to those who knew him well this was far from being the case. I have seen him smile with the most unaffected pleasure when he had succeeded in gratifying a friend, and I never knew him animated by any mean or ungenerous feeling. The petty jealousies and bitterness of politics or of literature were equally alien from his nature. His temper in public and in private life was calm and unruffled, and he bore no malice against any man. He was conciliatory in his demeanour to all, and his open frankness and candour were the genuine results of his personal character. All who knew him well will remember that his apparent gravity and thoughtfulness were really enlivened by a keen sense of humour, and a thorough appreciation of a joke.

No change in his own social or official position altered his cordiality or his affection towards his old friends, or made him more difficult of access. His manner was unchanged and his kindness undiminished. It was not in his nature to be affected by outward circumstances, and he was just as free from pretension when he was a cabinet minister, as he was when I first knew him as a young man.

The best testimony to Sir George Lewis's public worth was afforded by the universal sorrow occasioned by his death. There was a feeling that a statesman was taken from us whom we could ill spare: one to whom the country might have looked for sober thought and able guidance in the difficulties then impending. If we missed him then, we have good reason now to feel his loss quite as deeply, for those difficulties are greater now than they were last year. Domestic politics hang on a thread which grows weaker every day, and foreign affairs are in a more distracted state. In America the tide of war has gone on surging backwards and forwards without any decisive superiority to either side, whilst in Europe a gulf has opened, as it were, under our feet.

Sir George Lewis was listened to in the House of

Commons, not because he was eloquent, but because he never spoke unless he had something to say which was worth hearing. He expressed in plain and clear language an opinion which was founded on research, full consideration of the subject before him, and sound common sense. His mind had no tendency to exaggeration; he never made light of a danger, but, on the other hand, he never overrated an advantage for the purpose of producing an effect at the moment. His meaning was always clear, and his purpose honest and straightforward. The extent and variety of his knowledge was not more wonderful than its accuracy, and it is greatly to be wished that a collection of his smaller and miscellaneous writings should be published. His letters were full of information, and those which he wrote to me whilst I was absent from England in North America, were doubly interesting, because they narrated things which he would not have thought it necessary to write to a correspondent in England.

I cannot conclude this preface better than by adding a few extracts from some of these letters addressed to myself at different periods, which have been already printed.[1] The first of these are from letters written at Malta in the years 1836 and 1837.

At Marseilles we embarked on board a frigate, which had come from Smyrna, and therefore subjected us to the necessity of performing quarantine on our arrival at Malta. I found it a great mistake to suppose that there is no motion in large ships; a small vessel has moreover this advantage, that it is worked without there being a crew of 450 men to walk over one's head

[1] See *Edinburgh Review*, No. 241. Much of the substance of this preface will be found in a different form in that article.

during the chief part of the night. We had all kinds of foul winds and calms, and were ten days in reaching Malta. We saw the southern point of Sardinia, the north-west coast of Sicily, and a part of the coast of Africa near Cape Bon. We also remained about two days in sight of a hateful little island called Pantellaria.

Valetta is on the whole the most striking and beautiful town I ever saw; the indentations of the harbour, the extent and grandeur of the fortifications and their combination with the rock, and the terrace-like arrangement of the houses, form a collection of objects which no town that I know can equal. It resembles Edinburgh in some points—viz. the mixture of buildings and rock, and the rising of the streets in stories over one other. In other respects it is, of course, very different.

The French, of course, did much mischief in Malta, as in all other places which they occupied: among other things, they stripped the leaden roof off the '*Baraccas*'—large porticoes in which the knights used to walk in hot weather. They now serve for the same purpose in cold weather, as their uncovered walls exclude the wind while they admit the sun.

We found ourselves on our arrival much to our surprise floating down the full tide of popularity. We made a sort of triumphal entry (of course against our will) into the town. The streets were illuminated at night, and we were annoyed with all kinds of marks of respect. This state of things, however, has not been of long endurance, and we are already beginning to think of rotten eggs and dead cats. The people evidently thought, or were told, that we came out with a Maltese Magna Charta in our pockets; and when we summoned the chief complainants, and began to talk of enquiry, they were manifestly quite surprised, and seemed to think that we had merely to give a grind or two, and out would come a whole code of laws ready made. After three days of inane declamation on the part of the complainants, and of 'damnable iteration' on our part, they have at last begun to perceive that it will be necessary for us to investigate a subject before we report on it, and that in order to investigate we must take evidence. This sequence of propositions, which in England may seem tolerably clear, has only become manifest to our gentlemen by means of a long succession of the severest intellectual throes. It would have edified you to see the gravity which we maintained during the most ludicrous parts of the touching patriotic pathos addressed to us.

I have seen Hookham Frere, who found himself in Malta fourteen years ago at his wife's death, and has forgotten to return to England. He has translated four plays of Aristophanes and will, I imagine, publish them.

There is nothing in this island either ancient or remarkable in the way of art. The knights appear to have thought of nothing but building new forts, and enlarging the defences of Valetta. They have been so successful in this ambition, that the very extent of the fortifications is a source of weakness, inasmuch as it would take 20,000 men to man the works, if the town were regularly invested. This contingency, however, is most improbable, one may say almost impossible, so long as England retains the command of the sea. Nevertheless, the Ordnance are not satisfied unless they keep the place in a perpetual state of siege; and I hear that orders have lately come out from England to cut down some mulberry trees in one of the ditches. A well-fortified town may be an excellent contrivance in time of war, but it is an excessive inconvenience in time of peace. It takes between a quarter and half-an-hour of walking through narrow gates, and across ditches, and up steep steps, and under covered ways, to get clear of the defences, whenever one wishes to breathe some air. You can conceive Ehrenbreitstein on the scale of a town large enough to contain 50,000 people.

The native language of the Maltese is an Arabic dialect, which agrees pretty nearly with the Arabic spoken on the coast of Barbary, as far as Egypt. It has never been written and cannot even be said to have an alphabet. There are not, as far as I am aware, any literary compositions in it preserved by tradition.

The people are an Arab race descended from the Saracens, who obtained possession of the island. Their physiognomy bears a striking resemblance to the Jewish. They are a gloomy people; they never seem to laugh, or sing, or dance; their amusements, if such they can be called, are of a religious cast, such as processions on saints' days, &c. I hear that the country people pass the chief part of their Sundays and *giorni di festa* in the churches. They are exceedingly ignorant; and not unnaturally, as there has been no education for the poor, very little for the rich, and no free press. They are, however, by no means wanting in acuteness and ability. Their *practical talent* is, indeed, remarkable; and in this respect they appear to great advantage even by the side of the English, who (with their descendants) exceed all other nations in this quality. There is a pernicious race of nobles, who transmit their titles to all their sons, together with fortunes varying from 500*l.* to 40*l.* or 50*l.* a year, and a self-imposed inability to follow any money-making occupation. These people are ignorant, narrow-minded, stupid, and rapacious of public money; and it would be well if their titles could be abolished. As, however, they are now excessively poor, and they have no means of recruiting their fortunes by rich marriages: a few more descents, and divisions of property, must confound them with the middle and working classes. There is also a numerous body of priests, more than 1,000 (including the regulars), to a population of 120,000. The priests are for the most part bigoted and ignorant; but their influence has considerably declined of late years, and their incomes are most pitiful, varying from 10*l.* to 30*l.* or 40*l.* a year. The merchants, the advocates, the doctors, and the government employés form the really valuable part of the population. From the narrow policy of the government in discouraging education and discussion, there is a great want of *knowledge*, both of facts and principles, in these classes: but there is a very fair sprinkling of intelligence, and, on the whole, I should be very sanguine of the influence which might be produced upon them by a government which looked to improving the condition of the community.

The misery which prevails among the mass of the people is caused by the excess of their numbers. The great and unnatural commerce drawn into Malta by the Berlin and Milan decrees gave a stimulus to population, and also accustomed the working classes to a higher standard of living, from which they have now fallen. But the main cause of the over-population is the ignorant recklessness of the people, and the pernicious morality inculcated by the Catholic clergy as to the necessity of early marriage in order to prevent irregular intercourse. The world, always ready to find bad motives for every action, attribute this doctrine in Ireland and elsewhere to the desire of the clergy to augment their fees. In my opinion, their advice is perfectly disinterested; and is founded on a sincere conviction (however mistaken) that they are discharging an imperative religious duty. I am not at all clear that Protestant clergymen would not give just the same advice if the practice of confession afforded them the means of enforcing it.

The government has lately been making some changes in their charitable institutions, which we had recommended. The expenditure in charities is now 16,000*l.* a year out of a revenue of less than 100,000*l.* One of the institutions which we recommended to be gradually abolished was what in Italy is called a 'Conservatorio,' that is, a charity-boarding school for girls, who remain in it till they can get places or are married. On examining the girls in the conservatorio somewhat more closely than had hitherto been done, it has recently turned out that, although they have been regularly taught to read Italian, they never learnt the meaning of the words; and although there are some (who have been undergoing this process for several years) who can pronounce Italian to perfection, they cannot understand or speak a word of it. I hope this is not the way in which English is taught in Welsh schools.

The following extract is from a letter dated March 18, 1855, announcing his appointment as Chancellor of the Exchequer. It is eminently characteristic of the writer, and those who knew him well will not suspect him of any affectation when he professes his indifference, or rather his reluctance, to accept the high office then placed at his disposal.

Events have succeeded one another so closely with me of late, that I really have had no time to write to you. Soon after my return to London after my election, I received quite unexpectedly the offer of the office of Chancellor of the Exchequer in Lord Palmerston's Government. I had just returned from the country: I had had no time to look into my private affairs since my father's death. I had not even proved his will. I had the *Edinburgh Review* for April on my hands, and the last part of my volumes on the Roman History. I had been out of Parliament for two years, and I did not know the present House of Commons. I had to follow Gladstone, whose ability had dazzled the world, and to produce a war budget with a large additional taxation in a few weeks. All these circumstances put together inspired me with the strongest disinclination to accept the offer. I felt, however, that in the peculiar position of the Government, the office having already been refused by ——, refusal was scarcely honourable, and would be attributed to cowardice, and I therefore most reluctantly made up my mind to accept. I remembered the pope, put in hell by Dante,

> Che fece per viltade il gran rifiuto.

My re-election passed off without difficulty. I went down to Harpton for two nights and made a speech in the Town Hall at Radnor. Since my return to London I have been engrossed with the business of my office, and have hardly had a moment to spare. There is an awkward question about the newspaper stamp, which I have had to plunge into. There are also all the preparations to be made for the impending budget, and measures to be taken for providing sufficient sums to meet the enormous extraordinary expenditure which the war in the Crimea is causing. Gladstone has been very friendly to me, and has given me all the assistance in his power.

In 1856 I had sent him a lecture of Dana's on Mr. Charles Sumner, and his reply is most remarkable. It shows very plainly how thoroughly he understood the position of affairs in America. Many men had foretold the separation of the Northern from the Southern states, but very few appreciated the significance of the assault committed within the walls of the Senate House at Washington. He saw clearly, not that the storm was possible, but that the first blow in the great quarrel had already been struck.

Dana's lecture on Sumner is very interesting. It illustrates the relations of the South and North, and their feelings to one another. People here speak of the outrage on Sumner as a proof of the brutal manners of the Americans, and their low morality. To me it seems the first blow in a civil war. It betokens the advent of a state of things in which political differences cannot be settled by argument, and can only be settled by force. If half England was in favour of a measure which involved the confiscation of the property of the other half, my belief is that an English Brooks would be equally applauded. If Peel had proposed a law which, instead of reducing rents had annihilated them, instead of being attacked by a man of words such as Disraeli, he would probably have been attacked with physical arguments by some man of blows. I see no solution of the political differences of the United States, but the separation of the Slave and Free States into distinct political communities. If I was a citizen of a Northern State I should wish it. I should equally wish it if I was a citizen of a Southern State. In the Northern States the English race would remain unimpaired. But I cannot help suspecting that it degenerates under a warmer sun, and that a community formed of Anglo-Saxon masters within the tropics, and of negro slaves would degenerate. I see no reason why the pure English breed should not be kept up in the Northern Provinces and the Northern States. It may also be kept up in Australia, which has a climate suited to our race, and has fortunately been kept untainted by the curse of coloured slavery.

A similar view of the subject is expressed in a later letter (November 5) of the same year, 1856:

The United States seem to me to have come nearer to a

separation of North and South than they ever were before. I take for granted that Buchanan will win. The Southern States are thoroughly in earnest. They are fighting for their property. The Northern States have only a principle at stake; they will be less united and less eager. At the same time it is not at all clear that they can continue to form one State, or rather one political body; and they may reach a point when, like a married couple who cannot agree, they may part by common consent. Each may find his account in a separation.

At a much later time (May 15, 1861), he wrote as follows: —

The Northern States have drifted or rather plunged into war without having any intelligible aim or policy. The South fight for independence; but what do the North fight for, except to gratify passions and pride? —— in his curious letter talks of averting anarchy, but if the North had remained quiet they had nothing to fear from anarchy.

In an earlier letter of the same year, before the war had broken out, he said:

The refusal of Tennessee and Arkansas to join the new confederacy may give some hopes of a compromise, but I cannot see how men who have committed themselves so far as the leaders of the Secession movement, can be expected to come back except upon such terms as they themselves would dictate. They would not only lose their present position, but they would scarcely be safe from proscription, if they acquiesced in the re-establishment of the old Union, and thus to a certain extent put themselves in the power of a republican executive.

With these extracts I must close this preface, which contains a most imperfect record of Sir George Lewis's personal qualities and merits, written by one who had full opportunity of knowing them, and who lives to lament a loss which can never be supplied. His literary labours speak for themselves in his published works, and the small specimen contained in the following pages is offered to the general reader only as a sample of their excellence.

E. W. H.

CONTENTS.

ESSAYS

ON THE

ADMINISTRATIONS OF GREAT BRITAIN

FROM 1783 TO 1830.

I.[1]

ADMINISTRATIONS OF LORD NORTH, LORD ROCKINGHAM, LORD SHELBURNE, THE COALITION, AND MR. PITT.

THESE two publications throw so much light on the political history of England during the latter part of the last century, that, although they are both unfinished, we think it right to give our readers an account of their contents, without waiting for their completion.

The late Lord Holland, having abandoned his original design of writing the life of his uncle, Mr. Fox, made a full compilation of authentic materials for his biography, partly consisting of letters and other documents, partly of records of the recollections of his surviving friends. Lord Holland, unhappily, left this compilation unfinished at his death; but it afterwards passed into the hands of his

[1] Review of—1. *Memorials and Correspondence of Charles James Fox.* Edited by Lord John Russell. 2 vols. 8vo. London: 1853.—2. *Memoirs of the Court and Cabinets of George the Third, from original Family Documents.* By the Duke of Buckingham and Chandos, K.G. 2 vols. 8vo. Second edition, revised. London: 1853.

confidential friend, Mr. Allen, who was in every way qualified to complete the work which had been thus begun. Mr. Allen appears to have brought the materials into a state fitted for publication — but the MS. was not sent to the press, and it passed into the possession of Lord John Russell by the bequest of the late Lady Holland. Lord John has now given it to the world in the state in which it was left by Lord Holland and Mr. Allen, but with the addition of some ably-written and judicious comments of his own. As the work consists of a substratum of original materials, illustrated by the independent annotations of three commentators, which are distinguished by certain typographical marks, it presents (as Lord John observes) 'a disjointed and irregular appearance.' It has the form of a collection of Fox manuscripts, with *variorum* notes. Nevertheless it contains so much authentic information, accompanied with criticism so intelligent and so candid, that no Englishman who desires to understand the history of his country between the years 1768 and 1792 can fail to read it with advantage and pleasure. Lord John, indeed, says of the work which he edits, 'that its greatest value will be found in the letters of Mr. Fox to Lord Holland, written between 1790 and 1805. *These letters are more literary than political*, and show how keen was Mr. Fox's enjoyment of poetry, especially Greek and Italian.' Of the series of letters thus described only a few appear in these volumes; but we think that Lord John scarcely does justice to the value of the documents and papers which he has already published; for many of them are highly important, and the period to which they relate comprises the most active and prominent portion of Fox's political life.[1]

[1] There exist two biographical accounts of Mr. Fox. One is entitled *Memoirs of the Public Life of the late Right Honourable C. J. Fox*, by R. Fell,

The materials for the publication to which the name of the Duke of Buckingham is attached are family papers which have been preserved at Stowe. There are some interesting letters written by Mr. Thomas Grenville when employed in diplomatic service on the Continent; but by far the most valuable portion of the work consists of the letters of Mr. William Grenville (afterwards Lord Grenville) to his elder brother, the Marquis of Buckingham. These letters were evidently written in the strictest confidence, without premeditation, and with no idea that they would ever be given to the public. For this reason they cannot fairly be compared with official or semi-official letters, which are composed in a guarded and reserved style. But, on account of their familiar and unstudied character, they afford the stronger evidence of the sagacity, judgment, and undeviating good temper of their distinguished author. The task of editing the valuable materials which he had extracted from his family archives has been committed by the Duke of Buckingham to some person whose ignorance of the events and persons of the period, and whose consequent incapacity for the work, almost exceed belief. Most of the errors of this scandalously incompetent editor have been already pointed out by a contemporary;[1] but are nevertheless, with a few exceptions, faithfully reproduced in the new edition.[2]

in 2 vols. 8vo. 1808. The other is *Memoirs of the latter Years of the Right Honourable C. J. Fox*, by J. B. Trotter, Esq. late private secretary to Mr. Fox. 1 vol. 8vo. 1811. Neither work is at all satisfactory.

[1] Thus the strange blunder that the Marquis of Rockingham 'was succeeded in his title by his nephew, the Earl Fitzwilliam,' stands uncorrected in vol. i. p. 48, of the new and revised edition. Seeing that the present Earl Fitzwilliam is the son and immediate successor of the Earl Fitzwilliam who is supposed to have inherited the title of Rockingham, it might have occurred to the editor to doubt the accuracy of his statement.

[2] Even after the rich harvest of blunders gathered in by the *Quarterly* reviewer, a few still remain to be gleaned. Thus in vol. i. p. 185, Lord

Before the continuation of this work is published, we trust that an editor may be found who has heard of the

Grenville, in giving a rumoured list of the Coalition Cabinet, says: 'Lord Keppel to return. Query, whether he is by this means to be in the Cabinet with Twitcher? I think he should appoint *St. Hugh* a Junior Lord.' By *Twitcher* is meant Lord Sandwich, who was supposed to have instigated the court-martial against Lord Keppel. *St. Hugh* is evidently a misprint for *Sir Hugh*; that is, Sir Hugh Palliser, whose bitter feud with Lord Keppel is well known. At the end of the letter, the quotation 'amicitiæ sempiternæ, inimicitiæ placabiles,' is used sarcastically in reference to Fox, who had cited the sentence in the House of Commons as a justification of the Coalition (February 17, 1783).

In vol. i. p. 372, the following passage occurs in one of Lord Grenville's letters: 'We are a little uneasy on account of Tippoo, who had made peace with the Mahrattas, and was collecting his forces with a view of attacking the Nizam, or the Rajah of *Gravancore,* whom we must protect, or the *Camatre* itself.' For *Gravancore* read *Travancore,* and for *Camatre* read *Carnatic.*

Again, in p. 416: 'You have never sent me any answer about the Cranbourne *chair* proposal, by which means that business is delayed;' where for '*chair*' read '*chase.*'

In vol. ii. p. 52, William Gerard Hamilton is, by the interposition of a comma, divided into two persons, Gerard and Hamilton.

In vol. ii. p. 393, Lord Grenville writes on May 25, 1798: 'O'Connor's acquittal is imputed to *Miller's* charge, and *that* to his being completely exhausted, so as to omit some of the most material points in the evidence.' Who ever heard of Judge *Miller* at the end of the last century? The reference is to the celebrated case of O'Quigley, Arthur O'Connor, and three others, who were tried for treason at Maidstone, on May 21 and 22, 1798. The judge who summed up was Mr. Justice *Buller*; O'Quigley was convicted, and afterwards hanged; Arthur O'Connor, and the three others, were acquitted.

In the following sentence from a letter written by Lord Grenville, in November, 1788, a negative appears to be wanting: 'The party in general are so hungry and impatient, that I think they will [? not] act upon the better judgment of their leaders, and prevent them from doing anything which allows a moment's delay' (vol. ii. p. 24).

While the editor details at length those well-known events which may be found in the *Annual Register,* or any ordinary history of the time, he omits to explain those less obvious allusions on which a reader is most likely to desire explanation. Thus in vol. i. p. 258, Lord Grenville writes, on May 7, 1783: 'I am in some doubt what to do about coming over to you, as on account of *the prince's death,* there is no levée to-day, nor, I fear, on Friday.' The prince here alluded to is Prince Octavius, son of George III.

duel between Pitt and Tierney, and who knows that Cuxhaven is not in Ireland.

Mr. Fox was first returned to the Parliament which met on May 10, 1768, being then only nineteen years and four months old. He sat for the borough of Midhurst; his seat having, as it appears, been purchased by his father, Lord Holland. He came into Parliament as a supporter of the Government, of which the Duke of Grafton was then the head; and was, following his father's politics, an eager opponent of Wilkes. He began, even at the age of twenty, to show his remarkable powers of parliamentary debate; and some of his earliest speeches, as we learn from the unwilling testimony of Horace Walpole, produced a strong impression upon the House.[1] In February 1770—being in his twenty-first year—he accepted the office of a Junior Lord of the Admiralty, shortly after the appointment of Lord North as First Minister, upon the resignation of the Duke of Grafton.[2] In the Session of 1772, Mr. Fox

who died on May 3, at Kew Palace, of inoculation for the small-pox, aged four years.

In vol. ii. p. 63: 'I was a little mortified at finding our friend Sir P. P. among them.' Sir P. P. is Sir Peter Parker, as appears by a list in a subsequent page, p. 83.

Vol. ii. p. 139: 'Pitt authorises me to say that he could find the means of opening a ten shilling government for him in England immediately.' A ten shilling government is a small military command with a pay of ten shillings per diem.

Vol. ii. p. 377: In a letter of May 3, 1797, Lord Grenville says to Lord Buckingham: 'Have you seen *my prince*? He is sensible and well-informed, though not exactly the picture of a young lover.' The prince alluded to is the Prince of Wirtemberg, who was married to the Princess Royal on May 13, 1797, and whose figure, of extraordinary obesity, was certainly not that of a young lover.

[1] Both Fox and Pitt showed their uncommon powers of parliamentary speaking from their earliest attempts. Sir R. Walpole, on the other hand, who for courage, readiness, and dexterity in debate, was afterwards second to none, failed in his first speech. See *Lord Mahon's History*, vol. i. p. 265. Ed. 12mo.

[2] The popular belief that Lord Bute continued to exercise a secret influ-

1772. made a motion for the repeal of the Marriage Act; on which occasion Horace Walpole—a witness whose language must not always be construed strictly—gives the following account:—

When he had moved this repeal, he had not read the Marriage Act, nor did he till some days after. A few evenings before he had been at Brompton on two errands; one, to consult Justice Fielding on the penal laws, the other to borrow 10,000*l.* which he brought to town at the hazard of being robbed. As the gaming and extravagance of young men of quality had arrived now at a pitch never heard of, it is worth while to give some account of it. They had a club at Almack's, in Pall Mall, where they played only for rouleaus of 50*l.* each, and generally there was 10,000*l.* in specie on the table. Lord Holland had paid above 20,000*l.* for his two sons. Nor were the manners of the gamesters, or even their dresses for play, undeserving notice. They began by pulling off their embroidered clothes and put on frieze great coats, or turned their coats inside outwards for luck. They put on pieces of leather (such as are worn by footmen when they clean the knives) to save their laced ruffles; and to guard their eyes from the light, and to prevent tumbling their hair, wore high-crowned straw hats with broad brims, and adorned with flowers and ribbons; masks to conceal their emotions when they played at quinze. Each gamester had a small neat stand by him to hold their tea, or a wooden bowl with an edge of ormolu to hold their rouleaus. They borrowed great sums of Jews at exorbitant premiums. Charles Fox called his outward room, where those Jews waited till he rose, his Jerusalem Chamber (*Mem. of Fox*, vol. i. p. 70).

ence over the King, after his retirement from office, is, we may remark, conclusively refuted by the evidence adduced in vol. i. pp. 65-68, of the *Memorials of Fox*. [Yet Mr. John George Phillimore, in his recent *History of England in the Reign of George III.* vol. i. p. 387, n. asserts his firm belief in the continuance of Lord Bute's secret influence, certainly till the death of the Princess Dowager on September 3, 1764. I confess that the suppressed passages from Lord Chesterfield's letters, quoted by him, seem to me to afford very insufficient reasons for doubting the conclusion arrived at by Sir George Lewis in this note.—Ed.]

On the 20th of February 1772, Fox, being then in his twenty-third year, resigned his seat at the Admiralty Board. His resignation was due, partly to some personal discontent with Lord North, but chiefly to his intention of opposing the Royal Marriage Act, a measure then in preparation, much desired by the King, but reluctantly adopted by his Ministers. While the Bill was pending in Parliament, the King wrote to Lord North in the following terms: 'I expect every nerve to be strained to carry the Bill. It is not a question relating to administrations, *but personally to myself;* therefore I have a right to expect a hearty support from every one in my service, *and I shall remember defaulters.*' It is evident from the King's language that no person who voted against this Bill could continue to hold office under the Crown. Fox took an active part in opposing it during its passage through the House of Commons. 'In the course of the debates (says Horace Walpole) I have given very inadequate ideas of the speeches of Burke, Charles Fox, and Wedderburne, three excellent orators in different ways. Burke's wit, allusions, and enthusiasm were striking, but not imposing; Wedderburne was a sharp, clever arguer, though unequal; Charles Fox, much younger than either, was universally allowed to have seized the just point of argument throughout with most amazing rapidity and clearness, and to have excelled even Charles Townshend as a Parliament man, though inferior in wit and variety of talents. 1772.

Fox afterwards introduced his Bill for amending the Marriage Act: it was opposed by Lord North and by Burke, and was ultimately thrown out. Walpole's account of Burke's speech against this Bill is remarkable with reference to his subsequent career:—

Burke made a fine and long oration against the motion. Burke was certainly in his principles no moderate man; and

1772. when his party did not interfere, generally leaned to the more arbitrary side, as had appeared in the late debates on the Church, in which he had declared for the clergy. . . . He spoke with a choice and variety of language, a profusion of metaphors, and yet with a correction of diction that were surprising. His fault was copiousness above measure; and he dealt abundantly, too much, in establishing general positions. *Two-thirds of this oration resembled the beginning of a book on speculative doctrines, and yet argument was not the forte of it.*

This first breach between Mr. Fox and Lord North was not of long duration; for in December of the same year, 1772, an arrangement was made, by which the former returned to office and became a Junior Lord of the Treasury. His habits of deep play, however, unhappily continued unbroken, and in order to pay his gaming debts, he actually incurred liabilities to the enormous amount of 140,000*l.* which sum was discharged by his father from his own estate.[1] A strange story is likewise told by Horace Walpole (the truth of which is recognised by Lord Holland) of his having been at this time duped by an impostor calling herself the *Hon. Mrs. Grieve*, who undertook to procure for him as wife, a Miss Phipps,

[1] The following curious account of the occurrences of this time, given to Lord Holland in 1823, by Lord Egremont, is worthy of attention by all persons who are in the habit of high play: 'Lord Egremont was convinced,' he said, 'by reflection, aided by his subsequent experience of the world, that there was at that time some unfair confederacy among some of the players, and that the great losers, especially Mr. Fox, were actually duped and cheated; he should, he said, have been torn to pieces, and stoned by the losers themselves, for hinting such a thing at the time, and even now, those of them, himself excepted, who survived, would exclaim at such a supposition; but he was nevertheless satisfied, that the immoderate, constant, and unparalleled advantages over Charles Fox, and other young men, were not to be accounted for merely by the difference of passing or holding the box, or the hazard of the dice. He had indeed no suspicions (any more than the rest had) at the time, but he had thought it much over since, and he now had.'

recently arrived from the West Indies, with a fortune of 80,000*l.* 1774.

In the session of 1774, Mr. Fox, impatient of the restraints to which a member holding a subordinate office is subject, differed from Lord North and took an independent line with respect to the committal of Woodfall the printer for a breach of privilege. The King, who appears to have conceived a personal dislike to Fox on account of his opposition to the Royal Marriage Bill, was much displeased at his conduct on this occasion, and, on February 15th, wrote thus to Lord North :—

> I am greatly incensed at the presumption of Charles Fox in forcing you to vote with him last night, but approve much of the making your friends vote in the majority. Indeed, that young man has so strongly cast off every principle of common honour and honesty, that he must become as contemptible as he is odious. I hope you will let him know that you are not insensible of his conduct towards you.[1]

On a subsequent stage of the same proceeding, Fox repeated his insubordination to North, who, in consequence, sent him a laconic letter, informing him that he was no longer a Lord of the Treasury. Fox now put an end to his connection with Lord North, went into Opposition, and began to act with the Rockingham party,

[1] George III. commented very freely on the public men whom he disliked, in his letters to Lord North. Thus, in a letter of August 1775, he speaks of Lord Chatham's recent political conduct as 'abandoned;' he describes Lord Chatham as totally devoid of the honourable sentiment of gratitude, and calls him 'a trumpet of sedition' (*Mem. of Fox,* vol. i. p. 129). In letters of March 16, 1778, he speaks of 'Lord Chatham and his crew;' and calls him 'that perfidious man.' It seems to be ascertained that George III. had an attack of insanity (concealed from the public) so early as the year 1765. See *Adolphus's History of the Reign of George III.* vol. i. p. 175, ed. 1840; *Lord Mahon's History,* vol. v. p. 96. Nevertheless, the letters of Lord Grenville during the King's illness in 1788-9 (in the Buckingham Papers), convince us that the Ministers had, at that time, no suspicion of his having been previously insane. See particularly a letter in vol. ii. p. 5.

1774. though he did not formally join it till 1778 or '79. By this means he became the friend of Burke; a friendship which exercised much influence upon him. His independent political career, after he had broken through his original party ties, may be considered as commencing from 1774, when he was in his twenty-fifth year. This year, as Lord John Russell remarks, in an excellent review of our history from 1763 to 1774 (vol. i. p. 102–133), was the turning point of the American war. It was then that Lord North, though he had originally been adverse to the imposition of the tea duty, decided to maintain it, by closing the port of Boston, and altering the charter of Massachussets. 'In taking this course,' says Lord John, 'Lord North was warmly supported in the closet, and received the sympathy of the country. Yet it is impossible not to reflect that Lord North was the same minister who in 1768 had, by his voice in the Cabinet, prevented the repeal of the tea duty, and the abandonment of all taxation by Parliament for imperial purposes.[1] Had he supported that repeal in 1768, he would have prevented the American war; in 1774 he at least would have given a chance to peace; in 1778, after our armies had been defeated, the concession was useless and insufficient.'

Fox, from the time that he separated himself from Lord North, carried on an unremitting opposition to the

[1] The division in the Cabinet of 5 to 4, by which it was decided to maintain the tea duty, was not in 1768, but on May 1, 1769. See *Lord Mahon's History*, vol. v. p. 242, and App. p. xxxvii. The votes were as follow:—

For repeal.	*Against it.*
Duke of Grafton.	Lord President.
Lord Chancellor Camden.	Lord North.
Lord Granby.	Lord Rochford.
General Conway.	Lord Hillsborough.
	Lord Weymouth.

On such slight circumstances do great events sometimes turn.

American war. His speeches, always marked by decided ability, had hitherto been desultory and occasional; but he now (as Gibbon said) discovered powers for regular debate, which neither his friends hoped, nor his enemies dreaded. Mr. Grattan (as we learn from Lord John), who had heard Mr. Fox at various epochs, declared his preference for the speeches delivered during the American war, to all the other efforts of his eloquence. His denunciations of Ministers and their policy were conveyed in the strongest language. Thus in 1777 he described Lord G. Germaine, as 'that inauspicious and ill-omened character, whose arrogance and presumption, whose ignorance and inability,' had brought evil upon the country.[1] Horace Walpole says, that on the budget in 1778, 'Charles Fox poured out the bitterest and one of the finest of all his philippics against Lord North, taxing him with breach of honour in having declared that he would resign if his first conciliatory proposition had not the desired effect; that he had broken his word; that he had this year brought measures of the same kind, at which he confessed he felt humbled, though not ashamed; if such measures did not make him blush, what would? And in this style he spoke for above half an hour.' 1777.

The following curious account of a scene in an American debate in 1777 occurs in a letter of Mr. Crawford (better known by his prenomen of *Fish*) to Lord Ossory:—

Charles [Fox] spoke with great violence, but the House this

[1] On this occasion 'Lord North handsomely defended Lord George, and said he was glad Fox had abandoned him, an old hulk, to attack a man-of-war; but afterwards he perhaps hurt Lord George as much as Fox had done, for the latter coming up to the Treasury benches, Lord North said, in Lord George's hearing, "Charles, I am glad you did not fall on me to-day, for you were in full feather"' (*Mem. of Fox,* vol. i. p. 159). This anecdote proves the private familiarity which still subsisted between Lord North and Fox, notwithstanding their political differences.

1777. time went along with him. We were not shocked at his talking of bringing Lord George [Germaine] to a *second* trial, nor were we shocked at being asked if we could patiently continue to submit to see this nation disgraced by him in *every* capacity.[1] There were high words between Wedderburne and Burke, which so offended the latter that he went out of the House, and, I believe, intended to challenge Wedderburne, but was prevented by a letter from Wedderburne, and an explanation likewise, which he sent him through Charles. In the midst of Wedderburne's speaking, Burke burst into one of his loud hysterical laughs. Unfortunately at that moment there was a dead silence in the House. Wedderburne, in a very angry tone, said, that if that gentleman did not know manners, he, as an individual, would teach them to him; that he had not the good will of that gentleman, and did not wish for it, but he was ambitious of having even his respect, and would force it from him, &c. This the other construed into a menace. . . . . I have given this imperfect description of a quarrel, which is very well settled on both sides. Burke was originally in the wrong, because nothing could be more uncivil than his laugh appeared to be, from the accident of the dead silence of the House at that moment (*Mem. of Fox*, vol. i. p. 162).

The efforts of the Opposition in denouncing the policy of Lord North's Government were not unavailing, for in a letter to Lord Ossory of November 29,1777, Fox says, 'I am clear the opinion of the majority of the House is with us. I cannot help flattering myself that opinions will, in the long run, have their influence on votes.' A few months later (February, 1778) he uses the following remarkable expressions respecting himself in a letter to his intimate friend Fitzpatrick, who was then in America :—

I think I have given you enough of politics, considering I

[1] The allusion is to Lord G. Germaine's conduct at the battle of Minden, in 1759, for which he was dismissed by Mr. Pitt from all his military employments, and was declared by a court-martial to have been guilty of disobeying orders, and to be unfit to serve His Majesty in any military capacity whatever.

have nothing but reports and conjectures to give you. With respect to my own share, I can only say that people flatter me that I continue to gain, rather than lose, my credit as an orator; and I am so convinced that this is all that I ever shall gain (unless I choose to become the meanest of men) that I never think of any other object of ambition. I am certainly ambitious by nature, but I really have, or think I have, totally subdued that passion. I have still as much vanity as ever, which is a happier passion by far; because great reputation I think I may acquire and keep, great situation I never can acquire, nor, if acquired, keep, without making sacrifices that I never will make. If I am wrong, and more sanguine people right, *tant mieux*, and I shall be as happy as they can be; but if I am right, I am sure I shall be the happier, for having made up my mind to my situation.

1778.

The influence, however, which Fox had gained in the House by his speeches against the Ministry, and the waning popularity of the war since the reverses of our arms, especially after the surrender of Saratoga in October 1777, led to a negotiation with Fox in March 1778, to induce him to join Lord North's Ministry. This negotiation (to which the King's consent had doubtless been obtained) was conducted by Mr. Eden (afterwards Lord Auckland), whose account of his interview of three hours with Fox is now published. Fox is reported to have said, 'that except with Lord G. Germaine, he could act with the existing Ministers; but he disavowed every possibility of accepting singly and alone, and even doubted whether he could accept in any case.' 'I am convinced,' adds Mr. Eden, 'that he will make no bad use of the conversation, but in other respects will be as hostile as ever.' A similar overture was made at the same time, through Mr. Eden to Lord Shelburne, whose chief political connection was with Lord Chatham; and through him an attempt was made to ascertain the terms upon which Lord Chatham would join

1778. the Government. It is, however, evident that the King did not meditate any fundamental change of policy, or any real concession to the views of the Opposition. He was ready to engraft men of ability into the Ministry, but merely with a view of strengthening it, not of altering its measures. This appears clearly from a curious passage in Mr. Eden's account of his interview with Lord Shelburne. In the course of a discussion on certain changes of office, Lord Shelburne had made the remark, that, 'surely there would be some mode of doing everything right, without doing anything harsh.'

'This,' says Mr. Eden, 'gave me the opening I wished, to enter fully, and in the plainest language, into the narrowness, nonsense, and harshness of the whole proposition, so far as implied a wish and expectation in his lordship's friend at Hayes [Lord Chatham] to avail himself of the pressure of a moment in order to dictate terms to the closet, every part of which would imply a desertion and disavowal of servants who for many years had fought the cause of their master, of the Parliament, and of the whole nation, with the most cordial fidelity and zeal; and this, too, upon principles of the purest kind, the truth of which remains unimpaired, though mischances and circumstances may make it more difficult to enforce them. I added, that though uninformed and unauthorised as to any specific resolutions taken, I could argue safely from sentiments of honour which I knew to be firmly rooted, and could at once say *that no arrangement could or would ever be listened to one moment except on the ground of mere accession of capacity and business*; in a moment which would require great exertions, and that even such accessions could not be taken, unless made in a plan consistent with the honour of all that had passed heretofore' (vol. i. p. 185).[1]

[1] Concerning this negotiation through Lord Shelburne with Lord Chatham, see *Lord Mahon's History*, c. 57, vol. vi. p. 223-226. Lord Mahon remarks: 'It is certain that the object of the King was at this juncture wholly unattainable, that if Lord North retired as not willing or not able to carry his system further, *no other Administration on the same system could be formed.*' This opinion seems to us perfectly correct, but the plan of a coalition can

The limited extent of the King's views in consenting to these negotiations, and his resolution to continue the anti-American policy, so long as he could find Ministers who would support him, are fully displayed in his letters to Lord North at this period. In a letter of the 16th of March 1778, he thus expresses himself: 'I will only add, *to put before your eyes my most inward thoughts*, that no advantage to this country, nor personal danger to myself, can ever make me address myself to Lord Chatham, or any other branch of Opposition. Honestly, I would rather lose the crown I now wear than bear the ignominy of possessing it under their shackles.' On the following day he writes thus: 'My dear Lord, no consideration in life shall make me stoop to Opposition. I am still ready to accept any part of them that will come to the assistance of my present efficient Ministers; but whilst any ten men in the kingdom will stand by me, I will not give myself up to bondage. My dear Lord, I will rather risk my crown than do what I think personally disgraceful. It is impossible this nation should not stand by me. If they will not, they shall have another king; for I never will put my hand to what will make me miserable to the last hour of my life.' On the 22nd, the King says: 'I will never consent to removing the members of the present Cabinet from my service;' and on the 29th he puts this question to Lord North: 'Do you think it possible to strengthen the present Administration by an accession of some men of talents from the Opposition?' He then adds: 'If that cannot be effected, will you consent to continue, and try to exert yourself, and cooperate with me in putting vigour and activity into every department?' Again, on the 29th of January 1779, the King addresses Lord North in the same strain: 'I

1778.

hardly be called 'the King's object.' It was the King's aversion; and he was only willing to consent to it on terms which rendered it impossible.

1779. perceive, as I expected, that Opposition, when they talk of conditions, mean to dictate. I thank God, that whatever difficulties may surrouud me, I am not made of materials to stoop to that.' And on February 4: 'My conduct will show that I never am deaf to any apparent proposals of general union, though no circumstances shall ever compel me to be dictated to by Opposition.'

If George III. had understood his position as a constitutional king, he would at this time have consented to form a new Ministry from the leaders of Opposition, and have acquiesced, without querulous and undignified protestations, in a policy which in a few years was forced upon his acceptance by the general feeling of the country, and at the point of the parliamentary bayonet.

Lord Holland remarks upon these declarations, that 'the King was willing to employ any one who would concur with him in his efforts to reduce the revolted colonies to obedience, but would not accept the services of Opposition, because the Opposition thought that object unattainable, and were ready to acknowledge the independence of the United States. The result is, that it was the King at that period, and the King only, who prevented a coalition of parties, and peace with America.' From this view Lord J. Russell justly, as we think, dissents: 'I cannot,' he says, 'concur in this last remark. The King's determination to carry on the war in all quarters of the globe could have had no practical influence had not Lord North consented to remain Minister, to carry on a war of which he disapproved, and had not a majority of the House of Commons supported a system which they believed in their hearts to be fraught with danger to the country. The power of a single will was indeed conspicuous; but the Constitution afforded ample means of overruling that will, had the Minister obeyed his own convictions, or had the

House of Commons been true to the people they represented.' 1779.

In the summer of 1779, fresh overtures to the leaders of Opposition were made for the formation of a Coalition Government, in which Lord Weymouth was to be First Lord of the Treasury, and Thurlow Chancellor; Lords North, G. Germaine, Suffolk, Sandwich, Dartmouth, and some others, were to retire, and their places were to be filled up by Lord Rockingham and his friends, or they were to take in the Duke of Grafton and Lords Camden and Shelburne. This overture was rejected by Lord Rockingham's party, somewhat too hastily and peremptorily, in Mr. Fox's judgment: 'You think,' wrote Mr. Fox to Lord Rockingham, shortly afterwards, 'you can best serve the country by continuing a fruitless opposition; *I think it impossible to serve it at all but by coming into power*; and go even so far as to think it irreconcilable with the duty of a public man to refuse it, if offered to him in a manner consistent with his private honour, and so as to enable him to form fair hopes of doing essential service.' The wisdom of this refusal is most ably vindicated in an admirable letter from the Duke of Richmond to Mr. Fox, which its length prevents us from extracting, but which we strongly commend to the reader's attentive perusal (vol. i. p. 213).[1] The Duke of Richmond shows that the offer was too vague for acceptance; and that the Whigs, who might have joined the Government, would have had no security that their principles would be acted on.

[1] [This letter, which fully deserves the character given of it in the text, is too long for insertion even in this volume. It fills ten pages of Lord Russell's first volume. The principle laid down by the Duke of Richmond is: 'In a Ministry to be composed of men who have hitherto professedly differed in principles, as well as in the mode of conducting them, it is surely necessary, unless men look at nothing but employment, to begin by having a right understanding of the conduct to be pursued.'—Ed.]

1779. 'If,' he says, 'we are not to make the arrangement, and are yet to be supposed to have the management of affairs, it becomes surely not only fair, but necessary that we should have a specific description of that share of Government proposed for us, which is to give us the means, weight, and authority to carry our measures; or if it is not intended that we are to direct the measures, it is necessary we should have a precise idea of those to which we are called to accede. *Without one of these it is merely an offer of places without power, under a bargain to screen those whom we have been so long condemning.* Such an offer I am sure you will approve of our rejecting with indignation.' It is evident, from what we now know of the King's feelings, that if Lord Rockingham and his friends had met this overture with a less decided refusal at the threshold, and had shown a willingness to entertain the proposal, they would speedily have found that the King was only willing to admit them on terms inconsistent with their principles and personal honour, and that the negotiation would have immediately come to an end. Thus far we assent to the view so well enforced in the Duke of Richmond's letter; at the same time we think, with Fox, that it was a most important matter for the interests of the country at that moment to break up Lord North's Government, which object would have been accomplished, if several of the Whig leaders could have been introduced into the Cabinet without compromising their principles; and although we do not believe that the King would have allowed an Administration so constituted to remain in power for six months, we deem it highly improbable that, in the existing state of public affairs, he would have been able to resuscitate as bad a Government as that which continued in office until 1782.

In the summer of 1780, soon after Lord G. Gordon's riots, overtures for a junction were again made to Lord

Rockingham through Mr. Frederic Montague.[1] In a memorandum of instructions for this negotiation, found among Lord North's papers, it is stated: 'No difficulty about Dukes of Portland and Manchester, Mr. Townshend, Mr. Burke, and Mr. Fox; but Lord [North] advises that Mr. Fox should at first be proposed for an office that would not lead immediately to the closet.' The leaders of Opposition entertained this proposal, and offered to treat upon certain conditions, of which the two following were the most important:— 1780.

1. The American war requires no discussion, as they did not see how the troops could be recalled from thence, and the dependence of America need not at present be taken into consideration.

2. That some public measures must be admitted to enable them to coalesce with reputation, such as Mr. Crewe's Bill, the Contractors' Bill, and a part, if not the whole, of Mr. Burke's Bill.

As soon, however, as the King was made aware of these conditions, the negotiation received its *quietus* from the following remarks addressed by His Majesty, in his own royal style of composition, to Lord North:—

The evasive answer about America will by no means answer. Indeed, upon all constitutional points, the Opposition have run so wild, that it is absolutely necessary for those who come into office to give assurances that they do not mean to be hampered by the tenets they have held during their opposition. The second proposition is therefore quite inadmissible.

The Duke of Richmond and Mr. Fox have, more avowedly than any others of the Rockingham party, dipped themselves, for they have added shortening the duration of Parliaments, and

[1] Mr. Frederic Montague, of Papplewick Hall, in Nottinghamshire, sat for Northampton, and afterwards for Higham Ferrers. He was a prominent member of the Rockingham party, and was one of the seven commissioners named in Fox's India Bill.

1780. the former, by a strange conceit of changing the whole mode and right of election, would materially alter the Constitution. This added to his unremitted personal ill conduct to me, it cannot be expected that I should express any wish of seeing him in my service. *Persons must atone for their faults before I can attempt to forgive them.* The Duke of Richmond has not put his foot into my apartments for seven years, but not content with this, sent me a message by Lord Weymouth, that though he never came near to me, he, as a Lieutenant-General, asked my leave to go to France. As to Mr. Fox, if any lucrative not ministerial office can be pointed out for him, provided he will support the Ministry, I shall have no objection to the proposition. He never had any principle, and can therefore act as his interest may guide him.

The Duke of Portland I should with pleasure see in my service. Ireland, or any great Court office, would, I hope, suit him. The Duke of Manchester, in a lucrative office, I should not object to. Messrs. Townshend and Burke would be real acquisitions (vol. i. p. 252).

During all this time, Lord North was secretly disinclined to the policy on which his Government had been acting; he was desirous of resigning his post of Prime Minister, and only retained it in deference to the King's wishes. Ample evidence of this fact is furnished in the work before us. The following extract, from a letter of Lord North to the King, contains a most extraordinary confession of the state of his mind on the subject. The conversation took place on October, 1779; and Lord North remained in office more than two years longer: —

Lord Gower [President of the Council] came to Lord North to inform him that he had long felt the utmost uneasiness at the situation of His Majesty's affairs; that nothing can be so weak as the Government; that nothing is done; that there was no discipline in the State, the army, or the navy; and that impending ruin must be the consequence of the present system of government; that he thought himself obliged, as well in conscience as in wisdom, to desire an immediate dismissal from his employment; that he had no connection with any of the members of the Opposition, which he thought as wicked as the Administration is weak; that nothing can afford the least hope but a coalition, and he is afraid that even that remedy may be too late; that he feels the greatest gratitude for the many marks of royal goodness which he has received, but that he does not think it the duty of a faithful servant to endeavour to preserve a system which must end in the ruin of His Majesty and of the country. He is determined never again to take office, but to support Government in his private capacity. Lord North thinks that Lord Gower's resignation at the present moment must be the ruin of the Administration. In Lord North's arguments with Lord Gower, Lord North owns that he had certainly one disadvantage, *which is that he holds in his heart, and has held for these three years, just the same opinion with Lord Gower* (vol. i. p. 245). 1780.

In commenting on this remarkable declaration, Lord Holland and Mr. Allen 'lament Lord North's weakness, but enter into the *chivalrous feelings* of Lord North, which induced him, in opposition to his better judgment, not to abandon a master who expressed for him such confidence, affection, and regard.' From this opinion Lord John Russell dissents, and supports his dissent by the following just and discriminating remarks:—

The King held that the acknowledgment of the independence of America would place this country in a state of inferiority, and be tantamount to its ruin as a great and powerful State. Lord Chatham had held an opinion very similar to this. Lord Shelburne, following his leader, said in the House of Lords, that when America became independent the sun of England would set. *The Sovereign was only blameable for the obstinacy with which he clung to an opinion entertained by some of the most sagacious and eminent of his subjects.* Lord North's position was different; he was disposed to conciliate America, had sent commissioners for that purpose, and was quite ready to consent

1780. to peace. For three years he had been of opinion that his own Ministry was feeble, and would effect no good purpose. Why, then, did he remain? *To carry into effect the personal wishes of the Sovereign, which he preferred to the welfare of the State.* This may be Toryism; but it is not patriotic, still less is it constitutional conduct (vol. i. p. 247).

As the war proceeded, and its failures accumulated—moreover, as the ability with which its management was attacked by the Opposition, and the weakness with which it was defended by Ministers, became more conspicuous, a change in public opinion was gradually produced, which began to be felt in the votes of the House of Commons. The first decided symptom of this change was the result of the famous motion of Dunning—'That the influence of the Crown has increased, is increasing, and ought to be diminished'—which, after a hot debate, was carried, on April 6, 1780, by 233 to 215 votes. In the meantime, the pretensions of the Opposition, and their indisposition to such a compromise as they had recently been willing to accept, naturally increased. In writing to his friend Fitzpatrick, in September, 1781, Mr. Fox says: 'The more I think of the whole of the business, the more I feel averse to coming in upon any terms, unless on those of parliamentary condemnation of what is past.' Nothing of this sort was hinted at in the negotiation, through Mr. Fred. Montague, in the summer of the previous year.[1] A few days before the fall of Lord North's Ministry, Fox used language in the House of Commons which showed that he kept no measures with the Court. In the debate on General Conway's motion for peace with America, on February 22, 1782, Welbore Ellis, the new American

[1] [On January 23, 1781, Mr. Pitt took his seat for Appleby, a borough of Sir James Lowther's. January 23 was also the day of his death.—Lord Stanhope's *Life of Pitt*, vol. i. p. 49.—Ed.]

Secretary, made an unmeaning speech, which disclosed no decided views. 'Jenkinson,' says Horace Walpole, 'was less oracular, and Charles Fox accordingly applied a much harsher comment on him, as one who was the mouth of the oracle, of which Ellis was only the statue; but as if Fox had embraced all the notions that had been held about oracles (to which indeed he did not even allude), he mentioned the *infernal spirit* that really ruled and had nearly ruined the country.' But notwithstanding the increasing confidence of the Opposition, the King persisted, as long as he could keep a Ministry together, in refusing his consent to the independence of the revolted colonies. Thus even on December 26, 1781, he is careful to impress on Lord North that there is 'no change in his sentiments on the essential point, namely, the getting a peace at the expense of a separation from America, which no difficulties can get him to consent to.' Even when the overthrow of Lord North's Ministry, by adverse votes of the House of Commons, was imminent, the King still held to his intention of excluding the Opposition from power. 'Certain it is,' says Walpole, 'nothing could exceed the aversion of the King, not to parting with his Minister, but to accepting one by force. All his arts—little ones, indeed—were employed to avoid that humiliation; and though he succeeded in the only artifice in which he ever had succeeded—sowing division, yet he not only avoided no mortification, but laid a foundation for receiving much greater.' He even talked of returning to Hanover, and directions were given to prepare the royal yacht for his transport to the Continent. This intention seems to have been in his mind when, on March 17, three days before Lord North's resignation, he addressed to his Prime Minister the following mysterious words: 'I am resolved not to throw myself into the hands of Opposition, at all events, and shall certainly,

1781.

1782. if things go as they seem to tend, know what my conscience as well as honour dictates, *as the only way left for me.*'

Lord North's resignation, involving the dissolution of his Ministry, and the pacification with America, took place on March 20, 1782. The following lively account of the scene which passed that night in the House of Commons is left by Lord Holland:—

I have heard my uncle Fitzpatrick give a very diverting account of the scene that passed in the House of Commons on the day of Lord North's resignation, which happened to be a remarkable cold day, with a fall of snow. A motion of Lord Surrey's, for the dismissal of Ministers, stood for that day, and the Whigs were anxious that it should come on before the resignation of Lord North was officially announced, that his removal from office might be more manifestly and formally the act of the House of Commons. He and Lord Surrey rose at the same instant; after much clamour, disorder, and some insignificant speeches on order, Mr. Fox, with great quickness and address, moved, as the most regular method of extricating the House from its embarrassment, 'That Lord Surrey be now heard.' But Lord North, with yet more admirable presence of mind, mixed with pleasantry, rose immediately and said, 'I rise to speak to that motion;' and as his reason for opposing it, stated his resignation and the dissolution of the Ministry. The House, satisfied, became impatient, and after some ineffectual efforts of speakers on both sides to procure a hearing, an adjournment took place. Snow was falling and the night was tremendous. All the members' carriages were dismissed, and Mrs. Bennet's room at the door was crowded. But Lord North's carriage was waiting. He put into it one or two of his friends, whom he had invited to go home with him, and turning to the crowd, chiefly composed of his bitter enemies, in the midst of their triumph, exclaimed, in this hour of defeat and supposed mortification, with admirable good humour and pleasantry, 'I have my carriage. You see, gentlemen, the advantage of being in the secret. Good night' (vol. i. p. 295).[1]

[1] The same story is told in Wraxall's *Historical Mem.*, vol. ii. p. 607, ed. 1836.

The history of the formation of the new Ministry is not a little remarkable, and clearly explains its internal feebleness and speedy extinction. The King began by applying, through the Chancellor Thurlow, to Lord Rockingham, as leader of the principal section of the Whigs, in order to learn the terms upon which he would undertake to form an Administration.[1] These were, in substance, the independence of America, and measures for diminishing the influence of the Crown. Unwilling to capitulate on these terms, the King next made an attempt to induce Lord Gower to undertake the formation of a Government; but without success. In his letter authorising this application, he declared that 'he could never submit to a total change without abandoning his principles and honour, which he would never do.' The King then sent for Lord Shelburne, and asked him to form a Government; he declined the offer, and advised the King to prefer Lord Rockingham:[2] a fact which he did not then disclose, but which he stated in the House of Lords after Lord Rockingham's death,[3] and which was also mentioned at the same time by the King to Mr. Fox.[4] In the first interview nothing was arranged, but three days afterwards the King 1782.

[1] The particulars of this negotiation through Lord Thurlow are given in Lord Albemarle's *Memoirs of Lord Rockingham*, vol. ii.

[2] *Lord Mahon*, vol. vi. p. 307, gives the following extract from the Duke of Grafton's *Memoirs* respecting the failure of the negotiation with the Opposition in 1779, already mentioned: 'This circumstance cemented the Opposition into a more solid body, and furnished the means, that Lord Camden and I improved, by persuading Lord Shelburne not to contest with Lord Rockingham the Treasury, in case a new Administration was to be formed. Lord Shelburne yielded the point with a better grace than I had expected.'

[3] July 10, 1782.

[4] *Memorials of Fox*, vol. i. p. 436. Bishop Watson, in the anecdotes of his Life, says: 'Lord Rockingham told me that Lord Shelburne had behaved very honourably to him in not accepting the Treasury, which the King had offered to him in preference to Lord Rockingham' (p. 93, 4to.).

1782. sent again for Lord Shelburne, who returned, bringing an offer of the Treasury to Lord Rockingham, and full powers to treat, both as to men and measures; he himself was to be a Secretary of State. Lord Rockingham at first hesitated as to the propriety of accepting an offer made in so indirect and mistrustful a manner; but upon consultation with Mr. Fox and other friends, he decided (perhaps unwisely [1]) not to reject it. He accompanied his acceptance, however, with a list of the Cabinet, in which he was himself First Lord of the Treasury, and Mr. Fox and Lord Shelburne the Secretaries of State. The office of Chancellor was alone left open. On the same evening a large meeting of members of the House of Commons was held at the house of Mr. T. Townshend, to which this list was submitted. The list, having been approved by this meeting, was sent to Lord Shelburne, who agreed to the arrangement, and communicated the names to the King. Lord Shelburne had a long interview with the King on the following day, and then went to Mr. Fox to inform him that the proposals were substantially adopted. At this interview Mr. Fox told Lord Shelburne that he perceived this Administration was to consist of two parts— one belonging to the King, the other to the public. Lord Thurlow continued as Chancellor, and Mr. Dunning, created Lord Ashburton, was added to the Cabinet, upon the sug-

[1] After the resignation of the Shelburne Administration, the King applied to Lord North, who declined to undertake the formation of a Ministry himself, and advised the King to apply to the Duke of Portland. 'Lord North, says H. Walpole, 'proposed to the King to see the Duke of Portland himself, but that the King refused, and told Lord North to desire the duke to send him his arrangement in writing. This was as positively refused by the duke, who sent word that if His Majesty condescended to employ him, it would be necessary for him to see His Majesty' (*Mem. of Fox*, vol. ii. p. 49). It ended by the King seeing the Duke of Portland, and his becoming Prime Minister. The above account is confirmed by Lord Grenville's relation of his interview with the King, who showed him the correspondence with Lord North and the Duke of Portland (*Buckingham Papers*, vol. i. p. 213).

gestion of Lord Shelburne, without previous communication with Lord Rockingham. 1782.

It thus appears that the King, though he prudently yielded to the pressure of a parliamentary majority, and abandoned his intention of retiring to Hanover, yet bowed his neck under the yoke of Opposition with visible reluctance. He refused to see his future Prime Minister until he was actually in office; and by giving his chief apparent confidence to another member of the Cabinet, he laid the foundation of discord and distrust in the Government from its very commencement. The seed thus carefully sown began soon to germinate. Even as early as the 28th of April—about a month after the formation of the Government, Mr. Fox writes as follows to Fitzpatrick:—

> Shelburne shows himself more and more every day; is ridiculously jealous of my encroaching on his department, and wishes very much to encroach upon mine. He hardly liked my having a letter from Grattan, or my having written one to Lord Charlemont.[1] He affects the Minister more and more every day, and is, I believe, perfectly confident that the King intends to make him so. Provided we can stay in long enough to have given a good stout blow to the influence of the Crown, I do not think it much signifies how soon we go out after, and leave him and the Chancellor to make such a Government as they can; and this I think we shall be able to do (vol. i. p. 316).

The practical working of our Government has undergone so great a change since 1780, notwithstanding the preservation of its forms, that it is important not to misunderstand the true character of the struggle which was terminated by the overthrow of Lord North's Ministry. It was a struggle of the King's personal will, supported by the influence of the Crown, against the independent

[1] As Lord Shelburne was Home Secretary, the Irish business was in his department.

1782. portion of the House of Commons. The war against the insurgent colonies had at first been highly popular; [1] but a succession of disasters turned the tide of public feeling, and the country were ready to adopt the views of all the ablest men in both Houses of Parliament, who recommended either large concessions or entire independence. But the King remained unmoved: he would not consent to a dismemberment of the Empire; and he found in Lord North and his colleagues Ministers who were ready to persist in the policy to which he adhered, even when it was contrary to their own convictions. Against this Ministry, Fox, Burke, and other powerful speakers, thundered night after night, denouncing their principles, conduct, motives, and capacity in the most vehement language, and sometimes directing their fire over the Treasury Bench at the Throne. When the battle was over, Fox openly treated it as a victory of the House of Commons over the King. On the night when Lord North announced his resignation, he said, that 'as the House had now proved their abhorrence of a Government of influence, the new Ministers must ever bear in mind that fact, and *remember that to the House they owed their situations.*' Moreover, before the list of the proposed Cabinet was presented to the King, it had been submitted to a meeting of the Whig party, and had received their sanction. By placing the question on this issue, George III. abandoned the secure, dignified, and neutral position of a constitutional king, and entered upon the perilous career of a party-leader. He protested against changing his principles, threw out obscure threats of abdicating the throne, and staked his political reputation against Fox and the leaders of Opposition. The result was, that he underwent the humiliation of a personal defeat; but he had

[1] See *Lord Mahon*, vol. vi. p. 68.

sufficient prudence to tolerate for a time a Ministry composed of men whom he regarded as his personal enemies, rather than attempt some act of unconstitutional violence, or bring the machine of Government to a stand-still. 1782.

The Rockingham Ministry lasted just three months. Lord North resigned on the 20th of March. Lord Rockingham died on the 1st of July.[1] Two days after his death, Mr. Fox advised the King to appoint as his successor some member of the Rockingham party. The King announced his intention of preferring Lord Shelburne, to whom Fox objected; but the King adhered to his resolution, and Fox, followed by Lord John Cavendish, with Burke, Sheridan, and others not in the Cabinet, resigned. Lord Shelburne then became Prime Minister, with Pitt as Chancellor of the Exchequer and leader of the House of Commons. Lord Keppel, General Conway, and the Duke of Richmond, the other three members of the Rockingham party in the Cabinet, retained their offices, and did not go out with Fox.

Among the Rockingham Whigs, the Duke of Richmond considered himself as having the first claim to the post of Prime Minister. He was, however, rejected by his friends on account of his extreme opinions on Parliamentary Reform; and Mr. Fox, as being his kinsman,[2] was employed to impart to him the unwelcome intelligence, which he executed thus: 'We must (he said) settle without delay whom to propose as the successor of Lord Rockingham; and as *you and I* are both out of the

[1] 'The King (says Horace Walpole) showed his aversion to Lord Rockingham so indecently and unfeelingly, that, though he had accepted him for his Minister, he did not once send to inquire how the marquis did when he was dying' (*Mem. of Fox*, vol. i. p. 440).

[2] Mr. Fox was the nephew of the Duke of Richmond. His mother was the duke's sister. The present Duke of Richmond is the great nephew of the duke in question.

1782. question, owing to the decided part we have taken about Parliamentary Reform, I think the Duke of Portland should be the man.' The Duke of Portland was, however, chiefly recommended for this post by his rank and respectable character; and in point of capacity and fitness for the office of Prime Minister he was decidedly inferior to Lord Shelburne.

We have been the more particular in describing this change of Administration, because we believe that Fox's decision to separate himself from Lord Shelburne was the turning point of his political life, and exercised an enormous influence upon the subsequent course of events. His motive for this decision was his distrust of Lord Shelburne, whom he believed to be systematically insincere, and whom he likewise suspected of intriguing with the King against his colleagues. This suspicion partly rested upon Lord Shelburne's general character, who had so early as the year 1767 obtained from the writer of Junius the nickname of 'Malagrida,' on account of his supposed Jesuitical habits of mind.[1] Its chief ground, however, was Lord Shelburne's recent conduct in the negotiation for peace with America, the details of which we will proceed to narrate.[2]

[1] It was given him in some anonymous productions by the author of *Junius*, which appeared under another signature (see Woodfall's *Junius*, vol. ii. pp. 472, 482). Gabriel Malagrida, an Italian by birth, and a Jesuit, resided in Portugal. He was accused of participation in a conspiracy against the King, and was burnt by the Inquisition for heresy in 1761. He seems to have been scarcely sane (*Biogr. Un. and Chalmers*. See also *Lord Mahon*, vol. iv. p. 263).

[2] Fox's resignation, says Lord Holland, was not the result of advice or persuasion: 'It was his own resolution adopted after much reflection, and founded on a general conviction that he could not conduct the public affairs under Lord Shelburne's treasury with safety, honour, or advantage; and from resentment at the duplicity with which his negotiations at Paris had been impeded by Lord Shelburne through Mr. Oswald, of which he thought Mr. Grenville's letters furnished him indubitable evidence' (*Mem. of Fox*, vol. i. p. 473; see some similar remarks of Lord Holland, *ibid.* p. 387).

The Secretary of State's office was formerly divided into the Northern and Southern Departments. The Southern Secretary had the management of home affairs, and of the correspondence with Ireland, the Colonies, and the States of Western Europe. The Northern Secretary conducted only the correspondence with the other European countries. This unequal and inconvenient division was discontinued upon the accession of the Rockingham Ministry, when the third or American Secretary was abolished, and the existing division of the Home and Foreign Departments was introduced.[1] The Home Office was formed out of the old Southern Department, and it therefore retained the Irish and Colonial business: the Foreign Office was formed out of the Northern Department, by the addition of the correspondence with those foreign countries which had previously been under the charge of the Southern Secretary. The Home Secretary, as the successor of the Southern Secretary, retained the seniority in official rank. 1782.

In the beginning of the year 1782, Franklin, who had been appointed one of the American Commissioners for negotiating with France, was staying at Paris. At the time when Lord North's Ministry was about to expire, Lord Cholmondeley passed through Paris on his road to England, and called upon Franklin, though previously

[1] It has been mentioned in a former number of the *Edinburgh Review*, that Lord Holland and Mr. Allen are mistaken in supposing that the division of the Northern and Southern departments subsisted at this time (*Mem. of Fox*, vol. i. pp. 345, 475). If Lord Shelburne had had the old Southern department, *both* negotiations would have been in his hands; for both France and the Colonies were in that department. Lord Shelburne's letter to Mr. Grenville, of July 5, 1782, begins thus: 'His Majesty having thought proper to entrust me with the seals of the Foreign Department, *upon the resignation of Mr. Secretary Fox*, I take the earliest opportunity of notifying it to you.' (S.P.O.) The seals of this department were immediately afterwards transferred to Lord Grantham.

1782. unacquainted with him. During his visit, he offered to carry a letter from him to Lord Shelburne; and Franklin accordingly wrote to Lord Shelburne a letter of civility, in which he referred to their former acquaintance, and took occasion to express a hope that the recent votes of the House of Commons might lead to a general peace. This letter was written in ignorance of Lord North's resignation, the news of which reached Paris immediately afterwards. When Lord Shelburne received this letter, he already held the seals of the Home Department; and as the American colonies were still considered as subject to the Crown of England, all affairs relating to them were under his official cognisance. Without delay, he took advantage of this accident to send Mr. Oswald, a London merchant, formerly resident in America, to Paris, in order to communicate with Franklin.[1] Oswald accordingly arrived in Paris near the beginning of April, and had an interview with Franklin, at which he delivered to him private letters from Lord Shelburne, and Mr. Laurens, an American officer then a prisoner in England.[2] Franklin, in his detailed journal of these transactions, states that Oswald, at this interview, described England as ready to concede the independence of America, and to treat of peace, but as prepared to continue the war if the terms

[1] [See supplementary note at the end of this article for an account of Richard Oswald.—Ed.]

[2] See *Franklin's Works by Sparks*, vol. ix. p. 240, where the letters are printed. [The term 'an American officer' hardly describes Henry Laurens. He was one of the signers of the 'Articles of Confederation' on the part of the State of South Carolina, and became President of the Congress as constituted under those Articles. He was on his way to Holland on a mission from the Confederate States, when he was captured on the Newfoundland station by the Fairy sloop of war and the Vestal frigate. On October 6, he was committed to the Tower by a Secretary of State's warrant. The nationality of the vessel in which he was taken became a subject of discussion at the time of the affair of the Trent. See *Annual Reg.* for 1780, October 2.—Ed.]

insisted on by France were too humiliating. The answer made by Franklin was, that he could only treat in concert with France; but he offered to introduce Oswald to M. de Vergennes, the French Minister for Foreign Affairs, and an interview accordingly took place between them, a few days afterwards, in Franklin's presence. Oswald was unable to speak French, and the conversation was carried on through an interpreter. The general effect of this interview is related in a letter addressed by Franklin to Lord Shelburne. The principal points were, that France could not treat without her allies, and that Paris was suggested as the proper place for the negotiations. Oswald returned to London to carry the account of his interviews; bearing likewise the expression of Franklin's wish, that there might be no other channel of communication between him and the English Government than Oswald himself. Franklin, as Mr. Allen remarks, had doubtless soon discovered that Oswald 'was a simple-minded, well-meaning man, on whom he could make the impression he chose.' Upon Mr. Oswald's return to London, a meeting of the Cabinet was held, at which the following minute was agreed to:— 1782.

April 23, 1782. Present, Lord Chancellor, Lord President, Duke of Richmond, Marquis of Rockingham, Duke of Grafton, Lord Ashburton, Lord J. Cavendish, Lord Keppel, Gen. Conway, Mr. Fox, Lord Shelburne.

It is humbly submitted to His Majesty that Mr. Oswald shall return to Paris with authority to name Paris as the place, and to settle with Dr. Franklin the most convenient time for setting on foot a negotiation for a general peace, and to represent to him that the principal points in contemplation are, the allowance of independence to America upon Great Britain's being restored to the situation she was placed in by the treaty of 1763, and that Mr. Fox shall submit to the consideration of the King

1782. a proper person to make a similar communication to Mons. de Vergennes (vol. i. p. 345).[1]

Before Oswald left Paris Franklin placed in his hands a paper, containing suggestions respecting Canada, for Lord Shelburne's consideration. It threw out the idea that Canada might be voluntarily ceded to the United States, as an indemnity for the losses occasioned by the war; and it concluded with these words: 'This is mere conversation matter between Mr. Oswald and Mr. Franklin, as the former is not empowered to make propositions, and the latter cannot make any without the concurrence of his colleagues.' Franklin afterwards regretted that he had allowed the paper to go out of his own hands. On his return to Paris, Oswald told Franklin that he had shown the paper to Lord Shelburne, and by his desire left it with him for one night; that he had conversed with Lord Shelburne about it, and it seemed to have made an impression. The paper was then restored to Franklin.[2]

Oswald returned to Paris early in May, with instruc-

[1] We observe that the peculiar mode in which the Ministers address the Sovereign in private communications, which is now in use, was observed by Mr. Fox at this time. '*Mr. Fox* has the honour of transmitting *to your Majesty* the minute of the Cabinet Council assembled this morning at Lord Rockingham's,' May 18, 1782 (*ibid.* p. 351). When this epistolary form was introduced, or by whom, we know not. The letters of Mr. G. Grenville to the King in 1765, printed in the Grenville Papers, vol. iii. p. 4–15, are in the ordinary form: 'I have but just now received the honour of your Majesty's commands on my return home from my Lord Chancellor's, where I have passed the greatest part of the evening.' According to the more recent etiquette, the Minister uses the third person, and addresses the Sovereign in the second.

[2] It is remarkable that Mr. Forth, who had been sent secretly by Lord North to Paris before the change of Government, appears to have offered the cession of Canada as the price of a peace with France (*Franklin's Works*, vol. ix. p. 210). An account of Forth's mission is given in a despatch of M. de Vergennes, in Flassan, *Histoire de la Diplomatie Française*, vol. vii. p. 322, ed. 1811, but nothing is there said about an offer to restore Canada to France.

tions from Lord Shelburne to arrange with Franklin the preliminaries of time and place for negotiating, and also the announcement that a proper person would be shortly sent by Mr. Fox, 'from whose department that communication is necessarily to proceed,' to treat with M. de Vergennes.[1] This person was Mr. Grenville, whose speedy arrival, by way of Ostend, was announced by Oswald both to Franklin and the French Minister. Mr. Grenville shortly afterwards arrived at Paris, and was introduced by Franklin to M. de Vergennes, with whom he had a long conference on the subject of his mission.[2] Oswald now returned to London, and soon after his arrival, the Cabinet advised the King to direct full powers to be given 1782.

[1] Lord Shelburne to Franklin, 20th April, 1782 (*Franklin's Works*, vol. ix. p. 265).

[2] 'The Count de Vergennes (says Franklin) received Mr. Grenville in the most cordial manner, on account of the acquaintance and friendship that had formerly subsisted between *his uncle* and the Count de Vergennes, when they were ambassadors together at Constantinople' (*ibid.* p. 273). The person referred to is Mr. Henry Grenville, brother of Lord Temple, who was ambassador at Constantinople from 1761 to 1765. M. de Vergennes was minister plenipotentiary at the same capital from 1755 to 1768. M. de Vergennes, in a despatch written at the time to the French ambassador in Spain, thus describes Mr. Grenville: 'M. Grenville est très propre à recommander la mission dont il est chargé; c'est un jeune homme de trente ans au plus, qui annonce beaucoup d'esprit et de sagesse, d'honnêteté et de modestie. Il appartient à une famille considérable, qui est liée d'intérêt avec le ministère actuel, et il n'est guère vraisemblable que celui-ci lui eût destiné un rôle aussi plat et aussi peu analogue à sa naissance et à son état, que celui de venir nous ennuyer et nous tromper' (*Flassan, ibid.* p. 339). Franklin, on making Mr. Grenville's acquaintance, says: 'He appeared to me a sensible, judicious, intelligent, good-natured, and well-instructed young man, answering well the character Mr. Fox had given me of him' (*Works, ibid.* p. 272). These early notices of Mr. Grenville will be read with interest by those who enjoyed the pleasure of his society in the later years of his long life, as well as by all who appreciate the value of the rare and well-selected library which he bequeathed to the public. Mr. Grenville was born in 1755, and therefore was, at this time, twenty-seven years old.

As the epistolary form in which Sovereigns address one another has lately

1782. to Mr. Grenville to make propositions of peace to the belligerent Powers upon the basis of American independence, and his formal commission was accordingly despatched without delay.

Mr. Oswald returned to Paris early in June, bringing with him a paper of memoranda by Lord Shelburne, which he communicated to Franklin. This paper announced that 'on our (i.e. the English) part, commissioners will be named, or any character given to Mr. Oswald, which Dr. Franklin and he may judge conducive to a final settlement of things between Great Britain and America; which Dr. Franklin very properly says requires to be treated in a very different manner from the peace between Great Britain and France, who have always been at enmity with each other.[1] As soon as Franklin received this communication, and foresaw the prospect of negotiating with Oswald, whom he describes as having 'an air of great simplicity and honesty,'[2] he became reserved with Mr. Grenville, and showed a reluctance to speak openly with him. Mr. Grenville combining this circumstance with the incident of the

been made a question of international importance, we subjoin a copy from the State Paper Office of the credential letter sent by George III. to Louis XVI. on the occasion of Mr. Grenville's mission:—

'Monsieur mon frère,

'Ayant fait choix du Sieur Grenville pour se rendre à votre cour en qualité de mon ministre, je vous prie de donner une entière créance à tout ce qu'il vous dira de ma part, et surtout aux assurances qu'il vous donnera de mon estime singulier pour vous, et de mon desir sincère de voir heureusement rétablie entre nous une amitié ferme et durable.

'Je suis,
'Monsieur mon frère
'Votre bon frère,
'GEORGE R.'

'à St. James,
ce 21 Mai, 1782.

[1] *Franklin's Works*, vol. ix. p. 314.

[2] We regret to find that Scotchmen, seventy years ago, did not find favour in Mr. Grenville's eyes: 'He spoke of Mr. Oswald (says Franklin) as an odd kind of man, *but that indeed his nation were generally an odd people*' (*ibid.* p. 334). We may hope that Mr. Grenville lived to change his opinion.

Canada paper, of which he had been informed by Oswald, came to the conclusion that he was crossed by a concurrent negotiator, and that the treaty could never be satisfactorily arranged with such a division of powers. He likewise appears to have thought that there was a deliberate intention of encroaching upon Mr. Fox's province, which he, as Mr. Fox's envoy, resented. Under the influence of these feelings, he wrote to Mr. Fox the important confidential letter of the 4th of June, of which the public were first made aware by the two publications reviewed in this Article. In this letter Mr. Grenville points to the promise of Lord Shelburne to appoint Oswald a commissioner, and to the Canada paper, as evidence that a separate and independent negotiation was proceeding which destroyed his utility. He therefore requests that he may be recalled, and that Lord Fitzwilliam, or some peer of sufficient importance to render it impossible to associate Oswald with him, should be appointed in his place. This letter led to an answer from Fox, asking for 'further proofs of this duplicity of conduct,' and speaking of 'the clandestine manner of carrying on a separate negotiation which we complain of;' but particularly inquiring how far Fox and his friends are at liberty to make use of the contents of Mr. Grenville's letter in order to call Lord Shelburne to account. Mr. Grenville replied to Mr. Fox in a letter which seems to have left Paris on the 21st; but before any steps could be taken upon it, Lord Rockingham's fatal illness and death brought the Government to an end. As soon as the news of this event reached Paris, Mr. Grenville resigned his mission, and returned to England.[1]

1782.

[1] The entire private correspondence between Mr. Grenville and Mr. Fox, during this mission, has now been published in the two works named at the head of this Article. The official correspondence is preserved in the State Paper Office, but has never been printed; a brief outline of it is given by Mr. Adolphus in his *History of England during the Reign of George III.*

1782. The editor of the 'Buckingham Papers' (who seems to have been wholly ignorant of Franklin's detailed account) thus characterises this transaction:—

It is clear, from the singular facts revealed in this correspondence, that while an *ostensible* minister was despatched to Paris by the general action of the Government, with the sanction of the King, to negotiate terms with the *American* minister, Lord Shelburne had taken upon himself to appoint another negotiator, who was not only not to act in concert with Mr. Grenville, but *whose clandestine mission seems to have been expressly intended to thwart and embarrass him, and whose appointment was without the approval, or even the knowledge, of the Cabinet* (vol. i. p. 26).

Horace Walpole's account is not very different:—

While Fox thus unfolded his character so advantageously, Shelburne was busied in devoting himself to the King, and in traversing Lord Rockingham and Fox in every point. If they opened a negotiation, he commenced another underhand at the same Court. Mr. Fox despatched Thomas Grenville to Paris. Lord Shelburne sent *one, two, or three* privately to the same place, and addressed them to different Ministers or persons of supposed credit (*Mem. of Fox*, vol. i. p. 321).

Now, it is quite clear from our narrative of the facts, and from the testimonies which we have cited, that Oswald's first visit to Paris arose out of a letter accidentally addressed by Franklin to Lord Shelburne, before the change of Ministry was known to him; that Oswald returned to Paris with the full knowledge and approbation of the Cabinet, and as bearer of a message that he would be speedily followed by Mr. Grenville, as minister plenipotentiary, to

(vol. iii. c. 44). This correspondence (which we have perused) is conducted with great ability on both sides, and we regret that it still remains in manuscript. We may also remark that the discussion of the questions examined in the text would be more satisfactory if the entire documentary history of the treaty of 1783 were before the public.

treat with the French Court; that he communicated with Mr. Fox when he was in London, and that Mr. Grenville knew he was at Paris, and communicated with him almost daily when he was there.[1] Mr. Oswald's mission had nothing *clandestine*, in the ordinary sense of the term. It was open and avowed on both sides of the water. It was known to Fox and the Cabinet; and it was recognised in the communications of Mr. Grenville with Franklin and M. de Vergennes. Neither can it be said, with Horace Walpole, that Oswald was sent to thwart Mr. Grenville; for Oswald's mission preceded Mr. Grenville's. Mr. Fox gives this account of the origin of Mr. Grenville's mission, in a letter to Mr. Fitzpatrick, April 28:— 1782.

Shelburne has had an answer from Dr. Franklin, who seems much disposed to peace, if general. M. de Vergennes has, it seems, expressed the same sentiments, and wishes to have some opening from hence; in consequence of this, Shelburne's man is to go back this day to Paris, and upon the pretence of the business having begun with the American Ministers, he had a great mind, if I would have consented, to have kept even this negotiation in his own hands; but this I would not submit to, and so Grenville is to set out for Paris to-morrow or next day, in order to state our ideas of peace to M. de Vergennes (vol. i. p. 346).[2]

These remarks imply that Fox was fully aware of the

[1] Mr. Fox's letter of instructions to Mr. Grenville (April 30, 1782) begins thus: 'When you arrive at Paris, you will endeavour to see Mr. Oswald as soon as possible, who will probably have announced your arrival.' In a subsequent letter to Mr. Grenville, of May 21, Fox speaks of having received his letter by Mr. Oswald, and of having heard from Mr. Oswald an account of the state of affairs at Paris (*State Paper Office*).

[2] See in *Flassan*, *ibid.* pp. 328-59, the despatches of M. de Vergennes, describing his interviews with Mr. Oswald and Mr. Grenville. It appears that he understood perfectly the state of the case, for he says of Oswald:— 'Envoyé par Lord Shelburne, il n'avait point de commission pour moi, parceque ce secretaire d'état n'ayant dans son departement que l'Amérique et l'Irlande, c'est M. Fox qui est chargé uniquement des affaires de l'Europe' (p. 333).

1782. negotiation with Franklin having been begun by Oswald. Mr. Grenville was then sent by him to treat with the French Government, and he had a regular commission and credentials from the Crown for this purpose; but Oswald had no legal authority to treat, and had merely directions from the Secretary of State.

Let us now consider how far the two points raised by Mr. Grenville deserve to be considered in the serious light in which he and Mr. Fox regarded them. The most important of the two was the announcement, brought back by Oswald on his second visit to Paris, that Lord Shelburne was prepared to appoint him commissioner to treat with the American agents, his intention to make this appointment not having been previously communicated to Fox and his other colleagues. It is impossible not to see that if a proper cordiality had subsisted between Lord Shelburne and the rest of the Cabinet, he would have mentioned this intention to Lord Rockingham or Mr. Fox, before he announced it to Oswald. Nevertheless, his omission to take this step does not seem to us to have rendered it necessary to disturb the course of the negotiation by the strong measure to which Mr. Grenville resorted. If Mr. Grenville found by experience that a separate negotiator for America was likely to interfere with the rest of the negotiation, he could have represented this conclusion to his own Government, and the Cabinet would have then decided the question with the advantage of his opinion. Oswald had not as yet been appointed; and the appointment might still be arrested, notwithstanding Lord Shelburne's announcement, if the Cabinet thought fit to commit the entire negotiation to one person.[1] It is, however, to be observed

[1] A similar misunderstanding arose between the two Secretaries of State about a negotiation at Paris in 1723. George I. was desirous of obtaining a dukedom for a French gentleman, who was to marry a daughter of his

that when the bill then pending in Parliament, for enabling the King to conclude a peace with the American colonies, had passed, Oswald eventually received, under Lord Shelburne's Administration, a formal commission to negotiate with the American commissioners.[1] Mr. Fitzherbert (afterwards Lord St. Helen's) was appointed to succeed Mr. Grenville, with full powers to treat with France, Spain, and Holland. It appears from the correspondence in the State Paper Office that Oswald corresponded with Mr. Townshend, the Home Secretary, and Mr. Fitzherbert with Lord Grantham, the Foreign Secretary; so that the division of the negotiation between the two Secretaries and their envoys continued to the signature of the preliminaries, and, so far as we know, did not produce the inconvenient results which Mr. Grenville anticipated, and about which he so much alarmed Mr. Fox. It may be added that M. de Rayneval, a confidential subordinate of M. de Vergennes, and also M. de Heredia, a person 1782.

mistress, Madame de Platen. Lord Carteret accordingly instructed Sir Luke Schaub, the English ambassador at Paris, to make interest for this purpose. 'This affair (says Lord Mahon) belonged to Carteret, as Secretary for the Southern Department, in which France was comprised, and the other Secretary had no claim to interlope in his province. Nevertheless, Lord Townshend, unwilling to see an affair of so much interest in the hand of a rival, determined, if possible, to draw it from his management. With this view, and at the instigation of Walpole, he despatched his brother Horace to Paris, under the pretence of settling the accession of Portugal to the Quadruple Alliance, but in reality to watch the movements and counteract the influence of Schaub' (vol. ii. p. 57). This intrigue led to an open breach between the two Secretaries, and to the dismissal of Lord Carteret.

[1] The intention to appoint Oswald as commissioner to negotiate with the Americans had, however, been communicated to him by Lord Shelburne, in a letter dated June 30, the very day before Lord Rockingham's death. In this letter he states, that as soon as the Act had passed he lost no time in taking the King's commands for directing a commission to be made out conformable to the powers given to His Majesty (*MS.* State Paper Office. A portion of the letter is printed in *Franklin's Works, ibid.* p. 345). He does not, however, say that he took the King's pleasure upon the appointment of Oswald.

1782. connected with the Spanish embassy, came over to London, and negotiated with Lord Shelburne; and that Mr. Strachey, the Under Secretary in the Home Department, was sent to Paris to assist Mr. Oswald; so that even other negotiators were added before the preliminaries of the treaty could be settled.[1] When the change of Government took place, the Duke of Manchester was sent by Mr. Fox in the place of Mr. Fitzherbert, and Mr. David Hartley in the place of Oswald; and their names appear respectively at the foot of the definitive treaties with France, Spain, and the United States, signed in September, 1783. Both, however, as appears from the letters in the State Paper Office, corresponded with Mr. Fox. Lord North seems to have waived his right of instructing Mr. Hartley. No result, however, was obtained by Mr. Hartley's negotiation. The definitive treaty with the United States was identical with the preliminaries: so that Mr. Fox ended by adopting the precise results of Oswald's negotiation.

There was undoubtedly a great want of cordiality between Lord Shelburne and Fox, amounting to distrust and dislike; and a mutual jealousy of power, very undesirable in two Secretaries of State. Lord Shelburne may have acted, in his instructions to Oswald, without sufficient reference to the Foreign Secretary; but there is no evidence of any *intrigue* on Lord Shelburne's part, or of any attempt to negotiate through Oswald upon terms more

[1] Concerning M. de Rayneval's secret mission, see *Flassan, ibid.* p. 344; *Franklin, ibid.* p. 420. He is mentioned in the *Mem. of Fox*, vol. ii. p. 9, under the name of 'M. de Rennervalle.' A correspondence between M. de Rayneval and Lord Shelburne is preserved among Lord Shelburne's papers. M. de Rayneval first came to England in September, 1782, under the assumed name of Castel; he returned shortly afterwards, and made a second visit in December. A short notice of him will be found in the *Biogr. Universelle*, Art. *Gérard de Rayneval.* Mr. Strachey was sent over by Mr. Townshend to assist Oswald, on October 23, 1782 (*Letter in State Paper Office*; *Franklin, ibid.* p. 422).

acceptable to the King, or less favourable to America, than those prescribed by Fox to Mr. Grenville.[1] The King, as we have seen, only a month or two before, had been meditating a retirement to Hanover rather than consent to the independence of America. Yet this principle was conceded from the moment of Mr. Grenville's mission; and Franklin was so well pleased with Oswald, and so satisfied of his desire to settle the peace on terms favourable to America, that he expressed a strong wish that Oswald should be appointed to negotiate with him. Franklin's anxiety to secure Oswald's appointment is a decisive proof that 'Shelburne's man' was not desirous of promoting the views which the King had so fondly cherished; but, on the contrary, that he was desirous of promoting the views which the King had quite recently held in the utmost abhorrence.[2] So far was Lord Shelburne from yielding, like Lord North, to the King's prejudices on this subject, that his friends took credit to him for having persuaded the King to acquiesce in American independence.[3] 1782.

[1] 'There was (says Lord Holland) great mistrust and jealousy on both sides, much mystery and concealment on that of Lord Shelburne, which Mr. Fox and Mr. Grenville attributed, *perhaps too hastily*, to a secret understanding with the King. It is possible, and not improbable, that Grenville suspected more concealment, intrigue, and counteraction than really subsisted' (*ibid.* vol. i. p. 475, 477). Franklin makes the following remarks in his journal: 'Lord Shelburne seems to wish to have the management of the treaty; Mr. Fox seems to think it in his department. I hear that the understanding between these Ministers is not quite perfect. . . . I imagine we might go on very well with either of them, though I should rather prefer Oswald; but I apprehend difficulties if they are both employed, especially if there is any misunderstanding between their principals' (*Works, ibid.* p. 336).

[2] A portrait of himself, which Franklin presented to Oswald, when the treaty was concluded, was given by his nephew, the late member for Glasgow, to Mr. Joseph Parkes, in whose possession it now remains in London.

[3] General Conway made this statement in the House of Commons, in the ministerial explanations after Lord Rockingham's death, July 9, 1782. See also the expressions in Vaughan's letter, above.

1782. That Lord Shelburne did not use Oswald as the instrument of any royal intrigue, or for the purpose of inculcating any peculiar views of his own, is evident from Franklin's complaints of the scantiness of Oswald's communications. In writing to Mr. Laurens, on April 20, 1782, he says that Oswald had brought him a letter from Lord Shelburne assuring him that Oswald 'was fully apprised of his (Lord Shelburne's) mind.' Mr. Oswald, however (adds Franklin), could give me no other particulars of his lordship's mind, but that he was sincerely disposed to peace.'[1] On his second visit to Paris Franklin says: 'On the whole, I was able to draw so little from Mr. Oswald of the sentiments of Lord Shelburne, who had mentioned him as entrusted with the communication of them, that I could not but wonder at his being sent again to me, especially as Mr. Grenville was so soon to follow.'[2] In writing to Mr. Adams, on May 8, Franklin says that Lord Shelburne informs him that Mr. Oswald is instructed to communicate to him his lordship's thoughts. 'He is, however (Franklin adds), very sparing of such communication.'[3] On May 10, Franklin 'found him in the same friendly dispositions, and very desirous of good, and seeing an end put to this ruinous war. But (he says) I got no further sight as to the sentiments of Lord Shelburne respecting the terms.'[4]

Mr. Grenville is reported by Franklin to have expressed at Paris the opinion that 'Mr. Fox's resignation would be fatal to the negotiation.' Lord Shelburne, however, instructed him to repeat every assurance of the King's desire of peace, 'and not to leave any impression on the minds of those with whom he is in treaty of the least relaxation from the intention and spirit of the negotiation as hitherto

[1] *Works, ibid.* p. 254. [2] *Ibid.* p. 269. [3] *Ibid.* p. 270.

[4] *Works,* p. 276. Oswald disclaimed to Franklin all personal views, and all wish to remain at Paris. *Ibid.* p. 316.

carried on.'[1] Mr. Oswald seems to have lost no time in treating with Franklin: on July 10, he reports the first distinct proposal of terms made on the part of America; and the negotiation proceeded in an uninterrupted manner. It may be added, that the negotiation with America, and that with France and Spain, seemed to have proceeded independently of each other, and the preliminaries were signed with America without the knowledge of the French Government. 1782.

With regard to the Canadian paper, the other point brought forward by Mr. Grenville, we confess that we cannot regard it otherwise than as a very trifling affair; and we are unable to understand how Lord Holland and Mr. Allen could have viewed it in so serious a light. When Oswald received the paper from Franklin, he was not invested with the formal character of a negotiator. He had no commission from the King; and Franklin gave it to him, not as a proposition during a negotiation, but as a suggestion, or matter for consideration. The paper was treated as confidential; and Franklin evidently did not intend that it should go further than Lord Shelburne himself. It required no answer, nor was any answer sent to it by Lord Shelburne; but the original paper was returned. There was, in our judgment, nothing, either in the contents of the paper or in the manner in which it came into his hands, which rendered it incumbent on Lord Shelburne to communicate it to his colleagues. It may be observed too that Oswald did communicate its purport to Mr. Grenville, with whom the conduct of the main negotiation rested; so that no possible inconvenience could have arisen from Lord Shelburne's silence on the subject.

Lord Holland speaks of Franklin having been 'encouraged by the prospect of some new concessions, and

[1] *Franklin, ibid.* pp. 366, 367.

1782. *especially of Canada*, to hold aloof from the overtures made to him through Mr. Grenville;'[1] and Mr. Allen says that 'it is impossible to justify Lord Shelburne for his *favourable* reception of so important a paper as the one he had received from Franklin about Canada.'[2] There is nothing in Franklin's account to justify the inference that Lord Shelburne had expressed any opinion upon the paper brought by Oswald; he certainly sent no message to Franklin respecting it. We are, however, able, by the favour of the Marquis of Lansdowne, to lay before the reader a documentary proof that the 'favourable reception' of the paper in question must have proceeded from Oswald's imagination. In a volume of miscellaneous papers relating to the peace of 1783, collected by Lord Shelburne—now in Lord Lansdowne's possession—is a set of notes by Lord Shelburne for a conversation with Oswald, dated April 28, 1782, and therefore written shortly before Oswald's second visit to Paris. Among these notes are some remarks on the Canada paper with reference to the passage in which Franklin says: 'I do not know that the Americans will insist on reparation; perhaps they may.'[3] We annex a copy of the notes in question, premising only that the Cabinet minute, mentioned at the beginning, appears from 'Franklin's Journal' to have been communicated to him by Oswald, but without any copy being given. 'He showed me (says Franklin) the Minutes of Council, but did not leave the paper with me.'[4] As to the remark on the West Indies, it should be observed that Rodney's action took place on April 12; so that it had already occurred when this memorandum was written, though the news had not reached England.

[1] *Mem. of Fox*, vol. i. p. 469.

[2] *Mem. of Fox*, vol. i. p. 384.

[3] *Franklin's Works*, vol. ix. p. 251.

[4] *Ibid.*, p. 266.

MEMORANDUMS TO MR. OSWALD IN CONVERSATION, APRIL 28, 1782.

Memorandums of General Instruction.

A copy of the Cabinet Minutes to be shown to Doctor Franklin, but he must have no copy of it.

A fleet of upwards of forty ships in the West Indies—highly probable we shall intercept the reinforcement of the three ships for De Grasse.

The French islands in great distress.

A blow or two at sea may decide a great deal.

Insist, in the strongest manner, that if America is independent she must be so of the whole world. No secret, tacit, or ostensible connection with France.

If the negotiation breaks off, all our rights in America to stand as before.

Remarks on the Private Paper.

1st. Why does he say that he does not know of the Americans having any intention of making claims of indemnification, he and others having full powers. That is not open. No reparation to be thought of. The money spent in America is more than sufficient indemnification for all particular losses. Lord Shelburne has a manuscript of Sir William Petty to send in return for this paper. The title of it is to show that Ireland would have been in a state of poverty and uncivilised savageness if it had not been for the money expended by the English in their wars in that country.

All ideas of a supposed justice in claims of indemnification to be disowned; and if started, to be waived as much as possible.

It is reasonable to expect a free trade, unencumbered with duties, to every part of America.

Make early and strict conditions, not only to secure all debts whatever due to British subjects, but likewise to restore the Loyalists to a full enjoyment of their rights and privileges. And their indemnification to be considered. Lord Shelburne will never give up the Loyalists. The Penn family have been sadly

1782. used, and Lord Shelburne is personally interested for them, and thinks it his duty to be so for all.

The private paper desires Canada for three reasons:—

1st. By way of reparation.—Answer. No reparation can be heard of.

2nd. To prevent future wars.—Answer. It is to be hoped that some more friendly method will be found.

3rd. Loyalists as a fund of indemnification to them.—Answer. No independence to be acknowledged without their being taken care of.

A compensation expected for New York, Charlestown, and Savannah. Penobscott to be always kept.

These observations on the Canada paper show that, if Lord Shelburne had sent any answer to it by Oswald, it would not have been a favourable one. The probability is, that he made no remark upon it to Oswald, fearing that he might offend Franklin; and that Oswald construed his silence into approbation. There is likewise another paper of similar notes, which ends with the following passage: 'Tell him (Franklin), candidly and confidentially, Lord Shelburne's situation with the King: that he was sent for to form the Ministry:

'That his lordship will make no use of it but to keep his word with mankind, and is under as little apprehension of being deceived himself, as unwilling to deceive others. In short, that he knows the bottom to be sound.'

The purpose of this projected communication was to satisfy Franklin that the King was not secretly hostile to the negotiation, and that the American negotiators need not fear that the treaty would be ultimately defeated by the King's interference.

It should be added that the cession of Canada was afterwards formally proposed by Franklin to Oswald, when the latter had been appointed commissioner, and was reported to his own Government, in a letter of

July 12; but that the proposition was not assented to.[1] 1782.

Lord Holland remarks that, 'this resignation of Mr. Fox is unquestionably one of the *two* passages of his public life most open to animadversion, and most requiring explanation.'[2] The wisdom of this decision resolves itself into a question of *general* mistrust of Lord Shelburne; for Lord Shelburne's accession to the Treasury would have placed another person at the Home Office, who would have had the control of the American negotiation. Mr. Fox thus

[1] The story of Franklin's coat (the truth of which has been denied by Sparks) is traced by Lord Mahon to the signing of the treaty with France in 1778 (see his note, vol. v. p. 329). Mr. Allen remarks that, 'the anecdote rests on authority not slightly to be rejected. It was related to Lord Holland by Lord St. Helen's, one of the plenipotentiaries employed in negotiating the treaty, and the lasting impression it made on Lord St. Helen's leaves little doubt of the accuracy of his recollection. He could not speak without indignation of the triumphant air with which Franklin told them he had laid by and preserved his coat for such an occasion' (*Mem. of Fox*, vol. i. p. 385). Lord St. Helen's, then Mr. Fitzherbert, was sent to Paris to negotiate with France, when Mr. Grenville resigned. He had no personal concern with the treaty between France and America in 1778; and therefore, if his testimony is not rejected, we must suppose that Franklin wore the coat *twice*. Mr. Fitzherbert signed the preliminaries with France and Spain, but Oswald signed those with America; the definitive treaty with America was signed by Mr. Hartley for England. Mr. Fitzherbert could not have been present, *officially*, when any signature with Franklin took place.

Mr. Fitzherbert, in a letter to Lord Grantham, of February 9, 1783 (preserved among the Shelburne papers), has the following passage: 'Dr. Franklin seems anxious to return to America, which I am sorry for, being persuaded that he will do his utmost, when there, to prevent all revival of goodwill and cordiality with the mother country; his rancour and inveteracy against which are as violent as ever. I could mention to your Lordship instances of this which would be almost ludicrous, if anything can deserve that name which is likely to produce such serious consequences.' The letter from Mr. Hartley to Mr. Fox, of September 3, 1783, S.P.O., reporting the signature of the Definitive Treaty with America, describes the existence of a very friendly feeling with the American Commissioners on that occasion.

[2] Vol. i. p. 472. The *other* passage alluded to by Lord Holland is the coalition with Lord North (see vol. ii. p. 62).

1782. describes his motives for resignation, in a letter to Mr. Grenville of July 5: 'I am sure my staying would have been a means of deceiving the public and betraying my party; and these are things not to be done for the sake of any supposed temporary good. I feel that my situation in the country, my power, my popularity, my consequence,—nay, my character, are all risked: but I have done right, and therefore in the end it must turn out to have been wise.'[1]

Lord Shelburne had held office in the Duke of Grafton's Administration, and had been a Secretary of State at the age of twenty-nine. He was a man of ability, and was eminent as a speaker; he belonged to the Whig party, but his more immediate political connection was with Lord Chatham. During the American war, he continued in active opposition to the Government, and he had never been a favourite of the King. Before he left the Duke of Grafton's Cabinet in 1768, 'instigations to remove him (as we learn from the Duke's memoirs) fell daily from the King.'[2] Ten years later, in March 1778, the King,

[1] *Buckingham Papers*, vol. i. p. 55.

[2] Cited by Lord Mahon, vol. v. p. 202, 3rd ed. See his character of Lord Shelburne. *Ibid.* p. 209.

Lord Shelburne seems to have been a strong free-trader, at a time when such opinions among statesmen were almost unknown. The following passage occurs in a letter from Benjamin Vaughan to Franklin, of February 1783: 'The boldness of my friend's (Lord Shelburne's) conduct has done infinite service to men's minds, as his conversation has done to the royal mind. You will take pleasure in hearing that he talked of making England a free port; for which, he said, we were fitted by nature, capital, love of enterprise, maritime connections, and position between the Old and New World, and the North and South of Europe; and that those who were best circumstanced for trade could not but be gainers by having trade open' (*Works, Ibid.* p. 489). According to Lord Holland, Bentham always said, that 'Lord Shelburne was the only Minister he ever heard of who did not fear the people' (*Memoirs of the Whig Party*, vol. i. p. 41). M. Dumont, on coming to England in 1785, acquired the friendship of Lord Shelburne,

writing to Lord North, thus expresses himself: 'I am 1782.
willing, through your channel, to accept any description of persons that will come avowedly to the support of your Administration; and, as such, do not object to Lord Shelburne and Mr. Barré, *whom personally, perhaps, I dislike as much as Alderman Wilkes.*' [1] In December 1779, Lord Shelburne made a speech in the House of Lords, in an American debate, which Mr. Fitzpatrick describes as 'excellent, very violent, *and very personal to the King.*' [2] It may be added that the King's aversion for Lord Chatham, with whom Lord Shelburne had acted, was latterly not less than his aversion for Fox. If, therefore, the King showed any preference for Lord Shelburne in 1782, it must have been, not because he liked him much, but because he disliked Fox more. Lord Shelburne, indeed, according to Lord Holland's testimony, 'always complained that the King had tricked and deserted him in 1782 and 1783;' and 'he always suspected the Court of secretly conniving at his downfall.' [3] On the other hand, the King complained of Lord Shelburne for resigning the

and was entrusted with the education of his sons (*Dumont, Souvenirs sur Mirabeau*, p. ii.).

[1] *Lord Mahon*, vol. vi. App. p. lvi. A story is told of Wilkes, after he had given up the trade of a patriot, having been present at a party with the Prince of Wales, and having joined in singing 'God save the King.' The prince called to him, and asked how long he had sung that song. 'Ever since I have had the honour of knowing your Royal Highness,' was the answer.

[2] *Memorials of Fox*, vol. i. p. 239.

[3] *Ibid.* vol. i. p. 479; vol. ii. p. 65.

'The late Earl of Shelburne told a friend of mine that the King possessed one art beyond any man he had ever known: for that, by the familiarity of his intercourse, he obtained your confidence, procured from you your opinion of different public characters, and then availed himself of this knowledge to sow dissension' (Nicholl's *Recollections and Reflections during the Reign of George III.*, vol. i. p. 389). The same writer states (*Ibid.* p. 51) that the King ordered 'the members of his household to express their disapprobation of the peace, and thus affronted Lord Shelburne.'

1782. Government too easily, and for not prolonging the fight against the Coalition. In an audience granted to Lord Temple, upon his return from Ireland, his Majesty 'recapitulated all the transactions of that period, with the strongest encomium upon Mr. Pitt, and *with much apparent acrimony hinted at Lord Shelburne*, whom he stated to have abandoned a position which was tenable, and particularly so after the popular resentment had been roused.'[1]

Lord Holland, in his 'Memoirs of the Whig Party,' has given a full-length portrait of Lord Shelburne, founded on personal knowledge. His character is there summed up in the following words: 'His chief merits were courage, decision of character, and discernment in discovering the talents of inferiors. Want of judgment was his great defect. An imperious character, and suspicion, with its consequences, his ruling vices.'[2] If habits of suspicion, and a persuasion of the general dishonesty of mankind, had prevented Lord Shelburne from being frank and open in his dealings, and had earned him the nickname of Malagrida, this fact was well known to Fox when he accepted office as his colleague. The arguments founded on this general presumption were not, as we have seen, greatly strengthened by the Oswald affair. It cannot be supposed that Fox was influenced by such appeals to his self-love as that administered by Burke, when he spoke of 'the utter impossibility of his acting for any length of time *as a clerk* in Lord Shelburne's Administration.'[3] If Fox had put forward his pretensions to the office of Prime Minister, he might consistently have resigned because they were rejected. But he proposed the appointment of the Duke of Portland to that office, and did not object to serve

[1] *Buckingham Papers*, vol. i. p. 303. The latter words allude to the incipient unpopularity of the Coalition.

[2] Vol. i. p. 42.

[3] *Memorials of Fox*, vol. i. p. 457.

under *him*. The objection, therefore, was not to the subordination, but to the person of the chief. 1782.

Mr. Fitzpatrick, in a letter of July 5, thus pointedly describes the opinions of the public upon Fox's resignation: 'All persons who have any understanding and no office, are of opinion that Charles has done right: all persons who have little understanding are frightened; and all persons who have offices, with some brilliant exceptions, think he has been hasty' (vol. i. p. 461). Lord Temple, in a letter to Mr. Grenville, written on the previous day, gives the following account of a conversation which he had had with Fox at the House of Lords:—

He stated his knowledge that Lord Shelburne would succeed to Lord Rockingham, and his idea of throwing up. I stated Lord Shelburne's promises to measures, which I found Lord Shelburne had made to him; but *the loss of the object*, which was evidently a favourite point with him, seemed to affect him much. I repeated my apprehensions that the people would not stand by him in his attempt to quit upon private grounds, which, from their nature would appear to be a quarrel for offices, and not a public measure. He saw all this, and said that it had been urged to him by several, but that he was not determined. . . . . . My opinion, from all whom I have seen, is, that Fox has undone himself with the public; and his most intimate friends seem of the same opinion (*Buckingham Papers*, vol. i. p. 51).

The step (says Lord Holland) was universally lamented, and very naturally censured, by many friends of freedom and peace, who were unacquainted with the personal character of Mr. Fox and his colleagues, and who saw in it nothing but a fatal division in a body of men, to whom they were looking for a restoration of the blessings of peace, and the re-establishment of a virtuous system of government at home. To them it seemed the result of mere personal jealousy and squabbles for superiority, in which the interests of the public were overlooked (*Mem. of Fox*, vol. i. p. 472).[1]

[1] Nicholls, vol. ii. p. 140, gives it as his opinion that Mr. Fox's separation from Lord Shelburne took place on *private* grounds.

1782. It appears that Mr. Fox had announced his intention of resigning, a few days before Lord Rockingham's death, in consequence of a decision of the Cabinet with respect to the recognition of American independence.[1] This fact was indeed publicly stated by him in the House of Commons, in answer to General Conway, who had intimated that his resignation had been determined by merely personal considerations.[2] It is indeed highly probable that, even if Lord Rockingham had lived, Fox would before long have seceded from the Cabinet. Mr. Fox, however, declared in the same debate, that the appointment of Lord Shelburne to the office of First Lord of the Treasury, instead of the Duke of Portland, was one of the reasons of his resignation. Mr. Pitt, like General Conway, attributed Mr. Fox's conduct to private pique, not to public grounds, and contended that he ought to have remained in office until he had seen Lord Shelburne abandont he principles upon which Lord Rockingham and his friends had acted.

In order to form a proper estimate of Mr. Fox's decision to refuse office with Lord Shelburne, it is necessary to consider his subsequent course, and to compare the political connection which he abandoned with that which he proceeded to form. Before doing so, however, it is right to advert to the fact, that, when Mr. Pitt formed his Administration in 1783, after the dismissal of the Coalition Ministry, he made no offer to Lord Shelburne, although he had, in the previous year, been Chancellor of the Exchequer, and leader of the House of Commons in his Administration. This circumstance seems to indicate that he, like Mr. Fox, did not wish for Lord Shelburne as a colleague.[3] Lord

[1] *Memorials of Fox*, vol. i. p. 389, 435, 438–9, 453.

[2] July 9, 1782.

[3] Lord Grenville writing to Lord Temple, on December 7, 1782, says:

Shelburne resented this exclusion, and Lord Holland says, 1782.
that he even hesitated about accepting the marquisate, which was offered him by Mr. Pitt and the Court, as a mark of approbation of the peace.[1] Although Lord Shelburne accepted this mark of honour from Mr. Pitt's Government, he continued in opposition; taking, however, little part in politics after his retirement from office.

We are now in full possession of the grounds upon which Mr. Fox acted on this occasion, derived from the most authentic sources, and we can pass judgment upon them without any of those personal feelings by which the minds of contemporaries are inflamed. If Mr. Fox, after a trial of three months, found that he could not act satisfactorily with Lord Shelburne, it must be admitted that he was justified in refusing to hold office in his Administration. But Lord Shelburne's Ministry was a Whig Ministry: it included even a portion of the Rockingham party; none of Lord North's party belonged to it; Mr. Pitt, the leader of the House of Commons, was a decided Whig, and had taken a strong part in overthrowing Lord North's Government. The leading principles of Lord Rockingham's

'I have said that the complexion of affairs here makes it more unpleasant. Lord Shelburne's evident intention is to make cyphers of his colleagues. Rayneval's arrival at his house at eight in the morning was not known to Townshend till twelve, nor to any of the others till after four. They cannot be much pleased, but still it is imagined they mean to remain' (*Buckingham Papers*, vol. i. p. 84). This alludes to the arrival of M. de Rayneval, who was sent by the French Government to London, under a fictitious name, on the business of the peace. The length of time mentioned by Lord Grenville does not seem very great. After Lord Shelburne's resignation, Lord Grenville, also writing to Lord Temple, says, speaking of the Coalition: 'Yet these are the men who accuse Lord Shelburne of duplicity, *without having produced one instance during a six months' ministry*' (*Ibid.* p. 205). Lord Grenville was probably by this time made aware of what had passed with his brother at Paris nearly twelve months before.

[1] *Memoirs of the Whig Party*, vol. i. p. 43. Some remarks upon this peerage will be found in the *Edinburgh Review*, vol. xxv. p. 212, in an article on Wraxall's *Historical Memoirs*.

1782. Government, and particularly the recognition of American independence, were avowed by Lord Shelburne. If, therefore, Fox could not make up his mind to serve with Lord Shelburne, we think that, looking both to his duty as a public man, and to his policy as a leader of the larger section of the Whig party, his proper course was to stand aloof, to watch the conduct of the Government, to support it when right, to oppose it when wrong, to observe an armed neutrality, but not, as he actually did, to form a league, offensive and defensive, with the enemy. When Lord Rockingham died, and the King made Lord Shelburne, and not the Duke of Portland, Prime Minister, there were three courses open to Fox. 1. To remain in Lord Shelburne's Government. 2. To resign with his friends, and to form a separate independent party. 3. To coalesce with Lord North and the Tories. Of these three courses the last was, in our judgment, incomparably the worst; and this was the one which Fox selected.

As soon as Lord Shelburne's Ministry was formed, a practical solution of the problem of the three bodies had to be found. Gibbon, writing near the commencement of the ensuing Session, mentions a calculation of the comparative strength of the three parties in the House of Commons, which gave 140 votes to the Government, 120 to Lord North, 90 to Fox, the rest unknown or uncertain.[1] In this state of things a combination of any two would defeat the third. The views of the Government were therefore naturally turned towards a junction with some portion of the Opposition. It was, however, laid down as a principle by Lord Shelburne and Mr. Pitt, that they would not admit Lord North into the Cabinet, though they were willing to negotiate with some of his

[1] Gibbon to Lord Sheffield, October 14, 1782. *Miscellaneous Works*, vol. ii. p. 261, 8vo.

followers.[1] Hence they looked in the other direction, 1783.
and on February 11, 1783, Mr. Pitt sought an interview with Mr. Fox, in order to invite him to join Lord Shelburne's Government. The following is Bishop Tomline's account of what passed on this occasion:—

Neither Mr. Pitt nor Lord Shelburne saw any reason why they should not act with Mr. Fox. It was therefore agreed that an offer should be made to him to return to office; for which purpose Mr. Pitt waited upon him by appointment. As soon as Mr. Fox heard the object of Mr. Pitt's visit, he asked, whether it was intended that Lord Shelburne should remain First Lord of the Treasury; to which Mr. Pitt answered in the affirmative. Mr. Fox immediately replied, that it was impossible for him to belong to any Administration of which Lord Shelburne was the head.[2] Mr. Pitt observed, that if that was his determination, it would be useless for him to enter into any further discussion, 'as he did

[1] It is stated in the *Memorials of Fox*, vol. ii. p. 30, that the Duke of Richmond, Lord Keppel, and Mr. Pitt were inclined to a coalition with Fox, but that Lord Shelburne leant to Lord North. Horace Walpole speaks of overtures by Lord Shelburne to Lord North (*Ibid.* p. 12). Lord Grenville, however, writing to Lord Temple, February 19, 1783, mentions among some facts, the authenticity of which he vouches, that 'Lord Shelburne never has made any offer whatever to Lord North.' This fact was probably stated by him on Mr. Pitt's authority (*Buckingham Papers*, vol. i. p. 158). Tomline says, that 'Mr. Pitt positively objected to any application being made to Lord North' (vol. i. p. 88). Mr. Dundas told Mr. Adam, that 'Pitt was ready to negotiate with Lord North's party, *on the basis of excluding Lord North personally*' (*Memorials of Fox*, vol. ii. p. 21). Lord Temple's private notes likewise mention a coalition with some of Lord North's supporters as practicable, but without Lord North himself (*Buckingham Papers, ibid.* p. 301).

[2] Mr. Fox did not put forward his own claims to that office, but still insisted on the Duke of Portland (*Mem. of Fox*, vol. ii. p. 12).

In the debates which followed the dismissal of the Coalition Ministry, Pitt publicly stated that he would not sit in the same Cabinet with Lord North; and after the dissolution (although he had then strong motives for standing well with the King) he spoke of the one virtue of the late Parliament, that 'it had put an end to Lord North's Administration, and to the calamitous and ruinous war which he had brought upon the country' (*Tomline*, vol. i. pp. 359, 478).

1783. not come to betray Lord Shelburne;' and he took his leave. This was, I believe, the last time Mr. Pitt was in a private room with Mr. Fox; and from this period may be dated that political hostility which continued through the remainder of their lives.[1]

There was nothing at this time, either in the public or personal relations of Mr. Fox and Mr. Pitt, which would have prevented them from acting together, and serving in the same Cabinet. Their political principles were similar; and Mr. Fox had spoken with high praise and admiration of Mr. Pitt's abilities and character upon his first appearance in public life. 'Fox,' says Walpole, 'had fondly espoused him, and kindly, not jealously nor fearfully, wished to have him his friend.'[2] It is probable that Fox would have now consented to this union, if his dislike of Lord Shelburne had not formed an obstacle.

The resolution of Lord Shelburne and Pitt not to negotiate with Lord North, and the refusal of Fox to join Lord Shelburne's Government, produced an attempt of common

[1] *Life of Pitt*, vol. i. p. 89, 3rd ed. The date of this offer is fixed by Lord Grenville's letter of February 11, 1783, where he says, 'Pitt told me to-day that it being thought necessary to make some attempt at a junction with Fox, he had seen him *to-day*, when he asked one question—viz. whether there were any terms on which he would come in. The answer was "None, while Lord Shelburne remained;" and so it ended. Upon this (Lord Grenville truly adds) I think one may observe that the one must be very desperate, the other very confident, before such a question could be so put and so answered' (*Buckingham Papers*, vol. i. p. 148). Tomline appears to refer this interview to 'the end of autumn,' which is clearly a mistake. We suspect, moreover, that the retort ascribed to Pitt, that 'he did not come to betray Lord Shelburne,' was never really uttered; though it doubtless correctly expresses Pitt's feeling at the time. See also Adam's account, *Mem. of Fox*, vol. ii. p. 33, which agrees with Lord Grenville's, and does not support Tomline's. Walpole, *ibid.* p. 12, says that Fox had been sounded by the Duke of Richmond and Lord Keppel *before* Pitt's visit.

[2] *Mem. of Fox*, vol. ii. p. 5. See also Lord Holland's account, vol. i. p. 262. 'Till the unfortunate breach between the Whigs and Lord Shelburne, when Mr. Pitt sided with the latter, Mr. Fox never lost an opportunity of extolling the talents and praising the conduct of young Pitt.'

friends to bring Fox and Lord North together. Fox wished to turn out Lord Shelburne. Lord North was resentful at being proscribed by him and Pitt; and the object was speedily effected. On February 14, three days after the interview with Fox, he and Lord North met for the first time since their estrangement; and their interview is thus described: 1783

They agreed to lay aside all former animosity, Mr. Fox declaring that he hoped their Administration would be *founded on mutual good will and confidence*, which was the only thing that could make it permanent and useful. They agreed, also, that nothing more was required to be done in reducing the influence of the Crown by economical reform, and that on parliamentary reform every man should follow his own opinion. Mr. Fox having urged that the King should not be suffered to be his own Minister, Lord North replied: 'If you mean there should not be a Government by departments, I agree with you; I think it a very bad system. There should be one man, or a Cabinet, to govern the whole, and direct every measure. Government by departments was not brought in by me. I found it so, and had not vigour and resolution to put an end to it. *The King ought to be treated with all sort of respect and attention, but the appearance of power is all that a king of this country can have.* Though the Government in my time was a Government by departments, the whole was done by the Ministers, except in a few instances' (vol. ii. p. 37).

Since the accession of Lord Shelburne's Ministry, the negotiations for a peace, on the basis of American Independence, had been steadily pursued. The preliminaries had first been signed with America, and subsequently with France and Spain. The settlement of this all-important question was announced in the King's speech, and the preliminaries were subsequently presented to Parliament. It was agreed that this question was a favourable field for a trial of strength between the coalesced parties of Fox

1783. and Lord North, and the Government. A motion of censure upon the Preliminaries of Peace was accordingly made by Lord J. Cavendish, and carried by 207 to 190 votes.[1] Upon this defeat, Lord Shelburne and his Cabinet resigned (Feb. 24, 1783).

After a long *interministerium* (as Walpole calls it), and an attempt on the King's part to induce Mr. Pitt to attempt the formation of a Government—an undertaking which he steadfastly declined[2] — a new Administration was formed, of which the Duke of Portland (as originally proposed by Fox) was the head, and in which Fox himself and Lord North were the Secretaries of State. The other Cabinet offices were chiefly filled with followers of Fox.

Whatever admiration may be felt for the abilities, the eloquence, the patriotism, the courage, and the public spirit of Mr. Fox, no judicious and impartial biographer will, as it seems to us, seek to justify, or even to palliate, his coalition with Lord North. Lord J. Russell accordingly condemns, and does not defend it. In every point of view, it was an ill-assorted union. The political principles of the two chiefs were diametrically opposed to each other. Lord North had been, as Minister, the passive instrument of the royal will; Fox had waged a vehement war against the King and his policy, and had, at last, achieved a victory over both. During the Parliamentary conflicts of the American war, there was scarcely a form of blame, or

[1] [The opposition majority on the amendment to the address had been 224 to 208. See Pitt's letter to his mother (Lord Stanhope's *Life of Pitt*, vol. i. p. 97). The motion of Lord John Cavendish was made on February 21.—Ed.]

[2] [Pitt appears to have wavered. The Lord Advocate, in his letter of February 27, says, 'I was with Mr. Pitt this morning from eight o'clock till eleven, and parted with him perfectly resolved to accept First Lord of the Treasury. He then encloses Pitt's letter, containing his final refusal. See Lord Stanhope's *Life*, vol. i. p. 108.—Ed.]

even of vituperation, within the compass of the English language, which Fox had not applied to Lord North : not only his conduct, and his policy, his principles, but his character, his honour, and his honesty, had been unsparingly denounced. Hints of impeachment had even been thrown out. These debates were quite recent in the beginning of 1783; the very words of Fox's terrible philippics against Lord North's profligate and ruinous administration must have been still ringing in the ears of the members who saw them take their seats, side by side, on the Treasury bench, as the two Secretaries of State. All the disgraceful events of the latter years of the American war, and the censures which they had entailed on the Ministers who then mismanaged public affairs, were fresh in every one's thoughts; it was scarcely necessary to resort to such reminders as the 'Beauties of Fox, Burke, and North,' which were printed and circulated by the enemies of the 'monstrous and unnatural Coalition.' These were matters of universal notoriety, and the nation was shocked by a union of parties, in which they could see so little of public principle, so little to justify that 'mutual goodwill and *confidence*,' of which Fox spoke in his interview with Lord North. There was, therefore, no disposition to make in favour of the Coalition the allowance suggested by Lord Holland; namely, that Lord North had been insincere in his American policy, that he had carried on the war in order to please the King, and that the difference between his *real* opinions and the opinions of Fox was not considerable.[1] For the public knew nothing of his secret opinions; they had not the privilege (which we now enjoy) of reading his private correspondence with 1783.

[1] See *Memorials of Fox*, vol. i. pp. 195, 254; vol. ii. p. 63. We think that Lord Holland's meaning is mistaken by Lord John in his note on the former passage. His object, as it seems to us, is to vindicate Mr. Fox, on the ground that Lord North *really* agreed with him in opinion.

1783. the King; they judged him by his acts and his avowed opinions; and they knew that his course and that of Fox had, on all the leading questions of public policy, for the last eight years, but, above all, on the great question of the American war, been diametrically opposed. They thought that if Fox was right in his invectives against Lord North in the years 1774 to 1782, he could not be right in coalescing with Lord North in 1783. Besides, it might be felt that there is a medium between rancorous vindictiveness, and a spiritless oblivion of injuries. Though Lord North's well-tried good nature would prevent him from cherishing resentful spite, there was something, in our judgment, inexpressibly mean in the tameness with which the King's late favourite, covered with the scars of Fox's mighty sword, hastened to accept office in what was virtually *his* Administration. Hence the public were more inclined to blame Lord North for joining Fox, than Fox for joining Lord North. Neither, however, escaped the unpopularity which attended their coalition: the public are, in general, sufficiently ready to believe that ministers are influenced in their conduct by a mere love of place. On this occasion, it was natural for them to assume that Lord North and Fox were actuated by this motive, when they saw two such determined opponents coalesce in order to obtain office. It may be noted that if Fox's principles, as to the colleagues with whom he acted, were as latitudinarian as his coalition with Lord North evinces, it is difficult to understand why he should have refused to serve with Lord Shelburne on the ground that he could not place entire confidence in him.[1]

While the nation disapproved of the Coalition on grounds of public policy, the King resented it still more

[1] Mr. Adolphus, *History of George III.*, vol. iii. p. 463, says of the Coalition, 'in no action of his life had Mr. Fox displayed less discernment.'

acutely on grounds of personal feeling. He had for some time entertained the strongest aversion for Fox, his rival, his enemy, and now his conqueror and master: and that aversion had been recently strengthened by the friendship which had grown up between Fox and the Prince of Wales, now in his twenty-first year. The King had never loved his eldest son;[1] but his hatred for Fox was aggravated by the belief that he had alienated the Prince's affections from him, and corrupted his principles. When the Coalition Ministry was formed, the Prince and Fox were on the most intimate terms. A series of notes from the Prince to him, of this date, beginning. 'Dear Charles,' and written in a tone of confidential familiarity, are printed in these memoirs.[2] The King was said to have called the Coalition Ministry, 'his son's Ministry,' and his dislike of Fox, combined with his jealously of the Prince, became, at this time, in Walpole's words, *a rankling ulcer*.[3] Nor 1783.

[1] Even so early as November 28, 1781, Walpole has the following entry in his *Diary*: 'The King, as if he had never used the Duke of Gloucester ill, opened his mind to him on his son, the Prince of Wales, and his other brother, the Duke of Cumberland, the latter of whom, he said, was governed by Charles Fox and Fitzpatrick, and governed the Prince of Wales, whom they wanted to drive into Opposition. "When we hunt together," said the King, "neither my son nor my brother will speak to me; and lately, when the chase ended at a little village where there was but a single post-chaise to be hired, my son and brother got into it, drove to London, and left me to get home in a cart, if I could find one!" He complained, too, that the prince, when invited to dine with him, came an hour too late, and "all the servants saw the father waiting an hour for the son"' (*Mem. of Fox*, vol. i. p. 269). When Lord North's Government was falling, the Prince of Wales made interest against him, 'though,' says Walpole, 'he only influenced one vote, that of Lord Melbourne, then recently made an Irish peer' (*Ibid.* p. 286). The prince gave his vote in the House of Lords in favour of Fox's Indian Bill, at the very moment when the King had been canvassing the peers against it (Tomline's *Life of Pitt*, vol. i. pp. 220, 223, 226). See also the account of Fox's intimate relations with the prince, in 1785, at the time of the marriage with Mrs. Fitzherbert (*Mem. of Fox*, vol. ii. p. 277).

[2] Vol. ii. pp. 106–111.

[3] *Ibid.* pp. 45, 46, 57. Lord Grenville, in describing an interview with

1783. were his feelings towards Lord North much more friendly. There were two ministers to whom, in the course of his long reign, George III. gave a cordial, sincere, and consistent support. Those two ministers were Lord Bute and Lord North. Even in the disastrous state of things which the country had reached at the beginning of 1782, the King was ready still to support Lord North, if the minister could have held up his head against the hurricane of censure which night after night he had to encounter in Parliament. In taking leave of Lord North on that occasion, the King had said, in the exuberance of his sorrow, that 'he ever had, and ever should look on Lord North *as a friend*, as well as a faithful servant.'[1]

It must, therefore, have been with feelings of poignant disappointment that he beheld the subject of so much royal favour, and even of royal affection, desert to the enemy, enlist in his service, and by his political influence assist in promoting the defeat and humiliation of his once partial but now deserted master.[2] If he meditated an

the King in March 1783, says that 'he loaded Fox with every expression of abhorrence;' and he added, that much as he disliked both Fox and Lord North, if he was to choose he must certainly prefer the latter to the former (*Buckingham Papers*, vol. i. pp. 190, 192). Walpole, indeed, states that, 'when the Coalition Ministry kissed hands, the King received Fox graciously, but received Lord North with the utmost coldness, and continued to treat him with visible aversion' (*Mem. of Fox*, vol. ii. p. 56).

[1] *Memorials of Fox*, vol. i. p. 289.

[2] Lord Grenville, in the letter already quoted, says that the King spoke of Lord North 'in terms of strong resentment and disgust' (*Buckingham Papers*, vol. i. p. 191). Lord Temple mentions the King's language, at a subsequent audience, respecting Pitt and Lord Shelburne, and adds, 'This was naturally attended with strong expressions of resentment and disgust of his Ministers, and of personal abhorrence of Lord North, *whom he charged with treachery and ingratitude of the blackest nature.* He repeated, that to such a Ministry he never would give his confidence, and that he would take the first moment for dismissing them' (*Ibid.* p. 303). In a letter to Lord Temple, of April 1, 1783, the King speaks of 'the uneasiness of his mind at having been thwarted in every attempt to keep the administration of public

escape to Hanover in the preceding year, when Lord North was expelled from office, it was still more natural that he should now again throw out threats of resorting to this extremity; of trying the effects of that royal secession to the Mons Sacer.[1] The iron of the Coalition had indeed entered into his soul, but there was another alternative besides Hanover, and he resolved to take the earliest opportunity of shaking off his hated Ministers. We shall see that no long time elapsed before this opportunity presented itself. 1783.

The formation of the Coalition Ministry was announced on April 2, 1783.[2] Mr. Pitt was pressed by Fox's friends to join it, retaining his office of Chancellor of the Exchequer: but he refused on the ground that he would not serve with Lord North.[3] Nothing remarkable occurred

affairs out of the hands of the most unprincipled Coalition the annals of this or any other nation can equal,' and he afterwards sneers at 'the *grateful* Lord North' (*ibid.* p. 219). We owe likewise to the kindness of the Marquis of Lansdowne the information that amongst his father's papers there is a report of a conversation between the King and Lord Ashburton (Dunning) about this time, in which the King is described as complaining in strong terms of Lord North's desertion of him. Lord North's *ingratitude* was doubtless what rankled most in the King's mind, and, it must be admitted, not without reason. Lord Mahon (*History of England*, vol. v. p. 253) remarks, that the King never forgot his obligations to Lord North. It would, perhaps, be more correct to say, that the King never forgot Lord North's obligations to him.

[1] Under March, 1783, Walpole says, 'His counsellors were as inveterate as His Majesty, but had less boldness; finding which, he told the Lord Advocate that sooner than yield he would go to Hanover, and had even prevailed on the Queen to consent' (*Mem. of Fox*, vol. ii. p. 44).

[2] Watson, Bishop of Llandaff, in the *Anecdotes of his Life*, vol. i. p. 173, says, that 'on the day the Coalition Ministry kissed hands, he told Lord J. Cavendish that they had two things against them—the closet and the country; that the King hated them, and would take the first opportunity of turning them out, and that the Coalition would make the country hate them.'

[3] This fact is stated by Tomline, *ibid.* p. 155. 'Both Adam and Dundas expressed their wish that Pitt could be included in the new arrangement [the Coalition Ministry]. Dundas said he had done all in his power to bring

1783. during the remainder of the Session, and the prorogation took place in July. Parliament met again on November 11, and the King's speech announced with satisfaction the signature of definite treaties of peace with France, Spain, and the United States of America. Mr. Pitt, now the leader of Opposition, reminded the Ministers that these treaties were substantially identical with the preliminary articles upon which they had turned out the Shelburne Administration. The negotiation of that treaty was chiefly the work of Lord Shelburne himself, and its result was a conclusive proof that he had no wish to make reservations in treating with the United States, and that he was prepared for the fullest recognition of American independence. Some concessions were made to France, and particularly to Spain;[1] but the really important feature of

it about, but he found it impossible. . . . . He afterwards said, Pitt is impracticable on the subject of union: he proscribes Lord North, and does not even express himself clearly disposed to unite with Fox. He has a high opinion of Fox's abilities, and had always wished to have him in the Government, because he thought it impossible to conduct great and difficult affairs with such abilities to criticise them. But now he seems much estranged from him' (*Mem. of Fox*, vol. ii. p. 41).

Mr. Fox thus expressed himself respecting Pitt, in a letter to Lord Ossory of September 9, 1783, written under the Coalition Ministry during the recess: 'Next session of Parliament will be a great crisis. *I own I am sanguine about it.* Nothing can go on so well as we do among ourselves, but in my particular situation it is impossible not to feel every day what an amazing advantage it would be to the country if it could ever be in such a state as to promise a permanent administration in the opinion of Europe. If Pitt could be persuaded (but I despair of it), I am convinced if he could, he would do more real service to the country than any man ever did' (vol. ii. p. 208). In speaking of 'my particular situation,' Fox alludes to his office of Foreign Secretary.

[1] The cession of Gibraltar to Spain was seriously in question at this time. A history of the negotiation respecting it is given in *Flassan, ibid.* pp. 345–353. Lord Grenville, in a letter of December 15, 1782, mentions a rumour that Lord Shelburne was outvoted in the Cabinet upon the question of Gibraltar (*Buckingham Papers*, vol. i. p. 89). On two former occasions offers for the cession of Gibraltar had actually been made to Spain by the English Government—once by General Stanhope in 1718, and again by the elder Pitt in 1757 (see *Lord Mahon's History*, vol. ii. p. 127; vol. iv. p. 111).

the treaty was the unqualified recognition of the American colonies as independent States. The preliminaries were unpopular, and Mr. Fox had taken advantage of that unpopularity in order to overthrow a weak Ministry; but the concessions made were necessary, and were wisely adopted by Mr. Fox in the definite treaties which were signed under his auspices. If any blame was due for the concessions, it should have fallen on those who by their mismanagement of public affairs reduced England to such a state of weakness as compelled her to yield, not on those who extricated her from a hopeless and ruinous war. When the vote of censure was passed, Lord North and the Ministers ought to have changed places.[1] 1783.

About a week after the beginning of the Session, Mr. Fox introduced his famous Indian Bill. Its principal feature was that it vested the government of India, for

Speaking of the negotiations for the treaty of 1783, Flassan says, 'Les ministres Anglais du moins, et particulièrement Lord Shelburne et Lord Grantham, montrèrent de la droiture, et une envie de la paix qui n'était balancée que par la crainte que le parlement ne la trouvât pas assez avantageuse:' *Ibid.* p. 365.

[1] It is curious to observe how general the belief was, both in England and on the Continent, that the power and greatness of this country had been ruined by the loss of the American colonies. 'The era of England's glory,' said Mr. Pitt, in defending the preliminaries of peace, 'is past; she is now under the awful and mortifying necessity of employing a language corresponding with her new condition. *The visions of her power and preeminence are passed away.*' Coxe, in describing the effects of the Treaty of 1783 says: 'The Bourbon Courts exulted in the success of their machinations, and confidently anticipated the speedy downfall of the British power' (*Bourbon Kings of Spain*, c. 75). Again he says: 'France exulted in having wrested the colonies from the mother country, and anticipated the advantages which she expected to derive from the diminution of the British commerce and power. The same opinion prevailed throughout the Continent, and *the Court of Vienna prophesied that England would ultimately sink in the unequal contest with the House of Bourbon.* Nor were there wanting even in England persons of enlightened minds who regarded this peace as the ruin of their country, and who predicted that "the sun of Great Britain was set for ever"' (*House of Austria*, c. 48).

1783. four years, in a commission of seven persons named in the Bill, and not appointed or removable by the Crown. As soon as the plan was disclosed, Pitt denounced it as dangerous to the Constitution, and as a violation of the chartered rights of the East India Company; and the most ambitious designs were imputed to its authors. The subject was properly in the department of Lord North, as Home Secretary,[1] for the same reason that the colonies were in his department; but the measure was introduced and managed by Mr. Fox, who had probably been assisted by Burke's advice in its preparation. The Bill, owing to the numerical strength of the Coalition, soon passed the House of Commons, and it was carried up to the Lords by Mr. Fox, at the head of a large body of members, on December 9. Here a different fate awaited it.[2] The King, assisted by the suggestions of artful counsellers, sagaciously perceived that his enemies had given him the opportunity for which he was waiting. The Coalition had rendered Fox unpopular; his Indian Bill had alarmed the country. A canvass of the Peers against the Indian Bill was set on foot by the King, partly or chiefly through the medium of Lord Temple. In the House of Lords, the 'King's friends' were numerous; and on December 17 the Bill was rejected by 95 to 76 votes. On the following day Fox and Lord North were required to deliver up their seals; and Pitt, seeing the change which had taken place since the spring, now consented to form a Government.

Pitt's Administration, though it lasted sixteen years, did not commence under happy auspices. However great his ability, his age was only twenty-five years; the majority

[1] Tomline's *Life of Pitt*, vol. i. p. 463.

[2] [The majority on the second reading in the Commons was 229 to 120 (Lord Stanhope's *Life of Pitt*, vol. i. p 141).—Ed.]

of the House of Commons was against him, and the Coalition had absorbed so many of the leading members, that he had not in that House a single Cabinet minister to assist him. The late Government had been upset by the use of the King's personal influence in soliciting the votes of the Peers against his own Ministers. This royal interference was notorious, and almost avowed; Tomline, in his 'Life of Pitt,' admits and defends it.[1] Pitt doubtless took no part in this intrigue, but he knew of it, and profited by its results to obtain power. Lord Temple, who had accepted the seals of Secretary of State, and who had been intended for leader of the House of Lords, found the feeling respecting his own conduct so strong, that he resigned his office in three days, in order that he might meet any charges against himself in a private station.[2] 'This,' says Tomline, 'was the only event of a public nature which I ever knew disturb Mr. Pitt's rest, while he continued in good health.'[3] At that moment Mr. Pitt no 1783.

[1] [Lord Stanhope, in his *Life of Pitt*, can scarcely be said to defend it. He says: 'Without denying, then, that the course pursued in this emergency by George III. was most unusual and most extreme, and one most undesirable to establish as a precedent, I greatly doubt whether it would be practicable to lay down, with perfect clearness and precision, the Constitutional rule which he is supposed to have infringed' (vol. i. p. 155). I conceive that very few rules can be laid down in our Constitution *with perfect clearness and precision*, and when the letter of a rule can be stated with precision, its spirit is easily evaded.—ED.]

[2] [This was the ground assigned for his brother's resignation, by William Grenville, in the House of Commons. Lord Macaulay thought, on the authority of Wraxall, that Lord Temple had resigned because Pitt would not dissolve Parliament immediately; but he admitted that he was wrong in this view, which however Lord Cornwallis, in a letter dated March 3, 1784, rather confirms. On the whole, the reasons given by Lord Stanhope seem to me conclusive against this reason. That writer's own opinion is that Lord Temple resigned because he had applied for a dukedom, or some other personal object of ambition, and had been refused. Compare Lord Stanhope's *Life of Pitt*, vol. i. pp. 159-164; Massey's *History of England*, vol. iii. p. 221.—ED.]

[3] Vol. i. p. 233. Mr. Fox, writing to Lord Northington, the Irish Chancellor, to inform him of Lord Temple's resignation, says: 'What will follow

1783. doubt felt uncertain whether the waters were not closing around him. So great did the chances appear against his success in his hazardous undertaking, that when his writ was moved, on his acceptance of office, the motion was received with loud and general laughter by the Opposition.[1] Fox was confident that the attempt would fail. In a private note written at the time he says, 'We are so strong, that nobody can undertake without madness, and if they do I think we shall destroy them almost as soon as they are formed.'[2] This opinion he openly declared, and it was doubtless shared generally by his party.

The siege was now opened in form; a series of general votes of censure upon Ministers, and addresses to the Crown for the formation of a new Administration, were passed by the House of Commons. The King, however, refused to dismiss his Ministers, and Mr. Pitt refused to resign unless some specific charge was brought against him. The contest was carried on with consummate skill and ability by Fox on the one hand, and sustained with extraordinary coolness, courage, and judgment by Pitt on the other. Fox, however, abstained from going to extremities, being restrained, probably, by the reluctance of some of his friends; and while the struggle was still undecided, an attempt was made by some independent

is not yet known, but I think there can be very little doubt but our Administration will again be established. . . . The confusion of the enemy is beyond all description, and the triumph of our friends proportionable.' Dec. 22, 1783 (*Mem. of Fox*, vol. ii. p. 224).

[1] Tomline, *ibid.* p. 237.

[2] *Mem. of Fox*, vol. ii. p. 221. Compare Tomline, *ibid.* p. 463. At this time it used to be the practice for Cabinet Ministers to appear in the House of Commons in full dress. Hence Lord North is always designated in the debates during the American war as 'the noble Lord in the Blue Ribbon.' We have been informed that, after Mr. Fox had crossed to the Opposition bench, he continued to wear his full dress, in order to mark that, though dismissed by the King, he was still the Minister whom the House kept in power.

country gentlemen to bring about a junction between the two combatants.[1] The King was even prevailed upon to send a written message to the Duke of Portland, to propose a meeting between him and Mr. Pitt.[2] Mr. Pitt consented to have a conference with the Duke of Portland, 'for the purpose of forming a new Administration on a wide basis, and on fair and equal terms;' but a discussion arose on the meaning of '*equal* terms,' and the negotiation was broken off. The Opposition demanded that Pitt should resign before any attempt was made to form a United Government; but Pitt refused this demand, saying, that he could not resign in order to treat for office. The contest had now lasted for two months; the necessary supplies had been granted, and a Mutiny Bill passed; the majorities, which had been forty or fifty at the beginning, had dwindled down to one; and at last, without an Appropriation Act, on the 24th of March the King came down to dissolve the Parliament.[3] Pitt had wisely 1784.

[1] In one of the debates at this time, Mr. Fox said that he respected what he had always understood to be Mr. Pitt's political principles, none of which did any one whom he had consulted wish him to renounce. The union he (Mr. Fox) wished to see take place was a union of principle (see Tomline, *ibid.* p. 356).

[2] *Mem. of Fox*, vol. ii. p. 234.

[3] The Duke of Richmond, who had separated from Mr. Fox when Lord Shelburne became Prime Minister, was a member of Pitt's Cabinet, and contributed essentially to support him against Fox on this trying occasion. 'His firmness during the memorable contest of 1784 is said to have prevented Mr. Pitt from following the example of his cousin, Lord Temple, by resigning in despair. It was on that occasion George III. was reported to have said there was no man in his dominions by whom he had been so much offended, and no man to whom he was so much indebted, as the Duke of Richmond' (*Mem. of Fox*, vol. i. p. 455). See also Tomline, vol. i. p. 235. His reasons for separating from Fox are stated in Lord Albemarle's *Memoirs of Lord Rockingham*, vol. i. p. 340. [Strictly speaking Parliament was prorogued on the 24th, and dissolved by proclamation on the 25th. The curious theft of the Great Seal from the Chancellor's house took place on the morning of the 24th, and the new one was not ready till the following day (*Annual Register*, 1784, p. 185).—Ed.]

1784. calculated the effect of time in turning public opinion in his favour. An earlier dissolution might have produced a balanced state of parties. As it was, the influence of general opinion upon the elections, even in the comparatively shackled state of the representation, was decisive. Above 160 members lost their seats, nearly all of whom belonged to the Opposition. The rout of the Coalition was complete, and after the long series of votes of censure carried against Pitt at the end of the preceding Parliament, the first vote in the new House gave him a majority of more than two to one. From that time Mr. Pitt's majority in the House of Commons remained unshaken.

Of this result, the principal cause was Fox's coalition with Lord North. Although it gave him, for the moment, a large parliamentary support, it turned public opinion against him, and rendered his union with Pitt impossible. If his party was not strong enough to stand alone, and *some* junction was necessary, he clearly made the wrong choice in preferring Lord North to Pitt. His India Bill added to his unpopularity, and had a large share in the consequences of the election of 1784. It is difficult now to understand how the declamatory denunciations of that measure could have produced so great an effect on the country, or how the alarm which was expressed could have been really felt. Pitt may have been under the influence of strong personal prejudice, but his general character forbids the belief that his opposition was insincere. He had doubtless persuaded himself of the reality of the dangers which he described with so much force. The interference with the chartered rights of the Company, so far as they concerned the Government, not the trade, of India, seems to us to require no justification. The Company could have no vested interest in a form of Government which was not conducive to the public welfare. The appointment of an Indian Commission by Parliament, the members of which held their offices on the same tenure as the Judges, and could not be removed either by the Crown or the Company, was unusual, and might be fairly deemed objectionable.[1] But to suppose that within the space of four years, and under the control of Parliament and public opinion, such a use was likely to be made of the Indian patronage as would destroy the legitimate influence of the Crown, and insure the permanent triumph of Mr. Fox's party, appears extravagant and unreasonable.[2] In the first Session of the new Parliament Mr. Pitt introduced his India Bill, which was carried by a majority of 271 to 60; this Bill, by creating a Ministerial Board of Control for the affairs of India, established the system of 'double Government,' which has now existed for seventy years, and which was deliberately continued, with certain amendments, in the last Session of Parliament.[3] 1784.

While the great struggle between Pitt and Fox after the dismissal of the Coalition Ministry was going on, the King's anxiety was great; and in his private letters to Mr. Pitt he recurred to his former intention of seeking a refuge in Hanover from the intolerable pressure of his

[1] A protest formally signed by Lord Rockingham, the Duke of Portland, Lord Fitzwilliam, and other peers, which was much quoted at the time, contained the following passage: 'The election of executive officers in Parliament is plainly unconstitutional, and an example of the most pernicious kind, productive of intrigue and faction, and calculated for extending a corrupt influence in the Crown. It frees ministers from responsibility, while it leaves them all the effect of patronage' (see *Adolphus*, vol. iv. p. 59).

[2] See *Lord J. Russell's Remarks on Fox's India Bill*, vol. ii. pp. 96–100. A good summary of the objections made to it at the time is given in *Tomline's Life of Pitt*, vol. i. pp. 192–201.

[3] [As Lord Stanhope says, 'it continued with some modifications until 1858.' *Life of Pitt*, vol. i. p. 221.—Ed.]

1784. Parliamentary foes. On receiving the account of the first defeats which awaited Mr. Pitt upon his re-election, the King wrote to him as follows: 'I am ready to take any step that may be proposed to oppose this faction, and to struggle to the last period of my life; but I can never submit to throw myself into its power. If they, in the end, succeed, *my line is a clear one, and to which I have fortitude enough to submit.*'[1] About the same time he addressed Mr. Pitt in a similar strain upon an impending motion in the House of Lords: 'Should not the Lords stand boldly forth, this Constitution must soon be changed; for if the two only privileges of the Crown be infringed,—that of negativing Bills which have passed both Houses of Parliament, and that of naming the Ministers to be employed,—I cannot but feel, as far as regards my person, that *I can be no longer of utility to this country, nor can with honour continue in this island.*' 'From this extract,' says Tomline, 'coupled with the conclusion of his former letter, as well as from other authorities, it is evident that the King had at this time serious intentions of retiring to Hanover, in case Mr. Fox and his party should prevail.'[2]

No such painful necessity, however, awaited the King. The fatal error of his great adversary, the dexterity of his secret counsellors, and the consummate parliamentary ability of his young Minister, gave him a signal triumph. Fox had emerged a victor out of the long struggle of the American war; he had passed the King under the yoke,

[1] *Tomline's Life of Pitt*, vol. i. p. 271. In a letter to Mr. Pitt, of February 15, 1784, the King used the following terms respecting Mr. Fox: 'Mr. Pitt is so well apprised of the mortification I feel at any possibility of ever again seeing the heads of opposition in public employments, *and more particularly Mr. Fox, whose conduct has not been more marked against my station in the empire than against my person*, that he must attribute my want of perspicuity, &c.' (*ibid.* p. 390).

[2] *Ibid.* p. 341.

and made him submit to a Ministry which he hated. But he could not convert a victory into a conquest: he had the force which enabled him to defeat, he had not the longsighted and patient prudence which could alone enable him to subjugate. By the unhappy Coalition he lost everything: he threw away his popularity, he destroyed his party, he weakened his moral authority, and he made an opening for the formation of a new combination, which speedily predominated in both Houses of Parliament. As it was said of Napoleon that he was the heir of the Revolution, so it may be said of Pitt that he was the heir of the Coalition. At the critical moment, he was able to satisfy the conditions of the practical problem, which had for so many years remained unsolved. Lord North had, during his twelve years' Ministry, been the favourite of the Crown, but after a time he lost the support of the country. Mr. Fox, up to the Coalition, was warmly supported by the country, but the King would not endure him. In Mr. Pitt was at last found a Minister whom the King would tolerate and the country would support. His Administration, when once formed, could not be shaken by Fox's opposition. It weathered the storm of the Regency, by the King's timely recovery; and the results of the French Revolution gave it additional strength. At last, it fell by an intrigue of secret advisers who alarmed the Protestant conscience of the King: it was stabbed by an assassin in the dark, not overthrown by the blows of Fox's broadsword in fair and open parliamentary warfare. Like most great political contests in this country, the contest between George III. and Mr. Fox ended in a compromise. The compromise was effected in the person of Mr. Pitt.[1] Mr. Pitt was too unbending to become an 1784.

[1] 'On Lord Rockingham's death, Pitt expressed his concern to Mr. Fox, under the gallery, at the report that government would break up. Fox

1784. instrument in the King's hands, and had too much principle to lend himself, like Lord North, to a policy of which he disapproved. On the other hand, the King was grateful to Pitt for rescuing him from the hands of Fox: he endured and almost liked him, though he ultimately tripped him up. Pitt's ascendency in Parliament was maintained by his own talents and conduct, and by the personal confidence which he inspired, not by the influence of the Crown, or the support of the King's friends. In this manner the conflicting elements, which Fox could not harmonise, were reconciled.

Lord John thus sums up the effects of the Coalition, and the disruption of the Whig party, which that measure of apparent union produced:—

> Thus was broken and dispersed, by its own dissensions, that great confederacy of freedom which, nurtured in the adversity of the American war, had revived the ancient virtues of Whiggism, and made the Senate shine with the lights of patriotism and eloquence. Thus vanished the hope of seeing a more brilliant Fox and a more consistent Pitt; the one adorning and advising his country in the conduct of foreign affairs, which he, above all men, understood; and the other applying to the management of our finances the economical principles of Smith, and the wise frugality of Sully. The Coalition prevented a consummation so desirable. * * * The rout of the Whig party, the Pitt Administration, and the war of the French Revolution were the results of this fatal event (vol. ii. p. 91).

said, "it would, and the old system be revived," adding, "they look to you, without you they cannot succeed; with you I know not whether they will or no." "If," replied Pitt, "they reckon upon me, they may find themselves mistaken." Fox, as he left the House, repeated this to Lord John Townshend, and Lord Maitland (afterwards Lauderdale), and probably many others; and both Townshend and Lauderdale told it me. Fox added "I believe they do reckon on Pitt, and I believe they will not be mistaken"' (*Lord Holland, in Mem. of Fox*, vol. i. p. 446). Neither of the parties in this curious dialogue were quite right in their anticipations.

The life of Mr. Fox is brought down in these volumes to the year 1792; the Buckingham Papers reach as far as 1799; and both works contain much curious and authentic information respecting the Regency debates in 1788–9: but the length to which this Article has already extended prevents us from following the events of that period in detail; we can only remark that much light is thrown upon it by both publications.

The period of our history from the decline of the American war to the commencement of Mr. Pitt's long Administration, is full of instruction with respect to the working of our Parliamentary Constitution. It was not, in fact, definitively and clearly established until the year 1784, that where there is a conflict between the personal opinions of the sovereign and those of a majority of the House of Commons, the latter, and not the former, is to prevail; unless, indeed, a dissolution and a new election should reverse the decision of the previous Parliament.[1]

[1] On the Constitutional right of the Crown to dissolve Parliament in this state of things, see the authoritative remark of Lord J. Russell (vol. ii. p. 245). [The reader may like to see Lord Russell's 'summing up' on the Constitutional question which was at issue in this struggle:—

'If Mr. Fox had maintained that a ministry ought not to continue, unless it should acquire the confidence of the House of Commons, and that doctrine had been practically overthrown by the decision of the country; the Constitution, as it had been understood since the accession of George I., would have been virtually set aside. But the doctrine set up went beyond this, and affirmed that the power of dissolution during a session, or, as Mr. Burke called it, 'of penal dissolution,' did not belong to the Crown. No advantage would have flowed from the establishment of this opinion; for had the King taken Mr. Fox back for the remainder of the session, it was not denied that at the end of it he might have sent for Mr. Pitt, and by his advice have dissolved the Parliament. On the other side, there was some appearance of assuming for an existing House of Commons power beyond that which had been assigned to them, of controlling the Crown by the votes of an ascertained majority.

'The precedent of 1784, therefore, establishes this rule of conduct. That if the ministers chosen by the Crown do not possess the confidence of the House of Commons, they may advise an appeal to the people, with whom

The lessons which this portion of our annals teaches are manifold; but it throws especial light on the two points which appear to us to form the characteristic difficulties of that form of Government which is commonly known by the appellation of 'limited monarchy;' that is to say, a hereditary King, associated with a parliamentary body. These are, 1. The desire of the King to govern as well as to reign, and his attempts, open or concealed, to defeat the policy of the Ministers in whom the majority of the Parliament, for the time being, confides. 2. The envies and rivalries of the parliamentary chiefs; their impatience of a superior, or even of an equal; their unwillingness to cooperate for public objects on account of their separate pretensions and personal ambition; and the consequent facility afforded to the King of ruling by division, of fomenting their discords and animosities, and ultimately, perhaps, of reducing them all to impotence and silence.[1] Parliamentary leaders of parties, in their more contracted sphere, are likely to indulge the feelings which animated the great party leaders of Rome in their contest for the mastery of the world,—

> 'Nec quemquam jam ferre potest, Cæsarve *priorem*,
> Pompeiusve *parem*.'

---

rests the ultimate decision. This course has been followed in 1807, in 1831, in 1834, and in 1841' (*Memorials of Fox*, vol. ii. p. 245).—Ed.]

[1] Aristotle enumerates want of mutual confidence as one of the three great means by which the Greek despots maintained their power (Pol. v. 11). The impatience of equals is well denoted in the expressive Greek term, *τὸ φιλόπρωτον*.

Mr. Fox, in a letter of May 1782, expresses a fear that Pitt will attempt to revive the system of governing by the influence of the Crown, and in defiance of the independent portion of Parliament. He then proceeds to say: 'I feel myself, I own, rather inclined to rely upon his understanding and integrity for resisting all the temptations of ambition, and especially *of being first*, which I know will be industriously thrown in his way, and contrasted with that secondary and subordinate situation, to which they will insinuate he must be confined while he continues to act in the general system' (*Mem. of Fox*, vol. i. p. 325).

But there is this important difference in their respective situations, that, whereas Pompey and Cæsar contended which should be chief, parliamentary leaders, who act singly, and embroil everything with mutual jealousies, end by being all put down under the feet of one common master.

We have no space now to dwell upon this theme at the length which it requires, but we wish that our feeble voice could induce the leaders of popular parties on the Continent to gather from our history the warnings which it contains with respect to the working of a parliamentary system. If the great Powers should continue at peace; if the quiet development of wealth and industry, and the amicable relations of individuals in society, should be permitted to advance without the interruption of destructive violence; we cannot believe that the fairest and most civilised portions of Continental Europe will remain under purely despotic forms of government. The trial of the American model, which has been made in some European States, has not proved successful; and though we are far from being exclusive in our attachment to constitutional forms, and are quite willing to admit that a system of government which is suited to England may not be suited to countries differently situated; we still think that, whenever the pressure of the despotic regimen is at all relaxed—looking to the fact that man is a historical animal—the parliamentary form of government, combined with a hereditary king, offers the best chance of permanent amelioration in the existing circumstances of the European States. If the time should ever arrive when an attempt should be made in the great Continental States to reach a popular system of government by this road, we earnestly exhort the parliamentary leaders to bear in mind, that the first object to be secured is *some* form of parliamentary or corporate government, *some* species of rule which is not dependent on the will of one man, but which lodges the supreme power in a body; *some* constitution which ensures public debate in a legislative chamber, freedom of the press, and security against arbitrary imprisonment. When this great and paramount object has been accomplished, and a habit of regular government, upon these principles, has been formed, the time will have arrived for deciding the proportions of the aristocratic and democratic elements in the constitution, and for raising questions on which the anti-despotic party are likely to be divided. But it is premature to stir those questions, and to dwell upon the refinements of a free Government, the *apices* of a constitutional system, before its foundations have been laid. It is premature to dispute about accidents before we have secured the substance. The leaders of liberal parties should bear in mind that despotism is the normal state of mankind, and free governments the rare exception; and that, in all unsettled states of society, the tendency to a despotic form of government is strong and constant.

We have made these remarks with a view to the future, not to the past; not for the purpose of blaming the popular leaders in the late movements on the Continent, but for the purpose of exhorting them to a different course hereafter. Much wonder has been expressed at the failure of parliamentary government in the recent experiments in the Continental States: and an opinion has even been promulgated that the Anglo-Saxon race are alone fitted for free institutions. The Republican Governments of antiquity and the middle ages—which, whatever may have been their defects, were the best Governments of their respective times—prove that Free Government is not the monopoly of a privileged race: and the failure of the late attempts may, as it seems to us, be completely explained by the neglect of those precautions which an intelligent study of the history of England during the reign of George III. is calculated to suggest.

SUPPLEMENTARY NOTE.

Since the above Article was printed, we have (chiefly through the kindness of Alexander Oswald, Esq. of Auchincruive) obtained some additional information respecting Mr. Richard Oswald, which we annex in a note, as there is no account of him in any of the ordinary books of reference.

Richard Oswald, of Auchincruive, in the county of Ayr (probably born about 1710), was a younger son of the Rev. George Oswald, minister of Dunnet, in Caithness. He was for many years a merchant in the City of London, and (through his wife, Mary Ramsay) was owner of considerable estates both in the West Indies and on the continent of America. During the Seven Years' War, he took extensive Government contracts, and not being satisfied with the manner in which his agents in Germany performed their duties, he went to Germany himself, and acted for several campaigns as Commissary-General of the allied forces under the Duke of Brunswick. In 1759, he purchased the estate of Auchincruive, and other estates in Ayrshire. On account of his connection with America, he was often consulted by the Government during the American war. He died at Auchincruive, November 4, 1784, without issue. His acquaintance with Lord Shelburne, which led to his being employed as a negotiator in 1782, originated in a letter of introduction from Adam Smith.

We have been favoured by Mr. Alexander Oswald with a copy of a Diary kept by Richard Oswald of his two journeys to Paris in 1782, as well as of a journey in September of a previous year (apparently on some private business of his own), in which, however, he had an interview with Franklin, and also with the Comte de Vergennes. The entries in this Diary are very brief. Franklin arrived in France in December, 1776, and as Oswald's first visit was before 1782, and in a year in which the 7th and 14th of September fell on a Sunday, it must have been in the year 1777. It is, however, remarkable that Franklin in his 'Journal' ('Works,' vol. ix. p. 240) speaks of Oswald as if he had seen him for the first time in April, 1782; he says that Oswald was then introduced to him by 'an old friend and near neighbour of mine many years in London:' Oswald also brought a letter of introduction from Mr. Laurens, as well as the letter from Lord Shelburne; nevertheless, Oswald describes himself as reminding Franklin of this first visit in an interview which probably took place before the 'Journal' was composed.

Subjoined to this Diary are full minutes of Oswald's conversations with Franklin on the 31st of May and 3rd June, 1782; between which days he states that he had an interview with Mr. Grenville. We regret that the length of the minutes prevents us from printing them entire: we therefore subjoin extracts of those portions which bear principally upon the question discussed in our Article.

1782. 'Arrived at Paris, Friday, 31st May, nine in the morning. Called on Mr. Grenville; delivered his packets. Then went out to Passy, and delivered to Dr. Franklin the sundry letters for him, and had a good deal of conversation with him about the affairs of the peace. He thought there should be separate commissions to treat, one for France, one for the

Colonies. Was not so positive as to Spain and Holland, although mentioned on several occasions. That though the treaties might go on separately, yet to be united in the final conclusion; meaning that there should be such correspondence between them that there should be no separate conclusion. That by treating separately, different interests and subjects not strictly relative to each other would not be mixed and involved in too much intricacy, and so might be separately discussed in the progress, and yet the final conclusion of the whole in one general settlement might be governed and made to be dependent upon those separate adjustments. Adding that the more we favoured them (meaning the Colonies) the more they would do for us in the conclusion of these separate treaties.'

June 3rd. 'I wanted to take my leave, having sat a considerable time, but he wished me to stay a little longer. And he fell into the subject formerly mentioned of the treaty going on by separate commissions for each party, and said he could see no objection to there being one commission for France, one for the Colonies, and perhaps one for Spain and one for Holland. That by this means, the business with each being separately discussed, they might more quickly and clearly come to a conclusion than when so many different interests must be jointly treated under the same commission. That, with respect to the Colony business, if my private affairs would allow of my absence, and that I would divert myself in the meantime, I might take up that commission. I told him, that if it was to trench on the character of Mr. Grenville's station, it would be the last thing I should incline to. That I believed him very capable and prudent, and had no doubt of his acquiring himself a reputation. As to my stay here, it was on account of various circumstances not the most agreeable. And with respect to my private affairs, they were in such situation that I should not suffer much by my attendance. At least, I should make no account of these matters if I thought that upon so critical an occasion I would be of any service to my country, &c.

'The doctor replied, that he thought the commission for the Colonies would be better in my hands than in Mr. Grenville's. That I understood more of Colony business than he did, and he himself had a longer acquaintance with me than with Mr. Grenville, and could not say but he esteemed me; and therefore not only thought the Colony Commission would be left in my hands, but he wished it might be so.

'I replied, that his wishing it was enough to determine, if I found it was a task I could go through with. That my coming here after the first time was entirely owing to the letters he wrote to Lord Shelburne, wherein he was pleased to express himself so favourably with respect to me, that I was ordered to return on the two succeeding occasions. That I was happy in the enjoyment of his good opinion. Was much obliged to him, &c.

'From thence we turned to a more general course of conversation, when I told him I could not but congratulate him in his present happy situation. Since I considered the settlement of a peace on fair and equitable terms to be entirely in his hands. Since, to speak the truth I could not help thinking, that when they as Commissioners of the Colonies were satisfied, they had it in their power to draw the line of such reasonable termination as ought and must content the other Powers.'

Mr. Oswald's record of the latter part of the conversation on the 3rd of June agrees substantially with Franklin's account of it in his 'Journal,' although the latter is more concise ('Works,' ib. p. 316). Both the conversations, as preserved by Oswald in his private notes, negative the idea that there was any disposition on his part to counteract Mr. Grenville, although they show that Franklin preferred negotiating with Mr. Oswald.

II.

ADMINISTRATION OF MR. PITT. THE CATHOLIC QUESTION.[1]

WE have, in a former number (Jan. 1854), given an account of the first two volumes of the Memoirs of Mr. Fox, edited by Lord John Russell, as well as of the letters published by the Duke of Buckingham, and with their assistance we followed the course of the important political changes which took place, in this country, between the American war and the commencement of Mr. Pitt's long ministry. Since the appearance of that Article the seventh volume of Lord Stanhope's History has been published, which concludes his useful and meritorious work, and brings down the narrative to the peace of 1783. As Lord Stanhope has completed the period of seventy years which he proposed to comprise in his history, we trust that he will undertake the succeeding period of thirty-two years, to the Peace of 1815, for no writer is

[1] Review of—1. *History of England from the Peace of Utrecht to the Peace of Versailles.* By Lord Mahon [now Earl Stanhope]. Vol. 7 (1780–1783), 8vo. London: 1854. 2. *Memorials and Correspondence of Charles James Fox.* Edited by Lord John Russell. Vol. 3, 8vo. London: 1854. 3. *Memoirs of the Court and Cabinets of George the Third from original Family Documents.* By the Duke of Buckingham and Chandos, K.G. Vols. 3 and 4, 8vo. London: 1855. 4. *Memoirs of the Whig Party during my Time.* By Henry Richard Lord Holland. Edited by his son, Henry Edward Lord Holland. Vol. 2, 8vo. London: 1854.*

* Mr. Justice Buller's name has met with an unlucky fate in the recently published memoirs. The editor of the 'Buckingham Papers' has converted him into 'Judge *Miller*,' while in Lord Holland's 'Memoirs of the Whig Party' his name appears twice as 'Judge *Baker*' (vol. i. pp. 122, 124).

more highly qualified to treat those memorable events dispassionately and effectively; and it is disgraceful to our literature that the long administration of Mr. Pitt should only be recorded in the platitudes of Gifford, the imposture of Tomline, or the superficial tirades of Mr. A. Alison.[1] Lord John Russell has recently added a third volume to the 'Memoirs of Mr. Fox,' which, with the exception of a few introductory remarks by the editor, consists exclusively of letters written by Mr. Fox to his nephew, Lord Holland, and to some of his personal and political friends, between the years 1792 and 1804. This was the least active part of Mr. Fox's political life. During these years he not only held no office, but he absented himself to a great extent from the House of Commons, and stood aloof from parliamentary conflicts. His letters are those of a bystander and an observer of political events, rather than of an actor in them. Hence the third volume contains fewer materials for history than the two preceding ones; but, on the other hand, it exhibits a fuller and more detailed picture of Mr. Fox's mind and thoughts, and is more interesting, as a biography, than its predecessors. Mr. Fox's natural tastes evidently inclined him to literature rather than to politics; and, notwithstanding the life of vehement excitement, both in private and public, which he led for many years—notwithstanding his eminent success as an orator, as a party leader, and as a tribune of the people—he retained an ardent fondness and a keen relish for literary pursuits not always to be found even in persons who have passed their days in seclusion, without aptitude for public life or experience of its agitations.

[1] [Lord Stanhope has now filled the blank so far as Pitt's life is concerned, and has given us a most agreeable and able book. Mr. Massey's *History of England* is another work of great merit which has appeared since this Article was written.—ED.]

The correspondence in the two concluding volumes of the Duke of Buckingham's publication is of the same character as that in the preceding volumes, and is continued to the year 1810. We are happy to say that the task of editing the two last volumes has been transferred to competent hands, and that they are free from the ridiculous blunders which deformed the earlier part.

The second volume of Lord Holland's 'Memoirs of the Whig Party' is principally occupied with an account of the formation, acts, and dismission of the Ministry of 1806; it contains likewise some interesting notices of events of an earlier date, to which we shall advert in this Article.

The character of the political period which occupied the active part of Mr. Fox's career, was that of a struggle between the Crown and the independent section of Parliament. This independent section consisted partly of peers and partly of commoners; nearly all of whom, in whichever House they sat, were Whigs. The Tories were in general at this time friendly to the King and desirous of maintaining unimpaired the influence of the Crown, which the Whigs, on the other hand, desired to restrict and diminish. The position of these parties had been completely inverted since the reigns of the two first Georges, when the Whigs were the main supporters of the Hanoverian interest and the Tories were Jacobites, forming the Country party, in active opposition to the Court. But during the American war George III. relied for support upon the chiefs of the Tories, while the Whigs, in both Houses of Parliament, carried on an unintermitting, active, and formidable opposition to his policy, his ministers, and his influence. We who witness the working of our parliamentary system in its maturity may think that the event of this struggle could never have been doubtful. But Fox, who had fought in the front ranks of the battle, and knew the strength and compactness of the phalanx against which he had to contend, was perpetually haunted with the fear of the King's predominance, and the triumph of the influence of the Crown. In alluding to the King, he recurs in his letters more than once to the pregnant words in which Dante expresses the Divine omnipotence: 'Vuolsi così colà dove si puote Ciò che si vuole.'[1]

During the reign of George III. the great Tory peers and patrons of boroughs, who, by their influence in counties, and their direct power of nomination, commanded the votes of a large section of the House of Commons, were willing, in general, to support any ministry which the King appointed, and to permit all the influence of the Crown to be exercised in its favour,

[1] Dr. Johnson, who was a professed Tory, and who used to speak of 'Whig dogs,' 'detested the idea of governing by parliamentary corruption, and asserted most strenuously that a prince, steadily and conspicuously pursuing the interests of his people, could not fail of parliamentary concurrence. A prince of ability, he contended, might and should be the directing soul and spirit of his own administration; *in short, his own minister, and not the mere head of a party*; and then, and not till then, would the royal dignity be sincerely respected' (*Boswell's Johnson*, under the year 1770). This passage contains a distinct expression of the view that a constitutional king, with limited powers, ought to govern as well as to reign. Johnson, however, did not see that if a king is his own minister he must be a party leader, and must abandon the neutral ground which is the true strength of a constitutional prince. In an article on the regency question, by Mr. Allen, published in the *Edinburgh Review* in 1811, is the following passage: 'It appears to us that the same expediency which has subjected our kings, in their judiciary and legislative capacities, to the guidance of others, ought to regulate their selection of the persons who are fittest to govern the State, and direct its affairs to the honour, safety, and advantage of the kingdom. We are sensible, however, that a contrary sentiment is very prevalent in the country; and, in our apprehension, the difference of opinion upon this point constitutes one of the chief distinctions between the Whigs and Tories of the present day' (vol. xviii. p. 4). We doubt whether this distinction can be said to exist between the Whigs and Tories of our day. The Tories seem to us to have adopted the Whig opinion.

provided that their own personal wishes respecting the distribution of patronage received due attention. They contented themselves as politicians with a barter of power for patronage; they gave the former, and received the latter. The great Whig lords, however, made a harder bargain with the Crown. They insisted upon selecting the King's Ministers before they consented to support them. They required that an Administration should be formed of members of their own party, whose names should be proposed by their own leaders. This pretension has often been denounced as an improper and unconstitutional assumption of power; and the Whigs are described as setting up an oligarchical dominion to overawe the King and Parliament. It is likewise alleged that, in confining their choice to members of the prominent Whig families, they showed a peculiarly aristocratic bias. Lord Stanhope, in his History, frequently exhibits the Whigs in this unfavourable light. Thus, after having described the arrangement by which the Marquis of Rockingham was made First Lord of the Treasury, in 1765, he points out that Lord Rockingham was one of the greatest landholders in England; that his talents were not above mediocrity, and that he was totally deficient in the power of public speaking, but admits that 'he had clear good sense and judgment, improved by the transaction of business. His character was without stain, marked by probity and honour, by fidelity to his engagements, and by attachment to his friends.' He then proceeds to make these observations:—

Such was the man whom the Whig party of 1765 selected from their ranks for their leader. Such was the man to whom they continued their allegiance in every variety of fortune during eighteen years. The selection might surprise us more were it not in some measure characteristic of that party. Since

1782. parties were formed anew, though under the old names, early in the reign of George III., *it has been the boast of the Tories that with them family and fortune have been no necessary qualities of leadership*, that many an esquire of no ancient lineage, or a younger son of no broad domains, and relying on no merits save his own, has been with joyful assent raised far above the heads of the wealthiest and proudest among them. The same boast, at least not to the same degree, could scarcely, perhaps, be made by their opponents. We find the Whigs most frequently prefer for chiefs the *Porphyrogennets*, as the Byzantines might have termed them, men born and bred in purple—the Marquis of Rockingham, or the Duke or Portland, or, in our own times, Lord Althorp—men, no doubt, of irreproachable character, public and private, and of excellent plain sense, but still without one single ray of eloquence or spark of genius. 'Thoughts that breathe and words that burn' have been far less sought in the selection than high-sounding titles and rich acres. Above all, it seemed to be imagined that a certain small cluster of great houses, as the original Whig junta, should have the first choice of honours and employments (vol. v. c. 44).

Again, Lord Stanhope speaks of the King, upon the formation of the Rockingham Administration, in 1782, as 'contemplating, with the utmost aversion, his return to the oligarchy of the great Whig houses' (vol. vii. p. 207). And he thus characterises the Tory and Whig parties of that time:—

On viewing the two principal parties then in conflict—Lord North's and Lord Rockingham's, we can scarcely call either generous and large-minded on every point, and so far as regards both men and measures. Lord North's party had some narrow views of national policy, *but it freely welcomed to its high places high ability, however unconnected.* Lord Rockingham's, on the contrary, was more liberal in its political opinions, but as to men of genius, if low-born, it would receive them only as its servants and retainers; it almost avowedly regarded power as an heirloom in certain houses (vol. vii. p. 210).

The choice of the Lord-Lieutenant of Ireland, under the Rockingham Administration, is thus described:— 1783.

Ireland at that time needed, beyond a question, for its Lord-Lieutenant a great statesman. The new Whig Administration sent thither only a great duke. They selected his Grace of Portland, not for ability, not for activity, not for knowledge, not for eloquence, *for of all these he was utterly destitute*, but for his rank and wealth, and, above all, as the head of one of their principal 'Revolution families' (vol. vii. p. 232).

Upon the death of Lord Rockingham, Fox objected to Lord Shelburne as First Minister, but abstained from urging his own claims to that post, and proposed the Duke of Portland to the King. Upon this step Lord Stanhope comments as follows:—

Had Fox desired to put himself in competition with Shelburne for the Treasury, his preeminent abilities and his well-won lead in the House of Commons would have warranted his claim. But to run all risks of discord and division by proposing another man whose main merit lay in this, that he was the Lord of Welbeck, and had married a daughter of the House of Devonshire; to put forward in his stead a mere ducal puppet, whose strings others were to pull, seems a course which, however conformable to the precedents of his party, was, and I trust ever will be, repugnant to the spirit of his nation (vol. vii. p. 271).

Again, after the King had been forced to submit to the Coalition Government of Fox and Lord North in 1783, he is described as 'chafing at the dominion, so long eluded, of the great Whig houses' (*ib.* p. 307).

It was quite natural that the King should, in 1782 and 1783, contemplate, with the utmost aversion, a return to the oligarchy of the great Whig houses, and should chafe at their dominion. What he desired was, to continue the oligarchy of the great Tory houses. Between these two oligarchies there was, as he well knew, this great difference,

1783. that whereas the Tories submitted themselves absolutely to his will, the Whigs gave him only a conditional support; they insisted on his Government acting upon their political principles, and being formed of persons who would carry those principles into effect, though they might be unpalatable to the Crown. Lord Stanhope seems to represent the leaders of the Whig party as dull men, with ancient families, and large hereditary estates in land; and the leaders of the Tory party as poor and low-born men of genius. We are at a loss to discover the facts on which this antithesis is founded. The Government of Lord North, which began in 1770 and lasted for twelve years, was a Tory Government. The Prime Minister (who also held the office of Chancellor of the Exchequer) was the eldest son of an earl; the three Secretaries of State were the Earl of Rochford, Viscount Weymouth, and the Earl of Hillsborough; the President of the Council was Earl Gower; the Earl of Halifax was Privy Seal; the Great Seal was in commission from Jan. 1770 to Jan. 1771, when Earl Bathurst was appointed Lord Chancellor. Sir Edward Hawke, a celebrated naval man, was, indeed, continued in the post of First Lord of the Admiralty for nearly a year; but he was then replaced by the Earl of Sandwich. During the twelve years of Lord North's Administration, the only commoners who held the office of Secretary of State were Lord G. Germaine, the son of a duke, and himself created a viscount upon his resignation; and Mr. Welbore Ellis, afterwards Lord Mendip, who retained his seals only a few weeks. The other Secretaries of State were, Viscout Weymouth (twice), Earl of Rochford, Earl of Dartmouth, Earl of Sandwich, Earl of Halifax, Earl of Suffolk, Viscount Stormont, and Earl of Hillsborough.[1] There is nothing in this cast of parts to

[1] 'Lord Weymouth had good natural abilities, and an easy flow of eloquence, which, combined with a graceful person, pleased the House of

betoken the ascendancy of plebeian genius and the exclusion of patrician mediocrity; or to show that 'Lord North's party freely welcomed to its high places high ability, however unconnected.' 1783.

When the King turned out the Coalition Administration in 1783, and brought in Mr. Pitt, the new Minister may not, in strictness, have been a Tory; but he had separated himself from the Whig party, and he came into power in direct hostility to Mr. Fox. With the single exception of himself, he formed a Cabinet of peers exclusively. He was at that time the only member of his own Cabinet in the House of Commons; and he himself was the son of an earl, though we do not mean to assert that he owed his position in Parliament to his rank. We presume that Lord Stanhope does not allude to Mr. Addington when he speaks of plebeian genius rising to the leadership of the Tories, and that he does not see anything creditable either to the nation or the party in the manner in which this favourite of George III. succeeded to Mr. Pitt's office in 1801.

Lord Stanhope severely blames the appointment of the Duke of Portland to the lord-lieutenancy of Ireland in 1782, a time which he justly characterises as one of great difficulty; and he attributes it to mere considerations of property and family connection. But it must be remarked that, although the Duke of Portland is described as utterly destitute of ability, activity, knowledge, and eloquence, Mr. Pitt was, notwithstanding these signal wants, glad to receive him into his Cabinet, and to confer upon him the office of Secretary of State for the Home Department, when with Burke he seceded from Mr. Fox and the rest of the Whigs

Lords; but he wanted steady application, and had injured his health by his taste for gaming and drinking' (*Lord Stanhope*, vol. v. p. 292). Earl of Suffolk, 'pompous and shallow' (*ibid.* p. 293).

1783. in consequence of the French Revolution.[1] The Duke of Portland held this office from 1794 to 1801, at which time he became President of the Council, in the Addington Administration; and he filled the same post for a time under the subsequent short administration of Mr. Pitt. Upon the fall of the Government of 1806, he became Prime Minister in a Cabinet of which Mr. Perceval, Mr. Canning, and Mr. Vansittart were the leading members; and he remained in this position until his death, in 1809. It is evident, therefore, that, whatever may have been the Duke of Portland's deficiencies, the blame of appointing him to high offices does not rest exclusively with the Whigs, and must be shared, to at least an equal amount, by the Tories; and that the strings of this 'ducal puppet' were pulled as much by one party as by the other.[2]

When we compare the Whig and Tory parties in the

[1] We learn, from the biographer of Mr. Windham, that the Duke of Portland was at first unwilling to become a member of Mr. Pitt's Cabinet, and that Mr. Windham (who formed part of the same secession) was to have been Secretary of State; 'but at length, the Duke of Portland's reluctance to accept office having been overcome, it was thought proper, *in consideration of his high rank and influence in the country*, to place him in the office which had been intended for Mr. Windham, the latter consenting to accept the inferior one of Secretary at War, with a seat in the Cabinet' (*Windham's Life*, prefixed to his *Speeches*, vol. i. p. 35). Lord Holland's account of the Duke of Portland may be seen in his *Memoirs of the Whig Party* (vol. i. p. 72). He says, that when the Duke joined Mr. Pitt, 'he felt great repugnance to accepting office, and at least as great to resigning it. He was the last of his set to give his consent to either measure.' George III. in a letter to Mr. Addington of Feb. 5, 1801, alluding to the Duke of Portland, speaks of 'the fair part he has acted since in office;' upon which Dean Pellew (who cannot be accused of any Whig tendencies) remarks: 'The author cannot let this opportunity pass without observing how well this compliment was deserved by the nobleman in question. The period produced politicians probably of greater ability, but of higher integrity none' (*Life of Lord Sidmouth*, vol. i. p. 295).

[2] From the important part which the Duke of Portland played in the politics of this country for a long period, it might have been expected that

reign of George III. we cannot perceive that the former was characterised by the scantiness, and the latter by the abundance, of its talent; and we certainly were under the impression that the Tories prided themselves on their connection with the land, and reproached the Whigs with their alleged preference for the manufacturing and commercial interests. Lord Stanhope, pointing out the unfitness of Lord Rockingham for the post of Prime Minister, remarks, that his panegyrists were frequently compelled to rely on the merits of his large estate; one of whom (Burke) bids us recollect 'his lordship's great interest in the public welfare, in quality of one of the greatest landholders in England.' For our own part, we agree with Lord Stanhope in thinking that large landed property is not a qualification for the office of Prime Minister; but we doubt whether that opinion was held by the majority of Englishmen in 1765, or, indeed, whether it is held by them at present. 1783.

But, whatever may have been the inclinations of the two parties, the King did not prefer the Tories on account of their democratic tendencies. He chafed at the oligarchy of the Whig houses, because the Whigs put a bit in his mouth; whereas the Tory party was a quiet beast of burden, which the King could ride or drive as he pleased. The real contest in those days was, not between aristocracy and democracy, but between aristocracy and monarchy. The Tories were, at least, as much aristocrats as the Whigs; but they submitted to the dominion of the King. The Whigs sought to maintain a Parliamentary party, independent of the King's personal influence, and to establish its supremacy over the royal will. This state

his papers, if they were regularly preserved, would have thrown much light on the history of the time. We regret, however, to learn that they were all destroyed by his son, the late duke.

1783. of things is marked in the following verses of the Rolliad:—

> When secret influence expiring lay,
> And Whigs triumphant hail'd the auspicious day.

The great Whig houses may have been an oligarchy, but they fought the battle of the people against the Crown; and where such vast means of corruption existed as the Crown possessed in the first twenty years of the reign of George III. the possession of rich acres, which Lord Stanhope holds so cheap as a political instrument, was of material assistance for carrying on the war against the Court and the Ministry combined. The pretension which they made, of naming the King's Ministers,[1] was, in our opinion, necessary for the due working of a Parliamentary Government; and, after a long struggle, it is now conceded to every political party which successively acquires the preponderance.

It appears that, when Mr. Pitt was nearly twenty-one years old, he wished to become a candidate for the University of Cambridge, and applied to Lord Rockingham for his support, but that Lord Rockingham civilly declined to give it, 'from the knowledge he had of several persons who might be candidates.' Lord Stanhope remarks, that these persons 'were, no doubt, of the right family connections—some nephews or some cousins of the great Whig houses' (vol. vii. p. 112). But in 1780, Pitt was as much a Whig as Lord Rockingham, and he certainly was the son of a great Whig house.[2] Mr. Pitt's remarkable

[1] Mr. Pitt, in his reply to Mr. Fox, December 16, 1788 (during the debates on the Regency), speaks of it as a fundamental principle held by Mr. Fox that the Ministers of the Crown were to be nominated by the prevailing party in Parliament.

[2] Compare Lord Stanhope's remarks with respect to the party divisions in the early part of the reign of George III.: 'The Whigs of 1763, no

parliamentary abilities would, under any circumstances, have been soon recognised; but his early confidence in his own powers, and the prompt recognition of his claims for leadership were due, in great measure, to his being the son of the great Lord Chatham.[1] 1783.

When Mr. Pitt entered public life, he certainly shared in the desire of the Whig party to diminish the influence of the Crown; and there is no doubt that the motion for Parliamentary Reform which he made in 1783, under the Coalition Ministry, and which he renewed in April 1785, when he was himself Prime Minister, had for its main object the reduction of the influence which the King exercised through the close boroughs. It appears that Mr. Pitt's plan (the whole of which was not disclosed to Parliament) contemplated giving four members to the parishes of Marylebone and St. Pancras, and six members

longer the Whigs of King William or Queen Anne, may be justly termed the founders of that distinguished party which bears their name at the present day. But they were split into sections, and it was between these sections, rather than between Whigs and Tories, that the battle for office raged. The Rockinghams and the Bedfords, Mr. Pitt and Mr. Grenville, all equally called themselves good Whigs, all would equally have declared that they never had been, that they never could be, Tories. Yet these were the chiefs of warring parties and of rival administrations' (vol. v. c. 44). But although different sections of the Whigs might oppose one another, they all agreed in the principle that the King was to reign without governing. George III. on one occasion told the Duke of Portland (who had been the head of the Whig party after Lord Rockingham's death) that he was an 'old Whig.' 'In speaking of the King, the duke said, on the Wednesday, February 18 [1801], before he was taken ill, His Majesty was quite himself, and talked to him most sensibly and judiciously on all subjects. *Said he was an old Whig;* that he considered those statesmen who made barrier treaties, and conducted the ten last years of the Succession war, the most able ones we ever had' (*Lord Malmesbury's Diaries*, vol. iv. p. 44).

[1] Mr. Pitt's power hung, throughout his life, upon the slender thread of his elder brother's life. The second Lord Chatham, though married, had no child; his death would at any time have transferred Mr. Pitt to the House of Lords, and put an end to his career as leader of the House of Commons.

1783. to Birmingham, Sheffield, Manchester, and Leeds.[1] Lord Stanhope truly remarks that, in the great division which turned out Lord North's Government, and settled the question of American independence, in 1782, the county members generally voted with the Opposition; while the Ministerial forces were chiefly composed of borough members. Speaking of Lord North's party, he says:—

> Their numbers were now in great measure derived from merely nomination seats. Take, for example, the very stronghold of the smaller boroughs in that age. The two members for the county of Cornwall voted against Lord North; but of its borough representatives who took part in this division there were eight opponents, and no less than thirty supporters of the Government (vol. vii. p. 206).

The plan of Parliamentary Reform proposed by the Duke of Richmond in the House of Lords, on the 3rd of June, 1780, was democratic in its character; it was founded on the principles of universal suffrage, annual elections, and equal electoral districts, each returning one member.[2] Mr. Pitt's main object, however, was to emancipate Parliament from the influence of the Crown, exercised through the nomination boroughs, and to prevent the King bartering patronage for seats. He sought to diminish the influence of the Crown upon the House of Commons, not to clip the wings of the great proprietors of boroughs. One of his reasons for abandoning the question of Parliamentary Reform undoubtedly was, that he considered that object to have been attained by other means. When the question of Parliamentary Reform was revived by Lord John Russell, after the Peace, and the Reform Bill was brought forward by

[1] Adolphus, *History of England during the Reign of George III.* vol. iv. p. 174.

[2] Adolphus, vol. iv. p. 145.

Lord Grey's Government, the object was changed; it had become anti-aristocratic instead of anti-monarchical. The influence of the Crown was no longer formidable; and the measure of 1831 was intended to diminish the power of the proprietors of close boroughs, by the same means which Pitt proposed to employ for diminishing the power of the Crown. 1783.

Lord John Russell examines the grounds for the supposition that the plan of the India Bill was prepared by Burke, and that it was adopted by Mr. Fox without adequate reflection. In rejecting this supposition he makes the following among other remarks:—

If Mr. Fox formed his union with Lord North in the deliberate exercise of a sound judgment, surely we must give him credit for a similar deliberation when, in the recess of the summer and autumn, he constructed the measure upon which alone he feared any danger to the continuance of his power. Nor do the facts at all bear out the supposition that Mr. Fox was betrayed by the rashness of Mr. Burke into a scheme of which he did not approve. There do not appear any traces in the papers of Mr. Fox of any outline drawn up by Mr. Burke upon which the India bill was framed, nor has any such plan been produced from the manuscripts of Mr. Burke. On the other hand, we know that the Bill was submitted to Lord North and Lord Loughborough, and probably to other members of the Administration (*Mem. of Fox*, vol. ii. p. 98).

Mr. Prior, likewise, in his 'Life of Burke,' takes a view similar to that of Lord John:—

The recess of Parliament was devoted to the concoction of the celebrated India Bill, of which Mr. Burke is said to have been a joint penman with the reputed author, though this has never been proved. It is certain, indeed, that he was the only one of the Ministry who knew much of the matter in progress previous to its coming before the public; and it is also certain that it

1783. was submitted to his revision; he might, likewise, have been the author of the second or supplementary Bill, ascertaining the powers of the new Government, and securing the rights and interests of the natives; but all the great and leading principles were undoubtedly those of Mr. Fox (c. 8. p. 275).

Now, in the correspondence of Burke, published in 1844 by Lord Fitzwilliam and Sir Richard Bourke, the following letter appears, addressed to Burke by Mr. Arthur Pigott, afterwards Sir Arthur Pigott, and Attorney-General in 1806:—

(Probably Oct. 1783).

Dear Sir,—I shall be particularly obliged to you to send me, as soon as ever you come in, so much of the Bill, or instructions of the Bill, as you have, in the state in which it is, as it will very much forward my work. Indeed, I cannot begin till I get it, and therefore shall expect it impatiently. I would leave my servant to bring it if I had one with me.

I am, dear Sir, ever yours,

Three o'clock. A. P.

Note, in Mr. Burke's handwriting:—

From Mr. Pigott, who finished the India Bill from my drafts.[1]

From this letter, and its endorsement, it is evident that the instructions for the India Bill were given to Mr. Pigott, the draftsman of the Bill, by Burke, and not by Fox; and, moreover, that Burke did not give his instructions in the form of heads, or notes, but that he prepared a draft of the Bill, which Pigott reduced into correct technical form. There is no reason to doubt that the plan was submitted to Fox, and maturely considered by him; but it may be regarded as certain that the conception and elaboration of it belong to Burke. Mr. Fox adopted it, and made it his own, so that he fully

[1] It is likewise stated in the life of Sir A. Pigott, in the *Annual Obituary*, that he assisted Burke in drawing the India Bill (vol. vi. p. 443).

deserved the splendid panegyric upon his motives and intentions with which Burke concluded his speech on the Bill; but the ambitious plan, by which the power of the Company was at once annihilated, doubtless proceeded from the man who had devoted so much time to the investigation of Indian affairs, and who was, in a few years, to be the author of the great impeachment of Hastings, which, though barren of penal consequences, constituted an epoch in the management of Indian affairs.[1] 1784.

'The general election of 1784' (as Lord J. Russell remarks) 'determined for more than forty years the question of the Government of England.' The party, of which Pitt laid the foundation when he defeated the coalition of Fox and Lord North, continued, with the short interruption of the Ministry of 1806, to govern the country until the year 1830. Of this period of forty-six years, not less than twenty-one were passed under the primacy of Mr. Pitt, whose long administration of eighteen years may be divided into two portions—that before and that after the French war. With respect to the first of

[1] The following account of the origin of the India Bill is given by Mr. Nicholls, in his *Recollections of the Reign of George III.*; his statement respecting Pigott is confirmed by the letter in the text:—

'When the Coalition came into power, Mr. Burke saw that much strength might be acquired for his party by the seizure of the Indian patronage. With this view Charles Fox was employed to bring in the India Bill, generally known by the name of Fox's India Bill. But I am firmly persuaded that Fox had nothing to do with the formation of this Bill. It was proposed by Mr. Edmund Burke, whose only assistant in it was Mr. Pigott, afterwards Sir Arthur Pigott. Mr. Lee, at that time Attorney-General, and Sir James Mansfield, at that time Solicitor-General, both assured me that they never saw the Bill until it was printed for the use of the House of Commons. They doubted whether Charles Fox himself had seen the Bill before the essential parts of it had been completely arranged by Mr. Burke. Lord North certainly did not see it until the Bill was completed, and when it was shown him he said, with his usual pleasantry and sagacity, that he thought it a good receipt to knock up an administration. But he supported it in the House of Commons' (vol. i. p. 55).

1784. these portions, Lord J. Russell makes the following remarks. After speaking of the India Bill, he says :—

> The other public transactions which occurred between 1784 and 1793 are, chiefly, the financial system established by Mr. Pitt, the commercial treaty with France of 1786, the invasion of Holland in 1787, and the regency question in 1788.
>
> However unjustifiable may have been the conduct of Mr. Pitt in making himself the instrument of a Court intrigue, candour must allow that his subsequent administration during peace was marked by large public views, was founded on grand principles, and led to happy results. The financial administration of Lord North had been a mere series of shifts and expedients to supply the wants of years of war and misfortune. Amid the losses of the empire, the old corrupt practices had flourished unchecked, if not increased, under that indolent and easy Minister. Mr. Pitt, with a vigorous hand, pruned the luxuriance of prodigality, and grafted on the ancient system the new maxims he had learnt in the school of Adam Smith. A reduction of the tea duties checked smuggling, and increased comsumption ; a prudent economy enabled the Minister to set apart a million a year as a sinking fund for the redemption of the national debt (vol. ii. p. 257).

The conduct of Mr. Pitt, in first defending Warren Hastings and then assenting to his impeachment in the session of 1786-7, has often been the subject of comment. Mr. Adolphus examines the question at length, and enumerates the various discreditable motives which were at the time assigned for this step. Jealousy of the influence of Hastings at Court, fear of his appointment to the presidency of the Board of Control, and a desire of diverting the attacks of Opposition from himself to a State-criminal, were supposed to have actuated Mr. Pitt. Mr. Adolphus says that if it is necessary to ascribe his conduct to a motive of mere party politics, unconnected with the merits of the question, it may rather be conjectured that 'he was pleased to see the members of Opposition engaged in a conflict where success could gain for them no accession of influence or popularity, while failure would by many be deemed to inflict disgrace."[1] Mr. Macaulay, in his Essay on the 'Life of Hastings,' supposes Pitt to have been influenced by the fear that Hastings, created a peer, and placed at the Board of Control, would soon draw to himself the entire management of Eastern affairs, and might even become a formidable rival in the Cabinet. Lord John Russell's remark is: 'Whether the Minister was convinced by the evidence which threw so full a light on the misdeeds of Warren Hastings, or whether he was glad to protect himself from *the ambition of a rival* by acceding to a prosecution against him, the effect was no less certain' (vol. ii. p. 255.); and he quotes the following passage from a letter of Lord Bulkeley to Lord Buckingham, in the Buckingham Papers, dated 27th April, 1789:— 1786.

On one of the adjourned questions on Hastings' trial in the House of Lords, Lord Maitland, standing next to Dundas, asked him what he thought would be the result of the enquiry, to which he replied in these words: 'I don't care what is done with him, *for you and your friends in Opposition have done our business by keeping him out of the Board of Control.*' Lord Maitland on this called up Colonel Fitzpatrick and Dudley Long, in whose presence Dundas actually repeated his words, and they, of course, trumpeted them all over town; and they have occasioned much conversation and much abuse of Dundas, in

[1] (Vol. iv. p. 261–3.) The following is the account in the *Annual Register*, which was probably written by Burke himself: 'The conduct of the Minister on this occasion drew upon him much indecent calumny from the friends of Mr. Hastings; they did not hesitate to accuse him out of doors, both publicly and privately, of treachery. They declared it was in the full confidence of his protection and support that they had urged on Mr. Burke to bring forward his charges, and that the gentleman accused had been persuaded to come to their bar, with an hasty and premature defence; and they did not scruple to attribute this conduct in the Minister to motives of the basest jealousy' (vol. xxviii. p. 136).

1786. addition to their former abuse on the part of Hastings' friends. The folly of such language, especially to these violent Oppositionists, was very absurd, weak, and ill-judged; but the fact is certain (vol. ii. p. 154).

It should be observed that this letter was written in April, 1789, and that the conversation with Dundas reported in it was then recent, whereas the speech in which Mr. Pitt assented to the impeachment of Hastings was delivered on the 13th of June, 1786, nearly three years before. It is certain that Mr. Pitt could not have regarded Hastings as a rival, or have entertained any feeling of jealousy towards him, with respect to parliamentary contests. Pitt was now in the vigour of his powers, and he must have felt that a retired Indian governor, who entered the House of Commons for the first time in his fifty-third year, could not prove a very formidable antagonist or competitor in debate. An encounter of oratory betweeen Pitt and Hastings would probably have been not very unlike the battle between Pyrrhus and Priam. It seems, moreover, that Hastings' ambition led him to desire a peerage, so that there was no question of his appearance in the House of Commons. Nor was it likely that Pitt should fear the influence of Hastings in the Cabinet, in which parliamentary considerations would necessarily preponderate.[1] The only

[1] Mr. Nicholls describes himself as having become acquainted with Hastings after the session in which the charges were brought against him by Burke: 'He appeared to me to be a man of a strong, vigorous, decisive mind, well acquainted with the character of the natives of India, and with the views and interests of its various princes. He seemed to me to be a man capable of extricating himself from difficulties by his great resources and dauntless courage. In one word, he came nearer to the idea which I had formed of an able statesman, than any other man with whom I ever had intercourse. But he was a statesman only for the affairs of India. He knew nothing of the various parties in England, their interests, their designs, their ability to effectuate those designs, or how far they were likely to be

fear which Pitt could reasonably entertain was, that if Hastings, through the King's favour, should obtain a seat at the Board of Control, he might be able to distribute the valuable Indian patronage according to the King's personals views; whereas, in the hands of Dundas, it was used for the general purposes of the Government. This argument was doubtless presented to Pitt by Dundas, who probably had a stronger personal feeling against Hastings than Pitt himself. To this extent Pitt may have been jealous of Hastings; and to a danger of this description, the words of Dundas, reported by Lord Bulkeley, appear to allude. Mr. Pitt had probably no desire to throw the shield of ministerial protection over Hastings; at the same time, we cannot but think that one of his leading motives for the unexpected course which he took was a reluctance to stop an impeachment supported by all the ability of Opposition, and relating to matters of which Englishmen in general had little or no knowledge, but of which some of Hastings' accusers were perfect masters. Mr. Nicholls, in his 'Recollections of the Reign of George III.' makes the following remark on the subject:— 1786.

There were people who thought that Mr. Pitt had adopted this line of conduct to prevent the King from employing Mr. Hastings in India affairs. But I do not believe that Mr. Pitt was actuated by so personal and so paltry a motive. I think he

influenced or restrained by moral considerations. These were subjects on which he seemed to me never to have formed an opinion' (*Recollections*, vol. i. p. 277).

[In the next article (that on Lord Cornwallis's *Memoirs*) the reader will find Sir George Lewis's opinion clearly expressed, to the effect that Dundas's letter of March 21st, 1787, contains the simple explanation of Pitt's conduct in Hastings' case—viz. the charges were so strong, and the defence so weak, that the Government were compelled to give way. This is, in fact, Lord Stanhope's conclusion also. The solution of the mystery was to be found in the nature of the case itself. Pitt's consent was given when Fox brought forward the charge respecting Cheyte Sing.—Ed.]

1785. consented to the impeachment, because he saw the control which he should obtain over the Opposition by such acquiescence, and his expectations were answered.[1]

In December, 1785, the Prince of Wales being then in his twenty-fourth year,[2] Mr. Fox addressed to him a friendly letter, earnestly dissuading him from a marriage with Mrs. Fitzherbert, chiefly on the ground of her being a Roman Catholic.[3] To this letter the Prince returned next day the following answer:—

Carlton House, Dec. 11. 1785:
Sunday Morning, 2 o'clock.

My dear Charles,—Your letter of last night afforded me more true satisfaction than I can find words to express, as it is an additional proof to me, which I assure you I did not want, of

[1] (Vol. i. p. 270.) Dean Pellew says, that the question of the abatement of the impeachment of Hastings, by dissolution of Parliament, 'furnished the only occasion on which, as Lord Sidmouth believed, Mr. Pitt and Mr. Fox were ever brought together in private life. They met at a consultation held in December 1790, to consider, with reference to the trial of Mr. Hastings, whether an impeachment by the Commons abated by a dissolution of Parliament. Mr. Pitt and Mr. Fox agreed in thinking that it did not, and nothing could exceed the ease and cordiality of their manner towards each other on that occasion' (*Life of Sidmouth*, vol. i. p. 80). Lord Sidmouth was certainly mistaken. Mr. Pitt had an interview with Mr. Fox, during the Shelburne Administration; and he had a subsequent interview with him in 1792, to which we shall advert lower down.

[2] He was born on August 12, 1762. He was thirteen years younger than Mr. Fox, who was born in 1749, and three years younger than Mr. Pitt, who was born in 1759. He survived them both twenty-four years.

[3] Mr. Fox was fully aware of the strength of the Prince's feelings with respect to Mrs. Fitzherbert, from communications recently made to him, as we learn from Lord Holland's account: 'Mrs. Fox, then Mrs. Armitstead, who was living at St. Anne's, has repeatedly assured me that he [the Prince] came down thither more than once to converse with her and Mr. Fox on the subject; that he cried by the hour; that he testified the sincerity and violence of his passion and his despair by the most extravagant expressions and actions, rolling on the floor, striking his forehead, tearing his hair, falling into hysterics, and swearing that he would abandon the country, forego the Crown, sell his jewels and plate, and scrape together a competence to fly with the object of his affections to America' (*Memoirs of Whig Party*, vol. ii. p. 126. Compare *Adolphus*, vol. iv. p. 217).

your having that true regard and affection for me which it is not only the wish but the ambition of my life to merit. Make yourself easy, my dear friend; believe me, the world will now soon be convinced that there not only is,[1] but never was, any ground for these reports, which of late have been so malevolently circulated. I have not seen you since the apostacy of Eden.[2] I think it ought to have the same effect upon all our friends that it has upon me: I mean the linking us closer to each other; and I believe that you will easily believe these to be my sentiments, for you are perfectly acquainted with my ways of thinking upon these sort of subjects. When I say my ways of thinking, I think I had better say, my old maxim, which I ever intend to adhere to; I mean that of swimming or sinking with my friends. I have not time to add much more, except just to say, that I believe I shall meet you at dinner at Bushy on Tuesday, and to desire you to believe me at all times, 1785.

My dear Charles,

Most affectionately yours,

GEORGE P.

(*Mem. of Fox*, vol. ii. p. 283.)[3]

This false, hypocritical, and canting letter was written on the 11th of December. On the 21st of the same month the Prince of Wales was privately married to Mrs. Fitzher-

[1] The Prince means to say, 'not only is *not*.'

[2] Mr. Eden, afterwards created Lord Auckland, seceded from the Whigs, and joined Mr. Pitt at this time. He was appointed a member of the Board of Trade, and Minister Plenipotentiary to negotiate the Commercial Treaty with France, on December 9, 1785 (*London Gazette*). 'Mr. Eden's nomination as negotiator occasioned some personal attacks. He had been the firm friend of the Opposition, and styled the father of the Coalition; by them he had been created a privy councillor, and appointed one of the joint vice-treasurers of Ireland; and he was now remarked to be the first who had seceded from that phalanx' (*Adolphus*, vol. iv. p. 203.) His removal from the Opposition to the Treasury bench was the subject of animadversion in the debate on the Address, Jan. 24, 1786: Lord Surrey pretended not to see him, and regretted that he was not in his place. He had previously held office under Lord North's Government.

[3] The letter of Mr. Fox to the Prince and the Prince's answer are likewise printed in Lord Holland's *Memoirs of the Whig Party*, vol. ii. pp. 127–37. Lord J. Russell has omitted two paragraphs in Mr. Fox's letter, which are printed in Lord Holland's *Memoirs*.

1785. bert, by a clergyman of the Church of England, in the manner prescribed by the Common Prayer-book, and the certificate was attested by two witnesses. It is in the highest degree improbable that the final resolution for this step should not have been taken, and the preparations for it made, on the day on which he assured Mr. Fox that the rumours respecting his intended marriage were wholly unfounded. The subject, however, is evidently embarrassing and painful to the Prince; for after having denied the truth of the reports to which Mr. Fox's letter referred, he escapes with great agility to the comparatively uninteresting subject of Mr. Eden's apostacy, and to protestations of his immutable fidelity to the Whigs, on which subjects Mr. Fox's long and argumentative letter did not contain a single word.

The exact truth respecting this marriage was carefully concealed, not only from the public, but from the most intimate friends of the Prince.[1] But rumours of it were soon in circulation, and an allusion to it was made in the House of Commons. In a subsequent debate, Mr. Fox took occasion to treat the report alluded to as a vile calumny; he 'denied it in toto, in point of fact, as well as law. The fact not only never could have happened legally, but never did happen in any way whatsoever, and had from the beginning been a base and malicious falsehood.' On being further questioned, Mr Fox declared

[1] It is stated by Lord Holland, *Memoirs of the Whig Party*, vol. ii. p. 124, that documents proving the marriage, after having been long in the possession of Mrs. Fitzherbert's family, were deposited in June, 1833, at Coutts' bank, in a sealed box, by agreement between the Duke of Wellington and Sir W. Knighton, as the executors of George IV. and Lord Albemarle and Lord Stourton, as the nominees of Mrs. Fitzherbert. Lord Brougham states that of Mrs. Fitzherbert's papers, 'one was a will, leaving everything to her disposal; another was a marriage-settlement of great length, with the certificate of the marriage annexed' (*Sketches of Statesmen*, vol. ii. p. 2).

that 'he had direct authority for what he had said.' (April 30th, 1787.)[1] 1787.

After this nuptial ceremony, wholly invalid in law, had been performed, the Prince had not the courage to avow that he had even gone through the forms of a marriage with a Catholic. He therefore authorised and instructed Mr. Fox to deny the marriage, not merely as to its legal validity, but as to its actual solemnisation, in his place in Parliament. That this authority was distinctly given is certain; for if Mr. Fox had spoken without authority, the Prince would unquestionably, either in public or in private, have disavowed his act, which he never did, except to one person. This person was Mrs. Fitzherbert. He appears to have assured her that Mr. Fox had made the statement without his authority; and her resentment against Mr. Fox for the supposed wrong was in consequence permanent. The unprincipled step which the Prince had taken (for he never intended the marriage to be binding[2]) placed him in a painful alternative, as soon as the rumours respecting it began to attract attention. He must either incur the public indignation by avowing his secret marriage with a Catholic, or he must deny a fact in the

[1] [This answer was given in reply to a question of Mr. Rolle's. See Lord Stanhope's *Life of Pitt*, vol. i. p. 334.—Ed.] Adolphus mentions a belief that shortly after this debate Mr. Fox had an interview with the King (vol. iv. p. 222). No allusion to such an occurrence occurs in the *Memorials of Fox*, or in Lord Holland's work; and it seems in the highest degree improbable that the King should have communicated with Mr. Fox on the subject of the Prince's marriage with Mrs. Fitzherbert, at this or any other time.

[2] Mr. Fox, in his letter to the Prince before the marriage, spoke out so plainly as to leave no doubt on this subject: 'In the meanwhile,' he says, 'a mock marriage (*for it can be no other*) is neither honourable for any of the parties, nor, with respect to your Royal Highness, even safe. This appears so clear to me, that, if I were Mrs. Fitzherbert's father or brother, I would advise her not by any means to agree to it, and to prefer any other species of connection with you to one leading to so much misery and mischief' (*Memoirs of Whig Party*, vol. ii. p. 134).

1787. truth of which Mrs. Fitzherbert was deeply interested. In this difficulty the course which he took was to authorise Mr. Fox to give it a solemn denial in the House of Commons, and afterwards to assure Mrs Fitzherbert that Mr. Fox had denied it without his authority. The duplicity of which he was guilty, both to his alleged friend and his alleged wife, did not, however, sit easy on his conscience, as appears from the following account by Lord Grey of an interview which he had with the Prince on the day on which Fox made his declaration in the House:—

In a long conversation which I had with him, in which he was dreadfully agitated, the object was to get me to say something in Parliament for the satisfaction of Mrs. Fitzherbert, which might take off the effect of Fox's declaration. I expressly told him how prejudicial a continuance of the discussion must be to him, and positively refused to do what he desired. He put an end to the conversation abruptly by saying, 'Well, if nobody else will, Sheridan must' (*Mem. of Fox*, vol. ii. p. 288).

Lord Grey adds, that at this interview the Prince confessed to him that the marriage had taken place. It is difficult to conceive a more humiliating and more dishonourable position than that in which the Prince now stood: denying his marriage to Fox, confessing it to Grey, and denying his denial to Mrs. Fitzherbert; treating it as a fiction to the first, as a nullity to the second, and as a reality to the third.

An account of the Prince's conduct on this occasion, and of his interview with Lord Grey, similar to that contained in the 'Memorials of Fox,' is given by Lord Holland in his 'Memoirs of the Whig Party,' who adds the following particulars:—

Mr. Sheridan did come down to the House and utter some unintelligible sentimental trash about female delicacy—which implied the displeasure of the Prince, and still more of Mrs. Fitzherbert, at what had passed in Parliament—but did not directly or even remotely insinuate that what Mr. Fox had spoken was either beyond or without the authority of the Prince of Wales. That Mr. Fox subsequently suspected, or rather knew, that some ceremony had taken place, I cannot doubt; but, never having spoken to him on the subject, I cannot assert it of my own knowledge. The exact date and circumstances of that ceremony have not come to my knowledge; but the account given of some part of the transaction by Mrs. Fitzherbert herself to a friend of mine, a man of strict veracity, is curious, and, I believe, correct. It was at the Prince's own earnest and repeated solicitations, not at Mrs. Fitzherbert's request, that any ceremony was resorted to. She knew it to be invalid in law; she thought it nonsense, and told the Prince so. In proof that such had been her uniform opinion, she adduced a very striking circumstance—namely, that no ceremony by a Roman Catholic priest took place at all—the most obvious method of allaying her scruples, had she had any. I believe, therefore, she spoke with truth, when she frankly owned 'that she had given herself up to him, exacted no conditions, trusted to his honour, and set no value on the ceremony which he insisted on having solemnised.' It was performed by an English clergyman. A certificate was signed by him, and attested by two witnesses, both, I believe, Catholic gentlemen, and one a near relation of Mrs. Fitzherbert—Mr Errington. Mrs. Fitzherbert, from mixed feelings of fear and generosity, tore off the names of the witnesses at some subsequent period, lest they should by possibility be involved in any legal penalities for being present at an illegal transaction. Before George IV.'s accession to the throne, or, as I believe, his appointment to the Regency, the clergyman was dead (for it was not, as often surmised, Parson Johnes who married them), and his name, I understand, remains annexed to the instrument purporting to be a register or certificate of the ceremony. If any corroboration were necessary to substantiate facts of which such proofs are extant, and to which there are so many unexceptionable testimonies, it would be found in the behaviour of Mrs. Fitzherbert on many subsequent

1787.

1788. occasions, and in the uniform respect and attention which she has received from nearly all the branches of the royal family (vol. ii. p. 140-2).

This account so far exonerates the Prince, that it shows Mrs. Fitzherbert to have been aware of the utter worthlessness of the ceremony which she went through for effecting a valid marriage. At the same time, as the Prince desired it, he must have intended it to afford her some satisfaction; and she probably thought that it would in some way bind his conscience, and that he would take some ulterior step, instead of treating it with the entire disregard which he afterwards evinced for this self-imposed obligation.

'The mental disorder which in 1788 afflicted the King (says Lord J. Russell) gave rise to a singular and deplorable contest.[1] Mr. Pitt, as the guardian of the rights of the Crown, Mr. Fox, as the champion of the rights of the people, the Prince of Wales, as a dutiful son, the Queen, as an affectionate mother, seem all to have deserted their proper posts, and given but too much reason for censure.' The nature of the controversy between Mr. Pitt and Mr. Fox respecting the appointment and powers of a regent is so well known, that it need not be here repeated: Lord John thinks that a regent with all the powers of a king ought, in the first instance, to have been appointed; and that such restrictions as were reasonable ought to have been subsequently imposed on him by Act of Parliament, to which his own assent would have been given.

[1] [It is worth while to remark that in the session of 1787 the repeal of the Test and Corporation Act was brought forward, and opposed by Pitt: the majority against it was 176 to 98. In this year, also, the Act establishing the colony of New South Wales was passed. Hastings' trial began on February 13, 1788. See Lord Stanhope's *Life of Pitt*, vol. i. pp. 337, 338, 354.—Ed.]

A full and authentic account of the events of this period is contained in the series of almost daily letters from Lord Grenville to his brother, the Marquis of Buckingham, Lord Lieutenant of Ireland, which is printed in the 'Buckingham Papers.' Lord Grenville, then Mr. William Grenville, held one of the offices of joint paymaster, and was in confidential communication with Mr. Pitt during the course of the King's illness and the arrangement of the measure for a Regency. His letters disclose all the views and feelings of the Government at this period. The 'Memorials of Fox' afford little information respecting the counsels of Opposition during the King's illness; but they contain some interesting documents drawn up by the leading Whigs for the vindication of the Prince and the Duke of York, after the King's recovery. 1788.

Lord Grenville first mentions the King's illness in a letter of the 23rd of October, 1788, as having begun in a violent spasmodic attack of the stomach, brought on by his remaining a whole day in wet stockings. The King subsequently appeared at a levée;[1] but his health became worse, and his recovery was spoken of as doubtful. The political effects of the accession of the Prince of Wales became an immediate subject of speculation. 'You may naturally conceive (says Lord Grenville on Nov. 5) the exultation, not even wearing the appearance of disguise, which there is in one party, and the depression of those who belong to the other.[2] At this time the King is

[1] 'Just as the King was taken ill in 1788, he said, after the last levée he held in the closet, to Lord Thurlow and the Duke of Leeds, on the first advising him to take care of himself and return to Windsor, "You, then, my Lord Thurlow, forsake me, and suppose me ill beyond recovery; but, whatever you and Mr. Pitt may think or feel, I, that am born a gentleman, shall never lay my head on my last pillow in peace and quiet, as long as I remember the loss of my American colonies." I had this fact from the Duke of Leeds, who was present' (*Lord Malmesbury's Diaries*, vol. iv. p. 19).

[2] 'I returned to London from Bath a day or two previous to the com-

1788. described as being in imminent danger;[1] his mental alienation, and its possible permanence if the bodily health should be restored, are also for the first time mentioned. Lord Grenville speculates on the course which Fox and his friends will take if the Prince should become either king or regent. His own opinion is (Nov. 7), that the whole of Mr. Pitt's Ministry will be at once turned out; but he describes the general feeling as being, that the Prince will negotiate with Mr. Pitt, from the fear of his popularity; in which case it is thought, that he ought not to decline all negotiation, but that he would be justified in refusing to accept any other than his actual office of Prime Minister. The King's bodily health now improved, but the mental alienation continued. This state pointed clearly to the necessity of constituting a regency during the incapacity of the Crown, a contingency for which the constitution makes no provision. Lord Grenville's letter of November 13th contains a full statement of the views of the Government with respect to this subject. It announces Pitt's intention to introduce a Bill appointing the Prince of Wales Regent, with certain restrictions; and it sets forth his own views of the course to be taken in case a proposal should be made to Pitt for the formation of a Coalition Government with Fox. Lord Grenville thinks that the most desirable thing

mencement of the session. The capital exhibited a scene of fermentation difficult to conceive or to depicture. Yet was it far exceeded during the last days of January 1793, on Louis XVI.'s decapitation' (*Wraxall's Posthumous Memoirs*, vol. iii. p. 178).

[1] 'The King was worse. His night had been very bad; all the fair promise of amendment was shaken; he had now some symptoms even dangerous to his life. O, good heaven! what a day did this prove! I saw not a human face, save at dinner; and then, what faces! gloom and despair in all, and silence to every species of intelligence' (*Madame D'Arblay's Diary*, Nov. 16, 1788). Tomline, on visiting Mr. Pitt at this time, found him in hourly expectation of receiving intelligence of the King's death (*Life of Pitt*, vol. ii. p. 363, 8vo.).

would be that Pitt should be at once removed; he believes that the difficulties of a real *bonâ fide* junction are insuperable, and that no such junction is in fact contemplated. He is convinced that their proposals, if any are made, will have no other object than that of satisfying the Prince, and of lessening the odium of Pitt's removal in the eyes of the public, and holding him out as a haughty and impracticable character. Pitt's popularity was (he says) never greater than at this moment; and he thinks that if the Prince should be so ill-advised as to dismiss him, the current would run at least as strongly in Pitt's favour as it did in favour of the King in 1784. A few days later Lord Grenville says that the language of the Opposition points to a coalition, but that the Prince's manner to Pitt shows that no such intention is entertained. Sir W. Young, a supporter of the Administration, writes to Lord Buckingham, in a similar tone, on the 25th of November. 1788.

Should the change of Ministry (too much apprehended) take place, it is thought that Fox's party—to temporise with the public opinion, too strong to meet in the teeth—will propose a coalescence of some sort; but so narrowed, and in regard to Mr. Pitt, moreover, placing him in such jar of official situation, that it cannot be in any manner listened to. The refusal of the insidious offer is then to be noised through the country, and a trial to be made to engage the people 'to join with those who proffered a sacrifice of enmities to Pitt for the public good.' My opinion is, that the trial will be abortive, and the present Administration retire (if so necessitated) merely to return to power on the shoulders of the nation ('Buckingham Papers,' vol. ii. p. 17).

The belief in a coalition was not of long duration. Mr. Pitt and his friends soon became aware that whenever the Prince of Wales was constituted Regent, he would dismiss the existing Ministers, and form a Foxite ad-

1788. ministration. That the intentions of the Opposition were not misunderstood is plain from the following passage in a confidential letter of Mr. Fox, dated the 15th of December :—

We shall have several hard fights in the House of Commons this week and next, in some of which I fear we shall be beat; but whether we are or not, *I think it certain that in about a fortnight we shall come in.* If we carry our questions, we shall come in in a more creditable and triumphant way; but at any rate the Prince must be Regent, *and of consequence the Ministry must be changed.* The manner in which the Prince has behaved through the whole has been the most steady, the most friendly, and the handsomest that can be conceived. You know when he sets his mind to a thing he can do it well; and in this instance he has done it most thoroughly. The Duke of York, who is steadiness itself, has undoubtedly contributed to help him to his good resolutions, and seems as warmly our friend as the Prince himself. In short, with regard to princes, everything is easy and pleasant, much beyond what I could form any idea of. In regard to other things, I am rather afraid they will get some cry against the Prince for grasping, as they call it, at too much power; but I am sure I cannot in conscience advise him to give up anything that is really necessary to his Government, *or, indeed, to claim anything else as Regent but the full power of a king, to which he is entitled.* The King himself (notwithstanding the reports which you may possibly hear) is certainly worse, and perfectly mad. I believe the chance of his recovery is very small indeed; but I do not think there is any probability of his dying (*Mem. of Fox*, vol. ii. p. 299).

On the 17th of December, when the King's symptoms had undergone a material improvement, and his speedy recovery began to be anticipated by some of the physicians, Lord Grenville writes to his brother as follows :—

It will be ridiculous if he should recover just in time to give the royal *dissent* to the Regency Bill; which is not impossible.

The more probable supposition is, that they will just have time to parcel out the spoils, to dismiss us, and to hold their offices about a month: and so will end (if this should happen) the third reign of King Charles III.[1] 1788.

In a subsequent letter of the 19th of February, when the King's convalescence was declared by the doctors, and the Ministers had decided to communicate to him the steps taken respecting a Regency, Lord Grenville expresses himself thus :—

If the experiment succeeds, you need not be told that we shall not feel ourselves disposed, nor indeed at liberty, to give up the King's authority (he being well) into the hands of His Royal Highness the Prince of Wales; and the less so, because we know that he and his friends, as he calls them, have taken the resolution of making the change at all events, and of taking all the offices of the country into their own hands, even (as they express themselves) if they are to hold them only twelve hours ('Buckingham Papers,' vol. ii. p. 116).

A report was circulated by the Prince's friends that he would refuse to accept the Regency unless it were wholly unfettered by restrictions;[2] but Lord Grenville doubts whether this intention was ever really entertained (letters of the 7th and 9th of December), and at all events it was subsequently abandoned. The first person consulted by the Prince of Wales, when he became aware of the King's malady, was Lord Loughborough; Mr. Fox was then in Italy, and he did not return till the deliberations of the Prince's advisers had made some progress. Lord Loughborough (as we learn from the documents published by

[1] By the two previous reigns of Mr. Fox, Lord Grenville means the Rockingham Ministry and the Coalition Ministry in 1782 and 1783.

[2] The Prince, on the receipt of the letter from Mr. Pitt proposing the restrictions, wrote a letter to Lord Loughborough, in which he calls them 'such restrictions as no dictator could possibly ever have been bare-faced enough to have brought forward' (Lord Campbell's *Lives of the Chancellors*, vol. vi. p. 210).

1788. Lord Campbell, in his 'Lives of the Chancellors') advised that the Prince should at once assume the entire regal power; that he should, of his own authority, call a meeting of the Privy Council, and take the necessary steps for convening Parliament.[1] A declaration, to be read by the Prince to the Privy Council upon this occasion, is preserved among Lord Loughborough's papers. As soon as Mr. Fox returned he condemned this plan; but he so far adopted Lord Loughborough's views, as to assent to the doctrine that the Prince of Wales had a right to exercise the royal functions during the incapacity of the King. Lord Campbell and Lord Brougham[2] think, that if Lord Loughborough's plan had been acted on, and if a *coup d'état*, such as he recommended, had been attempted, a civil war would have been the result. It appears to us, however, that the opposition of the Executive Government, backed by the opinion of Parliament, would have frustrated the plan at its outset. The Prince's summons to the Council would have been disobeyed, or would have been obeyed only by his personal friends; and the attempt would have proved a failure.

[1] The following passage occurs in the Prince's Memorial to the King, delivered to him after his recovery: 'I was urged, from an honourable opinion, I am sure, and one which was sincerely entertained by the person to whom I allude, to come forward much earlier in my own person to claim the Government, as falling to me of right during your Majesty's illness, and to take the lead out of the hands of your Majesty's Ministers into my own. Such was the opinion of my uncle, the Duke of Gloucester; and he pressed it on me with all the earnestness of a sincere and fixed opinion on a subject of such moment' (*Mem. of Fox*, vol. ii. p. 319). The Duke of Gloucester here alluded to was the third son of Frederic Prince of Wales, who married the Countess Dowager of Waldegrave. His son Prince William, afterwards Duke of Gloucester, married the Princess Mary, now Duchess of Gloucester, the fourth daughter and only surviving child of King George III.

[2] See Lord Brougham's *Historical Sketches of Statesmen*, vol. i. p. 178 (ed. 1855).

The Prince and the Duke of York openly canvassed for votes in the House of Commons against the Regency Bill of the Administration. 'Lord Lonsdale's people (says Lord Grenville, December 17th) were against us in consequence of a letter, written by the Prince of Wales himself, soliciting it as a personal favour. This, which I have from authority, may serve to give you an idea of the pains they had taken.' There can be no doubt that the Prince was privy to the claim of *right* which was made on his behalf by Fox, and that he fully approved of the claim being made. The feeling of Parliament did not support this pretension; and Pitt took instant advantage of the error committed by his adversary, exclaiming, as is well known, that 'he would unwhig the gentleman for the rest of his life.'[1] The following remarks of Lord Grenville, in a letter of December 13th, illustrate the manner in which this question was viewed by the House of Commons:— 1788.

I must refer you to the papers for an account of our triumphant day in the House of Commons yesterday. You will see by that, that I was not mistaken in my opinion that the doctrine of the Prince's right was not likely to be a very popular one. Fox found that by what he said before he had offended so many people, that he was obliged to take the very first moment of explaining it away; still, however, he has left it in such a shape, that we cannot fail of debating it with great advantage. He intends, as you will see by his speech, to move the previous question on Pitt's proposition, which he is afraid to attempt to negative. After this recantation was over, the day was closed by such a blunder of Sheridan's as I never knew any man of the meanest talents guilty of before. During the whole time that I have sat in Parliament, in pretty warm times, I never remember such an uproar as was raised by his threatening us '*with the*

[1] This debate is well described in Wraxall's *Posthumous Memoirs*, vol. iii. pp. 201-7.

1788. *danger of provoking the Prince to assert his right,'* which were the exact words which he used [1] (vol. ii. p. 56).

Again, in a letter of December 17th, he says, 'Fox's declaration of the Prince of Wales's right has been of no small service to us. Is it not wonderful that such great talents should be conducted with so little judgment?'[2] This celebrated difference between Pitt and Fox respecting the Prince's *right* to the Regency, will be found, upon examination, to be little more than verbal. When during the American War the *right* of taxing the colonies was so often insisted on by Lord North and his supporters, Burke argued, with true wisdom, that it was vain to talk about an abstract right; the question was, whether it was politic and expedient to exercise and enforce that right. By *right* in these discussions was meant a *legal power*. When, however, Fox spoke of the Prince's right to the Regency, he meant, not a legal power (the existence of which nobody thought of asserting), but a strong and overwhelming *moral claim*.[3] That the Prince of Wales

[1] Concerning this indiscretion see Moore's *Life of Sheridan*, chap. xiii. where the Regency question of 1788 is treated with judgment and impartiality.

[2] Wraxall has the following remark in his *Posthumous Memoirs*, vol. iii. p. 224: 'I cannot indeed too strongly repeat, that in mental endowments of every kind Fox equalled, if not exceeded, his antagonist. It was Pitt's superior judgment and correct life which principally turned in his favour the scale, which retained him in office throughout almost his whole career, while the want of those qualities excluded Fox from office.'

Lord Brougham tells an anecdote, that 'when the conversation once rolled upon the quality most required in a Prime Minister, and one said eloquence, another knowledge, a third toil, Mr. Pitt said, "No; patience"' (*Sketches of Statesmen*, vol. i. p. 278). We rejoice to observe that Lord Brougham has reprinted, with additions, his valuable sketches of the statesmen of the reign of George III. Many of them relate to contemporaries, who were his friends or his antagonists; and to events, *quorum pars magna fuit*.

[3] 'It is in this sense we understand the argument maintained in 1788, for the right of the Prince of Wales to the Regency, subject to the adjudication

possessed such a moral claim Mr. Pitt did not dispute; nor did he ever entertain an idea either of conferring the Regency upon any other person, or of associating the Prince with a Council. The real question at issue between Fox and Pitt on this occasion was, not as to the choice of the Regent, about which they were agreed, but as to the imposition of restrictions. Pitt proposed certain limitations to the Regent's power, whereas Fox maintained that he ought to possess all the regal powers and prerogatives undiminished. 1788

When the Prince of Wales was appointed Regent in 1811, the precedent of 1788 was followed; and the Opposition did not maintain the principle that the Prince of Wales, as heir-apparent, succeeded of course to the Regency during the King's incapacity. Mr. W. Lambe, however (afterwards Lord Melbourne), upon the resolution that 'the Regent should be laid under certain restrictions,' moved an amendment 'that the entire royal power should be conferred upon him without any restrictions.' This amendment was negatived by a majority of only 224 to 200 votes.[1]

When the King's illness was at its beginning and the dismissal of Pitt seemed imminent, Lord Thurlow, who

of the two Houses of Parliament. Strict legal right, which could be asserted and made good in a court of judicature, he certainly had none. It was observed, with more truth than decorum, by Mr. Pitt, that every individual of his father's subjects had as good a legal right to the Regency as his Royal Highness the Prince of Wales' (*Ed. Rev.* vol. xviii. p. 61. By Mr. Allen).

[1] See also the debate on Sir F. Burdett's motion for a Regency Bill, in the House of Commons, February 23rd, 1813; and the speech of Mr. C. Wynne, 6th July, 1830. Lord Brougham, *Sketches of Statesmen*, vol. i. p. 176, remarks that the two precedents of 1788 and 1811 'have now settled the constitutional law and practice in this important particular.' Mr. Addington had intended to follow the precedent of 1788 in February 1801, when the King was threatened with a return of insanity (Pellew's *Life of Lord Sidmouth*, vol. i. p. 347).

1788. had held the Great Seal, with the sole exception of the nine months of the Coalition Ministry, since 1778,[1] entered into a negotiation with the Prince, in order to make terms with him for retaining his high office in the new Administration. His position at this critical moment is thus described by Lord Grenville, in a letter of November 30th:—

You will have heard, in all probability, much on the subject of the Chancellor. His situation is a singular one. It is unquestionably true that he has seen Fox, and I believe that he has also seen Sheridan repeatedly,[2] and certainly the Prince of Wales. And of all these conversations he has never communicated one word to any other member of the Cabinet. Yet I am persuaded that he has as yet made no terms with them, and that whenever they come to that point they will differ. With this clue, however, you will be at no loss to guess where the Prince acquires his knowledge of the plans of Regency which are to be proposed, because, even supposing the Chancellor not to have directly betrayed the individual opinions of his colleagues,

[1] Lord Thurlow was first appointed to the office of Lord Chancellor in June 1778, in Lord North's Administration. He continued to hold the office in the subsequent Administrations of Lord Rockingham and Lord Shelburne. During the Coalition Ministry, from April to December 1783, the Great Seal was in commission. In December 1783, Lord Thurlow resumed the Great Seal in Mr. Pitt's Ministry, and retained it till January 1793, when Mr. Pitt insisted on his dismissal (see *Buckingham Papers*, vol. ii. pp. 207–8, and *Lord Campbell's Life*).

[2] Much information respecting Sheridan's negotiations with Thurlow will be found in Moore's *Life of Sheridan*, chap. xiii. See also *Lord Campbell's Life*. Lord Campbell seems to be mistaken in supposing that Thurlow's treachery to his colleagues was revealed to them by the well-known incident of the *hat* (vol. v. p. 586). Several versions of this story are given by Lord Campbell. The story (as we have heard it on authority which we believe to be conclusive), is that when the Cabinet held at Windsor was over, the Chancellor's carriage was called first, and a search was made for his hat, but it could not be found in the room where the Cabinet had sat. Thurlow hereupon growled out, 'Then I suppose I have left it in the other place:' the other place being the Prince's apartment. In Lord Campbell's *Lives*, id. p. 583, 'Capt. Rayne' is twice misprinted for 'Capt. Payne.'

yet still his conversation upon these points, in all of which he has explicitly agreed with the opinions of Pitt, must lead to the communication of the plans in agitation. . . . . Pitt has been induced, from his regard to the King, to dissemble his knowledge of Thurlow's conduct, and to suppress the resentment which it so naturally excites. . . . . There is no great inconvenience arising, in reality, from the communication of these intentions to the Prince. His intentions are sufficiently decided, and he has no means of traversing our schemes. 1788.

The anticipations expressed in this letter with respect to Lord Thurlow proved true. Lord Thurlow made some bargain with the Prince through the mediation of Sheridan; but the arrangement was disapproved by Fox when he returned from the Continent, and advantage was taken of a change of intention on the part of Thurlow to annul the treaty.[1] His colleagues were so fully impressed with a belief in his apostacy, that Pitt went to the House of Lords to hear his declaration in favour of the Prince; when Thurlow made a solemn appeal to the Almighty in witness of his fidelity to his King, Pitt, struck with the effrontery and falsehood of this theatrical display, allowed the exclamation, 'Oh, the rascal!' to escape from his lips as he stood under the throne.[2]

[1] The letter of Mr. Fox to Lord Loughborough, of December 26, 1788, in Lord Campbell's *Chancellors*, vol. vi. p. 206, proves that Thurlow voluntarily broke off the negotiations with the Prince. Mr. Pitt believed at the time that the negotiation was broken off in consequence of the claim to the Great Seal made by Lord Loughborough. Wraxall's *Posth. Mem.* vol. iii. p. 218. On the Prince's negotiation with Thurlow, see Gifford's *Life of Pitt*, vol. i. p. 386, 4to.

[2] This story is told by Wraxall, ib. p. 220, on the authority of General Manners, who heard Pitt's exclamation, and afterwards obtained from him an explanation of it. [Mr. Massey gives it on the authority of the 'Locker MSS.' in a stronger form: 'Pitt was on the steps of the Throne, and after Thurlow's celebrated imprecation, rushed out of the House, exclaiming several times, "Oh, what a rascal!" Massey's *History of England*, vol. iii. p. 488. Wilkes's more profane commentary on the Chancellor's speech is well known. Lord Stanhope, *Life of Pitt*, vol. ii. p. 10.—Ed.]

1788. The violence of Burke during the Regency debates is known to have produced a most unfavourable impression both upon his hearers and the public. Moore even supposes that the displeasure caused by his indiscretion during this transaction assisted in producing the subsequent alienation between him and Fox, and first opened the breach which the French Revolution widened and rendered permanent. Be this as it may be, it surprises us, who know Burke mainly from his speeches and pamphlets, to find a respectable member of Parliament writing, from the House of Commons, the following account of one of his great exhibitions on the Regency question:—

Edmund Burke arose a little after four, and is speaking yet (half past five). He has been wilder than ever, and laid himself and party more open than ever speaker did. He is Folly personified, but shaking his cap and bells under the laurel of genius. In speaking of our debate I had forgot Burke, who, after I finished my last night's letter, finished his wild speech in a manner next to madness. He let out two of the new titles; Fitzwilliam to be Marquis of Rockingham, and Lord G. Cavendish . . . .[1] His party pulled him, and our friends calling 'Hear, hear,' we lost the rest of the twenty-five new peers, who would all have come out (*Sir William Young to the Marquis of Buckingham*, 22 *and* 23 *December*, 1788, vol. ii. pp. 71, 73).

The distribution of offices believed at the time to have been agreed upon was—First Lord of the Treasury, Duke of Portland; First Commissioner of the Great Seal, Lord Loughborough; Privy Seal, Lord Carlisle; Home Secretary or President of the Council, Lord Stormont; Foreign Secretary, Mr. Fox; Chancellor of the Exchequer, Lord John Cavendish; and First Lord of the Admiralty, Lord Fitzwilliam; Burke and Sheridan were to be Paymaster

[1] The title intended for Lord George Cavendish is misprinted in the original, and unintelligible. We have stated already that the two first volumes of this publication were edited by an incompetent person.

and Treasurer of the Navy.[1] Of these Lord Stormont and Lord Carlisle had been adherents of Lord North; the others belonged to the party of Mr. Fox. Lord Grenville adds that the Duke of York was to be Commander-in-chief, and the Prince himself, the Dukes of York and Gloucester, and General Conway to be Field Marshals.[2] So certain, indeed, did the accession of the Prince of Wales to the Regency appear in the early part of February 1789, that medals, with his portrait and suitable inscriptions commemorating his appointment as Regent, were struck and sold at the time.[3] 1789.

The King's convalescence was announced to the House of Lords by the Lord Chancellor on February 24; that his restoration from his mental malady was for the time complete, appears from the following passage in a letter of Lord Grenville, written on that day:—

> Pitt has just shown me a letter which he received last night from the King, written in His Majesty's own hand, couched in the warmest terms, thanking him for his unshaken attachment to his interests, and desiring to see him this morning. He went accordingly to Kew, and was with the King above an hour. He says, that there was not the smallest trace or appearance of any disorder, that the King's manner was unusually composed and dignified, but that there was no other difference whatever from what he had been used to see. The King spoke of his disorder as of a thing past, and which had left no other impression on his mind than that of gratitude for his recovery, and a sense of what he owed to those who had stood by him. He spoke of these in such a manner as brought tears into his eyes, but even with that degree of affection of mind there was not the least appearance of disorder (vol. ii. p. 125).

That the popular feeling was strongly enlisted in favour of the King's recovery appears from an entry in the diary

[1] Adolphus, vol. iv. p. 393.
[2] *Buckingham Papers*, vol. ii. p. 104.
[3] Wraxall's *Posth. Mem.* vol. iii. p. 310.

1789. of Miss Burney, who was at this time attached to the person of the Queen, and an inmate of Windsor Castle. She describes a visit of Sir Lucas Pepys,[1] who informed her of the wish of the physicians to remove the King from Windsor to Kew (28th November, 1788).

The difficulty how to get the King away from his favourite abode was all that rested. If they even attempted force, they had not a doubt but his smallest resistance would call up the whole country to his fancied rescue. Yet how, at such a time, prevail by persuasion? He moved me even to tears, by telling me that none of their own lives would be safe if the King did not recover, so prodigiously high ran the tide of affection and loyalty. All the physicians received threatening letters daily, to answer for the safety of their monarch with their lives. Sir George Baker[2] had already been stopped in his carriage by the mob, to give an account of the King; and when he said it was a bad one, they had furiously exclaimed, 'The more shame for you' ('Madame D'Arblay's Diary,' vol. iv. p. 282).

The King's recovery was celebrated by a spontaneous illumination, which Wraxall calls the most universal exhibition of national loyalty and joy ever witnessed in England. 'London displayed a blaze of light from one extremity to the other; the illuminations extending, without any metaphor, from Hampstead and Highgate to Clapham, and even as far as Tooting; while the vast distance between Greenwich and Kensington presented

[1] Sir Lucas Pepys, Bart. M.D. was younger brother of Sir William Pepys, Bart. the father of the late Earl of Cottenham.

[2] Physician to the King and Queen, and afterwards President of the College of Physicians. He was born in 1722, and died in 1809. Dr. Johnson, in arguing against Dr. Taylor, a Whig, in 1777, asserted, that 'if England were fairly polled, the present King would be sent away to-night, and his adherents hanged to-morrow.' Dr. Taylor denied what Johnson said, and maintained, 'that there was an abhorrence against the Stuart family, though he admitted that the people were not much attached to the present King' (Boswell's *Johnson*, ann. 1777). A great change in the popular feeling towards the King had taken place in the eleven years from 1777 to 1788.

the same dazzling appearance. The poorest mechanics 1789.
contributed their proportion, and instances were exhibited of cobblers' stalls decorated with one or two farthing candles.'[1]

The prevalence of this strong feeling produced the greater displeasure at the conduct of the Prince of Wales and the Duke of York, who showed a striking want of filial duty, and behaved with remarkable indecorum and impropriety on this occasion. Their conduct was so much resented by their royal parents, that when a concert was given at Windsor soon after the King's recovery, the Queen sent them a message, informing them 'that they would be welcome to the concert, but that she thought it fair to let them know that the entertainment was intended for those who had supported the King and Queen on the late occasion.'[2] When the intelligence of the duel between the Duke of York and Colonel Lennox (which took place on the 26th of May following) reached the palace, the Queen received it with indifference, and Her Majesty shortly afterwards invited Colonel Lennox to a ball, where she treated him with marked attention. Colonel Lennox was nephew and heir to the Duke of Richmond, who was at this time a Cabinet Minister; and his second in the duel, who delivered the challenge to the Duke of York, was Lord Winchilsea, who was, and continued to be, a lord of the bedchamber, and therefore a member of the royal household. The King likewise wrote a letter to the Duke of Clarence, expressing his displeasure at the unkindness which he had met with from his two elder sons during his illness. In consequence of the reproaches contained in this letter, a long memorial,

[1] *Posthumous Memoirs*, vol. iii. p. 369.

[2] Lord Campbell says that George III. always believed that those 'who opposed the restrictions upon the Regent had formed a conspiracy to prevent his remounting the throne' (vol. vi. p. 209).

1789. in vindication of the conduct of the Prince and the Duke of York, was drawn up by Sir Gilbert Elliot (afterwards Earl of Minto), and delivered by the Prince to the King. This, and a letter to the King, likewise drawn up by Sir Gilbert Elliot, which was not sent, are printed for the first time in the 'Memorials of Fox' (vol. ii. pp. 308-355); they contain much curious authentic information respecting the course taken by the Prince during the King's malady, and exhibit the entire alienation from his parents which his conduct produced.[1]

It appears from 'Miss Burney's Diary' (Nov. 8), that early in November the Prince of Wales took the government of the house at Windsor Castle entirely into his own hands. Nothing was done but by his orders, and he was applied to in every difficulty. The Queen interfered in nothing; she retired to a separate apartment, and lived in seclusion with her daughters. We learn, however, from the Prince's memorial, that when the King had been removed to Kew, the Prince was, by the Queen's order, denied all access to him, and that the care of His Majesty's person was henceforth exclusively assumed by the Queen. The Prince attributes the change to her displeasure at his having, after the removal to Kew, taken possession of the money, jewels, and papers belonging to the King. This measure, as it is described by the Prince, appears, however, to have been quite proper; he confided the money and jewels to Lord Brudenell, the keeper of the privy purse,[2] and the papers were locked up in the

[1] The draft of a letter from the Prince to the King, in Lord Loughborough's handwriting, among the Rosslyn MSS. printed by Lord Campbell, vol. vi. p. 212 (beginning with the words, 'Thinking it probable') had been already printed by Moore in his *Life of Sheridan*, c. 13 (from the rough copy of Sheridan). Compare *Mem. of Fox*, vol. ii. p. 339.

[2] James Lord Brudenell, born 1725, succeeded his elder brother, the Duke of Montagu, as Earl of Cardigan, in 1790.

drawers where they were deposited, the keys being enclosed in a paper, sealed with the seal of Lord Weymouth, the Groom of the Stole.[1] We may remark that the King's papers are described by the Prince, who had on this occasion personally inspected them, as 'arranged with great regularity and method;' and they were left, untouched, 'exactly in the places and order in which His Majesty had deposited them.' George III. was now in the twenty-ninth year of his reign, and the accumulation of papers in his possession was doubtless considerable. It may be presumed that he continued, up to the time when he ceased to perform the regal functions (1811), to preserve his papers, and to keep them in order. The communications which he received from his successive Ministers would, if published, form a historical collection of the highest value. What was the fate of George III.'s papers, and whether they are still in existence, we know not. They must have been in the custody of the Duke of York at the time when he had the charge of the King's person. We have reason to believe that no part of them has ever come into the possession of Her present Majesty. No reconciliation between the Queen and the Prince took place until March, 1791; about two years and a half after the commencement of the King's illness.[2] 1789.

The King's sudden restoration to health, and the practical settlement of the Regency question which it effected, preceded, by a few months, the greatest political event of modern times—the outbreak of the French Revolution. On the 10th of March, 1789, Parliament was reopened by commission after the King's recovery. On

[1] Thomas Viscount Weymouth, eldest son of the Marquis of Bath, was Groom of the Stole (which corresponds to the present office of Mistress of the Robes) from 1782 to 1796, in which year he succeeded his father.

[2] It appears from Lord Malmesbury's *Diary* that the Prince of Wales was on excellent terms with the Queen in July, 1792 (vol. ii. p. 450).

1789. the 14th of July following, the Bastile was taken. Henceforth, until the peace of 1815, not only all the international relations of England with the Continent, but its domestic politics, continued to be influenced by the French Revolution and its consequences. It was believed in France, by the speakers of the Convention, that their revolution would destroy Pitt's power, and put an end to his political ascendancy.[1] No anticipation could be more false. Not many months had elapsed before the Whig party was divided by differences of opinion respecting the changes in France; after a time a large section of it openly joined the Minister, while that part which adhered to Mr. Fox lost its popularity in the country, and was dispirited in Parliament by the secession of its leader.[2]

The general feeling of England at the taking of the Bastile was doubtless one of joy and approbation. It was thought to betoken the advent of a more free and popular regimen in France, and to threaten the well-known abuses of its government with destruction. When Mr. Fox said, in writing at the time to Mr. Fitzpatrick, 'How much the greatest event it is that ever happened in the world, and how much the best!' (*Mem. of Fox*, vol. ii. p. 361) he probably went beyond the popular sentiment of his countrymen, but he coincided with its general direction. Burke, however, was from the very beginning hostile to the movement in France: and as the progress of events began to disclose its character, his opinions spread to many other Whigs, closely connected with Fox by personal and party

[1] 'Les inquiétudes du premier ministre Pitt, maître absolu de l'Angleterre depuis huit ans, et que les orages d'une révolution ou ceux d'une guerre menacent également de sa chute,' &c. (Kersaint, *Speech in the Convention*, Jan. 1, 1793, *Moniteur*, Jan. 3).

[2] [It will be remembered that in 1790 we had on our hands the dispute with Spain about Nootka Sound, which looked very threatening. See Massey's *History of England*, vol. iii. p. 431. Compare Lord Stanhope's *Life of Pitt*, vol. ii. p. 58.—Ed.]

ties. A meeting of the leading members of the Whig Party was held at the Duke of Portland's house on the 11th of February, 1790, when a discussion, stated to have been conducted on both sides with remarkable ability, was carried on from ten o'clock at night to three o'clock in the morning; but it failed in reconciling the opinions of Fox and Burke; and the breach remained as wide as before.[1] In the summer of the same year, Burke wrote his 'Reflections on the French Revolution,' and published them in the month of November. Of this work 30,000 copies are stated to have been sold; and it exercised an immense influence upon the opinion of the country. 'It, was,' Professor Smyth remarks, 'read by every man of intelligence in the kingdom.' The views taken by Burke contributed powerfully to mould public opinion into a form hostile to the movement in France; and this hostility was greatly strengthened by the deposition of Louis XVI. on the 10th of August, 1792, and by his execution in the January following. Burke had formally announced his separation from Mr. Fox, on account of his opinions respecting the French Revolution, in the strange scene which occurred in the House of Commons during the debates on the Quebec Bill in the spring of 1791.[2] A

1790.

[1] *Adolphus*, vol. iv. p. 542.

[2] A careful account of the controversy between Burke and Fox on the occasion of the Quebec Bill is given in the fifth and sixth chapters of the *Annual Register* for 1791. Burke ceased to write the historical portion of the *Annual Register* about 1788, but he probably retained some control over it until his death in 1797. See also Moore's *Life of Sheridan*, c. xiv. A tolerably fair view of the state of English parties at this time, and of the causes of the separation of Fox and Burke, is taken by Sir Archibald Alison in his *History of Europe*, c. vii. [On the quarrel of Fox and Burke the reader may now refer to Mr. Massey's narrative, *History of England*, vol. iii. pp. 445–448; vol. iv. p. 43. The Quebec Bill was in fact the occasion, not the cause, of their rupture. Lord Stanhope (*Life of Pitt*, vol. ii. p. 90) quotes Fox's remark: 'I am convinced that the only method of retaining distant colonies with advantage is to enable them to govern themselves.'

1792. partial junction of the Whigs with Mr. Pitt's Government began to be agitated in June 1792.[1] It was not, however, until 1794 that the great secession of the Whig Party from their leader took place. In that year the Duke of Portland, Lord Fitzwilliam, Lord Spencer, Mr. Windham, Mr. Grenville, and the majority of the parliamentary Whigs, joined the Administration, some of them with office. Lord Loughborough, the confidential adviser of the Prince during the Regency debates, had already accepted the Great Seal in January 1793. The grounds of difference between Mr. Fox and his seceding friends are thus stated by Mr. Grenville in a letter to him written at the time:—

> The main points of difference between us are two: the one is respecting the war with France, which you condemn and oppose, while I think it the greatest of all duties to support and maintain it to the utmost; the other respects an apprehension which I entertain of those principles and designs in this country adverse to the constitution of it, which makes me feel it to be my duty to resist whatever can give to such designs either strength, opportunity, or countenance, while you, on the other hand, believe in no such designs, and believe the danger to arise from there being too little spirit of free inquiry and resistance in the minds of the people of this country. Either of these subjects of difference existing between us would tell very much in public conduct, but both united extend very widely indeed, and must in their direct course, or at least in their bearings and consequences, pervade almost all measures of public discussion (*Mem. of Fox*, vol. iii. p. 63).

'The fervid writings of Burke,' says Lord J. Russell; 'the general alarm felt at the subversive doctrines and

Turgot had in effect said the same thing in his report to M. de Vergennes on the North American revolt in 1776.—Ed.]

[1] See Lord Malmesbury's *Diaries*, vol. ii. p. 453, where a meeting at Burlington House, of the Duke of Portland, Lord Fitzwilliam, Lord Loughborough, and Burke, held for the discussion of this subject, is described.

horrible massacres of the French Republican Government; 1792
the aid of more than half the parliamentary party which had hitherto followed Mr. Fox, and the entire confidence of the King, made Mr. Pitt far stronger in war than he had been in peace.' It seems that in 1792, before the acceptance of the Great Seal by Lord Loughborough, a general negotiation for the junction of the Whigs, including Mr. Fox, took place with Mr. Pitt. The negotiation was fruitless, so far as Mr. Fox was concerned; but Lord John thinks that 'if Mr. Pitt had offered directly to Mr. Fox the Foreign Office, with the leadership of the House of Lords, there can be little doubt that Mr. Fox, however reluctant, would have accepted the offer' (*Mem. of Fox*, vol. iii. pp. 21, 248). Lord Holland informs us that 'Mr. Fox about this time had a very secret interview with Mr. Pitt, in which the latter proposed a coalition of parties, with many conditions somewhat unpalatable, though not utterly inadmissible, or in the least dishonourable, except the exclusion of men, and particularly of Sheridan, to which Mr. Fox would not listen' (*Mem. of Whig Party*, vol. i. p. 30). Dean Pellew, in his 'Life of Lord Sidmouth,' says of this negotiation, that 'it was intended that Mr. Fox himself should be included; but he resolutely declined, unless Mr. Pitt would previously resign the premiership; a proposal which, of course, put an end to the whole arrangement.'[1] A similar proposition was

[1] (Vol. i. p. 89.) Dean Pellew adds: 'To this occasion an anecdote of Lord Sidmouth respecting Mr. Burke may probably be referred. Mr. Pitt was negotiating with Mr. Burke for the accession of the Duke of Portland and his friends to the Government; and in speaking of terms of adjustment with France, he observed that they ought to be founded on the basis of indemnity for the past and security for the future. On this Mr. Burke, who had no relish for any such arrangement, drew himself up, and pompously said, "Sir, I am authorised by the Duke of Portland to state that he abhors indemnity, and detests security."' Lord Malmesbury mentions in several places the demand of the Duke of Portland and Mr. Fox that Mr. Pitt

1792. made to Mr. Pitt, on behalf of the Foxite party, during the struggle in the spring of 1784, and it put an end to the negotiation which had been then commenced for a union of parties.

It is certain that Pitt was drawn reluctantly into the war.[1] He desired to observe a strict neutrality with respect to France; and he did, in fact, observe it so long as he was able. His policy was founded on the continuance of peace. We have reason to know that he, an early disciple of Adam Smith, contemplated at this time a larger measure of Free Trade than the National Debt, accumulated during the subsequent war, now permits;—we mean, an abolition of all Custom Duties, and a limitation of the public income to internal taxation.[2]

should resign the office of First Lord of the Treasury, in order to prepare the way for their junction (vol. ii. pp. 459, 465, 468, 472, 473).

[1] [Mr. Massey says: 'It was the discovery of the French plot, or the supposed French plot, to revolutionise this country by an armed intervention, which first shook the firm mind of Pitt' (*History of England*, vol. iv. p. 45). The quotation from Wilberforce given in the note, to the effect that Pitt supposed the war would be a short one, is curious, and puts us in mind now of Mr. Seward's 'ninety days.'—ED.]

[2] Pitt did not escape the sarcasms about exclusive attachment to pounds, shillings, and pence, and neglect of science and literature, which have been levelled at more modern Ministers:—

'*Author*. Pitt views alike, from Holwood's sullen brow
(As near-observing friendship dares avow),
The fount of Pindus or Bœotia's bog,
With nothing of Mæcenas, but his frog.
'*Oct*. Mere spleen to Pitt; he's liberal, but by stealth.
'*Auth*. Yes, and he spares a nation's inborn wealth,
Another Adam in economy;
For all, but Burke, escape his searching eye.
Stiff from old Turgot and his rigid school,
He never deviates from his wholesome rule:
"Left to themselves, all find their level price,
Potatoes, verses, turnips, Greek, and rice."'

(*Pursuits of Literature* (by Matthias), part ii.)

It seems that the seal of Mæcenas, attached to decrees for the collection of taxes, had the figure of a frog (*Plin. H. N.* xxxvii. 4).

His Sinking Fund scheme was proposed in 1792. 'At that time' (says Dr. Marsh, in his work on the origin of the French war), 'Mr. Pitt's favourite object was a diminution of the National Debt, the abolition of taxes, the promotion of commerce and of general welfare throughout the kingdom; the attainment of which would necessarily be impeded by the expenses of a foreign war.'[1] The leaders of the Convention, on the other hand, were obviously desirous of provoking a war with England, unless they could compel the English Government to bend to their policy. It may be argued that Pitt erred in refusing to acknowledge the Republican Government of France, after the dethronement and execution of the King; in recalling Lord Gower from Paris, and in dismissing Chauvelin from London. But we do not believe that a recognition of the French Republic, and a continuance of diplomatic intercourse on the new footing, would have sufficed to prevent the Convention from declaring war against England, unless our Government had

[1] Herbert Marsh, *History of the Politics of Great Britain and France, from the Conference at Pillnitz to the Declaration of War against Great Britain* (London, 1800, 2 vols.), vol. i. p. 54; and see p. 194. This work contains an elaborate examination, founded on documentary evidence, of the grounds of the French war. Dr. Marsh justifies the course adopted by the English Government, but we do not agree with Professor Smyth (Lect. xxxv. on the French Revolution) that 'it is the statement of a diligent and able advocate, the statement of one side of the question only; nothing is said on the other.' It appears to us, on the contrary, that the facts are fairly stated on both sides, though judgment is given in favour of England. We think it quite possible to arrive on many points at conclusions quite different from those of Dr. Marsh upon his own statement of the facts. Lord Malmesbury has the following entry in his *Diary*, under March 29, 1801, soon after the dissolution of Mr. Pitt's long ministry: 'Pitt, I am told from authority, encourages Addington in his pacific plans, states the finances of the country to be such as require peace. I always perceived these to supersede in Pitt's mind every other consideration, and that, even when he declaimed the loudest, and with the greatest emphasis, for a continuation of war, his real and genuine opinion went for peace' (vol. iv. p. 53).

1793. professed itself friendly to the principles of the French Revolution. As it was, the grounds upon which the Convention declared war against England (on the 1st of February 1793), were frivolous almost beyond example.[1] Mr. Fox and his few friends would have been prepared, with certain limitations, to have made such a profession of faith.[2] But neither Parliament nor the country would

[1] This is remarked in a previous number of the *Edinburgh Review*, vol. lxxvii. p. 353, where the subject is fully examined. A different view is taken by Professor Smyth in his thirty-fifth Lecture on the French Revolution.

[2] The following extracts from Mr. Fox's letters illustrate his opinions on the French Revolution and war, and certainly they are strangely at variance with the views now entertained by all parties in this country: '*I do not think near so ill of the business of the* 10*th of August* as I did upon first hearing it. If the King and his Ministers were really determined not to act in concert with the Assembly, and, still more, if they secretly favoured the invasion of the barbarians, it was necessary, at any rate, *to begin by getting rid of him* and them' (Sept. 3, 1792). 'I exactly agree with you, that for France alone Robespierre is worse than any other despotism; but that for the general good, considering the diabolical principle of the present war, *even his government*, or a worse, if worse can be, *is better than the restoration* of the Bourbons' (May 17, 1795). 'A greater evil than the restoration of the Bourbons to the world in general, and England in particular, can hardly happen. You will be happy, as I am, to hear of the ill success of the emigrants [at Quiberon], but you will be astonished to hear that Ministers are so far from being discouraged by it that they are more sanguine than ever in their hopes of reestablishing Louis XVIII.' (July 28, 1795). 'Everybody says that the country is nearly unanimous for peace, but they do nothing in consequence of their opinion, and the Ministers are, I believe, as warlike as ever. An expedition is, after all, gone to France, under General Doyle, consisting of 4,000 British, besides emigrants, &c.; it is supposed they are destined to Noirmoutier. I think nothing can show the complete infatuation of our Government so much as this desperate expedition, which, *I believe as well as hope*, has not the smallest chance of success' (Sept. 10, 1795). 'My letters tell me what I can scarce credit, that the Ministers have given a flat refusal to the Great Consul's proposition to treat. Surely they must be quite mad.' 'I approve of Bonaparte's letter very much indeed; and what an answer! *Surely they must think as meanly of the people of this country as I do.* Restore monarchy or show us that you can behave peaceably for some time before we can treat; and this experience of peaceable demeanour is desired during the war' (Jan. 1800). 'I cannot help thinking that Bonaparte will not be so rancorous as you apprehend, and that he will find it for the interest, both of his glory and of his power.

have supported a Ministry which announced its adhesion to the principles of the French Revolution; and the King would have viewed it with greater abhorrence than he had felt even for the Coalition Ministry at the time of the India Bill.[1] Such was the fanaticism about political forms which prevailed at this time—a fanaticism not less fervid than that which existed about religious tenets in the 16th century—that, while this country refused to acknowledge a Republican Government in France, the French Government treated every king, whatever his powers might be, as a tyrant. They accordingly placed England under the ban of their anathema, and regarded it as a country with which peace was impossible. The only part which Fox could play, consistently with his opinions on the French Revolution, was to continue an unavailing protest against the war; but even this course brought his party to so low an ebb, that, near the end of the century, the entire Opposition was said, in joke, not to have filled more than one hackney coach, when they left the House of Commons.[2] All struggle between Fox 1793.

to continue in the system of moderation' (Oct. 1800). 'The refusing Bonaparte's offers, first in January and then in October, are faults, in my judgment, without a parallel in history' (Jan. 24, 1801).

[1] This question is well treated by Moore, in his *Life of Sheridan*, ch. xvi. whose views on this portion of our history are remarkably sound and judicious. Lord Brougham, *Sketches of Statesmen*, vol. i. pp. 60, 280, is of opinion that Mr. Pitt entered upon the French war from motives of selfish ambition, merely in order to consolidate his power, and that by uniting with Mr. Fox he might have prevented the war. We doubt the truth of both these propositions.

[2] 'I heard old George Byng say, at the dinner given to him to celebrate the fiftieth anniversary of his having sat for Middlesex, alluding to those times, "It has been asserted that the Whigs would all have been held in one hackney coach. This is a calumny. We should have filled two"' (Lord Campbell's *Lives of Chancellors*, vol. v. p. 614). Mr. Byng sat for Middlesex from 1790. Lord Holland says: 'The war was as popular out of doors as in Parliament, and perhaps even more so. Even there the minority was small: in the Commons forty, and in the Lords only four'

1789. and Pitt had at this time ceased; and when Pitt resigned in February, 1801, and was succeeded by Addington, Fox saw no prospect of any return to power—except, indeed, from the favour of the Prince of Wales, in the event of a regency, which the King's state then rendered probable. In a letter to Lord Holland, dated April 19, 1801, he expresses himself thus:—

Seriously speaking, I cannot conceive what you mean by everybody agreeing that something may be now done. I beg, at least, not to be included among the holders of that opinion; for, as it appears to me, there never was a moment when all exertion on our part was more certain to be useless, if not worse. . . . My present notion is, that except for Tooke's business (which I could not desert without shabbiness), and the May Whig Club, I shall go to town no more this year. . . . . It must be from movements out of doors, and not in Parliament, that Opposition can ever gain any strength; I mean, of course, as Opposition. What the King's death or illness might produce is another question (*Mem. of Fox*, vol. iii. p. 189).

The views and conduct of the English Government with respect to war, in the early part of the Revolution, appear clearly from Lord Grenville's letters. On September 14, 1789, being then Home Secretary, he thus writes to the Marquis of Buckingham:—

We have no sort of news. The French Assembly is going on with endless disputes about their Constitution; but one ought to be much more interested than I feel myself in the event of these disputes, not to be heartily tired of hearing of them. The main point appears quite secure—that they will not, for many

(*Memoirs of Whig Party*, vol. i. p. 30). Lord Bexley gives the story of the coach as a matter of fact. In a letter to Dean Pellew, he says of Mr. Fox's secession from Parliament: 'By means of that secession Mr. Tierney became the leader of the Opposition, such as it then was. You may judge of their numbers by the circumstance that they generally went home to dinner with Tyrwhit Jones in his coach' (*Life of Lord Sidmouth*, vol. ii. p. 135).

years, be in a situation to molest the invaluable peace which we now enjoy.[1] 1791.

In May, 1791, Lord Grenville was transferred from the Home to the Foreign Department, and on the 17th of August of that year, he writes to his brother as follows :[2]—

I hope I shall now begin to breathe a little, which I have hardly done since April last. You can hardly form to yourself an idea of the labour I have gone through ; but I am repaid by the maintenance of peace, which is all this country has to desire. We shall now, I hope, *for a very long period indeed enjoy this blessing,* and cultivate a situation of prosperity unexampled in our history. The state of our commerce, our revenue, and, above all, that of our public funds, is such as to hold out ideas which but a few years ago would indeed have appeared visionary, and which there is now every hope of realising.

His long and interesting letter upon the war of Austria and Prussia against France, and the policy of this country with reference to it, written on the 7th of November, 1792, three months before war was declared by the Convention against England, proves conclusively that the English Government had hitherto abstained from all interference in the hostilities against France :—

The events you read in the newspapers, often before I get them, and they have been such as it could give me little pleasure to

[1] [Anticipations rashly formed at this moment with reference to the future capacity of the Government of the United States for injuring others may prove as fallacious as these confident hopes of Lord Grenville, or the sanguine predictions of Pitt in his speech on the budget of 1792. 'Unquestionably there never was a time in the history of this country when, from the situation of Europe, we might more reasonably expect fifteen years of peace than we may at the present moment' (see Lord Stanhope's *Life of Pitt*, vol. ii. p. 140.)—Ed.]

[2] [This took place on the resignation of the Duke of Leeds in connection with the Russian quarrel. Lord Grenville had been made a peer in November 1790. The reasons for this elevation are to be found in Lord Stanhope's *Life of Pitt*, vol. ii. pp. 73, 74, and strong arguments against it in the Duke of Richmond's letter to Pitt of November 24, p. 75 of the same work.—Ed.]

1792. detail. The causes have been hid *caliginosâ nocte*, and I have been among the guessers only, and not always among those who were luckiest in their guesses. I bless God that we had the wit to keep ourselves out of the glorious enterprise of the combined armies, and that we were not tempted by the hope of sharing the spoils in the division of France, by the prospect of crushing all democratical principles all over the world at one blow. But, having so sturdily resisted all solicitation to join in these plans, we have been punished for our obstinacy by having been kept in profound ignorance of the details by which they were to be executed, and even of the course of events, as far as that could be done, which occurred during the progress of the enterprise. . . All my ambition is that I may, at some time hereafter, when I am freed from all active concern in such a scene as this is, have the inexpressible satisfaction of being able to look back upon it, and to tell myself that I have contributed to keep my own country at least a little longer from sharing in all the evils of every sort that surround us. I am more and more convinced that this can only be done by keeping wholly and entirely aloof, and by watching much at home, but doing very little indeed; endeavouring to nurse up in the country a real determination to stand by the Constitution when it is attacked, as it most infallibly will be if these things go on; and, above all, trying to make the situation of the lower orders among us as good as it can be made. In this view, I have seen, with the greatest satisfaction, the steps taken in different parts of the country for increasing wages, which I hold to be a point of absolute necessity, and of a hundred times more importance than all that the most doing government could do in twenty years towards keeping the country quiet. I trust we may again be enabled to contribute to the same object by the repeal of taxes; but of that we cannot yet be sure. Sure I am—at least, I think myself so—that these are the best means in our power to delay what, perhaps, nothing can ultimately avert, if it is decreed that we are again to be plunged into barbarism (vol. ii. pp. 222-4).

Lord Grenville's view of the war, when it had been once begun, is expressed in a letter of September 17th, 1794:—

I have no other view of the contest in which we are engaged, nor ever have had, than that the existence of the two systems of government is fairly at stake, and in the words of St. Just (whose curious speech I hope you have seen), that it is perfect blindness not to see that in the establishment of the French Republic is included the overthrow of all the other governments of Europe. If this view of the subject is just, there can be [no] worse economy than that which spares the expense of present exertion, and incurs the probability of increased risk, and the necessity of protracted efforts.[1] 1794.

The following remarks of Lord Grenville, made in a letter of April 28th, 1797, with reference to the French war, whatever truth they may have had at that time, are not applicable to the state of the popular mind in this country since the commencement of the war with Rusia: —

It is a curious speculation in history to see how often the good people of England have played this game over and over again, and how incorrigible they are in it. To desire war without reflection—to be unreasonably elated with success—to be still more unreasonably depressed by difficulties—and to call out for peace with an impatience which makes suitable terms unattainable, are the established maxims and the regular progress of the popular mind in this country. Yet, such as it is, it is worth all the other countries of the world put together; so we must not too much complain of it.

After having described Burke's policy of a crusade against the revolutionary government of France, Lord John Russell proceeds to say: —

Happily his advice was disregarded. Mr. Pitt took a totally different view of the nature and objects of the war. He was ready to admit that we had nothing to do with the internal government of France, provided its rulers were disposed and

[1] Mr. Pitt, in a letter to Mr. Addington, of Oct. 4, 1795, speaks of opening his budget before Christmas, 'and if that goes off tolerably well, it will give us peace before Easter' (Pellew's *Life of Lord Sidmouth*, vol. i. p. 157).

1792. able to maintain friendly relations with foreign governments. He sought to confine France within her ancient limits, to oblige her to respect established treaties, and to renounce her conquests. He sought, by expeditions to the West Indies, an indemnity for the expenses of the war. In short, he treated Robespierre and Carnot as he would have treated any other French rulers, whose ambition was to be resisted, and whose interference in the affairs of other nations was to be checked and prevented (*Mem. of Fox,* vol. iii. p. 32).

In a letter addressed to Burke on September 6th, 1792, respecting the recall of the English ambassador from Paris, Lord Grenville marks the difference between their opinions on the policy to be observed towards France. 'If our opinions,' he says, 'do not on all points agree, I well know that we have the same object in view; that the King's conduct in this crisis should be such as may best tend to preserve these kingdoms from the contagion of the evils which have ruined France.'[1]

It was not, however, the question of peace or war with France, or the opposition of Mr. Fox, which was destined to bring Mr. Pitt's long administration to an end. Its termination was due to internal causes: to circumstances connected indeed with important subjects, but small in themselves. What great men, and great questions, and great parliamentary conflicts had not been able to effect, was done by a quibble about the Coronation Oath.

> Finem animæ, quæ res humanas miscuit olim,
> Non gladii, non saxa dabunt, non tela; sed ille
> Cannarum vindex, et tanti sanguinis ultor
> Annulus.[2]

---

[1] *Correspondence of Burke* (1844), vol. iii. p. 532.

[2] [The man, whose spirit stirr'd the world to strife,
No sword shall slay: no shaft shall harm his life:
For Cannæ's field and all our hosts laid low,
That little ring must deal th' avenging blow.
Juvenal, Sat. x. l. 163.—Ed.]

After the union with Ireland had been carried, Mr. Pitt decided on proposing that the exclusion of Roman Catholics from public offices and Parliament should be abolished. His main reason seems to have been that this measure, which might have been attended with danger in a purely Irish Parliament, could not fail of being beneficial when one Parliament was elected for the United Kingdom. The Catholic influence, which might have preponderated in an Irish Parliament, would be counteracted and reduced to safe dimensions by the Protestant majority of an Imperial Parliament. His convictions on this subject must likewise have been strengthened by the deplorable events of which Ireland had been the theatre during the recent rebellion, and by the prevalence in that country of a disaffected spirit, which facilitated the hostile designs of France. With the removal of civil disqualifications upon the Catholic laity was to be combined a State provision for the Catholic clergy, which, so long as their religion was subject to legal disabilities, they would necessarily refuse to accept; and also a change in the law respecting tithes. This great and healing measure was frustrated by the personal objections of the Sovereign, whose sensitive conscience rendered him an easy prey to artful and selfish counsellors, and whose reason, since his illness of 1788, afforded him but a feeble protection against their practices. Its failure at the time when it was proposed, has been an irreparable calamity to our generation. It retarded the measure of Catholic emancipation by a quarter of a century, and left it to be extorted by intimidation. It created O'Connell's power, and gave importance to the Repeal agitation; above all, it has left the Protestant and Catholic churches of Ireland in their present anomalous state, with little prospect of this great defect in our internal 1800.

1800. polity being removed by a fair and equitable adjustment.[1]

The secret history of the means by which this unfortunate result was produced, is now known to us from the documents published in Lord Campbell's 'Life of Lord Loughborough,' in Dean Pellew's 'Life of Lord Sidmouth,' and in the 'Castlereagh Correspondence,' illustrated by the entries in Lord Malmesbury's 'Diary.' The Act of Union received the Royal assent in July 1800. In the following month the Cabinet began to discuss the measures which Mr. Pitt intended to propose as the sequel of the Union; and in September he wrote to Lord Loughborough, who was then in attendance on the King at Weymouth, to request him to return to London for their consideration.[2] It appears that Mr. Pitt did not intend to submit the plan to the King at this stage of the business. His Majesty was known, since 1795, to have been disinclined to the removal of Catholic disabilities, on account of a supposed inconsistency with his Coronation Oath. Lord Loughborough, however, showed the King Mr. Pitt's letter before he left Weymouth, and thus disclosed to him Mr. Pitt's intentions. Lord Malmesbury had likewise heard that the Archbishop of Canterbury, Dr. Moore, at the suggestion of his brother-in-law, Lord Auckland,[3]

[1] We refer our readers, with great satisfaction, to the excellent remarks of Mr. Macaulay, in which he proves the utter emptiness of the fancy which took possession of the King's mind, and dwells on its disastrous consequences (*Hist. of England*, vol. iii. p. 117). [Lord Stanhope, with his usual regard for truth, says: 'I am far from denying, although I was not convinced by them, that there were several weighty arguments to allege against the Roman Catholic claims. But most certainly the supposed breach of the Coronation Oath is not to be numbered among these. It has been lon[g] since, and almost by common consent, abandoned as untenable' (*Life of Pi[tt]*, vol. iii. p. 264).—Ed.]

[2] See Lord Loughborough's narrative, written in 1801, and circulat[ed] among his friends, in Lord Campbell's *Lives of the Chancellors*, vol. v pp. 322–6. Mr. Pitt's letter is in p. 306.

[3] Dr. Moore was married to Miss Catherine Eden, eldest sister of William

wrote to the King, when at Weymouth, to inform him of the measure contemplated by the Ministers, and to warn him against its adoption.[1] Lord Loughborough, on his return to London, prepared a statement of his objections to the proposed measure, which he circulated among his colleagues, and of which he gave a copy to the King.[2] He likewise, at the same time, assured His Majesty, in answer to his inquiry, that the Cabinet had as yet decided nothing on the Catholic question. It appears, further, from authentic information furnished to Lord Castlereagh, that Dr. Stuart, the Archbishop of Armagh, had been confidentially consulted by the King during the winter, and had contributed to strengthen his feelings against the proposed measure of comprehension.[3] 1800.

Lord Castlereagh, the chief secretary to the Lord-Lieutenant, had attended the consultations of the Cabinet, in September, upon the Irish questions; and before the meeting of the Imperial Parliament in the beginning of

the first Lord Auckland. Lord Auckland had been Joint Postmaster-General since 1798. He retained the office under the Addington Ministry, and was turned out by Mr. Pitt upon his return to power in 1804. [I cannot say that I think Lord Auckland's motives clearly made out. Mr. Massey says that he 'felt himself aggrieved by the reserve of the Government' (*History of England*, vol. iv. p. 147). It is perhaps possible that Dr. Moore may have influenced his opinions in the first place. Compare Lord Stanhope's *Life of Pitt*, vol. iii. p. 267.—Ed.]

[1] *Diaries*, vol. iv. pp. 16, 20.

[2] This paper, which was in answer to a paper written by Lord Castlereagh, and circulated to the Cabinet, is printed in Pellew's *Life of Lord Sidmouth*, vol. i. pp. 500–512. It was communicated to the Lord Lieutenant. Lord Castlereagh's paper, marked 'most secret,' is printed in the *Castlereagh Correspondence*, vol. iv. pp. 392–400.

[3] *Mem. and Cor. of Lord Castlereagh*, vol. iv. p. 83. It seems from a letter of Lord Cornwallis that the Irish primate went to England in January, 1801 (ib. p. 21). The Lord Lieutenant was mistaken in believing him to be 'by no means an anti-Catholic,' and 'not disposed to do mischief in a certain quarter.' Dr. W. Stuart was son of the Earl of Bute, George III.'s early Minister.

1801. 1801, he was again summoned to London by the Duke of Portland, the Home Secretary, to confer with the English Ministers. Upon his arrival in London, at the end of December, he took alarm at the Chancellor's opposition; and he probably may have heard reports of the difficulty to be anticipated from the King. He accordingly, on the 1st of January, 1801, wrote a letter to Mr. Pitt, representing to him the disappointment which Lord Cornwallis would feel, if the views expressed in Lord Loughborough's paper were adopted by the Cabinet. In this important letter Lord Castlereagh recalls to Mr. Pitt's recollection the communications formerly made by the Cabinet, through himself, to Lord Cornwallis, in reference to the Catholic question. He states that he was in England in the autumn of 1799, and was in communication with the Cabinet as to the means of carrying the Union in the Irish Parliament, after the unsuccessful attempt of the previous Session. By Lord Cornwallis's desire, he represented to the Cabinet the facility which would be derived in Ireland from its being in his power to give to the Catholics such a promise with respect to their claims, as would obtain their support for the Union. Lord Castlereagh says, that at this time, the Cabinet were unanimous in favour of the principle of Catholic relief; and, although they anticipated considerable repugnance to it in many quarters, and particularly in the highest, they authorised him to assure Lord Cornwallis that he need not anticipate any difficulty in dealing with the Catholics, so far as the Cabinet were concerned; and that he was fully warranted in soliciting from the Catholics every support for the Union which they could afford. Of this authority, he proceeds to say, Lord Cornwallis availed himself; and, at the desire of Lord Cornwallis, he recalled the attention of the Cabinet to the subject when he was in England in the previous autumn of 1800. Upon his return to Dublin he apprised Lord

Cornwallis that sentiments unfavourable to the concession had been expressed by Lord Loughborough; and that the Cabinet were unable, in the King's absence from London, to take a final decision on so momentous a question; but that he had no reason to expect that the expectations formed by Lord Cornwallis would be disappointed. Lord Castlereagh finally impresses upon Mr. Pitt the regret which Lord Cornwallis would experience at the abandonment of the measure, and the painful position in which it would place him with respect to the Catholic body.[1] Shortly after this letter Lord Castlereagh appears to have received an assurance from Mr. Pitt, that he would adhere to his measure, notwithstanding the obstacles which threatened him; for, on the 14th of January, Lord Cornwallis writes to Lord Castlereagh:— 1801.

> Your letter, dated the 7th, afforded me very sincere satisfaction. If Mr. Pitt is firm, he will meet with no difficulty; and the misfortunes of the present times are much in his favour towards carrying this point, on the same grounds that the Rebellion assisted the Union.

On the 22nd of January, he writes again to Lord Castlereagh:—

> All your last letters have administered real comfort to me. We now shall turn that great measure of the Union to real profit, at the same time that we are adopting the only means of resisting the hostility of almost all Europe.[2]

Notwithstanding Lord Cornwallis's sanguine predictions, the last act of the drama was now at hand. Mr. Pitt's

[1] *Memoirs and Correspondence of Lord Castlereagh*, vol. iv. pp. 8–12.

[2] *Memoirs, &c.* pp. 20, 21. The battle of Marengo was fought in June 1800, the battle of Hohenlinden on Dec. 3, 1800. The maritime confederacy of the Northern Powers was signed on Dec. 16, 1800. The isolated and perilous situation of England at this time is described by Alison, *History of Europe*, vol. iv. p. 486. ed. 1842. [Compare Lord Stanhope's *Life of Pitt*, vol. iii. p. 238, Mr. Massey's *Hist. of England*, vol. iv. p. 512.—Ed.]

1801. firmness in maintaining the cause of the Catholics produced no impression on the unreasoning mind of the King, poisoned by secret advisers. On the 31st of January, Mr. Pitt addressed to His Majesty a long and elaborate letter, containing what may be considered his ultimatum on the subject. In this letter he submits to the King the conclusions of his confidential servants upon the important questions respecting the Catholics and Dissenters, which would naturally be agitated in consequence of the Union. Mr Pitt proceeds to say: —

> The knowledge of Your Majesty's general indisposition to any change of the laws on this subject, would have made this a painful task to him; and it is become much more so by learning from some of his colleagues, and from other quarters, within these few days, the extent to which Your Majesty entertains, and has declared, that sentiment.[1]

Mr. Pitt then states that the majority of the Cabinet concur with him in proposing the removal of the political disabilities of Catholics and Dissenters, and a public provision for the Catholic clergy of Ireland—that his views in favour of these measures are unalterably fixed; and, if he is not at liberty to bring them forward with the King's full concurrence, and with the whole weight of government, his first wish is to be released from his official situation. He terminates his letter with assuring the King of his readiness to remain in the discharge of his duties until a new administration can be formed. The King's answer

[1] These words are inconsistent with the circumstantial statement in the *Castlereagh Correspondence* (derived at second hand from the Archbishop of Armagh) that Mr. Pitt sent Lord Castlereagh's papers to the King in September, and had mentioned the subject to him on the 13th and 18th of December, and that the King had then said, that sooner than concede he would part with his life (vol. iv. p. 83); and also with the account of the 'long letter' to Mr. Pitt from the King, when he was at Weymouth, in Lord Malmesbury's *Diary*, vol. iv. p. 21.

puts forward the Coronation Oath as a bar to the proposed measure, but suggests, as a compromise, that both he and Mr. Pitt should agree to be silent on the subject. Mr. Pitt refuses to accede to these terms, and repeats the offer of his resignation, which the King, by a letter dated February 5, accepts.[1] 1801.

It is evident from the tone of Mr. Pitt's first letter, and from Lord Grenville's letter to Lord Buckingham, written on the next day but one before the King's answer had been received, that Mr. Pitt believed the King's resolution to be immovable, and expected, when he wrote, that his resignation would be accepted. The mutual conduct of the King and Mr. Pitt on this occasion, and the manner in which the King put an end to his connection with a statesman who had guided the helm during the storms of the Coalition, the Regency, and the French Revolution, is a remarkable proof of the want of cordiality and confidence which subsisted between this sovereign and his ministers.

Although the measures relative to the Catholics had been under the consideration of the Cabinet since the preceding autumn, no intimation of them was made by Mr. Pitt to the King until his formal communication of January 31, when the King's adverse decision had been virtually formed and promulgated. Even when this communication had been made, everything passed in writing, and Mr. Pitt's administration of above seventeen years' duration was brought to a close without any oral explanation between the King and his Minister upon the measure which formed the ground of difference, although the latter considered it of vital importance to the interests of

[1] Mr. Pitt's correspondence with the King on this occasion was published by Bishop Philpotts in 1827, and is reprinted in the *Quarterly Review*, vol. xxxvi. pp. 290–5. It was printed from copies taken at the time by Lord Kenyon, to whom the originals were communicated by the King.

1801. the empire, and the former considered it as involving a violation of his coronation oath. Lord Malmesbury attributes Pitt's conduct to indolence, or to want of respect for the King; but it seems unlikely that he failed in this matter from neglect; probably he distrusted the influence of reason upon the King's mind, and hoped to bear him down at the last moment by the authority of an united cabinet.[1] It may be observed that the relations of George III. with his political servants were in general distant and stiff. We will not assert that no minister of this King ever sat in his presence, but we believe that such occasions were extremely rare; none of that confiding and frequent intercourse which subsequent sovereigns have kept up with their ministers, to the great advantage of public business, existed in his reign. The King had known, since the autumn of 1800, that a plan for removing Catholic disabilities was under the consideration of the

[1] [Lord Stanhope has published two notes of George III. to Mr. Pitt, dated Feb. 18 and Feb. 20, never printed before (vol. iii. App. p. xxxii.). The first of these begins 'My dear Pitt,' and contains congratulations on the passing of the Ways and Means. The second shows that this departure from Royal etiquette was specially intended to mark cordiality at this moment, and concludes with the words 'They were only the effusions of the real affection His Majesty will ever have for Mr. Pitt.' I have referred to these letters because, as far as they go, they may be set off against the remarks in the text. In a conversation with Mr. Rose, Pitt evidently blamed himself for not having earlier endeavoured to reconcile the King to the measure in favour of the Catholics, or to prevail with His Majesty not to take an active part on the subject (*Lord Stanhope*, vol. iii. p. 287).

In truth the King never appreciated Pitt at his real worth. It is scarcely credible that in 1804, in writing to him, he should have used the following words:—'Mr. Pitt, of whose services none has been more predominant than the proposing Mr. Addington, then a young man, for Speaker of the House of Commons' (Lord Stanhope's *Life of Pitt*, vol. iv. App. p. xx.). The notion that after Pitt had been Prime Minister seventeen years, the King should single out as his chief service the early patronage of Addington, is scarcely consistent with sanity, and this may be the explanation of it. Ed.]

Cabinet; he had conversed upon it with Lord Loughborough at Weymouth in September, and had seen Mr. Pitt's letter on the subject; he had subsequently spoken to Lord Loughborough in London about it, had inquired as to the decision of the Cabinet, and had obtained Lord Loughborough's paper of objections; he had also received private communications from the Archbishops of Canterbury and Armagh. So well-informed was he of the intentions of Ministers, that his negotiation with Mr. Addington was commenced before Mr. Pitt's letter reached him. In writing to Mr. Addington on January 29, the King speaks conjecturally of Mr. Pitt's opinion; and in a subsequent letter of February 7, he says that the subject had not been communicated to him till Sunday, February 1—the day on which he read Mr. Pitt's letter. If, however, the King had acted openly to Mr. Pitt, he would, at the time when he was receiving objections and warnings from the Chancellor and the Archbishops, have questioned Mr. Pitt on the subject, and have invited him to explain his intentions.

1801.

Sir Archibald Alison, in his *History of Europe*, repeats a suspicion thrown out by former writers, that the Catholic question was merely the ostensible ground of Mr. Pitt's resignation, and that he withdrew from office in order to make way for a minister who should have greater facilities than himself for agreeing to a peace.[1] Lord Campbell and Lord John Russell concur in rejecting this hypothesis;[2]

[1] *History of Europe*, vol. iv. pp. 492–5.

[2] *Lives of the Chancellors*, vol. vi. p. 296; *Mem. of Fox*, vol. iii. p. 252. Southey, in the *Letters from England*, published near the beginning of the century, under the pseudonyme of Don Manuel Espriella, has an interesting chapter on the advent of the Addington Administration, in which he attributes the resignation of Mr. Pitt and his colleagues exclusively to the Catholic question. He adds:—'That this is the real state of the case, I have been assured on such authority that I cannot entertain the slightest doubt' (*Letter* 12, vol. i.). [Lord Stanhope says:—'The original documents

1801. and an attentive perusal of the various original documents which have of late been brought to light, convinces us of its utter groundlessness. No such idea can be traced to any authentic source; it is clear that Mr. Pitt conceived himself bound by his previous conduct to press the question upon the King; that he would gladly, if he had been able, have overcome the King's opposition; that he resigned reluctantly; and that after his resignation, he would have resumed office if Mr. Addington had withdrawn voluntarily in order to facilitate his return. Lord Grenville's confidential letter to his brother, written before the resignation had taken place, and describing the plan as formed by Mr. Pitt and himself,[1] is decisive as to the real grounds upon which the Ministers acted. There is also in the Castlereagh Correspondence, a paper by Lord Castlereagh, containing a statement of the reasons for the retirement of Mr. Pitt and his friends from office. These reasons are threefold. 1. Their conviction that such a comprehensive measure is necessary in order to enable the empire to reap all the benefits of the Union. 2. The expectations of support held out by them to the Irish Catholics, whose support was in consequence given to the Union. 3. The improbability that a postponement of the question would mitigate the King's opposition.[2] In this

bearing on the question, some of which have but lately come to light, must, I am sure, convince every careful and dispassionate reader that any such idea' (i.e. any idea that Pitt resigned because he did not choose to conclude a peace) 'is entirely unfounded' (*Life of Pitt*, vol. iii. p. 309). Compare also vol. iii. p. 353.—Ed.]

[1] *Buckingham Papers*, vol. iii. p. 128. The King, in a letter to Mr. Addington of Feb. 13, 1801, says: 'I think I am right (though it appears most extraordinary) that Lords C—— and C—— and Mr. C—— are the persons that led Mr. Pitt to the rash step he has taken' (*Life of Lord Sidmouth*, vol. i. p. 305). The persons here signified are Lords Cornwallis and Castlereagh, and Mr. Canning. We doubt the correctness of the King's supposition.

[2] *Memoirs and Correspondence of Lord Castlereagh*, vol. iv. p. 34.

full statement there is no allusion to any other ground for Mr. Pitt's resignation. 1801.

Lord Loughborough's conduct is more easily explained. The idea about the coronation oath had taken possession of the King's mind so early as 1795; he had then consulted Lord Kenyon and Lord Loughborough himself upon it.[1] It was known to the cabinet in the autumn of 1799 (as we learn from Lord Castlereagh's letter to Mr. Pitt, cited above), that the King was then adverse to the admission of Catholics to Parliament and office. Lord Loughborough had indeed concurred with his colleagues in approving of this measure before the Union was passed; but finding from his conversations with the King at Weymouth that His Majesty still retained strong feelings on the subject, he changed his course, and opposed the measure, doubtless with no other motive than that of ingratiating himself with the King and strengthening his

[1] The correspondence between George III. and Lord Kenyon, C. J., was published by his son Lord Kenyon, in 1827. Lord Loughborough, in his paper above referred to, says:—'In 1795, by his Majesty's express command, I delivered my written answers to some questions he was pleased to put to me upon this subject, which answers fell so short of the high sense of the obligation his Majesty felt to be imposed upon him, that they were rather displeasing to him' (*Lord Campbell's Lives of the Chancellors*, vol. vi. p. 326). Lord Malmesbury has the following entry in his *Diary*, Feb. 26, 1801:—'King at Windsor about the 6th or 7th instant; read his coronation oath to his family, asked them whether they understood it, and added, "If I violate it I am no longer legal sovereign of this country, but it falls to the House of Savoy."' It is very likely that this danger had been artfully suggested to the King. A passionate exclamation of the King at the same time, after having caused his coronation oath to be read to him, that 'he would rather beg his bread from door to door throughout Europe than consent to any such measure,' is reported by General Garth (*Pellew's Life of Lord Sidmouth*, ibid. p. 285). [In 1795 the King had consulted Lord Kenyon and Sir John Scott on the question, how far an alteration of the Test Act was consistent with the coronation oath and the Act of Union with Scotland. They had answered that it might be altered or repealed without any breach of either. Lord Loughborough had answered more doubtfully as to the coronation oath. See Lord Stanhope's *Life of Pitt*, vol. iii. p. 263.—Ed.]

1801. own position. As to the exclusion or admission of Catholics he was probably quite indifferent, and he had no intention of turning out Mr. Pitt's Government if it was to endanger his own tenure of the Great Seal. When the fate of the Government was announced, he was, we are told 'all consternation;' he placed himself in Mr. Addington's hands, and was ready to accept the office of President of the Council, which the new Minister destined for him.[1] The King, however, who doubtless had not forgotten Lord Loughborough's conduct during the Regency, was not so easily conciliated as his late Chancellor had flattered himself. Lord Loughborough was mercilessly excluded from the new administration; and when the King, upon his resignation, delivered the Great Seal to Lord Eldon, he drew it from under the left breast of his coat, where he had carefully lodged it, saying, that 'he gave it to him from his heart.'[2] That the King distrusted Lord Loughborough—notwithstanding his attempts to gain the royal favour—as much as he loved Lord Eldon, is proved by his well-known exclamation on hearing of Lord Loughborough's death, that 'he had not left behind him a greater knave in the king's dominions.'[3]

As soon as Mr. Fox is informed of the hands to which the King had entrusted the formation of a new Administration, he writes to Lord Holland: 'Addington, Chancellor of the Exchequer, as against Pitt! If I do believe it, it must be *quia incomprehensibile*.' The pure Tory

[1] Pellew's *Life of Lord Sidmouth*, vol. i. pp. 312, 315.

[2] Twiss's *Life of Lord Eldon*, vol. i. p. 251.

[3] The copy of a paper delivered to Mr. Pitt in 1795 by the King, with a memorandum in the King's writing, dated April 12, 1801, which was found among Lord Loughborough's papers, must have been given him by the King when he had his audience to surrender the Great Seal (*Lord Campbell*, ibid. p. 300). It is dated two days previously.

Administration which was now formed does not support the theory to which we have adverted above, as to the anti-aristocratic tendencies of the Tory party. The Cabinet consisted of nine persons, five of whom were peers. The four commoners were Mr. Addington himself, together with Lord Hobart, Lord Hawkesbury, and Lord Lewisham, all eldest sons of Earls. But before the arrangements could be completed an unforeseen obstacle arose. The King's mind had been so much affected by the late ministerial crisis, that the necessity for a Regency seemed imminent, and his life was even in danger. In a short time, however, this cloud passed away; and after an unsuccessful attempt on the part of Mr. Pitt's friends to restore him to office, in which the conduct of this statesman does not appear to advantage,[1] the 'Doctor' (as he was now universally called) commenced his inglorious ministerial career. 1801.

The publications of the Duke of Buckingham and Lord Holland contained much authentic information respecting events subsequent to the close of Mr. Pitt's first administration. The limits of an Article have, however, been already exceeded; and the completion of the 'Memoirs of Fox' may afford us an opportunity of reverting to the first decade of this century.

[1] [See on this subject the fourth Article of this series, and the notes to it.—ED.]

III.

LORD CORNWALLIS. THE IRISH UNION, AND THE CATHOLIC QUESTION.[1]

As soon as nations emerge from that childlike state, in which every narrative of past events is accepted as historical, as soon as they begin to doubt and to inquire after the evidence of occurrences related to have happened in former ages, the distinction between contemporary and traditionary history is speedily apprehended. The modern critical historian draws this distinction with still greater precision. He points out, for instance, how history, founded on a consecutive narrative of well-informed contemporaries, begins, for Greece, with the Persian war, and for Rome, with the landing of Pyrrhus in Italy; and how the accounts of Greece and Rome for the earlier periods, are derived from oral traditions, assisted by fragmentary records in writing, and popular poems. Even in some periods of later history, where barbarous communities are concerned, the traditionary element occupies a large space.

Mr. Muir, in his recent 'Life of Mahomet,' has shown how much of the accepted history of the Arab prophet rests upon the uncertain basis of oral tradition;[2] and M. Amédée Thierry, in his 'History of Attila,' has given a copious analysis of the legendary materials which have

[1] Review of *Correspondence of Charles, first Marquis Cornwallis.* Edited, with Notes, by Charles Ross, Esq. 3 Vols. 8vo. London: 1859.

[2] See vol. i. introd. c. 1 (2 Vols. 1858).

been accumulated around the exploits of the conqueror of the fifth century.[1]

The modern history of civilised nations is founded exclusively upon contemporary materials. It is derived from the written accounts of persons who lived at the time of the events which they narrate. But the contemporary materials of history are not all of the same character; they differ in value and authenticity, according as they emanate from mere spectators, or from actors in the events. The annals and chronicles from which the history of England and of other European states, for the period prior to the sixteenth century, is derived, were chiefly composed by monks or priests, who, living in retirement, knew no more of contemporary history than could be learnt by a spectator of passing events. A similar remark applies to such historians as Stowe and Holinshed, and even to Smollett. A contemporary writer cannot be mistaken about patent occurrences, such as a battle, a pestilence, a famine, a change of government. His accounts will be free from the obscurity and fluctuations of tradition; but they may be erroneous as to the springs of action and the causes of events; they may mistake the motives and characters of public men; they may adopt current popular prejudices and ignorant misrepresentations. Hence the superiority of history composed by the actors in the events narrated. Contemporary memoirs by persons who make as well as write history, may sometimes be apologies for the conduct of the author; sometimes they may be warped by the bias of the party to which he belonged; yet they have this great merit, that where they err, it is not through ignorance of the facts; and that the author was able, if he was willing, to state the events as they really happened.

The actors in events, however, who have lived in this

[1] *Histoire d'Attila et de ses Successeurs* (Paris, 1856), vol. ii. pp. 229-443.

age of writing, may be converted into historians without having intended it. Their private letters and public despatches, or other documents prepared for official purposes, may be collected and published; and thus, having been originally designed for the information of friends or the transaction of business, may become materials for history. A historical memoir may be compared with a medal, which is intended as a reminiscence; while an official despatch is like a coin, which is intended for currency in mercantile dealings. Nevertheless, a coin not less than a medal may be used as a historical testimony. Several authentic collections of this kind, as the correspondence of the Duke of Wellington, Lord Wellesley, Lord Castlereagh, Lord Nelson, and others, have been of late years published in this country: the correspondence of Joseph Bonaparte is of a similar character, and a collection of the despatches of Napoleon has been commenced. The most ancient example is the collection of Cicero's epistles. Letters and despatches, like journals entered day by day, have this advantage over memoirs, that they exhibit faithfully the impressions of the moment, and are written without knowledge of the ultimate result. They are, therefore, more trustworthy than any narrative composed after the whole series of events has been worked out, at a time when the narrator is tempted to suppress, or has learnt to forget, the proofs of his own want of foresight. In confidential correspondence, written without any expectation of publicity, weaknesses and minor defects of the writer will be disclosed; many transient feelings or thoughts will appear which his deliberate judgment would have rejected; but where there is genuine ability and true integrity, these qualities will be more apparent from their evidence being undesigned.[1]

[1] [These observations on the different kinds of materials for history, and their relative value, are eminently characteristic of that acute and critical

It is to the latter class that the work before us belongs. The correspondence of Lord Cornwallis has been brought together from a variety of depositories, both private and public: the Family Papers, the India House, the State Paper Office, Dublin Castle, and other sources, have contributed to the collection. The editor, Mr. Charles Ross, who is married to Lord Cornwallis's granddaughter, and whose father, General Ross, was his intimate friend and constant correspondent, has shown extraordinary diligence both in the formation and illustration of this collection; his work is a model to future editors of similar collections, and offers a remarkable contrast to the ignorance and carelessness with which the family papers published under the auspices of the Duke of Buckingham have been edited. Mr. Ross, indeed, is sometimes excessive in annotation, but where the main work has been done in so efficient and satisfactory a manner, we are not disposed to be captious about trifles: and the fault, if it be one, is on the right side.

Lord Cornwallis was neither a brilliant nor a profound man; he never took part in debate, and his public despatches are composed in a simple and unpretending style. But he seems to have possessed, in an eminent degree, those qualities which inspire confidence for the management of public affairs and for the transaction of public business. During the chief part of his life, he was in the service of the State; and he was employed at critical periods in positions of the highest importance. He commanded a division in America during the American war; he was the first Governor-general of India appointed by the Crown after the recall of Hastings; he was Lord-lieutenant of Ireland at the time of the Rebellion and the

spirit which analysed the groundwork of Roman history, and sifted the conclusions of Niebuhr.—Ed.]

1776. Union; and he negotiated the definitive Treaty of Amiens. The confidential correspondence of a general and statesman who has filled such posts cannot fail to possess great interest for the reader, and to furnish invaluable materials for the history of the periods in question.

Charles, first Marquis Cornwallis, was born in London, December 31st, 1738, and was sent at an early age to Eton. He did not go to the university, but, at the age of eighteen, he entered the army, having obtained a commission of ensign in the First or Grenadier Guards in 1756. Shortly afterwards he received permission to study at a military academy at Turin, to which he was accompanied by a Prussian officer. In 1758 he was appointed on Lord Granby's staff, who commanded the English troops in Germany during the Seven Years' War, and he was present at the battle of Minden. After a short absence in England, Lord Cornwallis (then Lord Brome) returned to the army in Germany; he became lieutenant-colonel of the 12th regiment, and was engaged with the enemy in 1761 and 1762. In 1760 he had been elected member for Eye, but in 1762 he succeeded to the earldom on the death of his father, and took his seat in the House of Lords. After the peace, he accompanied his regiment to its various quarters in the United Kingdom, and once to Gibraltar. In 1768 he married Jemima, the daughter of Colonel Jones, who died in 1779.

Lord Cornwallis, when a young man, took no prominent part in politics; he acted with the party which opposed the policy of the Government prior to the American war, but was nevertheless permitted to retain some sinecure offices. In 1776, he was sent to America in command of a division of the British army. There, with the exception of two short intervals,[1] he remained until the surrender at

[1] During one of these visits to England he was examined as a witness, by

Yorktown, in October 1781, when he and the troops under his command became prisoners of war. This reverse of fortune, which was attributed to the arrangements of his superior officer, Sir Henry Clinton, does not seem to have diminished the confidence felt in his character and efficiency; and, in 1782, Lord Shelburne offered him the office of Governor-general of Bengal, which he at first declined, but ultimately accepted, though the change of administration prevented the appointment from taking place. He seems, however, to have been willing to accept the office from the Coalition Government if they had renewed the offer. He expresses the following qualified opinion of Fox's India Bill, in a letter to General Ross, of November 21, 1783:— 1784.

Fox's Bill will be strongly opposed, perhaps more so than it deserves; for, although I think there are several objectionable parts, I cannot say that the *daring attack* of the *chartered rights*[1] has much weight with me. I think Jenkinson hit one principal blot which can hardly be got over. He supposed the Commissioners to be appointed for three or five years, as proposed by Fox, and that a change of administration ensued—what would then be the consequence? The directors of East Indian affairs would probably be acting in direct opposition to the government at home. After all, it appears to me to be adopting a system almost as exceptionable as the present, and as likely to be perverted to the most corrupt purposes.

In a subsequent letter to the same correspondent (December 21, 1784), he says, 'You know I was partial to a great part of Fox's Bill.'

In 1784, Lord Cornwallis was much displeased at being passed over in the appointments to the offices of Governor of Plymouth and Constable of the Tower. After an angry

a Committee of the House of Commons, on the conduct of the American war (May 1779).

[1] This ground of objection to Fox's India Bill was taken by Pitt.

1785. interview with Lord Sydney, the Secretary of State, he wrote a strong letter of remonstrance to Mr. Pitt, who lost no time in giving him satisfaction. The great Minister declared upon his honour that he intended no slight; that if he had inadvertently offended, he could only ask pardon, and offer any reparation in his power; and tendered the constableship of the Tower as the price of reconciliation. Lord Cornwallis took a few hours to consider, for the sake of appearances; and he then notified his acceptance, with an assurance of total oblivion of what had passed. The pacification was accomplished by the following letter to Mr. Pitt:—

Mansfield Street: Nov. 10, 1784.

Dear Sir,—The fairness and candour of your behaviour to me, and your obliging expressions of friendship, have determined me never to turn my eyes back to whatever fatality occasioned the disagreeable subject of our conversation. I shall most thankfully accept the Tower from you, and I shall erase from my mind every idea that I could have been slighted by Mr. Pitt. I have, &c.

Cornwallis.

In 1785, he served as member of a board of land and sea officers appointed to report upon the expediency of fortifying Portsmouth and Plymouth. The plan recommended by the majority of the Board was subsequently brought forward by Mr. Pitt, but was negatived by the casting vote of the Speaker. Early in the same year, he refused the office of Governor-general of India, which was pressed upon him by Mr. Pitt; but in the summer he was sent on a special mission to Frederic the Great, for the purpose of reestablishing more intimate relations between him and the Government of England. He sent to Lord Carmarthen, the Foreign Secretary, an interesting report of his conversation with Frederic at Sans Souci, in

Sept. 1785. Prussia was at this time the only continental power friendly to England. He returned in the autumn, and early in 1786, he consented to accept the office of Governor-general, which he had declined in the previous year. He embarked for India in May, and arrived at Calcutta in September. 1786.

Hastings had left India in February 1785, and was succeeded in the office of Governor-general by Sir John Macpherson, as senior member of the Supreme Council. This functionary held the office for the eighteen months which elapsed until Lord Cornwallis's arrival, and made some treaties with native powers, which were censured by the Court of Directors, and annulled by Lord Cornwallis. All that we hear in these papers respecting him is discreditable. He is described as having been intriguing and corrupt, and as having connived at the peculations of his subordinates. Lord Cornwallis had received an unfavourable account of him from Hastings, who probably was not a very severe judge of the delinquencies of another servant of the Company. On his return to England, he was admitted for a time into the intimacy of the Prince of Wales.

Lord Cornwallis was the first Governor-general appointed after the creation of the Board of Control; after the transfer of the real government of India from the Company to the ministers and nominees of the Crown. He was the first English statesman appointed to that office, who carried to India the morality of the public life of England. Before his time, whatever might be the policy or instructions of the Directors in London, the local government of India in the hands of the Company's servants had been characterised, with rare intervals, by extortion, rapine, corruption, and perfidy. Lord Cornwallis went to India with a firm determination to put a

1786. stop to this system, which had been already condemned by all parties in Parliament, and he succeeded in the attempt. Before Lord Cornwallis accepted his office, he stipulated with the Government that the Governor-general should be rendered independent of his Council, and that he should be armed with powers sufficient for overcoming any opposition of the local servants of the Company. This object was effected by a supplementary Act passed in 1786.

If (says Mr. Ross) a retrospective view be taken of the conduct of the Company's servants in India—of their rapacity, their corruption, the oppression they exercised, their utter ignorance in many instances of the country—no powers conferred upon the Governor-general could be considered too great. Nor had the Court of Directors been exempt from blame. Few had any personal knowledge of India, most were only anxious to promote their personal objects; all, it may be said, revelled in jobs. The investigation (he adds) of the gross jobs and corrupt practices which had disgraced former governments occupied much time, and the inquiries were not completed till the following year.

Lord Cornwallis sends the following confidential account to Mr. Dundas, the President of the India Board, in November 1786:—

You recollect that I am writing confidentially to you and Mr. Pitt, and to nobody else. I depend on your secrecy, and will not conceal from you that the late government had no authority, and the grossest frauds were daily committed before their faces; their whole conduct, and all their pretensions to economy, except in the reduction of salaries, was a scene of delusion. I suspect even that the opium and other contracts, the terms of which appear so advantageous, are not calculated to promote the real interests of the Company; and I am sure that the contractor for Oude cloths and Oude indigo was saddled with friends not very distant from the Government House (vol. i. p. 227).

In 1787, the attention of Lord Cornwallis was again

directed to the peculation and corruption of the Company's servants, particularly at Lucknow and Benares. Frauds had been committed in the purchase of silk, and a collusion existed between the contractors and some members of the Board of Revenue. Prosecutions were ordered against seven of the most culpable of the Company's servants. 1787.

It was not (says Mr. Ross) till Lord Cornwallis had himself visited the Upper Provinces, that he became thoroughly cognisant of the extent of these delinquencies, and of the excessive corruption prevalent among the Europeans when removed from the immediate supervision of Government.

Lord Cornwallis introduced and established the principle for the Indian Civil Service, of allowing liberal salaries to the heads of responsible offices, and of abolishing all perquisites and emoluments, whether undefined or defined. Writing to Mr. Dundas, in August 1787, he says:—

I have saved, since I came, upon the salt, upon the various contracts, upon remittances, balances, and jobs of different kinds, ten times, I may say fifty times, the amount of the salaries that are retrenched. I am doing everything I can to reform the Company's servants, to teach them to be more economical in their mode of living, and to look forward to a moderate competency; and I flatter myself I have not hitherto laboured in vain. But if all chance of saving any money and returning to England, without acting dishonestly, is removed, there will be an end of my reformation.

Lord Cornwallis likewise entertained an unfavourable opinion of the Directors as a body; he complained of the badness of their appointments; and in writing to Mr. Dundas, in March 1792, respecting some flagrant jobs which they had recently perpetrated, he says:—'If the Court of Directors cannot be controlled, I retract my opinion in favour of their continuance upon the expiration of the charter.'

1787. But notwithstanding Lord Cornwallis's opposition to many of the acts of the Directors, and notwithstanding the uncompromising integrity with which he cleansed the Augean stable of corruption in India, he conducted himself so as to avoid unpopularity both in India and in England. 'I have the satisfaction to think' (he writes to Lord Sydney in August 1787), 'that, in spite of our reforms, this government is not unpopular. It has, to be sure, the advantage of succeeding to one that was universally hated and despised.' On the other hand Mr. Dundas, in a letter to Lord Cornwallis, of July 1787, assures him that the Court of Directors are very much disposed to show every mark of attention to his suggestions, for he is a great favourite with them.' That the King's Ministers should put confidence in the government of Lord Cornwallis, and should rejoice in knowing that the Company's servants in India were for the first time placed under the control of a firm and honest hand, was natural.

We never before (Mr. Dundas writes to him, March 1787) had a government of India, both at home and abroad, acting in perfect unison together on principles of perfect purity and integrity; these ingredients cannot fail to produce their consequent effects.

The cause of the satisfaction felt by the Directors in the administration of Lord Cornwallis is to be sought partly in the economy and order which he introduced into Indian finance, and partly in his desire to act upon the pacific policy which Parliament had recently embodied in the Act of 1784. The Directors, looking only to their dividend, had consistently instructed their local agents to abstain from wars with the native powers, but they had not been obeyed. Lord Cornwallis intended to act on a different system; but in 1790 he was drawn into a war with Tippoo, which in 1792, when Seringapatam was on the point of being captured, was terminated by a treaty. Tippoo agreed to cede half his dominions, to pay 3,600,000*l.*, to release all prisoners, and to deliver two of his sons as hostages. In consequence of this success Lord Cornwallis was created a marquis. 1791.

One of the most important of his measures as Governor-general was the settlement of the land revenue of Bengal. It was desirable to protect the interest of the occupiers of the land by withdrawing this essential question from the dominion of uncertainty and caprice. The measure recommended by Lord Cornwallis was, as is well known, a settlement with the Zemindars and in perpetuity. The policy of this settlement has been much disputed, and other principles of determining the land revenue have been tried in the other presidencies: it is sufficient for us to say that they agree in adopting some principle of permanence, and that the system introduced by Lord Cornwallis was undoubtedly a great improvement upon the state of things which he found in existence. Lord Cornwallis's plan was sent home for consideration, with the remarks of Mr. Shore, who differed from him on the question of perpetuity. On the receipt of it, Mr. Dundas and Mr. Pitt passed ten days together at Wimbledon in examining and discussing the subject: during a part of the time Mr. Charles Grant stayed with them. The result was that they adopted the views of Lord Cornwallis, and that Mr. Dundas prepared a despatch, sanctioning his proposals, to which the Directors agreed. It appears that at this time the official members of the India Board took part in the business, and that they did not, as at a later period, leave everything to the President. In a letter to Lord Cornwallis of July 1787, Mr. Dundas says: 'Mr. Pitt is a real active member of the Board, and makes

1787. himself thoroughly master of the business.' In a previous letter of the same year (March 21, 1787), Mr. Dundas gives the following account of the motives for the celebrated change in the course taken by Pitt and himself with respect to the impeachment of Hastings:—

The only unpleasant circumstance is the impeachment of Mr. Hastings. Mr. Pitt and I have got great credit from the undeviating fairness and candour with which we have proceeded in it, but the proceeding is not pleasant to many of our friends, and, of course, from that and many other circumstances, not pleasing to us; but the truth is, when we examined the various articles of charges against him with his defences, they were so strong and the defences so perfectly unsupported, it was impossible not to concur; and some of the charges will unquestionably go to the House of Lords.

Whatever collateral motives may have contributed to the formation of this decision, we cannot but think that the preceding simple explanation affords the true key to Mr. Pitt's conduct.[1]

Lord Cornwallis, at an early period of his administration, recommended the amalgamation of the King's troops and the Company's European troops into one service. The King's final approbation of this plan was given in July 1787, but its execution was successfully resisted by the Directors and the Company's troops. A long memorandum upon this question, the practical interest of which has been revived by the recent mutiny, was transmitted to Mr. Dundas by Lord Cornwallis upon his return to England.[2]

The following opinions on the attempts to convert the

[1] [See above, p. 105, the second article of this series, and the references there given.—Ed.]

[2] Concerning this question, see vol. i. pp. 240, 329, 330; vol. ii. pp. 283, 314, 567.

natives to Christianity are expressed by him in a letter to the Bishop of Salisbury of December 1788:— 1789.

The pride and bigotry of the Mussulmen, and the dreadful consequences to themselves and their families for ever attending the loss of caste to the Hindoos, must, in my opinion, prove insuperable bars to any material progress in the propagation of the Christian religion. The success of the Portuguese missionaries on the Malabar coast does not hold out any very encouraging prospect to us, as their converts are the poorest and most contemptible wretches in India. It is likewise a matter for serious consideration how far the imprudence or intemperate zeal of one teacher might endanger a government which owes its principal support to a native army composed of men of high caste, *whose fidelity and affections we have hitherto secured, by an unremitted attention not to offend their religious scruples and superstitions.*

Lord Cornwallis's manners as Governor-general were simple and unostentatious; he discouraged all parade and pomp; and in the campaign against Tippoo his life was endangered by his practice of not allowing more than one or two sentries to mount guard at his tent. He rather resembled Lord W. Bentinck, of whom Jacquemont said that he was a Quaker on the throne of India, than Lord Wellesley, who was described by Sir J. Mackintosh as having 'sultanised his office.' In writing to his son, Lord Brome, in January 1789, he thus describes his daily life, which offers a remarkable contrast to that of an oriental Prince.

I can send you no news from hence that can either amuse or interest you. My life at Calcutta is perfect clockwork. I get on horseback just as the dawn of day begins to appear, ride on the same road and the same distance, pass the whole forenoon after my return from riding in doing business, and almost exactly the same portion of time every day at table, drive out in a phaeton a little before sunset, then write, or read over papers

1793. of business for two hours, sit down at nine with two or three officers of my family to some fruit and a biscuit, and go to bed soon after the clock strikes ten. I don't think the greatest *sap* at Eton can lead a duller life than this.

The confidential despatch of 4th April 1790, in which he conveys to Mr. Dundas his opinion respecting the terms on which the Company's charter ought to be renewed, is a highly interesting document. The plan originally contemplated by the English Cabinet for the renewal of 1793 seems to have been to leave the commercial monopoly to the Company, without control, and to transfer the government and territorial revenues to the Crown. To this plan Lord Cornwallis objects that if the Company were left to manage their trade without government control, the jobbing would be so great that they would speedily become bankrupt: he thinks that the export trade from Britain to India might be safely thrown open, but that to abolish the monopoly of the trade from India to Britain and other countries would be ruinous: and he recommends the course which was subsequently adopted — the renewal of the monopoly and the government for another term, both being subject to the control of the King's Ministers. The mistake which was made in 1793, as well as in 1783 and 1784, was that the reform started on the assumption that the Company was to retain its monopoly of trade. The proper course would have been to wind up the Company, to throw open its entire trade, and to transfer its governing powers to the Crown. But although Lord Cornwallis was too timid, and too little versed in the theory of commerce, to recommend this course, he betrays a deep-rooted distrust of the Directors. He went to India at a time when the misdeeds of the Company and of their servants were fresh and well understood; and neither in this nor in his other papers is there any trace of the sentimental admiration of the Company's government which has grown up since their period of independent action has been forgotten, and they have mended their behaviour under the ferule of ministerial control. 1793.

Lord Cornwallis left India in October 1793, after a residence of seven years and one month; and reached England in February 1794. In 1792 he had refused the office of Secretary of State, offered to him by Mr. Pitt: he grounds his refusal upon his deficiency in the powers and habits of parliamentary debate.[1] He was succeeded in the Governor-generalship by his friend Sir John Shore (afterwards Lord Teignmouth), who, though originally a servant of the Company under the old system, was a man of integrity, and had acted cordially with Lord Cornwallis.[2]

These volumes contain much curious information respecting the Regency proceedings in 1788, and other public events, which Lord Cornwallis received from his correspondents in England during his absence. Our space does not permit us to notice these collateral matters: we can only make room for an extract from a letter addressed, soon after the King's recovery, to Lord Cornwallis by the Prince of Wales, which exhibits plainly the state of his feelings towards the King and Mr. Pitt. It is dated Carlton House, May 30, 1789. The King's restoration to health was announced to Parliament on the 24th of February preceding.

How things have changed, and what a chequered scene of life I have been obliged to go through for the last six months! Ere this I suppose you will have heard of the King's indisposition,

[1] [This was after the transfer of Lord Grenville to the place of the Duke of Leeds. See above, p. 139. Lord Stanhope, *Life of Pitt*, v. ii. p. 121.—Ed.]

[2] [In February 1791, Philip Francis had moved resolutions concerning the war against Tippoo. They were opposed by Pitt and Dundas, and negatived without a division. See Lord Stanhope, *Life of Pitt*, vol. ii. p. 88.—Ed.]

1789. and how the Ministers attempted [not only] to destroy my rights, but to deprive every other individual of our family of the common liberties and rights of Englishmen. Supported I have been by some real and true friends, at the head of whom your friend my brother [the Duke of York] stood foremost, which has gained [him] immortal honour. Had you been here, my dear Lord, I doubt not that we should have had the happiness of meeting with a similar support from you, though I am sorry to say that your members[1] consulted the interests of the cause of Pitt, instead of the rights and independence of the constitution of this country, as well as of the House of Brunswick. Everything has fallen into very different hands. The King is convalescent; that is to say, he certainly is better. Everything is thrown into the hands of the Queen. Every friend that supported me and the common cause of succession in the family, if they had any place, have been dismissed; such as the Duke of Queensberry and our little friend Lothian. Queensberry has been dismissed by order of the Queen and Mr. Pitt from the Bedchamber. Lothian has left his regiment of Horse Guards.[2]

They have had the insolence to threaten the Duke of York with taking his regiment of Foot Guards; and when they at last did not dare do that, they have brought officers into his regiment, and committed towards him every species of indignity to force him to resign, which he has had prudence and coolness sufficient, as well as firmness enough, to resist. Not only these great officers, but numberless of a lower class, whose sole dependence in life and sustenance depended upon their places, have been disgracefully dismissed from their offices for their disinterested support of me and our family. You will forgive me, my dear Lord, for thus expatiating upon a subject which I would not have done but to such a friend as I consider you.

I cannot but confess that I feel for the dangerous situation in

[1] The Prince alludes to the members for the borough of Eye, who were returned through the interest of Lord Cornwallis.

[2] The Marquis of Lothian, in consequence of the active part which he took on the Prince's side during the King's illness, was deprived of the Gold Stick and the command of a regiment of Life Guards; but the King offered him the command of the Irish Dragoon Guards, which he refused.

which the rights and liberties of this nation are at present, as well as the very critical position in which every individual of our family stands at present. However, the very precarious state of the King's health renders some people a little upon their guard, who are not driven to a state of despair, such as not only pervades the Minister himself but his adherents in general. I will not bore you any further at present, as I suppose you will have heard by many letters of our critical situation in this country at the present period, but trust you will attribute my prolixity to the intimacy of an old friend. 1794.

To this letter Lord Cornwallis answers as follows from Calcutta, in August 1790:—

I can with the utmost sincerity declare that you will only do me justice in believing that no man can love and admire more than I do, your Royal Highness's amiable qualities and virtues; that I feel the warmest gratitude for your personal kindness to me; that I am a determined friend to the liberties of my country, the just prerogatives of the Crown, and the rights of the House of Brunswick; and that I should feel the highest gratification in being able to coincide on all occasions in political sentiments with the Duke of York: but, after having said this, I must honestly confess that if I had been in England in the winter of 1788–9, I should have thought it my duty, however painful it might have been to me, to have taken a different line from His Royal Highness in Parliament.

Lord Cornwallis, as we have stated, reached England, on his return from India, in the early part of 1794. In that year the Austrian, Prussian, and English armies were carrying on a joint campaign in Flanders against the French. Lord Cornwallis was sent in June to the seat of war, for the purpose of removing the jealousies and misunderstandings which prevailed between the three armies, and of imparting some concert into their operations. His attempts were unsuccessful; but his mission suggested a plan for placing the Austrian and British

1797. armies under his joint command. As this plan involved the removal of the Duke of York from the command of the British army, Mr. Pitt obtained with difficulty the assent of the King; but it was given, and Mr. Windham went to Flanders to communicate the decision to the Duke. Shortly afterwards, however, Valenciennes was surrendered to the French, and the plan of appointing Lord Cornwallis to the chief command was abandoned. Near the end of the year, Mr. Pitt represented to the King the necessity of putting an end to the Duke of York's command on the Continent. The King acquiesced, and he was recalled by a letter from Mr. Dundas.[1]

At the beginning of 1795, Lord Cornwallis succeeded the Duke of Richmond as Master-general of the Ordnance, and entered the Cabinet. In the meantime the plan which he had proposed for consolidating the European troops of the Company with the King's troops had caused much discontent in India, and the officers of the Bengal army carried their remonstrances so far as to intimidate Sir John Shore, and almost to create a mutiny. The English Government took alarm, and decided on sending Lord Cornwallis again to India; he was accordingly sworn in a second time as Governor-general on the 1st of Feb. 1797. Concessions were, however, made by the Board of Control and the Court of Directors, which calmed the disturbance, and rendered his return to India unnecessary.[2]

In the course of 1797, a question arose as to the appointment of Lord Cornwallis to the chief command in

[1] [Compare Lord Stanhope's *Life of Pitt*, vol. ii. pp. 257–8, 262.—Ed.]

[2] It seems that Lord Wellesley (then Lord Mornington) was, in April 1797, appointed Governor of Madras, with a promise of the reversion of the Bengal Government after Lord Cornwallis, in the event of the latter going to India. See Lord Mornington's letters in *Courts and Cabinets of George III.*, vol. ii. pp. 367–75.

Ireland; but in the following year, the outbreak of the rebellion rendered it necessary that the civil and military government of that country should be committed to the same hands. Lord Camden was accordingly recalled at his own request, and Lord Cornwallis was, in June 1798, appointed Lord-lieutenant and Commander-in-chief. The duties which Lord Cornwallis was called upon to perform, in this office, were in the highest degree arduous and responsible. The consequences of the long-continued misgovernment of Ireland were now, under the sympathetic influences of the French Revolution, visited on a generation which had begun to relax the ancient bigotry, and to adopt a more liberal and enlightened policy towards that country. In order to understand the position in which he found himself, on assuming the government of Ireland at this crisis, it is necessary to cast our eyes back for a few years. 1798.

Up to the year 1782, Ireland had been a dependency of England. The Irish Parliament had stood to the English Parliament in the same relation in which the legislature of a colony (such as Canada or Jamaica) stands to the same body. The English Parliament could, if it thought fit, legislate for Ireland, and its acts were valid in that country without the assent of the Irish parliament. But the military feebleness of England at the end of the American war led to the formation of the Irish volunteer regiments, and inspired them with courage to assert their own power; and in 1782 the legislative sovereignty of Great Britain over Ireland was renounced. The Acts declaring the dependence of Ireland were repealed; and from that time Ireland became legally independent of England, the only tie between them being that the King of England was also King of Ireland. After 1782 the relation of Ireland to England was, in a constitutional

1798. and legal point of view, similar to that of Hanover to England, so long as the English succession remained in the male line.[1] Even this tie, weak as it was, might have been still further weakened by the divergent action of the two parliaments; thus, during the King's illness in 1788, the Regency regulations adopted by the Irish Parliament differed from those adopted by the English Parliament. The substantial dependence of Ireland upon England was, however, to a great extent, secured by the intimate connection of the great body of the Irish landowners with English interests, by the close character of nearly the entire borough representation, and by the wholesale system of corruption with which the Government managed the Irish Parliament. During this period, therefore, the Irish Government may be characterised as a system in which legal independence was neutralised by corruption and religious intolerance. The governing power was in the exclusive possession of the party identified with Protestant ascendency; and hence there were two elements of disaffection which were called into active operation by the events of the French Revolution; the Presbyterians

[1] Lord North, in proposing in 1783 a measure relative to the postage of letters, acknowledged it 'to be very certain that Great Britain and Ireland had become to each other, in point of political power, as foreign nations.' [Compare Sir George Lewis's book on the *Government of Dependencies* (p. 154), and the quotation from Lord Abingdon's speech of 1783, and Lord Grenville's on the Union (*ibid.* pp. 362, 366).

The latter said, that 'if the parliaments were to remain distinct and separate, the bond of connection between the countries was null and void.' At first sight it appears that the expression as to Hanover in the text is inaccurate, inasmuch as the King of England was King of Ireland in his political capacity—because he was King of England. He was King of Hanover in his personal capacity and accidentally. But in fact the theory of the connection with Ireland between 1782 and the Union was utterly rotten and unsound. A King of England can act *as such* only in connection with the Parliament of England: therefore, to require him to govern *as King of England* and exclude the English Parliament is a contradiction in terms. ED.]

and the Catholics. The latter formed the great bulk of the population; but the former were the more energetic and enterprising politicians. The United Irishmen, consisting of Presbyterians and Protestants, and having their head-quarters at Belfast and Dublin, wished to convert Ireland into a republic, wholly independent of England, and connected with that of France. For this purpose they entered into treasonable communications with the French Directory, and organised an insurrection in Ireland, which was to be supported by a French invading force. The French Government are reported to have assured the United Irishmen, a short time before Lord Cornwallis's arrival in Dublin, that 'invasion should follow invasion, though defeat succeeded defeat, until Ireland was completely free.'[1] The conspirators, however, were not faithful to each other; the Government received full information of the plans which were in preparation, and in May 1798, Lord Edward Fitzgerald and the Sheares were arrested. These arrests, instead of suppressing the insurrection, were the signal for its outbreak. The Irish rebellion now began; but although it spread to the Catholic population of the south, its duration was short. The defeat of the rebels at Vinegar Hill took place at the 1798.

[1] Vol. ii. p. 349. In the early part of the French Revolution Lord Cornwallis had shared the opinion, then general, that France would be so weakened by internal discord as to prevent her from being troublesome to her neighbours. In a letter written from Calcutta to the Duke of York, and dated April 1790, he says: 'It is impossible to look without compassion upon the wretched state of France; but when we consider that the unprovoked and unjustifiable part which that nation took against us in the late American war has, perhaps, greatly contributed to produce the present convulsions, we cannot say that they are totally unmerited; and although it may be natural for your Royal Highness to feel disappointed at not having the means of improving yourself in your profession, I must candidly confess that I reflect with no small degree of satisfaction, that our tranquillity in Europe is not likely to be soon disturbed by that late powerful and restless neighbour.'

1798. time of Lord Cornwallis's arrival in June; in July, the majority of the state prisoners offered to acknowledge their offences, on condition that their lives were spared and that they left the country. In this state of things, the humane, prudent, and temperate disposition of Lord Cornwallis induced him to adopt a policy of clemency towards the defeated rebels.[1] In the adoption of moderate measures, he was supported by his chief secretary, Lord Castlereagh; but the subordinate agents of the Government, and the ascendency party by which it had been hitherto guided, urged partly by fear and partly by resentment, strongly insisted upon the necessity of severe punishment. Lord Cornwallis, therefore, in the summer and autumn of 1798, found himself in a position similar to that of Lord Canning during the late Indian mutiny.[2] The Irish Protestants, like the English of Calcutta, cried for blood. In both cases, the head of the Government had the firmness to resist this cowardly and savage cry. The passages in the correspondence which relate to this subject are too numerous for us to reprint; we will, however, lay some extracts before our readers, which will serve to exhibit their general tenor. The first is from a despatch to the Duke of Portland, of July 8, 1798:—

The principal persons of this country, and the members of both Houses of Parliament, are in general averse to all acts of clemency; and although they do not express, and perhaps are too much heated to see, the ultimate effects which their violence would produce, would pursue measures that could only terminate in the extirpation of the greater number of the inhabitants, and in the utter destruction of the country. The words Papists

[1] The excellent effects produced by Lord Cornwallis's arrival are described, in strong terms, by Plowden, *Historical Review of the State of Ireland*, vol. ii. p. 765. 4to.

[2] [Compare Massey's *History of England*, vol. iv. p. 322. Lord Stanhope's *Life of Pitt*, vol. iii. p. 251.—Ed.]

and Priests are for ever in their mouths, and by their unaccountable policy they would drive four-fifths of the community into irreconcilable rebellion;[1] and in their warmth they lose sight of the real cause of the present mischief, of that deep-laid conspiracy to revolutionise Ireland on the principles of France, which was originally formed, and by wonderful assiduity brought nearly to maturity, by men who had no thought of religion but to destroy it, and who knew how to turn the passions and prejudices of the different sects to the advancement of their horrible plot for the introduction of that most dreadful of all evils, a Jacobin revolution. 1798.

In a private letter to General Ross, of July 24, 1798, Lord Cornwallis says:—

Except in the instances of the six state trials that are going on here, there is no law either in town or country but martial law, and you know enough of that to see all the horrors of it, even in the best administration of it. Judge then how it must be conducted by Irishmen heated with passion and revenge. But all this is trifling compared to the numberless murders that are hourly committed by our people without any process or examination whatever. The yeomanry are in the style of the loyalists in America, only much more numerous and powerful, and a thousand times more ferocious. These men have saved the country, but they now take the lead in rapine and murders. The Irish militia, with few officers, and those chiefly of the worst kind, follow closely on the heels of the yeomanry in murder and every kind of atrocity, and the fencibles take a share, although much behindhand with the others. The feeble outrages, burnings, and murders, which are still committed by the rebels, serve to keep up the sanguinary disposition on our side; and as long as they furnish a pretext for our parties going in quest of them, I see no prospect of amendment. The conversation of the principal

[1] Lord Cornwallis here assumes that the ratio of Roman Catholics to Protestants in Ireland was at that time as 4 to 1. The population of Ireland in 1791 is estimated by Doctor Beaufort at 4,088,000. Of this number the Roman Catholics were probably about 3,000,000, and the Protestants about 1,000,000.

1798. persons of the country all tends to encourage this sytem of blood; and the conversation even at my table, where you will suppose I do all I can to prevent it, always turns on hanging, shooting, burning, &c., and if a priest has been put to death, the greatest joy is expressed by the whole company. So much for Ireland and my wretched situation.

A despatch to the Duke of Portland, of Sept. 16, 1798, contains the following remark:—

The principal personages here who have been long in the habit of directing the councils of the Lords-lieutenants, are perfectly well-intentioned and entirely attached and devoted to the British connexion, but they are blinded by their passions and prejudices, talk of nothing but strong measures, and arrogate to themselves the exclusive knowledge of a country, of which, from their mode of governing it, they have, in my opinion, proved themselves totally ignorant.[1]

In a letter to General Ross, of Nov. 16, 1799, in the year subsequent to the rebellion, the Lord-lieutenant recurs to the same topic:—

The greatest difficulty which I experience, is to control the violence of our loyal friends, who would, if I did not keep the strictest hand upon them, convert the system of martial law (which, God knows, is of itself bad enough) into a more violent and intolerable tyranny than that of Robespierre. The vilest informers are hunted out from the prisons to attack, by the most barefaced perjury, the lives of all who are suspected of being, or of having been, disaffected; and indeed every Roman Catholic of influence is in great danger.

The same humane and temperate policy which was adopted by Lord Cornwallis had been acted upon by Sir Ralph Abercromby, who had held the office of Commander-in-chief before his appointment. But as he did not, like Lord Cornwallis, unite the chief civil with the military

[1] See further on this subject, vol. ii. pp. 355, 359, 361, 386, 414.

command, the course which he took led him into serious 1798.
differences with Lord Camden, the Lord-lieutenant, who, though disposed to support Abercromby, had not sufficient firmness to resist the advice of his Irish counsellors. Lord Cornwallis, in a letter to General Ross, of March 1798, speaks of Sir Ralph Abercromby as having been 'exceedingly wrong-headed.' This expression refers to his misunderstandings with the Irish Government; but it is clear from the papers of the Abercromby family, which we have had an opportunity of perusing, that the conduct of Abercromby was highly creditable to his moderation and humanity, and that the principles on which he had acted were in substance followed by Lord Cornwallis himself.

Considering the existence of patent rebellion and of martial law for a considerable time, the punishments actually authorised by the Government appear to have been moderate. Lord Castlereagh, in defending Lord Cornwallis's 'ruinous system of lenity,' in the Irish House of Commons, in Feb. 1799, stated that since the landing of the French in Killala Bay (Aug. 1798) 380 rebels had been tried by martial law, of whom 131 had been capitally convicted, and 90 had been executed (vol. iii. p. 13, 70, 90). Lord Castlereagh appears, unlike the Chancellor and other high Irish functionaries, to have acted cordially with Lord Cornwallis, and never to have been the advocate of a sanguinary policy, notwithstanding the charges of cruelty which have been made against him for his conduct during the rebellion. As the eminence to which Lord Castlereagh rose was not anticipated at this time, it is interesting to observe the judgment of him formed by his chief. In a private letter to General Ross, of July 9, 1798, Lord Cornwallis says:—

I have every reason to be highly satisfied with Lord Castlereagh, who is really a very uncommon young man, and possesses talents,

1798. temper, and judgment suited to the highest stations, without prejudices or any views that are not directed to the general benefit of the British empire.[1]

In another letter to General Ross written at the same time, he remarks: 'Lord Castlereagh is a very able and good young man, and is of great use to me.' Later in the year, he strongly recommends Lord Castlereagh to the Duke of Portland for appointment to the vacant office of Irish Secretary of State (a different office from that of Chief Secretary to the Lord-lieutenant); and in answer to the objection that this office had always been conferred on an Englishman, he remarks that 'as Lord Castlereagh is so very unlike an Irishman, I think he has a just claim to an exception in his person' (vol. ii. pp. 428, 439). His reasons for making this recommendation are thus stated in a private letter to General Ross:—

The particular obligations which I felt to Lord Castlereagh, who had concealed nothing from me, had pointed out all the characters with which I had to deal, and shown me where my predecessor had failed, and had been obliged to sacrifice his own judgment in order to follow worse counsels, by suffering some dangerous persons to gain an ascendency over him; and in short his lordship's excellent character and truly faithful conduct towards me in every respect, rendered me very unwilling to part with him, especially when it was doubtful who would be the person to succeed him (vol. iii. p. 8).

In a letter to General Ross, of May, 1800, he thus describes Lord Castlereagh's parliamentary position:—

Lord Castlereagh has improved so much as a speaker as to

[1] Lord Castlereagh was now twenty-nine years old. He sat in the English House of Commons from 1794 to 1797. In the latter year he became a member of the Irish House of Commons, and was appointed Chief Secretary to the Lord-lieutenant in the beginning of 1798. [In the session of 1795 he seconded the Address in the English House of Commons. Lord Stanhope's *Life of Pitt*, vol. ii. p. 355.—Ed.]

become nearly master of the House of Commons; and the gratification of national pride which the Irish feel at the prospect of his making a figure in the great political world, has much diminished the unpopularity which his cold and distant manners in private society had produced. 1798.

The complete legal independence of Ireland since 1782, and the entire separation of the Irish and English Parliaments; the violence of the ascendency party in Ireland, and the impossibility of establishing religious equality between Protestants and Catholics, so long as the Irish Parliament remained separate; the existence of a large disaffected party in Ireland who were in treasonable correspondence with the French Directory; and the danger to England from a French invasion of Ireland, supported by a simultaneous rising of the population;—these, and other evils growing out of the existing state of Ireland and of its Government, which the rebellion displayed in their full force, appear to have convinced Mr. Pitt and his colleagues that the only effectual remedy was to be found in an incorporating union between Great Britain and Ireland, similar to that which had been formed nearly a century before between England and Scotland.[1] We collect from a letter of Lord Grenville, published by the Duke of Buckingham, that the views of the Cabinet on this question were communicated to Lord Cornwallis before he went to Ireland. In a letter to the Marquis of Buckingham, of about July 1798, Lord

[1] The grounds for a union are stated with remarkable ability and sagacity in an anonymous letter, dated Cork, November 12, 1798, which is printed in the *Castlereagh Correspondence*, vol. i. p. 436. The writer of this paper, whoever he was, thoroughly understood the nature of the change which the revolution of 1782 had produced—'the plaything of independence' (as he calls it), which England gave to Ireland, and the slippery supports on which the connection between the two countries rested. [Compare the quotation from Lord Grenville's speech on the Union in a previous note, p. 176.—Ed.]

1798. Grenville says, after expressing doubts whether Lord Cornwallis has not carried the system of lenity too far:—

The great point I wish to be assured of, if I could, is, that he has not suffered a nearer view of difficulties to discourage him from the pursuit of the only measure which can make it signify one farthing what he does in the present moment. Let him carry that, and I will willingly compromise for all the rest (*Court and Cabinets of George III.*, vol. ii. p. 405).

This passage evidently alludes to the plan of a union between the two countries, and it implies that the English Cabinet looked to Lord Cornwallis for carrying it. Lord Cornwallis alludes to the contemplated 'great measure,' in letters to General Ross, of August 1798 (vol. ii. pp. 381, 384); and in a confidential despatch to the Duke of Portland, of the 16th September following, he thus expresses himself:—

With regard to future plans, I can only say that some mode must be adopted to soften the hatred of the Catholics to our government. Whether this can be done by advantages held out to them from a union with Great Britain, by some provision for their clergy, or by some modification of tithe, which is the grievance of which they complain, I will not presume to determine. The first of these propositions is undoubtedly the most desirable, if the dangers with which we are surrounded will admit of our making the attempt; but the dispositions of the people at large, and especially of the north, must be previously felt.

Lord Cornwallis, however, speedily made up his mind in favour of the 'great measure;' and he wished that the Union should be accompanied by other measures for the relief of the Catholics—by their admission to public offices and Parliament—probably also by a public provision for their clergy, and by a settlement of tithes. The latter views he recommended to his principal advisers in

Dublin, but without success. Lord Clare, the Irish Chancellor, and the able and vigorous leader of the Irish House of Lords, though favourable to the Union, rejected its proposed accompaniments; and in a visit to London in October 1798, he impressed these opinions upon Mr. Pitt, who gave his assent to them.[1] About the time of Lord Clare's interview, Mr. W. Elliot, the Irish Under-Secretary, went to London, and carried to Mr. Pitt a letter to him from Lord Cornwallis, urging the combination of Catholic emancipation with the measure of Union (October 17). Mr. Elliot strongly disapproved of the plan of Union upon the 'narrow basis;' and even doubted whether he could continue in the Government if it was proposed without emancipation. He enforced this view upon the English Ministers; but the convictions of Mr. Pitt, who had previously entertained the same opinion, had been shaken by Lord Clare's representations as to the danger of offending the leading Protestants in Ireland.[2] Lord Cornwallis was supported by Mr. Dundas; and he even 1798.

[1] See *Cornwallis Correspondence*, vol. ii. pp. 415–6, and the letter of Lord Clare to Lord Castlereagh, from London, dated Oct. 16, 1798, reporting his interview with Pitt (*Castlereagh Correspondence*, vol. i. p. 393). It begins thus: 'I have seen Mr. Pitt, the Chancellor (Lord Loughborough), and the Duke of Portland, who seem to feel very sensibly 'the critical situation of our damnable country, and that the Union alone can save it.' It does not appear whether Lord Castlereagh supported Lord Cornwallis's views on this occasion. It may rather be presumed that, looking to his difficulties in the Irish House of Commons, he acquiesced in those of the Chancellor.

[2] See Mr. Elliot's letters to Lord Castlereagh of Oct. 24, Nov. 23, 28, 1798, *Castlereagh Correspondence*, vol. i. p. 403, vol. ii. pp. 9, 29. In the latter letter he says, 'I cannot be easily persuaded that, if more firmness had been displayed here at first, a Union might not have been accomplished, including the admission of the Catholic claims; but Mr. Pitt has, with a lamentable facility, yielded this point to prejudice, without, I suspect, acquiring a support in any degree equivalent to the sacrifice.' Lord Camden, writing to Lord Castlereagh, on Oct. 27, 1798, says, 'Mr. Pitt is inclined most strongly to the Union on a Protestant basis. We have made little progress in our deliberations' (*ibid.* vol. i. p. 412).

1798. thought that, if the latter Minister had been in London before Lord Clare went over, 'he might have been able to carry the point of establishing the Union on a broad and comprehensive line.'[1] In the middle of November, Lord Cornwallis, in answer to his application for instructions, received from the Duke of Portland the heads of a treaty of Union settled by the English Cabinet, which he was authorised to communicate to the friends of the Government in Ireland. The fourth head of this scheme was as follows: 'All members of the United Houses to take the oaths now taken by British members: but such oaths to be subject to such alterations as may be enacted by the United Parliament.' It seems therefore that the English Cabinet at this time contemplated Catholic emancipation as a sequel to the Union, to be subsequently enacted by the Imperial Parliament, and not by the immediate concurrence of the British and Irish Parliaments.[2] Mr. Pitt, writing shortly afterwards to Lord Cornwallis, refers him to this article, and adds:—

I own I think this leaves the Catholic question on the only footing on which it can be safely placed. Mr. Elliot, when he brought me your letter, stated very strongly all the arguments which he thought might induce us to admit the Catholics to Parliament and office; but I confess he did not satisfy me of the practicability of such a measure at this time, or of the propriety of attempting it. With respect to a provision for the Catholic clergy and some arrangement respecting tithes, I am happy to find a uniform opinion in favour of the proposal among all the Irish I have seen; and I am more and more convinced that those

[1] Mr. Elliot to Lord Castlereagh, Nov. 9, 1798, *Castlereagh Correspondence*, vol. i. p. 431; Lord Cornwallis to General Ross, Nov. 15, 1798; *Cornwallis Correspondence*, vol. ii. p. 433.

[2] The ninth head specified that 'the Lord-lieutenant was to remain, but was not to be mentioned in the Act.' This shows that the authors of the Union did not contemplate the retention of the Lord-lieutenancy as a permanent institution.

measures, with some effectual mode to enforce the residence of all ranks of the Protestant clergy, offer the best chance of gradually putting an end to the evils most felt in Ireland.[1] 1798.

Lord Grenville's opinion upon this question concurred with Mr. Pitt's. In a letter to his brother, the Marquis of Buckingham, of November 5, 1798, he says, in reference to Lord Clare's recent conversations with the Ministers in London:—

I am assured that he talks not only decisively of the necessity, but also very sanguinely of the success, of our measure; provided always that no attempt is made to change, as a part of the Union, the existing laws about the Catholics. And in this last point I am very much disposed to agree with him now, though before the rebellion I should have thought differently (*Court and Cabinets*, vol. ii. p. 411).

It cannot be doubted that the exasperation against the Irish Catholics which had been created by the rebellion, must have rendered it nearly impossible to carry at this moment, in the Irish Parliament, any measure for investing them with political power, and for giving them a large, if not a preponderating share, in the Government of Ireland, as a kingdom under a separate and independent legislature.

Lord Cornwallis proceeded to act upon the instructions respecting a Union transmitted to him by the Duke of Portland; though he entertained great apprehensions as to the efficacy of the measure in its limited form, and thought that it would not have been much more difficult to have included the Catholics.[2] The intention of the Government was communicated to various persons, and

[1] [This letter was written after a conversation with John Foster the Irish speaker, one of the violent opponents of the Union. Lord Stanhope's *Life of Pitt*, vol. iii. p. 160.—Ed.]

[2] Letter to General Ross of Nov. 23, 1798.

1799. speedily became known to the public: an official pamphlet, by Mr. Cooke, the Irish Under-Secretary of State, entitled 'Arguments for and against the Union considered,' was widely circulated, and discussion of the question was encouraged. A violent agitation against the projected Union instantly broke out in Dublin, the head-quarters of the classes interested in the continuance of the existing order of things; and was at its height in the months of December 1798 and January 1799. The bar, in particular, whom a Union would render incapable of combining a seat in Parliament with professional practice, were vehement and united in their opposition.[1]

There certainly is (Lord Cornwallis writes to the Duke of Portland, on the 11th of January) a very strong disinclination to the measure in many of the borough proprietors, and a not less marked repugnance in many of the official people, particularly in those who have been longest in the habits of the current system. The secondary interests of course look to it as the destruction of their authority, and the leading interests as exposing them to fresh contests.

The Catholics, on the other hand, held back, and, at first, took no part in the anti-Union agitation. The English Cabinet, conscious of the difficulties which obstructed the success of the measure in Ireland, authorised Lord Cornwallis to announce their intention of persisting in it until it should be carried, and of not being deterred by defeat from prosecuting it to a successful termination. In this state of things, the project of Union was simultaneously recommended by the Crown, on January 22, 1799,

[1] The letter of Mr. Cooke to Lord Castlereagh, in the *Castlereagh Correspondence*, vol. i. p. 343, dated 'Dublin, Sept. 10, 1798,' giving an account of the bar meeting, is misplaced and misdated. The meeting of the bar took place on Sunday, December 9. See *Cornwallis Correspondence*, vol. iii. p. 18.

to both Parliaments: to the Irish Parliament by the speech of the Lord-lieutenant, to the British Parliament by a Royal message. The ground stated was 'the unremitting industry with which our enemies persevere in their avowed design of separating Ireland from Great Britain.' 1799.

The question being thus launched, an expression of opinion, as was natural, first proceeded from the Irish Parliament. In the debate upon the address, in the Irish House of Lords, the paragraph in favour of a Union was carried by a large majority. But in the House of Commons, Mr. George Ponsonby moved an amendment to the address, condemning the project of Union, which, after a violent debate, was negatived by 106 to 105 votes, being a majority of only one for the Government. Upon a second division, there appeared for the address 107, against it 105. After the announcement of these numbers, Lord Castlereagh stated that, although the Government were unalterably fixed in their intention with respect to a Union, he should not persist in the measure for the present. This failure in the Irish Parliament did not prevent Mr. Pitt from pursuing his course in the English Parliament. He proceeded without delay to propose eight articles of Union, in the shape of resolutions, to the House of Commons; and a similar course was followed by Lord Grenville in the House of Lords. They were agreed to by large majorities; and were presented to the King as the joint address of both Houses.

The Government was checked, but not disheartened, by the result of the division in the Irish House of Commons.[1] They now saw exactly the place and the extent of their

[1] The important despatch of Lord Cornwallis to the Duke of Portland, Jan. 28, 1799, reviewing the position of affairs after the vote of the Irish House of Commons (*Cornwallis Correspondence*, vol. iii. p. 58), is erroneously printed as the despatch of Lord Castlereagh in the *Castlereagh Correspondence*, vol. ii. p. 139.

1799. difficulty, and they set about devising the means necessary for overcoming it.

The proposal of Union (says Lord Cornwallis, in a letter to the Duke of Portland, written a few days after the division in the Irish House of Commons) provoked the enmity principally of the boroughmongers, lawyers, and persons who from local circumstances thought they should be losers, but it certainly has not affected the nation at large, nor was it disagreeable either to the Catholics or to the Protestant Dissenters.

The country at large did not take up the question on patriotic grounds; but there was a compact interested opposition, chiefly connected with the House of Commons, which was able to defeat the measure.[1] An arbitrary government or a military despot would have resorted to a *coup d'état*, and would have used force for removing this impediment. Lord Castlereagh had recourse to a gentler, surer, more efficacious, but less rapid method. The plan which he proposed was to buy up the Irish Parliament, and to buy it up in due form of law. Lord Cornwallis, deeply impressed with the advantages of a Union, earnestly bent upon its accomplishment, and seeing no other means of success, assented to the proposal; but embarked most reluctantly in a policy which rendered it necessary that he should be the principal negotiator in a series of bargains for the purpose of purchasing votes and neutralising parliamentary opposition. He made up his

[1] The following description of the state of opinion respecting the Union is given by Mr. Cooke, in a letter of April 12, 1799 (*Cornwallis Correspondence*, vol. iii. p. 86): 'The public mind is, I think, much suspended on the subject. There is little passion, except among the bar and the few interested leaders in the Commons. The Protestants think, however, it will diminish their power, however it may secure their property. The Catholics think it will put an end to their ambitious hopes, however it may give them ease and equality. The rebels foresee it in their annihilation.' See likewise pp. 93, 110–11, 121, 138.

mind to enter upon a course of corruption in the interest of purity; but his disgust at this portion of his duties is expressed with great animation in his letters to General Ross, of May 20 and June 8, 1799, at which time the negotiations were in full progress. The Irish Government did not attempt to press the question of Union, or to bring forward any definite plan, in the session of 1799: while, on the other hand, they were strong enough to prevent the House of Commons from pledging themselves against its adoption. They occupied the remainder of the year in preparing their measures for the following session, and in weakening the opposite army before the day of battle should arrive. The measures which they employed for this purpose were of three kinds, and may be classed under the heads of—1. Compensatory and remuneratory; 2. Penal; and 3. Conciliatory.[1] 1799.

In the month of February, Lord Castlereagh transmitted to the English Cabinet a memorandum in which all the personal interests hostile to the Union were enumerated and classified, and a detailed plan was suggested for granting a pecuniary indemnity to the persons interested in the boroughs to be suppressed.[2] He assesses the pecuniary loss inflicted on each of the different classes affected by the measure, in as business-like a manner as a surveyor would value property to be taken under the compulsory clauses of a railway act. This plan became known in Ireland, and contributed powerfully to mitigate the opposition. Various changes of office were also made in favour of supporters of the Union; peerages and pensions likewise were promised to several persons as rewards for their defection from the anti-Unionist cause, and their transition to the opposite camp. This process is

[1] [Compare Lord Stanhope's *Life of Pitt*, vol. iii. p. 180.—Ed.]

[2] See *Castlereagh Correspondence*, vol. ii. pp. 144, 149.

1799. described by Lord Castlereagh as 'the buying out and securing for ever the fee-simple of Irish corruption, which had so long enfeebled the powers of Government and endangered the connexion.'[1] On the other hand, patrons of boroughs who persisted in their opposition, or their nominees, were deprived of their appointments; and the offices thus vacated were conferred upon Unionists.[2] Measures of a more ordinary character for conciliating parliamentary support were employed towards the Catholics. As soon as the vote of the Irish House of Commons had shown that there was not then a majority in favour of the Union, Lord Cornwallis renewed his instances to the English Government to make Catholic emancipation a part of the measure. He stated that the anti-Unionists were bidding for the support of the Catholics, and that it was desirable to give the latter such assurances as would prevent this junction from taking place.[3] The answers sent from England were, that emancipation by an Act of the Irish Parliament could not be conceded, and that it would only be possible in a United Parliament. Lord Cornwallis was satisfied with the explanations on this subject which he received at this time from the Duke of Portland.[4] But in the months of September and October, Lord Castlereagh made a visit to London, and during his stay came to an understanding with the Cabinet on the question. He represented to Mr. Pitt the difficulty of carrying the Union, if, in the existing temper of the Protestants, the measure was opposed by the united strength of the Catholics; he stated the unwillingness of Lord Cornwallis to mislead the Catholics

[1] To Mr. Cooke, June 21, 1800. *Castlereagh Correspondence*, vol. iii. p. 333.

[2] See the letter of Lord Cornwallis to the Duke of Portland, May 24, and the list of changes in the letter of June 26, 1799.

[3] Letters to the Duke of Portland, January 26, 30, 1799.

[4] *Cornwallis Correspondence*, vol. iii. p. 64.

by promises which he might be unable to fulfil, and he requested the distinct announcement of the views of the Cabinet on the subject, for the guidance of the Irish Government. We extract from Lord Castlereagh's narrative his own account of the answer made to him by the Cabinet:— 1800.

In consequence of this representation, the Cabinet took the measure into their consideration, and having been directed to attend the meeting, I was charged to convey to Lord Cornwallis the result, and his Excellency was referred by the Duke of Portland to me for a statement of the opinions of His Majesty's Ministers on this important subject. I accordingly communicated to Lord Cornwallis that the opinion of the Cabinet was favourable to the principle of the measure; that some doubts were entertained as to the possibility of admitting Catholics into some of the higher offices, and that Ministers apprehended considerable repugnance to the measure in many quarters, and particularly in the highest: but that, as far as the sentiments of the Cabinet were concerned, his Excellency need not hesitate in calling forth the Catholic support, in whatever degree he found it practicable to obtain it. . . . I certainly did not then hear any direct objection stated against the principle of the measure by any one of the Ministers then present. . . . So far from any serious hesitation being entertained in respect to the principle, it was even discussed whether an immediate declaration on the subject to the Catholics would not be advisable, and whether an assurance should not be distinctly given them, in the event of the Union being accomplished, of their objects being submitted, with the countenance of Government, to the United Parliament upon a peace.

The course taken by the Irish Government, in pursuance of this instruction, with respect to the Catholics, is thus described by Lord Castlereagh:—

In consequence of this communication, the Irish Government omitted no exertion to call forth the Catholics in favour of the Union. Their efforts were very generally successful, and the

1800. advantage derived from them was highly useful, particularly in depriving the Opposition of the means they otherwise would have had, in the southern and western counties, of making an impression on the county members.[1] His Excellency was enabled to accomplish his purpose without giving the Catholics any direct assurance of being gratified, and, throughout the contest, earnestly avoided being driven to such an expedient, as he considered a gratuitous concession after the measure as infinitely more consistent with the character of Government.[2]

The result was, that no express promise was made by the Irish Government to the Catholics that emancipation would be proposed in the Imperial Parliament as a sequel to the Union; but that both Lord Cornwallis and Lord Castlereagh believed, at the beginning of 1800, that the English Cabinet were unanimously in favour of emancipation, and that steps would be taken in pursuance of this policy, as soon as the Union should be carried.[3]

The various preparations for the Union campaign, on the part of the Irish Government, had now been completed; and the Irish Parliament commenced its session on the 15th of January 1800. The time had arrived when the Government would learn what success had attended their efforts to gain over a portion of their opponents

[1] The Catholics were at this time admitted to the electoral franchise, but the boroughs were all close and in the hands of the Protestants. Hence the allusion of Lord Castlereagh.

[2] Letter of Lord Castlereagh to Mr. Pitt, Jan. 1, 1801 (*Cornw. Corr.*, vol. iii. p. 326; *Castl. Corr.*, vol. iv. p. 8). This letter was written for the purpose of recalling to Mr. Pitt's mind the course taken with respect to the Catholics during the pendency of the Union measure, and of urging him to propose emancipation, according to the previous intention of the Cabinet, immediately after the Union.

[3] Lord Castlereagh to the Duke of Portland, Nov. 28, 1799; Lord Cornwallis to the Duke of Portland, Dec. 9, 1799 (*Cornw. Corr.*, vol. iii. pp. 146, 148). The policy of converting Irish tithes into a rent-charge is discussed in a letter of Lord Grenville to Lord Buckingham, of Sept. 15, 1800 (*Courts and Cabinets*, vol. iii. p. 14, where '*town* farmers' seems to be misprinted for '*lower* farmers').

to the measure of Union, and whether, consequently, this session of the Irish Parliament would be its last. The Lord-lieutenant's speech from the throne did not advert to the subject; but in the House of Commons a motion was made for adding to the address a resolution condemnatory of Union. This motion was negatived by 138 to 96 votes, giving to the Government a majority of 42; which number, as compared with the equal division of the previous session, was the measure of the change of opinion which had been effected by the arrangements made by them during the past year. Assuming that the Government commenced their operations with an equality of votes, this majority implied a transfer of 21 votes from one side to the other. A message from the Lord-lieutenant, recommending a Union, was shortly afterwards presented to both Houses; and Lord Castlereagh, after explaining the principle of the measure, proposed eight articles as its basis. On the 6th of February, the House of Commons divided on the question of taking the message into consideration; when the numbers were, 158 for the motion, and 115 against it. This, it seems, was the largest division ever known in the Irish House of Commons. In the corresponding division in the House of Lords, the numbers were 75 to 26. Before the end of March, the Union Resolutions passed the Commons, and were carried up to the Lords: this House speedily agreed to them, and they were presented to the Lord-lieutenant by an address of both Houses on the 28th of March. The address of the Irish Houses was communicated by the King to the British Parliament; and the Articles of Union having been agreed to by them, were remitted by the King to the Lord-lieutenant for communication to the Irish Parliament. Lord Castlereagh thereupon introduced a Bill of Union, which was agreed to by the Irish Parliament, and which,

1800.

1800. together with the English Bill, received the royal assent at the end of the respective sessions. On the 2nd of August 1800, the Irish Parliament was prorogued, never to sit again.

As a part of the measure for the completion of the Union, Lord Castlereagh proposed and carried a bill for compensating the patrons of the disfranchised boroughs. The sum allowed for each borough was 15,000*l.*, which was to be apportioned among the patrons, if there was more than one, according to their several shares in the interest. Commissioners were appointed under the Act, for making this appointment; and the total sum awarded by them was 1,260,000*l.* A list of the persons compensated, and of the amounts received by each, is published in this work (vol. iii. p. 321).[1] This sum, together with some official appointments, peerages, and pensions—all of which were as public as the Boroughs Compensation Act—constituted the real price paid by the Government for the parliamentary support which enabled them to carry the Union. It has been often supposed that some secret and unavowed means of corruption were used for overcoming the opposition to this measure; but the correspondence published in the ample collections of the Cornwallis and Castlereagh Papers refutes this supposition: there are several applications to the English Government for Secret Service Money; but the remittances made were insignificant in amount, and could only have been used for the payment of subordinate agents, who rendered literary or other assistance to the Government.[2] On the other hand, it may be mentioned, that at the opening of

[1] Concerning the Compensation Bill see Plowden's *Hist. Rev.*, vol. ii. p. 1067. [Lord Downshire received 52,000*l.*, Lord Ely, 45,000*l.* See Lord Stanhope's *Life of Pitt*, vol. iii. p. 227.—Ed.]

[2] See *Cornw. Corr.*, vol. iii. pp. 27–34, 156, 276, 308, 358.

the session of 1800, the anti-Union party offered 5,000*l.* in ready money for a vote in the Irish House of Commons.[1] There is no doubt that a majority in the Irish Parliament was obtained for the Union by purchase; by places, pensions, peerages, and compensation for suppressed seats; the transaction was a bargain, but it was a bargain in market overt. The means employed were not unobjectionable; but they were less objectionable than force, which was the only practicable alternative; and, such as they were, they all lie within the cognisance of history. 1800.

It should not be overlooked that the eighty-four Irish boroughs which were disfranchised by the Union were all nomination boroughs, and that their suppression increased the comparative weight of the popular voice in the Irish representation, by reducing the power of the great borough proprietors. Speaking of the projected Union, Lord Cornwallis says:—

> There cannot be a stronger argument for the measure than the overgrown parliamentary power of five or six of our pampered boroughmongers, who are become most formidable to Government by their long possession of the entire patronage of the Crown in their respective districts (*Letter to Mr. Dundas*, July 1, 1799).

Hence Lord Castlereagh, in his paper on Emancipation drawn for the Cabinet in 1801, designates the new arrangement of the Irish representation under the Act of Union, as 'a mild reform.'[2] The Act of Union was at the same time a reform act, and included a schedule A of portentous dimensions.

[1] Lord Cornwallis states this fact as being within his certain knowledge, in a letter of Feb. 8, 1800, to his brother the Bishop of Lichfield and Coventry. Lord Castlereagh likewise states it as a fact of which the Irish Government have 'undoubted proofs, though not such as they can disclose,' to the Duke of Portland, in a letter of Feb. 7 (vol. iii. pp. 182, 183).

[2] *Castl. Corr.*, vol. iv. p. 397.

1800. The following account of Lord Cornwallis's conduct with reference to the Union is given by Col. (afterwards Sir Thomas) Maitland, in a letter written from Dublin, in May 1800, to Mr. Huskisson :—

It has been most fortunate indeed for the interests of Great Britain that the Government of Ireland was put into the hands of a person whose moderation led him to draw a middle line between the extremes of party violence, whose good sense has induced him to discriminate and to see through all the views of the men with whom he had to deal, and whose firmness has not only kept in check all their absurdity, but for a time has completely put down all their hopes of following and succeeding in their own plans, which must either have ended in the extirpation of the inhabitants or the ruin of the country. If his plans be hereafter steadily followed, Ireland will be a jewel—if changed, a thorn—in the British Empire. It requires a person to be here only a day or two to be convinced of this; for though the Lord-lieutenant's measures may some of them not be popular in themselves, still, from the general opinion entertained of the perfect rectitude of his intentions, it is impossible any measure of his can be unpopular, because such has been the fairness of his conduct to every one, that all are convinced whatever he proposes is meant for the public good. The success of the Union is greatly to be attributed to his conduct, and not to management.

The skill and firmness which Lord Castlereagh exhibited as a parliamentary leader, contributed materially to the success of the measure. His Irish extraction rendered him familiar with the means of obtaining support, which he lost no time in indicating, and which he consistently employed, until a majority of members had been secured. The English Government likewise, having once announced their policy, pursued it with undeviating steadiness; and authorised the Irish Government to give every assurance which was calculated to confirm supporters and to discourage opponents.

Lord Cornwallis regarded the Union only as a preliminary measure: Ireland, he said, could not be saved without the Union; but there was no certainty that it would be saved by the Union. Much, in his opinion, remained to be done, in order to render Ireland a useful appendage to the British Empire. His main object was to bring about Catholic Emancipation, together with such other measures as should attach the Irish Catholics to the English connection, and should extinguish that spirit of disaffection which had recently led to such disastrous consequences.[1] In September 1800, Mr. Pitt brought the measures respecting the Catholics, which he contemplated as forming the sequel to the Union, under the consideration of the Cabinet. A paper by Lord Castlereagh, arguing that the Union, though it removed an impediment to a better system, would do little in itself, and recommending, as ulterior measures, the admission of Catholics to Parliament and to public offices, an arrangement of tithes, and a provision for the Catholic and Dissenting clergy, was circulated among the Ministers:[2] and Lord Castlereagh himself, who was in London in the autumn of 1800, pressed the question upon the Cabinet with a view to an immediate practical decision. Lord Loughborough, however, who had recently convinced himself of the King's repugnance to Catholic Emancipation, on the ground of his Coronation Oath, and who saw an opening for intrigue, began to

1800.

[1] See *Cornw. Corr.*, vol. iii. pp. 228, 237, 250, 294, 306, 313–14, 331.

[2] The paper is printed in *Castl. Corr.*, vol. iv. p. 392. The editor refers it to 1801; but there can be no doubt, from internal evidence, that it was drawn up in the summer or autumn of 1800, when the question was under the consideration of Mr. Pitt's Cabinet. With respect to Lord Cornwallis's instructions to Lord Castlereagh to press the question on the Cabinet at this time, see his memorandum to Mr. Pitt, written after the resignation of the latter, *Cornw. Corr.*, vol. iii. p. 344.

1801. raise objections; the King, moreover, was at Weymouth; and Lord Castlereagh was unable to obtain any final decision from the Cabinet.[1] At the beginning of 1801, Lord Castlereagh returned to London, in order to attend to his duties in the Imperial Parliament, and to press upon Mr. Pitt the measures which were to form the sequel of the Union. The anxiety of Lord Cornwallis and himself upon this point was now at its height: they had heard that difficulties were anticipated on the part of the King; and they earnestly hoped that no unforeseen impediment would prevent the fulfilment of the healing policy for which they had laboured so hard, and on which, without making any express promise, they had undoubtedly excited the expectations of the Catholics. Even so late as the middle of January, Lord Spencer entertained hopes that the King would give way:[2] but his conscientious scruples, fomented by artful advisers, were too strong for the influence of reason: and when Mr. Pitt made his definitive communication respecting his comprehensive plan of Catholic relief, the King was already engaged in a negotiation with Addington for the formation of a new Ministry. Why Mr. Pitt should have so long deferred an explanation with the King on this important subject, is not apparent; but it is certain that His Majesty had heard, through Lord Loughborough, the Archbishop of Canterbury, the Primate of Ireland, and probably other channels, of Mr. Pitt's intentions; and it

[1] See the account in his letter to Mr. Pitt of Jan. 1, 1801, cited above: the letter of the Duke of Portland to Lord Cornwallis of Sept. 25, 1800, alludes to these deliberations of the Cabinet. The opposition of Lord Loughborough is mentioned by Lord Cornwallis in a letter to Gen. Ross, Dec. 30, 1800. Lord Loughborough's account of the final decision of the Cabinet in Lord Campbell's *Lives of the Chancellors*, vol. vi. p. 324, agrees with that given by Lord Castlereagh.

[2] *Cornwallis Correspondence*, *ib.* p. 333.

is difficult to understand how he could, in writing to Mr. Dundas on February 7, have ventured to assert that 'he had learnt, to his greatest surprise, on Thursday, from Earl Spencer, that the question had been in agitation since Lord Castlereagh came over in August, but that he never had the smallest suspicion till within these very few weeks.'[1] It appears from the testimony of Lord Loughborough himself that he showed the King at Weymouth, in September, Mr. Pitt's letter requesting him to come up to a Cabinet for the consideration of the Catholic question; and that he sent to the King in an official box the papers on the subject of the Irish measures which had been circulated among the members of the Cabinet. It further appears from a note in the King's own hand that Lord Loughborough's answer to Lord Castlereagh's paper on the Catholic question was given by him to the King in December.[2] 1801.

Immediately upon his resignation, Mr. Pitt authorised Lord Castlereagh to inform Lord Cornwallis of his wish that

His Excellency, without bringing forward the King's name, should make the Catholics feel that an obstacle which the King's Ministers could not surmount precluded them from bringing forward the question whilst in office; that their attachment to the question was such that they felt it impossible to continue in Administration under the impossibility of proposing it with the necessary concurrence, and that they retired from the King's service considering this line of conduct as most likely to contribute to the ultimate success of the measure (*Letter of Feb.* 9, 1801, vol. iii. p. 335).

In consequence of this communication, and of a letter which he received from Mr. Dundas, Lord Cornwallis

[1] *Cornwallis Correspondence*, vol. iii. p. 333.

[2] Lord Campbell's *Lives of the Chancellors*, vol. vi. pp. 308, 323. For a fuller explanation of the transaction, see above, pp. 144–5.

1801. delivered to Lord Fingal and Dr. Troy two papers to be circulated by them among the principal Catholics in different parts of Ireland. These papers contained positive assurances that Mr. Pitt and his friends would do their utmost to promote the success of the Catholic cause; and even went so far as to say that the Ministers who had retired would not resume office without the prospect of carrying the Catholic question; a principle which, probably, even at that time exceeded their intentions, and on which they never attempted to act.[1]

Mr. Pitt was strong enough, with the assistance of Lord Cornwallis and Lord Castlereagh, to carry the Union, and to extinguish the Irish Parliament. But the success of the Union raised another question, which he was unable to settle; and at the moment of triumph, when the newly created Imperial Parliament was commencing its first session, his Ministry was brought down by the King's invincible objection founded on his Coronation Oath.

The important question (says Lord Cornwallis) which has overthrown the long Administration of Mr. Pitt, must now sleep; as any person who should attempt to bring it forward would be accused of wishing either to kill or distract the King (vol. iii. p. 349).

In a previous letter to his brother of Feb. 17, Lord Cornwallis speaks of 'an unexpected blast from St. James's having overset him;' and in another letter to Gen. Ross of Feb. 26, he alludes to 'the fatal blow being struck from the quarter most interested to avert it.'

[1] See these papers in *Cornwallis Correspondence*, *ibid.* p. 347, with the explanatory memorandum of Lord Cornwallis in p. 343. The statement as to the *pledge* was disavowed by Mr. Pitt at the time, *ibid.* pp. 346, 350. See likewise *Castlereagh Correspondence*, vol. iv. pp. 72, 76, and the correspondence respecting them in 1805 with Mr. Plowden, p. 372, and Plowden's *Historical Review*, vol. i. p. 944.

All doubt as to the true cause of Mr. Pitt's resignation in 1801, if any reasonable doubt previously existed—has been removed by the publication of the letters in the Cornwallis and Castlereagh collections. But his motives were distrusted and disbelieved at the time; his course was unintelligible to the public; they could not comprehend why he should resign on account of the Catholic question, but refuse to press it in opposition. 'Nothing is so difficult' (as Mr. Cooke wrote to Lord Castlereagh with reference to Pitt's course) 'as to play a refined game in politics. The person who plays it is never understood, and is soon deserted.[1] 1801.

The King's illness, produced by the agitation consequent on Mr. Pitt's resignation, retarded the ministerial arrangements; and Lord Cornwallis remained in Dublin till the end of May, when he was succeeded in his office by Lord Hardwicke. He then returned to England; and in July received the command of the eastern district, and took up his abode at Colchester. Preliminaries of peace with France were signed at London on the 1st of October, and Lord Cornwallis accepted from Mr. Addington's Government the post of ambassador for the negotiation of the definitive treaty.[2] He sailed from Dover in November, and went to Paris, where he was honourably received, and had an interview with the First Consul. The negotiation was conducted at Amiens with Joseph Buonaparte, and the definitive treaty was concluded in March 1802. We shall not attempt to follow the negotiations of this unpropitious and short-lived treaty: the account which Lord Cornwallis gives of Joseph Buonaparte is, that 'he is a very sensible, modest, gentlemanlike man, totally free from

[1] Letter of Feb. 22, 1801. *Castlereagh Correspondence*, vol. iv. p. 60. See also pp. 51, 61.

[2] [Lord Stanhope's *Life of Pitt*, vol. iii. p. 354.—Ed.]

1804. diplomatic chicanery, and fair and open in all his dealings.' A picture, containing full-length portraits of the plenipotentiaries and their suites, is preserved in the Hôtel-de-Ville at Amiens.

With respect to the movements of political leaders in the English Parliament during the Addington Administration, Lord Cornwallis expresses an opinion in August 1801, that Mr. Pitt, in supporting Addington at that time, was 'influenced by the purest and most public-spirited motives,' but that 'he had undertaken a very critical and difficult line of conduct, and one that would expose his character to much misrepresentation.' At the end of 1803, he thinks that Pitt was not justified in estranging himself from Addington, after the intimate friendship which had subsisted between them; and that the terms demanded by Pitt, in the negotiation with Addington on the previous March, were unreasonable. In February 1804, he condemns the coalition between Fox and the Grenvilles as unprincipled; he likewise thinks that the line of opposition to the Government which Pitt intends to take is 'very injudicious, and highly discreditable to himself. He knew the talents of the Ministers, or their want of them, as well when he recommended them to the public favour, as he does now; if they fail from weakness of head, he is bound in honour to them, to the King, and to the nation, to assist them, or at least to support them; if their failings proceed from the heart, and they have an intention to destroy the constitution of their country, as an honest man he ought to oppose them.'

At this time Lord Cornwallis wished for the chief command in Ireland, and complained that Lord Cathcart was preferred to him. His disappointment was destined to be of brief duration; for at the end of 1804, Lord Castlereagh, who was the President of the Board of Control, again offered him the post of Governor-general.[1] The ambitious and aggressive policy of Lord Wellesley had brought him into violent conflicts with the Directors, and was not approved by the Government; Lord Cornwallis, as the representative of a pacific Indian policy, was applied to in this emergency, and accepted the employment. Early in 1805 he sailed for India, at the age of sixty-six, and he arrived at Calcutta in July; but his bodily powers began shortly to fail, and he died on October 5, at Ghazipoor, on his way to the Upper Provinces. His memory was treated with unusual marks of respect. The Supreme Council ordered the army to wear mourning for three months; a mausoleum was erected to him by subscription at Ghazipoor, cenotaphs at Madras and Prince of Wales Island, and a statue at Bombay. The House of Commons, on the motion of Lord Castlereagh, voted a statue for him at St. Paul's, and the East India Company granted a sum of 40,000*l.* to his family. 1805.

Our illustrations of the successive stages of Lord Cornwallis's career have been so copious, that it is unnecessary for us to dwell on his character. His firmness, his integrity, his calmness and moderation, the rectitude of his judgment, his public spirit, and his superiority to petty jealousies and rivalries, commanded the confidence of his contemporaries, and enabled him, in the different spheres of administration to which he was called, to reconcile popularity with a consistent discharge of duty. His two great achievements were that in India he put down the corrupt system of the Company, and that in Ireland he put down the corrupt system of the native Parliament. If in the latter country his wise and beneficent

[1] [It seems that the Duke of Portland pressed the claims of his second son, Lord William Bentinck, at this time. See Lord Stanhope's *Life of Pitt*, vol. iv. p. 230.—Ed.]

intentions had not been frustrated by the unfortunate scruple of the King respecting his Coronation Oath, he would have been the instrument not only of carrying the Union, but also of removing the Catholic disabilities, and of connecting the Catholic clergy with the state; one of which measures was postponed for more than a quarter of a century, and the other has never been accomplished.

IV.

THE ADDINGTON, PITT, AND GRENVILLE ADMINISTRATIONS.[1]

THE publication of the last volume of the 'Memorials and Correspondence of Mr. Fox,' from the authentic materials edited by Lord John Russell, affords us an opportunity of reviewing our domestic history, in continuation of former articles, which we have devoted to this and other recent works on the events of the period between the American War and the Peace of 1815. 1801.

In a previous article,[2] we stated fully the evidence collected from different sources, which proves conclusively that the resignation of Mr. Pitt and his colleagues in the beginning of 1801 was caused by the refusal of the King to consent to the measures proposed by the Minister for the relief of the Irish Catholics consequent upon the Union; which event had taken effect on the 1st of January in that year. The policy which dictated this step was so much in advance of the general intelligence of the country, that the true explanation of the grounds of resignation has been generally received with incredulity by the popular historians of the period. During a visit which Sir J. Mackintosh paid to Mr. Dundas in the summer of the same year, the latter remarked that his experience in public affairs had taught him to place little faith in historians. 'For instance,' he said, 'the motives which I

[1] Review of *Memorials and Correspondence of Charles James Fox*. Edited by Lord John Russell. Vol. iv. London: 1857.

[2] See *Edinburgh Review*, vol. ciii. p. 305.

1801. and my colleagues have assigned for our resignation, drawn from the Popery question, no historian will believe; and, if any mentions it, he will treat it as a mere pretext to cover the real motive; and he will support his representation by very plausible arguments; yet nothing can be more true than that the reason we assigned was the real one.'[1] This anticipation has doubtless been, to a great extent, verified by the event; the documentary evidence published has, however, now manifested the truth, and shown that the distrust which Dundas, like Sir Robert Walpole, entertained for the accounts of historians, is, so far as it rests on this case, unfounded.[2]

It is, in our opinion, difficult to exaggerate the loss which the nation sustained in the frustration of Mr. Pitt's intended measure of Irish policy by the irrational resistance of the King. At that moment, it would, if proposed by the Government with the King's support, have probably obtained the consent of Parliament, and the country would have acquiesced in the danger almost without knowing what had been done. By its repression, the

[1] *Life of Sir James Mackintosh*, by his son, vol. i. p. 170.

[2] Mr. Canning's celebrated song of 'The Pilot that weathered the Storm' was written at this time. It is printed in the *Spirit of the Public Journals for* 1802, p. 246. It is remarkable that Mr. Canning here speaks of Pitt as if his ministerial career was run out, although his age was only forty-two, and he had voluntarily quitted office on account of a difference with the King.

> Unheeding, unthankful, we bask in the blaze,
>   While the beams of the sun in full majesty shine;
> When he sinks into twilight, with fondness we gaze,
>   And mark the mild lustre that gilds his decline.
> So Pitt, when the course of thy greatness is o'er,
>   Thy talents, thy virtues, we fondly recall:
> Now justly we prize thee, when lost we deplore;
>   Admired in thy zenith, but loved in thy fall.

This description seems rather to apply to an aged minister, dismissed from office by the mere act of the King.

civilisation of Ireland was retarded for a quarter of a century; and, after all, the settlement of the Irish Catholic Church, which Mr. Pitt designed to effect, has not been accomplished. We hold, therefore, that Mr. Pitt correctly estimated the importance of the question upon which he resigned office. But in order fully to justify the step which he took, when he found that he was betrayed by some of his colleagues, and that the consent of the King could not be obtained, two conditions were, it appears to us, necessary. First, that he should be prepared consistently to act upon the policy of bringing the greatest amount of Parliamentary pressure to bear upon the King, with a view of compelling him to readmit a Pittish Ministry to office without any restriction as to the Catholic Question.[1] Secondly, that, in the event of the King's resistance being forcibly overcome, he should be in a position which would enable him to use all the influence of Government for carrying this question, and to postpone all other considerations to its success. How far Mr. Pitt had formed a fixed resolution to attempt the fulfilment of these two conditions, his subsequent conduct speedily evinced. 1801.

Mr. Pitt's resignation, after an administration of more than seventeen years, was completed without any oral communications between himself and the King. It was

[1] Mr. Fox anticipated that this would be the effect of Mr. Pitt's resignation, without any ulterior pressure. In a letter to Lord Holland, of Feb. 8, 1801, he says:—'If the Speaker is employed, as is said, to make a new arrangement, it must be indeed a notorious juggle, and it seems to me not unlikely that it will proceed thus. The Speaker will converse with some men of consequence, possibly Grey, or others, and will report that he cannot find it practicable to make a Ministry upon the principle of rejecting the Catholic claims, &c., and then Pitt will be restored, *and the King will submit*' (*Mem. of Fox*, vol. iii. p. 188). See also the remarks in pp. 320, 325. Nothing, in truth, less resembled a juggle than this resignation. Pitt took the step reluctantly, and the King preferred Addington to Pitt too much to allow the latter a *locus pœnitentiæ*, even when he was willing to return.

1801. accepted by the King on the 5th of February, and the Addington Cabinet was provisionally formed. But before the outgoing Ministers had their audiences to deliver up their seals, the King, in consequence of the mental agitation produced by the Ministerial change, was, for the first time since 1788, seized with an attack of insanity. His malady manifested itself by evident symptoms on the 20th of February, and before the end of the month his life was in danger; but soon after the beginning of March, he began to recover, and by the 10th of the month his mental and bodily health was sufficiently restored to enable him to sign documents and to give audiences to some of his Ministers.[1] During this interval Mr. Pitt acted as Minister, and had interviews with the Prince of Wales and Mr. Addington for the purpose of discussing the question of a Regency.[2] It seems that the King, on recovering from his attack, ordered Dr. Willis to inform Mr. Pitt of his convalescence; adding the remark, 'What has he not to answer for, who is the cause of my being ill at all?' This remark was repeated to Pitt, and produced from him a contrite letter to the King, offering to abandon the Catholic question.[3] Already, he was not only willing,

[1] *Lord Malmesbury,* vol. iv. pp. 14–30. Pellew's *Life of Lord Sidmouth,* vol. i. p. 308. *Memorials of Fox,* vol. iii. pp. 328, 332. It was during this first attack that Mr. Addington is reported to have procured rest for the King by advising the use of a hop-pillow (*Life of Lord Sidmouth, ibid.* p. 309).

[2] [Mr. Pitt frankly stated his intention of proposing and pressing, if the necessity should arise, a measure of restricted Regency, as in 1789 (Lord Stanhope, *Life of Pitt,* vol. iii. p. 296).—Ed.]

[3] *Lord Malmesbury, ibid.* p. 31. We learn from Sir Samuel Romilly's *Diary,* that the physicians who were examined by a Parliamentary Committee in Dec. 1810, during the King's final illness, stated that his insanity in 1801 was caused by Mr. Pitt's resignation, and that this answer was expunged from their evidence before it was presented to the House (*Life of Sir S. Romilly,* vol. ii. p. 352). [Lord Stanhope (*Life of Pitt,* vol. iii. pp. 303, 304) gives good reasons for thinking that Pitt's assurance to the King was conveyed in a message through Dr. Willis, not by letter.—Ed.]

but desirous to recede from the ground which he had taken, and to remain, upon the terms dictated by the King, at the head of the administration. But he refused, in spite of the entreaties of friends, to make any forward motion in this direction; he wished that the offer should proceed from the King, and that Addington should spontaneously withdraw from his new position. Addington, on the other hand, secure of the royal favour, declined to make any concession, or afford any facility for Mr. Pitt's return, without the previous signification of the King's desire. He added, characteristically enough, that 'they (i. e. Mr. Pitt's friends) might open the matter to the King if they pleased, but he would not propose it; and he trusted they would think fit previously to consult the King's physicians as to the effect which such a proposition might have upon His Majesty in his present state of health.' Hereupon Mr. Pitt put an end to the negotiation, and declared himself prepared to support the newly-formed Government. The King probably knew what was in agitation, but no formal representation was made to him on the subject.[1] 1801.

Mr. Pitt's conduct, at this crisis, was as unintelligible to those of his contemporaries to whom it was known, as it is to us at present. Mr. Abbot, the confidential friend of Addington, who succeeded him in the speakership, and was in habits of constant intercourse with him, made this entry in his diary:—'It is still a mystery why Mr. Pitt and his colleagues retired upon a question which they

[1] See *Lord Malmesbury*, vol. iv. pp. 26–47; Pellew's *Life of Lord Sidmouth*, vol. i. pp. 334–341, 349. Lord Malmesbury was mistaken in supposing that the King wished Pitt to return, or that Addington was willing to give way. He himself records a conversation with Mr. Pelham on February 27th, who told him that the King had, for a long time, been dissatisfied with Pitt's, and particularly Lord Grenville's, 'authoritative manners' towards him, and that he had meditated placing Windham in Pitt's place in the previous August. Mr. Pelham was sure of the fact (*ibid.* p. 22).

1801. were not pledged upon to any one, which the Roman Catholics did not desire, and which they can now so readily forego.'[1] Lord Malmesbury, who lived in intimacy with Pitt's friends, is equally perplexed by his conduct. We can understand two adequate motives for Pitt's resignation: one a deep conviction of the importance of his plan, and a belief that, by resigning, he should promote its chances of success; the other, a point of honour, that having authorised Lord Cornwallis and Lord Castlereagh to obtain support for the Union from the Catholics, by the promise of ulterior measures of relief, he was bound, if prevented by the King from fulfilling this promise, to retire from power.[2] But neither of these reasons is consistent with his resigning his office in February, because the King refused his consent to the measure of Catholic relief, and his signifying his readiness to resume his office in March, although the King's consent is still withheld. After the events of 1788, it must be presumed that Mr. Pitt contemplated the possible effect of a political crisis in deranging the King's mind. We confess ourselves at a loss to justify, and scarcely even to explain, the course which he pursued.[3] Why, if he was so willing to remain

[1] *Life of Sidmouth, ibid.* p. 335. The evidence of Pitt's inconsistency is collected by the editor in a note, p. 336.

[2] Mr. Pitt stated in the House of Commons, February 16, 1801, in answer to Mr. Sheridan, that he and some of his colleagues desired to propose an important measure, as a sequel of the Union; that when circumstances prevented them from proposing it as a measure of Government, they felt it equally *inconsistent with their duty and their honour*, any longer to remain a part of that Government. 'I beg to have it understood (he added) to be a measure, which, if I had remained in Government, I must have proposed.'

[3] [Lord Stanhope, in his *Life of Pitt* (vol. iii. p. 310), refers to this and the former article in the following terms:—'I grieve to find myself at issue on this question with the eminent critic whom I just now cited. I allude to the author of two articles which appeared in the *Edinburgh Review*, of April 1856, and January 1858, and which treat of the period now before us. Many persons have thought that they here discerned the hand of Sir George

in March, he was so resolved on resigning in February; or why, if he was so resolved upon resigning in February, he was so willing to remain in March; we are equally unable to determine.[1] What made Mr. Pitt's conduct the less creditable at this conjuncture was, that he signified his readiness to remain, without consulting some of the most important of his former colleagues, and particularly Lord Grenville, by whom this fact was communicated to Mr. Fox. Pitt's concealment of his change of intentions is 1801.

Cornewall Lewis; and certainly both these essays, in their discriminating powers of inquiry, their large stores of information, and their calm and sustained judicial temper, appear well worthy of that distinguished man.'

His Lordship then disputes the opinion expressed in the text as to the course pursued by Pitt in the Catholic question. I differ so far from Sir George Lewis that I am prepared to admit Pitt's course to be intelligible, and the result of kindly and natural feelings; but I doubt extremely whether, in this country, it is any man's public duty to take office on condition of waiving, in deference to his Sovereign, a question which he himself deems to be one of paramount importance. Nor do I believe that such compliance is patriotism, or that such a principle will *in the long run* tend to promote the best interests of the people or the Constitution. The case before us was never stated better than it was in a few words of the late Sir James Graham's—'Mr. Pitt was prepared to do the right thing at the right moment: but genius gave way to madness; and two generations have in vain deplored the loss of an opportunity which never will return.'—Ed.]

[1] Mr. Canning, on October 20, 1802, having then recently returned from a visit to Pitt at Walmer Castle, gave Lord Malmesbury the following account of Mr. Pitt's reasons for resigning:—'He said that Mr. Pitt told him that he went out, not on the Catholic question simply as a measure in which he was opposed, but from the manner in which he had been opposed, and to which, if he had assented, he would, as a Minister, have been on a footing totally different from what he had ever before been in the Cabinet. This obliged him to resign; but, as his sincere wish was that his going out should neither distress the King nor the country, he had required no one to follow him. Those who did, did it voluntarily, and against his desire' (Lord Malmesbury's *Diaries, ibid.* p. 75). It will be observed that this account was given more than a year and a half after the event; and that it is inconsistent with Pitt's own letter to the King and his explanation in Parliament, which put his resignation exclusively upon general, and not on personal grounds. We confess that it seems to us to throw no additional light on Pitt's conduct.

1801. severely censured by the latter, in several of his recently published letters.[1]

After this singular Ministerial evolution, Addington and his colleagues were formally installed in their offices, and passed from a provisional into a definite tenure of power. But in the course of a week there was a fresh alarm, and the King continued in the hands of the Willises till the end of June, when his state was considered to be such as to justify their removal from his person.[2] However little fitted the King's mind, at this time, might be to undergo the agitation necessary for the discussion of difficult questions of policy, no doubt can exist as to his satisfaction with the compliant and commonplace Minister whom he had brought into power, and as to the relief which he felt at having disengaged himself from the haughty and dictatorial service of Mr. Pitt. 'The King (he now writes to his favourite) is highly gratified at the repeated marks of the sensibility of Mr. Addington's heart, which must greatly add to the comfort of having placed him, with so much propriety, at the head of the Treasury. He trusts their mutual affection can only cease with their lives. A few days afterwards he assures

[1] The statement is that Pitt concealed his intention from all his colleagues except Dundas (*Mem. of Fox*, vol. iii. p. 452; vol. iv. pp. 14, 20, 22). 'Lord Grenville confirmed to me the extraordinary fact of Pitt never having told him of his offer to continue without Catholic Emancipation, in the year 1801' (Letter of April 19, 1804, *ibid.* p. 45).

[2] Lord Malmesbury's *Diaries*, *ibid.* p. 49; Twiss's *Life of Lord Eldon*, vol. i. pp. 374–383; *Memorials of Fox*, vol. iii. pp. 337, 338, 342. In a letter to Lord Lauderdale, dated March 15, 1804, Fox says :—'That the Ministers will venture everything for their places, I always believed, and it now seems certain. Three years ago, after the King had recovered sufficiently to invest them in their offices, it is known, and now scarcely disavowed, that he had a severe relapse, and was for weeks at Kew, in such a state as neither to see Ministers or family; and yet these very men, from whose timidity so much is expected, ventured to conceal this relapse, and even to deny it, and went on just as if nothing had happened' (*Mem. of Fox*, vol. iv. p. 24).

Addington of his thorough satisfaction with the new administration.[1] The King likewise confers on his new Minister the endearing epithets of '*my* Chancellor of the Exchequer,' '*my own* Chancellor of the Exchequer;' thereby marking the contrast with his stately and comparatively unbending predecessor. 1801.

As soon as the Addington administration was established in office, a negotiation for a separate peace with France was commenced between Lord Hawkesbury, the new Secretary of State for Foreign Affairs,[2] and M. Otto, a French agent in London, who received his instructions from the First Consul. The negotiation begun in March and lasted through the autumn; on the first of October 1801, the preliminaries of a treaty of peace between Great Britain and France were signed in London; and on the 12th the ratifications of the preliminaries were exchanged. This event was received with an explosion of joy in England; the people were tired of the war, and wished to see it terminated by any reasonable settlement. When Colonel Lauriston, the bearer of the French ratification, set out with M. Otto for Downing Street, the people took the horses from the carriage, and dragged it to the Foreign Office.[3] At night all London was illuminated.

[1] *Life of Sidmouth*, *ibid.* pp. 408, 411.

[2] Lord Hawkesbury was the eldest son of the first Earl of Liverpool; he was at this time in the House of Commons, but was called up to the House of Lords during his father's lifetime, in 1803. He became First Lord of the Treasury, as Earl of Liverpool, upon the death of Mr. Percival. We should have thought it unnecessary to mention these well-known facts, if the editor of the Duke of Buckingham's Papers had not confounded him with his father (*Courts and Cabinets*, vol. iii. p. 144).

[3] Lord Malmesbury gives the following account of this triumphant procession:—'A Jacobin saddler, in Oxford Road, saw Lauriston pass in his way to Otto's, who lived in Hereford Street; he assembled the mob, persuaded them he was Bonaparte's brother, and Lauriston was drawn about by them in a hackney coach to all his visits' (vol. iv. p. 61). It is however certain, from

1801. 'Never, perhaps (says the 'Annual Register'), since the restoration of Charles II., was the general joy in England so high and extravagant. It was in proportion to the sufferings that had been so long endured from the war, and the miserable forebodings arising from its further continuance.' At the end of October Parliament was opened, and in the following month the preliminaries were debated in both Houses. In the House of Lords, Lord Grenville denounced the arrangement, as not securing one of the objects for which we had so long fought; he regarded the terms as disadvantageous to the country, and fraught with national degradation.[1] The address, however, was carried by 104 to 10 votes. In the House of Commons the address was opposed by Mr. Grenville, who, referring to Sheridan's dictum, that it was a peace at which every man rejoiced, and of which every man was ashamed, said that if Englishmen could rejoice at a bad peace, at a peace of which they could not be proud, the national character was totally lost. Mr. Pitt gave a qualified, but, nevertheless, a decided approbation of the peace. He preferred accepting terms even short of what he thought the country entitled to obtain, to risking the result of the negotiation by too obstinate an adherence to any particular point. Although everything had not been obtained by the preliminaries, yet it did not appear to him that the difference between those terms and what the country had a right to, was to be compared with the evils which might have resulted by being too peremptory

all the contemporary accounts, that the popular enthusiasm was great and universal.

[1] Lord Grenville wrote to Addington on October 14, 1801, to announce his intention of opposing the preliminaries, which had been communicated to him by Lord Hawkesbury. Addington sent his letter to Pitt (*Life of Lord Sidmouth*, vol. i. pp. 459–60). [Compare Lord Stanhope's *Life of Pitt*, vol. iii. p. 355.—ED.]

in our demands. He concluded by giving his sincere support to the motion, in which he was joined by Mr. Fox, who declared that, since he had been a member of the House, he never had assented with greater satisfaction to any measure, than he now did to the preliminaries of peace. The preliminaries were condemned by Mr. Windham and Dr. Lawrence, but defended by Mr. Wilberforce, and the address was then agreed to without a division.[1] 1802.

A month after the signature of the preliminaries, the Marquis of Cornwallis left England as ambassador, to negotiate the definitive treaty. Having visited Paris, where the First Consul gave him an honourable reception, he repaired to Amiens, the appointed seat of the negotiation. The progress of the treaty did not arrest Bonaparte in the course of foreign aggrandisement which he was pursuing; but the definitive peace was signed on the 27th of March 1802.[2] In the month of May motions of censure upon the treaty were made in the two Houses of Parliament by Lord Grenville and Mr. Windham; in the House of Lords, the numbers upon the division were 122 to 16 in favour of the Government; in the House of Commons they were 276 to 20. On this occasion Mr. Pitt was absent, but the policy of Ministers was supported by Mr. Sheridan. The feeling of Parliament and the country was still decidedly in favour of the peace; and the *new Opposition*—as they were called—the friends of Lord Grenville

[1] [There was a division in the Lords—114 to 10. Windham spoke on the report in the Commons, but no division took place (Lord Stanhope's *Life of Pitt*, vol. iii. p. 360).—Ed.]

[2] An offer of a Cabinet office was made by Addington to Mr. Grey, about January 1802, and was declined on the ground that the Ministry could not accede to any measure of Parliamentary Reform. This fact appears in the *Fox Correspondence*, vol. iii. pp. 351, 357. There is no trace of it in the *Life of Lord Sidmouth*. The pacific policy of the Foxite party doubtless led to this offer. [Erskine pressed himself on Addington. Lord Stanhope's *Life of Pitt*, vol iii. p. 367.—Ed.]

1802. and Windham, met with little or no popular support in their disapprobation of the pacific policy of the Addington administration.[1]

Much delay took place in renewing the regular diplomatic intercourse between the two countries. Although

[1] Lord Malmesbury seems to have agreed rather with Lord Grenville than with Mr. Pitt in his estimate of the peace. On October 1, 1801, he designates the 'exultation and joy at an event of which the issue at best must be doubtful,' as 'childish' (*Diaries*, vol. iv. p. 60). On March 26, 1802 (the day before the signing of the definitive treaty), he met the Duke of York in the streets, who asked him for news. 'Peace, sir, in a week, and war in a month,' was the answer. This saying was repeated to the King, who, at the next drawingroom, told Lord Malmesbury that he took the same view of the treaty (*ibid.* p. 69). Mr. Fox's views with respect to the peace of Amiens and its advantage to this country, appear in the following passages:—'However it may have happened, it is an excellent thing, and I do not like it any the worse for its being so very triumphant a peace for France, who, except Ancona, does not give up any part of her conquests. *Indemnity for the past and security for the future* [Mr. Pitt's phrase] are now evidently construed into Ceylon and Trinidad. I do not know why you should consider it, however, a mere truce; I hope better. The sense of humiliation in the Government here will be certainly lost in the extreme popularity of the measure. I expect there never was joy more universal and unfeigned, and this rascally people are quite overjoyed at receiving from Ministers what, if they had dared to ask it, could not have been refused them at almost any period of the war' (To Mr. Maitland, 1801, vol. iii. p. 345). 'In regard to the public opinion upon the subject, my belief is that there never was more genuine and general joy upon any public event. I know that in London, and I heard too in Liverpool, there are some who abuse it; but in general it is far otherwise. Even those who are most dissatisfied only say that every gentleman is against it, and every blackguard for it' (To Mr. Grey, October 12, 1801, *ibid.* p. 347). 'I fear that whatever happens, I cannot with propriety be absent from the House of Commons on the day when the peace makes the regular subject; and so I shall have two days instead of one, which is in itself bad enough, besides the increased chance of saying indiscreet things, which I feel to be very great; for the truth is, I am gone something further in hate to the English Government than perhaps you and the rest of my friends are, and certainly further than can with prudence be avowed. The triumph of the French Government over the English does in fact afford me a degree of pleasure which it is very difficult to disguise' (To Mr. Grey, October 22, 1801, *ibid.* p. 349). It is impossible not to regret that Mr. Fox's long exclusion from office should have so far soured his mind as to lead him to indulge the feelings which are expressed in some of these passages.

the Definitive Treaty was signed in March, Gen. Andréossy, the French ambassador, did not arrive in England till the 6th of November, nor did Lord Whitworth, appointed to the embassy at Paris, sail for France till the 10th of the same month. Addington, however, had lost no time in putting the establishments of the country upon a footing of peace. For the next year's army and navy estimates showed a reduction of more than 10,000,000*l.* compared with the expenditure of the last year of war. The income-tax, which Addington, in common with all the statesmen of that period, regarded exclusively as a war-tax, was repealed; the total annual saving of expenditure was estimated by him at 25,000,000*l.*; but a loan of 10,000,000*l.* was announced on the part of the year's finance.[1] 1802.

In judging the Peace of Amiens with the light afforded by a knowledge of subsequent events, it is difficult to put ourselves in the contemporary position from which alone a fair estimate of its policy can be formed. But we confess that we agree with those who considered its terms more advantageous to the country than a continuance of the war. If the treaty had led to a permanent pacification between France and England, the acceptance of its terms by the British Government, notwithstanding M. Thiers' opinion of the advantages which it secured to France,[2] would have been, in our judgment, fully justifiable. The true question however is, whether any lasting peace with France, whatever might be its conditions, was possible so long as Bonaparte was the chief ruler.

[1] *Life of Lord Sidmouth*, vol. ii. p. 100, from a statement prepared by Lord Bexley.

[2] 'Telles étaient les conséquences de cette paix si belle, la plus glorieuse que la France ait jamais conclue. . . . Jamais négociateur n'avait eu le bonheur d'assurer par sa signature tant de grandeurs à sa patrie' (*Hist. du Consulat et de l'Empire*, liv. xi.).

1802. Addington seems to have believed in the moderation of Bonaparte, and in the sincerity of his desire for peace. How far such a belief was at that time reasonable, is uncertain; but that it was utterly false, and that no treaty which could then have been made between the two countries would have restrained the ambition of the First Consul, or have prevented him from rendering the renewal of the war uncertain, few will now be inclined to doubt.

It may, however, be interesting to compare the confidential opinions which the statesmen who represented the extreme warlike and pacific parties respectively, expressed on the subject about this time. Lord Grenville, writing to his brother in May 1801, before the signature of the preliminaries, thus states his views of Bonaparte's policy:—

I certainly agree with you in thinking that Bonaparte has not the most remote idea of peace, but looks to the continuance of the war as his only salvation. Indeed, unless he can find a pretence to plunder Portugal, and perhaps Spain too, the machine of his Government cannot go on, now that requisitions in Germany and Italy are at an end. I could bring a thousand little circumstances which the long habit of watching that nest of robbers and assassins, called the French Government, teaches me to look to as decisive proof that their intentions, at this moment, are entirely warlike.[1]

Again, in another letter to his brother, of Oct. 26, 1803, written about six months after the rupture of the peace, he says:—

I have received intimation, from which I collect that there is some disposition to hazard in both Houses, from our side of the way, certain recommendations in favour of negotiations for peace; and I cannot reconcile to myself to leave my utter disapprobation of all such language to be guessed at merely from my absence.

[1] To the Marquis of Buckingham, May 26, 1801, *Courts and Cabinets*, vol. iii. p. 160.

Peace I desire most fervently: no person in the country, I am sure, desires it more than I do; and few have had such opportunities of knowing how necessary it is to us. But then I am confident that there is no hope of peace for Europe, or for England, but by raising up some sufficient barrier against Bonaparte's ambition, which aims at universal empire, not in the figurative, but in the most literal acceptation of those terms. This great work, I have long been convinced, could not be accomplished but by the union of the three great continental Powers. That the insolence of France would ultimately produce this union, I firmly believed; and until it took place I was always averse to wasting the resources of this country in separate and therefore ineffectual exertions. But now that this union is formed, and that these Powers seem really convinced that they are fighting their own cause, not ours alone, it would, I think, be no less impolitic than disgraceful for this country to be the first to hold such language, or to take such steps as may lead to the separation of the alliance. 1802.

I am not so sanguine as many are in my hopes of success, because I well know how much there is to do; but God forbid that I should persuade this country to desert the cause of Europe so long as there is any chance—and such there certainly now is—that Europe will fight for its own independence.[1]

On the other hand, Mr. Fox, in November 1802, about nine months after the signature of the Definitive Treaty, expresses an opinion that Bonaparte 'will do everything that he can to avoid war;'[2] and in the following month he says, 'I am obstinate in my opinion that Bonaparte's wish is for peace—nay, that he is afraid of war to the last degree.'[3] His views on Bonaparte's position and policy are further developed in a letter written at the same time.

My notion about Bonaparte's politics is this—that when I first went to Paris he was foolishly sore about our newspapers, but

[1] *Courts and Cabinets,* vol. iii. p. 331.

[2] To Lord Lauderdale, Nov. 12, 1802. *Mem. of Fox,* vol. iii. p. 372.

[3] To Mr. Grey, Dec. 12, 1802, *ibid.* p. 384.

1820. not ill disposed to the Ministers, and still less to the country. At this time he was out of humour with Austria, and determined, as I suspect, not to give way a little to her. Afterwards, when he suspected (whether truly or falsely) that we should interfere, he began to be terribly afraid of a war, which might in France be imputed to his rashness. In consequence of this fear, he did make concessions by no means inconsiderable to Austria, and immediately felt bitter against us who were the cause of his making them. But as that bitterness (according to my hypothesis) arises principally from the fear he has of our driving him into an unpopular war, I do not think it will for the present prevent peace; nor indeed, if pacific counsels and language are used here, that it is at all likely [not?] to be lasting. . . . . Whatever ridicule may be attempted to be thrown upon the title of pacificator, you may be sure that whatever hold he has (perhaps no great matter neither) upon the people of France, arises from the opinion that he alone could make the peace, and that he will be the best able to maintain it.[1]

Mr. Horner has the following entry in his journal, under the date of January 1806:—

Mr. Fox was of opinion, before the commencement of the present war, that the real intentions and wishes of Bonaparte, however hostile he was to this country, were to make his subjects a commercial people; to keep his own power, of course, as absolute as possible; but to reduce the military spirit and system to which he originally owed it.[2]

During the session of 1802, Mr. Pitt absented himself from Parliament.[3] Though, on the whole, he approved of

[1] To Mr. Grey, Dec. 1802, *ibid.* pp. 381–2. Mr. Fox went to France in July 1802, and came back to England in November. He returns to his idea of Bonaparte's pacific disposition in Sept. 1805: 'I feel quite sure that Bonaparte would like peace if we would give way in anything' (*ibid.* vol. iv. p. 116).

[2] *Life of Horner*, vol. i. p. 323.

[3] Mr. Fox, in a letter of Dec. 19, 1802, says, that although Pitt is supposed to be friendly to peace, the war-party are constantly calling for his return to power; and 'therefore he will find himself obliged, after Christmas, to say

the peace, he was dissatisfied with the general course of the administration; and he reconciled his two feelings by maintaining a neutral station; he discontinued his active support to the Government, but did not commence a declared opposition to its measures. The ambiguous state of his mind was known to his friends: and accordingly, near the end of the year (November 1802), an attempt was made by some of the more eager of his followers to force or induce Addington to resign, in order that Pitt might succeed to his place. A paper was drawn up by Mr. Canning, for presentation to Mr. Addington, the object of which was to bring about this substitution by voluntary means. Both Mr. Pitt and Lord Grenville were now prepared to abstain from pressing the Catholic question upon the King, and to accept office without making this measure an indispensable condition. Pitt himself thought the change desirable; but would not consent to any active steps being taken by his friends, or any canvass being made: he deprecated anything which could bear the appearance of a plot or cabal; maintained that if he stood aloof, an alteration in his opinions would be inferred, and if there was a general wish to restore him to office, it would soon be manifested. The result of this discouragement was that Mr. Canning's paper was suppressed,[1] and that no active movement for Pitt's restoration to power had been made when the session for the ensuing year commenced in November 1802. Pitt absolutely rejected any attempt to force him upon the King through a parlia- 1802.

something pretty decisive, or to make his retirement (for a time at least) a complete secession' (*Mem. of Fox*, vol. iii. p. 206).

[1] See Lord Malmesbury's *Diaries*, vol. iv. pp. 80–127. [On this attempt of Canning's compare Lord Stanhope's *Life of Pitt*, v. iii. pp. 408–410. Pitt, however, declined to give advice to the Government. Lord Grenville, in his speech on the address, pointed to Pitt as the only minister fit for the crisis (*ibid.* pp. 411–412).—Ed.]

1802. mentary motion; and in this view Mr. Canning himself concurred.[1]

The Opposition at this time consisted of two sections, the old and the new. The old Opposition, composed of Mr. Fox and his few remaining followers, had strongly supported the peace; the new Opposition, formed of the Grenville party, had as strongly condemned it. The restlessness of Bonaparte, and the improbability of maintaining pacific relations with France, began now to manifest themselves; and public opinion gradually inclined towards the new Opposition, who had from the commencement censured the treaty, and predicted its failure. For the same reason, the general feeling pointed to Mr. Pitt's resumption of office. The chief title of the Addington administration to confidence and support was the peace: if the peace should prove a failure, their principal hold on the good wishes of the public was gone: and if vigour and ability for the prosecution of war were needed, the superiority of Pitt seemed undeniable. These considerations did not fail to present themselves, in some form or

[1] Lord Malmesbury, *ibid.* pp. 117, 145. There is in Mr. Fox's *Correspondence* a letter to Mr. Adair, dated simply 1802, in which allusion is made to some offer to Pitt with the King's consent; the report resting on the authority of the Prince of Wales, but having been heard by Fox from other quarters (*Mem. of Fox*, vol. iii. p. 383). There is no trace of any such offer in Lord Malmesbury's *Diaries*, although he was in intimate and frequent communication with Mr. Canning and Mr. Pitt himself at this time. It is highly improbable that any proposal should have been made by Addington to Pitt to join his Government, either with or without the King's consent, in the course of 1802. In a letter to Mr. Grey of Dec. 12, 1802, Mr. Fox says: 'The King is supposed to be full as unwilling to restore Pitt as ever; and indeed, from his nature, I am sure it must be so' (*ibid.* p. 386). [In February 1802, after an attack by Tierney on the late administration, Pitt addressed an indignant letter to Addington, as if he thought that the ministry had failed to repel the censure cast on himself. This letter and Addington's answer will be found in Lord Stanhope's *Life of Pitt*, vol. iii. pp. 369–370. After this (June 26, 1802) he corrected the draft of the King's speech (*ibid.* p. 382). Ed.]

other, to the mind of Mr. Addington; and they soon produced a negotiation for strengthening the Ministry by the incorporation of his predecessor. 1802.

Mr. Pitt, in his way from Bath to London in December, 1802, visited Lord Malmesbury at Park Place, and Lord Grenville at Dropmore. At the former house, in answer to the remonstrances of Lord Malmesbury with respect to his inaction, he declared himself in favour of a pacific policy; he thought that the great question then under deliberation was, *how to bear and to forbear*: if peace could be preserved for four or five years, our revenues would be so far improved that we might again face such a war as was just ended; and that nothing but a gross national insult, or an open act of hostility, or such an attempt at aggrandisement on the part of France as would in effect comprise both, ought to divert us from this course.[1] The result of Mr. Pitt's visit to Dropmore is preserved in a letter from Lord Grenville to his brother.[2] He was better in health and spirits; his opinions were more alienated from the Government: although disposed to treat them with the utmost tenderness, he was prepared to attend Parliament after the Christmas recess, and to make his sentiments known to the world. On his way through London to Walmer, Mr. Pitt (much to Mr. Canning's annoyance) made two visits to Addington, at his house in Richmond Park.[3] The conversation which passed between Pitt and Addington at this time was considered by the latter 'extremely comfortable and satisfactory.' Addington

[1] *Lord Malmesbury, ibid.* pp. 152-57.

[2] *Courts and Cabinets*, vol. iii. p. 242. The dates and places are mistaken by the editor, p. 241, who represents Pitt as visiting Lord Grenville after he had been to Addington.

[3] This was the White Lodge, to which, after it had been conferred on Addington by the King, Mr. Canning gave the name of the 'Villa Medici.' Lord Sidmouth retained it till his death in 1844.

1803. took occasion to sound him on the subject of his return to office, and received from the great ex-minister an answer which he deemed encouraging.[1]

The months of February and March 1803, which Mr. Pitt passed at Walmer, brought the relations with France to a crisis. On the 8th of March, a message from the Crown, pointing to military preparations in France and Holland, and to pending discussions with France, the result of which was uncertain, and recommending to Parliament the adoption of precautionary measures, was brought down to both Houses. Addresses in answer to this message, which was regarded as the signal of renewed war, were unanimously voted both by Lords and Commons: the Government proposed the embodiment of the militia, and an addition of 10,000 seamen to the navy. From these debates Mr. Pitt was absent. Mr. Fox gave an unwilling support to a warlike address, and Mr. Francis commented upon the exclusion of the whole ability of the nation from the existing counsels of the sovereign. The message of the 8th of March gave rise to the celebrated explosion of Bonaparte, at a public reception at the Tuileries on the 13th, when he upbraided Lord Whitworth with the supposed desire of his country to revive the war, and their alleged infraction of the treaty. In this state of things, with the prospect of being driven from his pacific policy, and being compelled to play the part of a War Minister, Addington lost no time in seeking the assistance of Pitt.

Before the end of March, Lord Melville went down to Walmer, the bearer of a message from Addington, announcing his willingness to form a junction with Pitt.[2]

[1] *Life of Lord Sidmouth*, vol. ii. p. 113. [Compare Lord Stanhope's *Life of Pitt*, vol. iii. p. 431.—Ed.]

[2] [This was on Sunday, March 20 (see Lord Stanhope's *Life of Pitt*, vol. iv. p. 21).—Ed.]

The scheme originally proposed to Mr. Pitt was, that Mr. Addington and himself should be Secretaries of State (or, if Mr. Pitt preferred, that he should be Chancellor of the Exchequer), with a third person, agreeable to him, as Prime Minister, it being intended that this person should be Lord Chatham. Mr. Pitt instantly rejected this overture, chiefly on the ground that the proposed arrangement, by which the First Minister would not be the most important person in the Government, was objectionable.[1] Addington understood this objection to mean that Pitt insisted on being himself Prime Minister, and thereupon sent him, by Mr. Long, a verbal message to the effect that he might resume his former offices, and Addington would be a Secretary of State. Pitt acceded to the wish for a meeting with Addington, after Easter, which was at the same time expressed, but declined to give any assurance as to his own course without further explanations. At this stage of the negotiation Lord Grenville arrived at Walmer on a visit, and received from Pitt a full account of what had passed. Pitt likewise inquired of him whether he and his friends would form part of a Government formed by himself, and ascertained Lord Grenville's feelings on this subject. The meeting between Pitt and Addington took place in the early part of April, at Mr. Long's house at Bromley Hill. At this conference Pitt stated that the entire administration must be remodelled, and that Lord Grenville, Lord Melville, Lord Spencer, and Mr. Windham must be members of it. As soon as Addington received this ultimatum, he perceived that there was an irreconcilable antagonism between his views and those of Pitt. He wished to strengthen his own Ministry by engrafting Pitt into it, or, if necessary, by

1803.

[1] [See Lord Melville's letter to Addington, dated March 22, 1803 (Lord Stanhope's *Life of Pitt*, vol. iv. p. 24).—Ed.]

1803. placing Pitt at its head. Pitt wished to form a Ministry of his own, out of new materials, adopting only, from motives of private friendship and from deference to the King, some portions of the existing Cabinet. Addington made an attempt by letter, before he submitted the plan to his colleagues, to obtain better terms; but Pitt declined to alter his resolution. The proposal was then laid before the Cabinet, who, as might be expected, refused to be parties to a step which was a virtual dissolution of the Government.[1] Their refusal was communicated by Addington to Pitt, who returned a simple acknowledgment of the letter. Some further explanatory correspondence between them ensued, which ended by Pitt's requesting that all the letters might be laid before the King.[2] It appears

[1] Lord Grenville says, in a letter of April 18, 'The colour which the few friends of the present Government affect to give to the failure of the negotiation with Pitt is, as I understand, that his demands were excessive, and *that the King's repugnance could not be surmounted*' (*Courts and Cabinets*, vol. iii. p. 293). It is, however, clear that Addington and his colleagues rejected Pitt's terms before the King was consulted on the matter.

[2] An accurate and complete knowledge of this ministerial negotiation may be obtained by a comparison of Lord Sidmouth's *Life*, vol. ii. pp. 113–30; *Lord Malmesbury, ibid.* pp. 176–188; and Lord Grenville's *Narrative*, 'Courts and Cabinets,' vol. iii. pp. 282–290. An authentic account of the transaction, from information made public at the time, is also given in the *Annual Register* for 1803. In Lord Grenville's *Narrative* the words 'He (Pitt) desired Mr. Long to add, that he should *put* himself at liberty to communicate what had already passed to some of his friends; and particularly to myself' (p. 280), ought apparently to be, 'he should *feel* himself at liberty.' Mr. Wilberforce represents this plan as having originated with Lord Melville, and as having been carried into effect by him. 'Dundas undertook to bring Pitt into the plan, which was to appoint some third person head, and bring in Pitt and Addington on equal terms under him. Dundas accordingly, confiding in his knowledge of all Pitt's ways and feelings, set out for Walmer Castle; and after dinner and port wine, began cautiously to open his proposals. But he saw it would not do, and stopped abruptly. "Really," said Pitt, with a sly severity—and it was almost the only sharp thing I ever heard him say of any friend, "I had not the curiosity to ask what I was to be."'—*Life of Wilberforce*, vol. iii. p. 219). This is a remarkable instance of the manner in which historical truth is unintentionally

that the King's consent to the negotiation, however necessary an element in the business, had never been procured by Addington; so that, in fact, no distinct offer, by competent authority, was made to Pitt. Addington assumed to act as plenipotentiary, but had not full powers to treat. The consequence was, that unless he induced Pitt to assent to the precise proposal which he made, and which the Cabinet were likely to ratify, the negotiation could not lead to a successful issue. Looking to Pitt's experience and sagacity, and to Addington's dependence on the King, it is remarkable that the latter should have ventured to make the offer, or that the former should have been willing to entertain it, without the King's express authority being previously obtained. It was not a mere question of changing a Cabinet office, as to which a Prime Minister might properly make a preliminary arrangement, subject to the King's confirmation. It was practically a negotiation for a complete alteration of the character of the Government; and the whole discussion proceeded on the assumption that Addington and Pitt were between them to settle who was to be the new Prime Minister.[1] 1803.

Addington's first communication to the King on the subject is stated by Lord Malmesbury to have been made at an audience after the levee, when Pitt's final answer had been given, and the correspondence was nearly terminated. He represented Pitt's conduct in such colours as to rouse the King's wrath; who talked of Pitt's 'putting the crown

perverted for the sake of conversational antithesis. It is certain that Addington's message was fully delivered to Pitt, that it was deliberately considered by him, and that he gave a written answer to it, in which his reasons for refusing the offer were stated at length. Mr. Wilberforce, who disliked Fox's character and politics, and thought the Grenvilles too warlike, desired to see a union between Pitt and Addington effected (*ibid.* p. 156).

[1] [For the reasons given by Sir George Lewis in the text, I cannot agree with Lord Stanhope (*Life of Pitt*, vol. iv. p. 38) in thinking that 'both were right.' The king's concurrence ought to have preceded Addington's offer.—Ed.]

1803. in commission;' and said that he carried his plan of removals so far and so high, that it might end in reaching himself. A short time afterwards Addington gave the King copies of the correspondence, but the King refused to read the letters, or to take any notice of them, adding that 'it was a foolish business, which was begun ill, conducted ill, and terminated ill.'[1]

It soon appeared that the hopes of averting the war, which Addington had weakly cherished up to the last moment, were destined to be but short lived. On May 16, a message from the Crown was delivered to the two Houses, informing them that the King had recalled his ambassador from Paris, and that the French ambassador had left London. A declaration of war by England was issued on the 18th. Papers explanatory of the rupture were presented; and an address was moved by Ministers pledging Parliament to the renewal of hostilities. Public opinion, which two years before had been so strongly pronounced in favour of peace, was now equally decided in favour of war. The majority for the address was in the Lords 142 to 10; in the Commons 398 to 67. Pitt appeared on this occasion, and spoke with great energy in support of

[1] *Lord Malmesbury, ibid.* pp. 185–87. In Lord Sidmouth's *Life*, no mention is made of any communication with the King on the subject. Lord Malmesbury says nothing of the King having expressed any dissatisfaction with Addington's conduct; but the *Annual Register* makes this statement, which has much probability:—'It had, as is believed, never been authorised in the quarter from whence alone it should naturally have originated; it was, therefore, not followed up in that quarter; and some displeasure is even understood to have been expressed against the persons who had treated on matters of such moment without obtaining such previous warrant for it, as duty and respect were supposed to require' (p. 216). Lord Malmesbury thinks that 'Lord Grenville's visit at the end of March produced all the exceptionable part of Pitt's conduct in this negotiation' (p. 187). But Pitt was consistent from the beginning; he did not vary in his demands; and Lord Melville's letter, containing his answer to the first proposal, written before Lord Grenville's visit, in fact involves all his subsequent conditions.

a warlike policy. Fox made one of his most successful efforts in favour of pacific relations with France.[1] 'Every- 1803.

[1] Fox's own account of this debate is as follows:—'Pitt's speech was admired very much, and very justly. I think it was the best he ever made in that style; and there were several circumstances that rendered it peculiarly popular with the House. I dare say you have heard puffs enough of my speech upon the address, so that I need not add my mite; but the truth is, it was my best' (*Mem. of Fox, ibid.* p. 223). 'In the debate Mr. Fox spoke from ten to one; and in these three hours delivered a speech of more art, eloquence, wit, and mischief, than I ever remember to have heard from him' (Abbot's *Diary*, in Lord Sidmouth's *Life, ibid.* p. 182). 'Pitt's speech on the 23rd, the finest he ever made—never was any speech so cheered, or such incessant and loud applause; it was strong in support of war, but he was silent as to Ministers; and his silence, either as to blame or praise, was naturally construed into negative censure' (*Lord Malmesbury, ibid.* p. 256). 'Fox spoke three hours, very ingeniously, but very mischievous. Windham answered him. Addington spoke very poorly' (p. 257). Mr. Horner's report will also be read with interest:—'By all the accounts I have collected, both Pitt and Fox made a very great display. Pitt's peroration was a complete half hour of his most powerful declamation, not lowered in its tone for a moment; not a particle of all this is preserved in the report lately published, though said to be done by Canning. Fox's speech was quite of a different cast, and not at all in the tone which he usually adopts; no high notes, no impassioned bursts; but calm, subtle, argumentative pleasantry. He very seldom attempts to keep the House laughing; but in this speech, I understand, it was evidently his design throughout, and Mackintosh says he never heard so much wit. A good many of the points are repeated, none of which are in the newspapers, but I cannot pretend to give you them. I remember, however, the compliment he paid to Pitt's speech, that "if Demosthenes had been present, he must have admired, and might have envied"' (*Memoirs of Horner*, vol. i. p. 221). The following is the account of Sir Samuel Romilly, in a letter to Mr. Dumont of May 31, 1803:—'Pitt's speech is universally allowed to be one of the finest, if not the very finest, he ever made. His influence and authority in the House of Commons, shown upon the debate I have just mentioned, and still more on the day when Fox moved that the House should recommend the Crown to accept the mediation of the Emperor of Russia, exceeds all belief. The Ministry seem in the House of Commons, in comparison with him, to be persons of no account. An administration whose talents were generally thought so meanly of, or, I may say, who were so universally despised, was never before at the head of a great country' (*Life*, vol. ii. p. 106). [Compare Mr. Ward's (Lord Dudley) letter to Coapleston. Lord Stanhope's *Life of Pitt*, vol iv. p. 48. He says: 'But whatever may have been its comparative merits its effects were astonishing and, as I believe, unequalled.'—Ed.]

1803. body here seems to be of one mind (says Mr. Horner, in a letter written at the time) as to the justice of the war in respect of the case, as we lawyers call it, that this country can make out against Bonaparte; but the policy of war at the present juncture is a different question, of which people take various views.'[1]

The only step now taken by Mr. Fox in assertion of his pacific policy was to move an address to the Crown, recommending a resort to the mediation of Russia in order to re-establish peace with France; Mr. Pitt concurred in the principles of the motion, and it was not pressed to a division.[2]

Shortly afterwards, resolutions censuring Ministers for their submissive conduct towards France since the signature of the peace, and expressing a want of confidence in them, were proposed in both Houses, and negatived by

[1] *Memoirs of Horner, ibid.* p. 219.

[2] The views entertained by Mr. Fox at this time, with respect to the chances of maintaining the peace of Amiens, and the causes of its rupture, may be collected from the following passages in his letters:—'Everybody seems to think that peace is more and more safe; but yet what you say of ambiguous menaces, which is applicable to both sides, bad blood, &c., is very true, and till a language more friendly is adopted on both sides, there can be no safety: this is what I will work at as well as I can' (To Lord Holland, Jan. 1, 1803. *Mem. of Fox,* vol. iii. p. 210). 'Everybody now sees that Bonaparte's wish is for peace; nay, even the most warlike say he does not yet think himself ready. Everybody, too, now sees there was no violence on the part of France (which was at first supposed to cause the message), and I believe all indignant feelings are subsided, and the wish for peace as general as ever' (The same, March 29, 1803, *ibid.* p. 219). 'You know I have no great expectations of the gratitude of the country; but yet the wish for peace among sober-minded people is so general and so strong, that I cannot help thinking we should, in the feel of the country at least, be honourably distinguished from the other politicians and parties of the day, who so evidently make war and peace mere engines of attack upon a Ministry whom they dislike' (To Mr. Grey, March 12, 1803, p. 297). 'At present I am more convinced than ever, that, if it is war, it is entirely the fault of the Ministers, and not of Bonaparte' (The same, March 1803, *ibid.* p. 404).

large majorities. In the Commons, the motion for the removal of Ministers, made by Colonel Patten, was chiefly memorable on account of the line which was taken by Mr. Pitt. Their conduct had been condemned in several elaborate speeches, chiefly from members of the Grenville party, and it had been defended by Addington; when Pitt rose to deliver his opinion. The Opposition at this time, consisting as it did of two sections, was weakened by difference of sentiment. The old Opposition regretted the renewal of the war; the new Opposition applauded its renewal, and only regretted the peace by which it had been for a time interrupted. The policy of the Government had failed, and Ministers were admitted to be wanting in ability and vigour. If Mr. Pitt cordially approved of the conduct of Ministers, the immediate strength derived from his support, and the prospect of a more intimate connexion hereafter, would probably place them in a position which, backed by the King's influence, would defy all hostile attacks. On the other hand, if he gave a decided assent to the vote of want of confidence, it was plain that, whatever might be the numbers in the division, his open junction with the two sections of Oppositions would speedily force Addington to a capitulation. The curiosity therefore as to the sentiments which he would express, and the vote which he would give, was great. But the hopes of all parties were doomed to be disappointed. He declared that he could bestow neither approbation nor censure upon the conduct of Ministers; that he saw no such extraordinary exigency as justified a parliamentary interference for their removal, and that he could neither affirm nor negative the address. He therefore moved that the House should pass to the other orders of the day without coming to a vote upon the resolutions. Lord Hawkesbury followed Mr. Pitt, and, on the part of

1803.

1803. the Government, rejected the proffered compromise, insisting that the House should decide for a direct censure, or a total acquittal. Mr. Canning announced that though he had never hitherto voted against the opinion of Mr. Pitt, he must support the resolutions. The question was then put; when there appeared for Mr. Pitt's motion 58, against it 333. The minority was the exact measure of Mr. Pitt's followers in this division, as both sections of the Opposition voted with the Government. After this division Mr. Pitt, with his friends, and the old Opposition, went away; and upon the main question the numbers were, for the resolutions 36, against them 277; this minority consisting of the new Opposition.

The conduct of Mr. Pitt, though deemed feeble by Lord Grenville,[1] condemned as factious by the King,[2] and

[1] In the intercepted letter from Lord Grenville to Lord Wellesley (written soon after this debate), Pitt's proceeding is thus characterised:—'The measure which he has lately adopted (I allude to his motions of adjournment on the vote of censure, illjudged in itself, as I think it was, and unfortunate in its result, since it lessened his public influence) has at least the merit of expressing, in an unequivocal manner, his disapprobation of the conduct of Government' (*Annual Register*, vol. xlvi. p. 118). Mr. Grenville writes in a similar tone to Lord Buckingham:—'Of Pitt's failure in effect, and in numbers, on Friday last, you must have already heard; I fear that he has hurt himself much in public opinion, though probably he may still recover, if he should even now take any decided part' (June 7, 1803. *Courts and Cabinets*, vol. iii. p. 304). Mr. Fox's language in a letter to Lord Holland, of June 6, is still stronger:—'Both the substance and manner of Pitt were as bad as his worst enemy could wish; and Hawkesbury answered him extraordinarily well, showing both a proper spirit of resistance, and a proper feeling at being compelled to make it against an old friend. The contrast between the reception of that speech [viz. on the Address, May 23] and of his last was perhaps the strongest ever known' (*Mem. of Fox*, vol. iii. p. 223). In a letter of May 21, to Mr. Grey, Fox says:—'Pitt's mode of conduct will, I think, have a different effect from what he proposes, and will tend to add real strength to the Doctor, to whom nothing can be more favourable than a demonstration of the impossibility of any union of the parties out of office' (*ibid.* p. 411).

[2] See the King's letter to Lord Sidmouth, June 4 (*Life, ibid.* p. 143).

considered an error in parliamentary tactics by his own friends,[1] probably answered his object. Having voted for the peace, and having for some time supported Addington, he was unwilling to join in the vote of censure; but by refusing to negative it, he implied his disapprobation of Ministers, and evinced a disposition which would not fail soon to break out into open hostility. 1803.

No further attempt was made during the session to place the administration in different hands. Addington proceeded without delay to restore the army and navy to a war footing, and to re-impose the income tax—the objection being taken then, as subsequently, that it made no distinction between permanent and precarious incomes. His Ministry had now lived through three sessions. In the first, he negotiated; in the second, he concluded the peace; in the third, he declared war. The pacification lasted from the signing of the preliminaries, in October 1801, till the recall of Lord Whitworth, in May 1803, a period of twenty months.

But although the Ministry had reached the close of the session, and stood high in the royal favour, the course of events had destroyed all their prominent claims to popular support. It was evident that the beginning of their end had arrived. Mediocrity was in all things their characteristic. They were considered a middle-class Ministry; and their weakness in the House of Lords was more striking than in the House of Commons. Moderate in measures,

[1] 'Certainly not a judicious measure, though kindly intended towards Government by Pitt. Its effect is to furnish a plea for the many to desert Pitt and blame him' (*Lord Malmesbury*, *ibid.* p. 260). Pitt's own explanation of his motives, and justification of his step, as stated in a long conversation with Lord Malmesbury, on June 8, are given, *ibid.* p. 263. He admitted that it was not 'good generalship,' but said that one of the first points for him was 'to do nothing which could displease, irritate, or discompose the King.' This refers to the state of the King's mind.

1803. as in ability,[1] they hoped to escape by bending before circumstances, and to obtain safety in the midst of storms

[1] The first stanza of Canning's song of 'Moderate men and Moderate Measures' runs thus:—

Praise to placeless, proud ability
  Let the prudent muse disclaim;
And sing the statesman—all civility—
  Whom moderate talents raise to fame.
He, no random projects urging,
  Makes us wild alarms to feel;
With moderate measures gently purging
  Ills that prey on Britain's weal.

In a poem entitled 'Good Intentions,' the following verses occur:—

Others, with necromantic skill,
May bind men's passions to their will,
Raise with dark spells the tardy loan,
To shake the vaunting Consul's throne;
In thee no magic arts surprise,
No tricks to cheat our wondering eyes;
On thee shall no suspicion fall,
Of sleight of hand, or cup and ball;
E'en foes must own thy spotless fame,
Unbranded with a conjurer's name!
  Ne'er shall thy virtuous thoughts conspire
To wrap majestic Thames in fire!
  And if that black and nitrous grain
Which strews the field with thousands slain,
Slept undiscovered yet in earth,
Thou ne'er had'st caused the monstrous birth,
Nor aided (such thy pure intention)
That diabolical invention!
  Hail, then, on whom our state is leaning,
O minister of mildest meaning!
Blest with such virtues to talk big on,
With such a head (to hang a wig on),
Head of wisdom, soul of candour,
Happy Britain's guardian gander.

Lord Holland says of Addington:—'His empty and pompous manner exposed him to ridicule; and old Lord Liverpool justly observed that he was laughed out of power and place by the *beau monde*' (*Mem. of the Whig Party*, vol. ii. p. 211). It seems to us that it was the wits, rather than the *beau monde*, who made Addington ridiculous. Addington was indeed the favourite of the Court; but it must be confessed that the Court at this time was not *in fashion*.

by their resemblance to the reed rather than to the oak. They likewise flattered themselves that good intentions would supply the want of vigorous acts. But a new state of things had arisen, and positive qualifications in a Ministry were now felt to be necessary. Pitt's protecting arm, which had been for a time held over Addington's head, was now about to turn the sword against his breast.[1] The Grenville party had never joined in Addington's support, and since the announcement of the preliminaries, had kept up an active, unsparing, and determined opposition. Fox and his friends had warmly supported the treaty and the pacific policy of the Government; but the war had now been resumed, and in January 1804, an overture was made to him by the Grenvilles to join in a systematic opposition for the purpose of removing the 1804.

[1] 'Pitt, I hear, is more and more bitter against the Ministers, and feels strongly what he deems the embarrassment of his situation. I am told he even expresses this sentiment (an openness not very usual with him) to some of his friends' (Mr. Fox to Mr. Grey, Dec. 17, 1803; *Mem. of Fox,* vol. iii. p. 443). Lord Grenville made to Pitt, in January, the same offer which he made to Fox; but Pitt refused to engage with others in any systematic opposition to Addington. Lord Grenville reports the result of his interview with Pitt in a letter to his brother, of Jan. 30, 1804:—'The same ideas prevail, and nearly the same course will be pursued. The most decided hatred and contempt of those who have done so much to provoke both, but views of middle lines, and managements, and delicacies *où l'on se perd'* (*Courts and Cabinets,* vol. iii. p. 342). Pitt's own detailed explanation of his conduct at this time, as given in a long conversation with Lord Malmesbury, may be seen in the *Diary* of the latter, vol. iv. pp. 288–292. Mr. Fox's feelings towards Addington break out in letters of an earlier date. Thus in a letter to Mr. Grey, of Feb. 28, 1803, he says:—'The insipidity of the House of Commons is beyond conception, and I think it is catching; for the few times I have thought myself obliged to speak, I felt some way as if I was speaking like Addington, and I really believe I was' (*ibid.* vol. iii. p. 396). 'As to men, the folly and hollowness of Addington is, you know, my aversion' (March 12, 1803, *ibid.* p. 398). 'If one is to attend, it would certainly be a great relief to one's mind to allow oneself to abuse Addington's pompous nonsense as it deserves: it really is, on all occasions, both trifling and serious, disgusting, in point of taste, to a degree almost intolerable' (March 1803, *ibid.* p. 406).

1804. Ministry, and substituting one formed on a wide and comprehensive basis.[1] This overture was accepted, and the old and new Oppositions, as they were called, were thus combined in common action against Addington. Fox, indeed, as late as November 1803, had been using his best exertions in Addington's support, for the purpose of keeping out Pitt;[2] but his language with respect to Ministers, soon after this time, which he used in his private letters, was contemptuous and hostile in the highest degree.[3]

[1] See Mr. Fox's letter to Mr. Grey, Jan. 29, and his letter to General Fitzpatrick, Jan. 27, 1814 (*Mem. of Fox*, vol. iii. p. 449, vol. iv. p. 15), for an account of this overture. This junction is described in the *Life of Lord Sidmouth*, vol. ii. p. 254.

[2] See Mr. Grenville's lettter of Nov. 25, 1803, *Courts and Cabinets*, vol. iii. p. 333.

[3] 'I really think the next six weeks must bring matters to a crisis, both with respect to the King, and to the getting rid of these rascals' (Mr. Fox to Mr. Grey, April 2 (misprinted August), 1804. *Mem. of Fox*, vol. iii. p. 459). 'Let us first get rid of the Doctor, is my first principle of action, in which I reckon you as concurring with me as much as anyone' (Mr. Fox to Mr. Grey, April 13, *ibid.* p. 463). 'You will perceive that the Doctor is much weaker in numbers than one could have imagined; but it looks as if this was not so much owing to our strength, as to speculations among their friends concerning the King, and Pitt's ambiguous situation. However, it has this good effect, that it makes him (the Doctor) more and more contemned every day; indeed the contempt, both with respect to the degree and universality of it, is beyond what was ever known. Not one unpaid defender, unless you reckon Dallas, who is impatient for the Solicitor-Generalship' (Mr. Fox to Lord Lauderdale, March 15, *ibid.* vol. iv. p. 24). 'The Doctor has exceeded, if possible, all his former lies in what he said about the Russian business. It is, I own, an ignoble chase; but I should have great pleasure in hunting down this vile fellow' (Mr. Fox to Lord Lauderdale, March 25, *ibid.* p. 31). Within two years, this 'vile fellow,' however, held the office of Lord Privy Seal in Mr. Fox's own administration. The following passage from Mr. Wilberforce's *Diary* of Dec. 17, 1803, exhibits the feeling of the time:—'The general opinion of Government is, that it is sadly blundering and inefficient. Yet people are afraid of the old set entire. Windham and Co., strong in opposition. Fox manifestly drawing towards them. Provoked by *Cursory Remarks* [a party pamphlet, written by an Addingtonian]. 'Tis said Sheridan tried to pique him by

At the beginning of 1804, the course of political affairs was again disturbed by a recurrence of the King's malady.[1] As on the last occasion, his life was for a time in danger; but when his bodily health was restored, the mental derangement was such that the appointment of a Regent came seriously into question. The attention of Parliament was awakened; but after some weeks the bulletins ceased, and Ministers declared that no necessity existed for the suspension of the regal functions. It is however certain, that during a large part of this year the King's mind was in a state which disqualified him for the calm and attentive consideration of important political questions.[2] We need scarcely point out that this incapacity rendered negotiations for the reconstruction of the Government difficult; that it tended to make parliamentary opposition for the 1804.

saying, "You will get Pitt in again if you oppose." He peevishly says, "I can't bear fools, anything but fools"' (*Life of Wilberforce*, vol. iii. p. 142).

[1] The physicians who were examined by Parliamentary Committees upon the appointment of the Regency at the end of 1810, declared that the King's insanity in 1804 had been caused by the publication of the correspondence between the Prince of Wales and the Duke of York, relative to the offer of the former to serve abroad. See *Life of Romilly*, vol. ii. p. 352. This correspondence is printed in the *Annual Register*, vol. xlv. pp. 564–575. The Prince's last letter is dated Oct. 24, 1803. See *Adolphus*, vol. vii. p. 699.

[2] See Twiss's *Life of Lord Eldon*, vol. i. pp. 416–427, 446, 452; *Life of Lord Sidmouth*, vol. ii. pp. 246–250; *Lord Malmesbury*, pp. 286, 291, 310, 311, 318; *Mem. of Fox*, vol. iii. pp. 453, 463, vol. iv. p. 24. The following anecdote of the acuteness which the King retained in the midst of his mental derangement is related on this occasion by Lord Malmesbury:—'In the first illness, when Willis, who was a clergyman, entered the room, the King asked him if he, who was a clergyman, was not ashamed of himself exercising such a profession. "Sir," said Willis, "our Saviour himself went about healing the sick." "Yes," answered the King, "but he had not 700*l.* a year for it"' (*ibid.* p. 310). Another similar anecdote is related in the *Life of Lord Eldon*:—'The King, during one of his illnesses, complained to Lord Eldon, who related the story to Mr. Farrer, that a man in the employ of some of his physicians had knocked him down. "When I got up again," added the King, "I said my foot had slipped, and ascribed my fall to that; it would not do for me to admit that the King had been knocked down by anyone"' (*Twiss, ibid.* p. 426).

1804. purpose of compelling the King to acquiesce in a policy which he disliked, objectionable on the score of feeling, and thus gave an undue advantage to the Ministers in possession of office.[1] The painful and conflicting considerations which the King's illness suggested may be understood from the following passage in a letter from Lord Grenville to the Marquis of Buckingham, of April 19, 1804. Lord Grenville, after informing his brother of a message from Pitt to Addington, involving a communication to the King respecting a change of Ministry, proceeds thus :—

You will observe all this supposes the King in a state to receive such a communication from Addington, and to undergo all the fatigue of body and mind to which it must unavoidably lead, if even he should be disposed to act at once as reason, policy, and the real interests of himself, his family, and his people require. *I cannot say that I believe him to be equal even to the very first entering upon such a business*; and if the state of public affairs were such as would allow of our postponing the whole question, most willingly would I lend him my assistance (without his knowing I did so) for warding off from him the difficulties of such a scene. But this I know is impossible. To trust the country for another year, in such times as these, to such management as we are now under, would be, in all reasonable calculations, inevitable ruin; and if, in measuring one's conduct upon such a subject, one could look to the King's health alone, the only possible means of securing his peace of mind is to do the best for guarding the kingdom against the dangers now ready to burst upon us, and which, if not better provided against than they now are, must, when they come,

[1] 'The truth seems to be, that the moment the Doctor found that the King's madness took the turn of wishing war against Bonaparte, he was determined to humour that on which his sole existence depended, viz. the King's madness' (Mr. Fox to Lord Lauderdale, April 2, 1804. *Mem. of Fox*, vol. iv. p. 36).

infallibly overthrow his reason in the first instance, but probably, with that, destroy himself, his family, and his kingdom.'[1] 1804.

No long time, however, elapsed before Pitt, by independent attacks, and by giving support to the concerted measures of the two Oppositions, drove Addington to the necessity of resignation. He commenced his hostile operations before Easter by a motion for papers on the state of the navy, in which he was aided by the Foxites and Grenvilles. Upon this motion the Prince's friends voted with Ministers, and the Government had a majority of 201 to 130.[2] After Easter, the opposition was continued upon a bill for the augmentation of the Irish militia: on the third reading, when Pitt voted with Fox and the Grenvilles, the ministerial majority was only 21. A week

[1] *Courts and Cabinets*, vol. iii. p. 350. Mr. Twiss, in his *Life of Lord Eldon*, in describing the difficulty of forming a new administration at this crisis, says:—'In addition to the difficulty produced by the discordant nature of the materials, there was this further obstacle, that the state of the King's mind, though not sufficiently disordered to incapacitate him from the transaction of common business, was yet too much unsettled to admit the deliberation necessary for effecting a change in the counsels of the country' (vol i. p. 438). The following is the account of the King's state given by the Prince of Wales, in November 1804, after a visit to Windsor:—'He had found things at Windsor as bad as they had been represented; no cordiality (hardly common civility) towards himself; a power of restraining himself and talking rationally for some time and on some points, but no day passing without much of a different description, and many points very prevalent in his mind of a character extremely irrational' (Lord Grenville to the Marquis of Buckingham, Nov. 30, 1804. *Courts and Cabinets*, *ibid.* p. 381). ['On Sunday the 26th two documents were published by authority; the one a prayer composed by the Archbishop of Canterbury, and offering thanks to God for the hope and prospect of His Majesty's speedy recovery; the other a bulletin issued by the physicians, and announcing that "His Majesty is going on favourably, though any rapid amendment is not to be expected." It could not fail to be noticed that these two documents contradicted each other.'—Lord Stanhope's *Life of Pitt*, vol. iv. p. 123.—Ed.]

[2] Fox says, in a letter written at this time:—'Pitt is, I believe, as far as temper goes, completely exasperated against the present men, and consequently desirous of making, conjointly with us, as strong an opposition as possible' (To Mr. Grey, March 28, 1804, *ibid.* p. 458).

1804. afterwards, Fox brought forward an opposition motion on the defences of the country, which was supported in debate by Pitt and Windham.[1] In this division Sheridan and the Prince's friends voted with the Opposition, and the numbers were, for the motion, 204; against it, 256—showing a majority of 52 for the Government. Two days afterwards, on April 25, 1804, Mr. Pitt followed up this advantage by opposing the order of the day for going into committee on a Government bill for the suspension of the Army of Reserve Act. He objected to the system of military defence proposed by Ministers, and developed a plan of his own. On this question the division was 240 to 203, leaving a majority of only 37 in favour of Ministers. Taking into consideration the gradual decline in his own numbers, and also the weight of the Opposition, Addington now resolved to resign. He communicated his intention immediately to the King; and on April 30 the Chancellor informed Mr. Pitt that the Government was dissolved.

Soon after the division on the third reading of the Irish Militia Bill, on April 16, Addington sent a message to Pitt, desiring to know, through a common friend, his opinions on the state of public affairs, and the steps to be taken for carrying on the Government. Pitt, who doubtless bore in mind the unsatisfactory result of the negotiation with Addington in the previous year,[2] declined to accede to this

[1] In a letter to Lord Temple of April 11, 1804, Lord Grenville says:—'Pitt comes, I understand, in a day or two; and with dispositions, as I hear, of increased hostility to the Government, so that we may look to strong divisions' (*Courts and Cabinets*, vol. iii. p. 346).

[2] Fox, in a letter to a Mr. O'Brien, of January 22, 1804, says: 'Depend on it, there is no truth in any treaty at present (I mean these last nine months) with Pitt or for Pitt' (*Mem. of Fox*, vol. iv. p. 14). On which passage Lord J. Russell remarks, that 'Mr. Fox was quite mistaken.' Referring to the *Life of Lord Sidmouth*, Mr. Fox's statement is certainly correct; there had been no negotiation with Pitt since March and April 1803; and this transaction was well known to Mr. Fox, who says in a letter

proposal; but stated that if the King wished to learn his views as to the formation of a new Ministry, he would state them to any person nominated by His Majesty for that purpose. Addington's reply was that he would advise the King to charge Lord Eldon with this mission.[1] A few days afterwards Pitt, without receiving any communication from the King, sent to Lord Eldon an unsealed letter to be laid before His Majesty, declaring sentiments adverse to the Government, and explaining the course which he was about to take on Mr. Fox's motion. This letter appears not to have been submitted to the King until about the time when Addington tendered his resignation.[2] On May 2, Mr. Pitt sent through Lord Eldon a letter to the King, containing his plan for the formation of a new Government, which was to comprehend the leaders of all political parties; but the King, who was greatly troubled 1804.

to Mr. Grey, of April 1803, 'I have good authority for saying that the negotiation with Pitt is at an end, and in a manner not likely to bring on a renewal' (*Mem. of Fox*, vol. iii. p. 410). [The negotiations may be said to have ended with Pitt's letter of acknowledgment of April 14, 1803. The letters were laid before the King on the 27th of that month. See Lord Stanhope's *Life of Pitt*, vol. iv. pp. 35, 37.—ED.]

[1] This transaction was related by Pitt to Lord Grenville. Letter of Lord Grenville to Lord Buckingham, April 19, 1804; *Courts and Cabinets*, vol. iii. p. 348.

[2] Twiss, *Life of Lord Eldon*, vol. i. pp. 439–441. A conversation between Lord Eldon and Mr. Pitt had taken place in March, at the request of the former, but without leading to any result, *ibid.* p. 438. Pitt mentioned to Lord Malmesbury at the time the letter which he had written to the King through Lord Eldon, *Diary*, *ibid.* p. 295. Lord Malmesbury thinks, p. 296, that Pitt's letter (which was dated and sent to the Chancellor on the 22nd of April) was withheld by him and not delivered till the 27th. There seems no ground for Lord Brougham's view (*Hist. Sketches of Statesmen*, vol. i. p. 297, ed. 1855) that this communication through Lord Eldon was an intrigue. [Lord Stanhope thus prefaces his reference to this passage—'We may rather concur with a judicious critic in the *Edinburgh Review*, often supposed to be Sir George Cornewall Lewis. With a most upright spirit, such as that critic ever shows, he has given judgment as follows on the question' (*Life of Pitt*, vol. iv. p. 153). Compare, however, Dean Milman's letter in the Supplement, p. 279.—ED.]

1804. and disconcerted at Addington's resignation, and was most reluctant to readmit Pitt to office, gave him a discouraging answer.[1] Mr. Pitt now requested a personal interview. This request was granted, and on the 7th he was accompanied to the Queen's House by the Chancellor; but such were the reports of the King's state which he had heard, that he refused to enter the closet until he had received from the physicians a written assurance that his visit would not disturb the King, especially as His Majesty had not seen him for three years;[2] that is, apparently, not since his resignation in 1801. Mr. Pitt, however, found the King capable of discussing public affairs with him. He obtained with some difficulty permission to treat with Lord Grenville and his friends, as well as with the friends of Mr. Fox; but the King positively refused to admit Mr. Fox himself into the Cabinet, although his comprehension was pressed by Pitt.

Pitt received this communication of the King's wishes as final, and made no further attempt to resist them. As soon as the interview was over, he sent Mr. Canning to Lord Grenville, and Lord Granville Leveson to Mr. Fox, to acquaint them with what had passed. Lord Grenville said that the result was what he expected, and he must decline to take office. On the following day, after he had communicated with his friends, he addressed a letter to Mr. Pitt (which was made public at the time), in which he

[1] Twiss, *ibid.* p. 443; *Lord Malmesbury*, pp. 296–299. [A 'discouraging answer' is a very mild description of the King's letter, of which Lord Stanhope truly says, 'The great harshness and exasperation which it displays throughout are best explained or best excused by his recent malady' (*Life of Pitt*, vol. iv. p. 165. See the letter itself, App. p. viii.).—Ed.]

[2] Lord St. Helens was the authority for this fact. *Lord Malmesbury*, *ibid.* p. 304; *Life of Lord Sidmouth*, *ibid.* p. 286. It seems that the fact of the King having passed Mr. Pitt in the Park without notice in June, 1803, was commented on at the time (*Memoirs of Horner*, vol. i. p. 221).

objected to becoming party to a system of Government formed upon a principle of exclusion; and he declared his opinion, that as large a proportion as possible of the weight, talents, and character to be found in public men of all descriptions, and without any exception, ought to be united in the public service. Mr. Fox, on receiving the message, expressed no surprise, anger, or disappointment; said that he was himself too old to care about office,[1] but that he had many friends who for years had followed him, and whom he should advise to join the Government, and he trusted that Pitt would give them places. Fox, anticipating the King's personal objection to him, had on the day before Pitt's interview with the King left a note with Mr. Grenville, announcing that he did not wish to stand in the way of any arrangement, and expressing a hope that his exclusion would not prevent either the Grenvilles or his own friends from accepting office. This disinterested conduct on his part weighed much with Lord Grenville and his friends in declining to acquiesce in his exclusion and to join Pitt. 1804.

On the receipt of the two answers Pitt testified much anger at the conduct of Lord Grenville, and much pleasure at that of Fox. He made an appointment to see Fox on the following morning, to which Fox assented; but Fox's friends, in the meantime, agreed not to accept office without him, and the interview never took place.[2]

[1] Mr. Fox was at this time fifty-five years old.

[2] *Lord Malmesbury*, *ibid.* pp. 321–325; *Life of Wilberforce*, vol. ii. p. 158–161; Twiss, *ibid.* p. 449.; *Courts and Cabinets*, *ibid.* p. 352; *Ann. Reg.* for 1804, p. 124. Pitt informed the King of Lord Grenville's refusal on the receipt of the oral message, without waiting for his written communication. See his letter, *Life of Lord Sidmouth*, *ibid.* p. 287. A full and confidential account of the views entertained by Pitt, prior to the overthrow of the Addington Ministry, and of the communications of his intentions which he made to Fox and Lord Grenville, is contained in a letter to Lord Melville, of March 29, 1804, privately printed by Lord Stanhope (then Lord Mahon)

1804. Pitt was doubtless mortified at the decided refusal of the Grenville party, and disappointed at being compelled to form an administration without their assistance. The two principal parties were, for different reasons, closed against him. The Foxites, because their chief had been proscribed by the King; the Grenvilles, because Pitt had acquiesced in this proscription. The new administration, however, such as it was, was soon formed. Six of the existing Cabinet Ministers remained; viz. Lord Eldon, Lord Chancellor; Duke of Portland, President of the Council; Lord Westmoreland, Privy Seal; Lord Chatham, Master of the Ordnance; and Lord Castlereagh, President of the Board of Control. Lord Hawkesbury was still Secretary of State, but was moved from the Foreign to the Home Department. The new Cabinet appointments were Mr. Pitt, First Lord of the Treasury and Chancellor of the Exchequer; Lord Harrowby, Secretary of State for Foreign Affairs; Lord Camden, Secretary of State for War and the Colonies; Lord Melville, First Lord of the Admiralty; Duke of Montrose, President of the Board of Trade; Lord Mulgrave, Chancellor of the Duchy of Lancaster.[1] It will be observed that the only Member of

from the original at Melville Castle in 1852. In this letter Pitt declares his intention of informing the King that if he is resolved to exclude the friends both of Mr. Fox and Lord Grenville, he will be ready to do as he best can with his own friends, united with the most capable and unexceptionable persons of the existing Government, 'but of course excluding many of them, *and above all, Addington himself and Lord St. Vincent.*' He adds that Fox is prepared to support an anti-ministerial motion, 'under the full knowledge that if the result produces the removal of the Government, he (Pitt) holds himself at full liberty to form a new one without reference to him.' [The letter referred to in this note will now be found in Lord Stanhope's *Life of Pitt*, vol. iv. p. 139.—Ed.]

[1] An authentic account of the circumstances which led to the dissolution of the Addington Ministry, and to the formation of Pitt's Government, is contained in a secret despatch from Lord Castlereagh to Lord Wellesley, of May 18, 1804, in *Lord Wellesley's Despatches*, vol. iii. p. 570.

the House of Commons in this Cabinet, besides Mr. Pitt, was Lord Castlereagh. The result was that Pitt was driven, in substance, to the very arrangement which he had rejected when proposed to him by Addington a year before. Six of the old Cabinet remained; Pitt, with five new colleagues, was added. Of these five Addington was willing to receive Lord Melville, and therefore, all that Pitt gained was the substitution of Lord Camden or Lord Mulgrave for Addington himself, and the addition of the Duke of Montrose, a change which profited nobody.[1] It should, moreover, not be overlooked, that before a year was over, Pitt was glad to negotiate with Addington, and to admit him into his Cabinet. 1804.

The King consented reluctantly to this change of Government. He desired to retain Addington; he disliked the return of Pitt. In writing to Addington, after his resignation, he styles the late Minister 'his truly beloved friend, whose honour, truth, and personal attachment will ever be a source of the greatest pleasure and comfort His Majesty can enjoy.'[2] The King likewise offered him an earldom, a pension for himself, and another for Mrs. Addington (which honour and emoluments were declined); and in his parting interview expressed undiminished attachment and respect for the retiring Minister, and a strong disapproval of the means by which he had been supplanted.[3]

[1] Lord Grenville, in a letter to the Marquis of Buckingham, Dec. 20, 1804, says, in reference to an accident which compelled Lord Harrowby to resign:—'He [Pitt] will have a great loss in Lord Harrowby, who is, with the exception of Lord Melville, the only person he had in his Government capable of giving him any assistance' (*Courts and Cabinets, ibid.* p. 392).

[2] *Life of Lord Sidmouth, ibid.* p. 292.

[3] *Ibid.* p. 294. The King afterwards presented to Addington a copy of Beechy's portrait of himself on horseback, to be followed by portraits of himself and the Queen in their robes. This gift was accompanied by another flattering and affectionate letter' (*ibid.* p. 321).

1804. Addington, as we learn from his biographer, always considered his treatment by Pitt as unkind and unfair. Pitt, indeed, had not recommended him to office, but he had contributed more than any other man to his acceptance of it. He began by offering advice, and giving it; he then withdrew to a distance where he could not be consulted, and stood aloof from the Government; and, finally, he threw his weight into the opposite scale, and, in fact, brought about Addington's downfall.[1] It may be added that Canning's incessant

[1] *Life of Lord Sidmouth*, *ibid.* p. 298. Mr. Wilberforce has the following entries in his *Diary*, Nov. 20 and Dec. 1, 1801:—'Pitt supports, most magnanimously, and assists in every way.' 'Pitt and Rose dined with me quietly to-day. Pitt very pleasant, and we stayed chatting politics. What wonderful magnanimity! wishing to form for Addington the strongest and best possible administration.' This, it should be observed, was after the signature of the preliminaries (*Life of Wilberforce*, vol. iii. p. 20). The following passage respecting Pitt's relations with Addington occurs in Lord Grenville's intercepted letter to Lord Wellesley, dated July 12, 1803:—'Though he did not recommend Addington to his present employment (and indeed who is there that knows him would have done it?) he nevertheless gave him a certain portion of influence, more active than my opinion would have permitted me to grant, in the formation of the new administration. He advised their measures a long time after I had ceased to have any intercourse with them, and he approved of them in different points which appeared to me the most criminal, and which were indeed so, as proved by the event. He is consequently more hampered in his conduct than I am, and he does not at present enjoy the inestimable advantage which I possess, of never having concealed nor compromised my opinion in regard to matters of so much political importance; but I believe that his ideas on their political conduct are not much different from mine, if they differ at all, *and to all this must be added a resentment justly merited from the personal conduct of Mr. Addington towards him.* He does not endeavour to conceal his sentiments' (*Ann. Reg.* vol. xlvi. p. 118; *Adolphus*, vol. vii. p. 754). In a letter to Lord Buckingham, of March 12, 1803, Lord Grenville says:—'Pitt is still at Walmer. Messengers of all descriptions are going continually to him to bring him up. The prevailing opinion is, that he will come up next week, but I really can venture no conjecture. He has hampered himself to such a degree by his support of measures which he so totally disapproved, that I really hardly see what he has to do, and am glad the decision is not with me' (*Courts and Cabinets*, vol. iii. p. 263). Similar language occurs in a letter of Lord Grenville, of Oct. 20, 1802, *ibid.* p. 212.

artillery of newspaper attacks, both in verse and prose, against the whole Addington tribe, with all their medical apparatus, must have fostered a feeling of perpetual bitterness against Pitt, because Canning lived with him on terms of the utmost intimacy, and it could scarcely be doubted that his battery might have been silenced by a serious remonstrance, coming from his honoured and beloved patron.[1] Such was Addington's case against Pitt, but such was not the light in which the matter was viewed on the other side. 1804.

Dr. Addington had been the confidential physician of Lord Chatham. His son Henry and William Pitt were nearly of the same age;[2] they had been friends from

[1] The following political squibs against Addington and his Ministry, reprinted in the *Spirit of the Public Journals* for 1803 and 1804, appear to be by Mr. Canning:—

Proofs of Political Wisdom, vol. vii. p. 194; Dialogue, *ibid.* p. 196; The Doctor: an Ode, *ibid.* p. 197; Apothecaries' Hall, p. 200; Remarks on the Foregoing, p. 204; The Blocks, p. 205; Ambubaiarum Collegia, Pharmacopolæ, p. 210; The Doctor's Practice Justified by Precedent, p. 211; More of the Doctor, p. 212; The Doctor *versus* Cocker, *ibid.*; Good Intentions, p. 214; Parallel between Bonaparte and Addington, p. 219; Theatrical Intelligence Extraordinary; St. James's Park Ghost, vol. viii. p. 13–17; Symposium, *ibid.* p. 215; A Quintetto, *ibid.* p. 223; Douglas, p. 224; Hints to the Minister, p. 227; Political Song, p. 232; Axing Pardon, p. 233; More of the Doctor, p. 237; Quack, Quack, p. 245; The Doctor's Friends, p. 250; More of the Doctor, p. 251; Petition Extraordinary, p. 260; Farewell to the Doctor, p. 265; Advertisement Extraordinary, *ibid.*; The Doctor's Sale, p. 268; More of the Doctor, p. 272; The Doctor in Distress, p. 274; Advertisement Extraordinary, p. 324 (?); Counter-Theatricals, p. 382. (The two last are directed against the opposition to Pitt's Administration.) Most of these squibs appeared in a newspaper called *The Oracle.* This journal is alluded to by Lord Grenville in a letter of June 14, 1803, as showing a disposition to go over to the Government side. 'You will see that the "Oracle" *Philippizes*, and probably for the same reasons that produced that effect of old' (*Courts and Cabinets, ibid.* p. 303). It is remarkable that Mr. Pitt, in a conversation with Lord Malmesbury in February 1804, described himself as having been assailed in prose and verse by Canning, on account of his lukewarmness in opposition (*ibid.* p. 291).

[2] Addington was Pitt's senior by two years; he was born in 1757, and Pitt in 1759.

1804. childhood; and when Mr. Pitt had become Prime Minister, and Mr. Addington had obtained a seat in Parliament, intentions had been formed on several occasions of offering public employment to the latter. At length, upon the transfer of Mr. W. Grenville to the House of Lords, from the chair of the House of Commons, in 1789, the Speakership became vacant, and Addington was proposed and carried by the Government. He therefore owed his first elevation in great measure to the favour of Mr. Pitt:[1] his unexpected and (we may add) undeserved elevation to the office of Prime Minister he owed to the favour of the King. Pitt encouraged his acceptance of this post, and for a time gave him countenance, support, and advice. Whether Pitt considered him a mere *locum tenens*, who was bound to withdraw whenever he might think fit to return, it is hard to say; but it could scarcely be expected that even Addington, certain as he was of the King's support, would consent to hold his office on such a tenure. The appointment of Mr. Tierney as Treasurer of the Navy, in June 1803, was regarded by the public as a measure personally offensive to Pitt, and could not fail to occur to himself in the same light.[2] Pitt, however,

[1] These obligations are alluded to in Canning's sarcastic poem of 'Elijah's Mantle,' written after Pitt's death:—

> Sidmouth! though low that head is laid,
> Which called thee from thy native shade,
> And gave thee second birth;
> Gave thee the sweets of power and place,
> The tufted robe and gilded mace,
> And reared thy puny worth;
>
> Think how his mantle wrapt thee round.
> Is one of equal virtue found
> Among thy new compeers?
> Or can thy cloak of Amiens stuff,
> Once laughed to scorn by blue and buff,
> Hide thee from Windham's jeers?

(*Spirit of the Public Journals* for 1806, vol. x. p. 153.)

[2] 'If it were matter of universal notoriety, that to the hereditary friend-

though contentious in debate, and haughty in negotiation, was undoubtedly of a placable and forgiving spirit, and did not cherish personal resentments. A ministerial pamphlet, published in 1803, attacked Pitt with much asperity, and might be considered as disclosing those feelings and opinions which the Government dared not avow.[1] It is, however, uncertain how far Addington can be justly held responsible for the contents of Mr. Bentley's anonymous pamphlet, and, on the whole, we have some difficulty in accounting for the 'just resentment' which Lord Grenville (no partial judge of Pitt's feelings at the time) says that Pitt entertained at Addington's personal conduct towards him. The part which Addington played was undoubtedly mean, low-minded, and selfish;[2] he acted towards Pitt without generosity. He sought, by subser- 1804.

ship of Mr. Pitt, to his powerful protection, and unwearied solicitude for his interest, the present Minister owed his existence as a statesman, and even his present elevation; it was equally so, that in the course of that opposition we have already described the personal rancour of Mr. Tierney to the late Minister was on all occasions perceptible, and a species of opposition to the man was as apparent as that to his measures. Whether this appointment, therefore, was considered as galling and repugnant to Mr. Pitt, or as the gage of contempt and defiance thrown down by Mr. Addington, it was equally considered by the world as conduct at once ungrateful and unwise, and became the theme of universal reprobation' (*Ann. Reg.* vol. xlvi. p. 179).

[1] Concerning this pamphlet, see *Life of Lord Sidmouth*, *ibid.* p. 145. The biographer admits that 'it commented with some severity on Mr. Pitt's conduct.' Wilberforce describes it as a pamphlet, 'evidently written by some confidential man, which abuses Pitt with the most bitter malignity' (*Life*, vol. iii. p. 119). Mr. Grenville, writing to the Marquis of Buckingham, says:—'Have you read the manifesto of Addington against all the Pitts, Grenvilles, Spencers, Windhams, &c., in a pamphlet called "Cursory Remarks upon the State of Parties"? The authentic tone in which it asserts as facts the most audacious falsehoods, gives it a consequence beyond what it could derive from the style of writing, which is but very moderate' (*Courts and Cabinets*, *ibid.* p. 321). [It appears to have been ascertained that the pamphlet was sent to several persons by Vansittart, then Secretary to the Treasury (see Lord Stanhope's *Life of Pitt*, vol. iv. p. 89).—Ed.]

[2] [See Sir George Lewis's letter to Lord Lansdowne, printed in the supplement to this article, p. 280.—Ed.]

1804. vience towards him, and by thus obtaining the great leader's assistance, to retain his hold upon Parliament; and by subservience to the King, to retain the royal favour. In this manner he hoped, without any real merit or ability, to continue in office.

No man of spirit or independence would have played this shabby game. But on the other hand, the position which Pitt had made for himself was such as to deprive him of the right of severe criticism, to create dissatisfaction in the leaders of all parties, to expose him to blame from all sides, and to denude him of all cordial support except from his personal adherents. The part which he attempted to fill, of secret adviser of the measures of the Government, without real power or responsibility, was sure after a time to lead to disappointment and misunderstanding. His relations to Addington as a friend and counsellor in private, and an independent supporter or censor in public, were radically inconsistent. The middle line which he traced for himself, of tenderness and forbearance to Addington, and of abstinence from parliamentary pressure on the King, so much complained of by Lord Grenville,[1] satisfied nobody, and was intelligible to nobody. It alienated the Grenvilles and Foxites, with whom he refused to form an alliance in opposition, and who therefore would not join him when he was charged with the formation of a Government; it wounded Addington, who considered himself overthrown by a friend; it failed in mitigating the King, who regarded Pitt as the real author of his favourite's ruin. It reduced public

[1] Lord Grenville, in a letter to the Marquis of Buckingham, written on January 7, 1806, about a fortnight before Pitt's death, says that his hope of bringing about a Government formed of the ablest public men had been rendered desperate; 'Firstly, by the great misconduct of Pitt, who might have realised it, but refused to do so' (*Courts and Cabinets*, vol. iv. p. 9). This must refer to the formation of Pitt's Government in 1804.

duty to a question of private feeling and personal delicacy. 1804.
Whatever may be thought of Pitt's foreign and domestic policy during the war of the Revolution, it cannot be disputed that up to 1801 he showed all the qualities of a great parliamentary leader, and that he succeeded in inspiring confidence in a large body of followers. But by his ambiguous conduct during the three following years—by his policy of seclusion and mystery—he so far weakened his parliamentary position, that on being charged with the formation of a Ministry in 1804, he was unable to obtain the adhesion of any of the chief parliamentary parties. The Grenvilles, the Foxites, even Addington and his personal friends, stood aloof, and Pitt became in substance the head of the old Ministry, whose policy he had condemned in the most contemptuous language, and in whose overthrow he had taken the most prominent part. To such straits was Pitt by his own conduct reduced, who, powerful as he had been in Government, might, if he had acted a straightforward, resolute, and open part, have been still more powerful in opposition, and, in combination with Lord Grenville and Fox, have dictated his own terms to the King and Addington. When Demosthenes was asked what was the first, and second, and third qualification of an orator, he answered, 'Delivery;' in like manner, if we were asked what is the first, and second, and third qualification of an English statesman, we would answer, 'Intelligibility.' As in oratory, the most eloquent words and the wisest counsels will avail but little if they are not impressed in voice and manner on the minds of an audience; so integrity and public spirit will fail to command confidence, if the course adopted is intricate and inexplicable.[1]

[1] [Sir George Lewis, himself afterwards afforded an eminent example of the truth of the principles here laid down. His perfect 'straightforwardness' was one of the qualities which tended most to win for him the confidence of the House of Commons. To use the words of an able article in *The National*

1804. The unfavourable light in which Pitt's conduct could be represented by an antagonist, without any clear or conclusive defence being possible, may be seen from the following retort to which he provoked Sheridan, by a taunt on his support of the Addington Government:—

The right honourable gentleman (said Sheridan, in a debate on March 6, 1805), has thought fit to allude to the support which I gave to Lord Sidmouth, when that noble lord was Chancellor of the Exchequer. He represents it as an insidious and hollow support. I hope it is not my character to give any support of that description. I say I gave my support to the late administration with the most perfect good faith, and I know that the noble lord has always been ready to acknowledge it. But supposing I had not supported him with firmness and fidelity—what then? I never had professed to do so, either to that administration or to this House. I supported them because I approved of many of their measures; but principally was I induced to support them because I considered their continuance in office a security against the return to power of the right honourable gentleman opposite me, which ever appeared to me as the greatest national calamity. If, indeed, *I* had recommended the noble lord to His Majesty; if I had come down to the House and described the noble lord as the fittest man in the country to fill the office of Chancellor of the Exchequer, because it was a convenient step to my own safety, in retiring from a situation which I could no longer fill with honour; if, having seduced him into that situation, I had afterwards tapered off from a prominent support when I saw that the minister of my own choice was acquiring greater stability and popularity than I wished for; if, when I saw an opening to my own return to power, I had entered into a combination with others, whom I meant also to betray, from the sole lust of power and office, in order to remove him; and if, under the dominion of these base appetites, I had then treated with ridicule and contempt the very man whom I had before held up to the choice of my

Review for October 1863, 'Sir George Lewis could not have described his own sort of mind better if he had been trying to do so. He *could* not be intricate or perplexed.'—Ed.]

Sovereign, and the approbation of this House and the public, then indeed I should have merited the contempt of all good men, and should have deserved to be told that I was hollow and insincere in my support, and had acted a mean and perfidious part.[1] 1804.

Pitt took his seat after his re-election on the 18th of May. In proof of his efficiency as a war-minister, he soon afterwards introduced a bill for improving the defences of the country, which was known as the Additional Force Bill. It met, however, with an unfavourable reception in the House of Commons; its second reading was opposed by 181 to 221 votes; it was much contested in other stages, and on one occasion Mr. Pitt went so far as to complain of the opposition made to it by the Grenville party. At the end of July Parliament was prorogued,[2] and Pitt had now leisure to consider what steps he could take to strengthen himself before the beginning of another session.[3]

[1] Sheridan had not spared Addington in the early part of his administration, as is shown by his joke about Theseus leaving his sitting part behind him, which Gilbert Wakefield furnished to him from a story in the 'Scholia to Aristophanes' (Equ. 1368). It seems that the reporters did not catch the name, and that Nicias, instead of Theseus, appeared in the newspapers (see *Adolphus*, vol. vii. p. 590).

[2] [It was prorogued by the King in person, who looked well, and read his speech with animation, but turned over two leaves at once, and thus omitted one-fourth of it (see Lord Stanhope's *Life of Pitt*, vol. iv. p. 211).—Ed.]

[3] The following account of Pitt's state, soon after this time, occurs in a letter from Mr. Grenville to the Marquis of Buckingham, September 11, 1804:—'I have received a letter from very good authority, to tell me that latterly the manner and appearance of Pitt has been "absorbed, melancholy, and ailing," to the greatest degree; so much so, that the writer assures me Pitt's friends are made anxious by it to the greatest degree, not knowing whether to attribute it to his own health, to the accounts from Weymouth [i. e. of the state of the King's mind], or to the apprehension of some great political crisis to which the rest of the world are strangers. My correspondent leans to the latter opinion, and has some, though no certain grounds, for imagining that this extreme depression arises from an overpowering sense of the present public difficulties, and from a consciousness that things cannot go on as they are' (*Courts and Cabinets*, *ibid.* p. 370).

1805. This strength he sought in a quarter where it seemed least likely to be afforded, and whence it was most humiliating to him to accept it. Before the opening of the session, on January 15, 1805—a period at that time considered unusually late [1]—a negotiation was opened with Addington for prevailing upon him to be reconciled with Pitt, and to accept a seat in the Cabinet. The ejected Minister, though recently unsparing in his censure of his successor,[2] was found placable; he was raised to the peerage as Lord Sidmouth, because, as was believed, Pitt feared his rival influence in the House of Commons; and he became President of the Council, instead of the Duke of Portland. The arrangement was highly pleasing to the King, but was not agreeable to the friends of either of the high contracting parties, and did not benefit Pitt either in popularity or character;[3] at the same time Addington's friend, Lord Buckinghamshire, was made Chancellor of the Duchy, instead of Lord Mulgrave, who had taken Lord Harrowby's place.

The reconciliation was hollow, and its effects were not of long duration. The Tenth Report of the Commissioners

[1] [Lord Stanhope says:—'During the administration of Lord North, it had been usual to convene Parliament in the month of November; but under Pitt the custom was changed. Unless in special cases, the Houses did not meet till after the new year. Thus, in 1784, at the time of which I speak, the opening of the new session was appointed for January 20, 1785.' In 1787, when war was impending, the Houses met on November 25.—Ed.]

[2] 'Addington is more bitter than ever against the present Ministers' (Mr. Grenville to the Marquis of Buckingham, November 13, 1804; *Courts and Cabinets*, vol. iii. p. 375). 'The reconciliation between Pitt and Addington must have been sudden, as I know that only two days before, upon Pitt touching his hat as he passed by Addington, Addington observed to Dyson, who was riding with him, that even that greeting was new to him' (The same, Jan. 7, 1805, *ibid.* p. 404).

[3] See Twiss's *Life of Lord Eldon*, vol. i. p. 484; *Life of Lord Sidmouth*, *ibid.* pp. 326–40; Mr. Grenville, in *Courts and Cabinets*, *ibid.* pp. 399, 403, 406; Mr. Fox to Lord Holland, March 19, 1805; *Mem. of Fox*, vol. iv. p. 75. Lord Hawkesbury was the medium of communication between them.

of Naval Inquiry had brought forward certain facts impugning the conduct of Lord Melville, with respect to his alleged misappropriation of public money, as Treasurer of the Navy. Upon this report, a motion inculpatory of him was made in the House of Commons by Mr. Whitbread. Pitt was eager to save his friend, and manifested the most lively anxiety during Wilberforce's speech, whose adverse opinion and vote produced much influence upon the House. Upon the division the numbers were equal, when the Speaker (Abbot) declared himself in favour of the motion of censure. Abbot was Addington's intimate friend; and Addington, differing from Pitt, took an unfavourable view of Lord Melville's case.[1] A few days afterwards Mr. Pitt informed the House that Lord Melville had resigned the office of First Lord of the Admiralty, and, subsequently, that he had advised His Majesty to erase his name from the list of the Privy Council. In making the latter announcement, Pitt confessed that, however anxious he might be to accede to the wishes of the House, he felt a deep and bitter pang in being compelled to be the instrument of rendering the noble lord's punishment more severe.[2] The question then arose as to the appointment of Lord Melville's successor 1805.

[1] The strength of the feeling which prevailed at the time against Lord Melville, and the cry against Placemen and Scotsmen, is described by Mr. Horner in a letter to Sir James Mackintosh (*Life*, vol. i. p. 291). Lord Malmesbury speaks of the huzzas and shouts of the House of Commons upon Lord Melville's condemnation, Sir Thomas Mostyn giving a view hollo, and 'we have killed the fox' (*ibid.* p. 338). The question seems in both Houses to have been regarded rather as political than judicial (see Lord Campbell's remarks on his acquittal by the House of Lords, in the *Life of Lord Ellenborough*). [Compare Lord Stanhope's *Life of Pitt*, vol. iv. pp. 281–2.—Ed.]

[2] After his acquittal by the House of Lords, Lord Melville was restored to his place on the Privy Council, but he never afterwards held office. According to Lord Holland, Pitt said to Mr. Huskisson at Bath, a short time before his death: 'We can get over Austerlitz, but we can never get over the Tenth Report. Such is the nature of Englishmen' (*Mem. of Whig Party*, vol. ii. p. 48).

1805. at the Admiralty. The arrangement which Lord Sidmouth desired was that his friend Lord Buckinghamshire should be First Lord of the Admiralty, and that his brother-in-law, Mr. Bragge Bathurst, should succeed to the vacant office of Chancellor of the Duchy. Mr. Pitt declined to accede to this proposal; but appointed Sir C. Middleton, an experienced naval officer (now created Lord Barham), to the Admiralty. Hereupon Lord Sidmouth resigned; but upon the request of Mr. Pitt, and after full explanations and assurances, which he deemed satisfactory, he withdrew his resignation, and consented to remain.[1] Matters were thus patched up in April; but the further proceedings in Lord Melville's case brought on fresh disagreements, and finally dissolved the ill-cemented alliance. In a division on the question of Lord Melville's impeachment, near the end of June, some of Addington's followers, to whom Pitt had promised office, voted against the Government. Pitt said that their conduct must be *marked*, which language Addington regarded as a personal indignity, and a breach of the previous understanding that his friends should be at liberty to act as they thought fit on Lord Melville's case. He therefore tendered his resignation; and this time Pitt expressed no wish that it might be recalled. Such was Addington's version of this transaction.[2] Pitt's was somewhat different; namely, that he was prepared to fulfil his promise in a short time, but not at that moment, when the votes had been so recently given.[3] Be this as it may, Addington and his friend Lord Buckinghamshire now ceased to be members of the

[1] *Life of Lord Sidmouth*, *ibid.* pp. 356–364, 368; *Mem. of Fox*, vol. iv. p. 78.

[2] *Life of Lord Sidmouth*, *ibid.* pp. 367–375. [Compare Lord Stanhope's *Life of Pitt*, vol. iv. pp. 313–314.—Ed.]

[3] *Lord Malmesbury*, *ibid.* p. 338. According to Lord Malmesbury's account, Addington offended the King at his audience by awkwardly offering His Majesty the key of the cabinet boxes, and by forcing him to listen to an unseasonable explanation, which lasted an hour.

Cabinet: their places were filled by Lord Camden and Lord Harrowby, Lord Camden being succeeded by Lord Castlereagh in the Department of War and Colonies. On July 12, the session was brought to a close without any further ministerial change. 1805.

Although Pitt's Government survived the session, its weakness was apparent, and indeed admitted.[1] His political isolation, now increased by the humiliating reconciliation with Addington, and its speedy rupture, could not but fill his mind with anxiety, as the successes of Napoleon and the difficulties of the country multiplied. Being deprived even of Addington, he sought to obtain the King's permission to revive the negotiation with Fox and Lord Grenville. He appears to have made his first attempt in July, on the resignation of Addington, and to

[1] 'Pitt will certainly not go out yet, and I am not one of those who think it impossible that he should last some time longer' (Mr. Fox to Lord Holland, April 9, 1805. *Mem. of Fox*, vol. iv. p. 77). 'Pitt, though he may still have a bare majority, is too weak to carry on the Government as it is; at least we flatter ourselves so' (To Mr. O'Brien, July 7, 1805, *ibid.* p. 88). 'What is clearest of all is, that Pitt is very low, and does not seem to have any notion of what plan he can follow to raise himself' (To Lord Lauderdale, July 12, 1815, *ibid.* p. 99). 'I see no newspapers that speak of politics; but I think the tone of the paragraphs ought to be to treat with contempt the notion of Pitt's being able to carry on the Government as he is, or to gain any accession of strength; and Castlereagh's appointment [to the Department of War and Colonies] ought to be stated as complete proof of his weakness and impotence in either view' (To Mr. O'Brien, July 17, 1805, *ibid.* p. 102). 'I hear that to those who casually see him [Pitt], his appearance is just as it was in the House of Commons, that of extreme uneasiness, and almost misery. Most of his friends speak of the extreme desirableness of a junction, and some even of the absolute necessity of it' (To Mr. Grey, Aug. 28, 1805, *ibid.* p. 105). A letter from Mr. Windham to Lord Buckingham, of Aug. 3, also says that 'one of the persons holding office under Pitt, and pretty much in his confidence, has talked, within these few days, the same sort of language that has been held for some time; namely, that though they might maintain themselves, they could not go on with any confidence or comfort, and that a proposition of the most liberal sort would soon be made' (*Courts and Cabinets*, *ibid.* p. 437).

1805. have met with a refusal.[1] The arrangement just described was the consequence. Foiled in this endeavour, he meditated a second attempt upon the King at Weymouth; and a letter announcing this intention was written by Lord Camden, the new Lord President, to Lord Grenville.[2] Pitt followed the King to Weymouth in the month of September; again he sought, in a long interview, to overcome the King's objections to Mr. Fox, and again he failed.[3] The negotiation, desired by Mr. Pitt, and expected by Mr. Fox and Lord Grenville, never therefore took place, and Pitt resigned himself to the idea of meeting Parliament without any accession of administrative or parliamentary strength.[4]

[1] See Mr. Adair to Mr. Fox, July 7, 1805, *ibid.* vol. iv. p. 90; and Mr. Fox to Mr. Grey, July 9, *ibid.* p. 95. Lord Grenville to Marquis of Buckingham, June 25 and July 6. *Courts and Cabinets, ibid.* pp. 426, 427. There must be a misprint in the date of one of these letters: either Lord Grenville's letter should be July 8, or Mr. Fox's July 7.

[2] Dated July 10. *Courts and Cabinets, ibid.* p. 430. Mr. Grenville, writing from Worthing on July 24, to Lord Buckingham, says: 'I yesterday received a letter from town, of good authority, to state that "Pitt certainly does not consider the last arrangements as creating any difficulty in the way of what is so much wished for by the considerate men of all parties; and he certainly goes to Weymouth at the beginning of next month"' (*Courts and Cabinets, ibid.* p. 433). Pitt, in his letter to Lord Melville, of March 1804 (already quoted), speaks of the advantages which the King would derive, in an equal degree with the country, from the extension of parties, and the establishment of a Government uniting all the weight and talents of the day, and capable of commanding respect and confidence both at home and abroad.

[3] For the positive evidence of this fact, we are indebted to a memorandum of information from a gentleman then attached to the Court, who was at Weymouth when Mr. Pitt came, and who received an account of the interview first from Mr. Pitt, and afterwards from the King himself. The interview lasted three hours, and Mr. Pitt desisted from further pressure, lest he should disturb the King's mind. [Lord Stanhope (*Life of Pitt*, vol. iv. p. 334) refers to this note, 'ascribed to Sir George C. Lewis,' as an authority. This is confirmed by the passages in Mr. Rose's *Diary*. The King appears to have been perfectly impracticable.—Ed.]

[4] Fox's belief seems to have been that the King had consented to a nego-

It is, in our opinion, certain that a junction with Fox and Lord Grenville was at this moment sincerely, nay ardently, desired by Pitt, and that his disappointment at the King's refusal to admit Fox into the Cabinet, by which alone Lord Grenville's adhesion could be obtained, was great and genuine. His conduct, and the exigencies of his position, equally point to this conclusion. If Pitt seriously meditated such a junction of parties, it cannot be doubted that he had maturely considered the means by which it was to be effected, and that he was prepared with such an offer as it would be reasonable to make and honourable to accept. At the same time, it is difficult to perceive how this Coalition Government could have been arranged so as to satisfy the pretensions of the rival leaders. Mr. Pitt, in his letter to Lord Melville, of March 29, 1804—written a short time before the fall of Addington's Ministry—said, 'I do not see how, under any circumstances, I can creditably or usefully consent to take part in any Government without being at the head of it; and I should be very sorry that either Lord Moira, or, through him, the Prince, should suppose that there is any chance of my changing my opinion on this point.[1] On the other hand, Fox, in his letters written at the time when the offer was believed to be impending, declares that he will not belong to any Cabinet of which Pitt is the head, and that the existing Cabinet must be considered as annihilated, and the formation of a new ministry conceded, before he will negotiate; 1805.

tiation with himself and Lord Grenville, that Pitt went down to Weymouth to arrange with the King the terms of the offer, and that Pitt's subsequent silence was owing to his own reluctance to negotiate. See *Courts and Cabinets, ibid.* pp. 432, 438. *Mem. of Fox,* vol. iv. pp. 109, 111, 115. Lord Grenville became aware, early in October, that, as the result of Pitt's visit, there would be no offer (*Courts and Cabinets, ibid.* pp. 439, 443, 444). In the letter of Oct. 22, he says:—'Now that all hope of united Government must finally be relinquished.' See also Mr. Grenville's letter, *ibid.* p. 441.

[1] Lord Mahon's *Secret Correspondence*, p. 12.

1805. even if Pitt is willing to concede these terms, he is desirous rather of finding obstacles to an agreement than smoothing the way to a compromise.[1]

The following remarks of Lord Grenville, in a letter to Lord Buckingham, of this date, upon our war policy, and the existing state of our Continental alliances, will be read with interest:—

Let me only say to you once more, that I earnestly hope we shall keep clear of all pledges, expressed or implied, as to our opinions and conduct respecting the new state of things which has arisen on the Continent. There are, I fear, some, at least of the old Opposition, who hold opinions on that point utterly irreconcilable with our principles and practice. I think you and I long since agreed that, whether we got well or ill into the war, or rather, that because we got so ill into it, there was no possible way of getting tolerably well out of it, but by connecting our peace with that of the Continent. There were two ways of doing this, and they never could be entirely disconnected; these were, joint negotiation and joint war. To joint negotiation, Fox pledged himself, last year, in a manner perfectly satisfactory to me, and, as I think, very advantageous to himself. But the thing has now taken the shape of joint war, the propriety of which depends on an infinite variety of circumstances, of all which I am hitherto in ignorance. But on a general view of the subject, I must own I never had much hope that Bonaparte would enter into a serious negotiation for tying up his own hands from future acquisition anywhere, until the experiment of war shall have convinced him that he has no choice on the subject. I think it, therefore, much more probable of the two, that the alternative of war was that to which we (I mean all the Allies) were necessarily driven, and that in this determination it is highly impor-

[1] *Mem. of Fox*, vol. iv. pp. 96, 98, 101, 110, 114. Mr. Grenville says, in a letter to Lord Buckingham of Nov. 7, 'Strange reports are spread with the greatest confidence, and universally believed, that a fair proposal has been made to Fox and us, and that we have with him refused to hear of anything unless Pitt first went out of office. What desperate lies they are driven to!' (*Courts and Cabinets*, p. 449).

tant to the greatest interests that this country ever had at stake, to show that we are nearly unanimous. Then comes the consideration of the particular stipulations and arrangements for that purpose—a consideration of great moment most certainly, and on which it would be folly to attempt to reason in the total ignorance both of the facts themselves, and of all the circumstances connected with them. But all the leanings of my mind are favourable to measures of exertion and vigour in a case where I have attributed all our present difficulties to the want of those qualities on former occasions.[1] 1805.

The attempts of Pitt during this year to organise and support a European confederacy against Bonaparte, had resulted in the capitulation of Ulm on October 17th, and the battle of Austerlitz on December 2nd. The battle of Trafalgar had, indeed, intervened, and had in some measure counteracted the land victories by extinguishing the French maritime power.[2] The military prospects of the country were, however, gloomy, and could not fail to depress even the sanguine mind of Pitt, who, with a feebly organised Government, and with impaired bodily powers, was preparing to meet Parliament. That event, however, was destined never to occur. Pitt's health appears to have been in a failing state for some time past, though his age —he was now in his forty-eighth year—forbad the idea that his malady threatened his life. He went to Bath early in December, and returned to his house on Putney Heath about the 10th of January, 1806.[3] Even on the road his condition was so emaciated that Sir Walter Farquhar, his physician, pronounced complete rest and abstinence from business to be necessary to his recovery, and considered his life in danger. Upon his arrival at

[1] Oct. 3, 1805. *Courts and Cabinets, ibid.* p. 441.

[2] [October 21.—Ed.]

[3] [He was three days on the road (Lord Stanhope's *Life of Pitt*, vol. iv. p. 369).—Ed.]

1806. Putney his symptoms of debility were aggravated, and are stated to have assumed the character of typhus fever. On the 23rd of the month he died. Even at the last the fatal termination of his malady had been so little anticipated, that his usual official dinner at the meeting of Parliament took place on the 20th, at his house in Downing Street.[1] This premature death of a man who had, since 1782, occupied so prominent a position in the eyes of England, and of all Europe, and who now filled the office of Prime Minister, could not fail to make a deep impression on the public mind. At a meeting of Opposition leaders which was held when he was at the point of death, it was agreed to suspend for the moment all political hostilities. The generous mind of Fox was touched with feelings of sadness, not of joy, at the approaching end of his great rival; he could not endure the idea of going down to debate in the House of Commons when Pitt was in extremities. 'Mentem mortalia tangunt,' he said.[2]

An undue importance is often attached to the incoherent ramblings of eminent men upon their deathbeds. It seems certain that Pitt died with little warning of his danger, and that his mind was in a lethargic state, with occasional delirium, for some time before his death. The story of his patriotic exclamation, which has been denied, is however, in a certain sense, well attested. Lord Malmesbury states that Lady Malmesbury saw Pitt's physician,

[1] *Lord Malmesbury, ibid.* p. 345. Lord Grenville, writing from London, on January 13, says: 'There is much speculation here on the state of Pitt's health, which is said, however, to be mending, but he is still so weak as to leave hardly any prospect of his attending at the opening of the Session' (*Courts and Cabinets*, vol. iv. p. 12). Lord Wellesley, in his letter on Pitt's death and character, states that he communicated the fact of Pitt's danger to Lord Grenville. [At the official dinner Lord Castlereagh read the King's speech, in the absence of Pitt (Lord Stanhope's *Life of Pitt*, vol. iv. p. 388).—Ed.]

[2] *Life of Horner*, vol. i. p. 328.

Sir Walter Farquhar, three days after his death, and received from him an account of his last hours; and that almost the last words he spoke intelligibly were these, to himself, and more than once repeated—'Oh, what times! oh, my country!'[1] 1806.

The latter part of Pitt's life had been clouded by disappointments and mortifications. The King's objection to Fox, and the consequent refusal of the chief politicians to join his Ministry; his compulsory recourse to Addington's assistance, and the speedy defection of his ignominious ally; his failure in saving Lord Melville from forced resignation and impeachment;[2] and the defeat of his continental policy by the surrender of Ulm and the battle of Austerlitz;[3] must have come as successive blows to his

[1] *Diary, ibid.* p. 346. Wilberforce says, in a letter written at the time, 'He spoke very little for some days before he died, and was extremely weakened and reduced on the Wednesday morning, when he was first talked to as a dying man. He expired early on Thursday morning' (*Life*, vol. iii. p. 252). [The fact that Pitt's last words were, 'Oh, my country! how I leave my country!' seems now to be clearly established by the paper prepared by Mr. James H. Hamilton, and published in Lord Stanhope's *Life*, vol. iv. pp. 378–382, as corrected by his Lordship in a subsequent letter to 'The Times,' and in his second edition. The words thus become more intelligible and more consonant with Pitt's character and feelings.—Ed.]

[2] Lord Fitzharris, Lord Malmesbury's eldest son, who was a Lord of the Treasury at the time, gives the following account of Pitt's feelings with respect to the vote against Lord Melville: 'I have ever thought that an aiding cause of Pitt's death, certainly one that tended to shorten his existence, was the result of the proceedings against his old friend and colleague, Lord Melville. I sat wedged close to Pitt himself the night when we were 216 to 216, and the Speaker, Abbot (after looking as white as a sheet, and pausing for ten minutes), gave the casting vote against us, Pitt immediately put on the little cocked hat that he was in the habit of wearing when dressed for the evening, and jammed it deeply over his forehead, and I distinctly saw the tears trickling down his cheeks' (*Lord Malmesbury, ibid.* p. 347).

[3] Lord Malmesbury communicated to Pitt the authentic account of the capitulation of Ulm, and observed the effect which it produced upon him (*Diary, ibid.* p. 340). He expresses an opinion that Pitt never recovered from the news of Austerlitz, which was communicated to him at Bath by Lord Castlereagh (*ibid.* p. 344). Lord Holland says: 'Mr. Pitt's vexation

1806. spirit. This period was one of unusual care, anxiety, and depression; but his mind unquestionably possessed sufficient strength to bear the weight, if his body had not been undermined by physical causes.[1]

Shortly after Mr. Pitt's death, a motion was made in the House of Commons for a grant of 40,000*l.* to pay his debts. The motion was carried without opposition, and the money was afterwards paid to his executors, Lord Chatham and the Bishop of Lincoln. Mr. Wilberforce tried to induce Pitt's private friends to contribute this sum, liberally offering to bear his share, but he failed in the attempt. Mr.

at having sacrificed what appeared the last hope of Europe, coming upon his yet deeper mortification and grief at the misfortunes of his friend Lord Melville, no doubt hastened his death, though his constitution was so much shattered, that his life could not, under any circumstances, have been much prolonged (*Mem. of the Whig Party*, vol. i. p. 207). The account of Pitt's last illness in the *Ann. Reg.* vol. xlviii. p. 11, is stated by Lord Holland to be singularly precise, and to have been derived from Dr. Bayley, who was called in to attend him. Wilberforce says in his *Diary*: 'Pitt killed by the enemy as much as Nelson' (vol. iii. p. 245). Some details as to Pitt's last illness, and speculations as to the consequences of his death, may be seen in a letter of Mr. Horner, of Jan. 21 (*Life*, vol. i. p. 325). A song written by Walter Scott for the anniversary meeting of the Pitt Club of Scotland, in 1814, commences with the following stanza:—

> Oh, dread was the time and more dreadful the omen,
> When the brave on Marengo lay slaughter'd in vain,
> And beholding broad Europe bowed down by her foemen,
> Pitt closed in his anguish the map of her reign.
> Not the fate of broad Europe could bend his brave spirit
> To take for his country the safety of shame;
> Oh then in her triumph remember his merit,
> And hallow the goblet that flows to his name.

Marengo was the first step in Bonaparte's career of independent aggression; and in June 1800, the date of the battle of Marengo, broad Europe was not 'bowed down by her foemen.' Moreover, the Peace of Amiens, in which Pitt heartily concurred, was made in the following year; and this peace was generally considered (if Sheridan's dictum was true) to involve 'the safety of shame.' The allusion seems more appropriate to Austerlitz than to Marengo.

[1] [Lord Stanhope concurs in this view, and refers to this passage as 'the opinion of an accomplished critic, whom I have more than once already cited' (*Life of Pitt*, vol. iv. p. 364).—Ed.]

Pitt's friends had raised 12,000*l.* in the autumn of 1801, shortly after his resignation, in order to relieve him from embarrassment; and one of the subscribers to this sum wished it to be included in the grant; but to this proposal Mr. Wilberforce strongly objected, and it was in consequence abandoned.[1] From 1784 to 1801, Mr. Pitt had held the offices of First Lord of the Treasury and Chancellor of the Exchequer, the joint salary of which was then about 7,500*l.* a year, together with an official residence in Downing Street. Besides this, he had since 1792 held the sinecure office of Warden of the Cinque Ports, with a salary of 3,000*l.* a year, to which the use of Walmer Castle was attached. Wilberforce says, that he lived at the rate of 5,000*l.* or 6,000*l.* a year. The celebrated inscription under Pitt's monument in Guildhall, by Mr. Canning, records in his honour that, 'Dispensing for near twenty years the favours of the Crown, he lived without ostentation, and he died poor.' But if, being unmarried, and having no expensive tastes or pursuits, he was at the same time in the receipt of an ample income, it would have been rather natural that he should have died rich, than that he should have died poor. We can only explain the contrary result on the supposition that, being entirely indifferent about money, and engrossed with public affairs, he neglected to attend to his own expenditure, and was plundered by his domestics.[2]

1806.

At the time of Pitt's death there was a general disposition among the leaders of all political parties, on account of the critical state of our relations with the Continent, to sink minor differences in a general union, and to form a Coalition Government resting on a wide and comprehensive basis. This idea, promulgated and enforced by Lord

[1] *Life of Wilberforce*, vol. iii. pp. 244–54.

[2] [The first mortgage on Holwood was 4,000*l.* In 1797 he found it necessary to raise a second mortgage of 7,000*l.* See Lord Stanhope, *Life of Pitt*, vol. iii. pp. 5, 341.—Ed.]

1806. Grenville, was adopted by Pitt, and would have been carried into effect by him in 1804, if his attempt had not been frustrated by the King's refusal to admit Fox into the Cabinet. The result of this failure was, that even Pitt was only able to form a weak and struggling administration; and if he had lived, the King would doubtless have been compelled by Parliamentary pressure to allow his minister to seek strength in the quarters where alone it could be obtained. We propose, in another article, to trace the consequences of this state of parties, and to show how the project of a Coalition Government, including the ablest men of different political connections, was realised by Mr. Pitt's survivors.

SUPPLEMENT TO THE ARTICLES ON THE ADMINISTRATIONS OF ADDINGTON AND PITT.

By the kindness of the Very Reverend the Dean of St. Paul's, I am allowed to print the interesting letter which follows. It was addressed to Sir George C. Lewis, in 1858, and presents to the reader another view of the relations of Pitt and Addington. The second letter is one written by Sir George Lewis himself to the late Lord Lansdowne, and is, in fact, a commentary on what may be called Dean Milman's Defence of Addington. Copies of both were found among the author's papers, and they are here given to the reader as a fit and proper supplement to the articles themselves.—Ed.

Deanery, St. Paul's, *Jan.* 27, 1858.

My dear Sir George Lewis,—Before I begin my observations on your Article in the 'Edinburgh Review,' I am bound to explain my right and title to presume to do so. Lord Sidmouth and his family always kept up some-connection with the neighbourhood of Reading, where I lived many years, and I thus formed an intimate acquaintance with them. This intimacy was greatly increased by his marriage with the second Lady Sidmouth, Lord Stowell's daughter, a very near neighbour and great friend of mine. During Lord Stowell's long and slow decay, Lord Sidmouth and his wife were constantly at Early Court (close to Reading), and I saw them day after day. After that I was a very frequent visitor at Richmond Park. Lord Sidmouth delighted in talking over old days, and did so with the utmost freedom and without reserve. I was of course much interested in listening to him. During this familiar intercourse, I heard repeatedly the same anecdotes, which were told, as is the wont of elderly men, again and again, with but little variation, and I had no scruple in *pumping* where the stream flowed so willingly and copiously. I think, indeed, that there was hardly a sentence of his conversation, in Pellew's 'Life' of him, which was new to me. It is true that I have only my memory to trust to. I repeatedly urged Lord Sidmouth's daughter to *Boswellise* her father, as his stories seemed to me even more curious and instructive than the papers which he also communicated to me. I myself was too indolent and too scrupulous to do so. I am, therefore, in some difficulty as to the precise dates of some of the facts.

Lord Sidmouth has often said, that what finally overcame his reluctance to accept the Government, was the result of an interview with the King, at which Mr. Pitt and himself alone were present. On Mr. Pitt's persisting in his resignation, the King turned to Addington—'Now, Mr. Addington, if you refuse to stand by me, to whom can I turn?' This appeal was irresistible; from that time, whatever misgivings he might have of his own power and capacities, he thought himself bound to accept the office; and certainly supposed from Pitt's manner and words that he had full right to reckon on his cordial support.

As to Mr. Pitt's reason for resignation, I cannot but think that more is attributed to his difference on the Catholic question than really should be. This was the overt act, as regards the King; this was Pitt's pretext to the King, perhaps to himself. Yet I am persuaded that the common version of the affair which was current, and which I perpetually heard in my boyhood, was to a great extent the true one. It was then almost always said that Pitt put Addington into office to make the peace, which he could not or was unwilling to make himself. Of the necessity of peace, Pitt was firmly convinced. His mind, as Lord Sidmouth has often told me, was depressed almost to despondency by the failure of our Continental Allies, and by the French successes. He had not the indomitable resolution and inflexible firmness of Lord Grenville. He might possibly suppose that 'ce monstre Pitt, l'ennemi du genre humain,' as he was called in Paris, would negotiate with less advantage, and might obtain less favourable terms from the Republic, or from Bonaparte, then thought the child of the Republic. At all events, he might (I have a strong opinion he did) wish to avoid the difficulty and the responsibility of a peace, which nevertheless, though a hazardous experiment, he thought must be made. At all events, he could hardly hope to obtain terms which would satisfy the unyielding Grenville, and must hence probably have come to a collision in his own Cabinet. This view, I think, accounts for his wavering—for his wavering, without consulting his colleagues. He deemed peace inevitable; but he was not the man to make it. I confess that I do not suppose, from his own language, that Addington had on his part much belief, assuredly no confidence, in the stability of the peace. He was not a man to form an opinion of Bonaparte so different from that which prevailed throughout England. He, too, thought the peace precarious, but absolutely necessary. Both Pitt and he were in the utmost alarm about the financial difficulties: neither had a notion of the vast resources of the country. I wish that I could recollect with accuracy the precise date of, and the exact numbers, in a speech of Pitt's, which Sidmouth constantly repeated. It was during the war. 'I think,' said he, 'that I see my way to another loan of (I believe) twenty millions, and of adding the interest thereon to the budget of the year.' Beyond that, he intimated that our credit could not go. He lived himself (Pitt) to double the national debt of that time, and to raise a revenue of an amount in proportion.

All this, that Pitt put in Addington to make peace, that as yet there was no suspicion in Addington of the least estrangement, and that they understood each other, agrees perfectly with what you state so justly and accurately, that the peace was hardly made when Addington made overtures to Pitt to return to office.

But Addington having made the peace, being popular to a high degree in the country (more of this hereafter), strong in the King's favour, could hardly, with the self-respect which he ought to have felt, which I know from his conversation he did feel, permit himself to be treated as a mere *locum tenens*, a *pis aller*, to be put into the Government at Pitt's will, to undertake its responsibilities, and then to vacate it, or to sink to a humbler and subordinate position according to Pitt's convenience. This he could not do without degradation—without in a certain sense proclaiming himself to be unworthy of the position which he actually filled, of the royal favour, and of the public confidence which he undoubtedly enjoyed. No man could expose himself voluntarily, and as yet under no pressure of adverse circumstances, to such humiliation. Addington's fresh overtures to Pitt about his return to office were received in a way, as you justly say, considered by Addington 'encouraging.' Canning's annoyance at the visit, and apparently friendly intercourse between Addington and Pitt, is a further proof that others as well as Addington supposed that there was not the slightest breach in their amicable relations. Addington, perhaps, ought to have augured no good from Pitt's visit to Lord Grenville, who, he well knew, held him in utter contempt—who had gone at once, even on the peace, into stern, uncompromising opposition. He knew, too, that Canning, besides pelting him day after day, unchecked, it might almost seem encouraged, by Pitt, with his merciless squibs, was incessantly working, as I think I have heard Sidmouth say, in an underhand way in alienating Pitt from his old friend Notwithstanding all this, Addington had, a blind it may be, but surely no ungenerous confidence in the unaltered friendship of Pitt; and in this confidence, when the war began to threaten, he renewed those overtures, which at least on the former occasion had not been rejected; and supposing himself on such terms with Pitt, it does not appear to me so surprising that, without obtaining the formal consent and authority of the King, he should initiate such negotiations (I may be ignorant of the strict etiquette in such affairs) in order to ascertain on what terms Pitt would join him—how far they could amicably combine to make a strong Government. No one knew better than Addington the King's personal dislike to Pitt, his dislike of his stately and dictatorial manner, a dislike greatly exasperated by Pitt's conduct and manner on his resignation of office. However the King, on Addington's representation of the necessity of the case, might submit to that necessity, Addington might think it prudent, that it might save even the King himself some embarrassment, if he could propose such coalition in full confidence that it could be arranged without difficulty. If he could say that Pitt would join him on terms not dishonourable to himself and palpably advantageous to the nation, the King himself could hardly refuse, and perhaps would easily have pardoned Addington for sparing him the difficulties and perhaps humiliation of the previous negotiation. At all events, up to this time Addington's feeling of reverence for Pitt was still at its height, a feeling which was so lasting that even the sense of what he thought hard and unkind usage on the part of Pitt never extinguished it, and which led him at the last (I shall revert to this) to destroy every paper which could reflect on the conduct of Pitt.

The terms demanded by Pitt in his interview with Addington, you justly observe, were a virtual dissolution of the Cabinet, in fact, an admission by Addington of his own incapacity, according to his view an abandonment of the King and of the great party in the country who had so far supported him with the utmost fidelity. It is upon this point, 'that the course of events had destroyed all their prominent claims to popular support,' that I am inclined to join issue with you. I wish to be clearly understood. I think the country was much more with him than you suppose; whether the country was right, is another question. No one in the present day will differ much from you in your estimate of the *mediocrity* of Addington and his Government as to abilities and intellect. Sincere as was my regard and esteem for him, and however warm my gratitude for his kindness, hospitality, and friendship (I never in my life met with a more honourable, upright, generous man, one whose judgment I would sooner have abided by in any question of honour or principle), I must acknowledge that he never seemed to me, according to the phrase, up to the very high position which he had attained. I am bound to say so much, and wish to say no more. But however the higher and more intellectual class, perhaps London, might estimate him, Addington had a hold on the country of which you do not seem to me to be aware. The country gentlemen were for him almost to a man, and they had then a weight and influence which are now almost forgotten. They disliked the haughty and unbending Pitt and his contemptuous condescension; they hated Canning, who quizzed, satirised, and laughed at them; they held Fox for an irreclaimable Jacobin. The mediocrity of Addington suited their mediocrity. What Lord Holland no doubt justly described as his empty and pompous manner exposed him to the ridicule of such keen and clever observers as Lord Holland himself and the choice few; but in his ordinary and social intercourse with the country gentlemen, if any of them had the perception of it, this pompousness entirely or almost entirely vanished. He was with them easy, frank, jovial, loved Port wine as well as the most resolute fox-hunter. To the end he described himself as the sole survivor of the 'Port wine faction.' In the towns the No Popery cry was dominant, had never sunk to rest, and Addington and his friends were the champions of Protestantism. The volunteer system, of which he was very proud, had spread with great excitement throughout the country, was violently popular with all orders, and no doubt some part of its popularity was reflected back on the advisers and organisers of the plan. Lord Sidmouth has often boasted to me of this almost unanimous support of the country gentlemen. That he entertained serious thoughts of dissolving Parliament, that he believed he would have obtained an irresistible majority on that dissolution, I have no doubt whatever; he has told me so over and over again. What would have been the immediate pretext I know not; in fact, it would have been an appeal to the country on the stability of his Government. He was only deterred by the state of the King's health. He has more than once put to me the plain question, 'Could I, Milman, act otherwise? Could I, as a man of honour, as a friend of my country, as responsible head of affairs, advise the King, in his *precarious* state, when the next day he might be raving mad, to exercise the highest prerogative of the Crown (his own words) by the dissolution of Parliament?' I cannot doubt that, unless he misrepresented his own courage, which was great when he thought he was right, he would have done so, but for that insuperable objection. He may possibly in much of this have miscalculated his strength as his friends did in the city, where a motion for approval of his conduct in taking the Government was proposed and ignominiously defeated; but that was after he had abandoned the Government.

The country, as I have said, was more than is generally supposed in favour of Addington's Ministry, and of Addington himself: the King was with him, constantly urging him to be 'true to himself;' the majority of the House was with him. Under such circumstances I cannot but think that the terms which you apply to his conduct—'mean, low-minded, and selfish,'—harsh, and on your own statement undeserved. I see nothing *shabby*, nothing but what in his position was unavoidable. He was Premier, not of his own seeking; the Premiership had been forced upon him by Pitt and the King; he was so far a popular Premier. He had, as I have said, still a majority in the House; he had a great and powerful following; not a mere knot of personal friends, but a large party, respectable from weight, position, property. The unanswerable proof of this is, that after his fall no Government could go on without him. Pitt was obliged to submit to the humiliation—after he had ejected him, insulted him, proscribed him (see the letter which you have quoted to Lord Melville), of courting his support, of admitting him and some of his friends into the Cabinet. Even Fox himself was obliged to court in the same manner, and strengthen his Government with the 'vile fellow;' and even Lord Grenville, who always spoke of and treated him with contempt, to sit with him in the same Cabinet, and for the sake of his support, submit to the unconstitutional measure, the unpopular measure, of introducing the Chief Justice Ellenborough into the Cabinet. Was he not bound then, in justice to the King, in justice to himself, in justice to his colleagues in the Cabinet, in justice to his friends in the House and in the country, to attempt to stand alone? He did attempt, and, as far as I can judge, not in a 'shabby,' but bold and manly way. He failed, as it was inevitable that he should fail, as he himself felt that he must fail, with such an array against him—Pitt, Fox, Lord Grenville, Windham, Sheridan, Canning; with but few supporters as debaters in the Commons of weight and power; with what, I suspect, was but the dubious aid of Eldon and some others in the Lords; and what I admit in the fullest manner, his own inferiority, I believe his conscious inferiority, in debate. Having made the attempt, finding his majority diminishing, as a constitutional minister ought to do and must do, he resigned. He resigned without conditions, without after-thought of his own interests; he left the field clear and open for Mr. Pitt.

I am even more at a loss to discover his 'want of generosity' to Mr. Pitt. At every juncture he had made advances towards him—sincere, honest advances, without any distinct stipulations on his part; he had risked making those advances in an irregular and unusual manner without the King's previous sanction. When Pitt insisted on conditions which I think you yourself consider inadmissible, which were the virtual proscription of almost all his colleagues in the Cabinet, if not of himself, when he (Addington) urged by letter the reconsideration of those conditions, Pitt did not vouchsafe an answer. After Pitt had been obliged to form his Government, having abandoned his lofty pretensions and haughty dictation, and was reduced to seek Addington's support, the placable Addington (and here perhaps was the weakness of his character) consented at once to join him; afterwards to be compelled again by Pitt's ungovernable resentment on a subject (hereafter to be discussed) to recede from the Government. But notwithstanding all this, such was the gratitude, the affection, I may almost say the idolatry, of Lord Sidmouth for Pitt (they had been friends from boyhood), that at a late period of his life (by an excess of generosity I am persuaded damaging to his own memory) he selected and deliberately destroyed every paper and document relating to all these transactions unfavourable to Mr. Pitt. That he did so I have his own repeated assertion, that of his daughter Miss Addington, I think of Lady Sidmouth, and, if my recollection be accurate, of one or two friends who had partially seen them. To me (whether they were then actually destroyed, I am doubtful), while he freely showed other papers, some of them very curious and interesting, he never would produce one of these relating to Pitt. It was only from the tone of his conversation that I could discover the yet rankling wound inflicted by his friend.

I am afraid that I cannot quite acquit Mr. Pitt of 'cherishing personal resentments.' He never forgave Addington's conduct in the affair of Lord Melville. It is true that Dundas had been his dear, his most useful, and faithful friend. But if Lord Sidmouth's account of that affair be true (I have heard it often, and have no doubt of its truth), he was by no means to blame. The Commission of Naval Inquiry originated in Lord St. Vincent, a high authority in such matters. It was conceived, certainly assented to, by Addington in no spirit of hostility to Dundas. In the course of their investigations they *stumbled* upon the transaction which implicated Lord Melville, and on which the charges against him were founded. Something of this must have transpired, some foreknowledge or suspicion must have forced its way to Pitt to account for that curious passage, quoted by you from the letter published by Lord Stanhope, in which Pitt proscribed *Addington and Lord St. Vincent*, writing to Lord Melville. The enemies of Dundas, not a few, seized on the charge: the public accusation, the debate, and the impeachment followed. Addington himself believed the affair at least questionable; many of his friends were convinced of the guilt of Dundas, more that it was a subject for inquiry. Pitt insisted on *marking* the friends of Addington who voted for inquiry. Addington would indeed have been base if he had abandoned those friends, especially thinking as he did, to Pitt's unmitigated wrath, or accepted the paltry compromise offered by Pitt of *hereafter* condescending to admit them to pardon. This was the cause of the final rupture between them—a rupture of which I have heard Lord Sidmouth speak more than once with strong emotion, not so much blaming Pitt as deploring the unfortunate misunderstanding.

At the hazard of lengthening this statement, already too long, I wish briefly to advert to one other incidental point. I am not quite sure that Brougham is altogether wrong in his view of Eldon's conduct, though 'intrigue' is a hard word. The fact I apprehend to be, that the sagacious Eldon felt how near the House was to its fall. As he intended to remain Chancellor, he did not care to prop it up, and did not wish to do anything which might keep Addington in, possibly keep Pitt out. I think that I have detected soreness about Eldon's conduct and relation to him at this period; though in later times they were drawn much more closely together, and became nearly connected by Lord Sidmouth's marriage with Eldon's niece. Eldon felt too, that by the exclusion of Addington he became the one person in the new Cabinet in whom the King had perfect confidence. When *my own* Chancellor of the Exchequer was withdrawn, *my* Chancellor stood alone and supreme in royal favour.

I have written, my dear Lewis, at much greater length than I intended; at much greater length than I am justified at such a time to one with such important avocations. But if Chancellors of the Exchequer will find time (I marvel how) to write as men of letters, they must suffer the consequences, and endure the visitation of epistles concerning past affairs of state, of such unconscionable prolixity as the present. But as I had ventured, though at a private dinner-table, to make some animadversions on an article written, as it appears, by a friend—an article I must take the opportunity of saying, in my opinion, generally excellent, calm, candid, conscientious, of great research, and dispassionate judgment—I was bound to justify myself to you; and yourself expressed at the Museum a desire that I would state my objections in writing. I will only add further my perfect conviction, that as my friendship for Lord Sidmouth has not blinded me to his defects—to his confessed inferiority to many of the great statesmen of his day, so I think that I have not done more than justice to his better qualities, his high principle of duty and honour, generosity, kindliness of feeling, and perfect integrity,

Believe me, &c.

(Signed) H. H. MILMAN.

KNIGHTSBRIDGE, *Feb.* 4, 1858.

MY DEAR LORD LANSDOWNE,—I take the liberty of sending you the copy of a letter written to me by Milman, which, whenever you may have time to read it, would not, I think, fail to interest you. It contains the comments on my article on Addington's Ministry in the last number of the 'Edinburgh,' which his conversations with Addington on the events of his ministerial life suggested.

It is possible that I used rather too strong epithets in characterising Addington's conduct. What I meant to say was, not that he did anything dishonest, or even dishonourable, but that his conduct was the opposite of *high-minded.*

He would neither quarrel with Pitt for his fast and loose proceedings, and set him at defiance, nor resign and make way for him; but he tried to soothe him, and keep him in good humour; he bore his *superba fastidia* patiently, and only endeavoured to extract as much support out of him as he could.

He knew that the King would not bear Fox, but he offered office to Mr. Grey; he took Tierney into his Government; he made offers to Erskine, and he gave a sop to Sheridan; he was deficient in independence and self-reliance, and he sought to maintain himself by the King's favour, and by deprecating the hostility of strong opponents. This conduct may be harshly characterised by the epithets 'mean, selfish, and low-minded,' but it seems to me to come very near it.

It is also to be remembered that Addington encouraged or allowed his pamphleteers and writers in the press to attack Pitt with great bitterness at particular moments.

With respect to Addington's hold upon the country, and his patriotic abstinence from a dissolution in 1804 on account of the precarious state of the King's mind, I confess I do not quite see its bearing upon the facts. I observe that Lord Grey makes a similar statement in his recently published work on Reform. Addington did not resign because the country and the House differed in opinion. He was never in a minority, though his majority diminished. He resigned because Pitt openly joined the Opposition against him, and he did not choose to face a hostile combination of all the Parliamentary leaders and speakers. A dissolution would have been no remedy for this state of things, for it was the general opinion of the country that Addington, though an honest, well-meaning and respectable man, had not sufficient ability for carrying on the war with so powerful an opposition in Parliament.

Lord Harrowby told me that his father's view of Pitt's conduct at this period was, that he had given Addington an honest support, but had been forced back into office by public opinion. This is the Pittite view—but I cannot think that Addington would have been able to maintain himself in power, if with his actual colleagues he had appealed to the country against Pitt, Fox, Lord Grenville, Windham, Sheridan, and the other prominent men who were then in active opposition, and whom, in order to make this policy successful, it would have been necessary for him to set at defiance.

With respect to the real motive of Pitt's resignation in 1801, it is difficult to penetrate his heart and discover all he really felt. But it is, I think, proved by overwhelming evidence that the only ground which he alleged to the King, to his colleagues, and to his intimate friends was the Catholic question. If his real wish was to let in a minister to make peace with France, why was he so ready to return a month afterwards? I cannot help thinking that the point of honour about the assurance given to the Irish Catholics, and the pressure of Lord Cornwallis and Lord Castlereagh, not altogether unmixed with reproaches, weighed with him. His conduct in 1801 is strange upon any hypothesis; but I have a strong impression that, but for the King's scruple about the Coronation oath, he would have remained minister, and perhaps have quarrelled with Lord Grenville about negotiation with the First Consul.

Believe me, &c. &c.

(Signed) G. C. Lewis.

V.

THE GRENVILLE, PORTLAND, AND PERCEVAL ADMINISTRATIONS.[1]

In a former article we followed the history of the Ministerial changes which occurred in this country between the resignation of Mr. Pitt in 1801, and his death in January 1806; and we showed how, at the renewal of the war with Bonaparte after the Peace of Amiens, there was a general wish among the leading statesmen for the formation of a comprehensive Administration, independent of party connections; which wish was frustrated by the King's refusal to admit Mr. Fox into the Cabinet. As the exclusion of Mr. Fox from the counsels of the King involved the refusal of Lord Grenville and his friends to join the new Government, the second Administration of Mr. Pitt never acquired the strength which his first Administration maintained throughout its long existence, and at his death it lost not only its principal, but almost its sole element of vitality. 1806

The King, indeed, made an attempt to infuse a posthumous life into Pitt's Ministry after the death of its founder and chief. The first step which he took upon this event was to authorise the Home Secretary, Lord Hawkesbury, to form a new Administration. Lord Hawkesbury requested a short time for consideration, and then declined the task. But though he did not now feel himself equal

[1] *Review of Memoirs of the Court of England during the Regency*, 1811–1820. From original family documents. By the Duke of Buckingham and Chandos, K.G. 2 vols. 8vo. 1856.

1806. to the enterprise of succeeding Mr. Pitt in the more arduous and honourable part of his functions—though he could not claim the inheritance of Elijah's mantle—he secured for himself, during this brief interval, the lucrative sinecure of Warden of the Cinque Ports, which Mr. Pitt's death had rendered vacant. A statement has been preserved by Mr. Horner that Pitt's remaining colleagues endeavoured to induce Lord Wellesley, who had recently returned from India, to assume the office of Prime Minister at the head of the existing Cabinet, but that the offer was instantly refused.[1] Lord Wellesley was at this time under the threat of impeachment for his acquisitions of territory in India, and his acceptance of a high Ministerial office would probably have been the signal for a repetition of Hastings' trial. Whatever overtures may have been made to Lord Wellesley, it is certain that they were not backed by any royal authority.

The King was by this time too well aware of Lord Sidmouth's hopeless incapacity to entertain any idea of falling back upon his assistance; and his next step, taken by the advice of his late Ministers,[2] was to send for Lord Grenville, to whom the royal message was conveyed on the 26th of January, three days after Pitt's death. Lord Grenville repeated to the King his previous opinion as to the advantages of a comprehensive Administration, not founded on a principle of exclusion. In answer to the

[1] *Life of Horner*, vol. i. p. 332. In a letter to Mr. Wilberforce, dated January 24, 1806, the day after Pitt's death, Lord Wellesley states that 'he knows nothing of public arrangements, and all the reports in the newspapers respecting himself are utterly groundless.' He adds: 'Having no personal object of pursuit, I shall not easily be deluded from the solemn conviction of my mind, that our recent loss cannot be repaired, nor our imminent perils be averted, otherwise than by an union of the approved talents and highest characters of the nation' (Pearce's *Memoirs of Lord Wellesley*, vol. ii. p. 389).

[2] This fact is stated by Lord Sidmouth (*Life*, vol. ii. p. 414).

King's inquiry as to the persons whom he proposed to include, Lord Grenville stated at once that the person whom he should consult was Mr. Fox. 'I thought so, and meant it so,' was the King's reply.[1] The result of this interview must be considered as a conclusive proof that Pitt might have obtained the same concession from the King, if he had resisted the exclusion of Mr. Fox in 1804; and that, however strong were the King's objections to particular men or measures, he would, when his position became untenable, yield to constitutional pressure.[2] 1806.

On this occasion an entirely new Administration was formed, and it was composed in the following manner:—Lord Grenville was First Lord of the Treasury, with Lord Henry Petty (afterwards Marquis of Lansdowne), who had established an early reputation as a statesman and orator,[3] as Chancellor of the Exchequer. Mr. Fox was Secretary of State for the Foreign Department, and leader of the House of Commons; Lord Spencer and Mr. Windham held the Seals of the other two Secretaries; and the late Lord Grey, as Lord Howick, was First Lord of the Admiralty. The Great Seal was first offered to Lord Ellenborough, with the view of appointing Mr. Erskine his successor as Chief Justice, but was declined. It was then proposed to Sir James Mansfield, Chief Justice of the Common Pleas; but this great legal prize was again refused, and Erskine

[1] The account of this conversation given in Mr. Horner's *Journal* (*Life, ibid.* p. 331) agrees with that in the *Annual Register*, written by Mr. Allen.

[2] In a letter to the Marquis of Buckingham, of March 16, 1809, Lord Grenville says, in reference to the affair of the Duke of York and Mrs. Clarke: 'The King's mind is, I believe, more difficult to satisfy. He holds out, as he has always done, just as long as he thinks his perseverance is likely to be of any use in carrying his point; and when he sees there is no longer any hope of that, he will give way as he has always done in such cases' (*Court and Cabinets of George III.*, vol. iv. p. 333).

[3] See the very favourable opinions of him expressed at the time, recorded in *Horner's Correspondence*, vol. i. pp. 300, 330.

1806. ultimately became Lord Chancellor.[1] Lord Fitzwilliam was President of the Council, Lord Sidmouth Privy Seal, and Lord Moira Master of the Ordnance. These Ministers, together with Lord Ellenborough, the Chief Justice, formed the Cabinet. Lord Sidmouth was at this time the leader of a party in the House of Commons which numbered forty or fifty votes, and although the King did not venture to try the experiment of a second Addington Administration, and probably had no desire to see Lord Sidmouth's weight thrown into the scale of the new Government, yet Lord Grenville and Mr. Fox, like Mr. Pitt, found themselves compelled by parliamentary exigencies to admit him into their Cabinet, meanly as they thought of his abilities, and widely as they differed from his opinions. Lord Moira's appointment was acceptable to the Prince of Wales, and Lord Ellenborough was made a Cabinet Minister, as being the political friend of Lord Sidmouth.[2] It seems that Lord Sidmouth first proposed Lord Buckinghamshire, but that he was objected to by Lord Grenville and Mr. Fox, and that the other arrangement was substituted. The view taken of the position of the two latter Ministers in this Cabinet is expressed in the complimentary remark of one of Lord Sidmouth's correspondents, who likened

[1] See *Life of Romilly*, vol. ii. p. 135; Lord Campbell's *Lives of the Chief Justices*, vol. iii. p. 183; Palliser's *Life of Lord Sidmouth*, vol. ii. p. 414.

[2] In the *Life of Lord Sidmouth*, there is a letter dated January 31, 1806, written to his brother-in-law, Mr. Bragge Bathurst, in which he specifies the items of the bargain which he made for his friends. He describes it as a great point to have carried Lord Ellenborough into the Cabinet. He made a strong claim for 'Brother Bragge,' and obtained a promise of a situation of adequate importance when a vacancy should take place. The Joint Paymastership was promised to 'Brother Hiley,' and Vansittart was to resume the office of Secretary to the Treasury, provided the King would dispense with the punctilio arising from his rank as Privy Councillor, which he had obtained when appointed to the office of Chief Secretary to the Lord Lieutenant in 1805. Lord Buckinghamshire was to be Joint Postmaster and Bond Judge Advocate (vol. ii. p. 413).

him, with Lord Ellenborough by his side, to 'a faithful old steward with his mastiff, watching new servants, lest they should have some evil designs against the old family mansion.'[1] 1806.

The only terms which the incoming Ministers made with the King related to the management of the army. They appear to have contended for the principle that the army should cease to be subject to the direct control of the Crown, through the commander-in-chief. This proposition was resisted by the King; but his objection was removed by an agreement that no change should be introduced into the government of the army without His Majesty's approbation.[2] Notwithstanding the King's known scruple respecting his Coronation Oath, no attempt was made to come to any understanding with him on the subject of the Catholic Question. Like their predecessor, Lord Grenville and Mr. Fox were compelled by the King's obstinate prejudice, and by the general state of opinion in the country, to allow the question to remain in abeyance, and to abstain from all attempts at using the ministerial influence for removing the disabilities of the Catholics.[3] It seems that when Lord Sidmouth accepted

[1] *Life of Lord Sidmouth*, pp. 417, 418, 422.

[2] *Ibid.* p. 415; *Life of Horner*, *ibid.* p. 334.

[3] Mr. Fox's difficulties on the subject are explained in his letter to Mr. Grey, April 19, and to Lord Grenville, April 20, 1804 (*Mem. of Fox*, vol. iv. pp. 45, 47). In 1803, Lord Grenville stated to Mr. Pitt, as an essential condition to his friends' taking part in any Government, 'that we should be at liberty to explain to the King in the most distinct, though at the same time most respectful manner, that whenever the Catholic Question might be proposed in Parliament, we reserved to ourselves the full liberty to state and urge in debate our unaltered opinions in favour of that measure' (*Courts and Cabinets*, vol. iii. p. 286). This reservation of the right of speech implies that all idea of action was then abandoned. Mr. Grenville, in a letter of January 17, 1805, adverts to Mr. Pitt's defence of his own silence and inaction on the Catholic Question, on the ground of the King's objection, in his speech of the 15th upon the address, and declares it to be unconstitu-

1806. office in this Cabinet, he gave Lord Grenville and Mr. Fox express notice, that 'whether in the present or future reign, in or out of office, he would ever resist to his utmost the Catholic Question.'[1] They were therefore precluded by the very terms of their incorporation, from taking any active step in the matter.

There was another point which was made the subject of preliminary negotiation at the formation of this Ministry, though not with the King. Lord Wellesley had, as we have already stated, then recently returned from India; his aggressive policy, and his system of territorial acquisition, had involved him in a violent conflict with the Court of Directors, and some preparatory proceedings had been taken in Parliament with a view to his impeachment.[2] The person most active in these proceedings was a Mr. Paull, who had resided for some years in India, and had carried on trade in that country as a private merchant. On his return to England he purchased a seat in Parliament, and employed his Indian knowledge in attacking the late Governor-General,[3] who, having (to use the expression of Sir J. Mackintosh) 'sultanised' his office, had

tional, and inconsistent with his resignation in 1801 (*Courts and Cabinets*, *ibid.* p. 411). This criticism may be just, but the course which his own friends subsequently took was not different. Mr. Fox speaks of Pitt's hydrophobia upon the Catholic Question, to Mr. Grey, March 28, 1804 (*ibid.* vol. iii. p. 457). [It must be admitted that this abstinence of Mr. Fox and Lord Grenville may fairly be pleaded in mitigation of Mr. Pitt's promise. They probably thought that the King's mind would again have given way if the question had been pressed on him.—Ed.]

[1] *Life*, vol. ii. p. 416.

[2] See the debate on Mr. Francis's motion in the House of Commons, April 5; and Mr. Paull's motion for papers in order to criminate Lord Wellesley, June 25, 1805.

[3] Professor Wilson's *Continuation of Mill*, vol. i. p. 156; *Annual Register*, for 1806, p. 100; Pearce's *Life of Lord Wellesley*, vol. ii. p. 428. Mr. Paull stood for Westminster at the election in May 1807, and a duel in consequence took place between him and Sir F. Burdett, in which two shots were fired, and both parties were wounded.

now exchanged his imperial throne at Calcutta for the levelling and censorious atmosphere of London. Anticipating the prosecution of these charges, Lord Grenville (who had been the early friend of Lord Wellesley) stipulated with Mr. Fox that the accusation of Lord Wellesley should not be made a Cabinet measure, and that no person should be appointed President of the Board of Control who should promote it in his official capacity. Mr. Fox assented to these terms, but reserved the power of supporting the accusation if it were brought forward by a private member.[1] A resolution criminatory of Lord Wellesley was submitted to the House of Commons in the following April, by Mr. Paull; but it was opposed by Mr. Fox, and the motion was withdrawn. The subject was, however, followed up; further charges were made, particularly with respect to Oude; evidence was heard at the bar of the House; but the dissolution in October, 1806, deprived Mr. Paull of his seat. When Parliament reassembled, Lord Folkstone resumed the attack, with a view to censure, not to impeachment; and in the following session he moved resolutions which were negatived, and a vote approving of Lord Wellesley's conduct was agreed to by the House.[2] 1806.

Shortly after the announcement of the Ministerial arrangements, the appointment of Lord Ellenborough to a seat in the Cabinet became the subject of animadversion

[1] *Life of Horner*, iii. p. 335. Lord Minto was President of the Board of Control in the new Ministry, without a seat in the Cabinet. On his appointment as Governor-general in the autumn, he was succeeded for a short time by Mr. Grenville, and afterwards by Mr. Tierney.

[2] Lord Folkstone's motions were on January 26, 1807, and March 9, 1808. With reference to the Oude charge against the late Governor-general, Sir S. Romilly says in his *Diary*, that he had read the voluminous papers printed for Parliament, and that the conduct of Lord Wellesley appeared to him to be unjustifiable (vol. ii. p. 236).

1806. in both Houses of Parliament. The resolution of censure was negatived without a division in the Lords, and by a large majority in the Commons. Parliament, therefore, must be considered to have affirmed the doctrine which was then broadly laid down both by Mr. Fox and Lord Grenville, that the Cabinet has no organised or corporate character, that it is not a body recognised by the constitution; and that however complete the moral responsibility of each member for the acts of the Administration may be, yet legally and constitutionally each Minister is only responsible for his own acts, and for the management of his own department.[1] Opinion was nevertheless unfavourable to an arrangement which involved the Chief Justice, the highest criminal judge, in the party politics of the day; it has never been since repeated, and is not likely to be hereafter revived.[2]

The most memorable events in this short-lived Administration were the negotiations with France and the death of Mr. Fox. Shortly after Mr. Fox's accession to office, the offer of a Frenchman to assassinate Bonaparte caused him to communicate directly with the French Government, and the communication thus made presented an opportunity for opening a negotiation for the restoration of peace. This negotiation, which was subsequently pur-

[1] Lord Macaulay's description of the origin and character of the Cabinet (*History of England*, vol. i. p. 211) agrees with this view. He remarks, that 'it still continues to be altogether unknown to the law. The names of the noblemen and gentlemen who compose it are never officially announced to the public. No record is kept of its meetings and resolutions, nor has its existence ever been recognised by any Act of Parliament.' See also Mr. Bankes's speech, House of Commons, March 2, 1810. The joint moral responsibility of the Cabinet is however recognised by Lord Macaulay, *ibid.* p. 273.

[2] Compare the statements in Lord Brougham's *Statesmen*, vol. ii. p. 101, as to Mr. Fox's doubts, and Lord Ellenborough's own subsequent disapprobation of this measure.

sued by Lord Yarmouth, then a prisoner at Verdun, and by Lord Lauderdale, as plenipotentiaries, at Paris, led to no result;[1] the practical experience of Bonaparte's policy thus acquired convinced Mr. Fox that peace with him was impossible, and that the active prosecution of the war by England was inevitable.[2] Almost his last words to one of his most intimate friends and colleagues enjoined on his survivors the vigorous prosecution of the war. Near the end of the session his health yielded to the debilitating effects of dropsy. He was forced to withdraw first from 1806.

[1] Lord Malmesbury, a highly competent, but not a friendly judge, remarks of this negotiation: 'Lord Lauderdale acted well, and with spirit, and proved what I had ascertained at Paris and Lisle in 1796 and 1797, that though revolutionary France was ever ready to listen to pacific negotiation, it never meant, and probably never will mean, to conclude a just and equitable peace. That of Amiens was not so; it was scarce an armed truce, or cessation of hostilities' (*Diaries*, vol. iv. p. 353). It appears to us that it was not at this time the form of the French Government, but the individual character of Bonaparte, and his inextinguishable appetite for conquest, which constituted the real obstacles to peace. For comments on this negotiation, see Lord Holland's *Mem. of Whig Party*, vol. ii. pp. 73-81.

[2] The adoption of a warlike policy by Mr. Fox during this Administration is alluded to by Walter Scott in the introduction to the first canto of *Marmion*:—

> If ever from an English heart,
> Oh, here let prejudice depart,
> And, partial feeling cast aside,
> Record that Fox a Briton died!
> When Europe crouched to France's yoke,
> And Austria bent, and Prussia broke,
> And the firm Russian's purpose brave
> Was bartered by a timorous slave;
> Even then dishonour's peace he spurn'd,
> Her sullied olive branch return'd,
> Stood for his country's glory fast,
> And nailed her colours to the mast.

The 'timorous slave' is M. D'Oubril, whose treaty, signed at Paris with the French Government, was repudiated by the Emperor Alexander. In the words 'Prussia broke' there is an allusion to the battle of Jena, which involves an anachronism; for this battle did not take place until October 1806, after Mr. Fox's death.

1806. his Parliamentary, and next from his official, duties; and on the 13th of September he expired.

Lord Holland had heard that the King could hardly suppress his exultation at Mr. Fox's death.[1] But we happen to know from the certain testimony of the late Duchess of Gloucester, who was with her father when the message was delivered, that the King expressed not satisfaction, but regret; and that he added the remark, that the country could then ill afford to lose such a man. The assurances which Mr. Fox gave to the King on accepting office appear to have removed much of His Majesty's prejudice against him;[2] and his subsequent conduct to the King confirmed this favourable impression. The biographer of Lord Sidmouth, after inserting a letter written by him on the day after Fox's death, in a tone of regret and esteem,[3] proceeds to say:—

> Mr. Fox's powers of attraction must have been extraordinary indeed, to overcome, as they did, not only the feebler resistance of Lord Sidmouth's political prepossessions, but also the more deeply rooted predispositions which were believed to prevail in the royal mind. But that such was the case is unquestionable. 'Little did I think,'—said His Majesty to Lord Sidmouth, at the first interview with which he honoured him after that fatal event,—'little did I think that I should ever live to regret Mr. Fox's death.' His Lordship used to remark that 'Mr. Fox was always peculiarly respectful and conciliatory in his manner towards the King, and most anxious to avoid every question which did not harmonise with His Majesty's conscientious feelings. In proof of this, he mentioned that Count Stahremberg

[1] *Mem. of Whig Party*, vol. ii. p. 49.

[2] See Wilberforce's *Correspondence*, vol. ii. p. 76.

[3] In this letter Lord Sidmouth says: 'Of his talents there can be but one opinion. His natural disposition deserved, I really believe, all that could be said in its favour. I never knew a man of more apparent sincerity; more free from rancour or even severity; and hardly any one so entirely devoid of affectation.'

said to Mr. Fox, when he first came into office. 'Have you no difficulty respecting the Roman Catholic Question?' To which he replied, 'None at all; I am determined not to annoy my Sovereign by bringing it forward.'[1] 1806.

The death of Mr. Fox, not less unexpected than that of Mr. Pitt at the beginning of the year, completely altered the position of the Ministry. But the changes of office proposed by Lord Grenville, and assented to with remarkable graciousness by the King, preserved the balance of power in the Coalition Government.[2] Lord Howick succeeded Mr. Fox as Foreign Secretary and leader of the House of Commons; Mr. Grenville became First Lord of the Admiralty; Lord Fitzwilliam resigned the Presidency of the Council, and was succeeded by Lord Sidmouth; Lord Holland was appointed to the Privy Seal. In this state the Ministry met Parliament for the following session on December 15, 1806. Both Houses, after full debate on the recent negotiations with France, concurred unanimously and cordially in the vigorous prosecution of the war; and business was proceeding in its usual course, when in the month of February a series of communications with the King commenced which led to the fall of the Administration. The Cabinet decided to introduce into the Annual Mutiny Bill a clause enabling the King to confer military commissions on any of his subjects, without distinction of religion; the object being to permit Catholics to hold commissions in the army. The King first assented to this clause, but afterwards changed his mind and withdrew his assent. The Ministers acquiesced in his refusal; but he proceeded to require from them a written declaration,

[1] *Life of Sidmouth*, vol. ii. p. 435.

[2] The various arrangements which were under consideration at this time are fully explained in the letters in *Court and Cabinets*, vol. iv. pp. 41, 52, 59, 65, 67, 70; as to the King's satisfaction, see p. 77. Lord Grenville's fairness on this occasion is commended by Lord Holland, *ibid.* p. 50.

1807. that they would propose to him no further concession to the Catholics. This assurance they declined to give, and the resignation of their offices was forthwith accepted.

Thus ended, in March 1807, after a duration of about fourteen months, the nearest approach to a Whig Administration which was in power during the forty-seven years between 1783 and 1830. The King had never given it a cordial support, and he dexterously availed himself of the earliest opportunity which his Ministers afforded him for bringing about a rupture, and driving them to resignation. In the negotiation respecting the clauses in the Mutiny Bill, and the objections which he took, he appears to have received assistance from some skilful adviser; the letters which he addressed to the Cabinet were certainly not of his own composition; nevertheless he informed Lord Eldon and Lord Hawkesbury, in his interview with them on the 19th of March, that he had communicated with no one—not even with the Archbishop of Canterbury.[1] As no agreement with the King was made by the Ministers on their accession to office respecting the Catholic Question, they could not justly complain of his objection if it was confined to the present, and did not relate to prospective measures. They made, however, a large concession to his antipathy against the Catholics, in complying with his desire that their limited measure should be withheld; and

[1] For a history of this negotiation see Lord Holland's *Memoirs of the Whig Party*, vol. ii. pp. 173–205, with the documents in the Appendix. Any person who is acquainted with the peculiar style of George III. will perceive that his letters of February 10 and 12, and of March 17, were not composed by himself. As the King was at this time nearly blind, the letters were probably composed by Sir Herbert Taylor. Further information is also furnished by the letters of Lord Grenville and Mr. Grenville in *Court and Cabinets*, vol. iv. pp. 117–121, 134–140; the account in Wilberforce's *Life*, vol. iii. p. 306; and *Lord Malmesbury's Narrative*, vol. iv. pp. 357–374. The Duke of Portland addressed a letter to the King on March 12, advising him to refuse his assent to the Bill, and, in the event of the resignation of Ministers, offering to form a new Administration.

having deferred so far to the King's prejudices, they could not reasonably expect to be exposed to the test which he now required them to subscribe, or to be arrested by the barrier which he now erected across their path. This was the second Administration which the King had turned out upon the Catholic Question. The same question was destined, many years afterwards, in the consequences of its final settlement, to be fatal to a third Ministry. 1807

Lord Sidmouth had differed from his colleagues during the final negotiation with the King, and had tendered his resignation to Lord Grenville; but it was suspended, and he, together with Mr. B. Bathurst and Mr. Hiley Addington, accompanied the rest of the Government into retirement. The King made this distinction between Lord Sidmouth and his colleagues, that he gave him alone an audience of leave; and afterwards addressed to him a gracious letter, thanking him for his services. Lord Sidmouth, on this occasion, although he considered the newly formed Government as extremely feeble, remarked that 'it was the King's Government, and he would never be a party to a systematic opposition.' His course, he laid it down at the same time, would be 'to support the King, and to resist any motion the tendency of which would be to throw an imputation on His Majesty's conduct, or to control the just exercise of his prerogative.' [1]

Full explanations of the grounds on which the resig-

[1] *Life of Lord Sidmouth*, vol. ii. pp. 466, 469, 470. The undated letter of Mr. Grenville (*Court and Cabinets*, *ibid.* p. 197), in which he alludes to the defection of the friends of the Prince, Lord Sidmouth, Wilberforce, and Bankes, is misplaced by the editor; it must have been written before the dissolution on the 27th of April. The peerage of Sir T. M. Sutton, created Lord Manners, referred to in the letter, was gazetted on April 14. For a character of Lord Sidmouth, and an account of his straightforward conduct at this time, see Lord Holland, *Memoirs of the Whig Party*, vol. ii. pp. 210–214. [Compare Dean Milman's letter in the supplement to a previous article.—Ed.]

1807. nation of Ministers had taken place were given in both Houses; in the Upper House, Lord Melville stated that though Mr. Pitt had once entertained the opinion that the Catholic Bill was indispensable, he had changed that opinion in consequence of the King's conscientious repugnance; and it was on his declaration of this change of opinion that he returned to office in 1804.[1] A resolution condemning the acceptance of pledges by Ministers, which should bind them not to offer any advice to the Crown, was moved in both Houses. In the Lords it was supported by 90 against 171, in the Commons by 226 against 258; so that in the latter House the course taken by the King narrowly escaped a distinct censure.[2] Shortly afterwards, a motion, expressive of deep regret at the late change of Ministry, was made in the House of Commons, and supported by 198 against 244 votes.

The new Administration which the King now formed was constituted as follows: at its head he placed the Duke of Portland, formerly leader of the Whig party, and Prime Minister of the Coalition Government. He was one of the Whig secession, who, with Burke, joined Pitt after the French revolution, and was Secretary of State for some years in his Administration. He subsequently held office under Addington, and again under Pitt, and retired to make way for Addington in 1804. Though an upright and honourable man, he never, even when in the prime of life, possessed much vigour or ability; he was now in his seventieth year, and much debilitated by

[1] Lord Camden stated at this time 'that he conceived it to be a sort of pledge he had given to Pitt that the (Catholic) question should not be mooted during the King's life' (*Lord Malmesbury*, vol. ii. p. 370).

[2] The Opposition expected to beat the new Government in this division, and when they were in the lobby they believed themselves to be a majority; see *Memoirs of Romilly*, vol. ii. pp. 193–195, who gives an account of the debate.

disease.[1] The more efficient members of the Cabinet were Lord Eldon, who gladly resumed the great seal; and Mr. Perceval, who was Chancellor of the Exchequer and leader of the House of Commons; with Lord Hawkesbury, Mr. Canning, and Lord Castlereagh, who held the seals of the Home, Foreign, and War departments. Lord Camden was President of the Council, and Lord Westmoreland Privy Seal; Lord Mulgrave, First Lord of the Admiralty; Lord Bathurst, President of the Board of Trade; and Mr. Dundas—Lord Melville's eldest son—was President of the Board of Control. Lord Melville himself had undergone his impeachment in 1806, and had been acquitted by a majority of the Peers. He had subsequently made himself the organ of the East India Company with respect to the appointment of a Governor-general as successor to Lord Cornwallis, and had, in the House of Lords, attacked the recall of Sir G. Barlow and the appointment of Lord Minto. The new Government offered him office, which he did not venture to accept; they lost no time, however, in restoring him to his seat at the Privy Council, from the list of which he had been reluctantly removed by Mr. Pitt.[2] He remained out of office until his death, which

1807.

[1] Lord Malmesbury, who was on intimate terms with the Duke of Portland, gives the following account of his state in 1808: 'His complaint (the stone) was returning, and the excruciating pain this occasioned, joined to the worry and torment of his official situation, quite broke him down. I have been often with him when I thought he would have died in his chair, and his powers of attention were so weakened that he could neither read a paper, nor listen for a while, without becoming drowsy and falling asleep. But he never would let me go away after dinner, when the rest of the company went, but always urged me to remain on with him, which I often did for hours, when he was equal neither to talk nor to hear. About twelve or one o'clock he generally rallied, and he has made me sit up many nights after my usual hour of retiring, particularly two, the 18th and 19th of January, 1808, when he wished me to assist him in drawing up the King's speech for the opening of Parliament on the 21st' (*Diaries*, vol. ii. p. 405).

[2] See Lord Malmesbury, *ibid.* p. 103; *Memoirs of Romilly*, vol. ii. pp. 192,

1807. occurred in 1811, when he was seventy years old. His son, who now succeeded to his former post at the Board of Control, and who subsequently became First Lord of the Admiralty, was a man of respectable abilities, but inferior to his father.

An attempt was made to incorporate Lord Wellesley in the Cabinet. He hesitated for a time, and then declined; but, notwithstanding his obligations to Lord Grenville, he declared himself a supporter of the new Ministry, and received the Garter as the price and pledge of his adhesion.[1]

Lord Moira made to his late colleagues a formal announcement of his separation from them, and of his attachment to the Prince. 'Where he does not go with you (he said) I do not.' At the same time he expressed his desire of acting with them, both on public and private grounds, and he stated that he had no political connexion with the new Ministers.[2] The Prince's pecuniary extravagance kept him constantly in a state in which it was inconvenient to him to be on bad terms with the King and his Ministers, and therefore made it necessary for him to ride perpetually at single anchor.

This Ministry was weak in the House of Lords:[3] its

193. Mr. Grenville states that the King and Ministry were at this time intent on rescinding the resolution of the Commons against him (*Court and Cabinets, ibid.* p. 163). There is a full and interesting description of Lord Melville in Lord Holland's *Memoirs of the Whig Party*, vol. i. pp. 238–243). [See above, p. 257.—Ed.]

[1] Lord Malmesbury, *ibid.* pp. 376, 377; Lord Holland's *Mem. of Whig Party*, vol. ii. p. 222; Mr. Fremantle's letter of April 3, 1807, *Court and Cabinets, ibid.* p. 155. There is in *Court and Cabinets*, p. 194, a letter from Sir Arthur Wellesley to the Marquis of Buckingham, dated July 8, 1807, respecting Lord Wellesley's political position at this time. Sir A. Wellesley became Chief Secretary to the Lord Lieutenant at this change of Government.

[2] Lord Holland, *ibid.* p. 244.

[3] Mr. Fremantle writes to the Marquis of Buckingham, April 15, 1807:

strength lay in the other House, where it was represented by Perceval, Canning, and Castlereagh. Mr. Perceval was the second son of Lord Egmont, and was born in 1762. He became King's counsel and leader of the Midland Circuit in 1796, and in the same year obtained a seat in Parliament. Though he never had much success at the bar, he was, at the formation of the Addington Ministry in 1801, appointed Solicitor-general, and in the following year became Attorney-general, which office he retained until Mr. Pitt's death. The abilities which he had shown as a debater, while he held those high legal situations, together with his strong anti-Catholic opinions, determined his choice as leader of the House at this conjuncture, in preference either to Mr. Canning or to Lord Castlereagh. 'Though no great lawyer,' says Lord Holland, 'he was, without much genius, a spirited, ready, and forcible speaker; affectionate, frank, and generous in private; dangerous and formidable in public; he united to the most vulgar prejudices and virulent enmities in religion and politics, courage, integrity, and abilities, that fortunately very rarely accompany them.'[1] 'He was,' says Lord Brougham, 'a person of acute and quick, rather than of great, faculties. As Attorney-general to Mr. Addington, and bearing almost the whole burthen of the unequal debate, while the forces of Fox, Pitt, and Windham

1807.

'You can have no conception of anything half so bad as these exhibitions in the House of Lords; Lords Mulgrave, Westmoreland, and Camden attempting to put themselves forward as great Ministers; the Duke of Portland shrinking from the attacks made upon him' (*Court and Cabinets*, *ibid.* p. 167). In May 1807, Lord Malmesbury says: 'In the course of the last three weeks it has, from various little facts, struck me that the Duke of Portland's colleagues are swerving from him; that they take a great deal on themselves immediately belonging to him, and treat him more as a nominal than as a real head of the Ministry' (*Court and Cabinets*, vol. iv. p. 386).

[1] *Mem. of Whig Party*, vol. ii. p. 214.

1807. combined to assail the meagre Treasury bench, his talents sparkled with peculiar brightness. His dexterity in any great or any personal conflict; his excellent language, always purely but unaffectedly English, nor ever chargeable with incorrect taste; his attention constantly awake; and his spirit ever dauntless, nay, rather rising with emergency, gained him very great reputation as a ready and a powerful debater.'[1]

Mr. Canning was Mr. Perceval's junior by eight years; he had, under Mr. Pitt, filled the offices of Under-Secretary of State, and Treasurer of the Navy; and it had been Mr. Pitt's intention, if his life had been prolonged into the session of 1806, to give him a Cabinet office.[2] This intention was intercepted by his death; and Mr. Canning passed into Opposition upon the formation of Lord Grenville's Administration. A short time before its fall, however, overtures were made to him to join it, probably with a seat in the Cabinet; the negotiation with him was pending when the difference with the King arose, and the Government was overthrown.[3] The position of Mr. Canning, at the formation of the Portland

[1] *Statesmen of the Time of George III.*, vol. i. p. 324. A highly favourable account of Perceval's private character is given by Mr. Wilberforce, *Life*, vol. iv. p. 26. A severe, but not unjust, estimate of his public character may be found in the *Edinburgh Review*, vol. xx. p. 29.

[2] *Lord Malmesbury, ibid.* p. 343.

[3] See the letters in *Court and Cabinets, ibid.* pp. 125–127; *Lord Malmesbury, ibid.* p. 367. Lord Sidmouth alleged the pending negotiation with Mr. Canning as a reason for his resignation on March 11, 1807 (*Life of Lord Sidmouth, ibid.* p. 461). Lord Malmesbury says: 'In November [1806], and during the elections, Lord Grenville made several attempts to disunite Pitt's friends. He offered splendidly to Canning, and to any three or four friends he would name. Lord Wellesley was the intermediary, and negotiated ably; but Canning remained steady, and from principle' (*Diary, ibid.* p. 354). There is no trace of this offer in the *Grenville Correspondence*, or in Lord Holland's *Memoirs*. It can scarcely have gone the length which Lord Malmesbury describes.

Administration, is thus described by his intimate friend 1807.
and mentor, Lord Malmesbury. It will be observed that Mr. Canning was at this time the brother-in-law of the Duke of Portland's eldest son. Lord Titchfield and he had married sisters, the two daughters of General Scott:—

Canning spoke as if the choice of Cabinet places was to be at his refusal, and declared with a threat, that he never would sit in the same Cabinet with Addington. Canning possesses the peculiar talent of justifying ably and forcibly all he does, or wishes to be done, and that so rapidly and so eloquently, that it is very difficult not to be carried away by what he says. He is unquestionably very clever, very essential to Government; but he is hardly yet a Statesman, and his dangerous habit of quizzing (which he cannot restrain) would be most unpopular in any department which required pliancy, tact, or conciliatory behaviour. He is honourable and honest, with a dash of the Irishman, and all his plans and ideas of governing would partake of this; and might be as dangerous in practice as he makes them appear plausible by the eloquent way in which he expresses them. He is right, however, quite right, about Lord Sidmouth. Canning may be safely trusted, for, I repeat it, he is honourable and honest, and if Pitt had not forced him in his hot-house of partiality and *engouement* (for it amounted to that), but had left him to ripen gradually, and allowed him, in the early part of his political life, which began only eleven years ago, to experience some hardships, or even contradictions, his mind would have taken a better bend; but spoiled as he has been—feared and wanted as he finds himself—no place is now high enough for him; his ambition rises beyond this visible diurnal sphere, and I fear he may lose many real and cordial friends for uncertain political connexions (*ibid.* p. 367).

Lord Castlereagh was a year older than Mr. Canning.[1] He was the eldest son of Robert Stewart, Earl o

[1] It is a singular chronological coincidence, that Mr. Fox was born in 1749; Mr. Pitt and Lord Grenville in 1759; and Napoleon, the Duke of Wellington, and Lord Castlereagh in 1769.

1807. Londonderry, by his first wife, Lady Frances Seymour, daughter of the first Earl of Hertford.[1] His early career had been in the Irish Parliament, which he entered in 1790; he was appointed Chief Secretary to the Lord Lieutenant in 1797, and rendered essential service to the Government of Mr. Pitt and to his country, by the part which he took in promoting the union with England. As representative for the county of Down, he became a member of the Imperial Parliament in 1801; and in July 1802, was appointed President of the Board of Control in Addington's Administration. This office he retained when Mr. Pitt returned to the helm in 1804, and in the following year he was promoted to the Department of War and Colonies. He continued to discharge the duties of this office, retaining also provisionally the Board of Control, until Mr. Pitt's death, when he resigned with his other colleagues, and entered the ranks of Opposition.

Although Mr. Canning and Lord Castlereagh shared Mr. Pitt's opinions on the Catholic Question, and the latter had taken a peculiarly active part in urging Mr. Pitt to propose his measure of 1801, in spite of the King's reluctance, yet the new Ministers lost no time in dissolving Parliament (which had only been elected in the previous autumn) for the purpose of raising the cry of 'No Popery' and 'the Church in Danger,' and of profiting by this cry in order to increase their strength.[2] Lord Castlereagh and Mr. Canning adhered indeed to their opinions, and, under the Regency, rendered important assistance to the cause of Catholic emancipation.

[1] The Earl of Hertford was Lord Lieutenant of Ireland when this marriage took place.

[2] See *Court and Cabinets, ibid.* pp. 162, 163, 165, 174; *Memoir of Romilly*, vol. ii. p. 198.

At this time, however, the latter so far identified himself with the anti-Catholic clamour, that he is a prominent subject of attack, together with Mr. Perceval, in the inimitable letters of Peter Plymley, which appeared soon after the change of Government, and were intended to counteract the intolerant cry raised at their dissolution. 1807.

The new Parliament met on June 26, and sat till the middle of August. A resolution was moved in both Houses censuring the dissolution of Parliament, and the ground alleged for the appeal to the country. In the Lords it was supported by 67 to 160; in the Commons by only 155 to 350, showing a majority of 195 for Ministers.[1] It was, therefore, apparent that the country had responded to the appeal in the King's favour upon the Catholic Question, and that the new Parliament was much more favourable to the Ministry than the old one. On this occasion Lord Sidmouth supported the Government, and separated himself from his late associates.

The battle of Jena had been fought in October 1806, a short time after Mr. Fox's death. In the ensuing winter, Napoleon, having accomplished the ruin of the Prussian monarchy, advanced into Poland, and gained against the Russian army the sanguinary and dubious victory of Eylau (Feb. 8, 1807). The siege and capitulation of Danzig followed soon afterwards, and in June the battle of Friedland compelled the Russian Government to negotiate. The treaty of Tilsit, arranged personally between the Emperors Alexander and Napoleon, was the result (July 7).

It seems that information soon reached the English Cabinet that a secret article had been agreed to at Tilsit,

[1] An account of the debate in the Commons is given in Lord Temple's letter, written on June 27 (*Court and Cabinets, ibid.* p. 180).

1807. under which the neutral territory of Denmark would be occupied by Napoleon, and the Danish fleet seized for the use of France. Mr. Canning, impelled by the apparent designs of Napoleon, and by the information of this supposed fact, and desirous of signalising his advent to office by an act of vigour, determined on demanding the delivery of the Danish fleet into the custody of England, in order to prevent its falling into the power of France. Upon the refusal of Denmark, Copenhagen was bombarded, and the Danish fleet carried away. This extreme exercise of the rights of war took place after the prorogation (in September); and did not come under the review of Parliament until the following session, which opened on the 21st of January, 1808. Several motions censuring the measure, and denying its necessity, policy, and justice, were then made in both Houses, and supported by Lord Grenville, Lord Sidmouth, Mr. Ponsonby, Mr. Windham, and other speakers. In every division, however, the Government obtained a large majority of votes.

During the recess an event had occurred which materially changed the position of the Whig party in the House of Commons. Since the death of Mr. Fox, Lord Howick had been their leader in that House; but the death of his Father (Earl Grey), in November 1807, removed him to the House of Lords, and it became necessary to provide a successor. Windham, Sheridan, Tierney, Mr. Grenville, Lord Henry Petty, Whitbread, were, for reasons which were then deemed conclusive, rejected; and the choice, after mature deliberation, fell upon Mr. George Ponsonby, who, in 1806, had filled the office of Irish Chancellor. He was accordingly brought into Parliament at the beginning of the session, in order to lead a party to nearly all of whom he was personally unknown.[1] Mr. Ponsonby was related by marriage to Earl Grey;[2] and it was this relationship which, to a great extent, had determined this choice: for, as Lord Grey, in passing from the Lower to the Upper House of Parliament, ceased to act as leader, in consequence of the position held there by Lord Grenville, it was thought desirable to consult his feelings and personal claims as much as possible in the selection of a leader for the House of Commons. Mr. Ponsonby continued to act in this capacity until his death in 1817. 1808.

The Berlin decree, by which Napoleon's Continental system had been established, was issued in November 1806, and had been followed by the retaliatory Orders in Council of the British Government in November 1807. The wisdom of this policy, with which Mr. Perceval completely identified himself, was questioned by able speakers on the Opposition side, in the session of 1808; the other business requires no particular remark, and the prorogation took place on the 4th of July.

Thus far the Portland Administration had weathered the storms of Parliamentary attack and public criticism without material difficulty. Events, however, soon began to thicken, which put its capacity of resistance to a severe test.

[1] See *Lord Holland, ibid.* vol. ii. pp. 236–240, and the letters in *Court and Cabinets, ibid.* pp. 191, 209, 215, 223, 224. In a letter of Nov. 23, 1807, Lord Grenville gives his reasons for declining to write to Lord Grey to recommend a leader in his place. His first reason is: 'That a leader of an Opposition cannot be chosen and appointed as a leader of a Government party may, and that all the elections in the world would not have made Windham or Sheridan leaders of the Old Opposition while Fox was alive. In Opposition, people will follow like hounds (according to Lord Bolingbroke's simile) the man who will show them game.'

[2] Earl Grey married the sister of the first Lord Ponsonby, who was the niece of Mr. George Ponsonby.

1808. The power of Napoleon may be said to have reached its culminating point at Tilsit. The efforts which he subsequently made for extending and consolidating his dominion, though attended with partial and temporary success, were in fact the means by which he undermined his own empire, and prepared the way for his downfall. Foremost amongst these attempts of his restless and unscrupulous ambition were his designs upon Spain and Portugal, which began to manifest themselves in the autumn of 1807. A French army under Junot occupied Lisbon in November, and the royal family of Portugal took refuge in Brazil. In March 1808, Murat at the head of a French army entered Madrid; and in the same month the abdication of Charles IV., and the proclamation of Ferdinand VII. as King, took place. In May Ferdinand abdicated, and Murat was declared viceroy; in June Joseph Bonaparte was proclaimed King. So rapid was the succession of events by which the entire Iberian peninsula was conquered by Napoleon, both its royal families deposed, and a French titular King, of the Bonaparte family, set upon the throne of Spain. These rapid successes produced, however, an equally rapid reaction. The population of Spain and Portugal rose against the French domination. Juntas, as the local centres of the national insurrection, were formed all over the country; the French fleet at Cadiz was seized by the Spaniards, and a cooperation with the English fleet was established. Deputies were sent to England to solicit succour, and to arouse the popular sentiment in favour of the Spanish cause. The battle of Baylen and the surrender of Dupont occurred in July 1808, which was immediately followed by the flight of Joseph from Madrid to Burgos.

The news of the Spanish insurrection lighted up a

flame of sympathy in England,[1] and the popular feeling was warmly seconded by Mr. Canning, the Foreign Secretary, and his colleagues. The Government lost no time in sending out supplies of arms, stores, and money to the insurgent juntas, which were assisted by voluntary contributions; and in July 1808, an expeditionary force, under Sir Arthur Wellesley, sailed from Cork, and landed on the coast of Portugal. The battles of Roliça and Vimiero, fought on the 17th and 21st of August, placed Junot in a position in which he was glad to negotiate; and the result was the Convention of Cintra, by which the French army agreed to evacuate Portugal, and were to be transported to France, with their artillery and property, in British ships. 1808.

The Convention of Cintra was received with a burst of indignation both in England and the Peninsula; and the English Government accordingly found themselves compelled to appoint in November a board of enquiry, composed of general officers, with instructions to report upon its conditions, and upon the conduct of the officers by whom it was concluded. The board reported their opinion that no further military proceeding was necessary in the matter; but the King's disapprobation of the articles affecting Spanish and Portuguese interests was afterwards officially signified to Sir Hew Dalrymple, the officer first in command.

After the evacuation of Portugal by the French forces, the English army remained at Lisbon under the command of Sir John Moore. An advance into Spain was now decided upon, for the purpose of cooperating with the Spanish insurgent forces; and the English general penetrated as far as Salamanca and Sahagun; but Napoleon,

[1] There is a strong expression of this sympathy in Mr. Horner's letters of June 13 and July 8, 1808 (*Life*, pp. 424, 427).

x 2

1809. warned by the disaster at Baylen and the loss of Portugal, invaded Spain in person with an army of 300,000 men, and entered Madrid in December, when he replaced Joseph on the throne. His operations scattered the Spanish levies, and compelled the English army to retreat; he himself returned to Paris, and left to Soult and Ney the pursuit of Sir John Moore, who found a warrior's death at the battle of Corunna, on the 16th of January, 1809. The remains of the English army were here re-embarked and returned to England.

Parliament met for the session of 1809 on the 13th of January. The policy of the English expedition into Spain was severely condemned by Lord Grenville in the House of Lords; a motion of censure upon Ministers on account of the Convention of Cintra was soon afterwards made in the House of Commons by Lord H. Petty, and supported by 153 to 203 votes; it was shortly followed by a motion of Mr. Ponsonby for enquiry into the affairs of Spain, which was supported by 127 to 220 votes. The unpopularity of the Convention of Cintra was visited, as is usual, upon the Executive Government, and involved them in its consequences. Lord Castlereagh, as War Secretary, was in particular the object of this storm. Mr. Canning dissented from some decision confirmatory of the Convention, to which the Cabinet had agreed upon the advice of the War Minister;[1] and this difference was not confined to him;

[1] Lord Malmesbury says: 'The Convention of Cintra excited great dissatisfaction, and I think very justly. Canning protested against an opinion of Cabinet given when he was absent, and which went to confirm it. This was the beginning of all the subsequent disputes between him and his colleagues, and led to the more serious one between him and Lord Castlereagh' (*Diaries*, vol. iv. p. 411). In a letter to the Duke of Portland, dated March 24, 1809, Mr. Canning speaks of his desire to resign his office having first arisen 'out of that decision respecting the Convention of Cintra, which was taken by the Cabinet in my absence, and my reason for dissenting from which I felt it incumbent upon me most humbly to lay before the King'

for the existence of discord between different members of the Cabinet was a matter of general belief.[1] Lord Grenville, in his private letters, attributes the continuance of the Government in its existing state of weakness entirely to the support and influence of the King. Speaking of the Ministers, he says, 'If they change hands at all, it can only be because they are quarrelling among themselves; for I am persuaded, so long as the King chooses to continue them, these very men will command the majorities of both Houses with as much certainty as ever.' Again he says, deprecating any attempt of the Opposition to dislodge Ministers: 'I am satisfied these people, or any people, may command under the King's influence a majority in Parliament; and it would have the appearance of a struggle for power, at a time when a man must indeed be of a most depraved ambition, to wish for the appearance and responsibility of governing the country, with the certainty that a Court intrigue would be incessantly at work, with ample means of depriving him of all power to be of real use.'[2] 1809.

(Phipps, *Mem. of Ward*, vol. i. p. 243). What this decision was is not apparent: for the Convention does not appear to have required any ratification by the Government; and the King twice conveyed his disapprobation of parts of it to Sir Hew Dalrymple, through the Secretary of State for War (see *Ann. Reg.*, 1812, p. 282).

[1] See the letters of Lord Temple, *Court and Cabinets*, vol. iv. pp. 234 (probably written in May, 1808), 274, 277. Mr. Grenville, in a letter of Dec. 5, 1808, says: 'The Ministry, when they speak in confidence, speak of the English war in Spain as over; and each of the Ministers begins to extend the circle of his confidential communications, which are full of complaints of each other, and which announce, beyond all disguise, the bad opinion they entertain of their own permanence. They all agree in falling foul of Lord Castlereagh' (*ibid.* p. 283). By the 'English war in Spain being *over*,' Mr. Grenville means that all hope and intention of prosecuting further hostilities on the part of England against France, in Spain, was at an end. 'One hears much (says Lord Grenville in a letter of Nov. 4) of the squabbles among the Ministers, the usual consequence of embarrassments and disgraces, which each labours (in such cases) to throw upon his colleagues' (*ibid.* p. 276).

[2] Letters of Dec. 15, 1808 (*Court and Cabinets*, *ibid.* pp. 288, 289).

1809. In addition to the difficulties of foreign politics created by the necessity of prosecuting the war with Napoleon, there arose at this moment an unexpected storm, which directly concerned the government of the army, and of which the Ministers had to bear the brunt, though it threatened the Throne more than the Treasury bench. This was the accusation of the Duke of York, the Commander-in-chief, brought forward early in the session by Colonel Wardle, relative to the corrupt sale of military commissions by his former mistress, Mrs. Clarke. The scandal and confusion caused by the disclosures to which this enquiry led were extreme; but the Duke of York was defended by Mr. Perceval, who carried an amendment exculpating him from any guilty participation in Mrs. Clarke's proceedings. The Duke thereupon resigned his office; his resignation was accepted by the King, and Sir D. Dundas was appointed his successor. The following passages from a letter of Mr. W. Fremantle, dated Feb. 16, 1809, will convey an idea of the impression which these proceedings created at the time:—

The scene which is going on in the House of Commons is so disgusting, and at the same time so alarming, that I hardly know how to describe it to you. Every day and every hour adds to the evidence against the Duke of York, and it is quite impossible but that he must sink under it. . . . All power and influence of Perceval in the House is quite gone by; he speaks without authority and without attention paid to him; and Canning has made two or three such rash declarations, that he is little attended to. You may judge the situation of the House, when I tell you we were last night nearly three quarters of an hour debating about the evidence of a drunken footman, by Perceval suggesting modes of ascertaining how to convict him of his drunkenness; Charles Long,[1] near whom I was sitting, telling me

[1] The Right Hon. Charles Long was at this time one of the Joint Paymasters-General.

at the time what a lamentable proof it was of the want of some man of sense and judgment to lead the House. There is no Government in the House of Commons. You may be assured the thing does not exist; and whether they can ever recover their tone of power remains to be proved; at present Mr. Croker, Mr. D. Brown, and Mr. Beresford are the leaders. Of course, while this ferment lasts, and God knows when it is to end, no attention will be paid to any other subject.'[1] 1809

The course which the Prince of Wales took during these proceedings against his brother was characteristic. He began by writing a letter, to be shown in the House of Commons, in which he stated that he considered an attack upon the Duke as an attack upon himself.[2] Finding, however that the tide was setting with irresistible strength against his brother, he changed his course; he reprobated the Duke's conduct, who, he said, had brought this business upon himself by not paying Mrs. Clarke the allowance which he had promised her; and announced his intention of observing a strict neutrality. The King, hearing of this decision, sent to him in great agony of mind, to request him to reconsider it, on the ground that neutrality in his position was condemnation;[3] and the Queen wrote at the

[1] *Court and Cabinets, ibid.* p. 318. Mr. Horner, in letters of Feb. 11 and March 25, 1809, has some good remarks on the Duke of York's case. He wisely prefers an address for his removal to an impeachment, and afterwards rejoices that the minority was sufficiently large to render the Duke's resignation necessary (*Life*, vol. i. pp. 427, 452). Public opinion likewise contributed powerfully to this result. Lord Malmesbury's views, more favourable to the Duke, are in his *Diaries*, vol. iv. p. 410.

[2] *Mem. of Romilly*, vol. ii. p. 267.

[3] The state of the King's sight at this time was such as to incapacitate him from reading and writing; and, although he was provided with a Private Secretary (Sir Herbert Taylor) on this account, he preferred for the actual purpose sending a message through the Queen (see *Court and Cabinets, ibid.* p. 291). The last speech which he delivered personally in Parliament was at the beginning of the session of 1805. It seems that this speech was printed, in order that he might read it better (*Court and

1809. same time to say that the King's life and health, as well as the honour of the family, depended on the result. All that the Prince would do was to send down Colonel M'Mahon, of his own household, to vote for the Duke; but he declined to exercise any influence over the other votes which he could determine.[1]

The session of Parliament came to a close on the 21st of June, without any Ministerial change. But in the meantime Napoleon had not been inactive. The campaign of the Danube had commenced in the spring; the battle of Eckmühl had been fought in April, and Vienna had capitulated in May. The sanguinary conflicts of Aspern and Essling speedily succeeded, but the Austrians were unable to follow up their advantage, and the campaign was terminated by the finishing victory at Wagram in July.[2] While Napoleon was thus occupied in annihilating the last remnants of Austrian independence, he relaxed his exertions in Spain; and allowed Sir A. Wellesley, who had returned in April to Lisbon, and was in command of the main body of English forces, to advance into Spain as far as Talavera, where he gained a hard-fought victory over the French, under Marshal Victor, on

Cabinets, vol. iii. p. 411). All his subsequent speeches until 1811 were, on account of his blindness, delivered by Commissioners. Lord Eldon speaks of the King's 'want of sight' in a letter of November, 1806 (*Twiss, ibid.* p. 11).

[1] See Lord Temple's curious letter of Feb. 26, giving an account of a long interview with the Prince at Carlton House, and his subsequent undated letter (*Court and Cabinets*, vol. iv. pp. 325, 330). Mr. Fremantle says, in a letter of March 24: 'Every part of the royal family at Windsor, excepting the King, is overwhelmed with despair at the Duke of York's business. The Queen very ill, and two of the princesses dying. The King is said to bear it very firmly; but I have reason to believe he is indignant at his Ministers for having suffered it to come forward at all. The Duke of York, I am told by those who have seen much of him since, is quite sunk under it' (*Court and Cabinets, ibid.* p. 335).

[2] See Lord Malmesbury's remarks on this campaign (*Diaries, ibid.* p. 411).

the 27th of July. His advance, however, was unsupported, and the approach of other French divisions speedily compelled him to fall back upon the Portuguese frontier. 1809

The English Government had not sufficient confidence in the policy of their Spanish interference to make it their exclusive object; for in July they sent a great expedition to the Scheldt, under the command of Lord Chatham, with a view of destroying the French naval arsenals at Flushing and Antwerp. The expedition, through the inefficiency and feebleness of the commander, utterly failed in accomplishing its purpose, and returned to England early in September, after leaving a detachment in the island of Walcheren, which, on account of its unhealthiness, was evacuated before the end of the year.[1]

The failure of this expedition brought about an important change in the English Cabinet. Mr. Canning had for some time considered Lord Castlereagh unequal to the duties of the War Department; he had in April communicated this opinion to the Duke of Portland, and had tendered the resignation of his office unless a new arrangement should be made with respect to that department. The change which Mr. Canning desired to see effected was the substitution of Lord Wellesley for Lord Castlereagh, as War Minister;[2] and after some further negotia-

[1] The severe censure upon this expedition pronounced by Colonel Napier appears to be just (*History of the Peninsular War*, vol. ii. p. 354).

[2] The Duke of Portland, in a letter to Lord Eldon of June 7, 1809, thus describes Mr. Canning's demands: 'The great object, and, indeed, the *sine quâ non* with Canning, is to take from Lord Castlereagh the conduct of the war; and perhaps Canning may go so far as to wish that he may not keep the seals, but have some other Cabinet office. But if Lord Castlereagh gives up the War Department, I think Canning would be satisfied, for the present at least' (*Twiss*, *ibid.* p. 80). An abstract of the entire correspondence which passed between Mr. Canning and his colleagues on this occasion is given in Phipps's *Memoir of Ward*, *ibid.* pp. 222–246. See also the letters of Lord Mulgrave, who was a member of the Cabinet, *ibid.* pp. 206–217.

1809. tion, a promise to this effect was obtained by him from the Duke of Portland, and sanctioned by the King. Lord Camden, who was connected by marriage with Lord Castlereagh, was directed by the King to communicate to him a proposal for a new arrangement with respect to the War Department; but Lord Camden found reasons for delaying the performance of his unpleasant duty; and when, upon the failure of the expedition becoming known, Mr. Canning reminded the Duke of Portland that the time was come for transferring Lord Castlereagh's seals to Lord Wellesley, the Duke informed him that nothing had been done to prepare Lord Castlereagh for the announcement, and that he himself was about to retire from office. It had been for some time apparent that the Duke of Portland could not remain at the head of the Ministry, and Mr. Canning had put forward his claims for that post. He laid a foundation for this arrangement by affirming the principle that the head of the Ministry ought to be in the House of Commons. This, as he considered, reduced the question to a choice between Perceval and himself; [1] and he asserted his claims to a preference over Perceval. The King and the Cabinet, however, did not concur in this view; [2] and

[1] See Mr. Canning's letter to Mr. Perceval, of August 31, in Phipps's *Mem. of Ward*, *ibid.* p. 229.

[2] Concerning Mr. Canning's endeavours to succeed the Duke of Portland as Prime Minister, see Lord Eldon's letters (*Twiss, ibid.* pp. 88, 90, 93). In a letter of September 14, Lord Eldon says: 'Mr. Canning thinks proper that his determination not to act under a third person, or to do anything else, but be himself Minister, should remain unshaken; and his resignation is certain.' Soon after the Duke of Portland's paralytic stroke in August, the King informed his Ministers that they must soon look out for 'a new chief' (*ibid.* p. 78). A full account of Mr. Canning's movements at this time is also given in Mr. Dardis's letter in *Court and Cabinets, ibid.* 390–397. The double ground of Mr. Canning's resignation was also known to Lord Grenville at the time (*ibid.* p. 372). A part of Mr. Canning's plan was that Mr. Perceval should become Chancellor instead of Lord Eldon (*Twiss, ibid.* p. 90).

therefore, on the receipt of the Duke of Portland's answer, Mr. Canning, having failed in procuring the removal of Lord Castlereagh and in becoming the successor of the Duke of Portland, lost no time in resigning his office. No sooner had this step been taken, than Lord Camden found it necessary to disclose to Lord Castlereagh all that had passed respecting himself and his department. Lord Castlereagh, without hesitation, resigned the office, from which he considered himself to have been virtually dismissed without his knowledge.[1] Ten days afterwards he wrote to Mr. Canning to demand satisfaction; which demand was promptly complied with. On the 21st of September they met on Putney Heath, attended by Lord Yarmouth and Mr. C. Ellis as their respective seconds; two shots were exchanged, and at the second fire Mr. Canning received his adversary's ball in his thigh, and a button was shot off the right breast of Lord Castlereagh's coat. The parties then separated. The ground on which Lord Castlereagh demanded this satisfaction was, that Mr. Canning had concealed from him the promise which he had obtained for his removal, and had continued to act with him in the Cabinet, to the extent of allowing him to send out an important expedition, without communicating to

1809.

[1] The respective versions of this somewhat intricate transaction, given by Lord Castlereagh, Mr. Canning, and Lord Camden, with the letters between Lord Castlereagh and Mr. Canning, may be read in the *Annual Register* for 1809, pp. 504–509, 516–530. A commentary upon it, written at the time by Mr. Canning himself, or by one of his confidential friends, was inserted in the *Quarterly Review* for November 1809, vol. ii. p. 412, and attracted much attention at the time.

Lord Castlereagh addressed an explanation to the King in reference to this transaction, and the King sent him a full answer dated Oct. 3, 1809, in which His Majesty states that Lord Wellesley's name, as successor to Lord Castlereagh, was submitted to him in June, and that it was then intended that the proposed arrangements should be immediately communicated to Lord Castlereagh (*Memoirs and Correspondence of Lord Castlereagh*, vol. i. p. 18).

1809. him the step which he had taken. Mr. Canning's defence was, that the concealment had not been owing to him, and that he had repeatedly urged that the matter should be communicated to Lord Castlereagh. Without going into the merits of this dispute, we may be permitted to express our concurrence with the view of Sir S. Romilly, that, according to the strictest code of honour, Lord Castlereagh was not justified in sending a challenge, or Mr. Canning in accepting it; and that the case was not one which was fitted for the arbitrament of the pistol.[1] Mr. Wilberforce is doubtless right in attributing Lord Castlereagh's conduct on this occasion to his Irish education and habits.[2] At the same time we are bound to admit that the prevailing opinion of that period, more favourable to duelling than the opinion of the present day, justified Lord Castlereagh's conduct, and considered the provocation as adequate.

The Portland Administration was now dissolved, having lasted just two years and a half. The Duke himself only survived his resignation a few weeks. Early in August he had been seized by paralysis in returning to Bulstrode from a Council, and had been taken out of his carriage speechless and insensible.[3] The two principal members of the Cabinet, after Mr. Perceval, had likewise resigned. In this state of things the King authorised Mr. Perceval to communicate with Lords Grenville and Grey, for the purpose of forming an extended and combined Administration.[4] Lord Grenville, on the receipt of this commu-

[1] *Memoirs*, vol. ii. p. 293.

[2] *Life*, vol. iii. pp. 426–431. 'Manent' (he says) 'vestigia ruris.'

[3] Letter of Mr. Fremantle, Aug. 13, 1809 (*Court and Cabinets*, *ibid.* p. 348). He died of an operation for the stone.

[4] That the King consented with the utmost reluctance to this step, advised by his Cabinet, appears from Lord Eldon's letters in *Twiss* (*ibid.* pp. 97, 98).

nication, journeyed from Cornwall to London, and on his arrival, sent to Mr. Perceval a refusal to join the existing Ministers, alleging, as a reason, that his junction with them would be considered as a dereliction of public principle.[1] A similar answer was sent by Lord Grey from Northumberland. The letters of Lord Grenville, published by the Duke of Buckingham, show clearly that at this time he entertained a strong repugnance to office;[2] partly on account of its troubles and anxieties, and partly on account of his conviction that he would obtain no fair support from the King. It appears that the arrangement contemplated by Mr. Perceval was, that Lord Grenville should be First Lord of the Treasury, and himself Home Secretary.[3] Mr. Perceval next addressed himself to Lord Sidmouth, seeking, however, not his accession to the Government, but that of some of his friends. The reason 1809.

[1] Mr. Perceval to Lord Grenville, Sept. 23, 1809. Lord Grenville to Mr. Perceval, Sept. 25 and 29 (*Court and Cabinets, ibid.* pp. 374–376).

[2] It appears from a letter to his brother, the Marquis of Buckingham, March 7, 1807, that Lord Grenville was under an impression that 'he was not competent to the management of men.' 'I never was so naturally,' he adds, 'and toil and anxiety more and more unfit me for it' (*Court and Cabinets, ibid.* p. 133). In letters to Lord Buckingham, of March 26 and 27, he expresses his joy at his relief from office (*ibid.* pp. 148, 149). In a letter to Lord Buckingham, of Jan. 27, 1810, written at the time when the Government was defeated by the Opposition in the House of Commons on the Walcheren question, Lord Grenville says: 'You love me, I am sure, too well, to wish to see me embarked in such a project as that of carrying on a Government in these times, with a Court influence actively exerted, as before, to undermine me' (*Court and Cabinets, ibid.* p. 426).

[3] Mr. Grenville, Oct. 5, 1809 (*Court and Cabinets, ibid.* p. 381). Mr. Horner, in a letter of September 30, 1809, expresses an opinion that Lords Grenville and Grey must refuse the offer of Mr. Perceval. 'Their course is plain, and I rely implicitly upon their pursuing it from first to last. They cannot make a coalition with either set; nor can they become the King's Ministers without obtaining his consent to the immediate relief of the Catholics' (*Life,* vol. i. p. 468). By 'either set' Mr. Horner appears to mean either Mr. Perceval or Mr. Canning and their respective friends. Their refusal is approved by Sir S. Romilly (*Memoirs,* vol. ii. p. 295).

1808. assigned for this course was, that some of the old Pittite connexion entertained objections to Lord Sidmouth, and it was therefore feared that they would be alienated from the Government and determined in favour of Mr. Canning. To this overture Lord Sidmouth's friends turned a deaf ear.[1] In consequence of the failure of these applications, the old Government was renewed with as few alterations as possible. Mr. Perceval became First Lord of the Treasury, as well as Chancellor of the Exchequer;[2] Lord Wellesley succeeded Mr. Canning as Foreign Secretary; Lord Hawkesbury assumed the War Department; and Mr. Richard Ryder took his place as Home Secretary. In this state Mr. Perceval's Administration met Parliament for the session of 1810. In substance, it was nothing but the old Government with the substitution of Lord Wellesley for Mr. Canning and Lord Castlereagh. With respect to the debating efficiency of the Ministry in the House of Commons, this change must have been most important. The Cabinet consisted of ten members, seven of whom were peers, the three commoners were Perceval himself, Mr. C. Yorke, and Mr. R. Ryder.[3]

The hopes and prospects of England, in respect to the success of her struggle with Napoleon, may be considered to have been at their lowest point of depression at the end of 1809. The Convention of Cintra had for the time secured the evacuation of Portugal; but the French troops had carried away their guns and plunder, and had returned

[1] *Life of Sidmouth*, vol. iii. pp. 6–9.

[2] It seems that the office of Chancellor of the Exchequer was offered on this occasion to Mr. Milnes, the member for Pomfret, and declined (*Twiss, ibid.* p. 105). It was also offered to, and declined by, Lord Palmerston (Phipps's *Memoirs of Ward*, vol. i. pp. 249, 279).

[3] For a list of this Cabinet, see *Annual Register* for 1810, p. 425. Mr. Richard Ryder, brother of the late Lord Harrowby, was born in 1766, and died in 1832.

to France without any restriction as to their serving again during the campaign. After the unsupported advance and disastrous retreat of Sir J. Moore, Portugal had been again occupied by the French troops; the useless march of Sir A. Wellesley into Spain, and the barren victory of Talavera,[1] had been followed by his retirement upon Lisbon; and the ill-planned and worse-executed expedition to the Scheldt had produced nothing but failure and calamity. On the other hand, Napoleon was now at his highest elevation. Since Tilsit and Erfürt, he had been in strict alliance with Russia; Germany was subdued, Switzerland and Italy were in a state of abject submission, the States of the Church had been incorporated with France, and Rome declared the second city of the French empire; even Spain maintained no open resistance to the authority of King Joseph. The attempt of Austria to renew the contest with the mighty captain and conqueror had ended in new defeats and humiliations; the divorce of Josephine took place in December 1809, and was speedily followed by the marriage with the Austrian archduchess. With the exception of Russia, which was a compliant ally, and Spain, whose irregular turbulence was regarded with contempt, Napoleon was at this time absolute master of the entire Continent, and ruled it with unresisted sway. Accordingly he ceased to fight, from the want of any worthy opponent; he was present at no battle between Wagram in July 1809, and Smolensko, in the advance upon Moscow, in August 1812, a period of more than three years. 1809.

Owing to the frustration of all our recent military enterprises, and to the apparently irresistible ascendency of

[1] The speech of Lord Wellesley in the House of Lords, Jan. 26, 1810, contains his view of the advantages which he conceived to have accrued from the battle of Talavera.

1810. Napoleon upon the Continent, the public opinion of England was sunk in a state of inevitable despondency, and the leaders of Opposition gave expression in Parliament to the most gloomy anticipations, and to denunciations of the Ministers to whose mismanagement these national calamities were attributed. It is a just remark of Sir Archibald Alison, that both Napoleon and the French nation were misled by the debates of this time into a belief that the continuance of the war by England, on the Continent, was impossible. These debates were carefully reprinted in the 'Moniteur,' and form, according to Sir A. Alison, a third part of its contents for the year 1810.[1] Either it was thought the attempt would not be made, because Parliament would refuse the supplies necessary for prosecuting hostilities by land; or, if the attempt were made, the English armies would be destroyed. This is not the only instance in which important events have turned upon a misconception by foreign Governments of the character of our Parliamentary debates, and upon the belief that the desponding and censorious habits of English orators will prevent them from consenting to measures of vigour when the moment for exertion arrives. It may be added that Napoleon likewise mistook the natural hostility of a Parliamentary Opposition to the Government for attachment to himself.

The meeting of Parliament for the session of 1810 occurred on the 22nd of January. In both Houses a resolution of censure upon Ministers for the military operations of the preceding year was moved as an amendment to the address. In the Lords the motion was made by Lord Grenville and supported by Lord Grey; it was opposed by Lord Harrowby and Lord Liverpool: and, on a division

[1] *History of Europe*, chap. 59, vol. vii. pp. 807–821, vol. viii. pp. 268, 269, 370.

was negatived by 144 to 92. In the Commons the motion was made by Lord Gower, and seconded by Mr. Ward in a speech which ably sums up all the main arguments of the Opposition at this period. It was supported by Mr. Ponsonby, the leader of the Whig party; and opposed by Mr. Perceval and the two ex-Ministers, Lord Castlereagh and Mr. Canning. On a division, the Government numbered 263 to 167.[1] Shortly afterwards Lord Porchester, in the House of Commons, moved for the appointment of a committee to enquire into the expedition to the Scheldt; the Government resisted it, and sustained a defeat, the numbers being 195 in favour of the motion and 186 against it. The papers relating to this expedition laid before Parliament contained a narrative drawn up by Lord Chatham, and presented by him to the King. This proceeding was regarded by the Opposition as unconstitutional, and Mr. Whitbread accordingly followed up the first victory over Ministers by moving for copies of all papers relative to the late expedition, submitted by Lord Chatham to the King. This motion likewise was carried against the Government by 178 to 171.[2] Mr. Whitbread prosecuted 1810.

[1] The original address was on this occasion seconded by Mr. Peel, who thus came forward as a supporter of Mr. Perceval's Government at a critical moment.

[2] Feb. 23. Upon this division Lord Grenville says, in a letter to the Marquis of Buckingham of Feb. 24: 'I say nothing to you of our victory last night, as you will hear all the particulars from others. It will, I take it, be worse received at Windsor than any event that has happened this many a day. People are asking this morning whether Perceval will resign upon it. But I think it is clear that he must stay in for his own safety till the enquiry is over. Enough has been already proved to make it necessary for him and his colleagues to retain all the support which Ministerial situation can give; and even so, I much doubt whether they can shelter themselves from censure. Lord Chatham's situation seems quite desperate. He has got into a scrape from which I don't see how it is possible for him to extricate himself' (*Court and Cabinets, ibid.* p. 426).

1810. the campaign by moving resolutions of censure upon Lord Chatham for submitting a private narrative of the expedition to the King, which, with an amendment proposed by Mr. Canning, were carried by a majority of thirty-three (221 to 188), although the Government only met them by moving the previous question. In consequence of this vote Lord Chatham resigned his office of Master-General of the Ordnance.[1] Thus far the course of the Opposition had been victorious; but their successes were arrested at the critical point. The enquiry into the Scheldt expedition, which had been carried on by the examination of witnesses at the bar of the House, having now reached its close, Lord Porchester, on the 21st of March, moved detailed resolutions of censure upon Ministers; but these, after a debate, in which the conduct of the expedition was defended by Lord Castlereagh, Mr. Canning, and Mr. Perceval, were negatived by 275 to 227 votes. It appears that a different result was anticipated by some at least of the Cabinet, and much desired by Lord Wellesley, who expected that, as he had not been involved in the discredit of the Walcheren expedition, he should be called upon to form the new Administration. His plan of a Cabinet was matured, and he is stated to have been surprised and mortified at the actual result. The result was attributed, not so much to the exertions of the Government in influencing votes, as to the preponderance of their arguments in debate.[2] Later in the session a resolution of censure

[1] 'The Government are terribly afraid that I shall get them, and myself, into a scrape. But what can be expected from men who are beaten in the House of Commons three times a week? A great deal might be done now if there existed in England less party and more public sentiment, and if there was any Government' (Lord Wellington to Admiral Berkeley, April 7, 1810; *Gurwood*, vol. vi. p. 20). This example shows that complaints about weak Governments sometimes occurred in the period before the Reform Bill.

[2] See the letters to the Marquis of Buckingham, with the writer's name

upon Ministers, with respect to the military operations in Spain, was moved in the House of Lords by Lord Lansdowne (who had recently succeeded to the title by the death of his elder brother),[1] and a motion on the state of the nation was made by Lord Grey.[2] The business of the session having been transacted, Parliament was prorogued on the 21st of June. 1810.

Lord Wellesley appears to have been dissatisfied with the existing construction of the Cabinet, and to have chafed under the supremacy of Perceval. In order to strengthen it he proposed the incorporation of Lord Sidmouth, Mr. Canning, and Lord Castlereagh. Perceval consented somewhat reluctantly with respect to the two first, and overtures were accordingly made to them; but this arrangement was frustrated by the positive refusal of Lord Sidmouth to sit in the same Cabinet with Mr. Canning. Upon his refusal an application was made to Lord Castlereagh; but Lord Castlereagh, though considering his personal quarrel with Mr. Canning to have been settled by what had passed, thought nevertheless that it would be detrimental to his own character to serve

suppressed, of March 26 and April 2, 1810 (*Court and Cabinets, ibid.* pp. 427, 430). The editor's motive for concealing the name of this person does not appear. He seems to have been a Mr. Dardis, who is often mentioned in the correspondence; he furnished information to Lord Buckingham, and was in the confidence of Lord Wellesley, from whom his authentic facts were derived. Mr. Dardis says, in his letter of April 2: 'You will also see that there is one proposed way of determining these difficulties, to which it is strongly hoped that all concerned in this "give and take plate" will accede; viz. the putting Lord Wellesley at the head of the Government, when the hunger for place, competitorship, and pretensions may all, by falling in under his banners, be adjusted and satisfied, and thus a strong, consistent, and united government be formed' (p. 432). No doubt can exist as to the quarter in which this view originated.

[1] John, second Marquis of Lansdowne, died Nov. 15, 1809.

[2] Lord Grenville was prevented by illness from attending Parliament in the latter part of this session (see *Court and Cabinets, ibid.* pp. 443, 445, 447).

1810. in the same Cabinet with him, and therefore declined the offer. The Cabinet did not consider the accession of Mr. Canning alone desirable; Lord Wellesley refused to agree to any arrangement which should not include Mr. Canning, and therefore no further negotiation took place.[1]

The accession of Lord Wellesley to the Foreign department confirmed the policy of prosecuting the war in the Peninsula, which, though hitherto on the whole unsuccessful, met with much support and sympathy in this country, on account of its popular and patriotic character. Sir Arthur Wellesley (created Lord Wellington after the battle of Talavera) had not been inactive during the winter and spring: at this time he contrived and quietly executed the celebrated lines of Torres Vedras, which formed a complete circumvallation round Lisbon. When, therefore, Massena invaded Portugal in September 1810, he found, to his surprise, his progress arrested by an impenetrable barrier; and after exhausting the country of all its resources, and exposing his army to severe privations, he commenced his retreat in November, and finally crossed the frontier in March 1811. This may be considered as the first decided reflux in the tide of Napoleon's fortunes, for the French armies never again entered Portugal. Its evacuation by Junot was provisional; but its evacuation by Massena was definitive.[2]

[1] See Mr. Dardis's letters (*Court and Cabinets, ibid.* pp. 434, 438, 450; *Life of Sidmouth,* vol. iii. pp. 25–28; Phipps's *Memoirs of Ward, ibid.* p. 440).

[2] The following important remarks on the campaigns of the French in Portugal occur in a letter addressed by the Duke of Wellington to Lord Sidmouth in 1826:—

'It is a very curious circumstance, that the cause of their destruction in Portugal was the same as the real cause of their destruction in Russia. The contempt of all the ordinary rules of war, and of the means and gallantry of their enemy, the want and deprivation of food in their own army, and the consequent undisciplined disorders and sickness of the troops, and the hatred

At the end of October 1810, the King's mental malady returned in an aggravated form; the immediate predisposing cause being his grief on account of the alarming illness of the Princess Amelia, who died on the 2nd of November.[1] Parliament met, and after some delays caused by uncertainty as to the King's state, a Bill was proposed by ministers, and agreed to by both Houses, which constituted the Prince of Wales Regent, with certain restrictions of his prerogative; these were to cease at the end of a year, viz. on the 1st of February, 1812. The precedent of 1788 was closely followed in the Parliamentary course pursued on this occasion. 1810.

When the King's illness commenced, Perceval sought to strengthen his Government by offers to Lord Sidmouth and Lord Castlereagh to join, but Lord Wellesley insisted on the inclusion of Mr. Canning in any reorganisation of the Cabinet; and, as the same personal incompatibility still existed which previously prevented the accession of all the three persons, this negotiation again fell to the ground.[2]

The political connections of the Prince of Wales had hitherto been with the Whig party. With Mr. Fox he had pretty constantly maintained habits of close intimacy. Since the death of Fox, Lord Moira and Sheridan had been his political friends. He had always occupied a

of the inhabitants, produced, in both countries, the destruction of the French armies. There was in Russia, besides, the frost to aggravate all their distresses, although in some respects an advantage to them; and, moreover, the Russian armies were more equal in numbers to the French in Russia, both during the attack and the retreat, than I ever was to the French in Portugal' (*Life of Lord Sidmouth*, vol. iii. p. 25).

[1] See the accounts in *Court and Cabinets*, *ibid.* pp. 458–483 (Lord Grenville's letter in p. 475 is misdated Nov. 30 for Oct. 30). Full particulars as to the King's state at this time will be found in the evidence of the physicians before the Committees of both Houses (in *Hansard's Debates*). The physicians expected his recovery, notwithstanding his age, which was seventy-two. George III. was born on June 4, 1738.

[2] *Court and Cabinets, ibid.* p. 478.

1810. political position independent of the King and the Court, if not in antagonism to them; and the King's ministers had, as such, no title to his esteem. Perceval and Lord Eldon had, in fact, earned his bitterest hostility by espousing the cause of the Princess of Wales; a course by which they expected to ingratiate themselves with the King. The Regency restrictions left the Prince's power of changing and selecting his Ministers unlimited; and, while the measure was still pending, he took the resolution of consulting Lords Grenville and Grey upon the answer to be made to the address of the two Houses; and, moreover, of authorising the formation of a new Administration, in which Lord Grenville was to be First Lord of the Treasury.[1] Differences, however, immediately arose as to the preparation of the answer; Lord Moira and Sheridan were also consulted, and an answer prepared by the latter was preferred to that proposed by Lord Grenville and Lord Grey.[2] The Prince was likewise impressed, through reports of the physicians, with the probability of the King's speedy recovery, and his resumption of the royal functions. Under these circumstances the Prince, on the 4th of February 1811, the day before the Regency Bill received the sanction of the great seal, addressed a letter to Mr.

[1] See Mr. Horner's letter of Jan. 18, 1811 (*Life*, vol. ii. p. 74), and Lord Grenville's to Mr. Horner, of Jan. 22, informing him that there is a question of a new Administration, in which he (Lord Grenville) is to be first Lord of the Treasury, and Mr. Tierney Chancellor of the Exchequer, and offering him the office of Secretary to the Treasury. The offer to Mr. Horner was declined (*ibid.* p. 77). Sir S. Romilly confirms this account as to Lord Grenville, and adds that Lord Grey, Mr. G. Ponsonby, and Mr. Whitbread were to be the three Secretaries of State; Lord Holland, First Lord of the Admiralty; and Lord Erskine, Speaker of the House of Lords, with the Great Seal in Commission (*Memoirs*, vol. ii. p. 359). Mr. Wilberforce adds a report that Lord Lansdowne was to be Lord Lieutenant of Ireland (*Life*, vol. iii. pp. 492–494). Another report was that Lord Moira was to be Lord Lieutenant of Ireland, and Sheridan Irish Secretary (Moore's *Life of Sheridan*, vol. ii. p. 409).

[2] *Moore*, *ibid.* pp. 379–407.

Perceval, stating that it was not his intention to remove the existing Ministers from office. He added that this step was dictated exclusively by his filial duty and affection.[1] The Prince is related to have been informed by one of the physicians, that, when the King came to learn the change of Ministers, his malady would undergo so great an exacerbation as to put an end to his life, and that the Prince would thus virtually become guilty of parricide.[2] In the course of the year, however, the King's malady assumed a permanent form,[3] and his physicians, when examined by both Houses of Parliament in January 1812, declared that there was no hope of amendment.[4] 1810

The Parliamentary session of 1811—the first session of the Regency—was not eventful. The restoration of the Duke of York to the office of Commander-in-chief created a debate;[5] and the depreciation of the Bank of England

[1] The Prince's letter, and Mr. Perceval's answer, are printed in the *Annual Register*, 1811; *State Papers*, p. 279. There seems to be a mistake in the dates, for the Prince's letter is dated Feb. 4, and Mr. Perceval's letter, which speaks of the Prince's letter 'of last night,' is dated Feb. 11. The Prince's letter is stated to have been composed by Sheridan (*Moore*, vol. ii. p. 408; compare Phipps's *Mem. of Ward*, *ibid.* p. 376–384).

[2] *Mem. of Sir S. Romilly*, *ibid.* p. 361. It seems that Ministerial changes had even been arranged on the supposition of the King's restoration to health, and of his resumption of his functions in May (Duke of Buckingham's *Memoirs of Court of England during the Regency*, vol. i. pp. 51, 57). In a letter to Dr. Swire, of April 24, 1812, reviewing the previous eighteen months, Lord Eldon says of the Prince Regent: 'My own real opinion is, that, whatever motives his friends or foes may, in their conjectures, ascribe his late conduct to, he has been principally governed by a feeling that, if his father should recover, he would never forgive himself if he suffered him to awake to a scene in which the father should see the servants discarded by his son' (*Twiss*, *ibid.* p. 197).

[3] Twiss's *Life of Eldon*, vol. ii. pp. 174, 182. Lord Eldon did not despair of the King's recovery in June (*ibid.* p. 178); *Life of Horner*, vol. ii. pp. 88, 103.

[4] See the evidence in *Hansard's Debates*.

[5] The Duke at first declined the Prince Regent's offer to restore him; he expressed a wish that his brother should not risk his popularity by this

1811. note, under the system of inconvertibility, began to attract attention;[1] but the session closed on the 24th of July without any great party struggle.[2]

The campaign in the Peninsula for this year was not much more fertile in events. Portugal had now been finally liberated from the French armies by the battle of Fuentes d'Onoro;[3] but the capture of Tarragona by the French, Lord Beresford's battle of Albuera, General Graham's battle of Barosa, and the unsuccessful attempts of Lord Wellington on Badajos and Ciudad Rodrigo, left matters in Spain nearly in a state of equilibrium.

The month of February, 1812, was the period at which the restrictions on the Regent were to expire; and, although they did not limit his choice of Ministers, they included the officers of the household, and other branches of the prerogative, so that their cessation created an epoch in his authority. The first effect of this cessation came by anticipation, in the shape of Lord Wellesley's resignation, who, in January, announced to the Prince that he could no longer continue to serve under Mr. Perceval, and must withdraw from the Government as soon as the restrictions had expired. Lord Wellesley had, during the last year, been in frequent controversy with Perceval, and in almost open mutiny against his ascendency; in particular, he had urged the policy of making concessions to the Catholics,

measure, and that nothing should be done until the king resumed his functions (*Mem. of Reg.*, *ibid.* p. 51).

[1] The bullion report, drawn by Mr. Horner, was presented in June 1810, and the subject was brought by him before the House in May 1811 (see an account of the proceedings in Parliament on this question, in his *Life*, vol. ii. pp. 79–93).

[2] It seems that a negotiation took place near the end of this session for a junction of Lord Wellesley and Mr. Canning with Lord Grenville and the Whig Party (*Mem. of Reg.*, *ibid.* p. 103).

[3] As to the policy of continuing the Spanish war in Jan. 1811, see the comments of Mr. Horner (*Life*, vol. ii. p. 69).

in which, though resolutely resisted by Perceval, he had hitherto apparently carried the Prince with him. He likewise complained that Perceval did not prosecute the military operations in the Peninsula with sufficient vigour. Upon Lord Wellesley's resignation the Foreign seals were offered by Perceval to Lord Castlereagh, who peremptorily declined them, on the ground that the offer was merely temporary and provisional. Perceval likewise proposed overtures to Lord Sidmouth; but the Prince, who had at this time a personal repugnance to Lord Sidmouth, positively refused his consent.[1] 1811.

Such was the position of the Ministry when the restrictions expired. The King's state was at this time considered hopeless, and the Regent felt that, for all practical purposes, his reign had begun. Being now his own master, he took the step, which he was expected to take, of making an offer to the leaders of the Whig Opposition. How far he was sincere in this offer it is not easy to determine; on the one hand, he was influenced by his old political connections, and by the expectations of the Whig party; on the other, by the wishes of Manchester House, and by the resentment of Lord Yarmouth for his recall in 1807.[2] The course which he adopted was, however, so tortuous that he could hardly have entertained any strong desire of its success. He communicated to the Cabinet his wish that a proposition should be made to Lords Grenville and Grey; whereupon Mr. Perceval prepared the draft of a letter for his consideration, which was

[1] Letter of Mr. Dardis, Feb. 1, 1812, in *Mem. of Reg.*, *ibid.* p. 215; Lord Temple, *ibid.* p. 247: Pearce's *Life of Lord Wellesley*, vol. iii. p. 208. Lord Wellesley and his friends fully expected that the Prince would make him Prime Minister when the restrictions ceased (*Mem. of Reg.*, *ibid.* p. 170). Concerning Lord Wellesley's exaggerated opinion of his own importance at this period, see Phipps's *Memoirs of Ward*, *ibid.* p. 424.

[2] See Lord Grenville's letter, Jan. 6, 1812 (*Mem. of Reg.*, *ibid.* p. 781).

1812. submitted to him on the 12th of February. This draft was unsatisfactory to the Prince, on the ground that it was likely to cause the failure of the negotiation; and on the following day he produced the letter which was actually sent. It was shown to Mr. Perceval and to Lord Wellesley, the former of whom highly approved of it, while the latter warmly remonstrated against it.[1] The letter, dated February 13, was addressed to the Duke of York: it begun by a review of the events of the preceding year; the Prince attributes his continuance of the existing Ministers to a sense of duty to the King. He dwells with satisfaction upon the military events of the year of Regency, and announces his wish to persevere in the Peninsular war. After these preliminary observations, he arrives at the material portion of the letter. Having declared that 'he has no predilections to indulge, no resentments to gratify, no objects to attain but such as are common to the whole empire,' he expresses a wish that 'some of those persons with whom the early habits of his public life were formed would strengthen his hands, and form a part of his Government.' 'With such support (he adds), and aided by a vigorous and united Administration, formed on the most liberal basis, I shall look with additional confidence to a prosperous issue of the most arduous contest in which Great Britain was ever engaged.' He lastly authorises the Duke of York to communicate the letter to Lord Grey, who is to show it to Lord Grenville.[2]

[1] *Mem. of Reg. ibid.* p. 257.

[2] This letter was versified by Moore in his celebrated parody, 'At length, dearest Freddy, the moment draws nigh,' &c., which is perhaps the wittiest and most pungent piece of political satire in our language. The passage in which the Prince declares that he has no predilections was naturally that most resented by the Whig party, and is thus happily rendered by Moore:—

I am proud to declare I have no predilections,
My heart is a sieve where some scattered affections

The offer thus conveyed to Lords Grey and Grenville, through the Duke of York, was rightly considered by them not as an authority to form a new Administration, but as a proposal to them to join the existing Government with certain modifications. They, moreover, believed that the direction to communicate first with Lord Grey was intended to sow jealousy between the two lords, because Lord Grenville had since 1806 acted as leader of the Whig party in the House of Lords. The attempt, however, failed: they agreed without hesitation to decline the offer; and on February 15, addressed a letter to the Duke of York, in which they informed him of their decision. 'All personal exclusion (they said) we entirely disclaim. We rest on public measures; and it is on this ground alone that we express without reserve the impossibility of our uniting with the present Government. Our differences of opinion are too many and too important to admit of such a union.' They proceed to advert to the state of Ireland, and to express a firm persuasion of the necessity of a 'total change of the present system of government in that country,' and of the immediate repeal of the civil disabilities of the Catholics. The two lords waited on the Duke of York with their answer, who received them with cordiality, and expressed great solicitude for the success of the negotiation. As soon as he had read the letter he insisted strongly that the Prince's intention had been misunderstood; that he did not wish to confine them to junction with the existing Government, but invited them to rally round him. The Duke of York then urged Lords Grey and Grenville, upon this assurance

1812.

Are just danced about for a moment or two,
And the finer they are the more sure to go through.

The sensation which the appearance of this parody produced is described in a letter from Moore to his mother (*Memoirs of Moore*, vol. i. p. 267).

1812. from him, to take back their answer and reconsider it. This proposition they respectfully declined, though they entertained no doubt of the Duke's sincerity; stating as their reason that the language of the Prince's letter admitted of only one interpretation, and that they saw no prospect of removing their grounds of difference with Mr. Perceval and his colleagues.[1]

This answer was treated by the Prince as final, and he immediately informed Perceval that he would be continued as Minister.[2] On learning this result, Lord Wellesley hastened to Carlton House, in order to surrender his seals; and was with some difficulty induced to retain them for a few days. On the following day, Lord Wellesley sent through Lord Eldon a message to Perceval that his recent conduct towards himself had been unmannerly, disrespectful, and contrary to the tenour of his professions; but that, when out of office, he would cease to feel any resentment towards him, from gratitude at being relieved from the degrading situation of serving under him. At his audience of leave Lord Wellesley earnestly implored the Prince not to form a Government upon the principle of maintaining the Catholic disabilities, which would be the case if he continued Perceval; and he denounced in strong terms the blindness and selfishness of the statesmen who clung to this policy. The seals of the Foreign Office

[1] Letters of Lord Temple and Mr. Grenville (*Mem. of Reg. ibid.* pp. 235, 237).

[2] Twiss's *Life of Eldon*, vol. ii. p. 189; Lord Grenville to the Marquis of Buckingham, Feb. 17, *ibid.* p. 238. Mr. Grenville mentions that the Duke of York sent a verbal message from the Prince Regent to Lord Grey, to say that he trusted that what had passed would make no interruption in their private friendship; afterwards he adds: 'Canning's language is reported to be as violent as ever against Perceval, and to regret nothing in our conduct except that we did not sufficiently temporise with the Prince to have succeeded in turning out Perceval, which, Canning says, we might easily have done' (*ibid.* p. 209).

were now delivered to Lord Castlereagh, who held them for the ten years until his death in 1822.[1] Lord Camden resigned the presidency of the Council, and was succeeded by Lord Sidmouth; but he remained a member of the Cabinet without office. Lord Sidmouth, it seems, expressed at the time his satisfaction at this junction, on the ground that he would be associated with those who had acted under him as Prime Minister, and that he should not be exposed to the treatment which he had experienced from Mr. Pitt in 1805.[2] 1812.

On reviewing this transaction, we perceive that the Prince's proposal came in an indirect, ungracious, and suspicious form, and was calculated to deter the two leaders from acceptance, and even from negotiation. Neither of the latter was disposed to make a concession in order to remove difficulties. Lord Grenville, in particular, was strongly disinclined to office, and entertained a rooted distrust of the Prince's sincerity.[3] Lord Grey entirely concurred with him as to their joint answer. There can be no doubt that the words of the letter were inconsistent with the Duke of York's interpretation; that the Prince meant only to offer a junction is indeed obvious from the fact that he originally instructed Perceval to prepare his letter.[4] Whether if the two leaders had asked for an audience, and had come into personal communication with the Prince, a different result would have been obtained, is uncertain. It is clear that the Duke of York believed the

[1] *Mem. of Reg. ibid.* pp. 257–262, 268.

[2] *Life of Sidmouth,* vol. iii. p. 73.

[3] 'I have been betrayed once by the King, and I have no taste for affording to his son the same opportunity, when I have so little cause to doubt that he has the same disposition' (Lord Grenville to the Marquis of Buckingham, Feb. 13, 1811; *Mem. of Reg. ibid.* p. 224).

[4] Sir S. Romilly considers the offer for a coalition with Perceval, to have been insincere, and to have been properly rejected (*Memoirs,* vol. iii. pp. 10–12).

1812. Prince to have intended something more than to make an offer in order that it might be refused. The same was likewise Lord Wellesley's conviction. His animosity against Perceval was now at its height; and he seems to have thought that the Prince would have consented to the formation of a Ministry founded upon a junction between Lords Grenville and Grey on the one hand, and himself and Canning on the other. Perceval's only support came from Manchester House; and the Prince had until lately entertained a strong repugnance for Lord Eldon.[1] Even after the breach of the negotiation with the Whig leaders Lord Wellesley entertained hopes that he would be preferred to Perceval.[2] The Prince's anger at the answer made to his letter likewise seems inconsistent with the supposition that he meant nothing real; for if he had simply called forth the answer which he expected and wished to obtain, there was nothing to provoke his resentment.[3]

Mr. Perceval, however, was not destined to enjoy for

[1] In a letter of April 1812, Lord Eldon says of the Prince: 'I have his own authority for believing that the kingdom produced no man whom he more hated than your friend the writer of this letter' (*Twiss, ibid.* p. 297), which statement he repeats in another subsequent letter (*ibid.* p. 225).

[2] *Mem. of Reg. ibid.* p. 260.

[3] The Prince 'is furious indeed with indignation against the "early friends"' (Lord Eldon, March 30, 1812; *Twiss, ibid.* p. 193. Lord Grenville, Feb. 17; *Mem. of Reg. ibid.* 238). The language of the Prince against the writers of the letter was so violent at a dinner at Carlton House, that when the Princess Charlotte went away to make her first appearance at the opera, she rose in tears, and expressed herself strongly to Sheridan as he led her out, upon the distress which she had felt in hearing her father's expressions. It should be added, that when she was at the opera, seeing Lord Grey in the box opposite to her, she got up and kissed her hand to him repeatedly, in the sight of the whole house (Mr. Grenville, Feb. 24, 1812; *Mem. of Reg. ibid.* p. 250; Phipps's *Mem. of Ward, ibid.* p. 432). This incident seems to have given rise to the beautiful stanzas of Lord Byron: 'Weep, daughter of a royal line,' &c. Lord Byron, in his *Journal*, Feb. 18, 1814, describes them as 'the stanzas on Princess Charlotte, weeping at Regency's speech to Lauderdale, in 1812.' The Princess Charlotte was at this time sixteen years old. She was born Jan. 7, 1796.

long the fruits of the Regent's favour. On the 11th of May, just three months after the correspondence which led to the renewal of his lease of office, he was shot by Bellingham in the lobby of the House of Commons. The suddenness and atrocity of this act created much public sympathy, and stimulated the liberality of the House of Commons, who, in consequence of a message from the Prince Regent recommending a provision for his family, voted 50,000*l.* to his children, an annuity of 2,000*l.* to his widow, and an annuity of 1,000*l.* to his eldest son. They also voted a monument to his memory in Westminster Abbey. 1812.

The Administration of Mr. Perceval was now dissolved, having lasted two years and nine months. The Cabinet deliberated whether, with Lord Liverpool as Prime Minister, they were strong enough to carry on the Government, without making overtures either to Lords Grey and Grenville, or to Lord Wellesley and Mr. Canning. They decided this question in the negative;[1] and accordingly, by the command of the Prince Regent, Lord Liverpool, on May 17, invited the two latter statesmen to join the Administration. This offer was declined by both; by Lord Wellesley, on the ground of the hostility of the Government to the Catholic Question, and their want of vigour in prosecuting the Spanish war; by Mr. Canning, on the former ground alone.[2] The Prince would probably have been satisfied with this attempt at strengthening his Government, and have filled up the vacant offices with persons of second-rate importance, if his path had not been crossed by a motion of Mr. Stuart Wortley, who, on May 21, carried, by 174 to 170 votes, an address for the

[1] Twiss, *Life of Eldon*, vol. ii. p. 209.

[2] See the papers relative to Lord Liverpool's proposal to Lord Wellesley and Mr. Canning, in *Annual Register*, 1812, pp. 346–360.

1812. formation of a strong and efficient Administration. The result of this address was, that Lord Wellesley was authorised to prepare the plan of a Ministry, and to submit it to the Prince. His first step, in pursuance of this authority, was to enquire, through Mr. Canning, whether Lord Liverpool and his colleagues, or any of them, would join a Government formed by Lord Wellesley upon the principles of an early settlement of the Catholic Question, and a vigorous prosecution of the Spanish war. This application produced an immediate refusal on the part of Lord Liverpool and his colleagues. A similar communication was at the same time made orally to Lords Grey and Grenville; but this communication produced nothing but a memorandum, commenting on the two principles laid down by Lord Wellesley, promising a warm support to the removal of Catholic disabilities, and expressing a qualified and conditional opinion on the mode of prosecuting the war in Spain.[1] At this stage of the business, the Prince put an end to the unlimited commission which he had given to Lord Wellesley, and authorised him to communicate to Lords Grey and Grenville the following proposal: viz. that Lord Wellesley should be First Lord of the Treasury, and be charged with the formation of the Government; that Lord Moira, Lord Erskine, and Mr. Canning should be members of the Cabinet; and that Lords Grey and Grenville should recommend four other names if the Cabinet should consist of twelve, and five if it should consist of thirteen. This proposal was rejected by Lords Grey and Grenville, on the ground that it was proposed to construct the Cabinet on 'a system of counteraction

[1] Lords Grey and Grenville gave this memorandum to Lord Wellesley and accompanied it with an oral statement that 'it did not appear there was any authority from the Prince to communicate with them, and therefore they did not consider themselves as entered into a negotiation for making an Administration' (*Mem. of Regency*, *ibid.* p. 317).

inconsistent with the prosecution of any uniform and beneficial course of policy.' Their answer was sent on the 3rd of June, and Lord Wellesley's hopes of forming a Ministry thus came to an end; although the Prince had, as it appears, given him every assistance for accomplishing his object. Lord Moira now appeared as a principal upon the scene. On the 5th he addressed Lords Grey and Grenville, referring to a previous letter of his own, and requesting an interview with them for the purpose of removing misunderstandings. The two lords, however, in a note of the same day, courteously, but decidedly, refused to enter upon any unauthorised discussions. On the following day Lord Moira came forward with authority to form an Administration, and with special instructions to address himself to Lords Grey and Grenville. An interview thereupon took place, in which explanations were given respecting the Catholic Question, the differences with America, and other questions of urgency, which the two lords deemed satisfactory; Lord Moira likewise stated that he had received his commission without any restriction or limitation. All preliminary difficulty as to fundamentals was therefore removed; a question was, however, put to Lord Moira, whether the great offices of the household would be included in the political changes. Lord Moira declined to give a positive assurance on this point; but Lords Grey and Grenville considered it 'indispensable that the connection of the great offices of the Court with the political Administration should be clearly established in its first arrangements.' Upon this point of difference the negotiation was broken off, and was not afterwards renewed.[1]

1812.

[1] See papers relating to the negotiations of the Marquis Wellesley and the Earl of Moira, for forming a new Administration, *Annual Register, ibid.* pp. 363–378. Moore attributes Lord Moira's conduct respecting the household

1812. The Prince thought that the attempts which he had thus made sufficed to satisfy the address of the House of Commons, and he accordingly set about repairing the breaches in his existing Ministry, without the introduction of any leading statesmen into the Cabinet. Lord Liverpool became First Lord of the Treasury, and Mr. Vansittart Chancellor of the Exchequer; Mr. Richard Ryder resigned the Home Office to Lord Sidmouth; and Lord Harrowby became President of the Council. Lord Bathurst passed from the Board of Trade to the department of War and Colonies. The other Ministers remained as before; the lead of the House of Commons being now assumed by Lord Castlereagh.

This Ministry of Lord Liverpool, though formed under these unpropitious auspices, remained in power until its dissolution on account of the failure of his health in 1827. Its composition, however, underwent material changes, first by the introduction of Mr. Canning, as President of the Board of Control in 1816, and his succession to the Foreign seals and the lead of the House of Commons upon Lord Castlereagh's death in 1822; by the substitution of Mr. F. Robinson for Mr. Vansittart, in 1823, and of Mr. Peel for Lord Sidmouth in 1822; and by the introduction of the Duke of Wellington as Master-General of the Ordnance in 1818.

The history of this negotiation shows that the Prince was desirous of bringing about a junction of Lord Wellesley and Canning with the existing Ministers, and that he gave Lord Wellesley sufficient powers for effecting this object, if the personal and political objections could have been overcome. On the other hand, it is clear that the Prince, although he was willing to authorise negotiation with the

to a point of honour; his opinion being adverse to the line which he took (*Memoirs of Moore*, vol. i. p. 287).

Whig leaders, was determined not to communicate with them directly, or to give them powers for the formation of a Government.[1] They again were inclined to take advantage of every presentable ground for repudiating the advances made to them, and for justifying a refusal, unless they received a direct and unlimited authority for forming a ministry.[2] The offer made by Lord Wellesley. according to which Lords Moira and Erskine, together with five persons to be named by Lords Grey and Grenville, were to be members of the Cabinet, would have given the Whigs a majority in a Cabinet of thirteen.[3] The point 1812.

[1] In a confidential report of an interview of Lord Wellesley with the Prince Regent, on May 25, 1812, the Prince is represented to have said, that 'As to making a proposition for a junction with Opposition, nothing should ever induce him to employ them. That he had no objection to one or two of them individually; but, as a body, he would rather abdicate the Regency than ever come into contact with them.' The writer adds: 'It is useless to state the outrageous vehemence with which the Prince abused the Opposition (*Mem. of Reg. ibid.* pp. 322, 323). This conversation took place in the interval between the attempt of Lord Wellesley and the commission given to Lord Moira. During the first year of the Regency, frequent attacks had been made on the Prince, at meetings, in the press, and partly in Parliament, all of which emanated from Whig quarters; they could not fail to leave their sting behind. When this negotiation was at an end, Lord Moira was offered and accepted the Garter. What passed afterwards is related by Moore, who was on terms of friendly communication with Lord Moira, in a letter written at the time: 'On the Friday Lord Moira went to the levée, and was installed. The next day the Prince had a great dinner of what he called friends, to which Lord Moira was not invited. And three times that day, both before and after dinner, he declared that if Lord Grenville had been forced upon him he should have abdicated. This was his expression. A friend of ours was there, and asked if this declaration was to be kept a secret; and one of the princes who was present told him not; that the Regent wished to have it known. This is an absolute fact, and shows what a dupe poor Lord Moira was' (*Mem. of Moore,* vol. i. p. 296).

[2] In a letter to the Marquis of Buckingham, written on June 5, the day before the offer of Lord Moira, Lord Grenville says: 'I grieve to say it, but my opinion now is, that the thing must finally come to us in a shape in which we shall be compelled to look at it' (*Mem. of Reg. ibid.* p. 351).

[3] See Mr. Grenville's letter, *Mem. of Reg.* p. 344.

1812. upon which the final negotiation went off was not of any great importance, and must be considered to have been rather a pretext than a real motive; especially as Lord Yarmouth subsequently stated in Parliament, that he and the other high officers of the household would have resigned if the intended Ministry had been formed. This intention had indeed been imparted to Sheridan, in order that it might be communicated to Lords Grey and Grenville; but he concealed the fact, with the deliberate object of frustrating the negotiation.[1] We willingly recognise the high sense of honour and inflexible integrity which actuated the Whig leaders on this occasion, and which made them resent the very suspicion of accepting place without power; and of refusing office unless they could obtain it precisely on their own terms.[2] At the same time we cannot but think that the country suffered materially in its best interests by a decision which excluded from the Government, for a long series of years, some of the ablest, wisest, and purest-minded statesmen of the day, which retarded the passing of Catholic Emancipation by fifteen years, and which destroyed the only chance of averting the war with America. We may likewise remark that, when it is said that the Whigs were excluded

[1] *Moore, Life, ibid.* p. 426. His biographer considers this the only indefensible act in his public life.

[2] Mr. Horner, in a letter written at the time, describes the result of this negotiation as 'the triumph of inveterate duplicity, and the low arts of a palace, over an inflexible and proud integrity' (*Life*, vol. ii. p. 111). He expresses a similar opinion in another letter (p. 113). Sir Samuel Romilly approves of the refusal; and he thinks that the Prince was insincere in his negotiation, and that, if Lords Grey and Grenville had entered the Ministry, some pretext for their removal would soon have been found. On the other hand, the article in the *Edinburgh Review* for July 1812, maintains that the reasons assigned by the leaders of the Whigs for rejecting the Prince's offers were inconclusive and insufficient (vol. xx. pp. 32–35).

from power during the twenty-three years from 1807 to 1830, it should not be overlooked that offers were made to them by the King in 1809, and by the Prince Regent on two occasions in 1812, the latter of which, at least, might have led to acceptance upon honourable terms. 1812.

Of the four leaders with whom these negotiations occurred, Lord Grenville, although he took part in Parliamentary debate some years longer, never again filled any official position, or received any overture which was known to the public. Lord Grey continued an active member of Opposition until 1830, when he became the chief of the Reform Ministry. Lord Wellesley never again filled any Cabinet situation; but he was Lord Lieutenant of Ireland from 1821 to 1828; he held the Court office of Lord Steward in 1830, and was again Lord Lieutenant in 1833–4.

Mr. Canning received overtures to join Lord Liverpool's Administration immediately upon its formation. The offer made seems to have been that he should hold the Foreign Department, and that Lord Castlereagh should be Chancellor of the Exchequer, and leader of the House of Commons. Mr. Canning rejected this offer, because he would not consent to be led by Lord Castlereagh. It appears that the qualifications of Lord Castlereagh for the lead of the House were generally considered superior to those of his rival;[1] notwithstanding the undoubted pre-

[1] Stapleton's *Life of Canning*, vol. i. p. 67; *Wilberforce's Correspondence*, vol. ii. p. 232. Mr. Wilberforce remarks, in his *Diary*, June 8, 1812: 'How striking is Canning's example! Had he fairly joined Perceval on the Duke of Portland's death, as Perceval offered, he would now have been acknowledged head, and supported as such. But his ambitious policy threw him out, and he sank infinitely in public estimation, and has since with difficulty kept buoyant' (*Life*, vol. iv. p. 34). Mr. Canning's reasons for insisting on

1812. eminence of the latter in eloquence and ability. Mr. Canning remained out of office from 1809 to 1814, when he went on a mission as ambassador to Lisbon. In 1813 he dissolved his political connection with Lord Wellesley, and formally disbanded his party of followers in the House of Commons.[1] In 1816 he re-entered the Cabinet as President of the Board of Control, an office which he resigned in January, 1821. In 1822, he had accepted the office of Governor-general of Bengal, when the death of Lord Londonderry opened to him the much-coveted post of Foreign Secretary and leader of the House of Commons. On the resignation of Lord Liverpool in 1827, Mr. Canning succeeded him as Prime Minister, but died in a few months.

The leaders of the Whig party were at the time of this Ministerial negotiation so deeply pledged against the policy of the Spanish war, that, if they had acceded to power in June 1812, they might perhaps have arrested the career of Lord Wellington, which, after many checks and reverses, was now assuming a victorious and progressive character. But as the battle of Salamanca was fought in July 1812; and as Napoleon was already engaged in his fatal expedition to Moscow, it may be doubted whether any such result would have ensued. Certainly if Lord Wellesley and Mr. Canning had been included in the Cabinet, they would have done their best to prevent

the lead in the House of Commons are stated in his letter (*ibid.* p. 40). In October 1812, after his return for Liverpool, he stated that twice in the previous six months the seals of Secretary of State had been offered him, and that he had twice declined them (*Speeches at Liverpool*, p. 87). This refers to the offer, upon Perceval's death, in May, and to the subsequent offer in July, after the formation of Lord Liverpool's Government.

[1] See *Mem. of Reg.* vol. ii. p. 36; *Life of Sidmouth*, vol. iii. p. 106. It was, we believe, on this occasion, that Lord Dudley said of Mr. Canning's party, that they dined 14 and voted 12.

any relaxation of exertion in that quarter. On the other hand, it is certain that the success of the Peninsular war, and the part which England took, both in the first and second overthrow of Napoleon, threw a lustre over the Cabinet of Lord Liverpool, and over Lord Castlereagh as its Foreign Secretary; while the same events cast a certain discredit upon the Whigs, who had from the beginning condemned the policy of carrying on the war in Spain. As a party they were rendered unpopular on this ground at the return of peace; in the same manner, though not to the same extent, that they had been rendered unpopular twenty years earlier by the opinions of their leaders on the French Revolution. 1812

The popularity which the Cabinet of Lord Liverpool had reaped from the results of its foreign policy, from the successes of the British arms upon the Continent, and the triumphant career of the Duke of Wellington, was, after a time, dissipated by the illiberal and unprogressive character of its domestic policy. The financial incapacity of Mr. Vansittart, the coercive severity of Lord Sidmouth, the narrow-minded immobility of Lord Eldon, and the supposed sympathies of Lord Castlereagh with the despotic courts of the Continent, effectually shook the hold of this Ministry upon public favour; such popularity as it retained in 1820 was rudely demolished by the proceedings known as the Queen's Trial. But the transfer of the lead of the House of Commons to Mr. Canning, and the introduction of Mr. Frederick Robinson, Mr. Peel, and Mr. Huskisson into the Cabinet, mitigated the Toryism of the Government, and raised its standard of intelligence and ability. The semi-liberal phase upon which it now entered gave it fresh vitality; and new Cabinets formed substantially upon the same principle succeeded, until the passing of the Catholic Question in 1829 divided the supporters of the Duke of

1812. Wellington's Government, and, combined with the growing feeling in favour of popular reforms, finally brought about its overthrow. In the meantime, the Whigs, led by Lord Grey in the Lords and by Mr. Brougham in the Commons, had during these administrations been the steady advocates of sound, enlightened, and liberal principles, with respect to retrenchment of expenditure, taxation, currency, education of the poor, colonial slavery, religious toleration, mitigation of punishments, amendment of the law, and Parliamentary reform; and on their accession to office in 1830, they commenced a series of practical measures which have been continued to the present day, which the interposition of Conservative Ministries has not been able to interrupt, and which, on the whole, have been crowned with greater success than even their authors had ventured to anticipate.

Napoleon is reported to have said, in his conversations at St. Helena, that the Spanish war was the cause of his ruin.[1] It rarely happened that in statements respecting his own failures he was disposed to tell the truth, and this case was no exception to the rule. It is certain that the Russian expedition, and the consequent rising of Germany, were the main causes of his downfall. The insurrection in Spain, and the successes of the English under the Duke of Wellington, contributed to this end, but would not have alone sufficed to produce it. His motive for this perversion of the truth doubtless was, that the French armies in the Peninsula had been commanded by his generals, and that he himself had only remained in Spain for a few weeks; whereas the Russian campaign and the battle of Leipsic had been under his own personal superintendence, and he could therefore less easily resort

[1] *Las Cases, Mém. de St. Hélène*, vol. i. p. 693. Paris, 1842.

to his invariable resource of throwing the blame of failure 1812.
in these great operations upon subordinates.[1]

That the campaigns of the English in the Peninsula, by fomenting the national resistance to the French, by occupying large French armies, and thinning their ranks, and by destroying the conviction of the invincibility of the French arms, assisted materially in bringing about the downfall of Napoleon, will probably be admitted by impartial historians of all nations. But the successes achieved in these campaigns mainly sprang from Napoleon's neglect of his own rule, to crush one enemy by an overwhelming force before he attacked another. A portion only of the great army which marched to Moscow would have sufficed to annihilate the weak Spanish levies, and to drive within the lines of Torres Vedras, if not to reembarkation, any military force which England could have maintained in the Peninsula. It was the expedition to Moscow which enabled Wellington to win the battles of Salamanca and Vittoria, and afterwards to cross the Pyrenees and to enter France; but his operations had so little direct effect upon the first fall of Napoleon, that the battle of Toulouse was fought after the entry of the allies into Paris, and after the signature of the first abdication.

According to the course which events took, the English campaigns in the Peninsula gave an impulse to the overthrow of Napoleon; but as it was impossible to foresee that his ambition, however restless and insatiable, would lead

[1] M. Thiers, in the thirty-ninth book of his *History of the Empire*, makes the following remark: 'Masséna ne chercha pas à s'exonérer du résultat de la journée en accusant ses lieutenants, ni à exhaler son chagrin en vaines dissertations sur ce qui aurait pu être fait, *genre de plaintes dans lequel les âmes faibles trouvent un soulagement.*' We doubt whether M. Thiers can be said to have observed his own rule on this point.

1812. him into the gigantic error of the Russian expedition, it may be doubted whether England pursued a wise policy in making herself the ally of second-rate Powers, without military resources or apitude, such as Spain and Portugal. If, instead of pursuing her traditionary policy of confining her operations to maritime objects, which dictated the expedition to the Scheldt, she had sent an army to the assistance of Austria in 1809, the campaign of Wagram might have taken a different turn; and it is possible that the Duke of Wellington, at the head of a strong and well-appointed British force in Germany, in 1812 and 1813, might, by cooperating with Prussia, Austria, and Russia, have contributed more directly to Napoleon's downfall, than by the diversion effected in the Peninsula. The complete annihilation of the French maritime power, at Trafalgar, and the firm determination of England not to yield to the continental tyranny of Napoleon, doubtless strengthened the wavering resistance of Central Europe; but these causes would have exercised as much influence if the military operations of England had been in Germany, as they exercised under the measures which were actually adopted.

It is, in our opinion, difficult to overrate the evil effects which the policy of Napoleon, military, civil, and commercial, produced both in France and in the rest of Europe; on account not only of the enormous miseries which he inflicted on his contemporaries, but also of the rich inheritance of mischief which he has bequeathed to posterity. The full extent of his pernicious influence will, however, be never fully appreciated until some historian is found who will take a dispassionate and enlightened view of the true character of his rule. So long as our estimate of him depends upon apologists, such as Thiers, who identify his successes with the national honour of France, and consider

it patriotic to praise this type of military despotism; or 1812.
upon Tory champions of England, such as Alison, who judge everything by the narrow views of an expiring political party; it is impossible that such a severe condemnation of his odious and retrograde system as justice demands should be awarded with the impartiality which alone can command the general assent of a European public.

VI.

LORD LIVERPOOL'S ADMINISTRATION UNTIL 1822.[1]

1812. In a recent article, with the help of some modern publications, we followed the course of the Grenville, Portland, and Perceval Administrations; and we gave a succinct account of the negotiations which, in June 1812, led to the selection of Lord Liverpool as the successor of Mr. Perceval.[2] We propose in this article to continue our review of the events of this period from the accession of Lord Liverpool to the death of Lord Castlereagh in 1822 and on a future occasion to carry on our retrospect from 1822 to the resignation of the Duke of Wellington, and the advent of the Reform Ministry of Lord Grey.

The Administration of Lord Liverpool, like that of Mr. Pitt in 1783, was neither formed under happy auspices, nor was it upon its formation expected to be of long duration. Yet it lasted for fifteen years, and was at last only dissolved by the illness and resignation of Lord Liverpool himself, without any adverse parliamentary vote.

The negotiations with Lords Grey and Grenville on the one hand, and with Lord Wellesley and Mr. Canning on the other, had equally failed; and the Administration of Lord Liverpool was in substance a reproduction of the preceding Government, with such shiftings of parts as were rendered necessary by Mr. Perceval's death. In his

[1] *Review of Correspondence, Despatches, and other Papers of Viscount Castlereagh, Second Marquis of Londonderry.* Edited by his brother, Charles William Vane, Marquis of Londonderry. London, 1849–53. 12 vols. 8vo.

[2] *Edinburgh Review,* Oct. 1858, Art. 1.

character of the First Lord of the Treasury, Mr. Perceval was replaced by Lord Liverpool, who resigned the War Department to Lord Bathurst, previously President of the Board of Trade. In his capacity of Chancellor of the Exchequer he was replaced by Mr. Vansittart. In his capacity of leader of the House of Commons he was replaced by Lord Castlereagh. The other changes were caused by the retirement of Mr. Charles Yorke and Mr. Richard Ryder.[1] 1812.

The new Prime Minister was the son of the first Earl of Liverpool, who had filled numerous official situations, had taken a considerable part in public affairs, and was much distinguished by the favour of George III., but is now chiefly known as the author of the work on the 'Coins of the Realm.'[2] He was born in 1770, and entered Parlia-

[1] Mr. Perceval's Cabinet, in April 1812, consisted of ten members, of whom six were Peers and four were Commoners. Lord Liverpool's Cabinet, in September 1812, consisted of twelve members, of whom ten were Peers and only two were Commoners—viz. Lord Castlereagh and Mr. Vansittart. The following comparative lists of the Cabinet, as it stood in April and September 1812, will show the changes produced by Mr. Perceval's death, and the formation of the Liverpool Ministry. We have marked in italics those persons who were not in both Cabinets.

	April 1812.	Sept. 1812.
First Lord of the Treasury	*Mr. Perceval.*	Earl of Liverpool.
Chancellor of the Exchequer		*Mr. Vansittart.*
Lord Chancellor . .	Lord Eldon.	Lord Eldon.
President of Council .	Viscount Sidmouth.	Earl of Harrowby.
Privy Seal . . .	Earl of Westmoreland.	Earl of Westmoreland.
Home Secretary . .	*Mr. Richard Ryder.*	Viscount Sidmouth.
Foreign Secretary . .	Viscount Castlereagh.	Viscount Castlereagh.
War Secretary . . .	Earl of Liverpool.	*Earl Bathurst.*
First Lord of Admiralty .	*Mr. Charles Yorke.*	*Viscount Melville.*
Master-general of Ordnance	Earl of Mulgrave.	Earl of Mulgrave.
(No office)	Marquis Camden.	Marquis Camden.
President of the Board of Control	(Not in the Cabinet.)	*Earl of Buckinghamshire.*

[2] Reviewed with high praise in the *Edinburgh Review* for January 1806 (vol. vii. p. 265).

1812. ment in 1790, a few months before he attained his majority; and soon took a prominent part in debate as a supporter of Mr. Pitt's Government. In 1801, upon Mr. Pitt's resignation, Lord Hawkesbury, being still a member of the House of Commons, entered Addington's Cabinet as Foreign Secretary, and in that capacity negotiated the Peace of Amiens. In 1803 he gained much reputation by his spirited answer to Mr. Pitt in the debate on Colonel Patten's motion of censure; and at the beginning of the following session he was called up to the House of Lords, of which he became the leader. In this position he remained, with a transfer only from the Foreign to the Home Department, until Mr. Pitt's death, when he went into Opposition. Upon the formation of the Portland Administration he returned to the Home Office and the lead of the House of Lords. In the Perceval Ministry he held the Seals of the War Department, which he only surrendered in order to become First Lord of the Treasury in June 1812, having succeeded to the Earldom of Liverpool upon the death of his father in December, 1808.

As soon as the Government was formed, Lord Liverpool made an attempt to strengthen it by the incorporation of Mr. Canning without Lord Wellesley, his partner in the late negotiation. The offer made to him was the Foreign Department together with other subordinate offices for his political friends; but the lead of the House of Commons was to remain with Lord Castlereagh, who was, it appears, to become Chancellor of the Exchequer instead of Mr. Vansittart.[1] The Foreign Department must have had great attractions at this moment for Mr. Canning; he had held it from 1807 to 1809 under the lead of Mr. Perceval. The Peninsular war, of which he had been the originator, and in the prosecution of which he had from the beginning

[1] See *Wilberforce Correspondence*, vol. ii. p. 232.

taken a peculiar interest, had now entered upon a more hopeful stage of its course; Ciudad Rodrigo had been captured in January, and Badajos in April. Lord Wellington had already commenced the advance which ended in the battle of Salamanca. Napoleon had, moreover, crossed the Niemen, and had begun his perilous and, as it ultimately proved, fatal march to Moscow; so that some gleams of light could be seen to streak the dark horizon of Continental politics. Mr. Canning declined this offer because Lord Castlereagh, in yielding to him the Foreign Department, which he had now held since Lord Wellesley's resignation in February, did not at the same time yield to him the lead of the House of Commons. Mr. Stapleton, in his 'Life of Mr. Canning,' states that Mr. Canning referred the question to three members of the House of Commons, who were supposed to be peculiarly well qualified to form a judgment upon it; that they advised him to refuse the office without the lead of the House, and that he acted upon their advice, but against his own opinion.[1] Mr. Canning, however, in a letter written at the time to Mr. Wilberforce, dwells upon the importance of the post of leader, and warmly justifies his refusal upon the ground that he was right in insisting on it.[2]

1812.

One of the first acts of the new Government, though right in itself, and only censurable because it came too late to avert war with the United States, was the revocation of the Orders in Council with respect to American vessels, a measure which Lord Castlereagh announced on the 16th of June, upon a motion of Mr. Brougham for

[1] *Political Life of Mr. Canning*, vol. i. p. 67. The disappointment which the refusal of this offer subsequently caused to Mr. Canning is described by Mr. Stapleton, *ibid.* p. 292.

[2] *Life of Wilberforce*, vol. iv. p. 46.

1812. an address to the Prince Regent to recall or suspend them.[1] This decision, forced upon the Government by parliamentary argument, by the commercial distress, and by the voice of the country, involved an entire departure from the policy hitherto followed or supported by the existing Ministers, and therefore was regarded as additional evidence of their weakness.

Shortly after the formation of the Administration, Lord Wellesley and Mr. Canning brought the Catholic Question under the notice of both Houses, by motions for a consideration of the laws affecting the Roman Catholics, early in the next session, with a view to a final and conciliatory adjustment. This resolution was met in the House of Lords by Lord Eldon, not with a negative, but with the previous question; and in this subdued form, his amendment was carried only by a majority of one, the division in his favour being 126 to 125, and the peers present being equal. In the other House the success of the motion was still greater; for it was there supported by Lord Castlereagh and carried by a majority of 235 to 106. The result of these motions shows that if an Administration involving a strong Whig element, and one favourable to the Catholic claims, had been formed in this session, it might have succeeded in effecting a final settlement of the question. At this time the demands of the war with Napoleon, and the manifest impolicy of keeping Ireland in a permanent state of disaffection, as a bait for invasion, and a chronic cause of weakness, created a disposition among the intolerant party in Great Britain to

[1] Motions for the appointment of Select Committees to enquire into the operation of the Orders in Council, had been made in the early part of the session by Lord Lansdowne and Mr. Brougham, had been resisted by the Government, and had been negatived by considerable majorities (Feb. 28 and March 3).

listen to reason;[1] which evaporated when the enemy had been defeated, and when peace had been restored. The fear of the foreigner now produced that willingness to do justice to the Catholics, which, in 1829, was reproduced in a more practical form by the fear of civil war. 1812.

The business of the session having been completed, and all ministerial negotiations being at an end, Parliament was prorogued on the 30th of July. The repeal of the Orders in Council had been too long deferred: war against Great Britain had been declared by the United States—and the prospects of the Government were gloomy, when the news arrived of the battle of Salamanca, fought on the 21st of July, a few days before the prorogation. This event (which was followed by the entry of the English into Madrid on the 11th of August) infused a new life into the Ministry: but the development of the Moscow drama, which speedily ensued, placed it in a new and far more hopeful position. Napoleon, before he left Paris for the Russian expedition, seems to have felt some uneasiness about the state of things in Spain; and though he did not think the Peninsular war worthy of his personal interference, he attempted to extinguish it by a separate negotiation with England. By a despatch which the Duke of Bassano addressed to Lord Castlereagh, dated April 17, 1812, he proposed: 1. That the integrity of Spain should be guaranteed; that France should renounce all idea of extending her dominions beyond the Pyrenees, and that the existing dynasty should be declared independent. 2. That the independence and integrity of Portugal should be also guaranteed, and that the House of

[1] The argument derived from the danger of a French invasion of Ireland, in the disaffected state of the Catholic population, is repeatedly urged in *Peter Plymley's Letters*, and is varied with all the power of Sydney Smith's witty imagination. He calls the English Government an *anemocracy*, because it relies on nothing but the winds for the defence of Ireland.

1812. Braganza should have the sovereign authority. 3. That the kingdom of Naples should remain in possession of the existing monarch, and that the kingdom of Sicily should be guaranteed to the existing family of Sicily : and 4. That, as a consequence of these stipulations, Spain, Portugal, and Sicily should be evacuated by the French and English land and naval forces. Lord Castlereagh's answer, dated April 23, stated that if by the 'actual dynasty of Spain,' the brother of the head of the French Government was intended the Prince Regent could not negotiate on such a basis ; but that if the existing Government, which exercised the sovereign authority in the name of Ferdinand VII., was intended, the Prince Regent was ready to enter into negotiation. With this answer the correspondence terminated; inasmuch as Napoleon clearly designed Spain to be a French dependency, governed through his brother as satrap. In May Napoleon arrived at Dresden, and at the end of June the French army crossed the Niemen. The scenes of this great tragedy now succeeded each other with rapidity, as if under the control of the avenging Nemesis of the Greek theatre : the battle of Smolensko was fought in August ; that of Borodino in September. The French army entered Moscow on the 14th of this month ; on the 15th of October the retreat commenced ; the battle of Beresina fell on the 28th of November : on the 5th of December Napoleon abandoned his army ; and on the 18th of the same month he arrived at Paris, having, since he left it in the previous May, pulverised that empire which then seemed to be made of adamant.[1]

Before, however, this catastrophe had been accomplished, Parliament had again assembled. The speech of the Prince Regent, delivered on the 30th of November,

[1] The sanguine speculations of Mr. Horner, upon the event of the Russian expedition, may be seen in his letter of Dec. 8, 1812, *Mem.* vol. ii. b. 136.

alluded in sanguine terms to the defence made by the Russians; as well as to 'the glorious and ever memorable victory obtained at Salamanca:' to which was added the expression of regret at the withdrawal from the siege of Burgos and the evacuation of Madrid. The declaration of war by the United States was likewise mentioned as an unfortunate event. In the motion upon the address, Lord Wellesley severely censured the management of the Peninsular war by Ministers; he characterised their system as 'timid without prudence, and narrow without economy; profuse without the fruits of expenditure, and slow without the benefits of caution.' Lord Grenville repeated his views respecting the war in the Peninsula, and attributed the disappointments experienced in that quarter to the delusion of Ministers in trusting to the cooperation of the Spanish armies. No business of importance was introduced before Christmas; but the House of Commons, before it separated, voted 100,000*l.* as a relief to the sufferers in Russia. After the holidays (Feb. 1813) the war with the United States was brought under the attention of Parliament by Lord Bathurst and Lord Castlereagh; addresses were moved expressing approbation of the course taken by Ministers, and pledging Parliament to the prosecution of the war. The address was supported in the House of Commons by Mr. Canning, and in both Houses it was carried without a division. 1812

The suspense in which the country was kept by the events proceeding on the Continent prevented any concerted interference, by parliamentary motions, with the conduct of the war; and the session of 1813 was mainly occupied with two questions of domestic policy, namely, the removal of Catholic disabilities, and the renewal of the charter of the East India Company. The success of Mr. Canning's motion in the previous session had elicited

1813. from the country many petitions adverse to the Catholics; but Mr. Grattan's motion for a committee of the whole House to consider the laws affecting Roman Catholics was carried on the 2nd of March by 264 to 224 votes. After some other intermediate divisions, the Bill introduced by Mr. Grattan was read a second time by 245 to 203; when the Bill was in committee the Speaker (Abbot) moved the omission of the words 'to sit and vote in either House of Parliament,' in the first clause, and carried his motion by a majority of four (251 against 247). Mr. Ponsonby, the leader of Opposition, then announced that the Bill was abandoned. With respect to the debates upon the East India Company, it is sufficient for our purpose to say that the political powers and the monopoly of the China trade were renewed for twenty years, but that the trade with India was thrown open to the public. An amendment moved by Mr. Canning for limiting the monopoly of the China trade to ten years was negatived by 69 to 29 votes.

The position of the Princess of Wales, and her permanent separation from her husband, began to attract additional attention since he had become virtually king, and since the age of the Princess Charlotte was advancing to maturity. In order, however, to understand the events of this year, it is necessary that we should revert to the previous history of the Princess of Wales, and trace the steps by which she had been brought into her actual relations with the Prince.

The Prince of Wales had, at the age of twenty-three, gone through the ceremony of a marriage with Mrs. Fitzherbert, which, though it had no legal validity, produced the effect of satisfying her scruples and quieting her conscience. This remarkable event in the Prince's life, and his versatile though overpowering female attachments, strongly indisposed him to contract a binding and lawful marriage. At length, however, his pecuniary necessities —for his debts had reached a sum exceeding 600,000*l.*— induced him to comply with the wish of the King and of the country, and to consent to take a wife. The position of Princess of Wales, and future Queen of England, was naturally much coveted by the Protestant princesses of Germany;[1] but the two candidates who seem to have held the first rank in the estimation of the Prince and his advisers were Princess Caroline of Brunswick, and Princess Louisa of Mecklenburg. The former, now (1795) twenty-seven years of age,[2] was the niece of George III., being the daughter of his sister the Princess Augusta. The latter was the niece of Queen Charlotte; and subsequently became Queen of Prussia, the idol and heroine of the Prussian people, and the object of Napoleon's insults.[3] The Princess Louisa had the advantage both in youth and beauty: and her elevated character might, if she had become Princess of Wales, have exercised some influence in fixing the wayward tastes of the selfish and unstable husband.[4] The Prince, however, having made up his mind to swallow the bitter pill of a wife, resolved to do it in the manner most acceptable to the King; and, there- 1813.

[1] The Duchess Dowager of Brunswick, sister of George III., and mother of the Princess Caroline, told Lord Malmesbury, when on his mission to fetch the Princess in 1794, that all the young German princesses had learnt English, in hopes of attaining to the dignity of Princess of Wales. She added that she never would give the idea to her own daughter Caroline, and never thought that she would make that marriage, as the King had often expressed his dislike to the marriage of cousins-german (*Diaries*, vol. iii. p. 155).

[2] She was born in May 1768.

[3] She was born in 1776, and was, therefore, eight years younger than Princess Caroline of Brunswick.

[4] Lord Thurlow said of the Prince, that 'he was the worst anchoring ground in Europe.' This dictum, which Lord Thurlow applied to his political conduct, was equally true of his domestic connections.

1813. fore, to prefer the King's to the Queen's niece. One day in returning from hunting, he suddenly announced to the King his wish to marry, and to marry the daughter of the Duke of Brunswick. The King said he could make no objection to his own niece, but suggested enquiries about her person and manners. The Prince, however, whose resolution was already taken, expressed himself as satisfied.[1] In November, 1794, Lord Malmesbury was sent to Brunswick to demand the Princess Caroline for the Prince of Wales,[2] and in the following month the King announced in his speech to Parliament the conclusion of a treaty of marriage.[3]

At the first meeting between the Prince and Princess the Prince took an aversion to her appearance, which upon further acquaintance was speedily confirmed by her manners and conversation.[4] Their nuptials were solemnised at the Chapel Royal, St. James's, on the 8th of April, 1795. When the time arrived, the reluctance of the royal bridegroom was great; he drank so many glasses of brandy in order to strengthen his nerves for the marriage ceremony, that he could scarcely stand, and the Duke of Bedford, who walked in the procession by his side, had even some difficulty in preventing him from

[1] The account of this conversation was given by George III. to Lord Liverpool, and by him repeated to Lord Holland (*Mem. of Whig Party*, vol. ii. p. 145). It agrees perfectly with what is known of the Prince's views; it is believed by Lord Holland, and no reasonable doubt can exist as to its truth.

[2] Lord Malmesbury's *Diaries*, vol. iii. p. 151.

[3] A detailed account of her voyage, by the commodore who commanded the squadron which brought her to England, may be seen in *Annual Register*, 1821, p. 638.

[4] *Lord Malmesbury*, *ibid.* pp. 218–220. Lord Malmesbury was alone present at the first interview of the Princess with the Prince. The impression produced on the Princess by the Prince's appearance was likewise unfavourable. His reception of her was in the highest degree cold, repulsive, and rude.

falling.[1] Among other things, the previous marriage with Mrs. Fitzherbert weighed upon his mind; and disturbed a nature, vicious, false, weak, and self-indulgent, but not proof against remorse, or devoid of kindly impulses. 1813.

On the 7th of January, 1796, being exactly nine months, wanting one day, from the wedding day, their only child, the Princess Charlotte, was born. The Princess had continued to reside at Carlton House, and it was there that her delivery took place; but the Prince is understood to have broken off all intercourse with her almost immediately after the marriage; and during the first year he resided chiefly at Windsor and Brighton. In April, 1796, a more complete separation between the parties was arranged through the intervention of Lord and Lady Cholmondeley: and the Prince addressed to the Princess a letter, in which he defined their future relations in the following terms:—'Our inclinations,' he said, 'are not in our power, nor should either of us be held answerable to the other, because nature has not made us suitable to each other. Tranquil and comfortable society is, however, in our power: let our intercourse therefore be restricted to that, and I will distinctly subscribe to the condition which you required, through Lady Cholmondeley, that even in the event of any accident happening to my daughter, which I trust Providence in his mercy will avert, I shall not infringe the terms of the restriction by proposing, at any period, a connection of a more particular nature.' In her answer to this letter the Princess says:—'L'aveu de votre conversation avec Lord Cholmondeley ne m'étonne, ni ne m'offense. C'étoit me confirmer ce que vous m'avez tacitement insinué depuis une

[1] *Lord Holland, ibid.* p. 122. Lord Malmesbury, who was present, perceived that the Prince was unhappy, and that he had had recourse to wine or spirits, *ibid.* p. 220. The Prince's state on this occasion is well attested.

1813. année. Mais il y auroit après cela, un manque de délicatesse, ou, pour mieux dire, une bassesse indigne, de me plaindre des conditions que vous vous imposez à vous-même.'[1] Thus, at the end of a year, and when their child was little more than three months old, the Prince dismissed his wife from his house, and separated her from his bed and board, without any cause assigned; for the plea of mutual unsuitableness meant in fact only that she did not suit his taste. The Princess herself, as her letter shows, submitted reluctantly to his conditions, and only required that the intercourse, once broken off, should not be renewed at his discretion, and without her free consent. In consequence of this correspondence, the Princess removed from Carlton House, and took up her abode in a villa at Blackheath, where she remained in comparative obscurity for a considerable time;[2] she was received at Court on public occasions, but never met the Prince, and had little intercourse with the other members of the Royal Family. The King, however, partly on account of his dislike for

[1] These letters are printed in the *Genuine Book*, pp. 227–229, with some notes, doubtless added by the editor, Mr. Perceval, upon the authority of the Princess. The Prince's letter is dated Windsor Castle, April 30, 1796. The letter of the Princess is dated May 6, and was written from Carlton House. Lord Thurlow called the Prince's letter a 'letter of license.' The Princess Charlotte was baptized at Carlton House on February 11. On this occasion the Prince and Princess of Wales received their Majesties and the Princesses at dinner, probably the last occasion on which the two former sat together at the same table.

[2] ['The conduct of Her Royal Highness in her retirement at Blackheath was on some points disrespectful to the Prince, and on others, to say the least, unguarded. At Cuffnells, in October 1804, Mr. Pitt told Rose that he and the Chancellor had made to the Princess in the most earnest manner their joint remonstrances, which Her Royal Highness received in the coldest manner possible, and utterly unmoved for a long time. At last, made sensible of the absolute necessity of some change in her conduct, by the effect which would otherwise be produced in the public mind, she promised an alteration. But Pitt said he had little hope that the alteration would be really made' (Lord Stanhope's *Life of Pitt*, vol. iv. p. 229).—Ed.]

the Prince, but chiefly from a regard to his own niece, always felt an interest in her, and extended to her a certain protection. The infant Princess was permitted to remain in the care of her mother, and it was not until 1804, when his daughter was eight years old, that the Prince remonstrated against this arrangement, and required that she should be transferred to his sole management. The King, however, denied that the Prince could be properly trusted with the care of his daughter, and insisted, as guardian of the Royal Family, that she should remain in the custody of the mother.[1] 1813.

The following year was an important crisis in the relations of the Prince and Princess of Wales. It came to the knowledge of the Prince, through communications made by the Dukes of Sussex and Kent, that Sir John and Lady Douglas, who had occupied a house near that of the Princess at Blackheath, and had been admitted to her familiarity, were prepared to make disclosures seriously affecting her character. Lady Douglas, the principal informant, having been requested to put her testimony in writing, submitted to the Prince, in Dec. 1805,[2] a detailed statement of facts and conversations, the result of which was that the Princess had, in consequence of an illicit intercourse, become pregnant, and been secretly delivered

[1] In 1718, upon a question referred to all the judges by George I., it was resolved, by the opinion of ten against the other two, that the education and care of all the King's grandchildren, while minors, and the care and approbation of their marriages when grown up, belonged of right to His Majesty, as King of this realm, during their father's life (*Blackstone Com.* vol. i. p. 219). The latter part of this rule has been since superseded by the Royal Marriage Act.

[2] It seems that the Prince of Wales had, through Lord Moira, made enquiries in June 1804 respecting a visit paid by the Princess, with some ladies in a carriage, and a gentleman on horseback, to Lord Eardley's house at Belvedere; but that the information obtained was not such as to cast any suspicion upon her (*Genuine Book*, p. 191).

1813. of a male child near the end of 1802, which child was living in her house, under her protection. As this statement would, if supported by evidence, have affected the succession to the Crown, the Prince was undoubtedly bound to communicate it to the Ministers; and Lord Grenville at once perceived, that if a child had really been born, the fact must be declared to Parliament.[1]

The information thus obtained was laid before the King:[2] who issued a commission, under the sign manual, on the 29th of May, 1806, to Lord Erskine, the Lord Chancellor; Lord Spencer, Secretary of State; Lord Grenville, First Lord of the Treasury; and Lord Ellenborough, Chief Justice, to enquire into the truth of 'certain written declarations touching the conduct of H. R. H. the Princess of Wales.' The four commissioners charged with this 'delicate investigation,' as it was called, considered their enquiry as an *ex parte* proceeding; they therefore conducted it in secret and without the presence of the accused party or her counsel: but the evidence was taken on oath; and on the 14th of July, they made their report, in which they gave a decided negative to the allegation that the Princess had been delivered of a child in 1802, or had been pregnant. The child then with the Princess was, they found, beyond all doubt born in the Brownlow Street Hospital on the 11th of July 1802, of the body of Sophia Austin, and was first brought to the Princess's house in the month of November following.[3] So far

[1] See *Memoirs of Romilly*, vol. ii. pp. 142, 148.

[2] For an account of the transactions up to this stage of the business, see *Memoirs of Romilly*, vol. ii. pp. 123–126, 140.

[3] Sir S. Romilly entirely concurred in this conclusion (*ibid.* p. 144). Lord Campbell, in his *Lives of the Chancellors*, alludes to a report as to the foreign parentage of William Austin. The story to which he refers is one which was unquestionably countenanced by the Princess of Wales herself, namely, that Sophia Austin's child was subsequently exchanged for an illegitimate child of Prince Louis of Prussia by a Brunswick maid of honour.

the report was a clear acquittal upon the main charge, and relieved His Majesty and the country from the embarrassment which would have arisen if a male child had been born to the Princess in wedlock, which her husband would not have recognised as his offspring. But the commissioners proceeded to call the King's attention to certain particulars respecting the conduct of the Princess disclosed incidentally in the evidence, 'which must, especially considering her exalted rank and station, necessarily give occasion to very unfavourable interpretations.' They proceeded to specify the depositions of certain witnesses: they added their opinion that the circumstances referred to 'must be credited until they should receive some decisive contradiction; and, if true, were entitled to the most serious consideration.' A copy of this report, with the accompanying documents, was communicated by the King to the Princess, by whom it was placed in the hands of Lord Eldon,[1] Mr. Perceval, and Mr. Plomer. These advisers prepared a long controversial answer to the report, in which both the course of proceeding and the evidence reflecting on the Princess's conduct were impugned in the most unreserved manner; it was couched in the form of a letter to the King, and was signed by the Princess.[2]

1813.

How far the story is entitled to credit, we offer no opinion. That the child originally taken to Montague House was Sophia Austin's child is, we think, proved by perfectly conclusive evidence.

[1] On the part taken by Lord Eldon at this period, as the adviser of the Princess, with some of her letters to him, see Twiss, *Life*, vol. ii. pp. 23–28. In a letter to Lord Eldon of July 25, 1806, she speaks of the Ministers and the Prince in the following terms: 'The Princess is quite resigned to her cruel fate, from the period that her honour was in the hands of a pack of ruffians, and who are only devoted, and slaves, to her most inveterate enemy' (*ibid.* p. 25). The broken English of this letter shows that it was her own composition.

[2] The date of this letter was Oct. 2, 1806. It was drawn by Mr. Perceval, with alterations by Mr. Plomer (*Memoirs of Romilly*, *ibid.* p. 164). Lord Holland states that Mr. Perceval caused a hundred copies of it to be printed at the time (*ibid.* p. 154).

1813. The enquiry being now completed, and the Princess having been heard, the matter was ripe for decision, and the King desired the Cabinet to advise him as to the course to be pursued.[1] The result of this reference was that on January 28, 1807, the Lord Chancellor transmitted a paper to the Princess, containing a message from the King which recited the opinion of the Cabinet that no further steps should be taken in the business, unless the law officers should advise the prosecution of Lady Douglas, and their advice that the King should no longer decline to receive the Princess into his royal presence. The King proceeded to express his satisfaction at the decided opinion of the four lords upon the falsehood of the accusations of pregnancy and delivery, brought forward against the Princess by Lady Douglas; but added that there were circumstances in the examinations, and even in the answers of the Princess, which he could not regard without serious concern, and he cautioned her to be more circumspect in her conduct for the future.[2] At this point the Prince interposed, and requested the King to take no further

[1] An account of the deliberations of the Cabinet on this occasion, and of the King's desire to embarrass his Ministers with the solution of this question, is given by Lord Holland (*ibid.* pp. 151–154). Lord Sidmouth (he says) called the business 'a sad *blister*.' The views of the Cabinet were embodied in a minute, dated Jan. 25, 1806, from which Mr. Wyndham alone dissented. He sent in a separate minute, declaring his conviction of the entire innocence of the Princess.

Lord Brougham states that the King wished to avail himself of the delicate investigation, in order to turn out his Ministers (*Statesmen*, vol. ii. p. 246). There is, however, no published evidence of his having formed such a design. Lord Malmesbury describes his indifference to attempts to undermine them in October 1806 (*Diary*, vol. iv. p. 353).

[2] *Genuine Book*, p. 199. In the message as originally framed by the Ministers, the sentence ran, 'His Majesty sees with concern and disapprobation;' but the King with his own hand struck out 'disapprobation,' and substituted 'serious concern.' Sir S. Romilly considers the affair to have terminated in a manner not very satisfactory to any party (*ibid.* p. 179).

step until he submitted to him an additional statement. This remonstrance produced a delay in carrying the King's declared intention into effect; but while the matter was still pending, the rupture with the Ministry upon the Catholic Question had taken place, and the Portland administration was installed. Lord Eldon and Mr. Perceval, the main advisers of the Princess in her late contest with the Prince, and in her attack upon the Commission of Enquiry, were now in office; and the new Ministers speedily passed a minute of Cabinet, concurring in the opinion of their predecessors that the two main charges alleged against the Princess, of pregnancy and delivery, were completely disproved, and declaring their own unanimous opinion, that all other particulars of conduct brought in accusation against her, to which the character of criminality could be ascribed, were satisfactorily contradicted, or rested upon evidence undeserving of credit. They therefore recommended that she should be admitted to the King's presence, and be received at Court.[1] In consequence of this decision, apartments in Kensington Palace were assigned to her, and she appeared at Court receptions; but her private intercourse with the Royal family underwent no change. 1813.

The result of the enquiry of 1806 had been to give a triumph to the Princess. The four lords acquitted her of the charges of pregnancy and delivery; the minute of the Portland Cabinet acquitted her of the charges founded on the incidental evidence. The King received her at Court, and she obtained apartments at Kensington Palace: allusion was even made to a prosecution of Lady Douglas for perjury.[2] The Prince therefore thought it prudent

[1] This minute, dated April 22, 1807, is printed in Huish's *Memoirs of George IV.* vol. i. p. 549.

[2] Lord Eldon, who was the partisan and confidential adviser of the

1813. to abstain from further measures of aggression; while the Princess, having the custody of her daughter, was contented to observe the truce which circumstances seemed to have established. The Regency, however, disturbed this equilibrium; and the Prince, now master of his own child, subjected her intercourse with her mother to severe restrictions. The Prince was always unpopular, and the Princess was counselled to try an appeal to the public. Accordingly, in January 1813, the Princess, acting on the advice of Mr. Brougham, addressed to the Prince a long letter of remonstrance, in which she complained of the restrictions under which her intercourse with the Princess Charlotte was placed, now limited to an interview once a fortnight; of the imputation upon her own character, unsupported by proof, and negatived by the enquiry of 1806 which these restrictions implied; of the injudicious seclusion of the Princess Charlotte from the world, and her residence at Windsor, and of the improper delay in administering to her the rite of confirmation. This letter, sent to Lord Liverpool and Lord Eldon by Lady Charlotte Campbell, was twice returned unopened; at last an answer was obtained that the contents of the letter had been made known to the Prince, and after further delay and correspondence, Lord Liverpool wrote to the Princess that in

Princess of Wales in 1806, said to Lord Grey in April 1813, in reference to the delicate investigation: 'My opinion is, *and always has been*, that, though she was not with child, she supposed herself to be with child' (*Mem. of Romilly*, vol. iii. p. 104). The truth of Lady Douglas's statement is not now material, as the main fact to which she deposed was clearly disproved; but we are by no means satisfied that the Princess (who was fond of hoaxes and mystifications, not of the most refined kind), did not tell her what she related. Lady Douglas's manner impressed Sir S. Romilly with her veracity (*Memoirs*, vol. ii. p. 126). See also his statement as to the handwriting of the anonymous letters, *ibid.* p. 151.

Lord Malmesbury was consulted by the Princess of Wales in 1806, upon the subject of the charge made against her, and left a minute account of the transaction which the editor has not published (*Diaries*, vol. iv. p. 355).

consequence of her demand, her letter had been read to the Prince, but that he had not been pleased to express his pleasure thereon.[1] The result of this ill-advised and almost puerile attempt to avoid all notice of a letter which had evidently been written as an appeal to the people at large was, that the document soon appeared in the 'Morning Chronicle.' The effect produced by this publication was such that the Prince found himself compelled to take some step for bringing the matter in dispute to a formal adjudication. Accordingly, he referred the letter, together with all the documents belonging to the enquiry of 1806, to twenty-three Privy Councillors, including the Cabinet Ministers, the three Archbishops, the Bishop of London, and the principal judges, with an instruction to report their opinion whether it was fit that the intercourse between the Princess of Wales and her daughter, the Princess Charlotte should continue to be subject to regulations and restrictions. Twenty-one Privy Councillors signed a report containing an unqualified affirmative answer to this question.[2] Upon receiving from Lord Sid- 1813.

[1] See Twiss, *Life of Eldon*, vol. ii. pp. 230–232. In a letter to Sir William Scott, written at this time, Lord Eldon mentions the Prince's unkind treatment of him, because he would not comply with the Prince's wishes as to the conduct which he should pursue with respect to the Princess of Wales and the Princess Charlotte.

[2] The following passage in Sir James Mackintosh's *Diary* for April 1813 relates to this transaction. 'Brougham, who is out of Parliament, was at first the Princess's sole adviser. When she published her letter, everybody thought that he had ruined her; but it has since appeared that he was only wisely bold, and that he had calculated exactly the timidity of [the Prince], the weakness of his case, the value of the first impression, and the embarrassment of Ministers, of whom some had been the Princess's confidential advisers, and all had concurred in formally pronouncing her innocence. Though they deserted her, yet they could not openly annul their own deliberate judgment. The extreme unpopularity of [the Prince], and the natural interest inspired by a wife abandoned by her husband, had a great effect. The result of these causes, combined with the most stupid blunders on the part of the other side, have given her the most complete victory.

1813. mouth an official copy of this report, the Princess addressed a letter to the Chancellor and the Speaker, protesting against the vague aspersions upon her character which it promulgated; throwing herself upon the wisdom and justice of Parliament, and expressing her wish to be treated as innocent, unless she could be proved guilty.[1] The copy of this letter, transmitted to Lord Eldon, was returned by him, with a recommendation to her not to make it public, and also with an intimation by command of the Prince Regent, that her visits to her daughter at Warwick House were to be discontinued. The Speaker, however, took a different course. He read it to the House of Commons on March 2, 1813, and on the 5th Mr. Cochrane Johnstone brought forward the entire subject in a motion for a copy of the Report of 1806, with certain of the documents attached to it.[2] The motion was opposed by Lord Castlereagh, and was negatived without a division; but it gave rise to a debate in which Mr. Stuart Wortley (afterwards Lord Wharncliffe) made the following severe but just remarks: 'He had as high notions of royalty as any man, but he must say that all such proceedings contributed to pull it down. He was very sorry that we had a royal family who did not take warning from what was

All the world is with her, except the people of fashion at the west end of the town' (*Life of Mackintosh*, vol. ii. p. 258). It is to be observed that when Lord Eldon, Lord Castlereagh, Lord Liverpool, and others of the present Cabinet, had concurred in the minute of April 1807, they were the Ministers of the King, whereas now they were the Ministers of the Regent, which accounts for the change of their conduct.

By the 'blunders' of Ministers, Sir J. Mackintosh means the foolish attempt to refuse the Princess's letter. It is much to be wished that a new edition of Sir James Mackintosh's *Diaries* should be published, with the insertion of the names unnecessarily omitted in the present edition.

[1] The two letters of the Princess, and the report of the Privy Councillors, are in *Annual Register*, 1813, pp. 341–347; *State Papers*.

[2] See the account of this debate in *Sir S. Romilly's Memoirs*, with the full report of his own speech, vol. iii. p. 82.

said and thought concerning them. They seemed to be the only persons in the country who were wholly regardless of their own welfare and respectability. He would not have the Prince Regent lay the flattering unction to his soul, and think his conduct would bear him harmless through all these transactions. He said this with no disrespect to him or his family; no man was more attached to the House of Hanover than he was; but had he a sister in the same situation with her Royal Highness the Princess of Wales, he would say that she was exceedingly ill-treated.'[1] 1813.

A copy of the Report of 1806 had, as we have stated, been placed at the time in the hands of Mr. Perceval, who had prepared it, with other illustrative documents, for the press, and had caused a large number of copies to be printed. Their publication had not taken place when he accepted office in March 1807, and the edition was carefully suppressed.[2] Some copies, however, were

[1] Mr. Horner, in a letter to Mr. Hallam of March 7, 1813, says: 'What a hint to the Royal Family is conveyed by Wortley's speech; it is like some of the signs that appeared among the Tories, after the trial of the bishops' (*Memoirs of Horner*, vol. ii. p. 142). This allusion to the signs which prefigured the dethronement of James II., shows how serious was the view which Mr. Horner took of the Prince Regent's proceedings.

[2] It is stated that the number of copies printed was 5,000, and that (with the exception of a few) they were all delivered by the printer at Mr. Perceval's house. Some of the reserved copies, which fell into private hands, are said to have been bought up for large sums; and the Chancellor granted an injunction, in March 1808, to restrain the proprietor of a newspaper from publishing the contents of the volume (Lord Campbell's *Lives of the Chancellors*, vol. vii. p. 213; Huish's *Memoirs of George IV*. vol. ii. pp. 42, 43). Sir S. Romilly, vol. iii. p. 165, states that the injunction was confined to the letter of the Princess in answer to the Report. But Lord Campbell's fuller account shows that it included the Report itself and other documents.

From an account of an interview with the King in 1807, before the change of Ministry, which Lord Eldon gave to Lord Grey, it appears that Lord Eldon wished to dissuade the publication of the book, on which Per-

1813. preserved, and were communicated to the newspapers, in which extracts appeared at this time, and shortly afterwards a reprint of the entire volume was published.[1] These publications gave rise to further motions and debates in both Houses of Parliament; in the course of which Lord Ellenborough, Lord Erskine, Lord Spencer, Lord Grenville, and Sir Samuel Romilly defended the course which they had taken in reference to the enquiry; the results of which were now, seven years after the event, first made known fully to the public; but the matter was not pursued to any practical result. The Prince's conduct on this occasion brought upon him much obloquy, while the Princess became the object of strong and general sympathy. It was thought that an illustrious stranger, a woman and a mother, had been treated with harshness and injustice. The Common Hall of London, on April 2, 1813, almost unanimously voted an address to the Princess of Wales, declaring the indignation and

ceval was bent. It further appears that the King was privy to the design (*Mem. of Romilly*, vol. iii. p. 104; Twiss, *Life of Eldon*, vol. ii. p. 37).

[1] The following is a copy of the title-page: '*The Genuine Book.* An Inquiry, or Delicate Investigation, into the Conduct of H. R. H. the Princess of Wales, before Lords Erskine, Spencer, Grenville, and Ellenborough, the four Commissioners of Inquiry, appointed by His Majesty in the year 1806. Reprinted from an authentic copy, superintended through the press by the Right Hon. Spencer Perceval. London, 1813. 1 vol. 8vo. pp. 246+108.' Lord Holland says that all the Ministers of 1806, except Mr. Wyndham, thought that the publication of the Report or evidence would divert the popular displeasure from the Prince upon the Princess, and that the advisers of the Princess would be desirous of suppressing them; but that both anticipations proved erroneous, for that all the publications of the documents of 1806 had proceeded from the advisers or partisans of the Princess, and that they had added to the unpopularity of the Prince. 'A share of the odium,' he remarks, 'fell on all who either conducted or sanctioned any enquiry at the Prince's request or instigation' (*ibid.* p. 120). Sir S. Romilly, who, like the Cabinet of 1806, thought that the publication of the depositions would not fail to destroy her reputation for ever in the opinion of the public, says that they were published by newspapers in the interest of the Prince (*Mem.* vol. iii. pp. 86, 90).

abhorrence with which they viewed the foul conspiracy against her honour and life, and their admiration at her moderation, frankness, and magnanimity under her long persecution. The Common Council of London and other public bodies followed this example.[1] Such were the first public manifestations of a domestic strife, which was destined at a subsequent period to create a profound agitation in the country, and even to bring the Crown into peril. 1813.

Parliament was prorogued for the session of 1813 on the 22nd of July; and the Napoleon drama was now moving on rapidly to its termination. The rising of oppressed Germany had taken place since the retreat from Moscow; and the campaign was in progress which ended in October with the decisive battle of Leipsic. The battle of Vittoria had been fought in June; after some unsuccessful attempts at negotiation, the allied armies crossed the Rhine, and entered France; and Napoleon, having in vain attempted to arrest their advance by a short but brilliant defensive campaign, abdicated his imperial throne in April 1814. In the meantime Parliament had assembled on the 4th of November 1813, and at this crisis of affairs, with the prospect of a speedy and successful termination of the war, the utmost unanimity prevailed in both Houses with respect to the policy suited to the occasion. When the Houses rose before Christmas, the Ministers moved and carried the adjournment until the 1st of March, which was afterwards prolonged to the 21st of the same month.[2]

[1] Concerning these addresses, see *Mem. of Romilly*, vol. iii. p. 103.

[2] The following dates will serve to illustrate the proceedings of Parliament at this period:—

Oct. 8, 1813. Lord Wellington's army crosses the frontier of France.

Nov. 2. The French army retreats across the Rhine, and evacuates Germany.

1814. Shortly afterwards the abdication of Napoleon, his removal to Elba, and the restoration of the Bourbon dynasty were announced.[1]

Lord Wellington, now created a Duke, received on his return to England the thanks of both Houses in person, and a public provision was made for him, in reward of his distinguished services. The treaty with France, by which the war with that country had been concluded, was communicated to Parliament in July, and acknowledged by addresses unanimously agreed to by both Lords and Commons. Some discussion arose about a stipulation for the abolition of the slave trade, but to the arrangements embodied in the treaty no objection was made. The joy at the cessation of the war and restoration of peace was enthusiastic and universal. The prorogation took place on the 30th of July, and the Prince Regent, delivering his speech in person, congratulated the two Houses upon the success of his adherence to the line of policy which had been pursued before the Regency; upon the full accomplishment of all the objects for which the war had been undertaken or continued; and upon the final deliverance of Europe, by the combined exertions of this nation and its allies, from the most oppressive tyranny under which it had ever laboured. He proceeded to lament the continuance of hostilities with the United States, but recommended the vigorous prosecution of this war. The Prince Regent had been honoured by a visit of the Emperor of Russia and the King of Prussia, who, with Marshal Blücher and other distinguished persons, arrived at London in June: their

Jan. 1, Jan. 2, 1814. The allied armies cross the Rhine, and enter France.
March 31. The Allies enter Paris.
April 6. Abdication of Napoleon.

[1] Louis XVIII. embarked from Dover for France on April 24, 1814. He was accompanied to his embarkation by the Prince Regent.

public reception was highly flattering, and they remained in England nearly three weeks. 1814.

After these successes and triumphs, among universal rejoicings, amidst the noise of salutes, and the blaze of illuminations and fireworks, the Prince Regent's Ministry basked in the sunshine both of court favour and popular applause. No murmur was heard of any ministerial change. The existing state of domestic politics, with respect to the rival parties, may be collected from the following passage in a letter written by Lord Dudley to the Bishop of Llandaff in June, 1814 :—

I am very glad to hear that Lord Grenville's conduct has been so satisfactory to all parties. In spite of some faults, and some mistakes, he is altogether the ablest and most accomplished of our statesmen, and, moreover, a man of unimpeached honour and worth. You would do well to encourage in Oxford the notion of his coming into office, for the amusement of seeing how much he will rise in public opinion. It would be an excellent hoax; harmless, indeed, but as perfect in its kind as Lord Cochrane's. No person, I believe, is more completely out of the question than Lord Grenville at this moment. The present administration is triumphant at home and abroad. The principal individuals of which it is composed enjoy the highest personal favour with their master, who, let him pretend what he pleases, has for Lord Grenville the most rooted aversion. I see you so far give into the notion yourself, as to speak of its being natural that the Prince Regent should wish to strengthen his administration by the accession of so able a man. But then you forget that Lord Grenville is bound, by all the ties of honour and consistency, not to strengthen it. If he comes in, he must bring his party with him. He would disgrace himself for ever if he consented to a partial arrangement. The truth seems to be, that the present government has a lease of power coeval with the public prosperity. As long as the present favourable gale lasts, they will continue at the helm. But if a storm comes on, they will, in all probability, be com-

1814. pelled by the public voice to take some abler seamen and more skilful pilots on board. They are so miserably off in the House of Commons, that one does not see how they could get through any severe debates, when the public feeling was divided, even in a tolerably fair proportion, between themselves and the Opposition' (p. 48).

The feud between the Prince and Princess of Wales, which had been blown into activity by her letter respecting her daughter in 1813, was revived in 1814 by the visit of the Sovereigns. The Princess received from the Queen an announcement that her presence at the drawing-rooms to be given in honour of the illustrious visitors could not be permitted; inasmuch as the Prince Regent considered his own presence necessary, and he desired it to be distinctly understood, for reasons of which he alone could be the judge, that it was his fixed and unalterable determination not to meet the Princess of Wales upon any occasion, either in public or private. Against this decision the Princess remonstrated, in a letter addressed to the Prince, which concluded with the following paragraph :—

Sir, the time you have selected for this proceeding is calculated to make it peculiarly galling. Many illustrious strangers are already arrived in England; among others, as I am informed, the illustrious heir of the house of Orange, who has announced himself to me as my future son-in-law. From their society I am unjustly excluded. Others are expected of rank equal to your own, to rejoice with your royal Highness in the peace of Europe. My daughter will, for the first time, appear in the splendour and publicity becoming the approaching nuptials of the presumptive heiress of this empire. This season your royal Highness has chosen for treating me with fresh and unprovoked indignity; and of all his Majesty's subjects, I alone am prevented by your royal Highness from appearing in my place, to partake of the general joy, and am deprived of the indulgence in those feelings of pride and affection permitted to every mother but me.

Of this letter no notice was taken by the Prince; but the Princess sent the correspondence to the Speaker, to be laid before the House of Commons.[1] Upon this correspondence Mr. Methuen on the 3rd of June founded a motion for an address to the Prince Regent, requesting him to acquaint the House by whose advice he had been induced to form his fixed and unalterable determination never to meet the Princess of Wales, either in public or private, and what were the reasons upon which it was founded. The motion, after debate, was withdrawn: but the same member made a subsequent motion, which led to the passing of a bill for settling on the Princess a separate annuity of 35,000*l.* 1814.

In the existing state of the relations between the Prince and the Princess, everything which they had in common necessarily became a source of discord; and thus their daughter, as she grew up and began to play her part on the stage, instead of a bond of union, acted as an incentive to fresh differences. The intended marriage with the Prince of Orange, which the Prince Regent desired to promote, was not encouraged by the mother; and it was so effectually resisted by the daughter, that it was ultimately broken off. The repugnance of the Prince Regent to the influence of the Princess over her daughter was so great, that he at length altogether interdicted their intercourse; and his interference so much irritated the Princess Charlotte, that on the 12th of July in this year, she fled from Warwick House, where she resided, in a hackney-coach to her mother's residence in Connaught Terrace, and was with some difficulty induced to return to a house where she should be under her father's superintendence.

The popularity of the Princess of Wales was now at its height. The charges made against her character were

[1] It is printed in the *Annual Register*, 1814; *State Papers*, pp. 348–351.

1814. believed to have been dictated by malice, and disproved by conclusive evidence; and the conduct of her husband towards her was regarded as a course of cowardly and unfeeling persecution, prompted by his preference for his wife's illicit rivals. Nevertheless, she appears to have found that the public voice, however strong and unanimous, could not support her against the hand of power, which barred every entrance against her: and accordingly, in August 1814, she left England for the Continent.[1] She first made some stay in her native town of Brunswick, and then proceeded to Italy.

The Princess Charlotte, who was now eighteen years old, remained unmarried until 1816, when she became the wife of Prince Leopold of Saxe Coburg. The fatal termination of that apparently auspicious marriage in the following year, severed the last tie which connected the Princess of Wales with this country. She had never seen her daughter since her departure from England in 1814, and she remained upon the Continent until she returned as Queen in 1820.

The war with France, which was terminated in this year by the forced abdication of Napoleon at Fontainebleau, was the greatest in which this country was ever engaged. Compared with it, the wars with Louis XIV., the Spanish war of 1739, and the American war, were of limited dimensions. Including the twenty months during which the hollow truce of Amiens was in force, it had lasted from February 1793 till April 1814, being a period of more than twenty-one years. During the continuance of the French Republic, it had borne the character of a con-

[1] Mr. Canning stated in the House of Commons, June 7, 1820, that the Princess of Wales had consulted him in 1814 on the question of her living abroad, and that he had advised it, upon the supposition of permanent separation from her husband.

test against Jacobinism; since the accession of Bonaparte to the chief power, it had been a contest against his restless ambition and insatiable lust of universal conquest. It had required and produced in this kingdom the greatest financial sacrifices and the most strenuous exertions, both naval and military. *Toto certatum est corpore regni.* The great objects for which such long-sustained efforts had been made; for which so many thousands of lives had been annually lost; for which such heavy taxation had been patiently borne; for which so many hundreds of millions had been added to the National Debt—namely the dethronement of Napoleon, and the reduction of France within her ancient boundaries—having now been accomplished, it is natural to enquire how far England contributed to the first overthrow of Napoleon, to his downfall in 1814.

1814.

It is certain that the continued resistance of England to the power of Napoleon from 1803, her refusal to negotiate with him and even to acknowledge him as Emperor—her successful defiance of his attempts to invade her shores and to destroy her trade with the Continent—her encouragement of all his foes, wherever they were to be found, and her subsidizing and supporting the great military powers of Europe against him, exercised a powerful influence in creating and fomenting the spirit which led to his ultimate ruin. While the French armies had entered Lisbon, Madrid, Naples, Rome, Turin, Milan, Vienna, Dresden, Berlin, Moscow, Brussels, and Amsterdam, the wealthy city of London, the most tempting of all baits to the mighty robber, had not been approached by a French soldier. As a belligerent the naval successes of England had been decisive. Since Trafalgar, when the French navy had been annihilated, she had remained undisputed mistress of the seas. But England had never aspired to

1814. be a first-rate military power, and by land her operations had been on a smaller scale. Relying only on voluntary enlistment, she could not, even with the aid of a foreign legion, attempt to make head against the enormous armies which Napoleon levied by forced conscription. The Walcheren expedition had been a failure, the operations in Italy and Sicily had been insignificant, and the only quarter in which an English army had made its influence felt was the Peninsula. By the Convention of Cintra in 1808, the evacuation of Portugal by Junot had been effected; Massena was repulsed from the lines of Torres Vedras in 1810; while subsequently, from the capture of Badajos and Ciudad Rodrigo and the battle of Salamanca in 1812 to the rout of Vittoria in 1813, the career of the Duke of Wellington was one of nearly continual progress, until at last he crossed the French frontier in October of that year. The merits of the Duke of Wellington and the service which he rendered to his country in overcoming obstacles and difficulties of all sorts, in organising his own army, in dealing with the Spanish and Portuguese Governments, and in turning their levies to account, his unvarying prudence, forbearance, and firmness, and his high military qualities, illustrated as they have been by a hundred competent writers, can never be too highly estimated. The task which he was appointed to perform he performed admirably well; the question however remains, whether the system which he was employed to work out was well devised.

When the policy of assisting the popular movement in Spain and Portugal was adopted and persisted in by the English Government some calculation must have been formed as to the probable course of Napoleon. If, following his principle of crushing one enemy before he attacked another, he made the Peninsula his first object, and marched

into it himself at the head of an army of 300,000 men, 1814.
the English general, feebly supported by two nations destitute either of financial or military resources,[1] and relying only upon the limited numbers which his Government could have placed at his disposal, must have retreated behind the lines of Torres Vedras, and have ultimately re-embarked his army. If, on the other hand, as was actually the case, Napoleon made his main movement in a totally different quarter, and left a marshal, with an army of moderate numbers, to keep the Duke of Wellington in check, the Spanish campaign assumed a subordinate character, and became only of second-rate importance. It is true that the Duke of Wellington repulsed Soult, and that he crossed the French frontier nearly three months before the Allies invaded France from the Rhine; but he was unable to effect a junction with them, or to cooperate with their advance upon Paris; and the battle of Toulouse was fought after the abdication of Napoleon.[2]

The Peninsular war caused a perpetual drain of men from the French military depôts; we have heard the French losses, from all causes, estimated on authentic

[1] On the small value of the military assistance afforded by the Spaniards in this campaign, see Napier's *History of the War in the Peninsula*, b. xxii. c. 6. General Napier remarks, that in 1813 'the only bond of union between the two governments (of Spain and Portugal) was hatred of the English, who had saved both (vol. vi. p. 306). In this year the Cortes were on the point of passing a law excluding foreign troops from a Spanish fortress (*ibid.* p. 308).

[2] It appears that, after the battle of Vittoria, the English Government entertained some plan of transferring the Duke of Wellington and his army from Spain to Germany, in order to cooperate directly with the great military powers (see his despatches to Lord Bathurst of July 12 and Dec. 21, 1813, and of Jan. 10, 1814, in *Gurwood's Collection*). The scheme of removing the Duke of Wellington and his army to Germany at this stage of the Spanish campaign had not much to recommend it; but the fact of its having been entertained proves the conviction of the English Government, that he was not in the right place at the critical moment.

1814. evidence at 100,000 men a year. This source of weakness and the moral effect produced in the camps and councils of the Allies by the successes in Spain, doubtless contributed to the triumph of the cause for which England had been straining every nerve. The pressure of the conscription was the chief source of Napoleon's unpopularity in 1813 and 1814, and this was increased by the Spanish war. Still it cannot be denied that it was the advance of the Russian, Austrian, and Prussian armies to Paris which was the proximate efficient cause of the overthrow of Napoleon in 1814. If that advance had failed, the success of the Duke of Wellington against Soult, in the South, would have been unavailing. Without the aid of the great Northern Powers he could not have driven Napoleon to negotiation, much less to abdication.[1]

Napoleon is reported to have said in his conversations at St. Helena, that the Spanish war was the cause of his ruin.[2] It rarely happened that in statements respecting his own failures he was disposed to tell the truth, and this case was no exception to the rule. It is certain that if we are to look for the remote causes of his first downfall, its main reason is to be found in the Russian expedition, and the consequent rising of Germany. The insurrection in Spain, and the successes of the English, under the Duke of Wellington, contributed to this end, but would not have alone sufficed to produce it. His motive for this perver-

[1] Mr. Canning, however, in his speech at Lisbon in 1814, attributed the first overthrow of Napoleon to the influence of England, through the medium of the Peninsular war: 'The arm of England,' he said, 'was the lever that wrenched the power of Bonaparte from its basis; Portugal was the fulcrum on which that lever moved. England fanned and fed the sacred fire; but Portugal had already reared the altar on which that fire was kindled, and from which it mounted, brightening and widening, until the world was illumined with the blaze' (*Memoirs of the Life of Canning* (Lond. 1829), vol. ii. p. 260).

[2] Las Cases, *Mém. de St. Hélène*, vol. i. p. 603. Paris, 1842.

sion of the truth doubtless was, that the French armies in the Peninsula had been commanded by his generals, and that he himself had only remained in Spain for a few weeks; whereas the Russian campaign and the battle of Leipsic had been under his own personal superintendence, and he could therefore less easily resort to his invariable resource of throwing the blame of failure in these great operations upon subordinates. 1814.

But however we may partition the shares of merit among the different nations in producing the first overthrow of Napoleon, it is certain that the policy consistently supported by Lord Liverpool's Government, of prosecuting the Peninsular war with vigour, and of not negotiating with Napoleon, had in the end proved successful. Of this policy, Lord Castlereagh was the most prominent organ and representative; and though all the Ministers participated in the popularity which was the consequence of success, the public attention was concentrated upon him beyond any other of his colleagues.[1] Mr. Canning, who had been his rival for the leadership in 1812, found himself now completely eclipsed by the superior brilliancy of the Foreign Minister, and by the important part which he had borne in the resettlement of Europe. Accordingly, having in 1813 formally disbanded his party in the House of Commons, and dissolved his political connection with Lord Wellesley,[2] (by which step he left himself free for individual action), he was content at this time to accept the almost nominal post of ambassador to the court of Portugal, and he sailed to Lisbon in November. The

[1] On the personal eminence of Lord Castlereagh at this period, and on the general popularity of the Ministry, see the statements of Mr. Rush, the American Minister, in his *First Narrative of a Residence at the Court of London* (London, 1833), p. 45.

[2] See *Mem. of Reg.* vol. ii. p. 36; *Life of Lord Sidmouth*, vol. iii. p. 106; *Mem. of Horner*, vol. ii. p. 150.

1814. motive assigned by himself for this step was the state of the health of his eldest son, who died in 1820.[1] At the same time his friends, Mr. Huskisson, Mr. Sturgess Bourne, and Lord Binning, joined the Ministry; the former as First Commissioner of Woods, the two latter as Junior Commissioners of the Board of Control. He resigned his embassy in April 1815,[2] but remained abroad until the spring of 1816, when he returned to England and

[1] Lord Dudley, *Letters to the Bishop of Llandaff*, p. 50, states, that political disappointment was the real motive of this step. Mr. Canning offered to resign his seat for Liverpool, but his offer was declined by his constituents. Mr. Canning's conduct, in accepting this embassy, was attacked by Mr. Lambton in the House of Commons, in May 1817, in a formal motion of censure, but was successfully vindicated by himself (see *Lord Dudley's Letters, ibid.* p. 166). [The following note of Mr. Canning's to a private friend dated in 1814, will be interesting to the reader.

GLOUCESTER LODGE: *Aug.* 1, 1814.

MY DEAR SIR,—I thank you for your kind note. The only ground of congratulation to me (but that in my mind is a very substantial one) is that I am enabled to leave England with the reflection that no man who had done me the honour to commit his political fortunes with mine, has suffered by my necessary abdication, for a time, of my political and parliamentary duties.

As to my own personal share in the arrangements, it is very likely not to take place at all—and is at all events distant and contingent—but my anxiety was for others, and nothing would have kept me at home.

Yours, my dear sir, very sincerely

GEO. CANNING.

[2] General Napier states that Marshal Beresford had prevailed upon the Portuguese Regency to send 15,000 men of the old Portuguese troops, completely equipped, to the Duke of Wellington, before the battle of Waterloo; that the only real business which Mr. Canning had to transact in his embassy was to procure the execution of this agreement; and although nothing but an order for embarkation was needed, he frustrated the whole affair by making it the subject of diplomacy (*History of Peninsular War*, vol. iv. p. 140). As General Napier quotes no authority for this statement, his habit of decrying all civil, and of extolling all military officers, leaves us in uncertainty as to its credibility. A letter from Mr. Canning to Lord Castlereagh, dated Lisbon, April 22, 1815, in the *Castlereagh Despatches*, vol. x. p. 321, relates to this transaction.

entered the Cabinet as President of the Board of Control. 1814.

This accession of debating force must have been highly valuable in the existing state of the Government. The only changes which the Cabinet had undergone since its first formation were that Lord Camden had ceased to be a member of it, and his place had been supplied in 1812 by Mr. Bragge Bathurst as Chancellor of the Duchy of Lancaster. In 1814, Mr. Wellesley Pole was likewise added to it as Master of the Mint. The Cabinet now consisted of thirteen members, of whom nine were peers and four were commoners. The four commoners were Lord Castlereagh, Mr. Vansittart, Mr. Bragge Bathurst, and Mr. Wellesley Pole. This was its constitution when Mr. Canning joined it in 1816, in the place of Lord Buckinghamshire. What therefore Lord Grenville remarked of Mr. Canning, in a letter written to Mr. Horner in July 1813, was equally true in 1816; that 'he would be a very desirable 'acquisition indeed to a Government so unusually weak as this 'was in House of Commons debate.'[1]

While Lord Liverpool and his colleagues were thus reaping the legitimate fruits of a policy which they had consistently supported, and to which they had adhered at seasons of adversity and danger, the Whigs were lowered in public estimation by their apparently unpatriotic resistance to a war which had ended in triumph. There were, no doubt, among the Whig ranks persons whom Lord Dudley calls 'Whig Napoleonists;'[2] admirers of Napoleon, because they regarded him as the heir of the

[1] *Mem. of Horner*, vol. ii. p. 151.

[2] In a letter of Jan. 17, 1816, he speaks of 'the Whig Napoleonists, those zealots for freedom, who have fixed upon a military despot as their true ally and protector' (*Letters to the Bishop of Llandaff*, p. 127).

1814. Revolution, as the maintainer of its principles of equality, and as the enemy of the legitimate thrones. Some of these were probably captivated by his power; by his military genius, his extensive conquests, and his all-pervading despotism; in short, they belonged to that school of which General Napier, the historian of the Peninsular war, may be taken as a type.[1] But when Lord Dudley remarks in another letter that 'the Opposition had staked everything upon Napoleon's success, and were grieved at his failure;'[2] we cannot believe that he correctly represents the genuine feelings of those who opposed the Spanish war, because they thought it would be ineffectual for its purpose, but who were not on that account the enemies of their country. For example, Lord Grenville, whose voice was most loudly and most consistently raised against the campaigns in the Peninsula, was one of the most determined opponents of negotiation with Napoleon

[1] The following passages, extracted from the sixth volume of General Napier's *History*, will serve to illustrate his matured view of Napoleon: 'Napoleon's power was supported in France by that deep sense of his goodness as a sovereign, and that admiration for his genius, which pervaded the poorer and middle classes of the people; by the love which they bore towards him, and still bear for his memory, because he cherished the principles of a just equality. . . . To France he gave noble institutions, a comparatively just code of laws, and glory unmatched since the days of the Romans' (p. 241). Of the advance of the allies upon Paris in 1813, he says: 'The neutrality of Switzerland was violated, and more than half a million of armed men were poured across the frontiers of France *in all the violence of brute force*; for their military combinations were contemptible, and their course marked by murder and devastation' (p. 450). 'Great as these two men (Napoleon and Cromwell) were in the field of battle, especially the former, they were infinitely greater when they placed themselves in the seat of power, and put forth the gigantic despotism of genius essential to the completion of their holy work. Nor do I hold the conduct of Washington to be comparable to either of those men' (p. 458). 'Napoleon's ambition was for the greatness and prosperity of France, for the regeneration of Europe, for the stability of the system which he had formed with that end, *never for himself personally*; and hence it is that the multitudes of many nations instinctively revere his memory' (p. 516).

[2] Letter of June 22, 1816, *ibid.* p. 145.

and had condemned the Peace of Amiens when Mr. Pitt, 1814.
his late colleague, Mr. Fox, with whom he was about to act, and nearly the unanimous voice of the nation, approved of it. So far as the 'Edinburgh Review' may be considered as an organ of the Whig opinion of the day, its language does not at all bear out the statement of Lord Dudley. Thus in an article on the State and Prospects of Europe, published in April 1814, immediately after the first downfall of Napoleon, the following passage occurs, which seems to us to leave little to be said:—

We do not think that an ambitious despot and sanguinary conqueror can be too much execrated, or too little respected by mankind; but the popular clamour at this moment seems to us to be carried too far, even against this very hateful individual. It is now discovered that he has neither genius nor common sense; and he is accused of cowardice for not killing himself by the very persons who would infallibly have exclaimed against his suicide, as a clear proof of weakness and folly. History, we think, will not class him quite so low as the English newspapers of the present day. He is a creature to be dreaded and abhorred, but scarcely, we think, to be despised, by men of the ordinary standard. His catastrophe, so far as it is as yet visible, seems unsuitable indeed, and incongruous with the part he has hitherto sustained; but we have perceived nothing in it materially to alter the estimate which we formed long ago of his character. He still seems to us a man of consummate conduct, valour, and decision in war, but without the virtues, or even the generous and social vices, of a soldier of fortune;—of matchless activity indeed, and boundless ambition, but entirely without principle, feeling, or affection; suspicious, cruel, and overbearing; selfish and solitary in all his pursuits and gratifications; proud and overweening to the very borders of insanity; and considering at last the laws of honour and the principles of morality equally beneath his notice with the interests and feelings of other men. Despising those who submitted to his pretensions, and pursuing with implacable hatred all who presumed to resist them, he seems to have gone on in a growing confidence in his

1814. own fortune, and contempt for mankind—till a serious check from without showed him the error of his calculation, and betrayed the fatal insecurity of a career which reckoned only on prosperity. Over the downfall of such a man it is fitting that the world should rejoice.[1]

Napoleon being now at Elba, and the congress of Vienna about to meet, Parliament was opened again on the 8th of November by the Prince Regent, in a speech in which he deplored the continuance of the war with the United States of America. This unfortunate war, which had grown out of the British Orders in Council, and of which Mr. Canning's repudiation of the settlement made by Mr. Erskine in 1810 was the main provocation,[2] had been declared by the United States in June 1812. It had been waged with much animosity on both sides, and with alternate success, until it was terminated by a treaty of peace signed at Ghent on the 24th of December, 1814, and ratified on the 17th February, 1815. The attack on New Orleans, so disastrous to the British arms, occurred on January 8th, in the interval between the signature and ratification of the treaty. It may be fairly presumed that if a total change of government had taken place at Mr. Perceval's death, and if some of the strongest opponents of the Orders in Council from the beginning had become leading members of the new Administration, the American war would have been altogether averted, and at all events have been speedily terminated. The Orders in Council were the worst part of the war policy of the Tories, and led to the most pernicious consequences.

On the 2nd of December the House adjourned without

[1] *Edinburgh Review*, vol. xxiii. p. 3.

[2] Sir A. Alison says that this resolution, 'although fully justified in point of right by Napoleon's violence, and by Mr. Erskine's deviation from his instructions, may now well be characterised as one of the most unfortunate, in point of expediency, ever adopted by the British Government' (vol. x. p. 650).

having transacted any business of importance, and met again on the 9th of February, 1815. The deliberations of Parliament were proceeding in their regular course, and the House of Commons was considering a Bill proposed by Ministers for excluding foreign corn, intended to secure remunerating prices to the agriculturist on the return of peace, and independence of foreign supply to the country at large, when the news of Napoleon's escape from Elba, his triumphant march to Paris, and his reoccupation of the imperial throne, threw everything into confusion. He landed at Cannes on the 1st of March, and on the 20th, he entered Paris, which Louis XVIII. had only left on the previous day.[1] On the 6th of April a message from the Prince Regent informed the two Houses that in con- 1815.

[1] Lord Dudley's reflections and speculations on the return of Napoleon from Elba may be seen in his letter of April 15, 1815 (*Letters*, p. 93). His expectation is, that Napoleon will maintain himself on his throne against combined Europe. He thinks that the language of the eight Allied Powers in the Vienna declaration of March 13 is incautiously strong. 'It is most likely,' he adds, 'that before six months are past, four or five of them will have ambassadors bowing and intriguing at the court of this very outlaw' (p. 98). With respect to the duration of the Ministry, he writes thus: 'Can our Ministry continue to go on exactly in its present form? I am by no means sure that any blame attaches itself to them for what has just happened; *but I am considering the effect that may be produced upon the feelings of that half-reasoning animal, the public.* As the popularity of our Ministers (merited, perhaps, by the constancy and spirit with which they had carried on their own system) was certainly very much increased by frosts in Russia and good harvests in England, in occasioning which, I suspect, they had no great share, may they not suffer for unlucky accidents equally beyond their control?' (p. 96). The allusion in this passage is to the abundant harvest of 1813, thus described by Mr. Canning in his speech at Liverpool, in October of that year: 'The same sun which gilded the triumphal entry of Lord Wellington into Madrid, and which turned pale at the conflagration of Moscow, has ripened, during the present year, both in the north and in the south, one of the most luxuriant harvests that ever blessed mankind.' The harvests of 1809, 1810, 1811, and 1812, had been deficient. The harvest of 1813 was so abundant, that the prices of corn fell one-half compared with those of 1812 (see Tooke's *History of Prices*, vol. i. pp. 341, 373).

1815. sequence of the recent events in France, he had given directions for the augmentation of the land and sea forces, and had lost no time in entering into communications with His Majesty's allies, for the purpose of forming such a concert as might most effectually provide for the general and permanent security of Europe. The address in answer to this message was carried in the House of Lords without a division; in the House of Commons, Mr. Whitbread moved an amendment requesting the Prince Regent to exert his most strenuous endeavours to secure to this country the continuance of peace; which was negatived by 220 to 37 votes. Motions were afterwards made in both Houses, by Lord Wellesley and Mr. Abercrombie, censuring Ministers for the improvident arrangements of the preceding year, by which the sovereignty of Elba had been granted to Bonaparte, and the Italian duchies settled upon his wife and son: and for not guarding him in Elba with greater care. The defence of the Government was that they had acquiesced in the plan agreed to by the allied sovereigns, because they did not consider it justifiable to incur a great addition of hazard and bloodshed for the sole difference between treating with Bonaparte and making him a prisoner. These motions were negatived by decisive majorities. The treaty with Napoleon had been signed at Paris on the 11th of April, 1814, and bears seven signatures; namely, those of Metternich, Stadion, Rasoumouffsky, Nesselrode, Hardenberg, Ney, and Caulaincourt. Lord Castlereagh afterwards acceded to it on the part of England, but made two objections. 1. That it recognised the title of Napoleon as Emperor of France, which England had never done. 2. That it assigned him a residence in independent sovereignty, close to the Italian coast, and within a few days' sail of France.

On the 28th of April, Mr. Whitbread moved an address, entreating the Prince Regent to take such measures as might be necessary to prevent this country being involved in war on the ground of the executive power being vested in any particular person. This motion he supported by a speech condemning the celebrated Vienna declaration of March the 25th, by which Bonaparte had been placed out of the pale of civil and social relations, and which was signed by the four representatives of England.[1] It was opposed by Lord Castlereagh on the part of the Government, and negatived by 273 to 72 votes.[2] On the 22nd of May, a message from the Prince Regent was delivered to both Houses, communicating copies of treaties with foreign governments, by which England entered into certain engagements for the renewal of the war with Bonaparte. Upon the address in answer to this message, Lord Grey, in a copious and argumentative speech, stated his objections to the continuance of a warlike policy, and moved an amendment condemnatory of a war undertaken for proscribing the actual ruler of France. The principal feature of this debate, which ended in a majority of 156 to 44 for Ministers, was, that Lord Grenville differed from Lord Grey, with whom he had acted cordially for the previous eight years, and declared himself convinced of the necessity of war.[3] In the House of Commons, the same amendment to the address was moved by Lord

1815.

[1] *Annual Register*, 1814; *State Papers*, p. 366.

[2] An excellent summary of the arguments used on both sides in this debate, is given by Sir S. Romilly (vol. iii. p. 167), who voted in the minority.

[3] Sir S. Romilly (*Mem.* vol. iii. pp. 160, 162), and Mr. Horner (*Mem.* vol. ii. pp. 243–246) both concurred with Lord Grey, although the latter had thought his party wrong in opposing the war in Spain (*ibid.* p. 158). Lord Wellesley took the same line (see Lord Brougham's *Statesmen*, vol. i. p. 249). Mr. Canning, who was absent from England, could not take part in the debates on the renewal of war in 1815; but it may be considered certain that he would have supported Ministers.

1815. George Cavendish. Mr. Grattan and Mr. Plunkett, like Lord Grenville, differing from their political friends, spoke eloquently in favour of war; the majority for Ministers was 331 to 92. The decision being thus in favour of a concerted action with the European movement against Napoleon, the final preparations were made for the four days' campaign, which, in less than a month from these debates, ended in the battle of Waterloo. The rapidity with which events succeeded this battle is remarkable, and can only be explained on the supposition that France was thoroughly wearied of Napoleon's rule, and that Europe was thoroughly determined that it should cease. Napoleon himself brought the news of his defeat to Paris in the early morning of the 21st of June, on the third day after the battle. Within a few hours he became aware that his servile Chamber were in a state of rebellion, and were resolved upon his deposition; the rout and dispersion of his army had been so complete, and so little desire existed to organise a military force in his name, that no attempt at defensive operations was made by any one; on the 22nd he abdicated in favour of his son; on the 23rd, a provisional government was formed, and on the 25th he was transferred, virtually as a prisoner of state, to Malmaison; on the 3rd of July Paris capitulated to the English and Prussians; and on the 7th of July Napoleon surrendered himself to Captain Maitland of the Bellerophon, in the harbour of Rochefort. Thus in three weeks from the battle of Waterloo Napoleon was a captive on board an English man-of-war.

The English Government, profiting by the experience of Elba, determined to keep him in safe custody, and, without permitting him to land, transported him to the island of St. Helena, for which he set sail in August, and which he reached, never to leave it again, in October; having passed from his petty sovereignty in the Mediterranean, through the Tuileries and Waterloo, to his captivity in the island in the Atlantic, in eight eventful months. 1815.

The position of England as a belligerent was wholly different in June 1815, from that which it had been in April 1814. In the first overthrow of Napoleon she was only an accessory; in the second she was a principal. Minute military criticism may find grounds for blame in Napoleon's management of the short campaign of 1815;[1] and it is possible that, partly from the diminution of his bodily vigour, partly from his imperial station, and partly from his confidence in his own military genius, his habits had become less active than they had been in his early campaigns. But it seems to us that his operations in 1815 clearly display his consummate generalship. The object of Wellington and Blücher was to fight in combination: no jealousy or misunderstanding existed between them. Each was bent on assisting the other, and on defeating the enemy, in whatever way this end could be accomplished. Nevertheless, Napoleon succeeded in attacking Blücher separately at Ligny on the 16th, and in defeating him; while he kept the English general in check: and the chief part of the battle of the 18th was fought against the English and their allies, before the Prussians could come up. Nothing but the excellent defensive dispositions of Wellington, and the extraordinary courage and endurance of his small body

[1] See the interesting work of Colonel Charras on the campaign of 1815 (*Histoire de la Campagne de* 1815. Leipzig, 1857. 1 vol. 8vo). Although we cannot but regard Colonel Charras's judgment of Napoleon's management of this campaign as somewhat hypercritical, we fully concur in his opinion of Napoleon's moral and political character, and we respect the honest, impartial, and free-spoken spirit by which the work is animated, not less than we admire the conscientious labour which he has bestowed upon the historical accuracy of the narrative.

1815. of British troops, prevented Napoleon from reaping the fruit of his bold, skilful, and successful tactics; by the unexpected excellence of these troops, his confident expectation of victory was frustrated, and the Prussian cooperation in the afternoon converted what would otherwise have been an undecisive battle into a complete rout. If the American war had not drawn off a portion of the best English infantry, the fate of the day would indeed have been less dubious. The English army and general bore the brunt of Napoleon's formidable attack at Waterloo; and they obtained the chief credit for the ultimate result. Wellington and Blücher, with their moderate numbers, immediately marched upon Paris. No attempt was made to arrest their progress in this perilous advance; and Paris capitulated to them, on the 3rd of July, without firing a gun; before they had been joined by an Austrian or a Russian regiment. Not a hand was held out to save Napoleon; he was glad to take refuge on board an English man-of-war, in order to save himself from a worse fate at home; there was no question of negotiating with him in the character of a sovereign, as had been done in the previous year: he surrendered himself unconditionally to the pleasure of the conqueror.[1] Although the Prussian army had, on the whole, played a less important part than the English army, in the campaign of 1815; yet that part was necessary to success; without the Prussians, there could have been no victory, nor indeed any battle in Flanders. Napoleon must have occupied Brussels without resistance. It must also be borne in mind, that the Prussians had the

[1] Lord Castlereagh stated in the House of Commons, April 7, 1815, that it had never been the intention of the Allied Powers to treat Bonaparte as a prisoner, or to exercise a system of police or espionage with respect to him. They relied on the treaty of Fontainebleau, and upon the apparent determination of the French people to have done with him for ever, and to adhere to Louis XVIII.

largest share in the battle of Leipsic, and took a prominent part in the advance upon Paris in 1814. The King of Prussia rode into Paris with the allies after the capitulation of 1814, and the capitulation of 1815 was signed by a Prussian general. This was not the case with any other power. No English general had any share in the capitulation of 1814, and no Austrian or Russian general had any share in the capitulation of 1815. Viewing, as we do, the rising of Germany after the retreat from Moscow, as the ultimate cause of Napoleon's overthrow, and considering the line which Prussia took in this patriotic movement—looking likewise to the material assistance which Prussia rendered in both the marches upon Paris—we cannot but assign to her a share second to none in the successful termination of this struggle. When we read the lofty and soul-stirring effusions of Körner's martial lyre, we are forcibly impressed with Napoleon's error, in supposing that men capable of appreciating such sentiments would patiently remain his slaves; his attempt to revive the Roman system of universal conquest was inapplicable to so intelligent and sensitive a population as that of Northern Germany; and we must be permitted to think that Wellington and his English troops were better placed at Waterloo, in fighting by the side of the brave and enthusiastic Prussians, than when they were performing the hopeless and ungrateful task of attempting to infuse courage and discipline into the stupid, illiterate, Spanish peasants.[1] 1815.

Napoleon being now safely encaged at St. Helena, Parliament met on February 1, 1816, to make the settlement necessary on the firm re-establishment of peace

[1] Mr. Canning, in his speech at Liverpool, of Jan. 10, 1814, and Lord Liverpool, in the House of Lords, Nov. 4, 1813, consider a coalition of states, founded on the principle of national independence, as the cause of Napoleon's overthrow.

1815. after a war which had virtually lasted for twenty-two years. This settlement was chiefly of an economical kind; it consisted in the reduction of armaments, the remission of taxes, and the restoration of the standard of the currency after the Bank restriction. The income tax, imposed by Pitt in 1798, suspended for a brief period during the peace of Amiens, and raised to ten per cent., or two shillings in the pound, in 1806, had been patiently borne during the continuance of the war. But it had been imposed and maintained as a war-tax; and in the early part of the session of 1815, before the return of of Napoleon from Elba, the Chancellor of the Exchequer had announced its immediate abandonment. The revival of the war subsequently rendered its continuance necessary, and the decision as to its ultimate fate was reserved for 1816. On March 18, Mr. Vansittart proposed its continuance at five per cent., or one shilling in the pound, being half the rate at which it had stood since 1806. But the impatience of this heavy impost, combined with the expectation that it would cease with the war, proved too strong even for this strong Ministry; and the resolution of the Chancellor of the Exchequer was negatived by 238 to 201 votes. 'When the result was announced' (says a contemporary chronicler) 'a long and loud cheering arose in the House, which was re-echoed by the crowd that filled the lobby and avenues; and the event was felt in general throughout the nation as a relief from an oppressive burden.'[1] In this decision the Government acquiesced: they likewise voluntarily abandoned the war duties on malt. Lord Dudley, in a letter to the Bishop of Llandaff, expresses his satisfaction at this result, not because he is convinced that the income tax ought to have been repealed, but because he thinks that the Ministry wanted beating

[1] *Annual Register*, 1815, p. 26.

upon something. 'Their prodigious success,' he adds, which, without at all meaning to deny their merits and abilities, must be allowed by all reasonable men to have been vastly beyond their merits and beyond their abilities, had made their underlings insolent and the House too obedient; and a blow of that sort was necessary to remind the servants of the country that they are not its masters, and to give back to the constitution that spirit and activity which it was perhaps beginning to lose.'[1] 1816.

The summer of 1816 was the coldest and wettest which had occurred in England since 1799, and the harvest was both deficient in quantity and inferior in quality. Before the end of the year the price of wheat rose to 103*s.* a quarter.[2] Distress began to prevail not only among the agricultural, but also among the manufacturing population, together with its natural concomitant, discontent. Instead of meeting this state of things by a liberal and enlightened commercial policy, as recommended by Lord Grenville and other members of the Opposition, the Ministers resorted to restriction of trade for the relief of distress, and to coercion for the suppression of discontent.[3] In 1815 they had proposed and carried a corn law which absolutely prohibited the admission of foreign wheat when the average price was under eighty shillings a quarter.[4]

[1] *Letters*, p. 136.

[2] Tooke, *History of Prices*, vol. ii. p. 14. Sir S. Romilly describes himself as having seen the harvest still on the ground on the 8th, 9th, and 10th of October, in a journey through Herefordshire, Worcestershire, Oxfordshire, Berkshire, and Surrey (*Memoirs*, vol. iii. p. 264).

[3] The character of the domestic policy of the Government from 1815 to 1822 is expressed by Lord Sidmouth's biographer in the following *euphemismus*: 'The remaining seven years of his lordship's public life was one extended campaign between lawless aggression on one side, and the firm and temperate exercise of constitutional authority on the other' (*Life of Sidmouth*, vol. iii. p. 143).

[4] This measure had created much popular discontent, and had led to

1817. In 1817, such was the state of popular feeling that missiles were thrown at the Prince Regent's carriage in his way to the opening of Parliament. Secret committees of both Houses were appointed to enquire into dangerous meetings and combinations. The Habeas Corpus Act was suspended, and the suspension was renewed during the session.[1] Other restrictive measures were likewise carried; the employment of spies by the Government was admitted and justified; Lord Sidmouth wrote a circular letter to lieutenants of counties instructing them that publishers of blasphemous and seditious pamphlets and writings could be apprehended by the warrant of a justice of the peace, and held to bail. The trial of Watson for high treason took place in June, and ended in an acquittal.[2] Other persons involved in the same accusation were discharged by the law officers. The trials of Hone for two blasphemous and seditious libels in December had a similar termination. After a time the distress, the disaffection, and the alarms diminished. At the beginning of the session of 1818 the suspension of the Habeas Corpus Act was removed: but 1819 was again a year of disturbance and political agitation. Public meetings were held in the open air, at the large manufacturing towns, for the discussion of political grievances, at which inflammatory addresses were delivered by Hunt and other popular rhetoricians. After the close of the session a meeting was held at Manchester, at which a collision took place between

serious riots in London. Members were assaulted on their way to the House, and the houses of the chief promoters of the Bill were attacked (*Life of Sidmouth*, vol. iii. p. 125; *Mem. of Romilly*, vol. iii. p. 157; *Life of Wilberforce*, vol. iv. p. 244).

[1] See the articles in the *Edinburgh Review* for March and August, 1817, vol. xxviii. pp. 59, 516.

[2] See the excellent remarks of Sir Samuel Romilly on this trial (*Memoirs*, vol. iii. p. 297).

the yeomanry and the people, and several lives were lost. 1819.
This event, known as 'The Manchester massacre,' gave rise to the assembling of Parliament in Nov. 1819, when the Government lost no time in proposing, and speedily carried, six coercive measures, which acquired an evil reputation under the name of the 'Six Acts.' Lord Fitzwilliam was at the same time removed from the lord-lieutenancy of Yorkshire, for having taken part in the proceedings of a county meeting convened on this occasion.[1]

The Cabinet in 1818 consisted of fourteen members, of whom eight were peers and six were commoners. The latter were Lord Castlereagh, Mr. Canning, Mr. Vansittart, Mr. Bragge Bathurst, Mr. Wellesley Pole, and lastly, Mr. Frederick Robinson, who was brought into it at this time as President of the Board of Trade. He had been Vice-President since 1812. In 1819, the Duke of Wellington was added to the Cabinet as Master-General of the Ordnance, in the place of Lord Mulgrave, who retained his seat in the Cabinet without office.

While the Tory character of the Government remained substantially unchanged: the re-establishment of peace, and the necessity for the settlement of a domestic policy adapted to the economical and social state of the country, was gradually exposing the narrowness and insufficiency of the Tory creed, and exhausting the store of popularity

[1] The offence of Lord Fitzwilliam, as defined by Lord Sidmouth, was, that 'he took the leading part in calling a public meeting for a purpose the most disrespectful to the Prince Regent, and in utter disregard of his Royal Highness's admonition from the throne upon receiving the address of the City of London' (*Life of Sidmouth*, vol. iii. p. 271; Twiss's *Life of Eldon*, vol. ii. p. 437). Compare the article in the *Edinburgh Review* for Jan. 1820, entitled 'The Recent Alarms,' vol. xxxiii. p. 187. The letter to the Marquis of Buckingham, dated Bagshot Park, Oct. 5, 1819, and signed William Frederick, which the Duke of Buckingham's editor attributes to the Duke of York, and describes as proceeding from 'the highest military authority,' is the letter of the Duke of Gloucester (*Mem. of Reg.* vol. ii. p. 349).

1819. which the Ministers had justly obtained from the success of their war policy. 'Time was (says Lord Dudley) when the odds were ten to one against them; luckily for the country as well as for themselves, they have won the game; and they are now enjoying themselves in spending the stakes.[1]

Lord Dudley, in 1819, describes the Administration as having 'suffered itself to be dragged through the dirt the whole session;' as 'having fallen into a state of discredit and insignificance;' as being 'a Ministry, but not a Government.' He remarks that the majority of the House of Commons seems equally determined upon two points: first, that the Ministry shall always stumble; second, that it shall not fall.[2] The language used by Mr. Tierney, in a motion on the state of the nation, on May 18, 1819, shows his belief that the Ministry did not then stand high in public estimation. At an earlier period it had been remarked that the currycomb of the House of Commons had completely taken off the gilding and lackering which Lord Castlereagh had brought from the Congress.[3] The qualities which enabled Lord Castlereagh and his colleagues to shine as a War Ministry, were not such as to fit them for working off the long arrears of internal improvement which had accrued during the period when the attention of the Legislature and the public had been engrossed by the more pressing cares of military and naval preparations. The Opposition had at the same time undergone little change. Mr. G. Ponsonby, a leader who had been more respected and beloved than followed, and who never exercised any great personal influence, died in

[1] Letter of Feb. 14, 1818; *Letters, ibid.* p. 197. In a letter of Aug. 31, 1818, he remarks: 'The Government don't seem much beloved. It has quite spent the popularity of the war' (*ibid.* p. 206).

[2] Letters of May and June 1819, pp. 218, 223.

[3] *Life of Mackintosh*, vol. ii. p. 337.

1817.[1] Mr. Tierney was chosen as his successor.[2] In the session of 1816 Lord Grenville formally separated himself from Lord Grey, and announced in the House of Lords that he should cease to take any part in their debates.[3] 1820.

It was in this state of things, with a Ministry wedded to an unprogressive policy, and hostile to almost every sort of reform and improvement, which had recently proposed and carried a whole code of coercive measures, and whose popularity had fallen from its zenith at the peace to a low point of depression, that the death of George III. took place. This event, which occurred on the 29th of January, 1820, was not at the moment attended with any important political consequence. Since the commencement of the unrestricted Regency in February 1812, the Prince of Wales had been virtually king; a demise of the Crown, however, rendered a dissolution of Parliament necessary. After a short meeting for the transaction of provisional business, Parliament was prorogued on February 28, preparatory to its dissolution; the speech from the throne alluded in the following terms to the Cato Street conspiracy for the murder of the Cabinet Ministers, which was to have taken place on the 23rd of February, a few days previously, and which, from its bold and sanguinary character, had made a deep impression on the public:—'If any doubt had remained as to the nature of those principles by which the peace and happiness of the nation were so seriously menaced, or of the excesses to which they were likely to lead, the flagrant and sanguinary conspiracy which has lately been detected, must open the eyes of the most incredulous, and must vindicate to the whole world the justice and expediency of those measures to which you

[1] *Mem. of Romilly*, vol. iii. p. 307; Lord Dudley's *Letters*, p. 171.
[2] *Mem. of Romilly*, vol. iii. p. 365.
[3] Lord Dudley's *Letters*, p. 159; House of Lords, June 16, 1817.

1820. judged it necessary to resort, in defence of the laws and constitution of the kingdom.' How far this wholesale scheme of political assassination justified the measures of the Government for preventing public meetings in the manufacturing districts, and for curbing the press, may be doubted; but it created a feeling of sympathy with the Government, and, combined with events which speedily supervened, diverted public attention from the recent coercive legislation.[1]

Although the death of George III. did not directly produce any political change, yet one of the formal measures necessary at the commencement of a new reign, led incidentally to a step which entailed the most serious consequences; which convulsed the entire country, threatened the continuance of the Ministry, and even brought the Throne into danger. As soon as the Prince and Princess of Wales had become King and Queen, the passages in the Liturgy in which 'Their Royal Highnesses, George, Prince of Wales, and the Princess of Wales' were prayed for, became inapplicable. At a Council held on February 12, at which the Archbishop of Canterbury, Dr. Manners Sutton, was present, an order was made that these words should be omitted from the Liturgy wherever they occurred.[2] The

[1] Some curious details respecting the deliberations of Ministers upon the course to be taken, when they received the intelligence of the intended plot, are given by Mr. Rush (*Second Residence at the Court of London*, vol. i. pp. 287, 293, 319). Lord Castlereagh advised that the dinner should take place; the Duke of Wellington pointed out the needless danger of this course.

[2] See the Order in Council, in the *Annual Register*, 1820, vol. lxii. p. 748. A full account of the discussions between the King and his Ministers on the subject of the Queen, at this time, is given by Lord Castlereagh in his letter to Lord Stewart, of February 13, 1820 (*Castlereagh Despatches*, vol. xii. p. 210). The Ministers had consented to the omission of her name from the Liturgy, to denying her the honour of coronation, and to making her pecuniary provision contingent upon her perpetual residence abroad; but not to the divorce. The King declared that if they were not prepared to advise the divorce, he should change his Government; and his Majesty

result was, that the prayers of the Church were offered up only for the King and the Royal Family; that the specific mention of the Princess of Wales was omitted, but that no specific mention of her as Queen, as had been done with Queen Charlotte and former Queens, was inserted. The motive for this step doubtless was that the King was determined to avoid all express recognition of his wife as Queen; and he hoped by this apparently negative course, and by leaving her to be included under the general prayer for the Royal Family, to keep the door open for any active measures against her which might afterwards be adopted. 1820.

The Parliament, which was dissolved in March 1820, had been elected in the summer of 1818. Notwithstanding the policy which the Government had recently pursued, the House of Commons of 1820 was somewhat more favourable to them than its predecessor. This result was owing, not only to the close nature of most of the borough seats at that period, but also to the alarmist views which had possessed the minds of the proprietary classes.[1] Even before the Reform Bill, the freedom of election for the English counties and for some of the towns, was such as to enable a strong national feeling to change the character of the House of Commons, as was proved by the dissolution of 1784. The new House met on April 21, and business was proceeding in its regular course, when

added, that if he could not find a Government who would agree to that measure, he should retire to Hanover. In a letter to Prince Metternich of May 6, 1820, Lord Castlereagh says of the Queen: 'If she is wise enough to accept the *pont d'or* which we have tendered her, the calamities and scandal of a public investigation will be avoided. If she is mad enough or so ill-advised as to put her foot upon English ground, I shall, from that moment, regard Pandora's box as opened' (*ibid.* p. 259).

[1] In an article in the *Edinburgh Review* for Oct. 1819, on 'The State of the Country,' it is remarked, that 'the most alarming sign of the times is that separation of the upper and middle classes of the community from the lower, which is now daily and visibly increasing' (vol. xxxii. p. 294).

1820. the event happened whose gravity we have already indicated.

It seems that the Princess of Wales, who had remained on the Continent for the six years since 1814, had not intended to return to England when she became Queen: but when she found her treatment by foreign courts altered, and a sort of stigma cast upon her character in consequence of the omission of her name from the Liturgy, she decided not to submit to this act of the King's Government, which, as it was unsupported by any public allegation or evidence against her, bore the appearance of a wanton insult. Accordingly, after the failure of negotiations through Mr. Brougham and Lord Hutchinson, intended to prevent her return, she crossed the Channel in a common packet, landed at Dover on the 6th of June, and on the following day arrived at Alderman Wood's house in South Audley Street, in the midst of a popular ovation. The consternation which this movement of the Queen produced in the Ministry was extreme; daily, nightly, hourly cabinets (according to Lord Eldon's phrase[1]) were held; but the Government lost no time in commencing proceedings against her, by a measure, the nature of which requires a short preliminary explanation.

The death of the Princess Charlotte and her child in November 1817, had removed the one powerful motive of forbearance from the Prince Regent to his wife. Within two months from that event, he held a meeting of some of the principal members of the Cabinet at Brighton, in order to deliberate upon the means of obtaining a divorce from the Princess of Wales.[2] The Prince was at this time fifty-

[1] Twiss, *Life of Eldon*, vol. ii. p. 372.

[2] See the letter of the Prince Regent to Lord Eldon, of Jan. 1, 1818, in *Twiss*, vol. ii. p. 304, which, though given only in extract, shows clearly the Prince's intention. The fact that the Prince's plan of obtaining a divorce

six years old; and he probably contemplated a second marriage, from the same motive which induced his royal brothers, the Dukes of Clarence, Kent, and Cambridge, to marry in 1818. The result of this meeting was the issue of a commission for the purpose of collecting evidence of the adultery of the Princess. The persons composing the commission were selected by Sir John Leach;[1] who had advised upon a mass of papers relative to the Princess, furnished to him from the Foreign Office, in the autumn of 1817; and the selection was approved by the Lord Chancellor and Lord Liverpool. The commission was dated in March 1818; the members of it assembled at Milan in September; and in July 1819, made their report, which was immediately submitted to the Cabinet.[2] Upon the receipt of this report (which doubtless contained all the criminatory matter subsequently opened by the Attorney-General to the House of Lords) the Cabinet, though pressed by the King to take active measures, decided not to institute any public proceeding against her unless she should return to England. The intention of Ministers to adopt this course in the event of her return was communicated by Lord Hutchinson to the Queen when she was at St. Omer on her way to England; and the effect of this threat was to determine her instantly to 1820.

had been brought before the Cabinet was known to the Marquis of Buckingham, and communicated by him to Lord Grenville early in January (*Mem. of Reg.* vol. ii. p. 199). A rumour of the Prince's intention had at the same time reached Mr. Wynn (*ibid.* p. 201).

[1] The members of the Milan Commission were Mr. Cook, a Chancery barrister; Mr. Powell, an attorney; and Colonel Browne (see Lord Brougham's *Statesmen*, vol. ii. p. 25.

[2] See the statement of Sir J. Leach (*Twiss, ibid.* p. 400). Lord Castlereagh stated in the House of Commons (Feb. 6, 1821), that the death of the Princess Charlotte had nothing more to do in the way of influencing Government as to the time of constituting the Milan Commission, than any other circumstance. But whatever may have been the views of the Ministers, the motive of the King is apparent from his letter to Lord Eldon.

1820. cross the Channel. On the day that the Queen arrived in London, a message from the King was presented to both Houses, communicating certain papers respecting the conduct of Her Majesty since her departure from this kingdom, and recommending them to the immediate and serious attention of Parliament.[1] These papers were the evidence obtained by the Milan Commission. In the House of Lords, Lord Liverpool moved that they be referred to a Committee of Secresy: the motion was agreed to, the committee sat, and reported; and upon their report was founded a Bill of Pains and Penalties for the degradation of the Queen, and for her divorce from her husband, which Lord Liverpool immediately introduced.

In the House of Commons, the motion of Lord Castlereagh for a Committee of Secresy was met by Mr. Wilberforce with a well-meaning proposition, intended to stay further proceedings, and to effect a compromise; but the consequent negotiation with the Queen led to no result.

The basis laid down by the negotiators, 'that the Queen should admit nothing, and the King should retract nothing,' in fact rendered an agreement impossible; and the House of Commons subsequently adjourned the question, in order to allow the measure to proceed in the other House. The proceedings upon the second reading of this Bill in the House of Lords commenced on the 17th of August 1820, and after the examination of witnesses, and the arguments of counsel on both sides, terminated by a division on the 6th of November, when the second reading was carried by 123 to 95 votes, being a majority of 28 for the Bill. The proceedings in the Committee were

[1] On the difference between the King and his Ministers at this time, see Lord Eldon's letters, in *Twiss*, pp. 372–374. The account which Lord Dudley heard from Sir J. Leach, early in the year, likewise indicates the King's views (*Letters*, p. 241).

remarkable, and exercised a material influence upon the final stage of the measure. A certain number of the Peers, who were friendly to the Bill, were known to object to the divorce clause: it became therefore manifest, that if this clause was retained, the majority for the third reading would be diminished. The Ministers, nine in number, voted against the clause, whilst most of the Opposition Lords voted in favour of it. The result was, that the clause was retained by 129 to 62 votes. On the 10th of November, the motion was made for the third reading of the Bill, when there appeared, for the third reading, 108; against it, 99; being a majority of only nine in its favour. Upon the declaration of these numbers, Lord Liverpool rose, and announced the abandonment of the Bill. 1820.

Thus ended, amidst the general jubilation of the country,[1] this ill-advised and unfortunate proceeding. George IV. had separated himself from his wife, by a formal act of his own, in 1796; during twenty-four years they had lived apart; in 1814, he had declared his fixed determination not to meet her on any occasion, public or private; their separation had been sanctioned by George III. and a separate maintenance had been settled upon her by an act of the Legislature; he had used all his influence to exclude her from Court, and from the society of the Royal Family; he had encouraged her removal to the Continent, but even there she was pursued by his ill-will, for he caused the English diplomatic agents to be cautioned against showing her any respect, and to be instructed to urge a similar procedure upon foreign courts. The serious charges of pregnancy and secret delivery, which he had brought against her in 1805, had

[1] London was illuminated, more or less, for three nights (see *Rush*, p. 345 see also *Life of Wilberforce*, vol. v. p. 54).

1820. been conclusively disproved upon enquiry. Not only had he denied her the protection and support due from a husband to a wife, but his behaviour to her was considered to have evinced a spirit of active persecution. It was likewise believed that his own life had not been such as to entitle him to complain of his wife's infidelities. The country regarded his conduct as the oppression of the weak by the strong, accompanied with almost every conceivable circumstance of aggravation.

Under these circumstances, the promoters of the Bill had to contend against heavy disadvantages. The case for the Bill was managed by the Attorney-General, Sir Robert Gifford, and by the Solicitor General, Sir John Copley, who acquitted themselves of their difficult task with the ability of accomplished and experienced advocates. The Queen was represented by her two law officers, Mr. Brougham and Mr. Denman; there were other competent counsel on both sides. Mr. Denman's speeches were forcible and affecting, and produced a powerful impression; but the principal moving power in the whole proceeding was Mr. Brougham, who, by his eloquence, boldness, resource, and pertinacity, so effectually succeeded in throwing suspicion upon the witnesses, in discrediting the accusers, and in arousing the sympathies of the country, that his entire performance may be considered to have been one of the greatest achievements of legal advocacy known in our history.

The case against the Queen rested principally on the evidence of foreign servants, who were suspected of having been bribed by the King's agents to give evidence against their former mistress. Although the Ministers attempted to represent themselves as champions of public morality, yet the proceeding was regarded as a private divorce bill, promoted by the King; and (as Lord Eldon said), if

1820.

evidence of recrimination was not admitted, the effect of recrimination was produced.[1] In the state of popular excitement which had arisen, and the feeling which prevailed respecting the King,[2] the attempt to carry such a measure through the House of Commons, after the close division in the House of Lords, would have been almost an act of madness. Lord Liverpool had even proposed to his colleagues to abandon the Bill in the Lords before the third reading.[3] But, although the scandalous proceeding had roused the indignation of the country against the King and his Ministers, and had rendered the Queen an object of general sympathy and support, yet as soon as the Bill was abandoned, the interest about her subsided, and the country seemed not to have such a conviction of her purity as to induce them to insist upon her entire rehabilitation in her rights. The position of the Ministers had been full of embarrassment. They were doubtless not blind to the weakness of the King's cause, and they expected her to remain on the Continent: but believing, as they did, that she had promoted her Italian courier to her bed, it was hard for them to resist his instances to action when she returned to England and defied her accusers. Her conduct and his conduct rendered it equally difficult for them to remain motionless and to move. Probably, moreover, they did not anticipate that the accumulation of proof which had produced the effect of conviction on their minds would be of so little avail in promoting the success of the Bill for divorcing and degrading the Queen. But the public, whatever might be their opinion respecting the Queen's chastity, were insensible to

[1] Twiss, *Life*, vol. x. p. 386.

[2] Lord Brougham affirms that, 'No prince, in any age or country, was ever more universally or more deeply hated, than George IV. during the year 1820 (*Statesmen*, vol. ii. p. 45).

[3] Twiss, *ibid.* p. 398.

1821. the depositions of the witnesses, because they thought that the King was not entitled to throw the first stone.

When Parliament met, on the 23rd of January, for the session of 1821, it might seem that Ministers were not likely to stand their ground. They had begun the previous year without any large stock of popularity; the result of the proceeding against the Queen had been not only a defeat, but a humiliation. They had likewise lost one of their pillars in debate. Mr. Canning had declined to take any part against the Queen as an accuser; but he had remained in the Cabinet till the end of the year, when he resigned the Presidency of the Board of Control. This office was, in January 1821, provisionally transferred to Mr. Bragge Bathurst, who held it without salary, in conjunction with the Chancellorship of the Duchy of Lancaster.

It had been previously offered to Mr. Peel, who, for some reason which does not appear, was unable at this time to join the Ministry.[1] Mr. Canning's resignation is thus commented on by Lord Dudley, in a letter to the Bishop of Llandaff, of December 22, 1820 :—

Canning, you see, is out. He has, however, no sort of quarrel with his late colleagues. His reason for retiring is simply this;—he had from the beginning determined to take no share in the proceedings as to the Queen. Those proceedings, or at least questions connected with them, are to form the main business of the approaching session. He thinks that absence or neutrality of one of the King's principal servants would be disrespectful towards his master and discreditable to himself. . . . The loss of him will be severely felt in the House of Commons. Peel, I take for granted, is to be his successor. We shall witness a most obstinate struggle. The parties are more nearly balanced than they have been for many years. On the one hand is the immense power of the Crown; on the other a most decided superiority of parliamentary talent. The Ministers have the old

[1] *Life of Lord Sidmouth*, vol. ii. pp. 338, 339.

Tory feeling in their favour; the Opposition are aided by the cry against the late measures to the Queen, and by the great personal unpopularity of the King. I think the Ministers will stand their ground; but the first advance of the Saracens under their renowned Emir Brougham will be fierce and terrible' (p. 271). 1821.

At the beginning of the session of 1821, petitions were presented to the House of Commons complaining of the late proceedings against the Queen, and praying that she might be reinstated in her rights, and that her name might be replaced in the Liturgy. The Parliamentary campaign in the Queen's favour was opened by a motion of Lord Archibald Hamilton condemnatory of the omission of her name from the Liturgy. The resolution was met on the part of Ministers by a motion of adjournment, which was carried by 310 to 209 votes. Shortly afterwards Lord Castlereagh proposed that an annuity of 50,000*l.* should be granted to Her Majesty for her life. Mr. Brougham presented a formal message from the Queen announcing her intention to refuse the money unless her name was restored to the Liturgy. The Government, however, persisted, and the Queen accepted the annuity without the fulfilment of her condition. A formal motion of censure upon Ministers for the late proceedings against the Queen was then brought forward by Lord Tavistock, which led to a debate of two nights, and was supported on a division by only 178 against 324 votes, giving to Ministers a majority of 146. A motion in favour of the insertion of the Queen's name in the Liturgy was subsequently made by Mr. John Smith, but, though sanctioned by Mr. Wilberforce, it was negatived by 298 to 178 votes.

Thus ended the Parliamentary efforts to support the cause of the Queen after the abandonment of the Bill of Pains and Penalties. Great embarrassment would have

1821. been created by the accession to power of a Ministry pledged to treat the Queen as free from stain, and to reinstate her in all her rights and privileges. On the other hand, it can scarcely be doubted that if the constitution of the House of Commons in 1821 had been as popular as it was subsequently rendered by the Reform Bill of Lord Tavistock's brother, his motion of censure would have been carried, and Lord Liverpool's Ministry must have resigned.

Whatever may have been the prevalent feeling of the country respecting the Queen, the course now taken by Ministers met with acquiescence, and her claims were not revived, until the announcement of the King's intention to exclude her from his coronation (which was fixed for a day in July), called forth a memorial asserting her right to take a part in that ceremony. Her memorial was referred to a Committee of the Privy Council, who, having heard the arguments of her Attorney and Solicitor-General, decided against her right.[1] She afterwards applied to have a place assigned to her as a spectator at the King's coronation, and to be crowned separately herself; but both applications were ineffectual. On the day of the coronation she made an endeavour to gain admission to Westminster Abbey, but she was repulsed by the door-keepers, and the assembled multitude showed no disposition to assist her in forcing an entrance. Her reception by the people was cold.[2] Within a month from this time she was seized with an inflammatory malady, and died after a few days' illness.[3] By her directions her body was

[1] See Twiss, *Life*, pp. 420, 426.

[2] Twiss, *ibid.* p. 427.

[3] Lord Londonderry, in a letter written to Lord Eldon from Ireland, in August 1821, where he was in attendance upon the King, describes the Queen's death as 'the greatest of all possible deliverances, both to his Majesty and to the country' (*Twiss*, vol. ii. p. 432).

conveyed to Brunswick for interment: her funeral procession created a riot, at which the military interfered, and two lives were lost. It is stated by Lord Brougham that before her death she had come to the resolution of leaving England; and that if her life had been prolonged she would have removed to the Continent.[1] This decision shows that she was conscious of a decline in her popularity, and of the impossibility of creating any new interest in her favour. The country had supported her against the aggressive measures of the King; but they were not prepared to support her in aggressive measures against him. 1821.

Whatever (says Lord Holland) may be thought of the treatment to which she was exposed on her arrival in England, or of the malignity, and possibly the falsehood, of some of the charges subsequently brought against her, or of the somewhat vindictive prosecution of her when Queen, she was at best a strange woman, and a very sorry and uninteresting heroine. She had, they say, some talent, some pleasantry, some good humour, and great spirit and courage; but she was utterly destitute of all female delicacy, and exhibited in the whole course of the transactions relative to herself very little feeling for anybody, and very little regard for honour or truth, or even for the interests of those who were devoted to her, whether the people in the aggregate, or the individuals who enthusiastically espoused her cause. She avowed her dislike of many; she scarcely concealed her contempt for all. In short, to speak plainly, if not mad, she was a very worthless woman.'[2]

We shall not attempt to give any account of the general Parliamentary business of the sessions of 1821 and 1822, and shall only advert to the ministerial changes which occurred during that period. It seems that in July 1821,

[1] *Statesmen*, vol. ii. p. 30.

[2] *Mem. of the Whig Party*, vol. ii. p. 120. Lord Eldon seems to have doubted of the Queen's sanity (Twiss, *Life*, p. 366).

1821. a short time before the Queen's death, the differences between the King and Lord Liverpool, with respect to some proposed changes in the Cabinet, were such as to render the duration of the Government precarious;[1] but the storm, whatever may have been its cause, passed away. In December 1821, Lord Wellesley went to Ireland as Lord-Lieutenant, with Mr. Goulburn as Chief Secretary, according to the system of balance which then prevailed; the former being favourable, the latter being hostile, to the Catholic claims. At the same time, Mr. Saurin was replaced by Mr. Plunkett, as Attorney-General for Ireland. Mr. Peel had, in 1810, during Mr. Perceval's Administration, been appointed Under-Secretary of the War Department. He had then recently entered the House of Commons: his age was twenty-two. In August 1812, he became Chief Secretary to the Lord-Lieutenant, after the accession of Lord Liverpool's Government, and resigned this post in August 1818.[2] He was accordingly out of office at the time of the proceedings against the Queen; and he declined to enter the Cabinet upon Mr. Canning's resignation, in the winter of 1820, when the sentence of the House of Commons, upon the conduct of Ministers, was still unpronounced. But, at the beginning of 1821, he became Home Secretary in the place of Lord Sidmouth,

[1] Lord Eldon, in a letter to Lord Stowell of July 1821, says: 'The bulk of the Ministers are, I think, convinced that the King means, and that my neighbour [Lady Conyngham] will induce him, to change them; and I should not wonder if, in a too great confidence that he has that meaning, they were to retire before he knew how to execute it. It is impossible but that the thing must fall to pieces' (Twiss, *Life*, p. 429).

[2] M. Guizot (*Life of Sir R. Peel*, p. 14) represents the office of Irish Secretary as having become intolerable to him, from the constant sight of the evils and abuses which he was called on to defend; and connects his resignation of it with his election as member for the University of Oxford, in 1817. We suspect the truth to have been that he had become tired of an office which he had held for six years.

who remained a member of the Cabinet without office. 1821.
Mr. Peel's political connections were, at that time, with the extreme section of the Tory party; he was a follower of Perceval rather than of Pitt. The anti-Catholics wanted an organ in the House of Commons; not only all the Whigs, but Lord Castlereagh and Mr. Canning, retaining Mr. Pitt's opinions, were advocates of Catholic emancipation; and Mr. Peel supplied that want. The 'Annual Register' for 1822, after eulogising Lord Sidmouth, and regretting the public loss caused by his retirement, remarks, as a ground of consolation, that 'Mr. Peel's political predilections, sympathies, principles, and prejudices, were very much the same with those of Lord Sidmouth; so that the substitution of the one for the other could have no effect on the course of administration.[1] Sir James Mackintosh has the following entry in his 'Diary,' respecting a debate on the Catholic Question in December 1817:—'Peel made a speech of little merit in point of substance, but so clearly and elegantly expressed, and so well delivered, as to be applauded to excess. He is a proof of the great value of the mechanical parts of speaking, when combined with industry and caution. He now fills the too-important place of spokesman to the intolerant faction.[2] The small party, likewise, who had followed Lord Grenville, and who, at that time, occupied a middle position, somewhat similar to that now occupied by the Peelite party, joined the administration at the end of 1821; as the price of this junction, the Marquis of Buckingham was created a duke, and Mr. C. Wynn entered the Cabinet as President of the Board of Control.[3] The Cabinet

[1] Vol. lxiv. p. 6.

[2] *Life of Mackintosh*, vol. ii. p. 342.

[3] A vain attempt seems to have been made to induce Lord Grenville to join the Government at this time (*Life of Sidmouth*, vol. iii. p. 382).

1822. now consisted of fifteen members, nine peers, and six commoners. The six commoners were Lord Londonderry,[1] Mr. Peel, Mr. Vansittart, Mr. F. Robinson, Mr. C. Wynn, and Mr. B. Bathurst.

With certain modifications of his Cabinet, Lord Liverpool had now weathered the second session since the failure of the Bill for degrading the Queen, and the resignation of Mr. Canning. The latter had, in the spring of 1822, accepted the office of Governor-General of Bengal, rendered vacant by the recall of Lord Hastings; notwithstanding his extraordinary, and, perhaps, unsurpassed oratorical powers, he preferred this imperial exile to exclusion from the Cabinet, with which the personal repugnance of the King now threatened him. Parliament was prorogued on the 6th of August, 1822, by the King in person; and His Majesty, who had, in the previous year, paid a visit to Ireland, embarked at Greenwich for Scotland a few days after the prorogation. On his arrival at Edinburgh he received the melancholy intelligence of the death of Lord Londonderry, who had, in a fit of insanity, put an end to his own life.[2] Upon the King's return to London, the choice of his successor was made. The person whose claims stood first was, without question, Mr. Canning But he was not acceptable to the King, on

[1] Lord Castlereagh became Marquis of Londonderry by the death of his father, April 8, 1821.

[2] Lord Eldon says, in a letter written at the time: 'I learn, upon the best authority, that for two or three days he was perfectly insane; and the medical men attribute that fact to the operation on his head of the unceasing attention to business, which the last harassing session to him called for' (*Twiss*, vol. ii. p. 464). Lord Londonderry's state may perhaps be more correctly described as mental delirium, extending over several days, than insanity (see also *Life of Wilberforce*, vol. v. p. 134).

According to an anecdote preserved in *Raikes's Journal*, Dec. 25, 1832, Lord Londonderry had exhibited symptoms of madness previously to his departure for the Congress of Vienna, in 1814.

account of his attachment to the Queen's cause: and Lord Eldon, with a portion of the anti-Catholic section of the Cabinet, wished for a person of their own politics.[1] But the Queen was dead; and Lord Liverpool, with the concurrence of Mr. Peel, insisted on the appointment of Mr. Canning, who was accordingly called to the office of Foreign Secretary, and the lead of the House of Commons.[2] Mr. Canning, without hesitation, but with considerable regret for the pecuniary sacrifice which he was making, relinquished his Indian throne, and accepted the offer.[3] Great as were the attractions of the post of 1822.

[1] See Lord Dudley's *Letters*, pp. 350, 356. Lord Eldon's animosity to Mr. Canning, and his regret at his introduction into the Cabinet, are plainly shown in a letter to Lord Stowell of September 1823 (*Twiss*, vol. ii. p. 484). According to M. de Marcellus (whose reminiscences are not of much historical value), Mr. Canning described himself as forced upon the King in 1822 (*Politique de la Restauration*, p. 15).

[2] M. de Marcellus, in a letter to M. de Châteaubriand, of Sept. 15, 1822, stated that Mr. Canning was first offered the office of First Lord of the Admiralty, to which he objected, as inconsistent with the functions of leader of the House of Commons (*ibid.* p. 90). We believe that the arrangement to which M. de Marcellus refers was in agitation, but that it was not offered by Lord Liverpool to Mr. Canning.

[3] See Stapleton's *Life of Canning*, vol. ii. pp. 120–130; Twiss, *Life of Eldon*, vol. ii. p. 464. Mr. Canning said, in the House of Commons, May 1, 1827: 'In the year 1822 I was appointed to an office fraught with wealth, honour, and ambition. From that office I was called, not only not on my own seeking, but contrary to my own wish; and I made a sacrifice—a sacrifice, be it remembered, of no inconsiderable nature to a poor man.' On May 13, 1828, upon a motion for a grant of a pension to one of Mr. Canning's sons, Mr. Huskisson made the following statement: 'I regret to be obliged to make reference on such an occasion to information derived from the privacy of confidential intercourse; but I can state, from my own personal credit, that, whatever were the feelings of others, who were justly near and dear to Mr. Canning, it had for years been his own warm and anxious wish (owing to circumstances that were likely to press upon the acute and sensitive mind of such a man) to be placed in some public situation, however it might sacrifice or compromise the fair and legitimate scope of his ambition, which, while it enabled him to perform adequate public services, would enable him also to place upon a better footing his wife's private fortune, which he had lessened, and the inheritance of his children, which he had impaired.'

1822. leader which he was invited to fill, the feelings with which he regarded it had probably undergone a considerable alteration since 1812.

Lord Londonderry had, for ten years, been the most prominent and important person in the Cabinet of Lord Liverpool, though he did not hold the office of First Lord of the Treasury, and was not called Prime Minister. Mr. Canning occupied after him a similar position. Here, therefore, we suspend our review of this administration. In another article, we shall resume the subject at this new phase; which will afford us an opportunity of estimating the change which the transfer of power from Lord Londonderry to Mr. Canning produced.

VII.

ADMINISTRATIONS OF MR. CANNING, LORD GODERICH, AND THE DUKE OF WELLINGTON.[1]

SINCE the appearance of our article on the first period of 1822.
Lord Liverpool's administration (Jan. 1859), two more volumes have been published from the family papers in the possession of the Duke of Buckingham, which comprise the ten years of the reign of George IV. In continuing our review of events from the death of Lord Castlereagh in 1822, to the accession of the Reform Ministry in 1830, we shall avail ourselves of the materials contained in these volumes. At the same time we must express our opinion that the editor has shown a culpable disregard of the feelings of living persons in publishing at length the private and confidential letters addressed to the late Duke of Buckingham, by his near relations and intimate friends; many of those letters contain passages relating to events in private life, of a comparatively recent date, which it was improper and unbecoming to give the public, and which are utterly valueless for any question of political and historical interest.

Adopting an American metaphor, we may say that the administration of Lord Liverpool, after the second and final downfall of Napoleon, began the peace with a large balance of popularity at their banker's in their favour,

[1] Review of *Memoirs of the Court of George IV.*, 1820–1830. From original family documents. By the Duke of Buckingham and Chandos, K.G. London: 1859. 2 vols. 8vo.

1822. formed out of their accumulations during the last years of the war; while the account of the Opposition had been overdrawn, and exhibited a balance against them. Owing to their policy respecting the war with Napoleon, the latter party had an arrear of unpopularity to cancel, before they could set themselves straight with the country; but this object was gradually effected, and before long they converted their deficiency into a surplus. The Whigs were not only more liberal and tolerant than the Tories; less desirous of maintaining a monopoly of power and of permanently excluding the unprivileged and the heterodox; but their opinions on financial, economical and commercial subjects, on questions of law reform, and on colonial and international policy, were more enlightened and philosophical. As the succession of debates and motions in Parliament, and the changes in public affairs, developed this antithesis, and disclosed the true character of each political party, the Ministry lost its hold upon the country, while the Opposition steadily advanced in public estimation.

It should be observed that the progress of legislative reform had been unnaturally retarded in this country during the interval between 1792 and 1815 by the circumstances of the time, and that a vigorous and somewhat enterprising spirit was required of a ministry at the commencement of the peace, in order to bring our legislation into harmony with the growing wants of the country, and the advanced state of intelligence.[1] This state of things had been owing partly to the war, which engrossed the attention of the Government and the public, and diverted men's thoughts from internal improvement; but principally to the French Revolution, which had

[1] Mr. Sydney Smith gives a striking description of this stagnant period in the preface to his collected writings.

engendered a morbid horror of all innovation, and had produced a vindictive mistrustful feeling in the upper classes towards their inferiors in social rank. 'If any person,' said Sir Sam. Romilly, writing in 1808, 'be desirous of having an adequate idea of the mischievous effects which have been produced in this country by the French Revolution and all its attendant horrors, he should attempt some legislative reform on humane and liberal principles. He will then find, not only what a stupid dread of innovation, but what a savage spirit it has infused into the minds of many of his countrymen.'[1] The storm which, on the Continent, had swept away all ancient institutions, even those which were beneficial, had in England rivetted even our ancient abuses to the soil. While Jacobinism had, in France, borne down its opponents, and had therefore been eminently destructive, it had in England only served to rouse a spirit of reactionary alarm, and had therefore been eminently conservative. 1822.

The almost unbroken tenure of power which the Tories had enjoyed for so long a period likewise produced its usual corrupting influence, in creating a sense of irresponsibility, and in separating their interests and sympathies from those of the people at large. This state of things is disclosed in the letters contained in the Duke of Buckingham's new publication. In admitting us behind the scenes of the Liverpool Cabinet, they show how much its movements were determined by petty personal motives;

[1] *Mem. of Romilly*, vol. ii. p. 247. Professor Smyth, in addressing his class in 1826, made the following remark: 'You, who have not exactly lived during the times of the French Revolution, cannot at all imagine how long and how deeply it affected the thoughts, the feelings, and the interests of every human being, without any exception, that then existed in the civilised world' (*Lectures on the French Revolution*, vol. i. p. 144). The publication of the *Anti-Jacobin*, and its success, is a striking proof how the public attention of England was engrossed with French politics, and what were then called French principles.

1822. how many arrangements were in progress in which the public interests was a secondary consideration; how much certain families and sections and interests had learned to consider the Government as a machine to be worked for their benefit, or at least under their direction. Although the feelings and opinions expressed in familiar letters, written without the idea of publicity, cannot always be taken as the deliberate views of the writer, yet it must be admitted by the most prejudiced Tory that the picture of the administration of public affairs, during the first years of the reign of George IV., presented by these letters, is anything but creditable or respectable.

Besides the stationary and unprogressive character which the Liverpool Ministry maintained at a moment when the inaction of twenty-five years demanded of a government a spirit of active improvement; and which therefore tended to lower the esteem in which it had been held; there was another circumstance which operated against the Ministry at this time, as compared with the previous reign. George III. always exercised a considerable influence, independent of his Ministers. His shrewdness and insight into men's motives, his moral and respectable life, his sympathies with the prejudices of the country, and his genuine wish to be a good king, according to the measure of his understanding, gave him this position. If he wished to undermine or weaken his Ministers, he used this influence against them; if he wished to support and strengthen them, he used it in their favour. But it was a substantive influence, which made itself felt throughout the greater part of his reign. Mr. Fox and Lord Grenville, in their private letters, equally bear testimony to its reality. George IV., on the other hand, was always unpopular; even before he became Regent, his debts, his profligacy, his quarrel with his wife, and his general character, had alienated the people from him. During his regency and reign, the eloquence of statesmen, the wit of poets, and the scurrility of newspapers and pamphlets, were equally employed in rendering him contemptible and odious. Lord Byron and Moore vied with one another in lampooning him in verses which the present generation learn by heart. When at length he secluded himself from the public view, the popular imagination regarded him almost as a Tiberius, who had found a Capreæ in the Cottage in Windsor Park. It may therefore be said that, from the beginning of his Regency in 1811 to the close of his reign in 1830, the regal influence was limited to the strict exercise of the prerogative. George IV. had no personal influence; instead of his popularity supporting the Ministry, the difficulty was for the Ministry to support his unpopularity, and to uphold the respect for the Crown when it encircled the head of such a sovereign. 1822.

The only popular triumphs which George IV. achieved, were his state visits to Ireland and Scotland; which were the more remarkable as they followed close upon the Queen's Trial. The following remarks of Lord Dudley upon the former visit, in a letter of November 1821, are, however, worthy of notice: —

I cannot help suspecting that His Majesty's late journeys to see his kingdoms of Ireland and Hanover will not on the whole redound much to his honour or advantage. His manners no doubt are, when he pleases, very graceful and captivating. No man knows better how to add to an obligation by the way of conferring it. But, on the whole, he wants dignity, not only in the seclusion and familiarity of his more private life, but on public occasions. The secret of popularity in very high stations seems to consist in a somewhat reserved and lofty, but courteous and uniform, behaviour. Drinking toasts, shaking people by the hand, and calling them Jack and Tom, get more applause at the moment, but fails entirely in the long run. He seems to have

1822. behaved not like a sovereign coming in pomp and state to visit a part of his dominions, but like a popular candidate come down upon an electioneering trip. If the day before he left Ireland he had stood for Dublin, he would, I dare say, have turned out Shaw or Grattan. Henry IV. is a dangerous example for sovereigns that are not, like him, splendid chevaliers and consummate captains. Louis XIV., who was never seen but in a full-bottomed wig, even by his *valet-de-chambre*, is a much safer model (*Lord Dudley's Letters*, p. 295).

The letters recently published by the Duke of Buckingham state that the King diverted himself and his companions during his passage to Ireland with revelry and singing, and that he arrived at the Phœnix Park in a state of intoxication. They likewise contain many details respecting his private life at Windsor which show that the popular feeling against him was anything but unfounded.

While the Liverpool Administration from 1815 to 1822, and in a less degree from 1822 to 1827, maintained on the whole a stationary course, and at seasons of disturbance resorted to measures of repression and coercion, the Whig Opposition steadily enforced measures of a liberal character. Though the practical success of the Opposition was not great, they prepared the mind of the public for political changes by discussion and debate; and by defending popular rights and popular interests, they acquired a popularity which speedily deserted their Conservative antagonists. On the questions of retrenchment, of the public expenditure, of Criminal Law Reform, of West Indian Slavery, of Popular Education, and of Parliamentary Reform, the Ministers were ranged on the unpopular, the Opposition on the popular, side. The commercial policy of the Liverpool Ministry was its brightest point; on the Catholic Question the Cabinet was divided.

The Administration of Lord Liverpool consists of two well-marked periods; the first of which may be designated as the nebulous, the second as the semiluminous, period. The first, which extends over the ten years from 1812 to 1822, is distinguished by the leadership of Lord Castlereagh in the House of Commons. The second, lasting for the five years from 1822 to 1827, is distinguished by the leadership of Mr. Canning in the same assembly. 1822

The post of ministerial leader of the House of Commons, to which Mr. Canning was promoted in September 1822, at the age of fifty-two, was one to which he had, some years before, aspired. When the Portland Administration was approaching its end, Mr. Canning had two rivals in the Cabinet, Lord Castlereagh and Mr. Perceval. To Lord Castlereagh he objected as unfit for the War Department, and the unfortunate issue of the Walcheren expedition rendered his competition innocuous. But Mr. Perceval was a more formidable rival; and when he was preferred by the King for the situation of Prime Minister, to which Mr. Canning advanced his claims, the latter retired from the Cabinet. If Mr. Canning had, at the Duke of Portland's resignation in 1809, retained the seals of Foreign Secretary, he would doubtless have become the political heir of Mr. Perceval, after his assassination in the spring of 1812. As it was, the office of Foreign Secretary, with the lead of the House of Commons, passed to Lord Castlereagh at the formation of the Liverpool Ministry; and although Lord Liverpool shortly afterwards proposed to Mr. Canning an arrangement by which he should resume the Foreign department, he refused the offer, because it was intended that Lord Castlereagh should retain the lead of the House of Commons. Those who now preferred Lord Castlereagh to his rival Mr. Canning as leader were influenced partly by the recollection of their quarrel in

1822. 1809, as to which the general sympathy was with Lord Castlereagh. Mr. Canning had been Foreign Secretary when the Spanish insurrection broke out; it was he who initiated the Peninsular war, and sent Sir Arthur Wellesley to Portugal: and if he had been Foreign Secretary at the time of Napoleon's fall, his political position in 1814 would have been one of great eminence and splendour although he might not have been ministerial leader of the House of Commons. The Peninsular war, which originated in his policy, would, under his official guidance, have been brought to a successful issue, and he might have concluded the peace.[1] As it was, Lord Castlereagh obtained the credit which accrued to the Ministry from the great events of 1814 and 1815; and he was raised to a pinnacle of fame and influence from which he looked down upon the comparatively obscure and powerless condition of his unsuccessful rival. Having, through a fortunate combination of circumstances, reached this elevation, his intrepidity, his directness, his firmness of purpose, his immovable calmness, the dignity of his personal demeanour, and his other moral qualifications for the post of leader, enabled him to retain in the House of Commons an ascendency which his abilities, knowledge, and eloquence would never have given him.[2] Lord Dudley considers the career of Lord Castlereagh, compared with that of Mr. Canning, to afford an illustration of Voltaire's saying, 'that a man's success in life depends less on his talents than on the force

[1] See on this subject the remarks in Mr. Stapleton's *Political Life of Canning*, vol. i. pp. 291, 292.

[2] A favourable, but not unjust, estimate of Lord Castlereagh's qualifications for the post of ministerial leader is given by Mr. Twiss, in his *Life of Eldon*, vol. ii. p. 462. See also Lord Brougham's sketch (*Statesmen*, vol. ii. pp. 109–117), which he concludes with this remark: 'Lord Castlereagh is certainly the most striking example of the effects produced by our parliamentary system of government, in most unjustly lowering the reputation of public men who happen not to succeed in debate.'

of his character.' Voltaire's examples are Mazarin and De Retz; to which Lord Dudley adds Bolingbroke and Walpole.[1] 1822.

Lord Castlereagh did not indeed possess those advantages which aristocratic birth and education have conferred on many of our statesmen. His knowledge, whether constitutional, historical, or classical, was of the most limited sort; he belonged to the illiterate school of politicians, and would doubtless have sympathised heartily with the modern dictum that more instruction is to be derived from one number of the 'Times' than from the history of Thucydides. His political life had however begun at an early age; he had been the Irish ministerial leader at the time of the Rebellion and the Union; his parliamentary and official experience had been extensive; and his mode of transacting the business of the English House of Commons was such as to satisfy that somewhat fastidious assembly even at a time when its intellectual standard was high. He navigated the ship of the State through the Syrtes of the distress and disaffection of 1817 and 1819; he withstood the shock of the Queen's trial, and when the short attack of insanity supervened which brought his life to a premature close at the age of fifty-three, he seemed to have taken a new lease of power.

Yet Lord Castlereagh's death, however firm his tenure of power may have seemed to be when it occurred, must be considered to have contributed materially to the duration of the Liverpool Administration. Like Mr. Canning, he was a supporter of the Catholic claims; and both belonged to the school of Pitt, rather than of Perceval. But Lord Castlereagh had, from his experience of the Irish rebellion, contracted a fondness for a strong coercive Government, at a period of disturbance; and his views of domestic policy, though sufficiently definite, were

[1] *Letters to the Bishop of Llandaff*, p. 301.

1822. founded upon this narrow basis. His views of foreign politics, on the other hand, were not clear or independent. During the eventful period from 1812 to 1815, he had administered the Foreign Office, principally as a War Minister. When peace returned, and the settlement of Europe was to be made, his judgment was chiefly guided by a view of the evils from which the country had just escaped; his main object, therefore, was to obliterate the traces of the French influence over Europe, and to build up dykes against the perils of another French inundation. Hence he adopted too implicitly the views of Metternich, and the other ministers of the great despotic courts, with which he had recently acted in the final struggle against Napoleon; and he saw no danger to Europe, provided the alliance of Russia, Austria, and Prussia maintained the combined action and military resources of those Governments. One of the most prominent feelings of the English statesmen who lived during the war with Napoleon, was a conviction of the advantages of peace, and a desire to preserve it unbroken.[1] In this laudable feeling Lord Castlereagh strongly participated,[2] but, in seeking to multiply the securities for peace, he

[1] Lord Liverpool stated in the House of Lords, Jan. 21, 1819, that 'he felt bound in conscience to affirm that, so far as he knew, there never was a time in the history of the world when so general an anxiety prevailed to preserve peace; when the causes of disturbance were so completely removed; when nations and sovereigns were more divested of ambition and the love of undue influence, andwhen the spirit of conciliation and the necessity for repose was more thoroughly acknowledged and acted upon over the whole European community.'

[2] At the birthday dinner to the diplomatic body in June 1819, Lord Castlereagh, in answer to a remark on the satisfactory aspect of a peaceable meeting of representatives of all the States of Europe, instead of the recent state of mutual hostility, said: 'Yes, and may the happy tranquillity we are speaking of long continue. Europe requires repose; each State has had enough of war and enough of glory, and ought to be content' (Rush's *Second Residence at the Court of London,* vol. i. p. 100).

overlooked the incidental evils which these securities engendered. The Congress of the three despotic Powers, which had been instituted for the purpose of keeping France within bounds, and of maintaining the peace of Europe, began to be used for the purpose of suppressing popular movements in other States, on the plea that revolutionary excesses might tend to war, and that Jacobinism might light up a conflagration in Europe. Hence the Holy Alliance (the principles of which Lord Castlereagh had tacitly favoured) became a military league, not so much for the preservation of European peace, as for the suppression of European freedom, and the confirmation of European despotism. In this armed conspiracy of despots against the liberties of Europe, Lord Castlereagh was believed to be an accomplice; and it is certain, that if he did not actively promote its operations, he did not actively remonstrate against its policy, or throw the influence of England openly into the opposite scale. It may be added, that at the Congress of Vienna, he disregarded the assurances which had been given by the German Governments, in appealing to the spirit of national independence against Napoleon. When the despotic Governments were weak, and wished to rouse the popular feeling against the common enemy, they encouraged hopes of the establishment of free institutions at the restoration of peace: but when peace was restored, these promises were forgotten. Lord Castlereagh, though the representative of the principal free Government in Europe, did nothing to recall the memory of these promises. He even allowed the pledges of English officers in Italy to be violated by the annexation of Genoa to Piedmont. Justice to the weaker States was overlooked, in deference to his avowed paramount object, the re-establishment and re-organisation of the two great monarchies of Austria 1822

1822. and Prussia, which (as he truly said) had been nearly destroyed by the war. The military position of these two States was the canon which determined the readjustment of boundaries, under his auspicies, in 1815.[1] Owing to this policy and these opinions, Lord Castlereagh became in the last years of his life a highly unpopular Minister: he continued, however, to enjoy the favour of George IV. and to receive the support of the large and still unbroken Tory party, as well as of the unreformed House of Commons, in which the direct popular element was weak.

Mr. Canning had been, from his first introduction into Parliament, a follower of Pitt, and had no political connection with the Whigs. He was a determined opponent of Parliamentary Reform, and had defended the existing constitution of the House of Commons in some of his most elaborate and effective speeches. But he was a man of far more knowledge and capacity than Lord Castlereagh; of a more elastic understanding, and of a more independent judgment. He could appreciate more quickly and truly the changes in the circumstances of the time, and adapt himself to them with greater readiness.[2] His views of foreign politics were more national, and less identified with those of the great despotic courts—with that system which, in the phraseology of the day, was called the Holy Alliance. His political connections, moreover, lay among persons of more liberal views in commercial

[1] See Stapleton's *Life of Canning*, vol. i. pp. 11, 14, 61, 62. Mr. Stapleton thus characterises Lord Castlereagh's foreign policy after the peace: 'Certain general ideas as to the advantages of preserving peace, coupled with a bias against liberal opinions, were apparently the springs which regulated each separate determination, on which the force of circumstances compelled him to resolve' (p. 63).

[2] The popular leanings of Mr. Canning, and his disposition to seek for support from the Whig party, are pointed out in a letter of M. de Marcellus to M. de Chateaubriand, of Jan. 30, 1823 (*Politique de la Restauration*, p. 129).

and financial affairs. At the beginning of 1823, soon after his assumption of the lead, Mr. Vansittart was created Lord Bexley, and succeeded Mr. B. Bathurst as Chancellor of the Duchy of Lancaster. His office of Finance Minister devolved on Mr. Fred. Robinson, who resigned the Presidency of the Board of Trade to Mr. Huskisson. The latter entered the Cabinet in the autumn of the same year.[1] In 1814, the Liverpool Cabinet had been represented in the House of Commons by Lord Castlereagh, Mr. Vansittart, Mr. Bragge Bathurst, and Mr. Wellesley Pole; in 1823, it was represented there by Mr. Canning, Mr. Peel, Mr. Fred. Robinson, Mr. Huskisson, and Mr. Charles Wynn. This alteration in the cast of parts betokened a great advance towards a more liberal composition of the Ministry. Mr. F. Robinson and Mr. Huskisson held sound economical opinions, and were disposed to move as far and as fast in the direction of free trade as the protected interests would permit. Mr. C. Wynn had been a member of the Grenville party; he had once acted with the Whigs, and was a friend of Catholic Emancipation. Mr. Peel, though the leader of the anti-Catholics in the House of Commons, and addicted to a narrow creed on all religious questions, was enlightened and liberal in his economical views. When out

1823.

[1] See *Biogr. Mem. of Mr. Huskisson; Huskisson's Speeches*, vol. i. p. 86. Lord Eldon, in a letter to his brother, in Jan. 1823, complains bitterly of the apprehended introduction of Mr. Huskisson into the Cabinet, and the violation of the King's promises as to the exclusion of 'the connections of a certain person'—Mr. Canning (*Twiss*, vol. ii. p. 468). In the same letter we should read: 'Whether Lord Sidmouth has [resigned] or not, I don't know.' We have adopted the statement as to the time of Mr. Huskisson's entrance into the Cabinet from his *Biographical Memoir*, which was, we believe, written by his private secretary, Mr. Leeves. His statement is confirmed by a letter of Mr. C. Wynn in *Mem. of Court of George IV.* vol. i. p. 494. The lists in the *Annual Register* do not bring him into the Cabinet till 1825.

1823. of office, he had been Chairman of the Bank Committee, and had introduced and carried, in 1819, the Bill by which the convertibility of the bank note was re-established, although he had entered on the enquiry with opposite opinions to those he was led by the evidence to adopt.[1] On questions of criminal jurisprudence, likewise, his opinions were far in advance, not only of Lord Eldon, and the Crown lawyers, but also of Lord Liverpool and Lord Castlereagh; and, as Home Secretary, he gave practical effect to the doctrines which Sir Samuel Romilly and Sir James Mackintosh had in vain attempted to enforce.[2]

The policy pursued by Mr. Canning as Foreign Minister likewise served to give a more liberal character to the Ministry, and to bring it more into accordance with the general feeling of the country. The first principle which Mr. Canning laid down on receiving the seals of the Foreign Department, and upon which he consistently acted, was to destroy the power of the Holy Alliance, to separate England from the union of continental sovereigns, and to

[1] On the Report of the Bank Committee, see Lord Dudley's letter of June 1819 to the Bishop of Llandaff, who had written a pamphlet on the subject (*Letters*, p. 222). Mr. Canning said that this triumph of bullionist opinions was 'the greatest wonder he had witnessed in the political world.' In introducing the measure, Mr. Peel declared himself to have been converted, not by theoretical argument, but by the evidence of the practical men examined by the Bank Committee. 'From the nature of that evidence, and of the other information he had received, he felt himself called upon to state, candidly and honestly, that he was a convert to the doctrines regarding our currency which he had once opposed' (House of Commons, May 24, 1819, on moving resolutions for the resumption of cash payments). He made a substantially similar declaration in 1846, with respect to his change of opinion on the Corn Laws.

[2] Mr. Peel said in the House of Commons, May 1827, in his explanations of his grounds for refusing to join Mr. Canning's Ministry: 'Tory as I am, it is gratifying to me to reflect, that no law stands on the Statute Book in connection with my name, which has not for its object the mitigation of the severity of the Criminal Law, and the prevention of any abuse in the administration of justice.'

make the maintenance of British interests the main consideration of his policy. The remonstrances of England were disregarded at the congresses of Laybach and Verona; but by the open exercise of the influence of England, Mr. Canning succeeded in dissolving the alliance of the great despotic courts. Though he was not able to avert the French invasion of Spain, for the sake of suppressing the Spanish constitution, he succeeded in making it an exclusively French operation, and in preventing it from being a joint act of European police. The Portuguese expedition prevented the invasion of that kingdom. He resisted the attempts of France and Russia to assist Spain in recovering her American possession; and he recognised the independence of the Spanish colonies on the mainland of America, as well as of Brazil. The latter was the principal positive result of his administration of the Foreign Office; he carried it against the general opposition of Europe, without causing a war: and Mr. Stapleton informs us that he met with so much resistance either from the King, or in the Cabinet, that he was twice on the point of resigning the seals of his office before the final decision to recognise the independence of the new states was taken. The treaty of London, which secured the final liberation of Greece, and united this country to France and Russia for the emancipation of the Hellenic people, was also the work of his bold and far-sighted diplomacy; and no English statesman of modern times has left on the continent of Europe a name so identified with a great and generous policy. 1823.

The Tory Government, having successfully encountered the discontents and disturbances engendered by the distress in the first years of the Peace, and having outlived the terrible earthquake of the Queen's trial, had at this time arrived at a period of prosperity, and (with the exception of Ireland) of internal tranquillity. It rested on the united

1827. strength of its party, now consolidated by a nearly continuous tenure of office for forty-three years. It was moreover represented in the House of Commons by leaders of undoubted ability, whose opinions were as enlightened as their party connections permitted. In this state of things, Lord Liverpool was on February 17, 1827, soon after the opening of the session, seized with an attack of paralysis, from which he never recovered, and which terminated his political life.[1] Although Lord Liverpool was not an important man, he filled an important position, and his death was immediately attended by important consequences. Without being the capital of the column, he was the keystone of the arch. Lord Castlereagh, and after him Mr. Canning, may, each in his turn, have been the leading man in the Ministry; but Lord Liverpool's death showed that he was necessary for reconciling the personal rivalries and political differences of a Cabinet which was divided on the principal question of the day—Catholic Emancipation; and that he performed the most important function of a Prime Minister, that of keeping his cabinet together.[2]

In order to explain the state of parties at this crisis, it is necessary that we should trace the recent history of the Catholic Question, upon which the ministerial negotiations mainly turned.

The partial successes in favour of the Catholic claims which had been obtained under the pressure of the war in 1812 and 1813, had not been followed up in the two anxious and agitated years of 1814 and 1815; but in 1816 resolutions in favour of the Catholics were negatived in

[1] He died on Dec. 4, 1828, aged fifty-eight years.

[2] See the character of Lord Liverpool in Twiss's *Life of Lord Eldon*, vol. ii. p. 587. There are likewise estimates of him in the *Annual Register*, 1827, p. 90; and in Rush's *First Residence at the Court of London*, p. 46, the latter of whom remarks of Lord Liverpool's Cabinet, that, 'if he was not the ablest man of the body, he was essentially its head.'

both Houses. The return of peace had given fresh confidence to the anti-Catholic party, by diminishing the dangers of internal discord, and removing the fear of an invasion. 'As the fear of Buonaparte subsided' (says Mr. Stapleton), 'the dread of the Pope arose; and when Mr. Canning accepted office in 1816, the opinions of the great mass of the population of England had become, more than they had been, hostile to emancipation.[1] It was not, however, so much an increased fear of the Pope, as a diminished fear of the consequences of Irish misgovernment, which produced this change of opinion in Great Britain. Mr. Canning, conscious of the strength of the anti-Catholic feeling in England, declared that the Catholic Question must 'win, not force, its way.' Unluckily, however, it was destined not to win its way by reason, but to force its way by threats. The prospects of the measure somewhat improved in the following years, as in 1821 a Bill for the relief of the Catholics passed the Commons, and was sent up to the Lords. In 1825, after both Houses had agreed to a Bill for suppressing the Catholic Association, which had commenced its agitation in 1823,[2] three Bills were introduced into the House of Commons; the first, removing the disabilities of the Catholics; the second, including a provision for the Catholic clergy of

1827.

[1] *Life of Canning*, vol. i. p. 117. Among the many sagacious remarks in Peter Plymley's Letters (written in 1807), there is a distinct prediction of this result: 'We are told, in answer to all our arguments, that this is not a fit period; that a period of universal war is not the proper time for dangerous innovations in the Constitution. This is as much as to say, that the worst time for making friends is the period when you have made many enemies; that it is the greatest of all errors to stop when you are breathless, and to lie down when you are fatigued. *Of one thing I am quite certain: if the safety of Europe is once completely restored, the Catholics may for ever bid adieu to the slightest probability of effecting their object*' (Letter X).

[2] See Wyse's *Historical Sketch of the Catholic Association of Ireland*, vol. i. p. 198.

1827. Ireland; the third, disfranchising the Irish 40*s.* freeholders. The first of these Bills passed the House of Commons; but was rejected in the Lords. The other two measures had made progress in the Commons, but were abandoned in consequence of the loss of the main Bill in the Lords. Sanguine hopes had been entertained in this year, that the increased knowledge of the state of Ireland, and the progress of reason, would have led to the peaceable adjustment of the entire question. Mr. Peel, the anti-Catholic leader in the House of Commons, tendered to Lord Liverpool the resignation of his office in consequence of the decision to which that House had come, in order to facilitate the settlement of the question.[1] The assent of Parliament to the measure for suppressing the Catholic Association, and the refusal of the House of Lords to pass the Bill for the relief of Catholic disabilities, indicated a determined spirit of intolerance, injustice, and coercion, which could not fail to extinguish all hopes of conciliation, and to exasperate the Irish leaders. The animosity, the virulence, the menaces of the Catholic agitators were redoubled by this decision of the House of Lords.[2] But though statesmen might see that this ex-

[1] This fact was stated by Mr. Peel in the House of Commons, March 5, 1829, and was the subject of further explanation, on June 19, 1846, in consequence of the charges made by Lord G. Bentinck and Mr. Disraeli. Sir Robert Peel then showed that, in consequence of his political position after the third reading of the Catholic Relief Bill by the House of Commons, he signified to Lord Liverpool his wish to resign, soon after May 10, 1825; and that he was induced to abandon this resolution, in consequence of the rejection of the Bill by the House of Lords. Lord Grenville, in letters of April and May 1825, expresses a confident opinion that the settlement of the Catholic Question is at hand, and cannot be long delayed (*Mem. of Court of George IV.*, vol. ii. pp. 245–263).

[2] As to the decisions of the House of Commons in favour of the Catholic Question in the five parliaments, from 1807 to 1829, see *Mem. of Peel*, vol. i. p. 288.

acerbation of symptoms was only an additional reason for a gentle and soothing treatment, the spirit of the English people rose against threats; and when the Catholic Question was brought forward in March 1827, by Sir Francis Burdett, his motion, contrary to Mr. Canning's expectation, was lost; it was negatived by a majority of 276 to 272.[1] This retrograde movement was doubtless the effect of the reaction of English opinion against the increased violence of the Irish agitators. At this moment, therefore, the breach between Great Britain and Ireland was wider than it had been at any time since the Union; and the prospect of a tranquil settlement seemed more remote than ever. Ireland was becoming more stubborn, insulting, and disaffected; Great Britain, more intolerant, angry, and oppressive. 1827.

It was in this state of things that the negotiations for the reconstruction of the Cabinet were to be commenced. Partly from a temporary uncertainty as to the effects of Lord Liverpool's seizure, and partly from the indecision of the King and the political difficulties of the moment, there ensued a long ministerial interregnum, during which the business of Parliament was to a great extent suspended. The main obstacles to an arrangement arose from the threatening state of Ireland, the repugnance of the King[2] to the removal of the Catholic disabilities, and the division of

[1] See Stapleton's *Life of Canning*, vol. iii. p. 312. Sir R. Peel, in his speech in the House of Commons, of June 19, 1846, likewise mentions that the majority against the Catholic Question, in 1827, was a surprise to every one. In an article in the *Edinburgh Review* for June 1827, it is remarked that, as to the Catholic Question, 'the difficulty is neither with the King nor with the Cabinet; neither with the Commons nor with the Lords. It is with the people of England (vol. liv. p. 253). It must be remembered that this is the admission of an unwilling witness.

[2] Two instances, in which the King's hostility to the Catholic claims was expressed in 1826, are mentioned on the authority of Lord Lansdowne in the *Memoirs of Moore*, vol. i. p. 88.

1827. opinion on that question among the leading members of the Tory party. As soon as Lord Liverpool's state was ascertained, negotiations were commenced between the chief members of his Cabinet respecting the choice of a person to supply his place. Mr. Canning aspired to the post of Prime Minister; and his political standing, his unrivalled eloquence, his ability in counsel, and his political experience, pointed him out as the natural successor of Lord Liverpool. But his opinions on the Catholic Question were distasteful to the King, and to the bulk of the party by which the late Cabinet had been supported. It may be added that, except in Ireland, they were unpopular; they were not shared by any large class either in England or Scotland; and they were adverse to the religious sentiments of the people. The two most important persons in the anti-Catholic party were Mr. Peel and the Duke of Wellington: the former as being their ablest speaker and their leader in the House of Commons; the latter on account of his high rank, his splendid military reputation, his force of character, and his honesty of purpose. Since the death of Lord Londonderry, the Duke of Wellington had been the leader of the high Tory section of the Cabinet, which was hostile to Mr. Canning, and which represented the traditions of the foreign policy of his predecessor. The personal relations of Mr. Peel with Mr. Canning were more friendly; but the inconsistency of their positions as leaders of the pro-Catholic and anti-Catholic parties in the House of Commons, respectively, produced an active feeling of political rivalry and jealousy between them.[1]

[1] Mr. Fremantle, in a letter to the Duke of Buckingham, of Sept. 29, 1823, says: 'I conceive that nothing can be more unfriendly than the footing on which the Duke of Wellington and Canning stand; for, independent of the measure of Lord Maryborough, the whole foreign diplomacy and policy

In an interview with the King on the 27th of March, Mr. Canning, being asked for his advice, had counselled His Majesty to form a government composed exclusively of persons hostile to the Catholics, and signified his own willingness to resign in order to facilitate such an arrangement. This offer the King rejected, declaring his wish to retain Mr. Canning in the service of the Crown; but he proposed that a peer of anti-Catholic opinions should be made Prime Minister. Mr. Canning then declared that he could not consent to be excluded from that post on account of his opinions, and that he could only retain office on condition of having the substantive power of First Minister. He objected to what he styled 'the superinduction of an anti-Catholic First Minister over his head.' With this mutual explanation, they parted; and nothing was then decided.[1] It appears that some days afterwards a plan was discussed between Mr. Canning and the Duke of Wellington of raising Mr. Fred. Robinson to the Peerage, and of placing him at the head of the Treasury. Mr. Canning's object in making this suggestion 1827.

is carried on without the Duke's intervention, whereas in Lord Londonderry's time not a step, even of the smallest import, was taken without his participation and concurrence' (*Mem. of Court of George IV.*, vol. ii. p. 7). In another letter of June 19, 1824, he says: 'The language of the Tory party, both of the old and present Court, is universal and undisguised abuse of Canning' (*ibid.* p. 91). Mr. Plumer Ward, in a letter of Sept. 28, 1824, says, in speaking of the superiority of the Duke of Wellington's party in the Cabinet: 'Neither he (Mr. Canning) nor Lord Liverpool conceal their feeling as to the preponderance; a feeling that breaks out into downright complaints of personal impropriety and unfairness. From this, however, Canning always excepts Peel, who, he says, though he has opposed him, has always done it in a fair, open, manly manner. On the other hand, the Duke says, he (Canning) is not to be trusted, and the great *corpus delicti* is not only his disposition to run counter to Lord Londonderry's policy and system, but his seeming personal run at his individual acts, schemes, and friends' (*ibid.* p. 126).

[1] Stapleton's *Life of Canning*, vol. iii. pp. 315–317, 374.

1827. seems to have been to keep the office of Foreign Secretary, which he preferred to any other; his intention, however, as he subsequently explained it, was, that he, and not the First Lord of the Treasury, should be the 'First Minister.'[1] As Mr. Robinson's opinions respecting the Catholic Question agreed with Mr. Canning's, the end which the King and the Duke of Wellington had in view would not have been attained by this arrangement. Mr. Peel did not put himself forward as a candidate for the office of Prime Minister, and apparently did not wish to become Lord Liverpool's successor; he deferred to the prior claims which seniority at least gave to Mr. Canning,[2] but he informed Mr. Canning of his intention to resign, if a person favourable to the Catholics should be placed at the head of the Government.[3] One reason which he alleged for this decision was the necessity of an agreement between the opinions of the Home Secretary, who was responsible for the government of Ireland,[4] and the Prime Minister, on

[1] Stapleton's *Life of Canning*, vol. iii. pp. 365, 373, 375.

[2] Mr. Peel was Mr. Canning's junior by eighteen years.

[3] Stapleton's *Life of Canning*, vol. iii. p. 219.

[4] The reason was stated by Mr. Peel in the House of Commons, in his speech of May 1, 1827. It also appears in one of his letters to Lord Eldon, of April 9, 1827 (*Twiss*, vol. ii. pp. 589-592). In these letters he says: 'My earnest wish is to see the present Government retained in His Majesty's service, on the footing on which it stood at the time of Lord Liverpool's misfortune. I am content with my own position, and wish for no advancement or change.'—'My first wish is to see the present (perhaps I should say the late) Administration reconstituted precisely on the footing on which it stood when Lord Liverpool was its head. If this be impossible, can it be reconstituted by Canning, I alone retiring?'—'I certainly did say to His Majesty that I could not advise the attempt to form an exclusive Protestant Government, that I could not be a party even to the attempt, should it be contemplated; but His Majesty was, I am confident, of the same opinion. I said also that I was out of the question as the head of a Government, under that arrangement which I consider by far the best that could be made, namely, the reconstitution of the late Administration; because it was quite impossible for Canning to acquiesce in my appointment.'

the Catholic Question; but Mr. Canning obviated this difficulty by an offer of the Foreign Department.[1] On the 9th of April Mr. Peel, having had an interview with the King, came to Mr. Canning, and by His Majesty's command proposed the selection of the Duke of Wellington for the post of Prime Minister as a solution of all difficulties. To this proposal Mr. Canning refused to accede;[2] so that the negotiations of nearly two months had only brought matters between the two persons, who were the real party leaders, to this point: namely, that Mr. Peel would not serve under Mr. Canning as Prime Minister, and that Mr. Canning would not agree to the Prime Minister proposed by Mr. Peel.[3] 1827.

The time was now come when the knot which could not be untied must be cut; and the King solved the

The second letter seems to have been written in answer to inquiries of Lord Eldon, received after the first letter had been despatched.

[1] Stapleton, *ibid.* p. 347.

[2] Stapleton, *ibid.* p. 322; compare pp. 321, 376. The Duke of Wellington stated in the House of Lords, on May 2, 1827, that he was prepared, when Mr. Canning invited him to join his Ministry, to propose the name of another person as Prime Minister. It does not appear who the person intended by the Duke of Wellington can have been (see Stapleton, *ibid.* p. 365). [See, however, the next note.—Ed.]

[3] Sir Walter Scott, in a letter dated Abbotsford, May 10, 1827, says: 'I understand Peel had from the King *carte blanche* for an anti-Catholic Administration, and that he could not accept it because there was not strength enough to form such' (Lockhart's *Life of Scott*). Sir Walter Scott had good political information from his Tory connections in London; but there is no reason to suppose that the King gave Mr. Peel any such authority, or that His Majesty ever seriously entertained the idea of a Ministry formed on this principle. In *Raikes' Journal*, July 7, 1836, the following statement occurs: 'In the year 1827 Lord Grey had nearly joined the Tory ranks; he used to meet the Duke of Wellington frequently at Lord Lauderdale's, and, after the death of Lord Liverpool, was absolutely proposed to the King as Premier, the Duke remaining Secretary for Foreign Affairs; but George IV. would not forget his personal antipathy to him, and sent for Canning.' It is certain that there was no question of Lord Grey as Minister after Lord Liverpool's seizure, and that no overture of any kind was then made to him.

1827. problem by giving to Mr. Canning, on the 10th of April, a commission to propose a plan for the reconstruction of the Ministry. Upon receiving this commission, Mr. Canning lost no time in communicating to each of his late colleagues the commands which he had received from the King: at the same time he announced to them his wish of adhering to the principles on which Lord Liverpool's Government had so long acted together. In a short time Mr. Canning received from the Duke of Wellington, Lord Eldon, Lord Westmoreland, Lord Bathurst, Lord Melville, and Mr. Peel, refusals to join a Ministry of which he should be the head. The Duke of Wellington likewise resigned the office of Commander-in-chief, which he had held in connection with the Master-Generalship of the Ordnance. The only members of the late Cabinet who consented to form part of a Canning Administration were Lord Harrowby, Lord Bexley, Mr. Fred. Robinson, Mr. Huskisson, and Mr. C. Wynn. In consequence of the refusal of junction from nearly all the anti-Catholic members of the late Government, Mr. Canning opened a negotiation with Lord Lansdowne and the Whigs which, however, for the present led to no result. His Cabinet was then formed in the following manner: Mr. Canning himself (after the example of Pitt, Addington, and Perceval) held the offices of First Lord of the Treasury and Chancellor of the Exchequer in conjunction. Sir John Copley, created Lord Lyndhurst, became Lord Chancellor: Lord Harrowby, Lord Bexley, Mr. Huskisson and Mr. Wynn retained the offices which they had held under Lord Liverpool. The Duke of Portland became Privy Seal. Mr. Sturgess Bourne received the Seals of the Home, and Lord Dudley those of the Foreign Department. Mr. Fred. Robinson, created Lord Goderich, became Colonial Secretary; and Lord Palmerston, as Secretary-at-War, which office he had held in Lord Liverpool's Government, obtained, for the first time, a seat in the Cabinet. The office of Lord High Admiral was not put in commission, but was conferred on the Duke of Clarence, without a seat in the Cabinet. As a proof of the resistance which Mr. Canning experienced from the Tory party, we may mention that a paper signed by eight dukes was presented to the King by the Duke of Rutland, remonstrating against Mr. Canning's appointment as Prime Minister, and notifying their organised opposition to any government of which he should be the head. 1827.

Upon the resumption of business after the recess, the explanations of the outgoing and incoming Ministers were given; the most important part of which related to an unfriendly correspondence between the Duke of Wellington and Mr. Canning, originating, as we feel satisfied from an attentive consideration of the circumstances, in a sincere misunderstanding on both sides.[1] Before the end of the session, Lord Lansdowne became a member of the Cabinet: Lord Carlisle and Mr. Tierney likewise were appointed First Commissioner of Woods, and Master of the Mint, and entered the Cabinet. After the session, Lord Lansdowne, became Home Secretary; Lord Carlisle succeeded the Duke of Portland, as Privy Seal, the latter retaining a seat in the Cabinet; and Mr. Sturges Bourne succeeded to the office of Woods. In this manner, a junction was effected between Mr. Canning and a section of the Whig party: the Home Office, which was confided to Lord Lansdowne, had a peculiar importance at this moment, on account of its connection with the Government of

[1] The Duke of Wellington, in his Private Explanatory Letter to Mr. Canning (published by Mr. Stapleton, *Life of Canning*, vol. iii. p. 384), says: 'I am not in the habit of deciding upon such matters hastily or in anger; and the proof of this is, that I never had a quarrel with any man in my life.'

1827. Ireland. The principal events of the fragment of the session which succeeded the formation of Mr. Canning's Ministry were the personal alienation of Mr. Peel from the Government, who, as Mr. Canning declared, 'openly raised the standard of opposition;' and the insertion of a hostile amendment in the Corn-law Bill, upon the motion of the Duke of Wellington, which led to the abandonment of the Bill by the Government. Lord Grey, likewise, to whom the King had conceived a personal objection, and with whom there had been no communication on the negotiation which had taken place with the Whigs, made a speech containing a severe censure of Mr. Canning's foreign and domestic policy. Parliament was prorogued on the 2nd of July, at which time Mr. Canning, though his constitution was impaired, enjoyed his usual health; but on the 3rd of August he was seized with a severe inflammatory attack, and on the 8th he died. We shall have occasion, in following the course of events till the end of 1830, to estimate the effects produced by Mr. Canning's sudden and premature death, at the moment when his ministerial arrangements had been completed, and his Cabinet had assumed a definitive form. We will only remark, that as an orator, he has never, in our opinion, been surpassed, if he has ever been equalled, among the statesmen of this country. Burke's diction may have been more copious and vehement; but we know that his speeches were marred in the delivery.[1] Mr. Canning's voice was

[1] Mr. Rush, in his *First Residence at the Court of London*, thus reports a conversation with Lord Erskine, no mean judge of oratorical delivery, respecting Burke: 'Desiring to hear something of Burke's delivery from so high a source, I asked him about it. "It was execrable," said he. "I was in the House of Commons when he made his great speech on American Conciliation—the greatest he ever made. He drove everybody away. I wanted to go out with the rest, but was near him and afraid to get up; so I squeezed myself down, and crawled under the benches like a dog, until I

clear, flexible, and harmonious, though not powerful; his manner was animated and impressive in the highest degree.[1] 1827.

The contest for the post of Prime Minister which took place upon Lord Liverpool's resignation was substantially a struggle for personal ascendancy.[2] Mr. Canning advised the King to form an exclusively anti-Catholic administration, believing such a government to be impossible, and also convinced that if possible it would be ruinous to the state. When he received from the King the answer

got to the door without his seeing me, rejoicing in my escape. Next day I went to the Isle of Wight. When the speech followed me there, I read it over and over again; I could hardly think of anything else; I carried it about me, thumbed it, until it got like wadding for my gun' (p. 237).

[1] The following anecdotes occur in Mr. Rush's *Second Residence at the Court of London*, under the years 1819 and 1820: 'After dinner I had renewed conversations with Sir James Mackintosh. Alluding to the style of speaking in the House of Commons, he characterised it by saying that the true light in which to consider it was as animated conversation on public business; and he added that it was rare for any speech to succeed in that body which was raised on any other basis.' 'I converse with Mr. Canning on the speaking in the House of Commons. I mention to him Sir James Mackintosh's remark: he accedes to it; says it is true as a general rule, that their speaking must take conversation as its basis, rather than anything studied or stately. The House was a business-doing body, and the speaking must conform to its character; it was jealous of ornament in debate, which, if it came at all, must come as without consciousness. There must be method also: but this should be felt in the effect, rather than seen in the manner; no formal divisions, set exordiums, or perorations, as the old rhetoricians taught, would do. First and last, and everywhere, you must aim at reasoning; and if you could be eloquent, you might at any time, but not at an appointed time. To this effect he expressed himself, though I do injustice to his language' (pp. 44, 306). A well-written and discriminating character of Mr. Canning, including a full account of his oratory, is in Mackintosh's *Miscellaneous Works*, vol. ii. p. 455. An offer was made to Moore, by the authority of Lady Canning, to write the Life of Mr. Canning, but it was declined (*Mem. of Moore*, vol. vi. p. 106).

[2] Sir Walter Scott was told by Lord Melville, in July 1827, that Mr. Canning had said that 'the office of Premier was his by inheritance; he could not, from constitution, hold it above two years, and then it would descend to Peel' (Lockhart's *Life of Scott*).

1827. which he expected, and was told that there was no wish to dispense with his services, he made conditions which were inconsistent with any other person being appointed Prime Minister. Mr. Canning would not consent to an anti-Catholic Prime Minister because it was a proscription of his opinions in his person; Mr. Peel would not consent to a pro-Catholic Prime Minister, because it was inconsistent with the part which he had taken in the Catholic Question and with his position as Home Secretary. Neither of these two arguments could properly be reconciled with the doctrine of making the Catholic Question an open question, to which nevertheless each of the leaders adhered, though Mr. Canning could urge, with truth, that if the Cabinet were to be strictly neutral on the Catholic Question, it was a violation of the principle of neutrality to insist upon an anti-Catholic Prime Minister. It appears to us that if Mr. Peel believed in his own arguments on the Catholic Question; if he really thought that the removal of the Catholic disabilities would be productive of the evils which he described; and that the existing system of exclusion ought to be permanently maintained as an integral part of the British Constitution; then he ought to have urged upon the King the formation of an administration upon the principle of resistance to the Catholic claims, and to have himself offered to take a leading part in it. If, however, he had a lurking consciousness that his arguments were unsound, and his policy mischievous; and that a case of necessity for conceding the Catholic claims might speedily arise, then he ought, notwithstanding the eminence which he had achieved as anti-Catholic leader, to have openly renounced his advocacy of a cause which he felt to be untenable. If Mr. Peel and the anti-Catholic members of Lord Liverpool's Cabinet were sincerely persuaded of the goodness of their cause, they ought to have set Mr. Canning at defiance, and to have formed an anti-Catholic government; if they had not that sincere conviction, they ought not to have refused to join his Ministry.[1] In a conversation which Lord Eldon had with the King in March 1829, while the Catholic Relief Bill was before Parliament, His Majesty stated that when Mr. Canning was made Minister, he engaged that the Catholic Question should never be brought forward, and he blamed the Ministers who retired upon Mr. Canning's appointment for having thrown the power into his hands.[2] Sir Robert Peel, however, in the memoir left by him for posthumous publication, states that the King must clearly have been mistaken in supposing Mr. Canning to have given any such engagement:[3] and it may be added that if the King wished to exclude Mr. Canning from power, he ought to have attempted the formation of an anti-Catholic government. 1827.

Upon Mr. Canning's death, Lord Goderich, who had been the ministerial leader of the House of Lords in the

[1] Sir Walter Scott, in his letter of May 1827, already cited, thus comments on the members of the Liverpool Cabinet who refused to join Mr. Canning: 'They ought either to have made a stand without Canning, or a stand with him; for to abdicate as they have done was the way to subject the country to all the future experiments which this Catholic Emancipation may lead those that now carry it to attempt, and which may prove worse, far worse, than anything connected with the question itself. Thus says the old Scotch Tory. But I for one do not believe that it was the question of Emancipation, or any public question, which carried them out. I believe the predominant motive in the bosom of every one of them was personal hostility to Canning, and that with more prudence, less arbitrary manners, and more attention to the feelings of his colleagues, he would have stepped *nem. con.* into the situation of Prime Minister, to which his eloquence and talent naturally point him out.' See Sir Walter Scott's further remarks on Mr. Canning's alliance with the Whigs, and its probable effects in promoting an anti-Tory policy, in his letter to M. Morritt, June 10, 1827—(Lockhart's *Life of Scott*).

[2] Twiss, *Life of Eldon*, vol. iii. p. 82.

[3] Vol. i. p. 275.

1827. late administration, was promoted by the King to the post of Prime Minister. The following additional changes were now made; the Duke of Portland was appointed President of the Council instead of Lord Harrowby, who retired on account of ill health; Mr. Huskisson succeeded Lord Goderich as Colonial Secretary, and was intended to be leader of the House of Commons; Mr. C. Grant was his successor at the Board of Trade; Mr. Herries became Chancellor of the Exchequer; and Lord Anglesey entered the Cabinet as Master-General of the Ordnance.[1] During the recess, a difference of opinion arose between Mr. Huskisson and Mr. Herries respecting the selection of a chairman of the Finance Committee, which was to be moved for in the following session; neither would yield his opinion, and Lord Goderich, declining to become the arbiter of this dispute between his two colleagues, tendered his resignation, which was accepted.[2] The King, apparently reluctant to fall back at once upon the ultra-Tory leaders, attempted to induce Lord Harrowby to form an administration, who declined on account of the state of his health:[3] it seems likewise that His Majesty would have

[1] Lord Lansdowne's reasons for retaining office in the Government of Lord Goderich, after Mr. Canning's death, are stated in *Mem. of Moore*, vol. v. p. 198. He tendered his resignation to the King in September, but consented to remain, on condition that he might have the royal authority for stating that it was solely in submission to the express desire of His Majesty that he did so.

[2] Some member of this Government, who regretted its dissolution, remarked at the time that he had never before joined so heartily in the prayer against 'false doctrines, *heresies*, and schisms.' A letter from Lord Goderich to the Duke of Buckingham, of Jan. 18, 1828, informing the Duke of the dissolution of his own government, and of his feelings towards the new government, is printed in *Memoirs of the Court of George IV.* vol. ii. p. 358.

[3] Lord Harrowby was now sixty-six years old. The interview of Lord Harrowby with the King took place at Windsor Lodge, on Dec. 18, 1827. The King tried to tempt Lord Harrowby by an offer of the Garter: a

been willing to entrust the same commission to Mr. Huskisson, if he could have ventured to accept it,[1] however, Lord Goderich having tendered his final resignation on the 8th of January, the King, on the following day, sent for the Duke of Wellington, and authorised him to form an administration. The account of his interview with the King which the Duke wrote to Mr. Peel on the same day was as follows: 'He (the King) said that he thought the government must be composed of persons of both opinions with respect to the Roman Catholic Question; that he approved of all his late and former servants; and that he had no objection to anybody excepting to Lord Grey. He afterwards expressed a wish to retain the Duke of Devonshire[2] and Lord Carlisle in his service, and he spoke highly of Lord Lansdowne and Lord Dudley; but upon the whole he left me *carte blanche*, with the single exception above mentioned; and he repeatedly desired that I would form for him a strong government. . . . The King said it was understood the Roman Catholic Question was not to be made a cabinet question: that there was to be a Protestant Lord Chancellor, a Protestant Lord Lieutenant, and a Protestant Chancellor of Ireland.'[3] 1828.

circumstance alluded to in one of the squibs of the day, which, describing the endeavours vainly made to find a coachman for the state coach, mentioned '*an experienced rider*' as one of the persons applied to, but added that he declined to 'handle the ribbons.'

[1] *Biogr. Mem. of Mr. Huskisson*, p. 145.

[2] The Duke of Devonshire had held the office of Lord Chamberlain since May 1827.

[3] Letter to Mr. Peel, of Jan. 9, 1828; *Mem. of Peel*, vol. i. p. 11. The objection made by George IV. to Lord Grey, like that made by his father to Mr. Fox, is likewise mentioned in *Biogr. Mem. of Mr. Huskisson*, p. 156. Mr. Raikes, in his *Journal* for Sept. 24, 1843, reports the following passage from the conversation of the Duke of Wellington at Walmer Castle: 'When he sent for me to form a new Administration, in 1828, he was then seriously ill, though he would never allow it. I found him in bed, dressed in a dirty silk jacket and a turban nightcap, one as greasy as the other; for,

1828. The effect of Mr. Canning's premature death began now to show itself in a reactionary tendency, at a moment when a progressive movement in the Liberal direction was peculiarly desirable. The Coalition Administration, which he had formed, and which had not time to acquire cohesion and firmness during his life, naturally fell to pieces soon after his death; and the King, resolved before all things to avoid a Whig Government, had recourse to the Duke of Wellington, whose main reliance must necessarily be upon Mr. Peel. His Majesty, however, announced from the beginning that there was to be no attempt at unanimity in opposition to the Catholic Question. The new Cabinet was thus formed. The Duke of Wellington became First Lord of the Treasury. The Whig members of the two late administrations, viz. Lord Lansdowne, Lord Carlisle, and Mr. Tierney, withdrew. They were accompanied by Mr. Wynn. Mr. Peel returned to the Home Office, and his friend Mr. Goulburn was made Chancellor of the Exchequer, Mr. Herries being transferred to the Mastership of the Mint. Lord Bathurst replaced the Duke of Portland as President of the Council. Lord Ellenborough was appointed Privy Seal, Lord Melville, President of the Board of Control, and Lord Aberdeen, Chancellor of the Duchy of Lancaster; the latter in the room of Lord Bexley. The Lord Chancellor and the four Canningites remained.

notwithstanding his coquetry about dress in public, he was extremely dirty and slovenly in private. The first words he said to me were, "Arthur, the Cabinet is defunct;" and then he began to describe the manner in which the late Ministers had taken leave of him on giving in their resignations. This was accompanied by the most ludicrous mimicry of the voice and manner of each individual, so strikingly like, that it was quite impossible to refrain from fits of laughter.' There must be some confusion in Mr. Raikes' notes or in the Duke's recollection; for the outgoing Ministers could not have had their audiences of leave before the Duke of Wellington's first interview with the King.

Parliament was opened on the 29th of January, and explanations were afforded respecting the dissolution of the Ministry of Lord Goderich, and the formation of that of the Duke of Wellington. The only important measure of the session was the repeal of the Test and Corporation Acts, which cast a stigma upon Dissenters, though without practically excluding them from offices, as their omission to take the sacramental test was healed by an annual Indemnity Act. The question was brought forward by Lord John Russell; his motion was opposed by the Government, but was carried by a majority of 44. The Bill was read a second time without a division; a declaration was inserted by Mr. Peel in the Bill in Committee—and in this shape it passed the House of Commons without any further opposition. The House of Lords agreed to it with some unimportant verbal amendments, and the measure became law. Later in the session (May 8th), Sir Francis Burdett moved a resolution for considering the laws relative to the Roman Catholics; which motion was carried by a majority of six, the numbers being 272 to 266. This resolution was communicated to the House of Lords, and the question was fully debated in that assembly. The Duke of Wellington, as Prime Minister, expressed himself as decidedly hostile to the removal of the Catholic disabilities, though his tone was conciliatory; and the motion was negatived by 181 to 137. The votes of this session, therefore, showed that the House of Commons was favourable to the principle of religious liberty; and that, though nearly divided on the Catholic Question, there was a bare majority in its favour; whereas a large majority of the House of Lords still held firmly to the anti-Catholic code. It is clear that at this moment the House of Lords, and not the House of Commons, was the main obstacle to the settlement of the Catholic 1828.

1828. Question.[1] The Corn-law Bill, establishing a sliding scale of high protective duties, was revived by the Government, and passed in a form substantially identical with the dropped Bill of the previous session, though less favourable to the consumer.

While a Bill for extending the franchise of East Retford to the hundreds, proposed in this session by Mr. Peel, was in Committee, Mr. Huskisson voted for a clause transferring the franchise to Birmingham. This vote was given on May the 19th. On his return home, at a late hour, after the debate, Mr. Huskisson, before going to bed, wrote a letter to the Duke of Wellington, stating what he had done, and tendering his resignation. The Duke, upon receiving this letter at ten o'clock on the following morning, wrote back an answer, expressing his surprise and concern at the contents of it, and stating that he had laid it before the King. Mr. Huskisson, not prepared for so sudden and absolute an acceptance of his offer, sent Lord Dudley, and afterwards Lord Palmerston, to explain to the Duke that he had mistaken the meaning of the letter. The Duke, however, replied, that 'It is no mistake, it can be no mistake, and shall be no mistake;' and refused to make any overture towards an amicable settlement of the question. A correspondence ensued between Mr. Huskisson and the Duke, but it led to no result. Mr. Huskisson would not request permission to withdraw the letter; the Duke would not ask him to withdraw it; and the resignation consequently remained unrevoked.[2] Judged upon moral grounds, the conduct of the Duke of Wellington on this occasion is unobjectionable; Mr. Huskisson's letter certainly conveyed the meaning which

[1] On the views of the two Houses at this time respecting the Catholic question, see the remarks of Sir Robert Peel (*Mem. of Peel*, vol. i. p. 183).

[2] *Ann. Reg.*, 1828, pp. 14–21; *Biogr. Mem. of Huskisson*, pp. 170–173.

he attributed to it, and he was justified in acting upon a letter which Mr. Huskisson expressed no wish to recall. But as a politician, he showed (as we think) a remarkable narrowness of mind and want of foresight, in permitting so trifling a ground of difference, and one which could have been removed without any real loss of dignity or honour, to be the means of expelling the more liberal section of his Cabinet, in the existing state of affairs. With Mr. Huskisson, the other Canningites of the Cabinet, namely, Lord Dudley, Lord Palmerston, and Mr. C. Grant, likewise resigned. Mr. W. Lamb (afterwards Lord Melbourne) also resigned his office of Irish Secretary on the same ground. In consequence of these resignations, Lord Aberdeen was advanced to the Foreign Department; Sir George Murray became Colonial Secretary; and Mr. Vesey Fitzgerald, President of the Board of Trade. The offices of Secretary-at-War and Chancellor of the Duchy of Lancaster were filled by Sir Henry Hardinge and Mr. Arbuthnot, but without seats in the Cabinet. 1828.

The resignation of Mr. Huskisson and the Canningite section of the Cabinet, was important, not only in its necessary and contemplated result, of giving to the Ministry a deeper and more unmixed Tory hue, but also in an accidental and unforeseen effect, which illustrated the saying of Aristotle, that revolutions, though they are made for great objects, often spring out of trifling circumstances. Mr. Vesey Fitzgerald, by accepting the office of President of the Board of Trade, upon the resignation of Mr. C. Grant, vacated his seat in the House of Commons, as member for the county of Clare. When he presented himself for re-election, he was opposed by Mr. O'Connell, who, though as a Roman Catholic unable to take the oaths at the table of the House of Commons, was not

1828. disqualified by law for election as a member. The poll took place at the beginning of July; the excitement and violence of language were great; the small freeholders, almost universally Catholics, were led to the hustings by their priests, in order to vote for Mr. O'Connell; and Mr. Fitzgerald, though backed by all the gentry of the country, was defeated by a large majority. Mr. Fitzgerald had always been a friend to Emancipation; but this availed him nothing. 'The time is come,' said Mr. O'Connell to the Clare electors, 'when the system which has been pursued towards this country must be put a stop to. It will not do for the future to say, "Sweet friend, I wish you well;" but it must be shown by acts that they do wish us well. It is time that this system should be put an end to; and I am come here to put an end to it.'[1] After the long parliamentary agitation of the Catholic Question, and after the obstinate resistance of the dominant party in England to the claims of the Catholics, Mr. O'Connell had now arrived at the conviction that nothing was to be hoped from the justice of England, and that the relief which he sought could only be extorted from her fears. He therefore resorted to a method of remonstrance, which, without a resort to violence, or a breach of the law, was practically a defiance to England. He approached the portals of the Constitution with a demand, not a petition, for admittance. We think that he was right: the patience of the Irish Catholics had been long tried, and had borne much; but the intolerant

[1] A full account of the Clare election—the lever by which O'Connell undermined the resistance of England to the Catholic question—is given in the *Annual Register* for 1828, pp. 123–129; see also Mr. Vesey Fitzgerald's Letters, written at the time to Mr. Peel (*Mem. of Peel*, vol. i. pp. 109–115); and Wyse's *Historical Sketch of the Catholic Association*, vol. i. pp. 371–399. The objects of the Catholic leaders in the Clare election are well summed up by Mr. Wyse (p. 392).

spirit of Great Britain seemed equally proof against time and reason. 1828.

Quam neque longa dies, pietas nec mitigat ulla.

Something more effective than annual motions in the two Houses of Parliament was required, in order to remove the civil disabilities of six millions of British subjects. As the Catholics, though they could not sit and vote in Parliament, could exercise the elective franchise, the experiment which Mr. O'Connell had tried in Clare, could manifestly be repeated with success in a large number of the other counties in Ireland.

Parliament was prorogued on the 28th of July. The lesson taught by the Clare election was so decisive, that before the Duke of Wellington and Mr. Peel parted at the end of the session, they agreed that the Duke should send Mr. Peel a full statement of his views on the state of Ireland and the Catholic Question. On the 9th of August, the Duke of Wellington communicated to Mr. Peel (who was at Brighton), a memorandum on the state of Ireland, which he had sent to the King, with an accompanying letter; the King's answer; a memorandum on the Catholic Question, containing a plan for its settlement, which he had since drawn, and a letter to the Lord Chancellor. Mr. Peel returned these papers on the 11th, with a letter and memorandum, containing a full and unreserved exposition of his views. The conclusion at which he arrives, after a statement of his reasons, is that there would be less evil in making a decided effort to settle the Catholic Question, than in leaving it an open question; but that its satisfactory adjustment would not be promoted by committing the charge of it in the House of Commons to his hands. He promises to resign at whatever time may be found most convenient, and to co-operate cordially

1828. with the Duke's Government in supporting the measure to be introduced into Parliament. In his memorandum he discusses the nature of the legislative measure to be proposed. The Duke communicated Mr. Peel's papers to Lord Lyndhurst, but not to the King; and the matter rested here for the present.[1]

The problem which the Cabinet were now called upon to solve, is correctly stated by Mr. Peel in the papers which he drew up at this time. It was properly a national and not a religious question; not merely the removal of disabilities from a body of religionists, but the pacification of Ireland was at issue. The Catholic Association had brought matters to a pass which rendered it necessary for England to choose between the concession of the Catholic claims and the reconquest of Ireland. A Cabinet neutral upon the Catholic Question was no longer a possibility. 'Such is the extraordinary power of the Association' (said Lord Anglesey, the Lord-Lieutenant, in a letter of July 2nd, 1828), 'or rather of the agitators, of whom there are many of high ability, of ardent mind, of great daring—that I am quite certain they could lead on the people to open rebellion at a moment's notice; and their organisation is such that in the hands of desperate and intelligent leaders, they would be extremely formidable.'[2] 'I have little doubt' (said Lord Francis Leveson, the Chief Secretary, in a letter to Mr. Peel, of December 2nd, 1828), 'that the peasantry of the south at present look forward to the period of O'Connell's expulsion from the House of Commons as the time of rising, but any occurrence in the interval which should appear to be ad-

[1] *Mem. of Peel*, vol. i. pp. 177–202. His views on the impossibility of the Catholic question remaining an open question are repeated in his memorandum of Jan. 12, 1829 (*ibid.* p. 291).

[2] *Mem. of Peel*, vol. i. p. 147.

verse to the interests of the Roman Catholic body might precipitate this result.'[1] 1828.

The menaces were not, however, confined to the Irish Catholics. The Irish Protestants, a high-spirited body, accustomed to command, and ignorant of fear, had been roused by the violence of their opponents; they had converted their Orange Lodges into Brunswick Clubs, and were ready, at a moment's notice, to take the field against their Catholic countrymen. 'The Orangemen' (Lord Anglesey writes to Mr. Peel, in September), 'or, I suppose I am now to call them the Brunswickers, are rivalling the Association both in violence and rent. Two Associations and two Rents are rather formidable.'[2] 'It is clear' (said Mr. Shiel in a speech delivered at this time to the Catholic Association) 'that the division between Catholic and Protestant is widening. They were before parted, but they are now rent asunder; and while the Catholic Association rises up from the indignant passions of one great body of the community, the Brunswick Club is springing out of the irritated pride and the sectarian rancour of the Protestants of Ireland. The Catholic Association owes its political parentage to heavy wrong, operating on deeply sensitive and strongly susceptible feelings. Oppression has engendered it. The Protestant Association has its birth in the hereditary love of power, and inveterate habits of domination; and thus two great rivals are brought into political existence, and enter the lists against each other. As yet they have not engaged in the great struggle; they have not closed in the combat; but as they advance upon each other, and collect their might, it is easy to discover the horrible passions by which they are influenced, and the full determination with which they

[1] *Mem. of Peel*, vol. i. p. 253. [2] *Ibid.* p. 208.

1828. rush to the encounter.'[1] The Protestant movement was not likely to be long confined to Ireland. The Protestants of England soon began to express their sympathies with their Irish brethren, and a great county meeting for Kent was held on Penenden Heath, in October, for the purpose of supporting the Irish Brunswickers. In this state of things, Lord Anglesey (who had hitherto been an opponent of the Catholic claims), pressed upon the Cabinet the necessity of immediate legislation.[2] He predicted a quiet winter, and told Mr. Peel that the English Government would have time to legislate before the Irish Government began to fight; but he declared that he could not answer for the tranquillity of Ireland beyond the meeting of Parliament; and that things could not remain as they were.[3]

The Duke of Wellington and his colleagues—assuming that they continued in office, and faced the difficulty of the moment, had three alternatives presented to their choice: namely, the Reconquest of Ireland, Repeal of the Union, and Catholic Emancipation.

It appears from Sir R. Peel's memorandum of January 12th, 1829, that out of the 93 members for Ireland, 61, in the session of 1828, voted in favour of the Catholic Question, and that out of 61 county members, 45 voted

[1] *Annual Register*, 1828, p. 141.

[2] *Mem. of Peel*, vol. i. p. 165.

[3] In a letter of Sept. 9, 1828, to the Duke of Buckingham, Mr. Grenville expresses himself thus: 'The measure of Catholic Emancipation is fast approaching, and that irresistibly. I know from the most unquestionable authority, that very many of the Orange Protestants in Ireland are now so entirely alarmed at their own position, that they express, in the most unqualified terms, their earnest desire for any settlement of the question at issue on any terms; and Dawson's recantation, which the papers will have shown you, has been the signal for a more undisguised display of the same opinions. It must take place, as I believe, before many months shall pass' (*Mem. of Court of George IV.* vol. ii. p. 380).

on the same side; and he shows that an attempt to govern Ireland by an English majority, while the Irish Catholics were so strongly represented in Parliament, would render the transaction of business in the House of Commons impossible.[1] In order to govern Ireland in defiance of the opinions of the Irish Catholics, a re-conquest of the country and its permanent treatment after the fashion of Poland and Hungary, would have been necessary. We are not prepared to say that the majority of England, if their pride, their passions, and their religious feelings had been gradually and skillfully inflamed, might not have sanctioned this course, so far at least as the preliminary steps were concerned. But neither the Duke of Wellington nor Mr. Peel were politicians of the stamp of Strafford or the Duke of Alva. They were both essentially humane men. The Duke of Wellington, in the most impressive passage which he ever delivered to a deliberative assembly, assured the House of Lords that he knew too well what were the evils of civil war ever to inflict them voluntarily upon any country. Mr. Peel, though he had played too long with the Catholic Question, and used it as the instrument and ladder of his ambition, had the views of a statesman, and saw too clearly the inevitable results of a further denial of equal laws to Ireland, to be able to advise the reduction and the subsequent government of that country by a Protestant army, composed of Englishmen, Scotchmen, and Irish Orangemen. No great amount either of perspicacity or of public virtue was in truth requisite in order to 1828.

[1] *Mem. of Peel*, vol. i. pp. 289–291. The more intelligent of the Irish Protestants seem to have been aware at this time that the state of affairs was perilous, and that some concession was necessary. Mr. Leslie Foster, a steady opponent of the Catholic claims, in a letter to Mr. Vesey Fitzgerald, of Nov. 14, 1828, says: 'I have not a doubt that a majority even of the Brunswickers are friendly to a settlement upon proper terms' (*ibid.* p. 266).

1829. foresee and to avoid this extremity. A repeal of the Union, and a permanent separation of Ireland from Great Britain, was a course which no English Minister could entertain; consequently there remained only the alternative of Catholic Emancipation, and that without loss of time.[1]

The subject had not been brought before the Cabinet at the end of 1828; and early in January 1829, the Duke of Wellington communicated with the Archbishop of Canterbury and two of the Bishops, with a view of obtaining their consent to an adjustment of the Catholic Question; but he received from them a decided refusal.[2] There was a fear at this time that the King might make a public declaration of his intention to maintain the disabilities on religious grounds, and thus assume a position similar to that formerly occupied by his father. In order to guard against this danger, Mr. Peel, on the 12th of January, addressed a letter to the Duke of Wellington, offering, if he desired it, to remain in office, in order to assist in carrying the contemplated measure; and at the same time sent him a memorandum, setting forth the reasons why the Cabinet should be authorised by the King to take the whole state of Ireland into

[1] The following anecdote is related in *Raikes' Journal*, Dec. 25, 1832: 'When the Duke had made up his mind that he could no longer refuse Catholic Emancipation, without endangering the loss of Ireland, he told the late King, who was decidedly averse to the measure, that only one of three alternatives remained to him—either to reconquer Ireland, to make the concession, or to resign. Constituted as the army then was, the first was impossible; the choice must then fall on one of the other two. The King demanded time to consider. In the meantime the Duke applied to Peel for his concurrence in carrying the measure.' The anecdote rests on the authority of Sir Alexander Grant, who had heard it from Sir R. Peel. The allusion to the constitution of the army refers to the number of Irish Catholics which it contained.

[2] *Mem. of Peel*, vol. i. p. 276.

consideration, with a view to the settlement of the Catholic Question. The memorandum was submitted by the Duke of Wellington to the King, who gave the authority which it advised; and the Duke accepted Mr. Peel's offer of retaining his office, which indeed was a necessary condition for the success of the measure in the hands of the existing government.[1] The Cabinet agreed unanimously and without delay to the principle of the settlement proposed by their two chiefs;[2] and, on the 17th of January, Mr. Peel communicated to his colleagues a memorandum containing his plan of a measure, which was little more than a simple repeal of the existing disabilities.[3] A passage was inserted in the speech from the throne, recommending a consideration of the whole condition of Ireland, and a review of the laws imposing civil disabilities on Roman Catholics, to which the King gave a reluctant consent; on the 5th of February Parliament was opened by commission, and the King's speech was read by the Chancellor. 1829.

The uncertainty in which the Cabinet had remained up

[1] *Mem. of Peel*, vol. i. pp. 278–299. [2] *Ibid.* pp. 300, 308.

[3] Sir R. Peel, in a speech in the House of Commons on the Reform Bill, Dec. 17, 1831, gave a narrative of the circumstances which led to his undertaking to carry the Catholic Relief Bill in Parliament; and described an imaginary conversation between himself and the King, in which the King pointed out to him the inconsistency of calling on him to sacrifice scruples which he would not sacrifice himself. It is clear from Sir R. Peel's published *Memoir* that no such conversation could have actually taken place; and that he only meant to put in a dramatic form the respective positions of the two parties. All his communications with the King at this time were made through the Duke of Wellington; his only interview with His Majesty between the two sessions of Parliament was that together with the Duke and Lord Lyndhurst, the character of which was of a wholly different nature. In fact, the King objected to the concession; he had no wish to assist the Duke of Wellington, and would have been glad if Mr. Peel had resigned. Sir Alexander Grant, who related the anecdote, in an incorrect form, to Mr. Raikes, understood that this retort had been actually made by the King (*Raikes' Journal*, Dec. 25, 1832).

1829. to the meeting of Parliament, in consequence of the recency of their own conversion, and of the resistance made by the King, rendered it necessary for them to observe a strict secresy as to their intentions; they even went further and created by their acts a belief that they adhered to their declared opinions on the subject. The Lancashire progress of Mr. Peel in the autumn, the Duke of Wellington's letter to Dr. Curtis in December,[1] and the subsequent recall of Lord Anglesey (who had been appointed Lord Lieutenant of Ireland, at the beginning of the year, upon the resignation of Lord Wellesley,[2] tended to produce an impression that the leaders of the Cabinet were still staunch to the Protestant cause. Their declarations in the session of 1828 likewise negatived the idea that their convictions on this subject had undergone any change. This secrecy lulled the Anti-Catholic party into a false security; it masked the battery until the guns were in position, and ready to play upon them. It therefore promoted the success of the measure; but their conviction that they had been defeated by a stratagem, created a strong vindictive feeling, which was destined to produce important political results.

The proceedings of Parliament were commenced by a motion of Mr. Peel for a Bill to suppress the Catholic Association; which was allowed to pass unopposed, as being a prelude to the repeal of the Catholic disabilities. This association had in fact gained its object; the Government had yielded to its menaces, and therefore its advocates might reasonably consent to its suppression. We may

[1] Concerning this correspondence, see *Annual Register*, 1828, p. 148.

[2] The grounds of this step were explained in the House of Lords, May 4, 1829. The office of Lord Lieutenant was offered to Lord Bathurst and refused (*Mem. of Peel*, vol. i. p. 273). The Duke of Northumberland was appointed Lord Anglesey's successor.

here remark that the three great questions of the last 1829.
thirty years—the Catholic Question, Parliamentary Reform, and the Repeal of the Corn Laws,—have been all carried by political associations, whose object was rather to intimidate that to convince the Legislature. The existence of the Catholic Association, the Political Unions, and the Anti-Corn-Law League may prove the freedom of our constitutional system, and the safety of its working even when its machinery is deranged by external influences; but it speaks little for the wisdom of the leading statesmen who had made so long and so stubborn a fight in defence of the established institutions; and rendered each of these three great settlements a capitulation to a victorious enemy rather than a grant of an acknowledged right. In each case the Legislature had the appearance of passing a wholesome measure upon compulsion, not because it was wholesome, but because it could no longer be withheld. The existence of the Catholic Association produced moreover the ulterior mischief, that it engendered a spirit, and gave rise to hopes, which called forth the Repeal Association; and thus Ireland was for several years kept in a state which threatened its forcible disruption from Great Britain.[1]

The Bill for the suppression of the Catholic Association passed the House of Commons on the 17th of February. On the 29th Mr. Peel accepted the Chiltern Hundreds, and vacated his seat for the University of Oxford. His re-election was successfully opposed by Sir Robert Inglis,[2] and on the 3rd of March he took his seat as member for

[1] Mr. O'Connell declared for Repeal of the Union at the first Clare election (*Annual Register*, 1828, p. 127), and again in the following year (*ibid.* 1829, p. 127). He formed an Anti-Union Association in 1830 (*ibid.* 1830, p. 148).

[2] Sir Robert Inglis was returned by 755 to 609 votes.

1829. Westbury. On that day he gave notice that on the 5th he would call the attention of the House to that part of the speech from the throne which related to the state of Ireland and Catholic disabilities; but in the meantime an event happened which nearly frustrated this intention. On the evening of the 3rd, the Duke of Wellington, the Lord Chancellor, and Mr. Peel were summoned to attend the King at Windsor on the morrow. When the three Ministers were admitted to an interview, the King appeared to be in a state of uneasiness; he stated the pain with which he had assented to their advice on the Catholic Question, and announced his wish to receive a more complete explanation of the manner in which they proposed to carry their object into effect. This explanation was given by Mr. Peel; but it failed to satisfy the King, who, in a rapid and earnest tone of voice, objected to the proposed omission from the Oath of Supremacy, of the words relating to the spiritual and ecclesiastical jurisdiction of the Pope. To this objection, notwithstanding the further explanations of his Ministers, the King adhered;[1] expressed his regret that he had misunderstood their intentions, and retracted the consent which he had given to the measure. He then asked Mr. Peel what course he intended to take on the following day, for which his notice stood. Mr. Peel's immediate answer was, that after the announcement in the King's speech, his vacating of his seat for Oxford, and the passing of the Bill for the suppression of the Catholic Association, the only course open to him was to resign his office, and to withdraw his notice. The Duke of Wellington and Lord Lyndhurst concurred in this course, and signified their intention to resign their offices

[1] It may be remarked, that the attaching of importance to declaratory oaths, as a political security, is an indication of minds of a certain stamp, and of a certain amount of intelligence, which is nearly infallible.

with Mr. Peel. The King said that he could not be surprised at their decision, and parted with them in a kind and almost affectionate manner, after an interview which had lasted five hours. On their return to London, the three Ministers joined their colleagues, who were assembled at a Cabinet dinner, and informed them, much to their surprise, that they were no longer in office. The King, however, soon discovered, upon reflection or consultation that he had gone too far to be able to recede; accordingly at a late hour in the evening, he addressed a letter to the Duke of Wellington, authorising his three Ministers to withdraw their resignations, and to proceed with the announced measure. Mr. Peel suggested a further reference to the King, with a view of obtaining a distinct written authority from him, that the measures were proposed with his entire consent and sanction; which was given without further hesitation.[1] The conduct of George IV., on this occasion exhibits a remarkable contrast to his 1829.

[1] The account of this singular transaction, given in *Mem. of Peel* (vol. i. pp. 343–350), has been followed. An inaccurate representation of what passed on this occasion was made by the King to Lord Eldon a few weeks afterwards, when the bill was before the House of Lords (see Twiss, *Life of Eldon*, vol. iii. pp. 82–87). Lord Eldon's description of his interview on March 28, 1829, in which the King repeatedly expressed his strong repugnance to the measure, ends thus: 'Little more passed except occasional bursts of expression—"What can I do? What can I now fall back upon? What can I fall back upon? I am miserable, wretched; my situation is dreadful; nobody about me to advise with. If I do give my consent, I'll go to the baths abroad, and from thence to Hanover; I'll return no more to England; I'll make no Roman Catholic peers. I will not do what this Bill will enable me to do. I'll return no more! Let them get a Catholic king in Clarence." I think he also mentioned Sussex. "The people will see that I did not wish this." There were the strongest appearances, certainly, of misery. He more than once stopped my leaving him. When the time came that I was to go, he threw his arms round my neck and expressed great misery' (*ibid.* p. 86). The King was mistaken in thinking that, before the Catholic Relief Bill passed, he could not create Catholic peers. He could create them; but when they were created they could not sit and vote in the House of Lords.

1829. father's character. George III. was obstinate in resisting a measure which he disliked, and artful in turning out Ministers whom he wished to remove, but he took care to object at a moment when the country would support him; he knew when he was beaten, and never exhibited himself in the undignified attitude of attempting resistance when it was too late.

On the 5th of March Mr. Peel moved the first step of a Bill for the relief of the Roman Catholics; his motion was carried by 348 to 160, the Bill was read a second time by a majority of 353 to 183, and a third time by a majority of 320 to 142. In the House of Lords, there were 217 to 112 votes for the second reading, and 214 to 109 for the third reading. On the 13th of April the Bill received the Royal Assent. Subsequently the Government proposed and carried a Bill for raising the freehold franchise in the Irish counties from 40*s.* to 10*l.* a year. The Catholic Relief Bill, therefore, after so many legislative miscarriages passed both Houses by majorities of about two to one. This result of so important a parliamentary conflict, amidst so many shoals and breakers, was mainly owing to the patriotic conduct of the Opposition. To their support Sir Robert Peel bears witness in words not less honourable to himself than to the independent members of both Houses. 'I cannot advert to that conflict' (says Sir Robert Peel in his Memoir), 'even after the interval of twenty years, without placing on record my grateful acknowledgement of the cordial support which we received in both Houses of Parliament, not only from all those with whom our official connection had been then recently interrupted, but from those also who had never had any political connection with us, and might be considered, so far as the interests and ties of party were concerned, our decided opponents. It was not merely that they supported our measures, but they cautiously abstained from everything which might have thrown obstructions in our way, and in many instances forbore from pressing objections strongly felt to portions of the plan, in order that their general support of that plan as a whole might be cordial and effective.'[1] 1829.

From the singular conduct of the King in attempting to recede from his promise after the measure had been announced to Parliament, it may be inferred that he gave the royal assent with reluctance, and that he viewed with dislike the Ministers who had compelled him to make the concession. Mr. Grenville thus describes the King's feelings in a letter of April 14, 1829 :—

'The royal assent was yesterday given by commission, I believe, with a very reluctant mind; and many rumours are abroad of the King being persuaded by the Duke of Cumberland to look about for the means of forming a new Administration; but this practically will be found so full of difficulties that I hesitate to give faith to it, and attribute the report only to the harsh language in which the King is said to indulge himself, whenever he speaks of the Duke of Wellington. The King, however, is fonder of abusing his Ministers than of changing them; for a few hard words cost him nothing; but a great political change could not be made, if at all, without much more trouble, fatigue, and worry to the King than he will like to expose himself to.' (Vol. ii. p. 395.)

The following characteristic letter of the Duke of Wellington, in explanation of the motives of his duel with

[1] *Mem. of Peel*, vol. i. p. 356. See also the remarks on the conduct both of the Government and the Opposition on this occasion, in the article in the *Edinburgh Review* for March 1829, entitled, 'The last of the Catholic Question' (vol. xlviii. p. 268). The *Memoirs of the Court of George IV.* vol. ii. p. 391–394, contain two interesting letters of Lord Grenville, in which he expresses his deepfelt satisfaction at the success of a measure for which he had made such great exertions and such great political sacrifices. He speaks of the strange revolution of conduct, though not of opinion, on the part of the Government.

1829. Lord Winchilsea, and of the success with which that duel had been attended, is printed in the recent Memoirs of the Court of George IV. It is dated 21st of April, 1829, and is addressed to the Duke of Buckingham, who was then in Italy. The duel had taken place on the 21st of March.

I am very much obliged to you for your letter of the 6th, which I received this morning.

The truth is that the duel with Lord Winchilsea was as much part of the Roman Catholic Question, and it was as necessary to undertake it, and carry it out to the extremity to which I did carry it, as it was to do everything else which I did do to attain the object which I had in view.

I was living here for some time in an atmosphere of calumny. I could do nothing that was not misrepresented, as having some bad purpose in view. If my physician called upon me, it was for treasonable purposes. If I said a word, whether in Parliament or elsewhere, it was misrepresented for the purpose of fixing upon me some gross delusion or falsehood. Even my conversations with the King were repeated, misrepresented, and commented upon; and all for the purpose of shaking the credit which the Parliament was inclined to give to what I said.

The courts of justice were shut, and not to open till May. I knew that the Bill must pass or be lost before the 15th of April.

In this state of things Lord Winchilsea published his furious letter. I immediately perceived the advantage it gave me; and I determined to act upon it in such a tone as would certainly put me in the right. Not only was I successful in the execution of my project, but the project itself produced the effect which I looked for and intended that it should produce. The atmosphere of calumny in which I had been for some time living, cleared away. The system of calumny was discontinued. Men were ashamed of repeating what had been told to them; and I have reason to believe, moreover, that intentions not short of criminal were given up in consequence of remonstrances from some of the most prudent of the party, who came forward in consequence of the duel. I am afraid that the event itself shocked many good men; but I am certain that the public interests at the moment required that I should do what I did. 1829

Everything is now quiet, and in Ireland we have full reason to be satisfied. We must, however, lose no time in doing everything else that is possible to promote the prosperity of that country. (Vol. ii. p. 397.)

This description of the position in which the Duke of Wellington was placed affords a remarkable exemplification of the evils which attend upon sudden changes of political opinion, and the obstacles which beset the path of a statesman who undertakes to carry a measure which he has previously opposed.

Sir Archibald Alison has a peculiar theory upon the means by which Catholic Emancipation was carried, which we will give in his own words. 'It was (he says) a victory gained by a large portion of the aristocratic, and the greater part of the highly educated classes, over the sincere conviction and honest resistance of the vast majority of the people. . . It was carried by the liberal opinions of the holders of a majority of the close boroughs, *which brought the government into such straits as compelled it to force through the measure.* Catholic Emancipation was the greatest, as it was the last, triumph of the nomination system.'[1] It must, we think, be evident to every one who has read the preceding review of events, that Catholic Emancipation was carried because the Catholic Association and the Clare election had convinced Sir Robert Peel and the Duke of Wellington that Ireland had become ungovernable, and that the choice lay between concession and civil war. If the members for close boroughs had as strong a sympathy with the Catholic cause, as Sir Archibald Alison attributes to them, it is not likely that the patrons of these boroughs in the House of Lords would have been so

[1] *History of Europe from* 1815 *to* 1852, vol. iv. p. 185.

1829. adverse to the repeal of the disabling laws. The House of Lords had constantly shown itself less favourable to the Catholic claims than the House of Commons: in 1825 it was the House of Lords which alone prevented a peaceable settlement of the question, and frustrated the hopes of the Catholics, which were then worked up to a high pitch.

It might have indeed been expected that the House of Lords would have redeemed its adherence to the interests of its order by its exemption from popular errors and popular fanaticism. Unhappily this has not been the case; on the contrary, it seems to have sought to atone for its maintenance of the interests of the aristocracy by embracing the prejudices of the democracy. Thus it has too often happened that when the people have been right, the House of Lords has been oligarchical, and that when the people had been wrong, the House of Lords has been democratic.

The justification which Sir R. Peel makes for his change of opinion and that of his colleagues in 1829, is, in our opinion, triumphant. No sane statesman, who had any regard for the interests of the country, could have advised a further resistance to the measure of Catholic Emancipation at that crisis. The objection against which Sir R. Peel was really called to justify himself, at the bar of posterity, and not in a meeting of angry and disappointed partisans, is of a wholly different kind. 'If' (he remarks near the conclusion of his memoir) 'it had been alleged against me that the sudden adoption of a different policy had proved the want of early sagacity and foresight on my part; if the charge had been that I had adhered with too much pertinacity to a hopeless cause; that I had permitted for too long a period the engagements of party or undue deference to the wishes of constituents to outweigh the accumulating evidence of an approaching necessity; if this had been the accusation against me, I might find it more difficult to give it a complete and decisive refutation.'[1] Our accusation against Sir R. Peel is, not that he changed his opinion in 1829, but that he did not change it sooner. 1829

There was nothing unexpected or unforeseen in the dangers of this crisis. They had all been predicted years before; nothing occurred in 1828 which is not prefigured in Peter Plymley; the impossibility of permanently governing Ireland on a system of Catholic proscription had been well understood, not only by the Whigs, but by Mr. Pitt and all the principal statesmen of his party; by Lord Grenville, Lord Melville, Lord Wellesley, Lord Harrowby, Mr. Canning, and Lord Castlereagh. The arguments by which Sir R. Peel justifies the concession of Catholic Emancipation in 1829 are very sound; but they are likewise very obvious; and had been obvious to all the more intelligent statesmen of both parties for the previous thirty years.

If Sir R. Peel had been an essentially narrow-minded man, like Mr. Perceval, Lord Sidmouth, and Lord Eldon, we could forgive his obstinate persistence in error: but looking at his subsequent history, we cannot but think that (as he says himself) he allowed 'the engagements of party and an undue deference to the wishes of constituents' to determine his course long after the scales had fallen from his eyes. This remark applies particularly to the manner in which he insisted on this question, as of paramount importance, at the time when he refused to serve under Mr. Canning.[2]

The alliance between the Wellingtonite Tories and the Liberal Opposition for the purpose of carrying the Catholic Question, though sincere for the time, was limited to its temporary object. The Whigs had never formed

[1] *Mem. of Peel,* vol. i. p. 364.

[2] Compare the remarks on Mr. Peel's conversion in the *Edinburgh Review,* vol. xlviii. p. 222.

1830. any political alliance with the Duke of Wellington; the Canningites had left his Government; while his sudden conversion on the Catholic Question, and the manner in which he had surprised and defeated his party, had inspired the ultra-Tories with feelings of bitterness and resentment against him. The session of 1829 was closed without difficulty; but in the session of 1830, which was opened in February, the isolated position of the Government began to be made manifest. Mr. Huskisson and the Whigs showed their hostility; and a section of the Tories were angry and discontented. The pressure upon the Government for reforms of various sorts, parliamentary, fiscal, and economical, began to be more urgent; but they gave no symptoms of any intention of following up the course of liberal policy in which they had reluctantly made one great step. While the session was advancing to its close, an event occurred which exercised an important influence upon the fate of the Ministry. On the 26th of June, George IV. died, at the age of sixty-eight, after an illness which had lasted some weeks; he was succeeded by the Duke of Clarence, who had held the office of Lord High Admiral from May 1827, to August 1828; at which time he was removed by the Duke of Wellington. Parliament was prorogued on the 23rd of July, and at the same time dissolved, in consequence of the demise of the Crown. Soon after the prorogation, the revolution at Paris, by which the elder branch of the Bourbons was deposed, and Louis Philippe placed on the throne of France, took place. The elections were held

[1] See *Mem. of Peel*, vol. i. p. 269. The office of Lord High Admiral was again put in commission, in August 1828, with Lord Melville as First Lord of the Admiralty. Lord Ellenborough, who held the Privy Seal, succeeded Lord Melville at the Board of Control; and he retained the Privy Seal till June 1829, when it was transferred to Lord Rosslyn, a Whig.

under the sympathetic excitement caused by the 'three glorious days of July;' and produced a House of Commons unfavourably disposed to the Wellington Ministry, and prepared for ulterior measures of reform. It was reckoned that out of 256 English members who then sat for counties, and for boroughs more or less open, only 79 were ministerial votes; 141 were in avowed opposition, and 16 were neutral.[1] 1830.

The melancholy death of Mr. Huskisson at the opening of the Liverpool and Manchester Railway, occurred in September, 1830,[2] and removed the chief personal objection which the Duke of Wellington entertained to a junction with the Canningite party. Accordingly, soon after that event the Duke addressed himself to Lord Palmerston as the leading member of that party, and requested him to join the Cabinet, offering at the same time to admit into it two of his political friends. Lord Dudley, Mr. Charles Grant, and Mr. William Lamb, were the persons named by Lord Palmerston as those with whom he then considered himself as mainly acting; but he declined to join the Cabinet unless Lord Grey and Lord Lansdowne were included in the arrangement. This condition put an end to the negotiation, as it involved a complete remodelling of the Cabinet, which the Duke did not contemplate.[3]

Parliament assembled for the first session under the new reign on the 26th of October, 1830. The Government appear to have been prepared to meet their fate with resignation, and they speedily laid their head upon

[1] *Annual Register*, 1830, p. 147.

[2] Mr. Huskisson was born in 1770, and therefore he died at the age of sixty. He and Mr. Canning were born in the same year.

[3] The fact of this negotiation (the details of which are here given from authentic information) was known at the time (see Twiss, *Life of Eldon*, vol. iii. p. 118).

1830. the block. Sir R. Peel was at this moment the real head of the Ministry; the most perfect understanding existed between him and the Duke of Wellington,[1] and in his knowledge of civil politics he was so superior to the Duke, that he could not fail to be his guide in all domestic questions of importance. It was by his advice, authority, and management, that the Catholic Question had been carried; and he was, doubtless, unwilling to repeat in 1830, for Parliamentary Reform, the process through which he had passed in 1828 for the Catholic Question. The Government therefore decided to yield nothing to the rising spirit of reform; and the Duke of Wellington made, on the first night of the session, a declaration of ultra-Conservatism on the subject, which seemed almost intended to provoke opposition and to court defeat. 'I am not only not prepared'—he said, in allusion to Lord Grey's remarks on a measure for reform of the representation—'to bring forward any measure of this nature, but I will at once declare that, as far as I am concerned, as long as I hold any station in the government of the country, I shall always feel it my duty to resist such measures when proposed by others.' On the same night Mr. Brougham, who had been elected for Yorkshire, gave notice of a motion on Parliamentary Reform, for the 16th of November. Another event at this time likewise served to precipitate the fall of the Wellington Ministry. The King had accepted an invitation from the Lord Mayor of London to dine at Guildhall on the 9th of November, but the fears of a popular tumult in consequence of the

[1] Sir R. Peel says in his *Memoir*: 'From the moment of his appointment to the chief place in the Government, not a day had passed without the most unreserved communication personally or in writing; not a point had arisen on which (as my correspondence with the Duke will amply testify) there had not been the most complete and cordial concurrence of opinion' (*Mem. of Peel*, vol. i. p. 279).

attitude assumed by Ministers,[1] induced them to advise His Majesty to postpone his visit to another occasion. 1830.

On the 15th of November, a motion to refer the Civil List estimates of Ministers to a select committee was made by Sir H. Parnell, and carried against the Government by a majority of 29, the votes for the motion being 233 to 204. Sir Edward Knatchbull and a section of the discontented Tories voted for the motion. On the following day the Duke of Wellington and Sir R. Peel, in their respective Houses of Parliament, announced that the resignations of Ministers had been tendered and accepted. The vote was not of such a nature as necessarily to entail the resignation of Ministers; but they doubtless took it as an indication of a spirit which would soon find an opportunity for a declaration of a more decisive character. They likewise stated subsequently that they were influenced in their decision by the prospect of the vote upon Mr. Brougham's motion on Parliamentary Reform. No personal objection existed on the part of William IV. to Lord Grey, and he was accordingly authorised, as head of the Whig party, to form a new Administration. Before undertaking the task, he obtained the King's consent to make Parliamentary Reform a Government measure. The Cabinet was speedily formed, and consisted of fourteen members, of whom nine were Whigs, four were Canningites, and one was a Tory. Lord Grey was First Lord of the Treasury, Lord Brougham received the Great Seal, Lord Lansdowne was President of the Council, and Lord Durham Privy Seal. Lord Melbourne had the Home, Lord Palmerston the Foreign, and Lord Goderich the

[1] The desire of creating a disturbance was materially strengthened by the dislike of the thieves and disorderly classes of the metropolis, to the new metropolitan police, which was introduced at this time under Sir R. Peel's Act, passed in the session of 1830; a measure for which he deserves the gratitude of the country.

1830. Colonial Department. The three Secretaries of State were therefore Canningites. Lord Althorp was Chancellor of the Exchequer and Leader of the House of Commons. Sir James Graham, who had distinguished himself as a speaker in the session of 1830, became First Lord of the Admiralty, Mr. C. Grant, President of the Board of Control, and Lord Auckland, President of the Board of Trade. Lord Holland was Chancellor of the Duchy of Lancaster, the Duke of Richmond was Postmaster-General, and Lord Carlisle had a seat in the Cabinet without office. The Cabinet consisted of ten peers and four commoners. The four commoners were Lord Althorp, Lord Palmerston, Mr. Charles Grant, and Sir James Graham.[1]

Such was the result of Mr. Canning's premature death, and of the attempt of George IV. to establish a reactionary administration under the primacy of the Duke of Wellington.[2] If Mr. Canning had lived, the coalition which he had effected with the Whigs would probably have been consolidated and have acquired strength, instead of falling to pieces soon after his death and making room for a Ministry which, after the quarrel with Mr. Huskisson and the resignation of the Canningites, became more Tory in

[1] Mr. Tierney and Mr. Huskisson, who had both died in 1830, would probably have been members of this Cabinet if they had been alive. If Mr. Fox, Mr. Pitt, Mr. Perceval, Lord Castlereagh, and Mr. Canning, had been alive in 1830, their respective ages would have been as follows: Mr. Fox, 81; Mr. Pitt, 71; Mr. Perceval, 68; Lord Castlereagh, 61; and Mr. Canning, 60. Lord Sidmouth, who was born two years before Mr. Pitt, died in 1844.

[2] Sir Walter Scott foresaw clearly the probable failure of such an attempt. The following reflections occur in his diary of Aug. 11, 1827, the day after he heard the news of Mr. Canning's death: 'A high Tory administration would be a great evil at this time. There are repairs in the structure of our Constitution which ought to be made at this season, and without which the people will not long be silent. A pure Whig administration would probably play the devil by attempting a thorough repair' (Lockhart's *Life of Scott*).

its character than even Lord Liverpool's Government had been since 1822. The year 1830 was the nadir of the Tory party, as the years 1814 and 1815 had been its zenith. It required fifteen years of peace to exhaust the popularity which the Tories had reaped from their triumphant conclusion of the war; but the work was effectually accomplished. The Duke of Wellington showed as much skill in leading a political party to defeat, as he had shown in leading an army to victory. His very success in carrying the Catholic Question helped to undermine his power. He had taken a step in the Liberal direction, which he refused to follow up by any subsequent movement of the same character. The consequence was that he gave mortal offence to a section of his own party, without strengthening himself by an alliance with any detachment of the opposite camp. The night of the division on the Civil List, a few days after the day when the Duke of Wellington was unable to appear at Guildhall for fear of creating a tumult, and was forced to interdict a new and popular sovereign from attending on the same occasion by reason of the unpopularity of his Ministers, was the lowest point of the Tory depression. Even the Reform Bill, though it abolished many Tory boroughs, nevertheless gave strength to the party by enabling it to close its ranks, and by healing the disunion which weakened it in 1830.[1]

1830.

[1] These sheets were already in the press when we received Mr. Augustus Stapleton's last publication, entitled *George Canning and his Times*—a volume of very high interest from the correspondence of Mr. Canning which it contains, and especially from the light it throws on the foreign policy of his administration.

INDEX.

CPSIA information can be obtained
at www.ICGtesting.com
Printed in the USA
LVHW101337160422
716387LV00003B/78

9 783752 590975